I0778986

Masks and Mirrors

By

Samara Williams

ISBN (PAPERBACK) : 978-1-962380-27-0

ISBN (HARDCOVER) : 978-1-962380-98-0

FOREWORD

Unmasked

When I was little, I would play in my imaginative playground with my pretend friend 'Tangkrid' – and her green hair.
I used to hand my mother pages I had written, as 'books'…..
and demand to know why they couldn't **be published <u>now?!'</u>**….

Later in my teens, I used to skip school and sit in the city park with the homeless, as they drank scotch and played chess. I would drink wine and express my dark side with depressing poetry.

Years on, and I still haven't developed my mother's admiral traits of poise, patience and perseverance, ~ worse luck. Nor her remarkable altruism.
Contrastly, I want it all and I want it now…..

Moderation too is a concept I still haven't grasped, sadly. Its extreme, and its all or nothing.
However, I am *aware* of my **weaknesses**, and have tried to harness them, and direct them towards learning power and strength.

One of them, is that through my expression, I am 'an open book'….
to my detriment at times, ~ what you see is what you get!
For I detest dishonesty more than anything. Allow exposure.
No hiding behind masks….the mirror bares it all……
Writing in all its forms: poetry; stories and prose helps one to deal with often disturbing realities, and I adopted this method.

My life has sent me unusual subject material; apparently I attract them (!)

~this collection of raconteur ramblings <u>are</u> *inspired* by my interpretations of several. Observation of people and life provides the seeds to stories. The imagination flourishes when you step outside the square…

Bukowski put it so well in 'tales of ordinary madness':

"….there is at least one madman on every job, a pest, and they always find me. "every nut in the joint likes you" is a sentence that I have heard on job after job. it is not encouraging"

1

When you write a book, you expose yourself to a serious roasting from the public; regardless of content, generally. It's just human nature!
I have no doubts I will be clubbed to death.....(incidentally, the same titled song resonated strongly whilst writing these stories)

*Answer to an English exam paper:

As I journeyed through phases of youth,
I listened to peers and discovered the truth:
that most would succumb to what they felt compelled
while stubborn me wondered what my future held

Amidst all societies' chaos and stress,
they thrive on TV, radio and press;
those marvellous minds that create what we see
through carefully crafted imagery

In the search for what I should pursue,
I looked all around and suddenly knew:
that to use and express my mind creatively,
the world of WRITING beckoned me…

Among others, I have used several further quotes from *Charles Bukowski* throughout this tome. I respect his work as the style is a total reflection of who he is at any given time. He is flawed, but fearless. He bends, and often breaks the rules.

"He is not a mainstream author and he will never have a mainstream public" says publisher John Martin referring to Bukowski.
"The kind of writing he does offends too many people. It's too honest and too direct"

Bukowski utilises a very *laconic* writing style; -brief, succinct and terse.
His writing is dynamic, and indicative of his mental state and life experiences at the time of expression.
The methods he uses to emphasize his opinions (and often twisted logic) are evident in that *style and tense* with which he writes
(Even the format of *font* I have found to be expressive of certain issues.)
He wears no masks.
It is an honest mirror into his soul……

"The guy just says it right for me. I do believe that it takes a strong dose of alienation to be a good artist or writer in the modern world. You can't be too well adjusted and have anything interesting to say"
(The artist R. Crumb, in reference to advice given to him by Bukowski on negative feelings about society. They worked in collaboration together and fame prevailed.)

'As Carl Rogers taught: "that which is most personal is most general"
~Ie: the more authentic you become, the more genuine in your expression, particularly regarding personal experiences and even self-doubts, the more people can relate to your expression and the safer it makes them feel to express themselves" '
(By Stephen R. Covey. The 7 habits of highly effective people.)

However......adhering to the TITLE of this book and all that it represents, I as the author wish to remain masked beneath a pseudonym.....to protect against the risk of an eponomous outcome eventuating from this potential tome.

Samaran....

We are complex beings. Comparing us to a computer, *Linus Pauling* quotes in **'THE NEW ORTHOMOLECULAR NUTRITION'**:

"People are programmed by life *instead of by a detailed set of instructions or software. Life experiences are our software, with the term education denoting those experiences. Our education begins at birth and never ceases"*

In my youth, a trip to the local library with my Dad to borrow 3 books was the ultimate joy and highlight of my school holiday memories!.......I always wished that I had acquired my father's extroidinarily expansive knowledge and intellect (encyclopaedic) ~ luckily, he did pass on his passion for flying; adventurous exploration; epicurian fancy; reading and languages however (And more recently, sleeping!)
And it is mostly through life experiences that one gains true, valuable knowledge.

And so.....I continue to learn.........

DEDICATION

First WORD UP

May tortured souls rest in peace…….

With love to all my extended family: blood and chosen.

~and dedicated to all the criminals; gangsters; whores and paranoid scitzofrenic geniuses I have known and loved. You know who you are.

Xoxoxoxoxoxoxooxo

"I have always known that the pursuit of excellence is a lethal habit"

(The world according to Garp. By John Irving.)

*two additions I never imagined id have to add:

In honour of my darling doppelgänger bro: grizzly silverback bodyguard. My Boo. I miss you every single day; you took such a large part of my heart with you. What remains is a daily work in progress…I fail often. But I am a survivor.

And then my father left to find you and join you….my utterly indescribable warrior Viking Dad. Who fought so hard for so long… Sun tzu values reigned right till the bitter end. So strong and yet so enigmatic .

Look after each other. As you did in this life. And for so many people represented such virtuous attributes as to amaze and warrant enormous respect.

You both accepted me on face value with no secrets; still loving the misfit sis I was; supporting me on every level.

You allowed me to take off my mask…

You were my mirror.

Table of Contents

Chapters 8, 9, & 10 (a trilogy series)
FAITH, IRONY, PERCEPTION, BIRTH AND DEATH

Chapter 1:
THE FIRST PHASE....

Who so neglects learning in his youth loses the past and is dead to the future.
Euripedes

You are only young once, and if you work it right, once is enough.
John E Lewis

Carpe diem...

<u>'Embryonic progression'</u>~ *by the author:*
Down the tunnel, towards the door
the oblivious journey to what lay in store.
From fusion to freedom, here was the source
-an introduction to life's bumpy course.

Riding the time capsule through phases of youth
a kaleidescope of fear; misconceptions and truth
I reached out to touch wondrous colours in sight;

but restrictions were laid down in black and white

The lessons began, aimed to guide and direct
all awareness controlled; a free spirits' neglect
For more craters than crests there appeared to be
in those earlier conflicts with conformity

Ideas were issued to adopt and pursue
-a shocking reception to anything new
But I blocked one ear, and opened my mind
in a quest for unique inspiration to find

As the wheels rolled relentlessly on down the track,
I savoured each moment, no time to look back
~dissolved all regrets and admonished the past,
for events may be over, but memories last

Now, at this point,
my mind realises the truth ~
that we only develop through journeys from youth
And so I keep travelling in search of my goal:
to stay individual and express my soul

'Topeng dan Cermin'. (Bahasa Indonesia)

Masquerade...the game with **masks** and **mirrors.**

1:

* Jack and Jill - Retro Rangers
* The decade that dominated
* Up, up and away
* Roman candle
* Ten reefs and sharing time
* Fear fetish and the fellow

1/ part 1:

Jack and Jill – retro rangers...... (Danny and Lovisa)

Jack and Jill they took a pill
to gain a new perspective....
But then whoops, they TRIPPED
and Jill believed, 'till now, she'd really not lived.....

It was like opening her eyes for the very first time.
Waking up from a coma.
This was what it was about!
It all made sense now.
L.
S.
D

He had a carefree blonde mane; like a lion. A golden Swede, with beautiful arms that would engulf; and a wild streak that would enrapture her with that irresistible combination of desire and fear.
She found him terribly sexy. He oozed a slinky appeal she had not encountered before.
At least not in a man. And yet......they were constantly asked if they were siblings or twins!
Lovisa wondered: why is it that sexy guys always have a penchant for peril?!
She didn't question the attraction, or where it was going; she just went with it.
She had held his hand and literally jumped, with sheer abandon into the abyss below......the unknown.
Where Russian roulette was the only description for the games that they played. Risky. Dangerous. Intoxicating.

Danny.

I guess sometimes in life, you choose certain partners to fulfil certain roles/ play out various chapters with. For Lovisa, he was the one to experiment all in *sex and drugs*........a wild, passionate entanglement that can only be had during the robust courage of youth.
One of the definitions of 'dancing with the devil' is :
taking a great risk/ sacrificing your soul to get one's desires.
-It seemed to be an ongoing theme for her. This chapter should hence come of less surprise.
To this day, she still keeps terrifying, albeit fond memories. The fear/adoration fine~line was definitely achieved with him. The standard had been set; would never be reached again.
It was never to be a permanent union, for it would have killed them both.

At the time of occurrence, she was impervious to the 'fleeting' aspect of life's thrills, and took them for granted; expected it to be the norm.....such is the oblivion of sweet youth (as most can attest.)
It was something that, once found, is expected to continue.
At this magnitude, sadly, in life you get one shot only. But of course you never know that at the time! Savour it and pay attention is advice that is only ever given in *hindsight*.....
For little did she know that he was the one.
 Sexual attraction was never the same again.
In fact, it was pretty much null and void. She endured lonely celibacy and abstinence thereafter, so *this* was her chapter of hedonism, debauchery and hell-bent madness. She had tested the boundaries and tasted the forbidden fruits, but when she left the garden of Eden, all she had was memories..

She existed in a tingly world with him.
Pheromones......
He carried his signature smell of musty aftershave and carnal desire.
Their kisses were deep and unconscious; swept on by waves of lust and intrigue.
    His body was perfect to her, and his face ?....
~ if you can visualize Richard Gere with *golden* Samson locks, then that about captures it.
He ignited a fire deep inside her, that has since lay dormant;
buried and forgotten with charred embers of sorrow and regret.

They were the puzzle pieces that fit together so snugly to become one whole.
It was a strength and a weakness rolled into one.
Alas there was a time-limit to their union; as with all the best things in life.

It was the golden *ages* too......the edge of the eighties, and a time of the parties that remain in the memory banks of so many: rat, bacchanalia, trance, ...
(Well......for those who can still actually access the memory bank after the pursuits of pleasure that were administered. There is always a price. Quantum physics.......)
It was a time of sheer madness......but then.....she'd always felt mad. Alien.
Time to shine. Bend the rules, or better still break them.

They used to play with fire. Using the most valuable toy they had; deep in the grey-matter zone. The risks were high of......never returning.....(enterprite this as you will).
Stimulants of all kinds were engulfed:
pills'n'caps taken; powder snorted; mixtures smoked; paper swallowed.
It was a cocophany of experimentation, and they were the labrats of the ages. Designer drug testers. It was madness, mayhem and hedonism like never before!
(In fact, they were actually recruited as private testers for a drug-lord associate as he considered his serious 'business deals'. He would rock on over with the goods and throw a few their way, then sit back and enjoy the rendition)
And they had no fear.....courage of a cowboy. Indestructible.
Enhanced to a state of heightened glorification.
They didn't think about taking the crown off some day, nor what damage it may cause in the potential aftermath.....for now they wore it.
And they owned it.

Even to this day, her most daring of comrades professed : it was the bravest of times. The live for now; fuck tomorrow era.
....they didn't know it back then. But it was crossing the threshhold of safety to its ultimate. For, as I already impressed upon you, there were big risks of never coming back....
And she encountered many who didn't. Or, who lost more than simply their sanity.
In her own close social circle alone, one was arrested, one was admitted to a psych ward,... and one killed his girlfriend in a road accident after a party was shut down at the precise point when all participants were high as a kite.

Quote Charles Bukowski in 'tales of ordinary madness- a bad trip' :

"
    did you ever consider that lsd and colour tv arrived for our consumption about the same time? here comes all this explorative colour pounding, and what do we do? we outlaw one and fuck up the other...

...it is true that the more you get the more you chance. any explorative complexity - painting, writing, poetry, robbing banks, being a dictator and so forth, takes you to that place where danger and miracle are rather like Siamese twins. you seldom go wire to wire, but while you're going the living is fairly interesting.

... a trip calls for a man who has not yet been caged, who has not yet been fucked by the big Fear that makes all society go.

the free soul is rare, but you know it when you see it - basically because you feel good, very good, when you are near or with them.
an lsd trip will show you things which no rules cover.
grass only makes the present society more bearable; lsd is another society within itself.

a bad trip? this whole country, this whole world is on a bad trip, friend.
but they'll arrest you for swallowing a tablet.   "

These were experiences that would never have been pursued later in life – they are for the young and reckless. Even the mere THOUGHT of living right on the edge to this degree now sent waves of intense anxiety and fear coursing through her veins.

She had kept a diary of her first trip abroad with him. Those wild and carefree adventures represented the most profound phase of 'zero responsibility' in her life to date. Upon reading it, the sense of liberation is most evident, and obviously something that was expected to be the norm in life….

The lovers' only concerns were survival – basic necessities and each other's company….(plus a constant quest for the next laugh, joint, acid trip or ecstacy!) The pleasure they derived from each other was the most fervent issue though. NOTHING mattered except that they were together.
It was pure love.

Her drug of choice in those days had always been LSD. Everyone was embracing the E craze. GENERATION X was going hardcore. It was like seeing Aldous Huxley's 'brave new world' performed live…albeit self-<u>pre</u>scribed meds vs administered by the powers that be.
But she preferred the more cerebral *retro* danger zone.

Acid came in kitsch emblem paper format mostly, but was also in pills and glass-like 'prisms'. One had to have complete faith in the dealer for these babies…..it was as courageous as it got. Their most reliable source, and a close comrade at the time kept an 'album' of all the different types of acid trips he had encountered; sold; tried etc. it was like a photo album of memories they would occasionally flick through and discuss
      – like going back down memory lane……

She couldn't really understand the whole point of knocking yourself into an ecstacy-ridden zombie state of delirium; somewhat labotomised. Cheshire cat. Smiley faces, (like their recognised yellow logo) abound;~ with the additional bonus of teeth-grinding; jaw tension and verbal slurring. It was also not a glamorous look by any means. It reminded her of the heroine-chick in the movie 'christian F' – which she was made to watch at one of her rough schools as 'mandatory education'. She remembered thinking 'wow, that's what a *real* junkie looks like – skinny, pale, with eyes rolling in the back of the head….i'll never go there'…..
The general perception, she found was that:
'injecting' meant junkie, but the rest was all fine and permissible…….

Groups of youths would meet at these parties and dance themselves stupid, then collect in groups sipping water; smoking joints and massaging each other like an orgy foreplay scene.
The craziest time was in south France, where she went to a trance party held in a quarry. She was surrounded by a foreign language, and French boys…..and they took the cake for insatiable partying and risk. No question. They scared even her!

E was a horny drug.
Not that she wasn't innately sensual and sexual, for she was.
 But it wasn't something she needed *stimulants* to enhance. It was already there.
Her brainbox on the other hand, was one worth investigating for all its hidden glory.
Open up doors that usually remain hidden and in the recesses of the subconscience.
For anyone remotely creative, it was utter nirvana…way too much fun!

The E generation was going strong around the time that the AIDS epidemic swept through the masses like a grim reaper. And this is precisely how it was portrayed in ads and whatnot designed to scare people out of its luring call. It backfired bigtime, as they wished to hide behind a wall of drug-induced oblivion from the fear of the scourge that had been pronounced. AIDS statistics rose substantially.
The prohibition debate…….we all know that forbidden fruits taste far sweeter!
So weekends were spent engulfing the smiley pills with gusto at all the parties over town. Floppy dolls on designer drugs…..their self-prescribed means of escape.

Contrarily, she loved more to turn on those hidden buttons of the mind and get **verbal**. Different chemistry.
Acid and Charlie mainly. (And many years later, the pinnacle: a personalized designer drug they christened 'perception'; ~ courtesy her doppelganger mate) Good grief, the mental euphoria….
She understood why Aldous Huxley wrote about them in 'the doors of perception' for it is only something that those who have dabbled with glee and get to see the promised land of mindscape nirvana – can understand.
(He was referring to mesculin of course, but being a psychedelic hallucination-inducer, it was in the the same league.)
It was off with the mask, and true insight to the personal *wiring* portrayed in the mental mirror. Like entering a mansion of marvels…
It sped things up. Amped life, so to speak, no question.

And then…….to calm from the excitement without too much melancholy?…..(for what goes up must inevitably come down) :
let's not forget the pharmaceutical grade medication. They had many a self-prescribed weekend as such, on Zanax; Quaaludes (mandrax) or Rohypnols (and sometimes Valium of course) ~ to soften the blow and provide a smoother 'landing'.
To begin she engulfed the 'ludes', which were later superceded by the more available version of (sort of) the same in the form of 'rohies'.
There was always a doctor contact willing to write prescriptions as a favour swap. (Alternatively, just steal one of your father's prescription pads from his surgery and write your own! The private school boys were masters of this technique).
Particularly if they were diagnosed in the unique (and handy) categories of obsessive compulsive disorder, and/or hyperactivity attention deficit disorder. Muscle relaxants were up for grabs for these guys. It was often a sideline business for them too, as people without the affliction had the reverse affect if it was stimulated in the right direction: instead of calming them down, it heightened aggression; always a fabulous enhancement for say football games and the like. Dexamphetamines to incite rage and

gladiator tendencies…..(her own brother had the handy sideline trade going of : 'dexies for a dollar')………..But we are getting off track here now (so to speak).

Her darling Danny had given her an uncharacteristic need for hydroponic weed too; an addiction she looked back on now with mystery. It was part of the package of him though, so she took it on with love and insatiability.
She remembered once being in a party of lads for 'happy hour' (only female present as usual) – and all sampling these massive 'cocktail' capsules called 'golden dreams'. They were said to have a bit of everything: speed, cocaine, heroine, liquid acid, ecstacy…..the works. Wild and carefree…….several days elapsed. Normal life and the real world was null and void.

She loved to dress up too. It portrayed so much about the individual at the actual time……a wardrobe must be expansive and extroidinarily diverse to express the ever-changing moods of one!! And shoes, shoes shoes……
Masks and Mirrors, masks and mirrors……

Generation X and its antics doesn't seem that long ago to those engulfed in the era, but it is another world to the modern GEN Y lot. The X-ers were never into the whole **Emo** phase and its' associated self-harming with razors and whatnot. Yes, they too were nocturnal beasts, (albeit tanned vs vampish!) ~but their form of self-abuse was a more intellectual and cerebral kind. And it was way more fun.

The Y's of today are troubled souls….or is it just the current fashion? As for their wave of suicides, this is beyond comprehension. X-ers were a mad lot, but the Y kids of now are an utter mystery. In a sense, though, it is all suicide. But It was more *incognito*……~in disguise back then than it is now/today.
You would die with a smile there, whereas now it is apparently more sinister and morbid. With a sorrowful frown.
One evidently only tries to hold onto a precious future when older……
in adolescence, it holds no weight. The concept is **Now. Only now**……
(Buddhist training wheels perhaps, for the detox phase of maturity!)

She had lived with her prince in several places. The 'home' was a small apartment in the north of the city, where the balcony views expanded the meagre internal size of their abode (and dreams!) enormously.
They were often amazed how many folk would squeeze happily into such a small confine for hours; days on end……and all gather on the porch to look out into the horizon; collectively dreaming of futures that were beyond description.

It was here that they planned the travelling adventure…..and on a whim raced off to the agency to book a flight soon thereafter. (these were the days before booking online became the norm).

Down with an acid trip then off to sit on a cliff-face and plan *the* trip. She wanted to be by his side on everything. It was mutual infatuation….and as you know, crazy decisions will always ensue……
They were each other's entire world…and they decided to explore the other vast world out there together.
They both abandoned their difficultly acquired jobs; packed up and took off. Just like that. A phonecall to their respective families on the drive to the airport was pretty much the only notice given.

And so for Danny and Lovisa the adventure began……
She was a diary addict amidst the other cacophony of addiction, and expression was her thing! So when not talking she was going with the ink routine.
This is her tale……

Excerpts taken from the British evening standard magazine - 24/2/17:

'Its no coincidence that many of today's tech titans and captains of industry hail from generation X - the generation that graduated in the early days of rave, a world before digital, when secret gatherings in fields and warehouses took place entirely illegally and away from the gaze of the police and the public. Organised through word-of-mouth, pirate radio or simply at service-station meet-ups, these gatherings were all about joining up people with similar mind-sets, forming communities of individuals who emerged intent on changing the way everyone said we should live our lives.'

…'Like a growing number of influential gatherings, it is under the radar, offline and invite-only'

'The decade that dominated'....

How would you describe the '80's and early 90's era and what it meant to you?...

"

    Its 1988,

and me 'n my go-to *boy-girlfriend* Ricardo are in the depths of embracing all things fashion;~ including the bang on-trend (or is it bong-on?) trend drug capers of the mo.
He was a budding photographer (and apprentice advertising creative) at the time, and I was his muse.
The Edie Sedgewick to his Andy Warhol.
(the verdict was always out on his sexuality as is often the case with gifted arty types......I knew first hand though that whatever the preference, he was happy to do the *straight* and narrow too.....for one must love and embrace their subject)......

Ah, the eighties.....
Of course it goes without saying that everyone's personal memory bank is different, but for me, the decade spanned the time of :

FASHION: ripped faded levi's denim 501 jeans; chunky cross chains and body embellishments; bandanas; leg warmers; ski pants ! ~perms and other horrid head fashion phases; midriff tops; songs with actual lyrics.....
and fashion shoots in New York style loft apartments with fan-blowing props for the 'windswept hair' look. Lots of mono and sepia tone prevailed vs colour.

AUDIO: Madonna rocked solid and Whitney Houston was far from the savaged victim she became. Eurythmics were at their peak; Duran Duran represented heart-flutter; Prince had us yearning for the Dove's cry, and Michael Jackson was, quite simply God. On the camp spectacular front, Jimmy Somerville reached the high note; Wham inspired teeth whitening; and the creatively confused Boy George produced a fanclub of *sexually* confused. (I even made a ragdoll of this idol)

Playlists consisted of INXS – (Michael Hutchence was *the* master sex-symbol)…Depeche mode…..the Cure…
Soft cell's *'tainted love'* was, im sure, responsible for many eighties pregnancies.
Tears for Fears had sadly become mainstream; their primordial original 'the hurting' was the recital of my youth.
Phill Collins' unforgettable 'In the Air tonight' was a classic for testing audio speakers everywhere. Accessory car stereos with psychedelic boom boxes that were detachable to counteract thiefs.
It was the time where *sony walkmans* were a swanky new device.

TRENDS: Cindy Crawford was our supermodel ~natural and healthy was still a desired look, but impossibly skinny was now becoming a challenge for the perfectionists crew. Actual models bore the covers of magazines; not airbrushed celebrities. Plastic surgeons were for the elite and privelidged few rather than for every man and his dog…..
 Late night café nachos was the snack of choice; chupa-chups the party favour. Intake consciousness did not exist like today; it was more liberated, autopilot consumption! The health industry was yet to accelerate. Fitness junkies were on the verge of inception. Aerobics was the go; just fun dancing and prancing basically….
The lingo deemed everything as 'wicked' or 'cool' and puke-worthy drinks of 'passion pop' and mixer spirit cans abounded in riotous events everywhere.

It was the time when wankers reigned supreme….there was much unabashed arrogance and showmanship….(an example being one of my ex-lovers and his heart-shaped water bed with red satin sheets, and ceiling mirror. Hello…)..it was generally a time where it was WHO you knew, rather than what you knew.

VISUAL: Image-speaking, it wasn't a *glamorous* time; conversely it was cringe-inducing in hindsight on many levels….but it was definitely the most *fun* decade ever!
 People were into smiling and laughing vs pouting…..*a la natural* was the theme du jour; not fake.
The social masks of today weren't necessary. It was more flamboyant; fresh faced and spontaneous.
Undoubtedly a privelidged, healthy time to prevail.

My god it was another world from the one we now know…….

It is definitely an era to blame for the current wave of nostalgiaholics….

My most profound smell memory was Ricardo's *Calvin Klein Obsession* aftershave, mingled with the chemical fumes of the dark room lab to develop the prints of his pride. Oh the nausea and headaches……I don't know how he persisted! So many hours; days and nights he would dedicate to his photography craft.

Weekends were spent at wild parties about town – with pill-popping in its ultimate heyday. Ricardo and I were hooked up with the best drug dealers; hippest crowd; DJ

Celebs and event planners. As previously noted, it was a courageous time of experimentation......
And let's talk about courage on Ricardo's behalf: having had multiple brain tumours recently, he partook with the most vigour of all in the chemical lab of party favours......now that's scary......ultimate danger and risk was the theme du jour..

I was in a 'serious' relationship at the time, with a really solid, loyal, 'marriage worthy' guy.
But alas, timing was oh so wrong. (Forgive me but I was into the phase of 'cool and chaotic' vs 'calm and diligent' lovers.)
Bad boys only....the ideal ones were just not appreciated one iota.

It was around this time that I was introduced to a new boy in the arena.
Danny represented the first time I felt extreme magnetism that *insisted* on unification.
He and Ricardo were friends......both in the advertising game.
His quest was for copywriting. With me having just done a reputable course in graphic design, it was a symbiotic combining of creative forces worth reckoning with. There was no denying: Imagery and words go hand in hand ~ as did we, almost from the point of introduction. We were an inseperable team.
I helped him apply for award school; - did all the sketches for his script.
He got in.
At first, Ricardo was all in favour of our mutual attraction. Encouraged it even. But slowly, he started to alter his tune....

Danny and i ached to be together at all times......pain and pleasure were interchangeable. It was masochistic; primal; urgent; passionate;....
once-in-a-lifetime stuff.
[These are the ones that you ache to be with; dream about; fantasize about.......
but can never have a 'forever' relationship with, or marry.]
You know what im talking about.
(If you say that you married the one that is described, then either it is doomed, or you are lying/kidding yourself. Sorry. Fact.)
He forever more refers to me now as 'the one who got away'

The party years.....

There was an arrogance in those that partook in the non-legal poisons on offer.
And the normal lot looked at them as rebellious outcast freaks.
It was a kind of segregation of social play. There wasn't a lot of interaction between the two.
There were the mainstreamers vs the alternate, hip lot.
There was the alcohol bunch on one side, and the pot smoking; class A engulfing mob on the other. Surprisingly, the latter (of which we fell into) was more the privelidged, educated private school kids. Go figure...

We were of the mindset that weekend binge-drinking in pubs was :
'repugnant; low class; - a coward's refuge......opiate of the masses'....

I remember not having a single alcoholic beverage in such a long time…
it was all about passing the bong; chopping the lines and dropping the pills.

The druggies had a different style of expression: a separate parlance, fashion and musical preference. The music was designed in conjunction with the altered mind activities – it was not something that was appreciated by the headbanger beer-swilling lot. They had their hard rock; we had our house; acid & trance; designed to enhance the dance, and heighten the sex. Jack to the sound of the underground…….and aceeeed……
It was almost like two different countries; cultures and beliefs!
They both looked on at the other with a degree of distaste..
whatever.
It is what it is……(or should I say was what it was)

"

Its all another WORLD ALTOGETHER compared with today…..

Lovisa looked back on at her notes on the decade that dominated with melancholy.

Zeitgeist

It was like another life away. Such a glorious and taken-for-granted time to have flourished, and then find replaced by a world of technological non-human living.
Her mind drifted back to the day the next chapter started….

Ricardo had 'cornered' her; taken her up to the 21st floor of the advertising building he worked *'to discuss something in private'*.
The panoramic views of the city were astounding from this vantage point; she had always loved to accompany him to this workplace he inhabited for most of his time.
They had done many a photo shoot up here. He dabbled in her makeup; hair; fashion as well as manning the lense. It was like his playground for any creative project that took his desire. He was king of the castle here, and she was his princess, and they reigned supreme. He was her go-to best friend; boyfriend/girlfriend package deal and the adoration was mutual.
 This time however, the agency was quiet, empty and forboding. The other advertising staff had taken off for their wild weekend pursuits.
Ricardo had once introduced her to the solid, stable guy she had a long-term serious relationship with, until now, and encouraged that. (Oh he looked good on her resume by his sheer patience and diligence in his dull job!) He had been a staff-member from this very building.
But now Ricardo was seething at the prospects of the 'lusting alternative' she was in the process of choosing, and inevitably replacing him with.
Danny.
Their silent rivalry was becoming apparent.
It was a concoction of jealousy and rage, that she couldn't quite fathom. He and Danny had been close friends when he introduced *them* too; why had he changed his tune ?
He tried to convince her "he was dangerous and toxic……it will end in doom"

But love is blind and evidently deaf too.

She realised that she exhibited her rebellious streak in the form of the *lovers* that she chose.
Her own mother had a nack for choosing **incredible looking** gents.
No point having a solid, stable….DULL AND BORING partner with no blessings on the genetic front visually (unless they were multi millionaires of course)…life is too short to endure repulsion!
It was something inherently instinctive; the same pattern emerged with each of her encounters.
So there was no solution to the programming…..its who she was. Paradigm.

So, Lovisa was heart-broken when Ricardo confronted her with an altumatum:
'its either him (Danny) or me, make a decision'….
For sadly, she recognized the fact that….
(though few will admit it):
lust *will* **always** *win* over moral duty and comrade commitment…….

Up, UP and away.......!

It has to be about as carefree as it gets:
......meet a fellow model friend who inspires you with her personal travel adventures; get her hand-drawn map of the said location, and literally head straight over yourself. No research. No ponderings or hesitations. Just pure, sweet glorious spontainaeity on every level imaginable.
Who **does** that these days?? There is so much nervous doubt and fear in the youth of today....simply acting on a whim is something only read about in books or seen in dreamy movies.

Anyway, that's precisely how the Tenerife chapter began!

Mystique had issued them with a mini map of the island, including all the 5-star resorts that she worked for in her timeshare heyday. The girl was a master sales-bitch; no question, and a gifted actress to boot.
 A true pommy conwoman, she could sell snow to a snowman *to be fair*; ~ that's how convincing she was. The striking looks didn't go astray either, naturally!
 And she had convinced them both to *"go see her contacts there for a job, and fund your global adventure thereafter".....*

Quite literally, she professed - it was a case of :
introduce themselves to Travis, (the boss); mention Mystique; get thrown a *'tenerife royal gardens'* t'shirt to don, and straight to work, pronto!
They would work the streets as **timeshare** tyrants; - you know the ones......they are notorious 'holiday wreckers' for the hours they insist you stay on tedious tours designed to coerse you into investments you can't afford.
Lovisa spoke German too, so Mysty informed her that the rates were to be higher. Multi-lingual capabilities were always an asset in the trade: the more nations you could pitch to, the better your odds. It was a numbers game......like so many chapters in her life.

Danny and Lovisa were so in raptures with their union at this point, that it would have been inconceivable not to pursue an adventure of passion together and create more magic memories. This opportunity presented itself and was seized in an instant.
As outlined, the physical attraction they shared was the once-in-a-lifetime kind.

Everybody has some character encounter in their life who reappears in the subconscious when in slumber and dreamscape mode...often repeatedly for years or even a lifetime afterwards.

Most people have a list of characters in their life-books that tick certain boxes.

Be it love; security; inspiration; fun; intellect; lust; adventure; sex etc.....he ticked the latter three.

But this equation inevitably comes with a degree of danger as every girl knows.....as it is the ultimate foreplay seduction recipe.

For the fact remains: all good sorts love a bad boy!

The term 'sex appeal' doesn't seem to exist without it.

Always a price.

It is to the detriment of peace and security....one is always wildly on the edge of danger and risk with these types. But it is an uncontrollable urge to be with them. Despite the fact that you know it is the worst decision for health, future wellbeing or safety.

Burnout is imminent.....(read *guaranteed*)

There is a use-by-date.....but like a product with only a short shelf-life that you impulsively crave and lust for, you seize the item and indulge in all its glory to maximum indulgence; regardless of the internal voice that knocks on your subconscience:

' *you may regret this tomorrow !'*.

But it was the carefree time of 'fuck tomorrows and focus on todays'.

And so the story continues.....

Even as they took off on the Garuda flight the games had begun.

A friend (dealer associate) who had farewelled the pair at Sydney airport threw a surreptitious 'gift' down both their throats; in the form of a paper acid square.

(L.S.D for those needing clarity due to innocence)

'Enjoy your trip' he smirked and stood to the perimeters of the gathering family throng who embraced them and wished them well at the entrance.

A few hours beforehand, they had felt very self righteous: waking to an alarm and brewing a coffee like a 'normal person' as they anticipated the months ahead.

Quick showers; baggage collection and following a morning 'time list' for a change. Normal stuff!

Well done.... ✓

Aside from the required work *routine* based in advertising, ~ which they had both sought and treasured as *pleasurable,* not laborious (she in graphic art and he as a copy writer), their world external to that was also of their own design. Mostly stimulant infused; chaotic; outrageously creative and insanely sensual.

 Artistic and expressive beasts at heart, they were entitled to a different view to the norm, and refused to fall victim to the borders. They repelled the norm and embraced the free-flow of their desires, devoid of usual protocol restrictions.

This had caused a degree of confusion in their families, colleagues, associates... (and themselves!)

Why would you down tools on the valuably granted vocation of choice, risking future re-employment and just take off like a vagabond escapee?

The answer was simple. Love takes you to places you never think you will go....
Often at tremendous risk.

This was deliciously spontaneous! A dying art now, for sure...

Plus she had dyed her hair a deep auburn colour. Something done on a whim one day of debauchery no doubt. Or to keep herself occupied while the boys told 'war stories' from school and passed the ceremonial bong 'around the campfire' in their city apartment; surrounded by open travel bags and lists.
She knew maintaining the blonde might be a challenge when abroad.
And besides, their hair was almost identical in colour style and length. This change gave her a degree of individuality in the pairing. Didn't look so much like an incest situation (!)

It was her first big stint away from the country of birth.
And who knows when or where or for how long it might take her beyond the rainbow....
That was the whole point.
Exploration. No restrictions. Just pure survival and live in the moment as it unfolds....
 (A concept of bygone eras now sadly, in this modern technological cesspit we inhabit. I feel sorry for the youth of today. They have no dreams or aspirations.... or indeed *imagination* beyond whatever screen they are holding and tapping on wildly with attention span fireworks)

His hair was long and and tied back like Tarzan. Swedish ancestry had done him proud in the looks department. Most guys should not grow hair as they do, for it does them no favours. But for him it would be a crime to chop such marvellous flowing golden locks. Like Samson to her Jane...
They held hands and boarded the plane.
Pupils now starting to dilate mildly and their perception of everything becoming more surreal.
And familiar.
Being sober and straight gave them a degree of anxiety. Particularly in normal protocol parameters. The whole family farewell thing was stressful....but now they were off.

She took out her brand new diary to start the ball rolling on the initial review. As the plane ascended and her stomach did a mini backflip, the pen she was using exploded and ink splattered her page like a jackson pollock before her eyes. She sulked momentarily, biting her lip, as she saw how her pristine clean slate had been assassinated in harsh black splatter. But then as she blew the ink and it took on a cavalcade of erupting tributaries from the centre she realised it was a work of art to unfold creatively before her eyes. From mess and mayhem to unique inspiration and spontaneous glory.....
"...as we left our familiarities to board the bird, it was a most awesome experience to fly high while flying high. Cant possibly explain the exhilaration of takeoff....."
They looked at each other and grinned. These acids were GOOD....but all his gear was.

Their travel inspiration was heightened further. Everywhere on the proposed agenda was foreign and new to them and the excitement was palpable!

First stop was an island break for a few days.
Bali in indonesia.
Then over to Roma, Barcelona, and finally migrate further south of Spain for flight to the canary islands.
The cash was going to be tight. Certainly a stressful concept of monitoring. But where there's a will there's certainly a way! They just had to get as far as the canaries before they could throw themselves wholeheartedly into the mission of earning more funding to continue their journeys. The rest was to unfold as new inspirations occurred.
And at this point of mind expansion thanks to their send-off sustenance, they had the courage of cowboys that as long as they were together they would make it work and have travel tales to relay.

For them, first priority was always 'good gear' to hand. (Going out with a drug dealer has its perks; - he would focus on that while she steered the moving ship).
He unfolded a map and they discussed the gameplan as they sipped on drinks being supplied by the Garuda staff.
The peanuts packet was tiny but as anyone on LSD knows well, even one nut in the mouth feels like the rock of gibraltar and a massive challenge to masticate!
And anything like bread was akin to chewing on the contents of a pillow.
Better not to eat at all. Just more stimulants are the go. Alcohol and soft drinks would fuel without discontent.
Their first encounter with air turbulence and 'seatbelt' sign on brought waves of anxiety. These were the days when the reputation of Garuda was grim.
(Anyone who worked in the airline industry would profess: 'fly **any** airline but garuda unless on a suicide mission!!'
But they were the cheapest tickets so it was their only financial option at this point.)

About halfway through the flight, they were both grinding teeth to a degree and feeling a bit restricted and scratchy. She had wandered around the plane a bit, and even had a chat to the pilot in the cockpit at one point. But now it was feeling restrictive in the small confined seats.
They looked out the window at the puffy clouds. It was a glorious image. And the sky beyond was so clear and blue.
He asked her *'do you think its time for US to land smoothly now?'* She knew what he meant and held out her hand with a nod of agreement. Down with a gulp of water went a **rohypnol** tab each. They sat back and waited to glide; sharing an earplug each from the walkman with their house music.
It felt like ecstasy when combined with acid. A perfect mix. In fact this was one of her favourite parts of the journey. When the racy phase was over they still got to hit cruise control and it was like coming home.
Comfort zone.

Years later she would dabble in the dangerous art of combining sleeping pills with class A stimulants. It resulted in the antithesis of normal reaction. Instead of sleep (as prescribed), she would be dancing on tables and in a mobile state of free expression

and joy. If you pushed past the barriers of the 'knock-out' element it was another medium of euphoria. But far from recommended for its danger element. Reports of people committing murder or jumping off buildings on the sleeping pills were becoming more frequent.
Eventually it was taken off the market and her games in that league were over.
Null and void.

For now, the rohys were easily accessible. His father was a surgeon so with one of his script books, Danny would hand-write and collect boxes whenever desired.
Qualudes were a dying fad now and the rohypnols had taken precedence.
Mandatory ammunition to allow one to come down from the psychotropic scratchy phase. What goes up must come down. Law of physics. Pure and simple. But if you could soften the downslide, it was like landing on a bed of soft grass vs a crash landing at high speed like a torpedo from the sky.

They floated off into dreamscape; the clouds powdering their vision, and allowing them to drift and glide in unison with the vessel they had boarded.
This was a time she enjoyed just as much as the initial high. For her mind opened; thoughts flowed freely and with no abandon, and the wonderful concepts that lay bedded in the subconscious grey matter came prancing out to play with clarity. She was deep in thought and ponderings, but blissfully happy in the mental garden of freedom. The meanderings of the mind are a marvelous thing…..but how often are we granted the access to the vagabond adventures without the intrusion of daily duties and demands?
She noticed, quite profoundly how being forced to sit still in an airplane seat enforced you to focus more inward and on self without other activities or time stresses.
You had to stay put for the duration of the journey which was always multiple hours. Your own access to cinema viewing, and service that arrives with refreshments and alcohol if desired. Without having to do a thing.
No doubt it could get frustrating and restrictive, but for now it was a most pleasant change from the usual chaos of her crazy life. Kind of a luxury - she could get used to this, she thought! The idea was to improve the quality of the conditions. Cattle class was a nice introduction, but the empty spacious sections at the *front* end of the plane beckoned her in the future…..

Some undefined time later, there was a tap on their shoulders from the airline hostess; announcing that
"the seatbelt sign is on - we are about to approach descent. Put your seat upright and stow your table please"
They glanced out the window at the massive expanse of crystal blue, that extended seamlessly from sky to ocean.
The island awaited. And they were so ready to get native pronto and lavish in the tropical conditions.
On exiting the plane at last the sudden wash of humidity permeated their bodies, warming them like they hadn't felt in a long time.
There was a distinctive smell about Asia too…..its a combination of spice and fragrance.
Musty. Enticing.

They couldn't be more eager to escape the confines (in all respects) of the other country of restrictions and spirit destruction - and explore what the exciting world had to offer.

Lovisa for one suspected that there may be no turning back for her now, having escaped like a prisoner on the run. The sense of liberty was so overwhelming it nearly took her breath away.

Bali would be the perfect start to the adventure they both agreed, aiming to acquire the summery windswept look with a golden tan glow. Better than the current insipid pale look to take to the *other* island destination so they would appear more at ease in the tropical conditions.

If they had arrived in Tenerife as they currently were, they would appear wildly foreign and vulnerable. It may compromise their reputation! For they reaked of 'inner city apartment nocturnal goth', and were no doubt desperately low in vitamin D. Australia forced fear of any sun exposure. Essentially because it KILLED YOU there. Ozone layer zero. Like the quality of life.

 Just another negative aspect of the propaganda-propelled nation of boredom.

Her current phase of auburn hair would suit Rome next - she wanted to get some chic photos in the ancient city of style and history.

Always planning ! Her life path, her veneer and her desires.

Spontainaeity is something she was not so adept at; which was why the assistance of stimulants guided her down the liberal path of go-with-the-flow. She was too much of a strategic planner and control freak otherwise!

Not an ideal path to the destiny.....but then, as the rest of her life unfolding would show, she never took the easy way out.

'Chilled out' was only acquired for her through numbing the senses. Blinding the normal vision, so to speak. Danny was the same with his overactive mind and intellect. Classified as 'obsessive compulsive disorder and attention deficit disorder' they really were like siamese twins.

Always, *always* pushing boundaries.....without reprimand.

As they walked towards immigration and passport control, Danny got out the folder with booking info of the humble accommodation they had acquired. It was truly bare basic; but ample to *go native*. Its what a first time backpacker traveller does, after all. They knew it wouldn't be glamour.......but vowed to up the standard next time they came once some finances were sorted and their safety assured. Lovisa knew in her heart she should perhaps embrace this starting phase. She would do whatever it took in her life to acquire standards of excellence, so this was to be an example of seeing/experiencing 'what the rest of society does'.......arrogance and hedonism was another thing they shared. The fact is though, they were narcissists supreme, and far from fearful to admit it!

They knew it and owned it.

He in particular had been brought up with a 'silver spoon' of privelidge and abundance. Lovisa hadn't in any regard, but spent her life craving and striving for the same.

Likewise, they both abhorred any threats to compromising their creative integrity. Which meant that authority in all its regards and restrictions was the antichrist.....

Not that they were religious in any sense. Although she loved the mockery Madonna flaunted with her crucifixes as **jewellery** adornment vs faith. The woman was an icon she truly respected and understood. She wanted to buy a leather jacket in Italy that embodied that vision. For who could forget the 'like a virgin' showreel in the Vatican City; flesh-baring and gyrating from a grand gondola.....it was akin to saying *yeah, you're powerful and cool - a mighty prop for a power performance.'* Embellishment to behold.

She herself had been brought up christian; - both christened and confirmed in the manner of *high* church of England, which was a different, more elaborate strain. The pomp and ceremony was akin to catholic drama, with the swaying of the incense and whatnot, plus guilty repentance for all sins. She defied the religious aspect of the rituals, but the supremely orchestrated artistry it embodied deserved applause and respect in her view. Bravo. Encore.....it made the skin tingle, and invoked emotion, like a dramatic movie of intrigue and mystery. Or an opera.
Her mind drifted back once more to contemplate.
Religion....Respect. From afar..... The third person, say.
Dance from the rooftops, join in the choreographed joy, but don't swim in the sea of it and get caught up in the torrents of mind manipulation and propoganda.
   She was stronger than that.......
   It was all fantasy after all! And an escapism crutch for needy souls.
   Each individual religion has its very own book of stories. Fables, if you will.
But applause and bravo to the authors.... - What fun they must have had formulating the codes of belief for the hungry masses.....it must have brought them a tremendous sense of power to manipulate so many with their creative scrawl....
No, she viewed the world according to her life to date. Her own bespoke empirical evidence.
Proof. Solid.
God was me; and my body and brain embody the temple. Enough said.
** (It should be noted that this was the perceived opinion at the time of event....later, life awarded her tremendous respect for those worthy enough to maintain the faith and service to a higher being/god)*

"Once we're through the public punishment queues, we need to get a taxi to the hotel; - I don't think its too far out according to the travel agent " Danny pronounced, showing her the itinerary sheet. "First step will be a shower for me then an urgent 'shopping' mission for supplies.....I don't have much to last more than the night, and that will never do for our holiday!" - he was of course referring to the pot he had hidden in his hair.....a marvel of disguise. One that didn't scare them in the slightest right *now.* Nor the abundance of class A encased in the check in bags. Along with the bong, knives for cutting gear, papers and powders.
(**Time** would instil fears so rigid it would never leave her. But for now it was peace love and harmony.....)
Threats? Not a hint.

"While I'm on the search, you can go sus out our other 'sustenance' for the evening. By the time we get in and settled in it will be late afternoon - no time to waste! Find a nice cosy beachside warung. A sunset spliff *(joint)* will be the go...."
They were both impatiently enthusiastic to arrive. And sailed through unscathed or interrogated in any manner.
Sounds like a <u>miracle</u> now.
(Another airport era away from the current security smothered routine!) but one that can be relayed and reminisced upon as the 'good, liberal old days of travel'. Where privacy and respect remained intact. Imagine that!
And drug suppliers were in their heyday.....terrorists were a concept not intensely considered at this stage. That was more fantasy movie material.
Oh those were the days.....)

The taxi driver was an utter lunatic. Something she got used to about the place.
What was it with the roads; the seeming lack of rules, regulations or logic?
Thousands of crazy bike riders peppered the rough freeway like a game of dodgems. They neither looked before turning nor indicated half the time and drove within a centimeter of the vehicle in front.
Lovisa's heart was in her chest and pumping like crazy by the time she arrived at the cos - she needed a calming agent pronto!

They trudged up the stairs to the hotel room. She glanced skeptically at the 'puspasari beach cottages' brochure and its room rates. The options were:
 fan and cold shower; fan and hot shower; standard aircon and deluxe aircon......
Hmm...no porters in this establishment, dearest!
What do you expect for Aussie 10 dollars a night?!!
At that rate they were lucky to have a fridge, balcony and running water!
And just as well since they were a ball of sweat from the intense humidity of the place. But a welcome joy after the chill and pollution of the other land.
Heat.....bring it on.

They stuck to plans; he headed out on the 'shopping' mission, while she showered, unpacked, and got changed. They ended up at a funky warung right on the beachfront. She ordered.
He rolled.
(Spliffs while out; bongs back at the base. That was the modus operandi).
He had bought a unique bong-style pipe that he was somewhat proud of, and keen to christen later in their humble room.
The glorious sound of the rolling waves in the background was like a lullaby they would both seek to establish in their everyday existence evermore.
Must be near water.
Though big city babes, they knew this was what their souls would always crave for personal balance. Life was rocky enough.....

So the next few days continued - with beach tanning; ocean swims; meandering down jalans and gangs shopping; massages daily, and then sunset dining.
Could it get better ? This was paradise for the soul! Too much fun.

It was like a constant playground, and made you feel young and excited for life. No wonder so many gravitated to this island of magnetic equilibrium.

Although their accommodation was indeed bare basic, it mattered not as their days were spent out basking in the island on offer.

One day, fed up with the hideous murky coffee with sickly sweetened condensed milk provided at the complimentary hotel breakfast, they headed off to find a decent cup.

Discovering the 'Bali Padma Hotel', they sat down to a proper cappuccino at last in the vast exotic grounds. It was magnificent splendour compared with their room! They ventured over every day thereafter. She diary-wrote: '*a self-contained Bali in a dreamy resort.....So we've seen the best of both worlds now : poverty and paradise...*'

They even selected a fabulous outfit each for the next Sydney Mardi Gras!

 He : a sequined black and silver vest and she a bustierre of same; mini shorts and some wild jewelry. The vendor was CLEARLY a tranny; lady-boy. She took immense pleasure in serving and styling them and professed to try to get to the party herself. They were in hysterics. They loved these people - so engrossed in a fantasy world !!

Masks and mirrors abounded here....or '*topeng dan cermin*' in bahasa.

Their ceremonies were so colorfully vibrant and joyous as the processions marched through the streets, and the stories behind the unique fusion hindu-dharma religion were the most inspiring they had heard.... These people won the imaginative artistry hands down.

They could dance, sing, paint and draw. Creativity oozed through the blood of the balinese.

She wished to be trapped here and compelled to never return to the other toxic wasteland!......one day she promised herself. The whole island life not only appealed, it felt right for the body and the soul.

 Balance.

On the beach she became engrossed in learning the local bahasa.

She wanted to converse with the people; be emerged in every aspect of their joyous life. She got the basics down, but was hungry for more fluency. But not enough time...the days flew.

She learnt that in Indonesian schools, they are taught in Bahasa Indonesia from 9-12am, and then return to learn English from 6pm - 9pm. That equal time on both - she surmised it was a smart system considering it was a tourist island and the foreign dollar was what funded their existence! There is no bigger incentive to learn another tongue, than for the means of survival. And improving ones' quality of life experience...

 He would languidly lie beside her with his increasingly golden glow and sexy mane, and roll numbers on the sand, while she practiced her local speil. They were a great pair like that. She took over the comms department while he provided the stimulants required for any given time. Team effort. It was to form the pattern platform for the travels to follow in fact.

Yes, it was a sign of respect to adopt the native tongue. This she firmly believed. Folk who defied that in their travels were ignorant.

When in Rome.......
which was just around the corner next, incidentally.
A few random folk had stopped to take photos of them together. They didn't mind being caught on film; were more than comfortable with it. It was another issue that didn't exert panic and fear of exposure as later decades did.

They had upgraded the modelling portfolios just weeks before embarking on the trip, being muses for a most bizarre photographer who diversified their looks to another level.
Katrina was well known in the gay and alternate communities. She was akin to the Bukowski behind the lense! This decade was already one of liberation and free expression compared to others, but she was perhaps the most extreme they had encountered. She constantly broke all the rule parameters of acceptable; pushing boundaries and testing the subject matter to comply.
They had acquiesced to her often weird requests, and now had postcards, framed prints in galleries for sale, and unique portraits to prove it.
She began by dressing Lovisa up like a doll in her outrageous lycra catsuits and kinky attire at her inner city studio, before she had them model together in different circumstances at different venues and dates. They would get calls from her:
'I want you to come and play in a stable'....for example.
It added an extra 'flavor' to the usual array of looks from various other shoots and photographers. Europeans were also notoriously more flamboyant when it came to erotica and carnal desire. It was second nature to them and natural, not considered risqué or daring. These new looks may serve them well outside the more conservative country of origin.
The shock category was well and truly ticked here!
From erotic kissing on horseback, to naked bod shots with cats at their feet, she saw the intensity between them and fully grasped it in visuals. The extremes to which love will take you....
The very night before their flight they had to graciously decline her invitation to a 'VIP party at midnight - orgy under the stars'..

In any case, Lovisa regularly checked to see she had the book safe in her bag as fallback work plan in Europe. Nothing was certain in their month ahead....they had basic plans, but life can always throw you curve-balls! Always have a plan B.....mandatory.

Sad to leave this glorious spiritual island but it was a fabulous entree taster and a wonderful start to their adventure. She vowed to return.
Nevertheless, time to repack and head to the other side of the earth....globetrotter fashion.

It was the day just before departure that panic struck.......

They had packed up the majority of their limited possessions and secured the backpacks so they could enjoy the final time remaining on the paradise island of promise.

Reluctantly they wandered down to the beach again to soak in as much of the island life experience as possible before European big cities took hold.

Knowing to take minimal here for safety, they had a small backpack only with the wallets, documents and so forth, plus hotel card in case they got lost in their meanderings, or were misplaced by the crazy cabdrivers here and so forth.

Down on the beach Lovisa decided to succumb to the constant vendor harassment, and got her pedi done while she sat with diary and the bahasa notes. Danny was doing what he does best: assassinating the public. Which had them both in fits of laughter. It was at the expense of some of the hideous examples of Australian wildlife scattered on the beaches of Legian and Kuta.....my god they are a species all of their own.

She in particular felt somewhat embarrassed by them, and decided to claim her heritage as British, as per her *other* passport.

Going to her bag to retrieve it and prove a point, she suddenly got flustered and nervous. Both her passports, and his, had been kept all together in one folded carrier, but were nowhere to be found now. Entire bag contents strewn all over the sand before her in panic, she turned to him and bit her bottom lip. "Oh fuck.......I can't find the passports"......

He puffed on the joint slowly and glanced over at her with a relaxed 'they're in there somewhere hon - keep looking.....or did you hand them over to reception for safe-keeping again?" ....she knew she hadn't.

All vital items were collected the very day before and kept in the backpack to carry around with them at all times now before the flight. They didn't want to leave anything to chance, and they certainly didn't trust the room security. The doors didn't even lock properly!

It was a step up from a tent.

Retrieving all her stuff, she threw the bag over her shoulder and wailed "we've got to go back and report it to the staff! The cleaners must have taken them from our bag.....we can't go anywhere without them"....the woman painting her nails started to rant about her ruined artwork and outstanding 'bill', but was ignored entirely in the midst of this panic and drama.

They virtually ran back to the hotel, and while he went to the front desk to complain wildly about the 'lack of security and safety in this dump'.....she raced back to the room to see if it had slipped out of the bag or god knows - but cover all bases, nevertheless.

Easy to say don't panic when the most important vital items to do ANYTHING had suddenly disappeared.....

Freaking out, they searched all the hiding spots; like behind the tv ~(where Danny had stashed the mull and bong); at the back of cupboards and so forth. But nothing.

The room had obviously still not been made up, so she couldn't point the finger at cleaning staff today; perhaps it was the day before's?

'Lay every fucking item we own on the bed now to check more intensely' he yelled with an escalating degree of fury.

As they were frantically unpacking all travel bag contents and so forth, he picked up the pillows to toss out of the way and provide more viewing room, when there it

was. The passport pouch. Under the pillows! A smart thing to do for complete security while you sleep, but they felt foolish as hell now.
Pointing the finger each other in argument; their hearts racing and nerves on edge, they eventually wandered out again to try to decompress from the profound panic session.
Oh boy……
Self protection mode when traveling kicks in big time like an extra sense.
This was their first real episode of 'watch your back'….and the lesson had stuck.
With a lucky outcome.
Full awareness mandatory.
The rule number 1 in travel. And in life, lets face it…..
It had put a sour taste in their mouth for this place, but their minds were now intent on the next stop.

Rome.
The land of vespers and good coffee.
They were ready.

1/part 4:

ROMAN CANDLE

~burning both ends, like a true persistent explorer....

The very first taste of travel was far from a luxury bite by any means.

They had been ready for the next flight session that awaited them to a more far-flung destination, and the fact that it would be arduous and simple standard again.

No frills on flight numero uno……this they were aware of now, and starting to harness future plans of increased standard in all respects!

It proved to be bearable as they utilized the entertainment channel on offer, plus the alcoholic beverages to unwind their weary systems. So they coped once on board, but the prior airport pularva was a drain. The flight was delayed and they were forced to endure way too much frustratingly spent time in queues of pathetic public……oh the dreaded cattle-class standard travel! They both vowed to be business or first only from now on if they could wing it (no pun intended)

What they WEREN'T ready for, was the immediate attack of *Zingarelli* on arrival in Roma, like a blindsighted assault. Even though the 'lets go Europe' book had warned to look out for them.

Holding up cardboard shields, as they begged and swarmed, they had managed to swiftly unzip the backpack in the process and take some of the cash before she had managed to swat them away like flies. Under siege before one has time to process or prepare for the takeover. A scheme they had perfected.

Still tiny creatures and so young; this gypsy street life was evidently
trained from birth to rip off the innocent new arrivals as a means of income.
Being frazzled, frustrated and disorientated, fresh blood off every flight here
would be easy prey. Fruitful business assured!

Not a great deal of cash disappeared, but to Danny and Lovisa every cent
counted right now before more funds could be accrued and replenished. So
again, the blood boiled as they lost their cool with impatience for the stresses
of travel torment.

Desperate for a safe zone to camp for the next few days and catch up on
rest from escalating jet lag and post sun burn-out, they stopped for a coffee so
Lovisa could retrieve her researched info and attempt booking a place.

'Pensione Orlando' at 60,000 lira per night (around $60 at the
time),became the secured booking out of the list of maybes, and they headed
off to locate the said address. Sounded tremendously expensive when
compared to Bali, and probably not much different standard, but welcome to
European prices.

This would be a killer journey if they didn't have work prospects lined up
fast!

Even a coffee each was over $6; and cups so tiny they needed several to
feel the buzz. A traveller needed big pockets; that was startlingly obvious.

But tedium aside, the old history was visually evident here; it was like
being in another era. Cobbled streets; old brick buildings and evidence of
ancient ruins scattered everywhere. Exploring the ancient city by foot offered
a scenic tour in itself.

All the usual touristic sights were had - colosseum and the like. Gladiator
turf - it reminded her of her father thinking of the ancient roman history. It
was almost breathtaking compared to the mindnumbingly dull modern city
they had departed from.

There were lunatic drivers everywhere. It was a competition between Bali
and here on that score, and they were pushing even.

After nearly 8 hours of walking they reached the Pensione destination, and
were granted the key to their room on *piano 5*.

(Note to self: learn to pack LIGHT when visiting European cities; much lugging of possessions up flights of stairs always involved)

Diary notes on the cuisine here suggested extremely boring and overpriced…..as is often the way of 'big cities' which flourish off visitors.

One often has to venture out to the further terrains of the country to experience the authentic, memorable fare.

Even to receive the luxury of a SEAT to drink your coffee was almost double priced! Hence why you see folk drinking shots of coffee while standing at the serving counter in bars throughout.

After 2 nights here they decided to head off to FIRENZE by train. They took in the awe and splendor of the Uffizi gallery (which was shortly before it got bombed by the IRA) - all the glorious majestic works of the great Italian renaissance artists - including on vast ceilings, proved the dedication to the craft. She gazed up in marvel, considering that a fear of heights was not granted access in this hall of skyscaping creation! But all the Botticelli angels abounding ….. there was certainly no risk of her acquiring those proportions with the cuisine and tariffs here (!)

Moving on again, but realizing the trains had stopped the next night, they were forced to stay in the boring university town of BOLOGNA. Surely they would seek and find a fabulous pasta bolognese here at least?…alas no.

On inspection, the most appetizing meal visually turned out to be tripe, and neither did offal! So plain pizza with some tomato paste, a scattering of cheese and an onion ring had them most disappointed with the perception of Italian tasty fare.

Still unsatiated on the food front, they struck more travel tedium when forced to sleep overnight in a station terminal at Genova. This year celebrated the 500 anniversary of native son Christopher Columbus stumbling upon America. A boring detail they absorbed in the frustrating delay. She may have cared more had she the luxury of a 5 star suite to unwind her weary soul with creature comforts vs the concrete seat they were forced to recline on (!)

Entertainment prevailed though, as they witnessed a drunk derelict attempting to seize a woman's baggage, and being escorted to exit by police with batons.

They then got stuck on a train to Nice, as they crossed the border from Italy to France. Never had the concept of a warm shower appealed more!!

However the audio was already more melodious now...the Italian accent was lovely, but French took the gateau...

Even Danny who was not as linguistically inclined as Lovisa was more affiliated with the local tongue now, and vowed to learn the language of love. She felt it suited him- he would carry it off well. All style and arrogance iced. Her beloved chaos cake....

And as for the 'siesta' rituals abounding everywhere now, he had that down pat too. Sleeping in the day had always eluded her. A nocturnal beast at heart, even when drastically drained beyond belief.....but he on the other hand could quite easily take to the laid back European daily rituals.

She was saturating her devotion to art however, and on arrival they found accommodation, then went out to explore. The museum of modern and contemporary art didn't disappoint. A funky building with 4 marble towers connected by transparent footbridges housed a collection of over 400 French and American pieces dating from 1960 to the present, including works by her yanky faves Warhol and Lichtenstein.

Another train journey required to cross another border. This time heading to SPAIN - Barcelona was next on the menu. In a week they would have done Indonesia, Italy, France and Spain. The whole concept of commuting for under a few hours, and visiting new countries in the process was hard to fathom, and a luxury unheard of for folk from the remote land down under. Everything was so close and accessible here. It was like 'welcome to the rest of the world!' after being stuck so far away from it in one (albeit vast) country only. One virtually just needed their passport tattooed on and they were good to go.

Life certainly appealed more to Lovisa away from the original land. Everything was so different, new and exciting. And steeped in history and heritage. New flavors were always just around the corner or on your doorstep.

It expanded and invigorated the mind.

And tested it.....

She ascertained : she had no concrete ties to Australia. Other than family of course.

Finally seated on another delayed train, they gladly seized the comfortable seats; offloaded the cumbersome luggage and exhaled.

Alas, at passport and ticket inspection, they were fined £40 each for *accidentally* sitting in the first class cabin! The first distasteful dish of authority figure turmoil. The French inspector was muttering away in a tut-tut fashion as he tore out the fine sheets, and Lovisa felt compelled to belt the bastard.

Albeit not clearly marked as such, it was still a message in itself; despite being a massive hindrance to the funds tally. For when one is this physically drained and challenged from constant mobility, regular standard travel is for the dogs. Her natural gravitational pull was for more comfortable conditions…..she wasn't designed for the turbulence of mainstream life!

Exhausted, they finally took advantage of the expensively accessed luxury coach and crashed out completely for several hours with an alarm set for early arrival. More disaster struck when they awoke to discover they were *'on the wrong train'* !!
- During their slumber, the train had split apart, and typically, theirs was the half heading back to Rome!! So one step forward and ten back, they eventually re-boarded the right train to destination and set off again. Patience now dwindling in Danny and totally depleted in Lovisa. She was learning fast the advantages of being multi-lingual. Even the slightest misunderstanding costs precious time, cash, days and energy. All of which are vital.

It was more than a skill, it was a survival **tool**.

FROM PORT TO PORT….passports and portfolios.

Arriving in Barcelona at last, and desperate for a shower, they finally booked a basic *pensione,* with the annoying aspect yet again of being on an upper floor. The top one in fact.

The host was most hospitable however, and the location was perfectly situated with all conveniences close to hand. Prices much more reasonable in Spain too.

They were keen to feast on both the cultural surrounds and the local food.

Once settled they took in some of the sights, including a visit to the Museo Picasso.

As they continued to walk the streets, map in hand they came across the miraculous temple *'de segrada familia'* - church of the holy family. In fact all the other examples of Salvador Gaudi and his unique architecture were somewhat mind-blowing. Some of his buildings had the effect of a melting candle into the cement footpath below. It was very Dali-esque to Lovisa, whom she had always admired for his zany works.

Final excursion for day 1 was to the *'park guel'* also by Gaudi. Reminiscent of Alice in Wonderland, it was fantasy-like playground, which they ventured through like Hansel and Gretel.

So much more soul in all the countries they were sampling! True to her starsign, she truly was an archer at heart - born to roam the globe.

Realising the cash was dwindling quicker than they had anticipated, they acknowledged the importance of being more survival savvy in order to get to the desired location alone; let alone enjoy the journey on the way.

She reluctantly grabbed her portfolio and headed to some of the well-established modelling agencies here. An exhausting day had her trekking uphill for interviews at 'Salvador's, 'Francina's', 'Atlantic' and various others.

She was happily greeted and accepted on most of the books for the fact that her dimensions were a refreshing change in this town. The prevailing 'pear shape' of the Spanish women ensured that she was a stand out with comparatively petite hips in relation to her ample chest and small waist. They were admittedly exotic creatures here, but the derrière dimensions were more than ample in this breed!

She felt she held a better chance of a more swift opportunity with 'Salvador's of the group; since they were larger and broader in their castings (commercial modelling; catwalk; tv; video and catalogues) - not just the few and far between glossy glamour mags. The modelling industry is something requiring time and patience for castings and job opportunities. Cut-throat; competitive and prestigious it wasn't an over night access of cash......and besides the time was ticking fast here now while the funds were rapidly evaporating.

'El tiempo es Oro'.......time is money.

A few days passed with some scattered cattle-calls and interviews for her, but they decided to get mobile again nevertheless.

Next destination planning prevailed; it was time to get way south, and closer to the island of target.

Investigations proved that the most affordable way was by railing it to *Cadiz*, and then planning the Canary Island flight from there.

They secured *dos billette* for the worst train trip so far; their bags virtually splitting at the seams now from the constant lugging and tossing. Bored out of her brain she made use of the hours, learning the Spanish numbers to 20 and some basic phrases she might be able to utilize in the island as well.

They were both still hungry and tired, but their quest for cash and some stability superseded that now.

It was then another 50 minute train journey to *Jerez*, followed by a taxi to the small aeroporto.

A hairy small plane journey for less than 2 hours ensued, and finally had them touching down in *Playa de las Americas*, Tenerife at last.

Aside from presenting as ID for accomodation now, they were eager to lock the tired passports in a safe for a spell, unpack and settle at last.
With map and instructions in hand, and much nervous anticipation....
the next epic chapter commenced.

Ten reefs and sharing time.

~~~~~~
~~

(NB: 'Reefer' is slang for cannabis. It can refer to a joint, bowl, plant or sac of mull.)

Another island to call home…thankfully for as long as it took to accrue further travel funding. Time to unpack the torn bags; toss them and settle in an apartment. Sheer luxury after perpetual trains, planes and automobiles. Enough travel torment already…
Speaking of which, all the taxis here were limousines; the weather was always warm (being just north of Africa after all) and as a duty-free island, alcohol, cigarettes etc were half price! It was all looking quite attractive so far.
She really felt more at home in an island atmosphere vs a suburban cesspit; it didn't take a genius to figure that one instantly.
Big cities however, always lured for the sheer awe and anonymity they held. But for personal peace, a true island spirit was required for the bulk of existence. (To access a combination of the 2 would be an ideal formula in Lovisa's view)
Surviving and avoiding the tourist component was key - a constant influx of hedonism-seeking vacationers was the price to bear for paradise.
This one was perhaps more mountainous than Bali, but nevertheless another seismic zone to call home for a while. *'Volcanic'* was an apt description of their life in general!

She started to noticed the prevalence of German tourists here, amongst all the other nationalities, and began to reboot the brain back into some of her rusty Deutsch banter. Only a matter of days of travel, and already she had dabbled in Indonesian, French, and Spanish tongue. (Adaptable tastebuds are virtually mandatory for the eager traveller)
Aussies were a rare breed in these parts; they were instantly mistaken for South African wherever they went, which was most bizarre. She guessed the concept of somewhere so desperately far away eluded all these European folk. Not surprisingly! It was becoming startlingly evident that Australia was the most segregated island on the planet. Remote, and near nothing……. Literally the bowels of the earth. Who in their right mind would *willingly* consent to abiding there? Lovisa felt she had outgrown the country entirely and this was her very first taste of life external to it. Barren and boring
~~~~~~

as it was to her by this point. It would take a seriously attractive offer or deal to entice her back there now. *(That, of course, meant money. Hello)...*

They sent the convicts there; banished from their former lives.....kind of says it all really (!)

Danny was marginally more attached to the place, but they were both particularly aware of the prevailing 'tude within the country : *'the safest, best land to live'* etc....brainwashing and propaganda was on steroids there! (Doubtless many would disagree.....she knew that too. But her opinion <u>was per</u>sonal (to clarify) - and attained through experience. *No insults intended to patriots!)

Her emancipation felt so liberating; Lovisa knew in her heart, that all negative aspects aside (as ALL locations have them) - finding a way to create a new life away from the former hell was the future plan.

The sheet given to them over a month ago by their pommy skilled salesgirl Mystique - was so tired, worn and folded now, after constant referral to her hand written instructions for their immediate destiny and salvation. On a party night together back in their former flat, she had suggested: *"look, if you're ever stuck, I know an instant fund button strategy -* **Timeshare**"

Whenever they had felt uncertain and concerned for the vanishing finances available, this had been their power tool. Knowledge is strength after all, and they had been issued with as much as was possible to get established on the island of potential with this single sheet of paper.

Mon was a salesgirl, actress and model, - and most confident at that, so a pretty attention demanding vision! She had given them an example of her rendition in the duplicitous game of timeshare scams at their apartment weeks ago, and at the time it was hysterical to witness, and appeared a tremendously fun way to earn a quid!

Now, the pressure to succeed was not only a goal but a serious NEED....it was the only way to stay away from the former land, and without cash, immediate return would be imminent.

So, it was with much trepidation and anxious expectation that they took the phone number she had given them and sought contact.

What if it didn't work??!! What then?

Her only fallback plan then would be work in the mother land - her British passport gave her ticket to residence and employment. But she didn't want to reach that road yet.

She decided she would consider herself British from now on - it opened up a much vaster life in all regards. Her father's British heritage would be her salvation one day; she felt it in her bones and her heart. Dual nationality was a bonus not to be sneered at. *(*These were of course pre-Brexit days!)*

In any case, pressure to **survive** was a constant theme in her life of travels from then on. For there is no other greater incentive to seek, learn and conquer with victory.

They had succeeded at last in contacting the manager of the grand 'Tenerife Royal Gardens' and arranged to meet him after his morning meeting with the crew of scammers he herded.

The huge foyer of the resort was definitely 5star grand. They looked on in awe and could virtually smell the money here; - in all its denominations!

Name-dropping Mysty right off the bat had them thrown work shirts immediately; and hands were shaken in a welcome gesture to commence their new vocation. She was evidently somewhat part of the family crew here, and well liked amongst the other OPC staff.

Travis was a jovial rotund little pom from Essex, and he laughed at the memory..."Oh fook, how is the crazy bitch? I didn't think she'd ever go back to a normal life, to be fair!....she had it well sorted here! C'oom on then, lets get you acquainted with the master troops, and then take you to your new 'office' tomorrow morn to start....."

The **'O.P.C'** - or 'outside personal contact' was a unique breed of salesman, whose skills involved the use of a blend of convincing verbal scams, theatrical antics and award winning performances while jumping in and out of taxis to escort the victims to the tour of deceit.
Their initial opinion was: years of promotional/acting work would set them in good stead! It's how Lovisa had met Mysty after all, through agency work.

They all had their own 'patch' to pitch from; - a particular street corner or location that was 'their turf' so to speak; - to seek and destroy the naive touristic prey.
For the rest of this first day, they were to observe the inspiring performance tactics of the most successful sales guys, and then apply their own unique script the following one, at the allocated spot that was to be theirs now. Learn the ropes and the lingo and create your own craft from that. Think auditioning for Nida....
Oh but they were so convincing at the craft and made it look so graceful and easy!
One of the Scandi guys, Greg, who had been there since a youth and conquered the market here, was stationed right outside the resort. Prime position. He had earnt it.
Tall, handsome, confident; golden hair, blue eyes and dressed impeccably in stylish 'resort wear' he was a traffic stopper before he even opened his mouth. He literally shone. Like a star himself. A sight to behold.
He represented the 'golden opportunity' investment he was pitching to perfection.
Like most things in life, having an appeasing veneer always made the journey more destined for success....Aim for alpha.
Masks and Mirrors. Always.....
He was just so damn good and a sure thing in this game, that a day would have him recruiting and ushering in literally hundreds of vacationers to complete the system.
The proof was in the pudding in this numbers game. And his scores were indeed consistently epic. There was no better example to aspire to emulate.
Danny and Lovisa watched in awe and learned; so caught up in his spell and the evident income he acquired - eager as punch to replicate his talent.
They came to realize that from her time on the island; decadent lifestyle and reputation, Mysty herself had been somewhat in the same league.

Upon 'blagging' (or conning) the victims - (cue leaps and bounds in the air with excitement, that may involve the use of other languages for the emphasis):
'you have won the GRAND PRIZE for gods sake!' - or *'sie haben die drei sterner gewonnen!!').* After being swept up in the contagious theatrical excitement, they were then to be 'qualified' (this being the tough bit, as the list of requirement boxes the couple is obliged to tick to be eligible for timeshare purchase is a challenge, and they

often require further incentives to fabricate the facts (read lie) in order to 'pass the test for their prize' at the end)
Qualification was required for the O.P.C to be paid.
Simple.
It is akin to any form of insurance, no less.....designed to take your money only, not give back (!) They make it virtually impossible to claim a payout without a battle on the hands. The only chance of success is through deception! Truth **NEVER** pays!!
For example they must be married- (usually done by the OPC in the taxi on the way to the resort!) ; within certain age parameters (which usually entails giving them a new birthdate to memorize) ; have a certain income (cue new profession and annual salary) - and so forth. Upon agreeing to 'embellish' the facts facts to suit (since that was virtually *always* the situation) they were convinced of the imminent victory that awaited them, and were swiftly ushered into a taxi urgently to 'collect their prize' (before having time to think logically and change their mind).....

The OPC accompanies them to the resort in the limousine, and it is now impressed upon them most importantly at this stage that if they didn't stay for the whole duration of their *'brief meeting and tour'* at the resort, they would disqualify themselves from the reward that awaits (!) They are not in any way obliged to invest - but simply play the game of interest to exit with the goods! Patience is insisted upon, but knowing that they had 'won' made it an irresistible no-brainer.
(In short, you had to master the art of looking the genuine deal while faking it wildly.
Anyone who thinks this sounds like an easy task can think again.....)

In addition to that, **if** it was ascertained on the tour that lies had been told to complete qualification, (which was often the case), then the OPC responsible for recruiting them was fined heavily. A pay packet decimator! So the whole game was one of wit; manipulation talent; risky fact-fiddling and nervous tension. In short, a lunatics' domain! Most folk just wouldn't be able to handle the heat; preferring a less profitable albeit safe and stable income.
But....never ones to take the easy path. The concept of discomfort and uncertainty was familiar terrain to these two.
An antithesis of the norm. 'The new security.'
Guaranteed safety nets almost made them anxious.
Anomolies to be sure; that had found their kindred spirit in each others' twisted logic and idiosyncrasies.
Here, there were no guarantees. Like gambling. You win some you lose some.
As an obvious result, the personalities of the successful OPCs were also wild and erratic. The social scene here was something else. Never a dull moment, thats for sure.
It is a dangerous game, but like all others, the financial rewards existed for the courageous and convincing.

Upon arrival however, the snared victims were taken on the mystery 'tour' that entailed them being submerged in the depths of property salesman *hell* for the rest of the day, in a quest to receive the elusive prize. At the completion, they were tired; frustrated, and had often 'signed themselves up' in resignation, for the unaffordable deal on offer (when the small print is observed) - simply to stop the relentless pitch and get on with their damn holiday!!

And the grand prize? A toy watch and a logo t-shirt.

If they completed the tour, your commission was granted. They were considered a 'qualified 'up'. The OPC would then be paid accordingly.

Every day would require keeping the eyes open for re-emerging couples who come back to give you an earful for the torture they had endured the day before.

Their starter rates for the job were $140 per couple, and a lot more for Germans and the like. Not to be sneered at for the penniess traveler!

Timeshare........anyone who knows of, or has heard of the term knows to AVOID IT LIKE THE PLAGUE!!

The OPCs were sheer con-men; the sales folk guiding the tours were complete pressure merchants and deceitful lyers, and the final promised awards for loss of their precious holiday time was nothing but a sheer *waste of* time, energy, cash and patience.

It was one of the biggest legal scams they had witnessed.....and these two were no strangers to that world.

And yet, it was what the island was financially run by. Didn't the word get around that this was the trap? Evidently not, as fresh meat arrived in droves constantly.

Ah, the magical powers of a 'free gift' and 'first prize'.....everyone WANTS to believe that life does occasionally grant them. And in lazy 'holiday brain' these people were most susceptible, as the normal defence mechanisms were down. They had left their former lives of stress - even for only a week or less, and they didn't want to be on the defensive. It was time out. They were on vacation for god's sake!! Fantasy and fun prevails!

But anyone who's ever done a great lunch, knows that they are never, ever free......

The whole place here reaked of 'mafia'.....there were notorious stories of all sorts of gangsta activity; murders; mysteries and evil. Thats what comes with the 'money' turf.

As in most avenues of life, they were to discover as their lives unfolded.

"The timeshare trade, which sees hordes of luckless British tourists accosted by touts and often persuaded to part with money they can ill-afford, has become a multi-million pound business - and a magnet for the criminal underworld"

- This from the *'mirror'* reflected dozens of other articles similar. And yet, it never deterred!

This was big business. It was a timeshare island, and order had to be in place.

One such character, as legend had it, was the 'security service' for the resorts all-important cash takings. If the 'money makers' were taking days off work, or playing up in any fashion, (which of course was regular, since money breeds power and arrogance, and decadence gets out of control)....he would hang them upside down over their balconies in threatening warning of their shenanigans.

There would be murmurs of *"Dennis cracked his knuckles last night; there are a few in hospital now"*....

He was never actually seen.... Just infamous for his tasks of torment. Rumour had it he had left for Portugal, but there was always another heavy waiting in the wings, as another article confirmed:

It told of the murder of Andrew Winder- another timeshare tout baron, who was shot dead in a Tenerife apartment complex.

"Last Sunday, a small corner was lifted on the violent and secretive world of timeshare touting in the Canary Islands. It is a world where rewards are great for the ruthless and where Winder, a 17- stone British bodybuilder, was rising to the top using methods closer to racketeering and gangland feuding than estate agency.'......

He arrived from Darlington, where he had started a modelling agency with his topless model girlfriend.

Winder - who controlled groups of the timeshare sales folk (OPC's) had money in abundance; a Porshe with a number plate BAD and a reputation to match.

'One man returned to Britain for plastic surgery after a run-in with him......three other men were stabbed and one jumped from a balcony to escape from him'

A freelance journalist investigating the touts last year was knocked unconscious by a large Jamaican sporting a knuckleduster as he left a bar and spent 5 days in hospital. Another who tangled with the timeshare criminals was beaten about the head with a baseball bat.

'Sources say Winder and co wanted control of southern Tenerife. The area had previously been the fiefdom of Dennis Laws, renowned for biting off one rival's nose and hanging people from balconies by an ankle'

The most inspiring thing they witnessed in their quest for timeshare tyrant employment, was the advantageous tool of multi-lingual salesfolk......they had the market covered, and their quality of life plus bank balances proved it. The luxury cars and villas of villains....

For a start she noticed *Rolexes* on the majority, as they waved their hands; ushered folk to collect their prize and hugged the winners with such genuine conviction. Was there any greater indication of having 'made it' ?! It was a status symbol. One she in particular aimed to acquire for herself one day.....

Usually Scandies, these guys would swiftly ascertain the nationality of their prey, and switch from one language to the next with fluency. It was like a performance song, and a marvelous sight to behold! Sheer inspiration to aim to be up there on the linguistically flexible front. Particularly since all the other nationalities trumped the English for commission bonuses........in short, if you speak another language, your daily salary doubles. Forget the plain English; - the other tongues were where it was at here......the English may run the island, but for the most part, the European foreigners funded their income.

Mystique had managed to focus entirely on the English, but she was an anomaly to be sure.
Tenerife was to the poms, as Bali was to the Aussies.
Sadly, they tended to take the worst varieties of each species into their paradise trap.

So while the privelidged few were shopping in Monte Carlo; lazing on their yacht in Cannes or Menorca; luxuriating in their chateaus in France or indulging at their vineyards in France and Italy, the budget conscious English were raiding the tourist island here. With no respite.

Causing havoc while partying themselves silly; - recklessly 'boozing and shagging' the nights away.

It cast a somewhat hideous light on the reputation of the British abroad. But then, the Aussies in Bali took it to a whole new level……

Suffice to say, Lovisa had learnt to profess herself 'Australian in Tenerife', and 'British in Bali' to avoid the stigmas attached!

And so they left the first day exhausted by the absorption of information and assimilating the *facts vs the fiction* that was on display.

It was akin to a fantasy world with this caper; - which makes perfect sense when one considers that the *prey* were on their holiday, and the theme of existence here was 'escapism' ! Like most islands she supposed.

However, to get into the role required endurance on a personality and patience front…..not to mention the fact that it was outdoors in the elements here. A far cry on an energy quota when compared to a desk job in an air conditioned office! Both physically and mentally.

They were eager to start, but also nervous for the pressures of success.

Even the English language had variations to adapt to……

The uniform required shorts, a logo polo shirt or t shirt (issued by the resort), cap and trainers or *thongs*.

(Or as the pommys call them: ***flip-flops***. To them, it sounded like you were saying g-string..- a ridiculous image under the circumstances!)

In some ways it was like a foreign language; albeit still under the term 'English'. Obviously the Aussies had their own crafted version of the real language.

What the hell was a 'duvet'? -she wondered the first time she heard it mentioned. She realized they meant 'doona' - but nobody here understood or had heard that word ever. The slang of both countries must have made 'street talk' a serious challenge to anyone learning text-book English!

But then, the real language vs the abbreviated and 'spoken' one that evolves, are a totally different issue in virtually every language that exists. Theory vs practice.

(She marveled at the fact that the balinese had hundreds of idiolects specific to each village; ie a crafted version of 'Bahasa Bali' that only those in each location understood! Stick to the globally recognized Bahasa *Indonesia* she thought. Learning village speak would be a total mind-fuck!)

The next day, they donned the afore-mentioned attire and headed in to meet Trav for the location drop-off to start the hunt.

The plan was to be hauling tourists back in to the resort by taxi to go on tour, so they assumed they would always be in range of the Royal Gardens hotel.

'C'umon then, lets get you bloody Ozzies out of the pubs and into the workforce!'….

he herded them both into a limo with him and directed the driver to their designated pitching post.

As luck had it, it was a short walk from the apartment they had seized for the first 2 weeks so the morning trek to work would be easy.

Bonus.

Travis handed them a pile of cards each.

"Here's your weapon - as you noticed yesterday with the barons of the trade. They never leave home without these; you need to start thinking the same. Time is money; money is numbers; this is a numbers game. Get with the program kids"…..

With a *"Best of luck - do us proud, see you back there soon eh!"* he turned around and headed back in the luxury car.

They glanced down at the cards. **'Scratch and Match'** or in German *'Kratzen und unpassen'*. In French: *Grattez & Gagnez'*.

literally - scratch three boxes with a coin, and if they match - you've won! It was always the 3-star prize by the way. First prize!

This was either £1000; a gold watch or a video camera.

They stood on the corner to psych themselves for action. She was reminded of the times in promotional work that she had to dress up in some costume to hand out samples etc, and the fact that one could not be self conscious or shy to succeed. As the English would say, it could render one feeling like a 'total git' at times……but it was all showmanship.

Time to put the mask on.

It looked like enough cards for the first few hours, they figured they would have to restock again later in the day. There were plenty of tourists about, surely this lot would diminish fast. Anything for free right?! The fact was, actually getting someone to *take* the card, *listen* **and** comply was the work.

It took what felt like an eternity to get rid of 10 of the damn things with the spiel attached. 'At the end of the day' (as the poms say) - This was **not** a game!

They toiled away at their pitching post for the first week with several hopeful victims snared. Roughly two thirds succeeded in granting them rewards. But the challenge was indeed evident. People who make a task look easy are simply doyens at what they do!

One of the couples who didn't qualify for the tour, returned to see them anyway and bought the pair a huge new travel bag to replace their trashed one out of sympathy! A simple gesture, but indeed the most useful gift they could receive.

From a paying perspective, it wasn't rocket science…..the other nationalities held more weight than the English. But it required a lingual diversity.

Lovisa decided to focus on the GERMANS, and started to reboot the rusty Deutsch tongue learnt at school. But practice makes perfect….You don't use it you lose it! It was like muscle memory. But one can resume with perseverance.

She was complemented on her pronunciation and her confidence improved. Nerves tend to evaporate when one counts the extra cash in hand….(!).

But no substantial money gain appears without a degree of challenge. And discomfort. Plus often risk.

Adrenalin….

And with exercising new or alternate languages it was like being on stage and open to criticism....or self doubt.

But she had been shuffled around schools by her parents in the quest for a strong language department so she was used to feeling unsettled. It came more natural to her than most as a result......a strength she had utilised as a survival tool.

It was her opinion that other languages required 'practiced time in the field' and with the natives. None of this 'text book' hermit crap! No. Real life conversations differed quite substantially from the classic manuals.

You literally have to disregard the self-flagellation issues. Perfectionists have to stumble and fall before they can walk the talk with ease. But reward is there for those who persist. Her experience was that it opened doors; both made and saved money....incentive enough right there.

When their first fortnight was nearly up, which seemed like an eternity with so many hours in performance-playing mode, so too was their first accommodation deadline. It was time to reconsider a new abode that was more long term and affordable.

One of the larrikin OPCs who was another gift of the gab merchant, mentioned renting a room to them at her villa. Karina's enthusiasm was most contagious, like all the pomms that had lasted the distance in this seedy salesman pit. However trust was an issue to be questioned here; it was so dog eat dog that what you see is so often **not** what you get. So their skepticism was being honed for absolutely everyone now. Especially one such as her who pulled in £1000 a week from the mere skill of her convincing banter!

"Oh, you won't find better, I promise you! Its like you really are living on a beautiful island, away from all this toxic tourist shit....in this game you need a retreat to reboot, right!

I'm at a tiny fishing village called 'la caleta' right on the water and so private and exotic. Best kept secret here, I swear. Come see for yourselves! Im driving there after work. Ill take you there! I'll even drive you back as I'm into night pitching now to supplement the income, so ill be your chauffeur service".....sounded too good to be true.

But delightfully enticing nonetheless!

Realising now that fantasy and fiction here were an intertwined concept, they knew they would have to see it to ascertain the truth for themselves. But with the opportunity and transport landing in their lap, and the distinct wish for it to be true, it was an irresistible offer they couldn't refuse. And they were on a time limit for new digs anyway. Naturally they wanted a rewarding place to return to (or *'right pukka gaff'* as the brits would often say) after hours of stress and toil. Life here would just be too tedious if there were no rewards of a degree of luxury to call the home base.

The travel distance was considerable; 30 mins from the pitching post as opposed to the convenient walk each morning they had been doing. However, on arrival, it was love at first sight. They forgave all its misgivings. And they knew that anywhere else would fade in comparison. It was the most gorgeous location and address they had ever been to and the villa itself was clean, spacious and welcoming.

The sound of the ocean lapping against the rocks was like a lullaby; a soothing sound to behold. They felt all the work worries and cares of the world drip off them and transform into a sense of calmness. It was a far cry from the city apartment they had initially rented here. So private, remote and exquisite.

To add to the appeal, she sat on the porch outside with them rolling spliffs which she handed around as they gazed out at the bluest ocean. It was the first smoke they had done in 2 weeks now; - a record for them! And a sign of how focused they were on mere survival vs the usual lifestyle luxuries (*read habits*).

Nirvana. They could get used to this.....it made it all worthwhile.

That was it. Done deal! They went back into town with her to repack their stuff and plan the move almost immediately once their pay packet was granted.

She was happy to have the empty room occupied also and as she dropped them back in town declared: "*So roomies, I'll pick you up after work friday, yeah? Grab your stuff and you can settle in immediately. Ill be cooking a 'welcome' English roast with all the trimmings that night and some great wine to boot. Its been a grand week*".....

Sorted then.

It looked like they really would last the distance they had hoped to working on the island. Albeit still a daily challenge, the initial threat of immediate return had now disintigrated. They knew they would do what it took to make it all work out.

At least with such minimal possessions, moving and settling was a swift task.....

Such a picturesque little quiet village here. Sleepy seaside town.

A massive contrast from the hectic pitching post and tourist strip in town. It was like 'going on holiday' after work was finished each day! They even went for a few ocean dips on the rocky shores - treating it like a private mini beach sanctuary.

From the sandy shore, they could look up at their white cottage with its jolly vibrant flower embellishments on the porch. They had planted a rainbow of gorgeous blooms in pots outside the windows, and against the crisp white structure it added a harmonious glow, and was the prettiest sight. So calm.

Lovisa was usually diary or list-writing and planning; - her bizarre need to document epic moments in her life eluded even herself, but she knew one day she would look back on events and be reminded of her crazy life. Reminisce...as a writer does...

Danny would meanwhile write a few letters home to his folks and the guy minding the city apartment. "*I better tell him to stay the full 6 months now, as we have no intention of returning before then! Its the best deal for what he gets there, and he only has to feed the cat*"....

It had been a mere miracle to find a pet minder for his pedigree feline so last minute, but where there's a will, there's always a way. Most were so smitten by the vast city view from the balcony that they ignored the tiny confines of the place.

She personally didn't do pets. Or people most of the time! Just a hindrance and time waster in her books. She was a bit of a cat herself! Always preferring to remain a loner.

It was testament to the way she had felt about Danny. They preferred to spend more time in union than apart or with others.

If she had been single, without her loverboy? Her idea of the perfect life would be to live somewhere remote such as this, and write a book by the ocean breeze....

The evenings get quite cool; particularly here near the mountains. Never imagined we'd be getting out the winter jumpers packed for Europe! We walk to a nearby basic convenience store often, and Danny slips items up his oversized sleeve.....it halves our supply costs, and provides a degree of 'taxing triumph!' Watch the pesetas and the global ambitions shall increase....

In daily diary updates she would summarise the bonuses. Every little bit helped they supposed....

The days passed, with sunset unwinding at the quaint village retreat.

The first situation of concern however occurred when Karina was too busy working (or caught up in a pub somewhere more like)- to drive them home, and they had to resort to the **bus** to La Caleta. A more scenic journey perhaps....

It proved to be the most terrifying, death-defying ride they had ever experienced:

Winding hair-pin turns all the way down the steep mountain had the bus virtually fish-tailing along for over 20 mins. They were trapped with a kamikaze speed freak driver with zero safety sense and perhaps even devoid of a license at the helm. Lovisa virtually slid under the seat in the fetal position with eyes closed, convinced death was imminent and feeling her heart pounding wildly in her chest. Faaaaaaaaaaark.....

'How did they die'?....'they were propelled off the edge of a mountain near the fishing village they inhabited, by a lunatic suicidal bus driver...'

Danny feigned bravery, but she could see he was tortured with concern also.

On arrival, (a sheer miracle they were alive to tell the tale)...while shaking like a leaf with jangled nerves, Lovisa professed adamantly: 'I will NEVER get back in a bus here *ever*......if 'Rine doesn't drive us home, we're walking! End of discussion"...

Explaining it later that afternoon with the flatmate, Karina laughed while pouring them each a drink and announced : "Bollocks! it will take you 40 mins every day!"

Lovisa hardly cared. She was a daredevil at heart but this was pure suicide. Too much exciting life awaited to experience yet.

It would turn out to be a blessing in disguise: the walking was good exercise to decompress from the days' adrenalin load, and very quickly, they both acquired golden island glows.

Lovisa's hair was already sun bleached super white blonde naturally; stripped of its former auburn tint. They were starting to look and feel fab and they knew it.

To compound that, they had been 'clean' now for over 3 weeks......somewhat of a record for the pair. There was a definite degree of self-satisfaction at the realization. And such clarity. They had achieved it without trying.

Amazing how adrenaline and survival instincts supersede cravings and addiction!.....if you wanted to kick a habit in the bud, best to immerse yourself in more immediate concerns....like where the next peseta is coming from; how you will pay the rent and put food on the table.....guaranteed detox success !

Alas, it was short lived. For the usual reason. Influence and company.....

Karina proved to be a pommy pot head through and through. It was readily available at all times here now, and to add to the appeal, she had started dating a somewhat older drug lord on the island. So they were like kids in a candy store.

And the old habits kicked in once again.

The diary never lies.....

K was still buzzing this morn, and greeted us with a 'hash brown brekkie' (the smoked variety) compliments her party partner of passion - S. (Sonny) Joints and herbal tea made for a very unproductive, lazy day at work.....plans for class A parties on the pier may well ensue this weekend!.....

Like all underground style figures, Sonny always had some fascinating story to relay. You could rely on him for entertainment shows to accompany the stimulants he issued. He bounded in one afternoon with the grand entrance of:

"new shipments ahoy me darlings.....its snowing in la caleta-land!"....he commenced chopping up and sorting lines along the kitchen bench for them.

"So these recent gangs they speak of have been raising money by forging credit cards and organising fraudulent time-share deals - mostly with the brits and krauts. Check out the paper":

He underlined the quote from the mirror front page headlines:

And where there are gangs, there are drug cartels - cocaine is rife and the formerly idyllic island has earned the unwelcome nickname "the white island" among partygoers.

Sonny took full advantage of Karina's 'hospitality' (and physical offerings) - taking up camp in her bedroom most nights, after evenings filled with charlie-fueled meetings or messy speed-induced banter. One thing was for sure in Karina's kitchen: you may not be able to find a utensil or an appliance, but you could ALWAYS locate plastic straws.

And if outside; too delirious or lazy to get to the drawers there, then a rolled paseta note would do.

Their proud progress on the *clean* front was decimated entirely here at this deceptively tranquil village retreat. It seemed ironic that the city chaos had kept them pristine, and yet here in sleepy-ville they were anything but.

Danny was back into the bong. With a vengeance. The hardened former ways ensued and left them in a haze of delirium. And he introduced it to many a former spliff smoking foreigner; who became instant fans and converts.

Even the diary tone illustrated this:

We are collecting a pre-booked German up tomorrow morning.
Supposedly.....
***IF** they show. Which may or may not fulfil the rent owing.*
But experience has taught us : 'no counting your cones before they are packed!'
We should stay longer today but we are both still wasted from last night....Sonny is away a few days, and Dan needs to source some new gear. Priority.

On several other occasions when Sonny was busy with 'the biz' Karina would go out and pick herself up another 'shagging partner' behind his back.

The sounds from her room that emanated in the early hours were hideous; yet she would deny it with such conviction.

There was always a new occupant/bed partner if Sonny was detained in his nocturnal trade. It was the classic example of how so many people really can't stand their own company. But in her case, they understood, since she had become unbearable!

Danny and Lovisa reassessed now. Their fondness for her turned to repulsion. They were better than this.....

The walls were crowding in.

Her company was becoming overbearing and toxic and it became evident her initial appeal was just a mask for the selfish moronic nympho she really was.

Her lies steamrolled, and she forgot what piece of verbal garbage she had relayed to whom; contradicting herself constantly. How she functioned while in perpetual hangover and mess-mode was a mystery. But so many seemed to here.

Never trust a good salesman......(!)

So time again to seek an alternate habitation box.
As a final farewell gesture, they went on an exploration of the surrounding rock mountains to view la Caleta from further afar. From this angle they got to photograph the village in all its scenic splendor.
Such a shame it had been tainted by others. You open your door to external influence of any kind and poison arrives with it. Literally.....
that is life, and why so many folk prefer to remain completely alone. Understandably so!
Lovisa concurred with that view with much conviction now. For health and contentment it was virtually vital. People were toxic creatures.

'You're a strange guy. You stay alone a lot, don't you?'
Yes
'Whats wrong?'
I was sick long before that morning you met me.
'Are you sick now?'
No...
'Then what's wrong?'
I don't like people.
'Do you think that's right?'
Probably not.
'Have you ever been in love?'
Love is for real people.
'You sound real'
I dislike real people.
'You dislike them?'
I hate them....

Bukowski. Factotum.

Lovely as the islands secret corner had been on a vista front, it was definitely time to move back to the heart of Playa de las Americas again. Where all the action was. And the money to be made.
If they could resume their privacy alone, it would be a godsend.
The arguments between them were the first indicator of trouble in paradise.
The dynamics were changing as a result of this toxic addition, and they realised they needed to live alone together again; albeit the extra pressure it would exert on them fund-wise. But the alternative was unbearable now.
Karina and her entourage were poisoning their relationship.

'For each Joan of Arc there is a Hitler perched at the other end of the teeter totter.
The old story of good and evil'
Buk. Factotum.

Finding they could stand it no longer, they left earlier than the end of the month; a simple note left on the kitchen bench for the erratic fellow occupant:
'Dear Karina,
we have decided to move closer to work.
Thanks for everything.
Can you please reimburse us the rent we had paid for the next 3 weeks; we will need that urgently for bond.'
Sincerely,
D & L xx

They knew it was risky and perhaps a loss of precious pesetas, but their sanity and relationship was worth more! Trapped with a Tenerife tramp was far from ideal or conducive to harmony.
Naturally with her it would be lots of promises and *'mañana polo mañana'* attitude to ensue on that front. It was definitely siesta land here; particularly when it came to 'owed' money…..there was never any urgency on debts.

So goodbye village, hello apartment. Familiarity stakes.
There was an intermittent rental for a fortnight in one immediately, as they sought the ideal next move. They were in a hurry to change location, so no time to waste. They knew this one would be temporary, although they nearly reconsidered as it was a fabulous block. The location was ideal and convenient, the amenities were perfect (pool, sauna, laundry, cafe, bus stop out front) etc.
However, there was a price to pay for their sudden shuffle.
She remembered feeling uncertain on one of the first nights there. They were watching 'Midnight Express' on video; a haunting movie she had watched countless times before. Although a disturbing film, she felt another sensation. Nervous. In her core. Her gut indicated there was danger afoot. That internal feeling you get at times just before impending disaster.
The inevitable happened that very night as they slept. They got broken into and all their precious belongings (limited, but important nevertheless) were seized. Bags, jewellery, books, some cash and various other items went. The scary fact was it all lay at the foot of the bed they were asleep in! Too close for comfort.
It was on the ground floor. Accessible to danger; insecure from easy invasion.
(Never again…..apartments high up only! Pref with 24/7 security)…
The police reports and multiple trips to the station were tedious and fruitless. The chances of catching a perpetrator here was pretty much nil!
So learn, start again and move on. A theme on replay in life it started to seem.
At times like these, the concept of secure monotony seems almost a privelidged pain.

And so yet another hunt for safe domain commenced.
High up though….and they loved to get high!

Their previous apartment had been high and the view and safety factor proved a blessing.

They found one right in the heart of work terrain for convenience, and yet so many floors up that they sort of viewed the busy life around from a birds' eye vantage point. They could walk everywhere, and yet when the balcony door was closed, they felt far away from the peripheral action and devoid of disturbance.

A smashing panoramic view of the ocean extended from the sizeable porch. And below, the huge pool was constantly scattered with the usual touristic array of : golden Scandies; tanned Italians and Europeans; gold embellished *'frogs'* and white *'roast beef'*.

Nations unite.

As Aussies they were almost like some exotic foreign species from another planet, that instilled curiosity!

A destination so god-damn far away was a mysterious land. Most considered a flight more than 2 hours to anywhere a mega distance and an insane concept! They were globally advantaged; used to having it all easily accessible. Doorstep stuff.

The world seemed to come together here and converge, with the common denominator being sun and party-seeker escapism. Wallets always opened on vacation too. Normal discipline disintegrates. In all regards.

Holiday destinations can hence become notoriously messy for those who actually attempt to live there with any sense of sanity maintenance in mind. Expats beware….!

Aside from hermit-like activity, one is exposed to the evils that abound virtually without even trying. In this gangster-run industry, like most others, it was virtually impossible to protect yourself from the exposure.

Lovisa tended to shun all media. No news was good news in her eyes! It was all toxic stuff.

Danny, contrastly read everything to do with media he could get his hands on.

He sat scanning local rags on the porch one afternoon as she put costumes out to dry.

"Man, its gruesome press for the tourist trade - and our pay packet….Fuck, there's been a double murder of this wealthy couple here who made their millions running a highly lucrative timeshare business. It is believed hitmen were hired by rival operators"

He puffed on his joint; inhaled deeply and read on:

"Although this is the most likely murder suspect, Albanian, Kosovan and Romanian gangsters have been moving into the Canary Islands. At first they controlled the drugs, cheap labour and organised begging rackets, but have been trying to move into property and timeshare. They are also possible culprits"

The fact that this was all happening so close to home was a symptom of the money potential here. Murder is always a risk with ridiculous amounts of money.

"She was bludgeoned to death in her Mercedes, and he was slumped with his throat cut in the back of his new Porsche Cayenne. Oh, and he had been shot in the head. Jesus….

Ha! - The Morrisons had been working for the notorious timeshare conman John "Goldfinger" Pullman and still operated from an office he used.

Pullman - who earned his nickname after being cleared of helping to dispose of gold from the £26m Brink's-Mat robbery at Heathrow airport in 1983 - is living in Essex after being released last year halfway through an eight-year prison sentence for a £30m

fraud in which bogus timeshares were sold to 16,000 victims. The Morrisons were still in touch with him and had visited him in Britain to discuss the timeshare business"….
Danny shook his head and glanced up at her.
"Oh man…..the cats out of the bag - you kinda dread the new arrivals getting their hands on this blurb"….
She always rolled her eyes at the revelations he delivered regularly regarding world **news**. It was all usually so drastically out of their control, why ignite anxiety over it? There were always more pressing issues on your own doorstep to contend with in life. Best not to overload the system!
But this time Lovisa couldn't help sliding into intrigue too.
It was after all happening here and now. And the revelation would impact on their revenue scheme.
A bit of further research on the case informed them that Pullman's godfather was one of the notorious CRAY BROTHERS…..surprise us not!!
Danny continued: *"In the Independent here it also says : One of the latest correspondents on the Tenerife Mafia website believes the explanation is simple: "Tenerife has always been run by gangsters and mafia with fear long being the effective motivator for sales staff - so the murders of this couple are not a surprise. It you play with fire you get your fingers burnt. The fact he still had his Rolex on was a statement, not a mistake".*
She leant over his shoulder, unable to resist, and read from the article: 'THE NEW COSTA DEL CRIME' :
Away from the smart hotels, pristine villas and sparkling beaches, lurks another Tenerife, a dark and violent place of dirty deals and bloody murder.
While millions of British holiday makers top up their tans, a handful of international gangsters and London thugs have turned this Mecca into the dodgy timeshare capital of the world.
Local police believe the double murder is a brutal escalation of the tangled web of corruption, money laundering, extortion and even gun-running that has invaded their island….

They were the facts as they were here, but it always sends shivers when you actually read it in print. It kind of makes the 'subliminal knowledge' more a stark reality. Like so many island and holiday destinations, what one sees during the light of day is a far cry from what emerges as the sun goes down. There is always an underbelly to places of supposed glory and freedom. Man has a way of fucking up the good life of his own accord!
As further evidence of the haunts of hedonism here: an OPC friend they had become familiar with was sent home 'mentally ill' to recoup. The stakes were high here, but the meltdown levels were too.

They bumped Sonny out one night. Despite his shady character, he really was quite a likeable chap. He confirmed being well and truly over 'her royal *whoreness'* now. He had clearly used Karina all along as a convenient supplier of accommodation source plus 'action' on demand and whenever desired. The home-cooked meals (often English roasts as were her specialty) and our company didn't go stray either. All he had to do was entertain (be himself) and share some of his product range. Anyway, he was now bored with her and moving on.

He had bigger fish to fry on the illicit radar anyway. His courier sidekick Nathan had been 'nicked'. He was now facing 5 years in the hothouse. Sonny was growing a beard 'disguise' for his return trip to the UK to witness Nat's fate. Unlike with his partner in crime, he wasn't faithful to the motherland - he never quite fitted the expected 'vocational role'. And certainly couldn't discuss it in a family or social aspect.
They understood that concept.
Empathy.
On the 20ᵗʰ December, he left for the airport. Giving them a generous 'Chrissy cheer' package, he had a drink with them and promised to write, and return asap.

Her diary updates were indicative of their vices at the specific time:
'we were immersed in the black here, (hashish) while the accompanying drink of choice was cafe con tia. (Coffee with tia Maria).'
They weren't really into alcohol that much. Just smoking and class A was the preferred caper.

NYE 1992 update:
'We met these 2 zany French OPCs at the resort one day, and found them so entertaining; have become quite close friends. Maurille and Henri are as mad and hedonistic as we've ever encountered! Boy the French love to 'do zer party'. Relentlessly. Even we are having trouble keeping up. Maurille has been supplying Danny the bong fuel for the last few weeks. And we have arranged to meet them on the strip NYE. To kick start the evening into gear'....

They planned to serenade the year off with 'goey and strawbs' (translation = speed and LSD).
Plus some cocaine too to 'clear the air passages' as Maurille liked to say.
The diary confessed:
 'Once a few of the clubs had been dealt with on the club strip, (for collection of extra supplies to be precise) we headed back to the apartment for a rare cork-popping cheers session with the lads before they took off to seek even more hell-bent hedonism. The French were insatiable. They took the gateau when it came to self obliteration. They would no doubt go missing in action for the next week at least. Any excuse to get fucked up!.....'

Maurille's quote of the night had to be:
"Ahh....it would be travesty of justice not to combine the powers of the forces here, no?! Strawberries, cocaine and <u>champ</u>agne. The perfect marriage. Bien Sur! ...... *C'est bon; c'est cool...."*

Danny in particular felt a strong affiliation with the French, and their seductive methods of play. He had met his match.
They were all about quality indulgence; lots of fun; no sleep; and abundant blatant sex.
The ones that we met all seemed to be living off inheritance too. Privelidged princes.
The concept of wor<u>k elu</u>ded them.
'travaille?....no....!!' it was akin to an offence and a dirty swear word to them.
'Onculay!'

The fact that they called hash 'shit' was amusing. Literally! *'Ve need to get some more shit!!'....'This shit is MERDE!'*

They may have been a health hazard with regards to self obliteration, but the amusement factor that they supplied tended to outweigh the carnage! Again, sign of the times....fun trumped health......

So for Danny and Lovisa the next 24 hours ensued on speed, acid, charlie, hashish, champagne (French influence!), tia coffees....and lots of sex. Mostly in the shower. Clean eroticism. Hygeinic hedonism.
Thats what saw off '92 and welcomed '93.......
Indicative of the era it was.

They were profoundly optimistic about what the year ahead had in store for the 2 tyrant travellers. (Nothing to do with the stimulants of course).
They had utterly no intention of returning back to the original Australian hell-hole until it was absolutely vital from a financial perspective.
The motto they had devised one messy night with a fellow OPC became the new mantra:
'Work, work, earn, earn, move, move, learn, learn!'
It transcended to their efforts and results at work too. They were on a roll now.

1993 started off on a profoundly positive note!
Work was the most fruitful it had ever been : 6 ups. Bravo on the sales pitch.
A German; Italian; English; Spanish; Belgium flemish and French couple.
All qualified and all paying perfect!
A global effort....applause.

A few days later they scored a Norwegian couple first thing.
They couldn't help laughing with the quote from the woman: "I feel like I'm being kidnapped!" as they whisked them into the next cab.
The success scores continued through the next months and they had been encouraged to get more serious about the role.
They had reached a level of greater respect amongst fellow timeshare tyrants now; no longer outsiders in this scheme of scams.
Prior to this they had been 'ghosting' for Travis - with him paying them the proceeds to their efforts minus a small commission.
Now, Erik ('the viking' they called him) - an unstoppable German multi-lingual timeshare guru came to them and quietly took them aside:
"You guys really should start on your own number now. You are doing too well to 'ghost' - better pay and a proper cut of the deals that succeed at the resort! Don't waste your precious time putting cash in someone else's pockets anymore!"
It was sound advice. And tempting....Trav had been a great safety net up until now, and since the confidence had indeed propelled with performance scores, they concurred that they were worth more now. Lovisa was on a roll. The 2 were well known and liked amongst all expats on the island. Reputation sound.

But never rest on your laurels……..

In retrospect they learnt more of the situation they were immersed in….
They were working illegally, since you needed a work permit to be granted employment here. The alternative of 'ghosting' was a convenient, albeit potentially dangerous pursuit for anything more than short-term 'quick fix cash'. The pursuit of <u>ample, easy money</u> is never without risk; a danger element attached.
Though unaware of it at the time, it was a forecast for future employment in Lovisa's case. The expansion of the theme played out in real life….
No wonder they had been stopped and interrogated a few times! Trav had got them off the hook (no doubt paying fines on their behalf) but he never elaborated on the fact it was not ideal, and they had hence felt no concern for their safety whatsoever. It was a win-win for all concerned, after all! Literally…
Eric's advice to get their 'own number' was out of concern for them in fact….he never raised the alert with them either, but strongly suggested they consider alternatives.

Confidence had indeed increased for the two by this stage. It had been a challenge to establish themselves in this tough, competitive industry, but with the reassurance now of others top of this game, it looked like they could make it work in their favour here.
They started to relax more…..Oblivious to the evils that lurked. Cash counting was the reward for labours, and propelled them on, devoid of conscience.
Lovisa reminded Danny of the initial warning Mysty gave them months ago, and they both laughed at the memory:
*"Don't ever forget….it's the **magnetic** island. It's best to use it to your advantage and try to move on elsewhere with your life. It's evil….It'll suck you back just when you think you have escaped its evil grasp"…..*
There was a predominance of thrill-seeking poms on the island; that was immediately evident. The 'mainstream' Brits dominating the seedy side of this island were akin to the Aussies of the same calibre in the dregs of Bali, as already outlined. Comes with the territory of 'freedom'… all here was *'sound as a pound; dandy as a Deutschmark'*…..but where money seems easy, evil lurks…….

Lovisa continued to pull the German couples as priority, but with the influence of the two larrikins they had been spending most social time with, the French couples started to respond too.
She had picked up *'un petit peu francais'* - much stoned verbal had instigated the new tongue. They also noticed the marvellous memory of the French lads with their English as it improved in their company. No matter what state they were in, you only had to say something once to them, and they adopted it as part of their verbal; with their own humourously accented version. Maurille in particular. He was the quintessential street kid…..his entire survival strategy was dependant on the flexibility of his expression in any given circumstance. It was an inspirational enticement to acquire multi-lingual status in life. For with it came many extras.

In fact, it became like a game - they reversed too in competition and started pitching the English! Role reversal as the two nationalities combined forces. That was key: make it fun, and the learning just follows. No tedious textbook traumas.

Maurille and Henri had cooked for them several times. Lovisa helped chopping in the kitchen while Danny packed cones. Team effort!
As suspected, the French do cuisine so well.....it is always an event and akin to luxury with every bite. Much care and attention to detail goes in to their pride with table offerings.
(The rest of their life may by all accounts be an utter dogs breakfast, but meal times were sacred!)
   On one of those nights, Danny and Lovisa regaled the story of the *'perils of generous catering'* which had them all in tears of laughter:
A close dealer associate had just purchased a mighty load of E's for distribution, and on a rush to go out for a sting hid them in <u>his</u> oven. His girlfriend lived on takeout so it was a safe bet! However, they were having problems at the time, so she tried to do the romantic 'peace' gesture of cooking him a sumptuous meal...cue oven on....and the shock of smelling burnt plastic and billows of smoke emanating from the oven. Suffice to say that relationship went up in smoke (!)...the thousands of lost dollars and clients with it.

After a while the laid back approach lost it's midus touch though.
Henri was starting to slip on his timeshare former tally......when Maurille arrived on the scene, his work ethic went dramatically south, with more emphasis placed on the social chaos as opposed to work pride and performance. Prior to that, he had been somewhat of a legend on the French OPC front. But something always has to give........
Likewise, Lovisa and Danny felt the pull of lazy indifference. Minimal effort working and more concentrated focus on the *after hours* cavalcades. Their performance was slipping too. They felt themselves falling back into the trap - addiction and craving superseded sane judgement.
The initial adrenalin fear of where the next rent and travel stash was coming from was steadily evaporating day by day. And a paradigm shift began to occur in the relationship too.....
They were constantly told they looked like brother and sister with the flowing gold locks, but now they started to fight like rival siblings also.

Copious stimulants with the fog of heavy hashish cloud brought a sense of surreal to daily life, and with it logic and discipline are a distant blurry memory.
 Paranoia occurs as a matter of course with some mind mess, but it became more prominent now.
And it **was** based on truth..... albeit blown out of proportion; steroid-like.

Danny knew the shortcuts to making ends meet and providing cones on demand was to engulf himself into 'the business' as a money and supply aim. Old habits.
It used to be a sideline bonus for him while in the advertising industry. She knew that and accepted it. But now it was his whole focus. The influences and demands he was under here transformed him into a more ruthless player.

She detested the game, which by definition brought a whole host of extra pressures on life as it was. It meant late nights; an unhealthy existence on the consumption front (in all regards), and continual interference from others - the perpetual invaders in the home and interrupters of any time alone there was left.
All human contact was with addict types; - not the attractive specimens of life. People were business; business was money; seek only the weak and needy to supply the next fix.
Hardly conducive to mental health and agility. Or god knows, trust.
Wasn't this part of the reason they had embarked on the trip in the first place? To escape that life and start afresh while getting inspired about a brighter future?!

Danny and Maurille joined forces of sorts, and spent more time on the hunt, gather and supply than with Lovisa at the pitching post. The arguments escalated as a result; the intimacy dwindled and the harmony they held sacred faded.

A diary entry included:
Oblivious to his own demise, Maurille was often saying that 'all the people who should be in hospitals or mental homes seem to escape and find their way to Tenerife'.... Funny, but true!
Feels like a movie, with a persons' thoughts as a voice-over, for this crazy, loony-infested black market crime-ridden island of doom......

'It was my turn for a little good luck, not much but a little. It was true that I didn't have much ambition, but there ought to be a place for people without ambition., I mean a place better than the one usually reserved. How the hell could a man enjoy being awakened at 6.30am. By an alarm clock, leap out of bed, dress, force-feed, shit, piss, brush teeth and hair, and fight traffic to get to a place where essentially you made lots of money for somebody else and were asked to be grateful for the opportunity to do so?'
Factotum. Bukowski.

The Christmas season in the Canaries was **windy** season. Almost as disruptive as rainy season in other tropical zones....but the effect on the people was evident.
Rainy season led people to frustration and anger, but windy season here?.......it was akin to the effect on children in a playground, causing them to flip out in a manic manner.
It just sent people completely *insane*.......!

Maurille had been staying over some nights too now; crashing on their lounge after 'doing zer party' night after night on the Veronica's strip. He used the excuse of 'doing business' but the earnings were gone by the time he returned.
As for his relationship with Henri, it became virtually hostile; - Henri stormed off blaming him for the reputation and finance assassination he was now enduring. Their previous close bond established in France was now tainted with friction.

Lovisa felt sorry for the guy. She had witnessed his complete metamorphism, and watched him plummet into a dark hole from a once glorious height. He described Maurille's arrival on the timeshare scene as *"the beginning of the end for me"*. It had all escalated, and in the end he was forced to leave and return to Paris.

Maurille was now banned from 'global' timeshare, for dealing in drugs. His sidekick now gone, Maurille was feeling abandoned and low; like a wounded animal he was taking irrational risks with money and contacts. Usually at the expense of others' funds.

A few enemies and threats inevitably came into his arena. And his health was suffering - kidney pains and other physical side-effects were evident.

His influence was a toxic intrusion to the couples' already dwindling union. The roles played with him were changing from comrade to babysitter.....

He was often accompanied by a group of foreigners - taking up their lounge room and invading their privacy.

Lovisa spent much time now seeking solace at the pool, out, or alone in her bedroom.

The **diary** was her only sacred tool. She had no idea what compelled her to write so vigourously daily and document the minutiae of life......perhaps one day she would use it as a reminder or revisit it? All she knew was she was compelled to do it. Gut driven.

She treated it with the same respect as one would a vital assignment; obsessively pouring details into it constantly. But they started to become more private snippets of info now. Revealing all. It would not have been a welcome read for anyone else involved. This is when the habit of establishing different daily hiding spots for her book commenced.

Protection mode.

She wrote lots of mail home to family. Her mum saved her correspondence in a box. It was indicative of situations as they occurred......much was subliminally indicated at in *code*.

Cryptography.

Most folk would be totally confused - but her mum always worked it out. She had kind of accepted the fact that her firstborn was a puzzle, and had become adept at code-cracking (!)

Lovisa started to mentally prepare herself to move on now. Time to rock'n'roll.

She had lost track of the amount of hard earned cash she had saved and stashed away for their trip; and when she went to check it one day was horrified to find it all gone....

Danny was the only other one with access to it; the closest one to her.

And that's when the trust was officially trashed.

She was suspicious of everything now. Life was tainted.

Who was friend; who was foe?!

Don't ever fuck with her money....as a survivor she had established this as her

golden rule.

She internalised her pain and became increasingly more insular. Protect number one. Suspect everyone; trust no one.
Consider all people smiling assassins…….

She was trying to maintain focus and discipline to earn as much as possible now - time was ticking. And any earnings she would control herself entirely. No more delegation. Relying on self was key.
The problem of course was the external influence.

Maurille's charm had well and truly worn thin now. He was in a perpetual cloud of delirium and substance abuse, and was virtually squatting in their lounge room; unable to pay rent or support himself. His quests to do business nightly were fruitless since all profits went up his nose, or up in smoke. Literally.
One of her diary entries included a description:
"Later, he was back with 3 of his fellow French freaker friends. It was such a bizarre experience to sit there, positively clubbed and listen to missile convos in French spit firing between the 4. We realised how much you notice the eccentric hand movements and expression as you focus on other senses besides audio - ie visual.
Its quite comic! We no doubt look just as strange to foreigners when we speak English. Their attempts at English are twice as hilarious when in such a brilliantly bent state. God knows what we sound like with our attempts at French"….

His way to try to compensate for the hospitality and outstanding debts was to cook. Which he could do well; with his French influence and all. And offer the pills, powders and pot for them to partake in. Danny felt it evened the score. But Lovisa just wanted to count cash for the trip they were here on - the initial goal. And she not only felt annoyed at the constant temptations; she despised them now.
Danny loved the decadent fare Maurille brought to the table; (all created from ingredients Lovisa also had to provide at additional expense), but she just craved some privacy, peace and a more stable routine; not intruded by unbalanced individuals.
It is so true that you become a reflection of your immediate surrounds; toxic people in your arena are the most destabilising influence of all. Everything felt…….messy.

She and Danny had always been somewhat obsessed with perfection; it was part of the attraction between them. But now their life had sort of evolved into the more mainstream, careless attitude. And it was entirely correlated to the company they kept. Humans are intrinsically like chameleons.
They drifted further and further apart. Both were discontent, and naturally attacked each other.

The famous 'Carnivale' in Santa Cruz was looming. They intended all along to attend the event. Being veteran attendees at the Sydney Mardi Gras since forever, this had been a pinnacle aim in their social calendar. '**The**' annual event in the Canary Islands.
By this stage however Lovisa vowed it to be more of a final farewell and hurrah before they progressed to the next location and leg of the tour. Frankly party mode was the furthest thought from her mind.

But she wanted no regrets.

So they discussed getting tickets and transport sorted.

Typically, last minute Maurille managed to score a lift to Santa Cruz, so the pair caught the bus as planned to meet him there. They were compelled to stand the whole journey, in a sardine tin load of crazy costume-ridden Spanish. No mean feat, especially considering they were already part smashed before they took off, having indulged in ceremonial lines of Charlie to kick-start the carnival spirit. The public was a curse at the best of times....

The theme was 'circus' and virtually everyone was in outrageous costume. Its the worlds' second largest carnival crowd at this annual event, and the serious dedication to theme was impressive. Much attention to detail and party spirit in full swing.

They met up with Maurille at the designated spot.

'Our little french 'flatmate'; resident-dealer provided coke and hash, in addition to our already gobbled trips and speed. It remains his substitution rent payment at present'...

It was an all night affair as usual, and they watched the sun rise before heading back.

They had such a outrageous night, they decided to revisit a few nights later for the Spanish celebration *'the death of the fish*"...whatever that meant. The boys didn't need too much of a reason to put the party hat back on. Such is the endurance of youth! Recovery period? - No time for that....rock on.....

However, it was a much more lacklustre event than the previous one. Due to Maurille's delay, they missed the parades, and having downed more acid and snorted copious Charlie, they were on edge somewhat. Adding speed to the mix didn't help....such a messy drug. Grindy....

Maurille also lost the key to the apartment. No surprises there.....he lost his wallet last trip also.

Lovisa felt like she was in a private bubble of gloom most of the night; observing from within. The distance between her and Danny was becoming uncomfortable now.

What was happening to them..

The diary entries also indicated a pessimistic perspective on everything noted. The perpetual indulgence and delirium was evident.

'So much for celebration of the dead fish.....a sardine-sized effort'.

The preoccupation for the next plans for pot were always on the radar.

'Wanna go halves in some draw?'......Maurille was the master of paying 50% of something he consumed 90% of......but apparently only Lovisa noticed this fact.

On reflection of her written rendition, she was somewhat amazed at the clarity of expression amidst the prevailing haze of consumptive chaos......

The details of 'the addicts' life' were peppered throughout the diary. They were immune to the shock factor of their existence. So immersed in it, it was simply 'the norm'.

The mention of, for example:

while they waited they resorted once again to barrel hash (this entails scraping the inside layer from the bong cone and smoking that!) - or *we were left with the remnants of the other nights' party sachet, but it was looking damp and sad now....and a challenge to consume.......resorting to smoking the butts from the ashtrays while they were stationed waiting for home deliveries'......*

It was the 'where there's a will there's a way' attitude to drugs. Nothing was wasted; all was welcome; anything was possible. Again, the courage of fearless youth......one would shudder to consider the lifestyle now. How they maintained the momentum, and consistent busy days was a mystery. Fuelled by coffee, stimulants, hope and dreams....

But always a flip side. Coupled with joy comes pain. And what goes up has to come down.

But so much substance abuse; and potloads of pot.....the lack of luck on the pitching post was in direct correlation to indulgence.

At this point Lovisa officially reverted her mind into focus on escape from this evil place. Gather what fees they could now and flee.....

She had become annoyed at Maurille full time. With his debts to them having reached a staggering sum at this point, he was teaching Danny French lessons in a desperate attempt to allay the wrath of the pair. Their travel budget had been seriously compromised by this invader of their happy zone and home.

They were rapidly giving up hope of ever acquiring their debts.....lots of promises ensued to no avail.

'Tomorrow, I promise!'

Ah, mañana polo mañana.........

Again, it must be reiterated: **never trust the word of a salesman!**

This was a lesson she had been dealt repeatedly in her life....human nature is to really WANT to believe, especially considering the remarkably convincing pitch they are so adept at delivering with their 'craft'.........but if you fall victim, you only get stung in the end.

Danny tried to alleviate Lovisa's increasing temper over the debt matters, with even further promises that looked doubtful and unlikely. *"He has promised we can go and stay in his home when we go to the south of France later.....his mother is a fantastic chef, and he has many other friends to introduce us to in Toulon, Avignon and Marseille."*

France wasn't even on her list of destinations at this point, or it hadn't been. Being shuffled schools and gathering German consulate prizes, she had kind of hoped to get to Germany to practice the language she had been educated to use-in its native surrounds. They had already discussed this before departure. And Danny had been most encouraging and willing.

It appears their global aims were conflicting now too.....

How time can change all plans, people and prospects.

London was a definite. Danny's Estonian 'aunty' (by adoption) lived there, and had welcomed them to stay.

Amsterdam too was a given….(hello)

The other european destinations had focused more on Germany and Italy, but it appeared that France was the new hotspot. Her mother's latest letter informed her that her godfather (uncle) was in southern France on vacay and his door was open for her too. Serendipitous.

But she hardly cared now - *anywhere* but here. She needed to get out!

They returned from the pitching post one day to find Maurille still passed out in their lounge room; having done the party at carnival yet again…his aim at cashing in with the dealing potential had of course failed with his party spirit (a pro drug lord once told me *'never dabble in the shop fare…..if you don't keep your wits about you the business runs at deficit, not profit'……)*

On closer inspection Lovisa gasped. His face was grossly swollen, with shades of blue and black permeating his skin. Dried blood framed his face.

He had been bashed and mugged the night before. They had intended on confronting him that afternoon with a firm conversation regarding the loans and debts, but that hope now disappeared with the sad sight before them. She busied herself with icepacks and facecloths. *'It hurts to look at the guy, let alone push for pesetas'*…..

He was bedridden for days; barely conscious. As she washed the dried caked blood away from his face and his pillow, she noticed how swollen and misshapen one side of his head was. She was seriously concerned there may have been brain trauma.

 Plus she was virtually convinced his nose was broken. It was like a huge bulbous strawberry in shades of red and blue. If he recovered from this, he really should pay heed to the lesson learnt and follow a different path.

In desperate times, when one feels moments of despair, they gravitate towards the lifestyle tactics that preserve rather than decimate. Call it the 'Phoenix rising instincts'….survival mechanisms kick in. One develops tools for future use.

On reflection, Lovisa sensed that a few habits commenced for her during this trying period.

For one, she found that sleep and exercise was vital. It quite literally, changed the perception and management of EVERY facet of your life.

The brain and body function a million times more efficiently under the successful maintenance of both.

She noted too that obsessive compulsive behavioural activities are more profoundly played out under stress. Some sort of *routine* is the backbone to each day. Patterns prevail. Rituals emerge. Without it a sense of disarray and panic pervades the soul…..

She also became more pedantic about issues.

She found solitude was a godsend now; - space for self is not just a luxury but a must. It allows you to process and recalibrate. Unravel the tangled wires of mental torment….

Intake was an absolute key component. She sensed only **pure** nutrition helped enormously.

Abstinence of alcohol, drugs and nicotine combined with food such as home-made vegetable soups and fresh salads provided a total feeling of wellbeing and fuel for coping more efficiently. The body performs at optimum.

Quite simply, <u>you are what you eat.</u>

You eat crap, you are a loser!

Its not rocket science.

You can read all the health manuals in the world that you like, but the proof is ultimately in the pudding......its how you *feel* and *live.* And ultimately, cope.

Regardless of the daily trials and torments that may strike. You continue with much greater ease amidst the daily flying meteors of unexpected impact that strike.....

She was literally nursing Maurice for a while now, like a job. It tended to take precedence over the timeshare work during this phase of intense concern.

She woke him to feed him soup or healthy stir-fys she had made every evening, but other than that he was sleeping relentlessly to the point of a coma. The days merged into weeks. It/he was in a virtually critical situation. His face was distorted to the stage of unrecognition now. He really should have been in hospital.....

As annoyed as she was with his impact on their life, savings and privacy, this was a matter of survival. His ally from home, Henri had returned to France, so they were all he had for now.

His family. His life-force.

Conscience propels you to put your own needs aside temporarily when you see others not coping. You can't abandon a battered homeless dog!

Once he was strong enough to function again, they would travel onward as planned and get on with their lives.

The Island 'working holiday' had been a learning experience on so many levels. About life. About self. Where there appears despair is actually golden opportunities of growth...

You live, and you learn. So you prosper from the pain.

It is never wasted hell.....

For life has a way of dictating circular pattern periods.....one finds themselves being reminded of roads once travelled, and utilises the paths chosen during those times of challenge and hurt. The **tools** you develop are invaluable.

To this day, the lessons learnt have remained like a tattoo on the memory.

She wrote in the diary of developing *'leather Tenerife skin'*.....metaphorically speaking.

Though it may be shed, the tough exterior can return. Like muscle memory.

Metamorphism is nature evolving to exist. Subject to environmental and circumstantial aberrations.

Under her care and attention, Maurille slowly started to mend; vowing to abstain from the evils and 'start a new healthy life' in continuation of the simple healing measures administered. Lovisa was cooking; giving him healing books to read;

witnessing sunsets; watching videos with him and going for walks. It was a nurturing phase and he seemed to truly relish the rare experience and attention.
Slowly but surely he started to feel his stamina and life-force returning.
But.........as one eventually learns, despite their desperate need for reassurance of renewal, in retrospect all efforts are fast thwarted.
For most folk have limited (read selective) memory span, and the cliche *you can lead a horse to water, but you can't make it drink* is a true statement of human nature.

.....Or, at least, the stupid animal will eventually forget when temptation emerges.

The days before his flight back to France loomed closer ahead now.
He had been busy packing and contacting family. Predominantly his mother.

And so after all that rehabilitation success, how did he spend the day and night before?
He headed to the Veronica's nightclub strip for his final obliteration and indulgence!
Bien Sur....
Returning at 7am utterly delirious, he drank the remaining wine from the fridge; collected his gear; lit up a joint, and cabbed it to the airport.
And there departed another chapter of no hope. Plenty of potential.....but unable to reach the heights that were possible.
Like most, sadly.
Look around.........

Amidst her annoyance, disappointment and exhaustion from his impact on their life, Lovisa saw the light once more. As the diary confessed:
'My biggest psychological stress factor has just evaporated!! We've arranged to call him from England. So with a week or 2 only left to ourselves now, I have many other topics to concentrate on.....'

All conversations between Danny and Lovisa led to arguments and drama by this stage. The lovebirds' nest had been invaded and poisoned so it was an inevitable outcome.
Lovisa was just focused on mission exit now.

However, just to add insult to injury, she discovered that Danny had given permission to a girl they knew to stay with them for the remainder of their stay. It was an attempt at quick, extra cashflow from rent contribution, but the price was high.....
The new flatmate caused further friction.
A self-confessed junkie; stripper; prostitute; and shoplifter....who even tried to convince Lovisa to do a show for quick cash!
Lovisa was reluctantly compelled to put most of her stuff in storage at a friends house; also utilising her safe for passport etc.

The whole co-habitation issue was so toxic to her now - she craved to be left the hell alone and in peace! People only served to rock your boat and shake your foundations. And let's be honest……who the hell can you trust?!

Desperate to move on, she counted down the days till their departure.
Thank god they had accommodation lined up in London, that sounded civilised.
Danny's Estonian aunt Alice had a terrace in a quiet neighbourhood there, so the transition from 'party island' to (what was normally the antithesis of their desires)- <u>suburban privacy</u> sounded like a welcome change that would untangle the nerves and provide some sense of security…….well, in theory.

Meanwhile, back at the pitching post, they got chased by an irate French timeshare tour victim from the day before. After seeking a safe retreat and hibernating in a local tapas bar for a spell, Danny wrote a *dummy* postcard to London. Then they re-emerged to recruit one of their final 'ups' before their work time was complete. Only 3 days to go now…..
Semi traumatised yet again, they returned to the apartment, mulled up, and Danny set off to the post office to send his mail (strawberry acid trips with the card) to the Estonian aunts' address. Timing was of the essence with parcels as such…..he knew he would be there to receive it in person. Supplies assured.
Curiously, in his absence, Lovisa collected the *arriving* post and an envelope caught her eye….
A letter had been forwarded to them from their Australian address to here! But it was from London…..
The name and address of the sender was unidentifiable to her (S.R. Feldon - thetford, Norfolk…..)
The intrigue overwhelmed her and she seized a knife to open the aerogramme:

'Dear Danny and Lovisa,
I bet you never thought you would hear from me again. Im writing this from my prison cell in England. I don't know if you knew I was a wanted man back in good old Blitey. Well I was. You remember me leaving Tenerife to check out what happened to Nathan.

Lovisa gasped with realisation. It was from Sonny - Karina's part-time drug dealer beau back at la Caleta.
Good grief!
He had kept his promise and written. From a deep, dark cell no less.

….'Well I never got out of Gatwick Airport. Airport police came over while I was having my first cup of real tea. Asking to see my passport. Saying it was just a routine check. Well I didn't check out and was immediately arrested. Then taken from Gatwick, halfway across England to prison. "Talk about your luck!?"…..

Talk about your STUPIDITY more like, Lovisa thought. Why on earth would you STOP in the airport for a *cuppa* instead of getting the fuck out as quick as you can?! He knew his capers were so far from legit; he was a fool to think he could carry on a chilled normal life anywhere without watching his back…..

a wave of nausea overwhelmed her as she continued reading:

'Well folks, the prison, it wasn't bad. A new building and unlike anything ive ever been in before built on an American theme, with an open door policy. Which means we were only locked in a cell overnight. Whilst I was there, I was taken to Northampton which was 20 miles from the prison, for my trial. I was put in front of the worst judge on this planet. He found me guilty on two accounts of
1: possession of ecstasy
2: intending to supply E's to others.
I mean we're only talking 81 pills.....I screamed perso!
(personal)
But he wasn't having any of it. He deferred sentence, as he slapped me with a confiscation order for £97. The man must be mad. He also decided to move the rest of the trial to Peterborough, which meant I would have to move to another jail.
Now, this prison was totally the opposite to the first. It was like moving from heaven to hell. This dungeon was bad. It smelt, was cold and damp and had no toilets in the cells. So we had to use a bucket. To make things worse I had to share with a crazy man. I was there for 3 months. In between that time, I went back to court for the final part of my trial. The outcome of that was 4 1/2 years prison plus 6 months for skipping England and going to Tenerife. Plus the confiscation order. The judge accepted my offer of £20. But he gave me a further year in default of payment. So fuck him. Im not going to pay. That makes a grand total of 6 years. As I said earlier: 'what a nasty judge'....
Now I've been moved to a long term jail called Wayland, which is only 20 miles from my home town of Norwich. Its quite laid back here. Im quite happy here and time seems to go quickly. Also its handy for Nathan to come visit.
What happened to Nathan you ask? Well, thats another story, and as you can see ive run out of space. So until next time,
All the best
Sonny xoxo

Lovisa exhaled heavily and thought what a crazy life it was and what crazy folk she seemed to be embroiled with.
Danny would return shortly - she placed the aerogramme next to the bong for him to devour while he puffed, and got back to sorting her final packing duties.

Unbenownst to her, her life would see her amass an impressive collection of prison mail over the years.
Drugs......
Incarceration....and the characteristic outcomes that prevail from becoming institutionalised. She could write a thesis on the metamorphism.
These folk were never meant for the real world anyway.

How she managed to skip the experience herself was part of the 9-life cat luck she held.....
For now.

On the last day at the resort as they awaited a meeting with Trav for their final pay-packet, - the word had got around amongst staff of their ensuing departure, and they were bombarded with farewells and friendly advice for their travels:
Lars from Denmark, who was usually so work-focused and unsocial amongst fellow pitchers, even took time out for them today! Time was money and he never wasted a second, as they were about to understand better.
He spoke with much conviction about 'back home' and the high suicide rate, plus expense of the country. Their policy was to save 50c from each dollar out of fear....
Lovisa felt a rush of empathy for the hard working Dane.
He also warned them that Sweden and Norway were similarly expensive.
Neil chimed in and recommended Antwerpe, in Belgium. They made a mental note to factor in an **Amsterdam** stop if that destination eventuated! (Lovisa knew it would be foolish not to realise that Danny had full intentions of going there above and beyond anywhere......for obvious reasons.)
A whole host of other resort crew bid them farewells and hugs of luck and safety.
Evidently folk here had established a soft spot for them.
Both Danny and Lovisa realised in unison why it was nicknamed the 'magnetic island'...~ already in their hearts they knew that despite its evil underbelly, it was almost certain they would return *some* day......

1/part 6:

Fear fetish and the fellow....

A lone wolf in sheep's clothing.

So a cultural shock to the system was to take hold on reaching the mother land. London was very much a 'real world' location compared to island existence. Akin to speaking a whole new language; albeit on a total *living* front. Particularly environmental. (Excepting the very few summer days....so comparatively rare, that they have the poms flip out in utter rapture; filling every park and alfresco seat with excitement bordering on hysteria. It's most amusing to witness: the things us island folk take for granted).

For a start, the necessity for complete bodily coverage was instant; no more life in a bikini shenanigans! Insulation was vital.

Being a person of extremes, it felt right going from one to the other. This was her first taste of an ongoing theme throughout her life: the union of island meets city life.

Hot to cold.

Black to white.

Excess to deprivation....

Life's too short to become complacent or bored. Or take matters for granted.

[NB: this was written prior to climate change hysteria that has now got the globe in its grasp. London has more recently experienced heatwaves the likes of which she hadn't had since early childhoodm]

Danny's Estonian aunt Gladys greeted them at her huge house and urged them to make themselves at home. It was a very traditional London terrace, in a typical suburb of the inner city.

Intrinsic to the land, Lovisa noticed certain characteristics were uniform in any typically London abode it seemed. It was her first time here in the UK, and yet oddly familiar…and in keeping with many of the well known pommy series she had grown up with, under her father's patriotic influence.

And, indeed, her <u>grandparents'</u> traditional English existence on their stately property in Australia. She had spent much of her early childhood roaming their vast estate…. (though theirs was more 'Downton Abbey' than London terrace; in an area labelled as 'millionaire's drive' in an inner western suburb of the city.)

Like so much about Australia, it 'borrowed' most things from the Great Britain street names; traditions and lifestyle.

Being formerly a returned-war-veterans' hospital that they ran, it was immense and grand. She had known many of the now mentally challenged 'inmates' well as a tot, and used to chat to them (and all their *invisible* friends) on the huge lawns and around the fountains.

One in particular, Ron, was a crowd favourite. Everybody loved him and he was considered family. Bravery cost sanity and those men were living reminders of the futility of war.

(She reflected: this early exposure to madness would probably have helped her deal with many of the characters she later encountered in her life….a bit like watching 'the fisher king'. Long live Robin Williams. There was no comedy in the real man. The irony of comedians….the masks and mirrors.)

They were fond; old fashioned, family-focused memories, and she could virtually close her eyes and describe the interiors of a typical abode from recollection, exposure and senses:

Sofas; crocheted blankets, antique furniture and mis-matched pieces everywhere (described affectionately as 'shabby sheik' in many institutions of England) ; framed photos, mantle-pieces, crockery cupboards, priceless figurines and scattered tacky ornaments, corny souvenirs…..it appeared the nation had a reliance on surrounding themselves with 'stuff' for a level of security and comfort. Not surprising considering the harsh environmental conditions she thought as she shivered… 'cosy' was the theme du jour here, and for good reason!
Banisters; creaky hardwood floors and staircases; bathtubs instead of shower units, the perpetual ticking of cuckoo clocks and heater units.

And in an olfactory sense: the musty smells of mothballs, fabric softener, lavender, rosemary, sausages, pork chops and baked beans.

Australia had tried to mimic the same in certain **terraces** throughout the eastern suburbs of Sydney, deeming it to be a sign of prestige/privelige and attribute but it never worked well; particularly on a climate front. For they don't do summer well - the design is entirely focused on bitter winters as any architect worth his salt can attest. As is the general condition of where they arose.

When in Rome….

There lies method to the madness of various locational traits. Things that work in their homeland simply don't thrive when replicated elsewhere. It applies to all matters: lifestyle; design, food and so forth. Enjoy them where they reside, and leave them there where they belong.

Aunt Doris was embarking on the life-saving tactic of quitting smoking, so the motivation to do the same arose. For the reflection of indulgence quotas on all scores back on the island was mind-boggling, and bordering on burn-out phase - so a need to polish the routine felt necessary now.
The initial conversation while on acid mid-flight was a distant memory now… *"wouldn't it be great to just hook up to a trip-drip and be perpetually in the target zone!"*…. the concept of **cleanse** was the new replacement goal.

Contrast is always a joy…..avoid boredom in life.

After a few days, they were joined by a few of Doris' Estonian family members and the terrace was indeed a full house. They were well educated German speaking Estonians, and complimented her on her Deutsch.

Flattery was welcome in her flattened state; weary from months of hedonism. One was even considered royalty, and was often reciting life stories of shock and snippets of intriguing factual information. For one - his house had been taken over by the Russians for their headquarters during the occupation.

Interesting stuff.

He was a professor of course; - all were in the specs-donning intellectual category. The entire fam present were very reputable, degree-riddled nerds.

Quote Danny at the time: *"Fuck, these Estonians have nothing better to do than study!"*

They would all congregate in the kitchen most afternoons which was quite a novelty at first; - before the inevitable quest for solitude would take hold of Lovisa once again.

She was still in the state of immense relief at having landed somewhere that would guarantee more stability, and their intelligent company was refreshing. They taught her to make sauerkraut one day, and explained that meatloaf was called '*pikkpoiss*' in Estonian. Her tongue still naturally gravitated toward Spanish after the island, and they reminded her that 'hasta mañana' was '*bis morgen*' in Deutsch. Muscle memory was a curious thing. And it applied to language as well as body. Use it consistently or lose it.

The guests finally left, and aunt Gladys too had to go on a journey for a while, leaving the place completely to them. An exciting prospect! Left to their own devices.

Of course, it wasn't too long until Danny busied himself crafting a bong out of a plastic milk container. He had always been able to create one out of virtually any bottle contraption available…. a skill one perhaps shouldn't add to their resume.

The problem was, they had reached different stages; - for she was focused on maintaining the clean living change so their worlds were bound to conflict.

She had her sights set on a more routine based healthy life now, looking into part time work options and so forth with her British passport. She also realised she was eligible for the dole (which Danny too, insisted she take advantage of) - but she wanted to get some cheeky work on the side also….exploiting the system? Most would consider this so. She turned a blind eye to the fact. Survival will always trump logic.

Quite simply, money = safety. And she needed that in a big dose now. Justification enough….

Meanwhile <u>his</u> first priority was to enquire re travel to Amsterdam pronto. For obvious (addict) motives.

News on the former homefront in Australia, was that a couple who were friends of theirs were front page news. And not for good reasons. No news is ever good news….she would carry this knowledge for the rest of her life.

Coby and Sandy had joined them in many a raucous party on their apartment balcony and at big hardcore events. At the most recent drug party the day before, at a country location hours from the city centre, the cops had raided and shut the event down. All attendees were forced to slam the bag - and the majority left. In their cars.

The verdict on the guilty party was one of mixed opinion. Most felt that the police had a lot to answer for. For the events that inevitably ensued were unthinkable. (To handle machinery in that state was a potential death sentence. It didn't take a genius to work that out)….the careening car accident on the cliff killed Sandy and resulted in rehab for Coby. Destined to never recover from the worst trip of his life. No pun intended.

He would later face trial and manslaughter charges. So essentially, both their lives were over.

Meanwhile, in the land where they were, Danny contacted Donny Web; - in a British hospital recovering from a burst blood vessel in his brain. He had to be airlifted from Tenerife to survive; his family in a flummoxed state of shock. The once good boy had been seriously affected by the available candy.

Quite literally, his head exploded.

The memory that haunted them was the daily ritual he had of dancing around the resort with Santa cap on and a powder-tipped nose; high as a kite, pronouncing: *'its going to be a **white** Christmas my friends….. Embrace the white powder power folks…'*

In London itself, Lovisa's father called warning of the prevailing bomb blasts and urging her to stay safe. The IRA were rife. They were aware of the news but had both been oblivious to it in their outings. His words of warning now became a subliminal background voice.

Only days before they had caught the subway into town for a wander down hectic Oxford street; - (always a novelty at first and then an area well avoided thereafter, as any Londoner knows).
Complete chaos. Crowd and noise hell to the max. Assault of the senses. They had stopped for some respite from the impact at 'pizza for a pound' - which included free-range of the salad bar. The affordable belly fill for the cash-challenged traveller! (The price has since no doubt quadrupled. Sign of the times.)

On the subway journey back the station warnings of reporting any 'abandoned bags' were constant. The sight of so much as a plastic bag (an everyday item) caused mass panic.
It was the first taste of the power of terrorism to them. It's ability to instil fear on folk, and affect their lives in more ways than just a hindrance to lifestyle. Little did they know it was to become the norm of existence globally soon after. (Superseded only by pandemic fever decades later.)

Lovisa started to relish the comforts of normalcy for a while: peaceful days in the terrace followed by local walks to shop; cooking and videos. Simple stuff.

It was when healing and restoration occurred.

There was a degree of calm for a while, and the relationship began to mend the broken cracks. But then the diary indicated more distress as she realised that her happy hours of writing away meanwhile had Danny continuing in his prior patterns behind closed doors. He would retreat to one of the huge bedrooms 'for a siesta nap'. The dark moods re-emerged. As did the undeniable smells of smoke and red, glazed eyes. An addict always thinks he is skilled at the art of masking their secrets but a word of wisdom to all folk: look in the mirror……..nobody is fooled.

The silence gaps grew more frequent and lengthy. Her fear returned. Forget terrorism….keep your friends close but your enemies closer.

She wrote several more letters to her mum <u>in *cryptography,*</u> hinting at the dangers emerging. Some lines even quoted soliloquies from Shakespeare! Her paranoia evident. Her poor mum must have been at her wits' end worrying for her safety and sanity.

Statements interspersed in her letters such as: *'and the devil hath the power to assume a pleasing shape'*….(her mother followed the underlying semantics, being used to her daughter's wild mind; and kept the evidence, but it would be lost on most.)

In an odd twist of logic, she realised if you can't beat them, join them. Sometimes simply safer to do so.

So she agreed to go on the booked **Amsterdam** trip with him. Not that she had a lot of choice with the tickets already paid for placed on the bench one morning. The first smile she had seen on him in weeks.

It was a sad fact that the only way the man she loved could be happy was when in a state of inebriation. There was no sobriety or natural state of peace for him. Or if so it was fleeting.
A tortured soul.

They are usually the ones who try to self-medicate: distinguish the torture of the inner demons. But it's futile. A bandaid for the **now**. The fires and wounds still remain tomorrow.
These are the ones to beware of. Virtually impossible to love.

As they can't be held accountable for their actions when the manic swings take hold. Uncontrollable. It had them capable of personality transforming actions to the degree of Jekyll and Hyde altitudes. Ones that even they don't understand….

A fine start to the journey: at Heathrow they set off the alarm in customs, which instilled paranoia in Lovisa considering the acid trips hidden in Danny's wallet. She had lost some of her prior 'courage of a cowboy' in the trafficking regard. Visions of the movie she used to be obsessed with kept springing to mind - *midnight express.* Perhaps one of the most haunting true accounts of incarceration ever made. It was the loss of trust that was taking her mind down these dark alleys.

Upon arrival they immediately jumped the tram to the Liederspleen. It felt like a toy town; cruising around on these high tech coloured mobile monsters.

But it was like Christmas for Danny; perusing the vast menu at the 'sensi seed bank' and he excitedly purchased a robust bag of sincinilia.

They sat in the bulldog cafe and he rolled a pile of joints, with obvious glee. Lovisa still had her trusty diary with her; the updates in Amsterdam bound to be peppered with delirium.

They met a character who offered them accommodation and use of a bong which had always been their preferred device over the spliff option. He was qualified as a negative option however, with the underlying scary aggression they witnessed:

He was a bodyguard who carried on about killing people, most recently stabbing a guy in the lung (!) Even though he offered to sell them 1000 Escher trips, which was tempting, they reluctantly moved on; scurrying down some dark alley side street to escape the freaker.

Her camera constantly to hand, Lovisa took photos of the surrounds that unmistakably indicated the region: tulips, clogs, wild graffiti, trams, cobblestone streets, canals etc. The days there were spent walking and tramming around in circles it seemed, amidst the carnival atmosphere. She had her hair plaited in a Scandi 'Heidi' frame of mind. Meanwhile he read 'the mellow pages' - a smokers' guide to Holland.
Days went up in smoke. Literally.

On the second day dinnertime had them on the hunt for hash cake. It was kind of a must-do action in this terrain. Cue giggles and hooded eyes.

Their budget accommodation looked like a prison cell; bunk beds and tiny confines with minimal furniture to speak of. However, they paid no mind as it served as their dutch oven, and they were out on the perpetual cafe puff-crawl anyway. They dragged the mattresses on the floor, and signed the walls.

Then made a beeline to the grasshopper cafe and dropped a strawberry trip. As it kicked in, they perused a potential purchase at a place called the 'dungeon'. Pressing a button for a neon menu to appear behind glass, purple sinc was the decided choice.

Clouds……Ciao…….

Danny also made a call to the big time dealer in Sydney they knew well, and arranged a seed purchase for him. She was so wasted by that point that she hardly cared for the risks of this prospect. Huge pupils; singed synapses. As the diary succinctly professed: *'mass mental mutilation'* ensued.

Translation: numbed to danger.

They returned to the UK with bountiful bud souvenirs. Danny's stoned courage here was to mark the first of many a risky commute for ensuing chapters of re-stocks and Amsterdamage.

Appearing from Aunt Doris' cellar one day, he joyfully announced that it would be the perfect place to grow a crop! Little did his poor aunt know, that her property would harbour continued criminal activity. He always presented as the perfect private school boy when in her presence (or *public* as labelled area appropriate.) Sons of kings….the brainwashing of the priveliged is cell deep…

Danny continued to seek company that gravitated to the same evils; there was always a willing party partner to partake in all the poisons with. He befriended some fellow travellers in London who were like-minded in their antics. And as insane as it may sound, it was actually safer for her to partake, even though she really wanted to continue with a routine of preservation vs obliteration. For somewhere in the recesses of her paranoia bank, the fear of illicit substances being hidden in her belongings if she wasn't careful was the underlying constant thought. A scratchy state to be in.

However….watch your back. And your stuff.
If you can't beat them, join them…. as already declared.

She reflected on Ricardo's classic, albeit frustrating quote to folk on any invitation: "Thanks…..Don't be surprised to see me… *And don't be surprised* **not** *to!*"

Non-commital genius she realised in hindsight. It was like a superpower of personal freedom; - the ability to please oneself at all times. Fuck compromise; its all me, myself and I!
She yearned for that now, but the situation did not allow it.

She vowed, one day….it would be **her** mantra too. Personal satisfaction; not protocol performance seal.

A group of them sat in aunt Doris' loungeroom passing the peace-pipe (read filthy bong); - her being the token female as usual. They all dumped acid, and as hers started to kick, she seized her diary once again for some

activated scrawl. Danny was by now used to her seizing pencil case and book as soon as chemistry evolved, while he meanwhile continued to pack cones and discuss all manner of topics with whoever was present.
Sketches and notes…..all were a reflection of the state of mind mayhem.

So much for the joys of healthy living……she was once again back into the addicts' boudoir of sin. She was pretty much qualified by now to write a thesis on psychotropic drug use….

"I try, with futility, to unravel the monstrous labyrinth of my mind on paper…."

She sent another cryptic code message to her mum to crack with 'read between the lines' weaved into its madness.
Updates of the time were a shock to read over. Of course they seemed incredibly vivid and lucid at the time of ink.
" She was woken by an instinct and a vision. In a window, a face was staring at her with demonic eyes. It held her captivated as it then turned to form a black wolf-like presence….and then to her. Herself.
Self -reflection.
Repugnant. And Divine…."
Always using the third party. Would it protect her from guilt?
Masks and Mirrors.

These were the days of camera FILM that, for the Y generation onwards, entails putting it in to be processed, and waiting with much anticipation to collect the expensive surprise images to appear. This was not a cheap way to obtain souvenirs of any memories. It was trial and error. You just clicked away and hoped for the best. But oh the excitement to glance through the tangible prints!

That element of mystery and surprise no longer exists nowadays with the instant nature of all things in life. The emergence of selfie-mania provided the ability to veto all outcomes and exposure- with the selecting and eliminating options. Almost like 'cheating'….a fake representation of reality. But more personally satisfying. Appease the narcissistic needs, of sorts.

These were the times of no delete button. More caution was taken - less snap everything in sight - including your damn toast and Vegemite - (as if the world cared)…..Facebook remains the opiate of the (read moron) masses. A necessary evil.

The black clouds continued in their dutch-oven inhabitance; green was virtually impossible to acquire. It wasn't as dense and obliterating as the hashish. There was evidence in her updates of a sinking into a personal pit of hermit solitude.

Dark.

Black.

No denying: You are what you injest……

They were living off her dole-cheques now from the british passport benefits. Danny was in perma-*'taxing daks'* for shoplifting…..spend a pound; come home with a showbag. Big pockets. Munchies mostly to supplement the chems. (Anyone who has succumbed to the bodily desires of pot can attest that any healthy diet ambitions are up in smoke….all cravings are as far on the 'crap' radar as possible…..)

Danny was also constantly tuning in to the toxicity of world news events. Lovisa heard in snippets that : 'after 10 years, terrorism is back to haunt Italy. 100kg TNT caused mass destruction in Florence - killing 6 and wiping out the Uffizi gallery'…..

This caught her attention since they had only recently been to see it themselves. Lucky they had. The Uffizi used to be plagued by tourism, not terrorism. (Amazing what big news this was then; - it hardly registers in the modern world terrorism activities. Prevalent perpetually. Suffice to say, in all fairness nobody is safe anymore; regardless of chosen zone)

A friend of theirs called while crying…..they were in a pub when someone let off a tear gas bom   b.

The world was going mad…..

Lovisa spent some time sun baking in their garden, while Danny attended to gardening duties: blooming bud babies. His pride and joy. The audio factor was somewhat lame in aunt Gladys' terrace, so when boredom struck they went shopping for Sony *Walkmans* to play their *cassettes* designed by DJ friends throughout their travels….sign of the times.

Lovisa scored herself some part-time work; not declaring her dole-cheque
system to assure double supplementation. Risky, but by the time it was
detected they would probably be gone.
A quirky little store with divine fashion on Bond Street tube caught her eye.
She applied for work and almost instantly left the premesis employed; set to
commence the following morn.

Rumours abounded that the Pakistani owner of the silk boutique was a
sleazy slimy creature who had assaulted many of the girls he had gleefully
hired.

She avoided his advances but agreed on his reputation. She knew his type
well. Repulsion comes at a price.....
So she took to bagging clothes after every shift as souvenirs of her torment.
They both acquired complete new wardrobes; Danny was suitably chuffed.
But she didn't mention the paki . With his proven notoriety she felt no shame
ripping him off stock. If he decided to pursue charges she figured she would
have had a line-up of women to back her, so was unphased by the rort.
(Obvs these were the days before the 'me too' movement!)

So the pay from this supported their existence, and meanwhile all dole
money went on drugs and clubbing. The best time was had on 'cali whites' at
the ministry of sound. (Funny - if you search the definition, it advises teeth
whitening products.....they were certainly flashing the pearly whites in wide
grins on these!)....
She jumped up onto the speakers to dance beneath the laser beams and was
joined by a throng of others; all moving to the beat in a massive unified drug-
bubble.
The bar there sold no alcohol...says it all, really.

From what one would gather from all the diary entries of the time, their
entire existence pivoted around the acquisition of dope and stimulants.
Sourcing it and smoking it. It ruled their daily lives. Addicts in denial....
(Her weight at the time had plummeted to 47 kilos, at nearly 6 foot tall.
Enough said.)

The basement had become Danny's shrine with lights over the leaves he
nurtured in anticipation of the crops they craved. Green would be a luxury
away from the only available bong filler here of hash. It was all black. Heavy.
A total downer and motivation killer. The other ever-available candy was of

course the London E's.

They got extra supply contact details off Danny Web, who still had a distorted swollen face from the explosions within his head. But a true addict never says die.....he was already focused on the next binge regardless of physical disfigurement.

Progressive house music was the audio du jour. And sex galore was an obvious bi-product. Danny and Lovisa's magic still shone in that regard. The mutual magnetism was undeniable. All other human traits forgotten temporarily when in the act of carnal desires. (People bang on about them being a necessary 'package deal', but in fact they are separate entities. One either gets the 'normal' stuff : security, comfort, future safety etc...or the sexual escapades penultimate. Take your pick; make your choice. They don't exist together baby.....)

On a personal level however, they were both in a world of pain. He would retreat to days of solitude and hermit behaviour, and she would feel the fear....   The contemplations of over-thinking and striving too desperately for perfection. It only leads to personal downfall.

A natural gravitation towards the balinese people and mindset was now evident in retrospect: 'not thinking too much'.....   But in the lowest points she wrote: 'scars teach us to never follow the same path on which we fell'. And a poem in reference to surviving any relationship. And never surrendering yourself completely:

'WORDS OF WISDOM'

Don't ever lose that solid grip,
or your emotions they will strip
And once you've reached the withered bone
you're twisted, hurt and left alone.
With love, pain is emotional rape...
'for the devil hath the power to assume a pleasing shape'   (*quote Shakespeare)
So on your own two feet stand tall
and then they can't push you to fall
For when it all is said and done
to survive, we must keep on the run.....

Of course the London parties continued. When in rome….but not.

They went to a Rave party 'Xtravaganza'….where they appropriately had the strongest X ever. The E's were called 'lemon and lime' and rendered them completely poleaxed at one point. Immobile. Hardcore and progressive music prevailed. (E's tend more towards the latter; (audio-enhancement wise), Acid the former).

Naturally, lots of Xperimental sex ensued also. The place was like a freefall orgie zone, but they always retreated home for theirs.

She was into reading Hunter S Thompson at the time. 'Fear and Loathing in Las Vegas'. Life imitates art…..or the other way around……

Meanwhile, the diary tally of freebies from the silk boutique had reached an impressive 30. At least they were stylishly attired for debauchery!

Danny had offered to play Amsterdam tour guide to a group of new acquaintances in London (no alternative motives at play of course!) What Lovisa didn't realise was that the travel didn't stop there…..they were to continue to other destinations after leaving the other fellow travellers. A lot was starting to happen without agreed conversations now. No doubt because he knew it would cause conflict, panic and alarm.

Deception radar buzzing hot…

Well, the trip commenced in a mad panic fashion: they arrived late; - 3 minutes before takeoff to be precise, and as a result the flight was delayed by an hour. (God they'd never do that nowadays for any passengers! The only exception would be terrorism. Different world….)

They stayed in a shared room; like a dorm (another thing she would never normally do; particularly in company of several in addition to partner) and all mattresses were put on the floor like camping again. There was a view of the river at least, which was perfect for window-ledge joints and to peruse the passing parade.

Limited luggage was a given for such hippy conditions obviously; but Lovisa's diary accompanied her at all times. Mandatory accoutrement.

No captured opportunity was to be left unchartered. It was her most trusty ally by now. She relied on it. It didn't lie. Nor deceive.

…. So the diary emphasised, yet again, self obliteration on a grand scale in a limited time; the addictive nature of the characters frighteningly evident.

It was akin to reading about Snoop's downtime in the doghouse, in modern terms. Hip-hop jargon. (His daily instagram updates are unabashed and refreshingly (albeit bravely) honest! Debauchery flaunted in all its guises. No reprisals.

When the Amsterdamage time was up and their friends were due to depart back to London, Danny took Lovisa's hand and they embarked on a mystery train ride. Through Belgium; to Toulon via Marseille. Four countries in 5 days. Zoom. Wizardry.

Justine and Maurille picked them up at six fours, toulon. She was exactly like the perceived Italian mamma; cooking daily and trying to stuff them like geese. There was never more than a few hours between table time; a somewhat degustation existence! The tantalising wafts of her cooking would permeate the place, and regardless of how full they felt, they were compelled and eager to sample her culinary delights. Each day had a few of the typical faves here: l'apin a la moutarde; coq au vin; boeuf bourguignon, confit de canard and so on. All hearty, flavoursome and decadent. And served lovingly by she with towering stiletto heels and full makeup! She had managed to maintain a svelte physique and pristine veneer despite the indulgence and imbibing quota of every day. The true French mystery.

Normal life in the south of France was pretty laid back: *'Perfect life of leisure surrounding. A pot smoker's dream really. Adapting to the good life'….*

They would rise daily to the wafts and array of French coffee and pastries; then wander down to the village by the water. Past the boulangerie; patisserie, supermarche etc and then to the corso for ice creams and drinks en 'le plage'. Mountainous surrounds abound; an idealic seaside sanctuary. The humidity appeased by the sea breeze and the friendly cicada audio backdrop.

'No wonder lads to the likes of Maurille looked for trouble elsewhere…..the risks of boredom evident after a tad too much of the good life'.

For Lovisa at this point it was a welcome change from work toils and
finance fears however. Safety was still a concern, but on the brain back-
burner for now; a reboot necessary. They practiced French with the local
lads; - certainly a more preferable and less urgent use of brainpower -
particularly for her with her passion for linguistic pursuits. Mind sponge time
must prevail when travelling; again, when in Rome…(or wherever you lay
your hat at the time). And if not in danger, the mind opens to observation on
a much more panoramic spectrum, unhindered by immediate survival
concerns.

They noted how well dressed the French folk are, even for casual
'beachfront' attire. The national pride in appearance (or was it narcissism?!)
was evident, and a refreshing change from the former land of lazy garb.
The gorgeous winding streets of the cobble-stoned corso, with quaint little
shops and cafes were so pristine and clean; - she understood the arrogance
more now. It seemed somewhat justified. *It is reminiscent of the imitation Los
Christianos (Tenerife) attempts to capture Europe; - albeit in a much more crowded;
hapharzard and cheap/dirty manner. The quality shines in comparison to Tenerife's
multi-cultural mess*

Authentic identity was always where the quality lay, Lovisa decided.
Australia didn't really have one other than the communal love of sports….
No wonder the masters all found serenity here: Van Gough, Toulouse
Lautrec and so forth.

They went to Kassisse; - emersed themselves in its exotic crystal-clear
water and basked in its breathtaking scenery. 'Camped' on the rockface and
absorbed the surrounding natural beauty at its best. Nirvana. Paradise in a
different sense to island style.

When not doing the outings, there was always the constant cooking by
Maurille and his mum; robust feasts several times a day. Dinners on 'le
balcon' bore witness to the most splendid skyline colours and slither moon
visions. *The days rotate from food to cones in a continuous, contented fashion*

It tends to numb the brain and slow one down…..coupled with the dutch-
oven like boudoir they inhabited below in 'the cave' it was a perpetual state
of : **je suis casseit** *Danny and I brought in abundant Dragon and Strawberry trips;
grass and hash across the borders thru France. Pab problem! Smoked 15 grams hash
within a few days….*

All good and well, but....*never let your guard down*.....

She realised this in retrospect. Perhaps some just weren't entitled to the inevitable sensations of relaxation if they were to self-protect.... for behind the scenes of serenity, evil was at play.

Danny was in planning cahoots with the Sydney contact for business. Danger money was always in proportion to risk, so Lovisa was kept in the dark with all details these days.

An avoidance of justification and conflict on his behalf. Is no information akin to lying? If so there was a lot of dishonesty going in in their world.

Miasma....

Her father used to always remind her of the quote:

'Behind every large fortune there's a crime against humanity'

Balzac

Meanwhile, they were 'summoned' to what was to evolve as an epic 7 day party schedule in Avignon. The hedonism of which would serve as a distraction from sideline evil; - what actually transpires behind the veiled facade of fact-fiddling. Trust no one...

The diary as always told the brutal truth however, at all times. Her private world was open book. She transcribed events as they occurred in all manner of their lives. Her trusty ally was always by her side, and it never lied....

Quote: *'I think ill write a diary till the day I die'*....

Which might not have been far off if they had continued in the same vein as the week that ensued. The trip was to prove an eye-opener. They had certainly met their match on the indulgence front. The French lads did indeed take the gateaux.   *'Which has added conclusive proof to our theory that the southern french are all completely mad'*.

It was a side-effect of their roots. **'Vous etes beaucoup fou!'**

For the rich French lads were destined to party from birth as most of their privileged associates of choice were also from a similar aristocratic stock to which they descended. A gravitational pull. Strength in numbers. The more money they had the more daring and risky their self-obliteration was. It was like a game. They were competitive by national nature. And they played to win.

Their arrogant hedonism was bordering on terrifying…….it was literally a supreme example of 'why? Because we CAN!'…..

Maurille had beckoned them to join in the shenanigans ahoy. First stop was at the place of one of his fellow Tenerife workers that the pair also knew vaguely. Emanuel was the son of the French ambassador of Botswana. His 'Maison', not far from Avignon bridge - where they stopped for photos, was a massive estate including guest house and outdoor 'forest'. They all drank pastis and played table tennis in the massive games room. One of his mates present was the son of the royal dentist in Monaco, who also designed a 'mind game'.

The star of the show this trip though, was the owner of 'domain de Torge' with incredible contacts and a family history to match. Walls dedicated to the family awards of excellence were on display in his palatial abode.
He was quarter finalist in the French open tennis for 4 years, and his father was the most famous jockey in France before being killed in a car accident.

The place he inhabited was mind-blowing. Akin to a suburb! The famous family wine distillery was underneath his house, and vineyards extended from the property perimeter for as far as the eyes could see. His mother was currently away on business, so he did his usual 'travail task' of planning an epic party event. Why? Because that's what the uber wealthy and elite do! It's almost an obligation of privilege….flying in DJs from Canada, London and Paris; inviting the famous and social elite; clicking his fingers for continuous catering and staff etc.
We were the first to arrive, but it proved to be a packed house full of glamour and underground activity. Surrounding audio verbal was predominantly French but they could switch any time to English when they wanted to direct conversation to them. Being hugely respectful of linguists, Lovisa found it bizarre but beautiful to bask in.
He had a tennis court, massive pool, garden akin to a football field, and a 20

room mansion that he insisted they 'pick any room they like' at any time that they required (heaven forbid) some shut-eye at any stage. Lovisa wandered through the vast corridors like goldilocks, opening doors to the most grand private rooms you could imagine.

Jerry was truly at home, sitting with arms folded behind his head from his favourite armchair (read throne), surveying the scene all around him. Always with a bottle of his vintage wine by his side.
'Ah its good to be the king' he purred.

And so his castle rocked on for days. Nobody appeared to retreat for sleep or even feel the desire to - they were relentless! Insatiable.
The quality catering was up there with Michelin star grade and never stopped. Nourishment assured. But fuck the shuteye! Waste of time, obviously….

They were reaching the dizzying heights of sleep deprivation now to the point that they were hallucinating.. and that was before the addition of the chemical enhancement on offer.

And once most of the guests had left, flown off etc Jerry took the gang down to the cellar for a tour of 'the medicine vault' - and to sample from the vats. Its a well known fact that the French exist on more wine than water. *Bien sur*. The musty, earthy smell and dank interior spoke volumes of the history contained beneath the home. Most of the bottles were older than the guests. (And would probably last longer!) All in attendance assisted in bringing up 30 bottles of the primo stuff - which was demolished poolside, within 4 hours. *Petit dejeuner*…..

Later it would be bucket bongs and a range of acid to choose from. They hung up decorations and banners in the trees, and blasted music on massive speakers, to share with all the land for several kilometres.
It was hedonism on steroids, the extremes of which most people never get to experience or witness. And Lovisa couldn't help but ponder: what would the lifespan of these folk be…? Mortality must be challenged, surely. For it was a rare, indulgent marathon event for Lovisa and Danny, (and they were no wimps on that front), but for their French friends here, this was not special. It was *the norm*….
One word:
terrifying.

And hence the French summary thus far: the degree of their (generally justified) arrogance was met / equalled only by the degree of hedonism they achieved. Always to the grandest scale.

Pinnacle.

The relentless maintenance of which could only lead to a devastating demise….

And yet whilst all this was occurring, in the heights of hallucinatory eclipse, plans were being devised and scheduled on 'business scheming pursuits'. One would question the validity of any decisions made while within this bubble of mental carnival capers, but it was all part of the game to Danny and greater courage (read insanity) ensued.

Even more terrifying.

The phonecalls he made during this time went unnoticed by Lovisa. Her attention was somewhat sabotaged with current chaotic matters at hand.

Nevertheless, things unfolded like a magic carpet before her. She was just trapped in the ride.

While on their French sojourn, Randy Clarson and his girlfriend Lia were staying at the London abode - still empty with aunt Gladys's absence. It had all been pre-arranged, evidently. Lovisa knew Lia well - (she had lingerie waitressed for her on her stripping shows; they had worked extensively in the industry together.) Lia had been lured by her boy to the lights of the big apple [they had just been there on 'business' prior to his London trip. It didn't take a rocket scientist to work out he was there for the London E's.]

Meanwhile, the local Marseille police were cracking down on drugs, so supplies there were scarce. Maurille and Danny went to a local festival and spent hours scouring the streets until they finally scored. Once back at the cave, they bonged on and planned 'future business' in Australia; Danny suggesting they should start a mini investment for him with sups for France, so he had a bank account there to survive on for a while.

It was all becoming unbearably toxic for Lovisa. As much as she participated in the games ahoy, she felt the walls were closing in….anxiety was the general sensation of her existence now. All the masks don't hide what the mirror knows to be the facts, after all. Even in smokescreens and blurred vision. She clutched her diary close to her; guarding it protectively. Her only truth and ally for now. Like a security blanket, she held onto it for dear life, and entrusted it with information the likes of which could be damning and expose several smiling assassins in the process……her weapon. A superpower. Honesty can be a curse however…she told it like it was.

It was while on 'Hoffman' trips (designed with respect to the founder of LSD himself - Albert Hoffman) at an underground Rave party that the news arrived to Danny that the cash Clarson had sent for a big business purchase in France hadn't come through. (You couldn't send money between Britain and France). Nevertheless, the deal went ahead. Danny funded the sale with his own credit card and he and Maurille headed off to Paris to do the business. She asked no further questions; remaining alone with her diary and postcard writing. He returned earlier than anticipated; pupils wired on MDMA and very chuffed with proceedings.

Lovisa felt sick to her stomach. Like stage fright. But the show must go on…..play the game. Don the mask. Do what you have to do, right. One can not be suspected to be weak or cowardly. The games were dark but the risks darker. They were joined by a gang of Maurille's street strays; the lads he hung and scored with for the most part. They all dumped E's and took off on a road trip to St Raphael. The bong was passed around the car creating a dutch oven vehicle of fog. After meeting others at a local bar for lots of hand passing and money exchange, they headed back to Nino's impressive place for games of pool, dancing and more indulgence. A brief crash out exercise must have ensued, for they evidently woke to huge bowls of black French coffee and the wafts of pan au chocolate for sustenance before the return journey.

This is how the life went there. It was just one rolling exercise of debauchery onto the next. Lovisa considered: the prevailing attitude was most certainly live fast and fuck what the future holds…..it was all about the here and now. To the ultimate hardcore degree in every undertaking. It was akin to borrowing the buddhist mantra of 'live in the moment' and screwing the underlying semantics of *peaceful existence* to the other spectrum of jaw-grinding masochism; - that was anything but.
Was it their form of rebellion and power?

Mortality was of no importance or consequence here. Suck it dry; live and die.

She would be lucky to escape the grasps of this mindset before it was too late and her own mortality was chopped into a fraction of the assigned duration on this earth...

They purchased cases of fresh fruit and sat on the rocks at the beach overlooking the bay as they gorged on the juicy joy. She stayed to sunbake while the lads had stone throwing competitions until bored, after which Danny and Maurille took off yet again to score in Toulon. The following day they went to 'la cride'; clambering down a steep rockface to a diving crystal blue haven below, where they went snorkelling. By normal accounts these would appear like healthy travel pursuits, were it not for the evil interludes of ingestion that took place.

The midnight trance party in a quarry was a most dark memory in her mind. Literally. There was a sense of impending doom; emblazoned further by the intense MDMA that was engulfed. A bizarre situation in the middle of nowhere with everyone floating around from one theme room to the next in this huge cave-like landpit. It was a hippy scene, and everyone blissed out and floaty, but she just wanted <u>out</u>....

What happened next, as I paint the picture for you, was the part that proved like a huge ink stain on an already tarnished canvas.

It was time for them to leave the south of silliness and head back to the land of the lost.....farewells to the French freakers ensued, and they departed.

So Lovisa reluctantly took the train with Danny from Paris to Amsterdam again. In Paris they had been joined by Randy Clarson as they awaited the TGV. Grins all round from the boys and veiled suspicions from Lovisa. She sensed a far from calm journey ahead.

He greeted and gifted them with some penguin trips. A double strategy ticker on his behalf. (He actually wanted them tested, and knew Danny would be more than willing as usual, so for the ensuing train journey he intended to sit back and observe)

In addition, and perhaps more importantly, it would serve to quell any nervous tension on *courier* duties to unfold….

While they had been in Toulon, Clarson meanwhile had spent the week in Paris; *'living the life of luxury and soaking up the sights and sounds of the city of romance'*. (While shopping extensively for 'stock'….and awaiting the order. …..the entire purpose of the sojourn.)

The humble luggage he carried contained no clothing or other items for instance. He had tossed those days ago to allow more room for purchases and alleviate any suspicions with bulk cargo. For he intended to offload it onto his two little 'transport vessels' anyway so he would no doubt return to London virtually empty handed; aside from a few deliberate postcards, souvenirs and so forth from the city of romance……deliberate decoy matter. If interrogation ensued. Etc.

Mr clever Clarson: always, always thinking and observing…..Always planning. Always a step ahead. Strategy devising; Visualising. Always covering his arse.

Always cutting off detection or suspicion. Focused.
And most importantly, never, **ever** partaking in any mind numbing purchases <u>personally.</u>
There were disciples; minions for that. Other vessels to infiltrate the grey matter of, in 'testing' mode.

Stay clean. Crystal clear.

That was how a professional dealer operated.

And by all accounts, his veneer couldn't be wiser. Created brilliantly.

First impression? The quintessential nerd. Possibly computer guru. Definately intellect. Loner. Ticks in all avenues.

Applause.
This 'vocation' can only <u>be succeeded</u> by obsessive/compulsive alpha types Lovisa realised. Way too many fine details for the average. The operative word here is 'succeed' though…..anyone could **do** it. But success and safety is always another story in life….

(An apt quote here, posted by Snoopdogg:)

'Drug dealers know more about running a business than 95% of college professors'

A few packages and envelopes were quietly passed to Danny who distributed them throughout both his and her bags, while Clarson chatted animatedly with Lovisa to try to distract her attention from the actions to hand. At one point Danny demanded she get out her lingerie, and made her stuff pills in the linings of it. She obeyed instructions but knew she had to seek exit asap.

During the train ride Clarson issued Lovisa with bribery chocolate bars and some jewellery - much to the amusement of Danny who knew his tricks. She was no fool but she graciously played along. Danny had obviously had a few quiet words with him to ensure plans went smoothly.

She took deep breaths and focused her mind on the mantras: Always watch your back….trust nobody but yourself. They were becoming like a cement encasing on her now. Some lessons always stay.
Like a tattoo brain scar.

Clarson calmly fixed his attention on her. *"Now, I hear you are a very clever lady in the expression field. A wordsworth. A gifted writer and so forth? Im impressed! I envy that talent."….*
t₀ be closely followed by : *"and I hear that you write a **very special diary** that lists every little minute detail of your travels and adventures abroad…..is that true?!"*

Leaning forward as if in confidence, and virtually whispering: *"You know, I would love to see that. Do you have it with you?!"….*

Queue rapid heart rate, panic alert sensations and self-protective urgency.

Lovisa remained calm, but she knew she was cornered and monitored. Every action, every move…..

"We wouldn't want such information getting into the wrong hands now, would we….let me help protect you with that"…..

So this was hell, she registered.

To offer analogy imagery: think caged animal; trying to protect its' offspring from attack.

For the fear of having her diary taken now superseded that of the drug trafficking antics. Go figure! And its amazing how patterns and cycles work

in life, like quantum physics. And she was definitely a creature of
'patterns'….destined to be a croupiere…..(but that's another chapter
for another time)…..

For the rest of her life cycles played out. Like an album on repeat. For she
would lose everything dear to her many times. She could never hold onto
things. But the one thing nobody could ever take was her writing. Because it
WAS her. Write what you know.
Just make sure you keep it safe and hidden.
The rest of the train journey, as utterly exhausted as she felt, it was crucial
she got no shuteye and kept guard. She knew that if she slept, her bags would
have been searched. So feigning period pain, she rumbled through her bag
and put the diary, with painkillers, tampons, and some clothes etc in another
bag and 'left for the bathrooms'…they probably even rummaged in her
absence. In any case, she found a hiding spot behind some huge heavy
luggage in the compartment near the toilet, and stashed it there to retrieve
before disembarking. Making several trips back and forth to ensure it was
safe.

Mr C kept prizing her with joints and chocolate in an attempt at sedation
but she was aware of all tricks and merely played along. Safety always first.
For the book had lots of intricate details; of no interest to the normal reader
but to the parties involved it risked exposure complete. She knew it, and they
had obviously become aware of the fact too and intended to eliminate any
threats.

They eventually arrived back to London and she was a jangle of nerves.
Sleep deprived and anxious. For she had guarded her diary around the clock;
never letting her defences down for fear of a property siege ….the threat had
been there and it was real; not imagined. For they knew that the contents of
her private journal were always of a brutally honest nature, and would leave
no stone unturned. It was a massive danger zone threat for their ensuing
activities. Corrupt as they were. She had unwillingly become an accomplice
to the facts, and that is something a serious dealer eliminates.

As she had returned to her hiding spot to retrieve her book, her heartbeat was so strong and fast. She nearly fainted. If she got out of this sitch unscathed, it truly would be a miracle. She wasn't religious but she said silent prayers.

She found herself grateful for London's security system: CTV throughout carriages and on stations etc. The eye in the sky was not usually an ally to a criminal, but in this case it felt like a lifesaving device.

So it was good to be back on some safe solid ground, and to exhale for the moment. The sight of Aunt Gladys and her presence in the home was a joy to behold at this time. Like a safety net, it calmed her jangled nerves.

Danny's 23 birthday arose. Family calls from Australia. Lovisa's dole cheque came through too, so it was cake and bong fuel provided, plus cash to process the French photos. Pretty epic visuals of debauchery. They hired a video and watched 'The crying game' - about the IRA and underground London. A somewhat camp element throughout; prompting Danny to sort the pre-purchase of their sleaze ball tickets for back in Sydney. It was one of the annual gay party events they attended, knowing many other fellow enthusiasts of debauchery; consisting of all gender preference variations and obscurities.

A visit to see some comrades however turned into disaster as she knew it would. Nat revealed a bundle of deceit and lies on Danny's behalf; including a tonne of consumption and substance abuse while she toiled working - which explained a lot regarding his prevailing dark moods and evil nature. It all resulted in a complete showdown, and calling the cops.

They were a well known couple in several cities now by the pigs; - becoming a bit like the boy who cried wolf.....it was another traumatic blur of an evening but she was pretty sure she would always remember the threats of having her "pretty model face scarred for life"

Days later he went to collect flight tickets to Amsterdam again to meet with mr C. The $65,000 he had made twice with a few small bags and stints would have been impressive to her a year ago, but now it just flooded her gut with nausea. She was so over the repetitive zone of sideline dealings, and dreading the whole risky exercises.....so while he was out she too found a payphone to contact her uncle, currently on vacay in France. She had spoken to her mother only days before, urging her to *"go straight to your uncle Jax in Montpellier…..he will protect you. Call me when you are there."* Shortly after that, Danny had seized the phone out of the wall and hidden it from her for good measure.

Things were getting a bit distorted; the walls were closing in around her……she needed an out, so carefully planned her exit. She would depart their little venture at the point of Paris (Clarson intended to head over to France for a few days 'holiday' with their contacts in the south - via Paris, so the 3 of them were to part ways in Paris.) Instead of accompanying Danny back to London, she would head to her uncle…….the convincing excuse still to be crafted in her busy mind.

She wanted to stash her diary somewhere safe while away, but as always, it was safer to <u>remain</u> with her at all times….life had taught her to never leave property unguarded. She was only attracted to brilliant minds; the caveat of which was, they were capable of so much on the *deceit radar* that it was paralysingly scary. Like her, they played to win. And they didn't suffer defeat mildly.

For she knew the beast she was aligned with, and the passion she felt for him went hand in hand with his evil alter ego. Love and danger were a parallel universe…..
~if she wanted 'safe' she would have opted for a balanced, mainstream; normal future and career-driven man. A protocol prince. Dull and predictable. Brain boredom. She'd endured a few and they weren't her thang. By contrast, the thrill and excitement was always stimulated with Danny…physically and intellectually. But the price to pay was fear. It was a tarif that only served to enhance the sensual magnetism further. Some would call it masochistic.

While in Amsterdam, they had gone on a few side street meanderings while stoned. He took her hand with a sexy, evil look on his face and said *'lets go on a walk babe….I want to show you the other side of this town'….*
Her anxiety level already heightened; acute paranoia was a natural bi-

product. Pot panic.   But it may have been
warranted….for you just couldn't predict the nature of this beast while under
the influence. She was intrinsically aware that his sideline 'business' schemes
would involve her somehow, without consent or knowledge so all trust had
officially left the building.

Now she was convinced he was planning to do her in on a dark, secluded
alleyway somewhere. She posed as a potential threat to his risky dealing
schemes, so was to be discarded….. Heart pounding, she resisted his leading
arm and pleaded nausea that required a swift return to the hotel. He folded
his arms with a tilted head and gave her the look of *'you can't be serious,
bitch'…..*
Real or imagined on the fear radar, their partnership had become one of
uncertainty and in her case despair. Worried for his mental state and her
mortality rating, she knew that a mission to divide them a while was utterly
vital now. Maybe it would heal the scar. Maybe not. But it had to happen.

So with more sleepless nights of scheming and planning her escapade solo,
the day to leave for Amsterdam arrived yet again with a gut feeling of
trepidation for her. The ensuing morning quarrels that were now everyday
activity, coupled with her intense weariness were impacting greatly on her
power for defence. She forgot to pack several items as a result of the
distractions.

Once on the plane, and then back once again in the wacky weed domain,
Danny was quite calm and pleasant; akin to 'returning home'.

To kill time on the train from the airport she had her tarot cards read by a
tripper dude. The forecast was predictable. He told that her 'present' was
open minded and experimental; her 'challenge' was to balance her aura and
energies, and her 'future' was proposed to be a duel (referring to the dual
aspects of her personality: good vs evil. The real her and her alter ego)

Masks and mirrors……

Petit déjeuner ensued at the grasshopper cafe as they met with mr C.
Complimentary cappuccinos from the barista there that knew them like
family by now; laced with 'la fraise' acid trips - courtesy the big C himself.

He simply popped them on top of the cappuccino froth to dissolve and
delight. A different method; albeit a novelty to be tried and tested.

Coffee and strawberries. Breakfast of champions.

His cousin was in tow, showing them how to roll primo tulip joints; a skill akin to origami - a true dutch delicacy!

She experienced waves of intense paranoia while tripping - (Danny's dangerous 'revenge plot' threats taking their toll in her sub-conscience)

A couple of mindless days of continual joints, coffee and munchies ensued, before the overnight train trip to Paris.

The boys were to head to Toulon in the south for 'la fete' and sideline business, while she would change-over for Montpellier, to the francofile uncle. (Unbenownced to other parties involved. Read escape plot)....

A few more petit dejeuneur sessions of debauchery occurred. Acid caffeine and croissants. Delicieux! Melt in the mouth moments of mental mayhem....

Finally reaching departure date, she felt a mixture of nerves and excitement.

Scoring a sleeper carriage, they were at least in a degree more comfort to do overnight travel. It wasn't spent sleeping though naturally; smoking joints and eating the usual cavalcade of munchies crap continued. The pot smokers' sin bin existence....... *(Far from pristine and those who have done it wonder how they ever coped with feeling so perpetually 'messy'; often parading down the **other** direction of perfectionist obsessive compulsive prison pattern behaviour **later**- almost as penance. Lovisa being no exception later in her life.....but back to the story.........)*

Finally in Gare du Nord, she managed to slip away to the public toilet and from there, sneak off swiftly to catch <u>her</u> other train to destination emancipation.While waiting she wrote him a message on the phone that she sent once safely on the journey to Montpellier. His reaction was bound to be one of fury, but being far away and safe by that stage, relief flooded her veins with a sensation of near-sedation after days of highly strung angst. She desperately longed to catch up on some sleep, but gripping her diary and belongings close, forced herself to remain alert.

Arriving in Montpellier to family; real sleep in an actual bed; a shower in a normal bathroom with privacy and proper hearty 'real' food was to be a joy beyond description. .....things normally taken for granted are like luxury gifts from the gods at travel times like these in ones' life.

St jean de la Blacqier…..a picturesque French village in the south of France. At the time it was still authentic and untouched by human modernisation/modern intervention. It was akin to stepping back in time to a commune from the 18 century. All charm and harmony.

A village consisting of a local bakery, butcher, fishmonger and fruit/vegetable vendor.

Or, more appropriately put: a Supermarche; Boulangerie; Bucherie; Patisserie; La Post, and Le Tabac.
A few other little industry shops laboured on, such as shoe repairs, tailors and so on also. It was refreshing quaint and peaceful; - and dare I say old fashioned, unlike modern impersonal shopping malls and centres on a grand and soul-less scale.

One can still see remnants of such villages in various areas scattered predominantly throughout Europe, but sadly they eventually get upscaled and trodden on.

(Cornwall was a UK example of this; the once village environment has now been superseded by the demand for the franchise monster store chains that now adorn the outskirts. It destroys the unique charm and peace of a place once consisting of a close-knit, healthy community atmosphere. More touristic money-making zones now.)

Local walks around the vineyards, olive and fruit trees after hearty breakfast fare; trying to rebuild an appetite for the ensuing lunch then pastis aperitifs, with saucisson, cheese etc followed by dinner ……the gluttony never ceased. How the French avoided obesity was a mystery that they touched on in animated conversation; settling on the notion that it was all the accompanying wines for digestion which they hence included also as a must (!). Any excuse. Bien sur…..

The clever manipulation of semantics was a skill she had well honed in her life thus far and would no doubt continue….

Her beloved Uncle and 'the godfather' her mother had chosen was an adorably jovial man. His rosy cheeks and twinkling eyes expressed sheer delight in the luxuries of life. He relished indulgence as the French themselves do, and was right at home here amongst the fine fare and frivolity of daily existence.

He was such a brilliant-minded specialist doctor that she wondered how
he could allow himself to be a victim of the chain-smoking variety. For it
wasn't just a francophilic action he had adopted..... It must have been the
stress and demands of his skill, she surmised. Much pressure to solve
mysterious health scares that he was renowned for eradicating and healing.
But then again, people would probably wonder how she let herself pursue
hedonism to death-defying degrees too....physician heal thyself (!)

There seems to always be a mirror image of contrast in all people of such
calibre. Think Jeckyl and Hyde. Mega intelligence = self-destructive
behaviour patterns. She knew all about it.

Although she hoped her evidently alpha bloodline would finally reveal
itself in her, she wondered what the downside tax would be if it did.. She was
already a hazard enough to herself. The prison walls of personal lifestyle
habits and rituals were growing taller brick by brick the more life threw at
her.

Stories relayed to her by her mother of her great uncle Ben; a scholar and
elite linguist who had chosen to live a life of complete seclusion in hermit
fashion in Madrid showed a similar pattern. He spoke 27 languages to their
knowledge and was worth a small fortune but was such a miser he studied
away relentlessly by candlelight to save on power bills; living in a most modest
Pensione with virtually no possessions; but for his work and his marvellous
mind.

Minimalism was another of the evident traits. Too much 'stuff' and
people interference disturbed the delicate mantras of their code. Self
containment and privacy was a distinct, vital necessity. Alien crew

With the prevailing pressures of his daily life, she could see why her uncle
had chosen his vacay in this terrain, The whole environment and daily life
here was conducive to much introspection and thinking time. Though a
natural action, it was a rare luxury when compared to the usual pace and
stressors of normal life in faster-paced zones. One realises this only in
retrospect however, as time to ponder anything is also not a normal allowance.
Auto-pilot actions prevail as one continues moving or gets squashed under the
pressures of life existence and, mostly, deadlines.

Being her <u>godfather</u>, this surprise (read imposing) trip she embarked
on to visit him as a self-rescue ploy proved to be the fulfilment of his role
entirely.

Sorted. Weren't godfathers supposed to ensure that one is religiously cared for if their immediate parents were deceased?! Well, she *wasn't* religious, by choice, so rescuing her from a drug-crazed; potentially dangerous maniac lover - while she was far from her own parents, would be more than the job description ticked in her books! And theirs, no doubt. Her mother had instructed her after all.

Much discussion time on character traits and human behaviour prevailed in comfortable, liberated free flow; akin to a psychiatrists' chair when in his company.

Almost every evening when the others retired for bed, she would sit with her uncle and have the most intense D & Ms - it was akin to such therapy. She sensed it served the same purpose for him; - he had a lot of secrets in his heart as well, she could tell.

(Generally, in those related by blood bonds it is rare; - or at least strained and 'monitored' expression. Often honesty tends to bite one in the arse where family is concerned! The mask remains intact; keep the peace.....save potential conflict etc)

But here they opened their hearts and souls in free flow liberation. Such a relief. Akin to communal dams bursting - they expressed their innermost feelings equally; in recognition of a trusting soulmate.

He was also an avid list-writer - definitely her blood uncle. The comparative character traits between them were now becoming much more obvious. He felt like her kindred spirit. She understood his private, hermit like ways now; -like a mirror to herself.

***** a few suspect family members were also discussed, and using a pseudonym for ease of detail, she opened up about the crazed partner she was embroiled with. He was the perfect sounding board. Reciting things she already knew implicitly, it was often better to hear it also stated by someone you respect, than listen to the voices in your own head. This she knew......often it just took a nudge of sound reasoning.

Regarding her crazed lover, he said that: *"whatever the scenario, it (he) is* **not going to change**......*this is the true nature of the beast of topic. All decisions must be made on that fact alone."*

This seemed contradictory to the person she met and fell in love with. Under evil influences he was another beast entirely. A suggestion: it was a lesson never to be forgotten....how drugs change a person. Entirely. Its like metamorphism on a grand scale. Who you once knew and loved suddenly becomes the enemy .....they don't realise it themselves, but it is those around them who suffer most with the transition and resultant fallout and distrust .....so many times and examples of this had played out in her life. It was like another tattoo. .....and yet one still always gives a new character the benefit of the doubt and replays the same old tune......

Play it again, Sam...history repeats itself. Why do people forget and repeat patterns of hell?? Human nature.

But the person who partakes in substance abuse will always be a tainted character. The poison is bigger than the man.

And until the day that abstinence becomes the mainstay, nothing will alter. The monster remains.

For at the end of the day, we really WANT to trust people will remain constant and faithful. Its never the case, but human nature is also to wish upon a star; dream, and what have you.

'Benefit of the doubt'. Like turning a blind eye to the character before you;

~in preference for the perception the mind, heart and soul longs to believe is true.

Fantasy solitude becomes inevitable after a while, and has proven the happiest path......(read ignorant bliss! A survival mechanism not to be scoffed at).

Protection from mankind and its masks becomes the modus operandi after repeated exposure and turmoil.

Lovisa was by no means a 'tourist sights' fan, but was of course compelled to accompany the family on their journeys of interest out of respect. Aunty Harriot: whose mother was descended from the Hugeunorts of France ; - persecuted for their protestant faith in a catholic nation and forced to flee to other terrain.

It made a historical journey to the town of Aigues Mortes more fascinating. Aunt H seemed to have a morbid fascination with graveyards too - and we visited a few in her company. She would read the tombstones and feel acquainted with the subject. Apparently she did this wherever she went!

- Each to their own, obvs……. respect, and all that jazz….We all have our own little idiosyncrasies after all.

Chateau Capion was more up Lovisa's alley on the touristic front however; - (a winery: thank god!)- sampling the local rouge and blanc vin, and learning about the *appellation controllee* in each region. It served to numb her senses somewhat for further touristic exploits.

Another trip had them off to the fortified city of Carcassonne, (with diary notes describing her joy at a new camera battery for the ensuing postcard shots.) Modern youth today wouldn't understand the 'camera device' concept.   Smart phones govern all aspects of life nowadays, including photography.

The highlight of her sight-seeing however was the ancient torture exposition *'inquisition et punition'*. Terrifying and difficult to view or imagine, but worth the insight to human monstrosity. What man was capable of was beyond comprehension. In another life she felt she would have been burnt at the stake; believed to be a white 'witch' for her alternate ways, surely! Mankind is brutal.

Finally her time to leave arrived with a mixture of fear and trepidation. She was now feeling so revived and relaxed after fab food, wine and excellent sleep; she was not the slightest bit eager to return to the former travel lifestyle of hedonism and self-abuse. But she was now better equipped with mental ammo..

The clean-living stint had rebooted her and reinforced the damage of the situation she was in. Physically of course, but psychologically mostly. (Excuse the French; albeit being in the zone, but it was a monumental MIND F*^K). Expressing herself with free abandon and merely having a sounding board of reason proved therapeutic on a grand scale. Bottling concerns brews potent poisons; it's a sure recipe for disaster. And so the sense of relief and relaxation gave her the impetus to return once again to the hazard zone; simply because there *was* no other choice. Stronger and better equipped.

So to speak.

She farewelled Montpellier and the uncle 'rescue' mission. Little did she know it went 2 ways……

It was to be one of the last times she ever saw the dear man.

(Only one other time - at his estranged daughters' wedding, where she held his hand throughout the entire reception for support. For the revelations of his private world of personal hell was revealed in his infidelity, and conceit to the family unit. In hindsight she realised that he was actually in a world of pain more than her and needed the vent more than she had. She hoped having an ally of sorts had helped with his lonely torment.)

[Lung cancer took him in the end. A gruesome, horrifying finale. Smoking…..the anti-stress tactic of many an intellectual.]

Back in Avignon, the hedonism pursued. Lots of farewell joints with the priveliged lads. Their life of leisure appeared by all accounts one of envy, but in reality, too much of a good thing is way worse than none at all…small doses work wonders but long term reaks havoc. Like any holiday, to be fair.

They endured the final time in toy land Amsterdam (thank god)…..then back to the UK. She swore if she ever went back to the place she would vow to experience it in a more glamorous light. Behind the hostels and pot-smoking dens she knew a world of quaint hotels; fine dining and proper Dutch joy awaited. At least life experiences set your future standards she thought. Nothing is ever wasted if you have the strength of mind to make it a lesson.

A word to the wise….

On the flight back to London, her Sony walkman was stolen from the side pocket of her bag, much to the fury of Danny. She'd only had it a few weeks; the item wasn't meant to be, obvs. (God knows they're like a museum relic piece now)

Once back, she knew the patterns would continue, so as a diversion of attention, she focused on packing again to visit her father's folks up north. Another sideline journey to break up the strained partnership sitch. She hoped it would help to mend it, but with more brewing business schemes in his mind, it remained strongly doubtful.

She had booked her coach trip ticket, but on the morning of travel, the predictable occurred and he had a tantrum rant; throwing her belongings across the room, breaking nail varnish, makeup etc and splattering her new bag and jacket. A total chaos scene, with much screaming and cursing for peppered effect. Her trip was hence delayed an extra day while she cleaned up the debris and fallout of his fury, with gritted teeth. "You should be thankful!….I could do a lot worse to you"….

Later he tried to console her "You know it's only because I care…1 have to be careful with you though. No physical marks or scars. No evidence….." Crafty was his forte. He always managed to cover his arse. Like most of the same league! But deep down, he was a loving sensual creature, she knew. It wasn't his fault the substances controlled his behaviour.

She closed her eyes and recalled her uncles' words of wisdom. In the afternoon while he was out to score, she passed Aunt Gladys in the hallway who asked about her wellbeing: *"I wasn't born yesterday you know"*.

Lovisa looked at her with the expression of 'what can I say?'….to which she emphatically replied : *"He is insecure;..dissatisfied with himself. Be wary: the inability to control and express emotions and behaviour is deep-rooted in his Scandinavian blood"*…..

He was obviously battling his own personal tug of war games, and she actually felt sorry for him, knowing that one always lashes out at the person closest to them. Worry struck her and she forgot her own concerns. She wasn't qualified for this degree of human damage.

Exhaustion constantly prevailed; he locked the door and spent most days now like a wounded animal. Was it wise for her to leave him at all in this state? Maybe it would be what he needed…hard to tell.

Damned if you do; damned if you don't…sometimes in life you just can't win either way, but need to move forward in one direction, so pick the path and pursue it. One thing is for sure: lost opportunities transcend as potential life-long regrets, so should be avoided at all costs. Proactivity must prevail….

And indeed it proved a memorable trip in honour of her paternal heritage, that she would be thankful she didn't miss. They made a colourful effort to welcome her with balloons and a party full of nobody she knew, but all of whom knew her it turned out (!) indicating her father's legacy lived on…he was a regular traveller to his hometown, and a well known friendly face. Their enthusiasm for imbibing passion was contagious; albeit exhausting. (Some of the poms have the constitution of an ox; it evidently comes with the heritage roots)

*'We are akin to **vikings**'* her father used to always preach, much to the mockery of her and her siblings. She now realised the semantics of his cries! Insatiable. The northerners she met were simple country folk though; their innocence evident and indeed refreshing to her.

She made him a photo album of all those surviving 'family plus' characters
that she was introduced to, and were true to his heart. She also included
photos of his childhood street; school; church and general neighbourhood. To
know that she had 'walked his streets' of origin was a bit of a privelege, and
insight into her roots of yore. The photo album was taken to London and
packed as a gift for him she would relish presenting.

Finally flight time again arrived. It was farewells and gifts to aunt Gladys
and off to Bali once more. As stated prior, these were the days where to fly
Garuda you had a death wish: their safety records weren't what they are
today. But cost trumped safety to them in the frivolity of youth…..as is the
case for most.

Cue severe air turbulence, to the likes of which mass panic ensued
onboard. Belongings went flying…..passengers started to think they were
going down for the count, and staff were busy trying to instil a degree of calm
throughout the cabin to little success. A few were medicating with alcohol for
nerves. Amidst the chaos Danny and Lovisa were oblivious to any dangers
and mildly amused through their sedation cloud. As far as Lovisa was
concerned, this was NOTHING compared to the likes of terror she had
endured with deceit. [Although, the author readily admits that years on, the
response to turbulence would be at times high anxiety; regardless of
frequency in the air.]

You can get high all you like, but it doesn't mean the fear disappears when
under threat. She learnt to visualise a 'white light bubble' encasing her in all
takeoffs and landings thereafter. Live and learn.

They finally hit Bali shores once more, and a sense of 'coming home' was
something Lovisa felt in her heart here.

The pursuit of wild sleaze ball party outfits ensued. The annual gay dance-
party in Sydney was a ritual event for them; as was the Mardi-Gras. (But
these were the days when they were more old-school original events with
alternate appeal as opposed to the present day 'tourist attraction spectacles'
they have become, sadly.)
Shops here filled with drag-style costumes proved wonder wardrobes to
explore. She met a multitude of beautiful lady boys, more than thrilled to play

barbie doll games. And while she played dress-ups, he meanwhile wandered the pantai to score again for bong fuel. Or in his case, read *medication*.

He already had some seaside comrades set up to assist; like a homing pigeon. Priorities always prevail…..wherever one lays their hat. Or their bong as is the case here.

Finally back at Denpasar airport for the grand finale leg of this wild ride. They were admittedly sunburnt to the extreme; albeit satiated on the great food, local lovelies and shopping joy success.

Oblivious to the dangers once again, Danny panicked at the airport when the joints he had stashed in his bumbag mysteriously disappeared. Retracing his steps, he noticed them under airport chairs and parts of the airport he had passed through. He retrieved them all and restashed them before joining the queue to board the plane. Being a risky antic which was much to his amusement, it invited a few smirks and knowing glares from fellow travellers. Fearless fellow. She was in a dangerous union of drama and deceit and she felt it intrinsically.

But then a wave of cautious anxiety swept over Lovisa like a current of warning. Her eyes caught sight of the fluorescent warning sign DEATH PENALTY FOR THOSE WHO BRING DRUGS INTO INDONESIA. Nausea flooded her system and she thought she would be sick. For she knew, the illegal substances he had sorted would be stored and locked in checkin baggage too. Hers *to her knowledge* were meanwhile just full of clothes and memorabilia. What about the times she had left the room for water and snack supplies though? There had been many backward and forward exercises for them both in the last 48 hours….. A huge amount of 'bag unattended' time. Lovisa sickeningly realised that he would quite naturally have stashed loot throughout her bag too. It had been done before and was an automatic action for him now. For the way an addict thinks: cover all options…….if *one* got busted? It may act as a deterrent of attention and the *other* could still sail through…..

Always devious plans afoot.

She knew her well-honed actions and mantra for when under threat, and yet when relaxed and in *'holiday mode'* one tends to forget their disciplinary strategies. It is a risky luxury in that regard. She berated herself for letting her guard down….She was supposed to be constantly protecting herself from the exposed identities.   Always watch your back…….self-protect and be ready to run.

Leave no room for error or blind-sighted attack.

There was a time when he wouldn't have exposed her to such dangers. One she remembered fondly. Now, however he was different in several ways. The cowboy courage capers had made him invincible; impermeable - which entails zero emotion or consideration to anyone or anything that posed a threat to his strategy plans. Often devised in a non-calculated or carefully thought through manner as a result of the noxious substances on free flow availability. His usual attention to minute details was now null and void. He had no fear of retribution anymore. A most dangerous personality trait to be amalgamated with.

On the packed plane, she sat through waves of the intense anxiety and nausea that paired sickeningly with the prevailing air turbulence on board.

She knew the desperate character traits of a user. They can trample on nearest and dearest, defying law and logic with a seemingly crystal-clear conscience. For when in the manic swings of addiction, nothing else matters! Trust issues for anyone in their radar are shot to shit.

The true description and volume of whatever 'souvenirs' had been cunningly packed were a mystery. Just the fact remained: it was there and he didn't waste chances. Never had and never would. Like her: all or nothing/black and white perameter restrictions in all aspects of life. The reason why they connected so well, but also, no doubt, the cause of their breakdown.

Eventually the announcements of descent emerged, and she focused intently on defying the hyperventilation at hand. Focus on breath. Normal bodily functions seem to need concentration when in a state of turmoil. A rough landing was par for the course. Her heart pounded wildly as the plane tick-tocked from one wheel to the other on tarmac.

People scrambled for backpacks and belongings in overhead lockers. It was disconcerting to be amongst the chaos all around when already feeling dizzy with despair.

Concerned her feet would buckle from beneath her, she walked off the plane with exaggerated concentration that must have garnered a few raised eyebrows. Could others notice she wondered? It reminded her of the guy in midnight express as he sweated profusely while chewing gum nervously. It drew security attention like waving a red flag to a bull. Could they hear her heart beating wildly in her chest?! Boom boom.

Forget strong coffee....live with a wild boy and your risks of heart attack must treble infinitely!

Speaking from experience: you burn out super fast in the realms of lust appeal. The types that enliven also destroy.

Longevity is only gained from the safety of a boring life and partner.....sigh.

Nothing comes for free. Bottom line.

Arrival entailed a bus from plane to airport terminal. This was no red carpet business class travel!.....and most flights to Bali were of the budget no frills variety, and have remained so.

The calibre of occupants were often rowdy and obnoxious too from party focused intentions from the moment they left their homes. Nothing has changed in this regard. The reputation of Australians in this holiday destination is generally not one to be proud of.

The airport security are wary of this fact too, and it is quite acute and strict compared to more civilised journey location arrivals. They swoop in force and prepare to arrest.

It feels like interrogation tactics are looming as soon as you disembark.

Upon collecting checkin luggage, all passengers were instructed to stand aside their personal bags in a line. Lovisa's fear radar hit red alert. What the hell was going on now? It felt like being amongst a throng of suspected criminals. What am I doing in this situation she thought with wild panic until she remembered the facts of her reality. She searched the expressions on the security staff and whether their focused gaze lay upon her or Danny in particular. Of course she was convinced they were prime targets, and went into some kind of mental shock as one probably does when arrested and incarcerated. Human nature is of course to suspect the worst. Mental preparation, if you will. Nothing could protect her now. The fun and games were over and the shit was now super real.

But the full assault hit when the sniffer dogs were led in to walk the length of the passenger queue slowly; instructed to stop at every bag and have a good whiff. Holy shit. Dogs can detect even the tiniest hint of contraband and illegal substances…..their craft is well honed and taught from litter birth. One may be able to defy human detection if cunning, but canine patrol? Not a chance….   On flights from Indonesia, Thailand and much of Asia, it is almost expected that they will catch a deviant intent on a little 'sideline business'….or merely for personal use. Attaining it was a walk in the park at these locales compared to Aussie shores, and the temptation too great for many. Indeed the very purpose of their journeys was sheerly for that fact.

When panic and fear hits peak crescendo and can't get any more intense, a sense of calm pervades the body like a wave…..its like you have embraced the ultimate it could be and have accepted worst case scenario.

So when the dogs stopped at Danny's bag for an extended period of time….. Like, **way** longer than anyone else's, Lovisa felt she had already experienced the aftermath. The staff serenaded them with "Good boy!…..what have you found ? Is there something there boy?" Cue some dog treats to encourage them further.

Lovisa felt the blood flow away from her face, and was sure her palor must have been grey like a ghost. Her legs turned to jelly and felt like they would crumble beneath her. Acid rose in her chest and waves of nausea mixed with cortisol overload. Adrenalin doll, a beacon of alert….could they see her about to pass out in front of them? Surely….

Difficult to plead 'bali-belly' at a crucial time like this. It took all her concentration to remain standing upright and not collapse from the sheer hell of it all. At that point she mentally promised herself that if she got out of this one free she would never forget it, and remain forever relieved and damn grateful for the liberty pass. And learn from it……there is no love worth the risk of your own freedom.

Miraculously, like a gift from a higher being, the dogs moved on and didn't hesitate for long at her luggage either. Maybe Danny had wrapped the contraband in a certain manner that disguised the smell of weed and narcotics. ?! With foil or toothpaste to mask the aroma? Maybe strong coffee even. Or was the dog having a lazy day? If all else fails, they can smell fear, can't they? Who knew…..and who the fuck cared. As long as they were nearly at the finish line of the survival quest.

Her internal sigh was an anticlimax of such cataclysmic proportions from the

terror, that her energy and functioning capabilities plummeted. To the point where she worried for the ability to withstand the simple distance from here to safety, which was the home run after all! A cortisol rollercoaster. Definitely a way to shorten your lifespan if constantly in that state.
Her parents were to collect her from the airport; pre-arranged. She craved curling up fetal in bed to recover. But knowing the relief she would later embrace at last, she also suspected a second wind of life-force that would beckon a toast for sheer gratitude.

They were eventually ushered through to the exit and the sheer relief was euphoric.

Never before in her life had she been so excited to see her folks. Virtually shaking, she walked arm in arm with her mother, who could detect the suffering she had lived through instinctively, and was there to catch her now if she fell. Her father carried all luggage and ushered them to the carpark in his usual serious, safety-focused manner, which was an absolute tonic to behold. He loved an airport and created any excuse to be close to, or in one! She knew flying would never be the same for her now however. She vowed to find a way to upgrade standards to the more..civilised and privelidged few. A mission statement that would colour her future.

Turning her head one last time she caught eye contact with Danny and nodded. He looked at her knowingly, with a sexy smirk and joined the guys who had arrived as his chauffeurs. The lads. The drug squad. They probably popped some acid in his mouth as a welcome-home toast, (just as they'd done for the 'bon voyage' so many months ago).....oblivious to cameras and airport staff.

No matter now- she was emancipated at last and the brain had no more power to process anything but that fact.

Other than she knew she would see him again someday. And she would never stop loving him.......for the line between love, hate and fear is wafer thin. And in time, the ultimate mental safety mechanism kicks in, which is to somehow remember only the *good* stuff.

"For the devil hath the power to assume a pleasing shape".....Hamlet forever.

Masks and mirrors.....the villain and the prince.

She would never know or experience real, passionate love and lust again in her life. This was her chapter for that.

But better to have loved and lost than never to have loved at all.

Words of wisdom:
*Don't ever lose that solid grip
or your emotions they will strip
and once you've reached the withered bone
you're twisted, hurt and left alone.
With love, pain is emotional rape
for 'the devil hath the power to assume a pleasing shape'
So on your own two feet stand tall
and then they can't push you to fall
For when it all is said and done,
to survive, we must keep on the run...
~Lovisa*

Chapter 2:

Rebekkah
and the
Valley Doll

*Hindu philosophers view wisdom as something beautiful and attractive, and therefore feminine...

Comparing girl-on-girl intimacy to 'straight' play is like the feel of <u>soft velvet</u> versus starched lace:
smooth~gliding and sensual to the touch; vs rough and fumbling.
*The **fabric** of society is based on an ingrained protocol; a code of social behaviour.*
Men, women, children, families.....its 'what one does'.....
Play
The
Game.
And adhere to its rules. For what....acceptance?

For those who dare to rebel, however, and jump over the walls of confinement;
seeking what the heart directs,
It's an instinctive....(read preferable) union;
~ not one formulated from masses of conflicting info and advice on 'the expected protocol procedure of play'.
Society dominates the drive and mindset of the 'norm'....whereas with gay encounters, it comes from instinct. Because there ARE no rules. Kind of goes with taboo terrain !!
Risky and exciting.....
*Conversely, it's generally a cocktail of confusing disaster in the **'straight**-lace' sector!*
Restricted and unsatisfying.
(You can dispute this all you like 'till you have jumped the fence yourself....)

Lesbian play is more like being in a trance and being on autopilot. Naturally.

Close your eyes and focus on the sensory guidance of the subconscious desires.
Let go…lose control…. Isn't that what good sex is?
People have lost touch with the whole point of the exercise! I guess that's why so many drugs are usually involved with <u>hetero</u> missions of lust.
How often do women really reach the ahh moment without faking a finale? Stop kidding yourself…..
Too many boundaries; rules; expectations and disappointments.
The moves 'here' come naturally. It's……understood.
There is no satnav required for familiar territory (!)

Why do I speak of all these things?
Because I know firsthand. I have fallen on/(off) both sides of the fence.
And I know which one has the thorny bushes of torment and which one comforts your fall with feathery rose petals…….
Not that i am strictly one-directional….for I usually fall victim to the protocol of society in that regard too.
Play the game….
But on the occasions I have leant to the direction we speak of….
Well, my sentiments have been expressed.
As best I can…..

Rebekkah and Barbara met while on a fashion photo shoot for a magazine spread. Barb was one of the line-up of girls to be puppetteered for the lense to gape in their wake, and Bekky was the stylist.

Bek was an obvious lesbian. A butch…but with undeniable beauty. When I say that, I'm talking the blokes' clobber; sexy saunter; strong, killer bod; mandatory piercings and shaved head. Think a young Shinead O'Connor in combat..

Barbara was the antithesis. She was all woman and displayed that in all avenues.

"Gawd…you are *such* a girl!" Rebekkah would chant as she flirtingly adjusted her attire or accessorized a look. 'Lippy fem' was the only category she could possibly veer towards.

But, as with all the most intense unions, opposites really **do** attract….and somehow it calibrates the score somewhat.

Balance…..

For Barbie, Bek would prove the perfect *boy*…..undeniably gorgeous; sensual; and yet masculine in an androgenous way, that she felt an instinctive yearning within. Like all the subjects of her affection, she was attracted to the great humour and fast wit of this new love interest. Essential ingredients.

Bek would deliver the goods and hit the zone like a bullseye every time. Without communication required. It was instinct. It was easy. Uncomplicated.

It made sense….

As stated, at this time, the resemblance of Bek was to Sinead O'connor; an icon of her times.
By today's standards: think classic Ruby Rose.
I don't know about you, but I've described my perfect gentleman..(!)

When one of the fashion changes required a boy look:
~complete with jeans; doc martins; black top tied; hair slicked with a cap on backwards; a can of coke prop and a wide-legged macho stance pose, Rebekkah held her chin in her hand and shook her head…"Nope, you're the valley doll honey….that look is better <u>on</u> me". She wrapped her arm protectively around Barb, putting her hand into her back jean pocket. "Although…..if I painted a mo on your lip"…she teased.
It was soon evident that they were misfits in the group. The two stuck together like siamese twins while the other girls coyly pouted and posed looking on at their union with female jealousy. It's amazing how women who profess to be totally straight can watch a lesbian coupling and then seek a taste themselves. For it will always be up there as a 'fantasy desire' - regardless of sexual preference.
Barbara had been in romantic entanglements with women before to varying degrees, but none reached the depth and degree of this one. She felt it deep in her core. It was like an ache.
One that can't be explained….except to say that it often takes one by surprise when they stumble across such a life experience.
It takes the usual protocol parameters of union behaviour and decimates them with the excuse of uncontrollable lust……and that is, after all, the only way to describe true **passion** adequately.

Barb wondered: was it *always* a naturally genetically-attributed scenario to fall into the realms of homosexuality? What if it was all someone had been subjected to; exposed to, and knew…?
Could they not then adapt to, and prefer it to the alternative ? Her mind drifted to analogies.

She thought of the documentary she had viewed, on human toddlers dumped in a forest and brought up by wild dogs. When older they were only able to move on all fours; they barked, scratched, and aside from external appearance were dogs 'personified' in a *copycat* fashion….
When later rescued by doctors, they then refused to accept human reintroduction. It was in their *soul* now….they escaped clinical captivity and fled back to the pack where their 'family' remained in the wild.
It just goes to show…you cant fuck with nature. Or intrinsic **programming** from birth.

The group meetings outlined the ensuing days of photography assignments. They were to be country, forest and waterfall shots. It had been sponsored by Calvin Klein, intimate lingerie and Guess jeans.
Bek rolled her eyes as the catty arguments started over 'who should be entitled to wear what' and so forth before the photographer himself intruded with the command of 'Enough squabbling! listen to what the stylist had designed for each of you individually. Any aggravation and you get sent home.' And then for good measure he added 'by hitch'….which had a squeak of horror amongst the group.
'Wow, he is pissed' Barb whispered to Bek.
'Oh, he's a teddy bear really' she grinned - 'I've know him….like forever it seems. We go way back. He's like a father to me in many ways'…..

Bek had been in the industry since a tot. She was swept up in its allure after her father, an artist himself had been working on paintings of naked women. She was virtually weaned on the concept of 'naked' - and naturally, became a naked model for artists herself from the age of around 12. From there it was modelling, fashion, styling and so forth.
Women women women. And gay men mostly. Like her Dad.
Its all she knew.

Barb got the impression that Bek had been through several rough phases of being like a homeless street kitten. She understood that. For she had been there several times in her own life. Interesting, albeit hardship chapters.
Character building.

The group were all allocated separate hotel rooms on the modelling mission outback. Identical rooms with the essentials: bar fridge, well-equipped bathrooms and comfortable beds. For those who opted to get the beauty sleep required.
Barb had *intended* on that.
Natural sleeping pills packed; lavender oil for the pillow and so forth.

They remained in her bag however. For as she shut her door and set her alarm for the following mornings' super early start, she heard the knock at her door.
Peep hole indicated it was someone with dark brown eyes. Evidence blinking right up against it - like showing a fingerprint for identity. Well that didn't exactly narrow it down since 4 of the 5 other girls had brown eyes!
'Who is it?' she asked as she prepared to open it.
'Your worst nightmare, dream girl'......
She let Bek in, albeit reluctantly; feeling self conscious with a bare face and pyjamas on.
'Don't be coy valley doll; you ain't got nothin'i ain't seen before. I got your back...'
Bek marched on in and sat cross-legged on the bed; intent on rolling a joint. 'This might help achieve dream-scape.....always helps me'.
Barb sighed. She had endured a long struggle herself with trying to quit the wicked weed, but was partly seduced by the thought of its calming powers now. She knew it wasn't conducive to the fresh-faced start required, but it was either that or stare at the ceiling most of the night as she often did....so what was the worst evil?!
Bek chatted away as she rolled and Barb glanced around for her morning gear, list and alarm clock. She knew it would be panic stations come sun-rise.
Mental preparation tick-off before she allowed the brain to melt down like a candle until it dimmed completely. She convinced herself that *some* shut-eye would assist. Even if it was induced artificially.
Natural sleep was an elusive concept to her but one that she hoped she could one day achieve. Maybe it took a clear conscience and no haunting past? In that case, she was fucked! Destined for eternal insomnia-ville.

They sat together and slowly unravelled as they chatted; the chemical toxins floating serenely to the mind-box.
"You wanna come on a road trip?" Bek asked languidly.

Barb glanced at her, unsure. "Oh relax, it's not to the bloody outback in a camper van princess!! Its a chilled out country trek, before hitting the slopes. I want to get some ski time in this winter. And besides….a girlfriend needs me to come rescue her on a stopover".....

Barb knew Bek was nothing but adventure, but she was kind of enjoying her quirky, twisted outlook on life. And her company so far had proved far from dull!

She had undertaken this assignment to enhance her portfolio parameters, but the motive had now altered for Barb;….she desired to spend every moment with this fascinating woman. She was certainly multi-dimensional. The type she was attracted to. On all levels…

She generally shunned people. Not only for self protection but also because they either bored her senseless; wasted her time with fake chitchat or just stole her precious **alone** time…..she cherished that.

Needed it.

"All the people in Los Angeles are doing it: running ass-wild after something that is not there. It is basically a fear of being alone. My fear is of the crowd, the ass-wild running crowd; the people who read Norman Mailer and go to baseball games and cut and water their lawns and bend over the garden with a trowel"
(Charles Bukowski from 'tales of ordinary madness')

Bek was doodling on a hotel notepad as she waited for Barb's response to the proposal. A profile portrait of Barb as she pondered the journey: its rewards and potential risks.

The thing that concerned her most she thought privately was that if the risks outweighed all else, then the appeal factor was heightened exponentially for her. Twisted for sure, but it was what it was and she was far from the society's norm.

Barb broke from her trance and bit her bottom lip as she surveyed the art: Quite amazing sketching - and actually very complimentary!

'Wow' - you do me gracious justice ! 'I used to love to sketch myself as a child….and then at art school'

Bek enquired 'what did you sketch?' …..

'Oh, still-life sometimes….no, wait I painted that in acrylic and oil paints.

Sketching……oh god always sexy women! Cliche style…..think Penelope Pitstop out of that old cartoon on tv!'

They both smirked. 'And exaggerated for sure: blonde; huge double D boobs, tiny waist, pert arse and fabulous long legs with killer heels on. And perfect makeup and hair'.

"God, no wonder you landed yourself where you are - this industry is smack, bang all about the stuff'- Bek looked at her with inquired interest. 'This is fake fiesta at its best''

Barb continued: 'and *horses* for some reason….god knows why. I'm the furthest thing from equestrian you could muster. I think it was their sleek outline and shape of their body, for the pencil. The curves and profound form'

'Then of course at art school it was the naked women they would bring in as models. They were never skinny. The accentuated curvature and muscle definition was always the factor in being chosen obviously…..in that way it was far removed from the visual physique required **here**'……

They both glanced at the uneaten pizza slices they had collectively bought with the whole group. There was evidence of Barb's apple cores, but the fast food remained untouched.

As if to prove a point, Bek defiantly grabbed one of the greasy triangles and began eating. The cheese dripped down her chin.

God she's such a boy, Barb thought as a pang of yearning hit her out of the blue. In fact, more man than many she had met!

She felt respect for Bek and where she had come from. Her survival instincts after turmoil. She was one of the rare few who convincingly grew stronger and wiser as a result of hardship; as opposed to withering in a world of self-destruction and blame.

'Ive always liked to ensure that I have a safe haven to gravitate from, and have done everything to secure that…..but confession : I'm pretty fucked up…. I have trouble concentrating on everything. I tend to continually scan and save stuff… hoping to do some day…." said Barbie.

" That's a shame! Life is for the here and now girl - you have to seize the moment and run with it ! Life is cruel…..you can't live with regrets…" Bek exclaimed in a slightly sombre tone.

Sage advice, Barb thought…

She felt certain she escaped the fate of prescribed drugs for her ADD condition - doctors handed out amphetamines like candy for the condition….her ex boyfriend and her own brother were 2 of the victims. The side-effects could be dire.

She had tended to deal with it on her own terms….a certain degree of 'self-medicating' involved. She knew from Bek's colourful and gregarious personality that she was one of 'them' too….no wonder they had both succumbed to pot. It was the only way to slow down the overactive brain……for they both loved the hyper aspects of life; their personality traits dictated that beyond their control.

"So what about you Barbie; whats your story?"…..her reverie was interrupted.

They then began to unravel the overview of their lives to date for each other. It was Bek in a more intimate light to her normal gregarious social persona. She always projected that usually and hid behind it like a mask.

Barb realised that she often did the same too.

They both shared the world of masks and mirrors…..

No imperfections allowed. Including weak traits, insecurities or flaws. It was a constant challenge to be the all encompassing picture of perfection. Despite what may be occurring on the inside.

"Sometimes I feel like an utter phoney" Bek admitted sadly…. "Everyone thinks I'm just the constant party starter. And the bubbly personality is all there is….i should have been an actress really! Reckon I would have blitzed it. Bravo. Encore. Academy award…….Would have been a better option than stylist I think. But hey - its never too late!! You just don't know where the road winds to, or what doors it may open!"

"Well……life is the ultimate stage when you think about it." Barb suggested. "But there are no rehearsals…..does that sound wildly cliche, or what ?!"

Bek all of a sudden jumped out of bed and ran to the door...."Hold that thought princess; back in a mo..." she left momentarily and returned with her makeup toolkit box. It looked like a tradesman's tools. Especially with her tomboy appearance; shaved head and androgynous physique. The classic model material really.

She opened pandoras box and began to play with the kit she knew best. Brushing Barb's hair aside and started the process of transformation.

Then she started with the makeup. Barbara wondered why she was doing this; she had freshly cleansed her face and settled in for an early night before shooting the following morn, but Bec was so in her element, focused and calm for a moment, that she just let her go for it. It was obviously the place she felt most at home.

The more they chatted, the more dramatic her touches became. The liquid eyeliner went from defined and neat to windswept, dramatic and interesting.....or scary! The only way to describe it in todays' terminology is that she was wildly channeling Amy....(Winehouse that is; with her signature winged lids that became profound emblems of fashion copied and adored worldwide.) of course this was way before her time however, so let's just say it was bordering on gothic horror story. Then came the fake freckles; beauty spots......

Barb had morphed into a canvas of no return.....

This went on way into the early hours, and before they knew it, they heard birds chirping and footsteps. A knock at the door heralded alarm, and the photographer himself was revealed on the other side. "Barb, I'm looking for Rebekah and........what the **fuck** has happened to your face?!"

Barb closed her eyes and gritted her teeth. "Oh shit I'm sorry - I'll cleanse it off immediately. She was just practicing...." Next thing she knew Bek ducked under his arm holding the door open into the hallway to retreat - not so much in shame but in quick situation-damage-control. Holding toolkit box in hand she raced off to her room with a "i know I know, but it's no drama....hang cool 'mr lense' we have situation averted....."

'What the hell were you thinking? Have you slept?'

No answer to that question hung in the air, and had him grunting off to knock on the other doors; a fierce temperament now starting to take hold.

Oh dear they were in for a long day........

Barb frantically scrubbed off the dramatic artwork adorning her face; quickly got changed and raced off to the bus for the photo shoot cavalcade ahead.

In the bus she sat at the back in the corner. The other girls crammed in the middle; chatting and giggling. Comparitively full of energy and fresh-faced after a recharging sleep.

Bek sat in the front next to the photographer who was driving, and was doing her best to subdue his tempered state from an anguished start to the day. She had accompanied him on a multitude of similar shoots, as his trusty sidekick and stylist mostly, but today she was to be involved in the photos too. And rightly so, barb thought. She was by all accounts a more attractive and fit-bodied physique than the rest of the crew in her eyes. Alpha material;~ androgyny promoting perfection.

She turned around and winked at Barb. The attraction pull between them was undeniable.

There were pangs of guilt, but all said it had been a worthwhile night.....in fact, fuck the shoot, she had enjoyed every minute in Bek's company! So hard for her to define or explain to herself, but it was like being with a boyfriend in every way...but *better.*
There were more relatable aspects to the affair too (not to mention the physical one)
They had covered some ground in learning about each other, too.
 Simple, quiet time is required to achieve that. It doesn't occur on the arranged meets or dates or 'diary-devised' rendezvous that so many people get excited or hopeful about. It's really not until you have the 'nothing time' in the same room with someone that their true colours and personalities start to show. It simply won't be revealed until then. Which is of course why so many initial meetings end up being abysmal failures thereafter, when communal time alone is eventually introduced.

While Barb was contemplating this concept in her current situation, Bek meanwhile was entertaining the whole entourage.
As the photographer, with clipboard to hand was verbally outlining the days' agenda and who was to be allocated to what outfit/role/shoot etc, the audible mumble was rendering him annoyed once more.
So she had reached for the glovebox and pulled out a gun. A very convincing looking one; despite the fact it was merely a harmless prop, and was now threatening the row seated behind her. "Listen up.....anyone out of line, and the car contents reduce. I'm talking body numbers.....So obey orders and sit pretty, or else, bitches"..
Given that the girls were somewhat terrified of Bek and her brutish bravado, it was a visibly effective threat.
Steven was in stitches himself now, and it eased the ride ahead for the moment. Always add a touch of comedy spice.....his co-pilot knew how to drive a situation in the right direction.
'That's my boy' Barb thought quietly, blushing beside herself. She knew that deep down Bek could be wildly passionate and vulnerable too. This display was self-protection tactics she had garnered through her life's hardships.
Familiar territory.
Bek looked out the window with a glazed expression....part sleep deprived; part tingly longing. How long was it since she had felt this way? she wondered. It most certainly was true: it always hit you when you least expect it!

The van became a pseudo 'mobile home' as the day wore on. It felt like they were on a movie set. From each assignment to the next, clothes were strewn through the back; quick touch-ups applied and props chosen from the middle seat. It proved a test of patience in such confinement; particularly among competitive ego-driven women. Without Bek's threatening gaze, Bek was sure it would have evolved into catfight city. Thank god for the 'security guard' patrol.

There was one shoot where all of them had to don Calvin Kline underwear; walk over slippery rocks to the focal point and stand under a waterfall. The temperatures this day were bitter; ~the freezing spray of the water a total shock to the system and challenge to defy visibly without shivering and nattering teeth! Such is the challenge of epitomising beauty through discomfort and pain. It was part of the game - and no doubt why it paid so well. The torment tally often truly deserved it, as any model subjected to discomfort can attest.

All the girls wore boy-style boxer shorts and briefs, and covered their breasts with their hands. Bek was included. Barb noticed for the first time what an utterly flawless body she had. Her breasts were small, which served to create her 'tomboy' look, but otherwise she had the sort of shape that all women envy and slave themselves to attempt to achieve. Bek was genetically blessed though - she didn't have to torture herself at all - takeaways for instance, were part of her existence - particularly when she was on the road, and didn't have the access to a kitchen to cook her healthy vegan fare. A rocking metabolism to be sure.

As could be expected, Bek took the initiative to amp up the image somewhat.

Winking at Steven, she turned to the girls and scooped water repeatedly at them; hurling it in a spray of shock and annoyance. The reaction to the scene was priceless; they squeeled; ducked and laughed. And naturally - therein was the money shot.

Steven was beyond thrilled with the grand finale wild water scene.

The girls were livid. Drowned rats.

Result (!)

She was such a fabulous stylist; - Steven always took her suggestions on board for shoots too, and usually followed them. But it was her spontaneous actions, such as this that he was ever-ready for. As that was the gold he was after.

Barb had to contain herself though - she had a hysterics fit at one of the final shoots on the first day. They had reached a farmhouse; which was intended to serve the 'cute country style cowgirl' look well with the rickety old fences and background barnyard. However, Bek was getting bored after a super tedious day of shooting with intermittent sulking and tantrums amongst the bitches.

She got fed up with one of the more surly models, and made her wear a polka dot flair skirt; put her hair in ponytails; and rouged up her cheeks - by all accounts it looked like the circus had come to town.

The magic moment was when she forced her plus 2 other girls stand knee high in mud in the pig pen with the squeeling beasts. They were all way too scared of Bek to defy her orders....even if it meant immersing themselves in squalor!

The following day was less punishing as Bek and Barb were so exhausted they really did get some shut-eye before it all re-commenced.

They left super early - before 5am to a misty looking forest area with abundant trees and a lake beyond the foilage.

Steven was insistent that one of the girls was to be brave enough to do a nude scene with a bow and arrow. Needless to say they all read their 'agency rights' act re not exposing flesh for the maintenance of reputation.

Bek started to strip and screamed 'Oh you sooks! What a pathetic lot of cowards!' - took the weapon and wandered into the chilly mist beyond. She was so perfectly sculptured; - it was more like art than anything vulgar. It almost seemed a shame to cover up such physical perfection. The girls' jaws dropped, and Barb could sense their jealousy at her cellulite-free; lithe frame.

Think erotic 'hunger games'.....

They were indeed the most outstanding photos, but served as part of Steven's personal collection obviously as the intention of the project had always been a fashion shoot. Later, Barb begged him to print her some for herself and he eyed her suspiciously. "Once the magazine spread with you all has been approved and released, you can come to my studio and we shall discuss it then".......
It didn't require a rocket scientist to fathom the undeniable connection between the 2 girls. The nature of which was sexually charged beyond belief.

Barb had butterflies in her stomach....she knew the time would come when they really would intertwine completely - it was just a matter of when. Considering that they were soon to be on the return back to the city after mission accomplished, she realised that not having the others in tow would mean the opportunity would arise and be irresistible. Nervous excitement flooded her gut. She felt all light headed and floaty and it was nothing to do with the prevailing sleep deprivation she was suffering.

With the shoots over and the packup process underway it was all a bit of an anticlimax. The few days away had been charged with nervous anticipation; anxiety; excitement; surprise and discomfort. It was a cocktail of sensations and emotions for all involved; regardless of whether close-knit bonding had ensued or not.
Barb had found it a fascinating opportunity for character analysis....a journey of anthropology if you will. She had always been fascinated by human behaviour; - conscious of her anomaly status, they served to intrigue her. Forever having been a loner and content as such. Most of the girls here were pretty naive; insecure and identity-screwed anyway, so in this industry it had just been about 'keeping immaculate face' under pressure. (Albeit cracking at regular interludes, but remaining in denial of their meltdowns). <u>Fake</u> in other, simplified terms. But Barb really found most people fake anyway and preferred to view from afar, and 'not get too close to the fire'.
Avoid the burn.
What had shocked her, however was that she had not expected lust, and now found herself attracted to someone for the first time in so long. The gender was a new experience for her too. Yet, it was somehow so right and natural compared to all her other encounters and affairs. It felt like she had woken up from a deep coma and all her cells were electrically charged.

The drive back to the city held more passive passengers than on the way. Everyone was pretty exhausted and most of the girls napped for the majority of the journey.
Bek was still up front with Steven but silent for a change, and gazing out the window in deep thought. When they hit a fuel stop, Bek filled the tank and then went in to stock up on some drinks and snacks. She threw a pack of crisps at each of the girls, and then walked to the rear window where Barb was seated. "And for you princess".....winking, she passed Bek the chips, a heart chocolate and an envelope. Barb surreptitiously hid the latter 2 items as the middle seat occupants all leaned over in curiosity as to the preferential treatment she was obviously receiving. A few raised eyes and smirks were made her way before they took off once again.
Barb quietly opened the envelope to read the note inside:

*"Can I make us dinner tonight? You said you had no urgent plans for the next few days.
My flatmate is away so we could have the place to ourselves. Maybe even discuss the
ski trip over a few wines! I make a smashing pasta "*
B xoxoxo

She felt her pulse quicken and butterflies in the stomach. Was this a date? Was she
ready for this after all? - The mention of 'few days' had her feeling anxious.....would
that be too uncomfortably long? She felt compelled to comply and quash her growing
curiosity - but if it felt wrong, how would she escape?
Awkward....
She shyly raised her eyes but all other passengers were blissfully unaware of her
actions at present.
She wasn't sure whether to write a personal reply; speak aside to her in person or just
let it ride until the topic was resurfaced.
In the end she instinctively just smiled and gave a vague nod in Bek's direction when
their eyes met. Thankfully nobody else noticed. The last thing she wanted was the
rumour mill to go awol…especially in this industry. Any gossip spread like wildfire and
this would be an irresistible one to flame.

As the roads became more familiar once the highway cruise came to its end, she
started feeling more edgy as each kilometre clocked down. They were so close to
Surry Hills now, and there was minimal traffic at this time. Her fate (or was it destiny?)
awaited her any minute now.
Either way, it was bound to be a chapter for her experience catalogue. One that had to
be ventured and explored for all its' worth.....opportunities like this were few and far
between in life.

Finally parked nearby Steven's studio, and close to Central station, they all alighted
while Bek provided the 'manpower' required to seize all luggage from the boot. The
camera and lighting equipment took up even more space than 5 womens'
luggage….go figure that one!
Semi-genuine embraces ensued amongst all the women and they possessively 'group
hugged' Steven; insisting Bek and Barb join in for a group photo on their phones.
Off they walked to the station while the remaining team offloaded the camera gear.

"Nonsense, We will all have this back in no time" Bek insisted, raising a dismissive hand
as Steven gave them permission to leave themselves. "But it might cost you a beer at
the local pub afterwards as reward!"…..
The studio equipment returned to its usual nest, the 3 of them walked arm in arm off to
the nearby pub. A beer was not quite Barb's thing, but at this point she was willing to
try anything - especially if it could quash some of her mounting nerves.
"Well, mission accomplished plus some!" Bek grinned while Steven eyed her
suspiciously in return. "What's going on with you miss B….i know you, and something
is definitely different"

"Oh, I think valley doll here and I are just super relieved to have you all to ourselves because we love you so much and get way too jealous when other women get involved!!"

She gave him a cheeky peck on the cheek. "Besides, we all know how f…'ing taxing on the patience women are. The model types Im referring to. The precious princess caper doesn't apply when I'm in lead, and it makes them ultra snooty and precocious"

Steven nodded knowingly and Barb had to admit she was right. She had always hated that most about any of these assignments. The fake catclaws; jealous competition and nasty bitching was the bit she could do without. The actual work itself; and camaraderie with photographer and crew was always something she relished, and did like it was second nature.

The 3 of them were propped up on barstools having a collective debriefing session of each of the topical shoots they had managed to conquer. Steven had a printed sheet out with pencil scrawled notes all over it. He went through ticking all listed with satisfaction. "I think, Sir Steven, we can call that a wrap" Bek slammed her hand on the bench like it was a gavel. He nodded approvingly as he raised his hand to order another round.

The lager proved to be a comforting tonic for Barb's stomach and head and allowed her to feel light and filled with anticipation of the hours beyond. She had to suffocate the doubts; - they couldn't deter her this time.

For she had nowhere to be in particular. The partner she lived with had taken off to New York on one of his 'missions'. She knew how that went with him, and she no longer wished to be involved. So it was just her with her city apartment that she had locked up. Nobody knew of her comings and goings and she was left free as a bird. What excuse did she have not to take opportunity when adventure prospects beckoned ? she pondered.

('**Bek'-**oned she thought in her now tipsy head with a grin. That was definitely the operative word here.)

The crowd was starting to get deeper towards the bar as the after-work boozers began to appear from the local trading businesses.

There was a big textile industry around here - loads of tailors; dressmakers and designers inhabited the area.

Barb had to get to many casting addresses around these parts for fashion parades and so forth, in the designers' work zones. She got to see where the creative juices were realised and don them to display. It allowed her to keep many of the outfits too, so her wardrobe was always evolving and she rarely had to shop for new pieces.

Needless to say, the area also housed a load of well known fashion photographers; stylists and film crew. It was the native stomping ground to her and she knew the streets; venues and many of the local folk well. Two of the agencies she had spent some time with were located here also; their headquarters in an adjacent street to Steven's studio.

As the volume started to ignite, and they could no longer speak without yelling, they up and left the pub - out into the already darkening streets. It looked like a storm was brewing too; you could feel it in the air. Barb shivered and Bek put her arm around her 'lets get you home and warm' she said comfortingly. Once in his studio the girls grabbed their bags; said their farewells and took off to flag down a taxi.

Barb said nothing as Bek gave her address and glanced surreptitiously sideways at her to gauge her reaction. So this was it, Barb thought - thankfully calmed somewhat by the previous beverages. She wasn't used to drinking these days. She had fallen into the habits of living with a pot dealer so her life was more a dutch oven than brewhouse.
  Bek opened her door and announced "the castle, my love.....may the princess be warmed by the fires of my humble abode". She did a sweeping gesture, ushering Barb inside and then passed her a towel and did a tour of the place.
The place smelt of a mixture of incense and fresh herbs. She noticed a herb garden on the window sill near the homely kitchen.
Without anything said, the few items of evidence of the 'flatmate' did indeed indicate he was also gay...(the male on male pvc framed photos in the hallway were a dead giveaway. Not to mention the phallic ceramic creations on the mantle piece, and so forth).
   "The bathroom upstairs has all the amenities you will need; freshen up, get comfortable and come down for supper".
Barb took a long, relaxing shower and dried herself off. What should she wear? All she had was her jeans and jacket as before, or her flannelette pyjamas! She hadn't packed 'lounge' wear or anything else for the shoot away. They had been on strict instructions to only pack the absolute minimum needed to keep luggage volume low.
She bit her nail in thought. Took a deep breath and shrugged. Pjs it was. And pink pin-striped at that. How embarrassing! Hardly sexy.....but she had no other choice.
She shyly tiptoed down the stairs in her slipper/socks and stood against the wall to the kitchen looking on at Barb in action. She was humming and singing along to the CD playing and grooving around the kitchen grabbing pepper grinders, knives, vegetables and so forth. She finally got wind of someone in her peripheral and stopped; turned and grinned back. "Ah perfect honey - I want you to totally relax. Here I want you to taste this" she handed a spoon of the pasta sauce to Barb and said "more herbs? Extra garlic? What do you think?" Barb closed her eyes as she swallowed with satisfaction. "Mmmm....That is the *perfectly* blended sauce - you have blitzed it. No further embellishments needed. Green light!"
Bek pulled her in close and embraced her with passion, whispering in her ear "ooh we love a green light" she teasingly brushed cheeks with her as she swung around to the open bottle of red wine and poured a glass. "Here have your medicine. I think we could do with a calming tonic after manic missions are complete."
They clinked glasses "To us." Barb looked at her directly with sparkling eyes "Indeed, to us".

They chatted away animatedly as Barbara assisted with the salad making duties while Bec grated romano cheese and put the pasta on to boil. The red wine was robust; full of depth and lingering flavour.
Barb felt so blissfully at home and content. She now wondered why she had stopped drinking for all those years, as she had experimented in other avenues with her partner at the time. None of which made her feel any better. Oh boy the stupid things you do for love....

She truly was a gourmand at heart. And certainly a wine buff. Or so she now thought as the powers of the vintage elixir took hold. This felt more relaxing and in her comfort zone than being wasted on weed; or polaxed on hydro or black.......what a decade up in smoke. Literally.....

The more cerebrally focused form of entertainment had been more up her alley; being a control freak by nature. (In other words class A - speed, coke, ice, crystal meth and so forth). This was way more preferable to her than the heroin chick; smacky, spaced out; delirious effect of the other relaxants.

This was her relaxant. Alcohol. The stimulants took another aspect of crystal clear clarity and brainbox boosting, but for time out, tonight was the most at ease she had felt in some time. And she had to confess she had surprised herself by the admission. In herself and in her company. She didn't want the evening and following few days to pass. If only you could freeze time.....

Being one of 'open book' tendencies she stopped chopping cucumbers momentarily and said "you know, this is the best I have felt in.......such a long time.....i can't even remember the last time. I usually shun company but I feel better here tonight than I would at home alone. And that's ......something for me....."

Bek beamed - evidently thrilled at the effect it was having on the girl she had quite suddenly become obsessed with. Maybe this one was the one?! She had certainly played the scene to date. And she herself had been rapidly approaching the end of her tether in the dyke n drama scene of Sydney. She was a lover of *girls*, not men parading around with a pussy. The overalls and hairy armpit thing was a major turnoff to her. And as for the dykes on bikes......fat chicks on fatboys grunting around in oversized leather kit. Shudder. It was scary even to her.....lippy fems were few and far between in this town.

She had even toyed with the idea of a trip overseas and the potential of a complete move abroad. A photographer had offered her the accompanying stylists' role. But after the last few days.....motivation to make a go of it here was boosted. Her life didn't seem so empty and pointless after all.

"You know girl, thats the best thing anyone has ever said to me. And you know why? Not just because I adore you, but because I know that dishonesty is the thing you detest most. You are an open book. What you see is precisely what you get." She sidled up behind her close and wrapped her arms around Barb's shoulders, kissing her neck. "And what I'm seeing has opened my tired eyes".....

Her hands wondered down to Barb's stomach and under her top. Skin. Barb shuddered internally. It took her breathe away for a moment. The hands crept up to her breasts as she cupped them and pulled herself so close behind Barb that there was no space between them. They stayed like that for a few seconds. The emotional depth of a seemingly innocent embrace meant more than frantic sexual activity. They were both more sensual creatures. It was rare that someone knew how to return the instinctive human need of simple touch in the same way. It was like they had finally found the missing factor...the puzzle pieces slotted so perfectly like it was meant to be.

"Okay beautiful, enough tease time, its tea time"

Bek reluctantly broke the union as she went about dishing up the meal for them both that she had laboured over. They would need it for energy. They would get to her room soon enough, and she intended to have them there for a long, long time........

"Sustenance my love. It shall feed the soul and ignite the fires of passion" she poured them both another glass of red, and checked there was another bottle in the rack in reserve. She didn't want any element of imperfection tonight. It was to be remarkable. One they both instinctively already knew, they would remember for the rest of their lives.

The music in the background was ideal for dinner ; Bek evidently still in stylist mode - even the lighting and candles throughout lent a soft candescent glow that was forgiving of their post adventure exhaustion.
(Not surprising after years in close cahoots with a range of Sydney photographers. The paramount importance of lighting in every aspect of life was obviously drummed into her from a very young age. It could make the difference between 'okay' and 'extraordinary'. And to say that she strove for perfection - and hence the latter, is an obvious aspect of her persona - and no doubt the reason Barb was attracted to her like a bee to honey. Like kindred spirits, the force was magnetic. They were synonomous minds in the concept of accepting nothing but flawless alpha traits.
Anomolous traits aside, it was still like a case of *narcissists unite…* as they do in life.

Barb's mind wandered - she had met a few lesbians with similarly flawless physiques to Bek's while embroiled in the <u>lingerie waitressing</u> world. Curiously, they never went so far as to do the associated stripping shows, as many of the straight girls eventually did for the cash bonuses acquired in comparatively minimal time. Too *'feminine* sexy' for them she supposed. However, they were perfectly equipped for <u>the</u> floor task, which involved having to don flimsy G's and cleavage-bearing attire while serving drinks. This was not an issue to them; they cared not. Nor their butch partners! For after all, they figured: it was only in view by a room of slobbering male idiots, and all groping aside, the risks of affairs and betrayal were obviously nil! The worst they ever got was washed with a spray of malty lager and a few obscenities thrown their way by hideous men who realised they didn't stand a chance with the fem in question. Either in romance or in battle!
Ego assassination in men they took on as a hobby, so often in the bathroom as Barb was doing the lingerie change for the shift and chatting with them, they had to calm themselves not to *"deck the dickhead in the west wing"* during their reign of the bar/club floor. Often while punching their hand and deep breathing in frustration.

Barb noticed Bek was observing her opposite, and her mind returned to the here and now.
Even in silence at intervals as they ate the soulful dinner, the level of natural comfort was undeniable. No forced conversations of ridiculous fluff as society generally dictates is the 'social grace's code'. What a crock of shit. They both had no time for polite banter, and most people were complete phonies. Talk was cheap.
"Oh god I was just thinking, I know a chalet in the snow we can stay at for a while when we go."
Barb put down her fork momentarily : "i have nothing with me to wear to the snow!"
Bek brushed the comment aside with a sweeping gesture: " it will be my pleasure to dress you AND keep you warm; dont fret!"
Barb knew she was making another exception to her usual rule of avoiding winter sports. She was by no means a slope girl. Slippery slope more like……(apres the only way to go)

She had been skiing with girlfriends in the past, but the mere conditions alone repelled her. She simply didn't do cold well - unlike many of her other European comrades who preferred it. And then the kit involved...oh the ridiculous amount of clobber they had to wear to hit the slopes. It was definitely not her style of challenging workout! No, she was an island girl at heart.

But now she found herself thinking it might be a cosy way to get closer to this fascinating new interest. That being Bek. She assumed the protective male role better than most of the guys she had been with, she could tell, even in this somewhat brief encounter time.

The image of a log fire; a glass of schnapps, and Bek's arms possessively clutching her close all of a sudden seemed nike a nirvana scene.

She stopped worrying about the lack of wardrobe she had to hand. She was with a stylist after all - she knew it would unfold seamlessly with this company. Bek ticked so many of Barb's desire-list wants that her mind was cloudy and calm anticipating every hour they had ahead together. Usually one made compensations for a partner's misgivings; accepting 50% or less in satisfaction mode. But her gut instinct here was a flawless specimen.

She sighed with contentment as she drained the rest of her glass and Bek reached over to ensure she was topped up. This hospitality was easy.....but what about the 'upstairs' chapter to unfold....her stomach felt sensitive with nerves and fluttering yearning.

It was so long since she had felt this way with anyone. When you are young and in the grasps of your first infatuation, you confidently believe that *'this is what it will always be like; ~what a wonderland lies ahead!'*....you may even make flippant decisions or actions to *abandon* the joy you are immersed in, *assuming* there is more of the same all around, and you will **always** find the abundant satisfaction you found with the said candidate.

 But then the stark reality hits that the terms 'the one' or 'the one that got away' held solid weight as the facts. People actually get very few chances to experience the pangs of real love. We are lucky to have even one.____

So, *Carpe diem....*

With the washing up done, and the last of the red drained, Bek turned her back from the kitchen while reaching for Barb's hand and guiding her up the stairs. She did feel like she was being led into a new world as she entered the cosy bedroom; this was new terrain.....akin to a new language she would have to get acquainted with. Little did she know she would be quite fluent very rapidly....she was a gifted linguist after all. Perhaps her strongest skill trait.

They experienced more sensual and satisfying mutual connection without penetration than any other straight episode Barb had been in. It felt real and right for the first time. 'Is this what I am now?.....should I consider myself a fully fledged lesbian, or am I just *testing the water?*' she wondered now. But if it felt so much more natural and she craved it; yearned for it to continue, then wasn't that her answer right there??!

Barb was surprised by the altitude of satisfaction acquired from body friction alone; embellished with the skill of touch and tongue….everything was exquisitely sensual. Far more than the majority of men have any concept of how to deliver or enjoy. Its definitely a femme trait. A woman knows implicitly what the other one wants or needs….or in any case steers down the right path if guided correctly. It was like seeing the same view on the horizon, rather than a case of 'blind leading blind'
And explains the reason why the heterosexual union is often like trying to drive in new terrain without a map or instinct to rely on. A harsh description, yes. But one anyone who has been on the same track as outlined here will no doubt attest to.

"I dont want this night to end"…Bek whispered as she put her arm around Barb - who was now snuggled up to her with their legs intertwined. The comfort rating was as good as it gets. "Yes, its so perfect….right here, right now" Barb cooed.
"How very buddhist of you hot lips!" Bek giggled. "Learning to smell the proverbial roses I see…..im glad to see you in a better mindset than a few days ago….nothing else matters but this moment in time you see….you can try to control all the external crap in your life, but the universe has your plans mapped out…..just go with them and make the best of them. And learn to jump the hurdles and dodge the bullets as they appear. Thats life, my sweet "
Bek was like an old SAGE…..obviously her life had taught her wise coping advice. And it was also evident that she really *did* love life and relish every aspect of it as a positive rather than a negative. She certainly walked the talk. Something Barb truly admired; so many people were full of shit!
Barb felt committed to recalibrate her mindset to think the same. For what was the point of living a life of misery?! It all comes down to your perception of every nanosecond…..the sink or swim mentality.

Survival.

They had dozed off to sleep in a spooned embrace till the early afternoon. It felt to Barb that they had been together forever….that sensation of familiarity, trust and complete relaxation.
The faint buzz sound of an electric razor started to bring Barb back to reality. Good grief - Bek was in the bathroom shaving her head. God, she'll need a beanie now for sure, with where we are headed, Barb thought. Sinead O'conner indeed! There are few that can do justice to the bald look; - it takes genuine beauty to uphold the look with appeal.

When they eventually got up for showers and a much needed coffee, they sat in the sunlight of the porch table, soaking up the glorious warmth of the gentle rays descending upon them. Barb was just thinking again how every moment she had spent since returning from the shoot had been instilled with a sublime comfort zone she had been devoid of for some time. So calm.
It was at that moment that Bek interrupted her thoughts with a flurry of excitement, grabbing her hand and dragging her inside and upstairs. "You know what - lets just do it. Today. Tonight….lets just **go!**"
Barb looked at her quizzically. "Why skiing of course!" there's a greyhound bus that runs in a few hours. Ive done this route before. Its the quickest way to get there. Its not

a limousine…. but not so bad, - if you score the back seat you can actually lie down and sleep most of the journey"
She started hurling skivvies, long pants, gloves and ski jackets into a large open bag.
"Ive got gear for us both, all you have to do is come along…..our first adventure together! The first of many, I hope, now that you are mine….at least I hope you are…."
She pulled Barb towards her and started kissing her neck. The electric buzz shot down Barb's spine, and she knew she would relent to anything this woman wanted from her. Even a trip she would normally avoid at all costs - (as outlined) The bitter cold of the slopes; the cumbersome clobber and the insanely early mornings were her idea of hell! But in this instance, she saw the opportunity to be cosy and held in rapture by this creature; even if it was to comfort her shivering and nattering teeth!
For one of the first times in her life, Barb threw herself entirely into Bek's hands and let her steer her on some wild and wonderful adventure. She was entirely out of control, and it felt great! So free….
That comes with supreme trust only. So she knew this was more than just an experimental union.
She even allowed Bek to pack for her! She had never experienced the liberty of pure spontaneity without spending weeks in a frenzy of planning; re-organising schedules; budgeting and so forth. Just 'coming along for the ride' was an entirely new concept to her. It did feel a bit like bravely skating on ice with no brakes or exit strategy….but they were going skiing after all! And as far as 'trusting the guide you are with', she was with a stylist who had proved infatuation towards her so……it felt like a wonderfully wild, natural thing to do.
What she did know, was that Bek didn't do anything (or know anyone) the 'normal' way - which of course was partly where the pure attraction and intrigue lay.
What she *didn't* was that normal bored the hell out of Bek too….they were in for a ride with risks and a definite element of danger with every step of life. Exhilerating was the only adjective to capture it.

Before they knew it they were at the bus station and boarding the empty vehicle to choose a seat. "I told you - its a great time to go. Virtually private travel - I guarantee we will literally be the only passengers." Bek marched up to the long back seat and pulled Barb in beside her.
"Whenever you're ready captain….we have mountains to conquer!" she instructed the driver.
Barb felt her stomach flip. Bek was obviously a veteran skier. Somewhat in the league of her own sister, who had just come back from Vale.
How was she going to manage accompanying her to such dizzying heights? She belonged somewhere back at a chalet; *apres* style. Ordering schnapps and gravitating towards an open fire.

[When she had been to the slopes with her sister and some model friends the year before it had been her first time, and she was over it after a few runs down! The novelty wore off almost immediately. It just wasn't her thing. Too many discomforting elements to the sport. She was a masochist, sure, but in a warmer, drier environment, with no public and so forth.
At one point she got totally fed up and went back to the room for a warm bath with a champagne in hand. The rest of the girls were apparently freaked with concern, and

even employed guys to go out on skidoos looking for her; scoping the vast snow fields to no avail. Her sister was beside herself with worry. And they were livid to find her back at the chalet; safe and sound - soaking in, and consuming bubbles like a rascal cheshire cat.]

The bus took off but within minutes the driver pulled in to a service station to fill up with gas. Bek got up; bounded off the bus and ran inside to seize some drinks, snacks and supplies. She returned with the loot just as they took off again. The two snuggled under a blanket she had wisely packed. Barb could already feel her fingers tingling. She would need gloves when mountain bound for sure. Gangrene was not on her bucket list!
"Okay we're sorted now till we get there. Supps and fun games at the ready"....she ring-pulled one of the cans of soda - "not that I usually drink this shit, but the sugar will be welcome for energy soon".....she then turned to Barb and popped a paper token on her tongue.
Barb rolled her eyes with familiarity. Here we go again she thought....this will be the test....
The next 24+ hours would take them on a different journey in addition to the one they were on in the real world. Acid trips ahoy......she hoped it was a fun one and not an anxiety inducing tab.
LSD....her land of grey matter familiarity and frivolous antics. She had tried to exercise restraint....but, when one must relent to be gracious, well......
But with knowledge comes power: the company you are in is the most vital component to ensuring that the ride was smooth. Nevertheless there always remains the slight stomach-flip anticipation of events to follow. She knew Bek was a guaranteed good time and ideal party partner but she hadn't expected things to ramp up quite so quick. And she hoped that her gut instincts were serving her well; - the company to go on this courageous albeit dangerous mind-game was on point.

They chatted until the first stop, where 2 more occupants boarded, but sat at the front of the bus. The waves of euphoria slowly began to flip their insides, and everything started to look mystical and surreal in the mysterious visions from the bus window. The fact that it was a boring highway became progressively obsolete as the city view was blocked by the invading toxin that took perception on a crazy route of other-worldly grandeur.....
Fantasy.
Barb had done the rounds, and these were super strong papers. She thought back to her drug baron associate, who had a **'collector's item album'** of all the different acid he had tried, sold etc and as they had perused the colourful pages she realised she was familiar with almost all contained. A pretty scary admission.

They smiled as they saw the penultimate adventure ahead on the road and felt brewing excitement and anticipation of every moment in store.
(What a way to enhance an otherwise boring-as-batshit bus ride, they both agreed!).
Bek pulled the blanket over their heads as waves of perceived chill led them to snuggle up for body heat sharing. Even though chilly, the truth was more like: all the skin cells were reviving and doing fluttering dances that tingled and travelled along their skin like electrical currents of receptive-revival.

Intimacy ensued under the veil of privacy; the blanket like their **mask**, and the kissing was the most sensual and smooth tongue entanglement they had ever experienced. They were insatiable for the compatibility of each other. And with each touch the intensity of feeling was enhanced to a whole new level of joy.
It just felt like two drifting puzzle pieces that got lost in the breeze but then found each other; reunited and connected with precise and comfortable ease..

The driver eventually called out the next stop approaching, but it had felt like an absolute eternity of entwined passion. They didn't want it to end, but with the comfort of the fact that for the here and now each other was all they wanted or needed, they gladly took off the blanket and the chatting began.
Relentlessly.
For the next 2 hours.
Like battery-driven bunnies they both expressed all their feelings and thoughts on every possible topic that occurred with freedom and sheer abandon. It felt great to have the body AND mind allowed to drift confidently down any path they chose. Such a rarity in life. In fact, this felt like waking up to a *real life*, they agreed. Akin to waking from a sad coma of survival and endurance in the mind.
There were no games to speak of here. It was free-rule funfair. And they both embraced it , and each other with open arms.

"Ah the absolute perfect nutrition of LSD...its like reconnecting with a long-lost friend internally.....a missing twin......it feels so *right*! Like coming *home*..." Barb bubbled with enthusiasm and virtual relief.
Bek just grabbed her and kissed her again.
And so the journey ensued until final destination......

The tingling skin sensation masked the plummeting temperatures on approach of the slopes. Barbs hands were like ice. Bek took the ski gloves out of her bag and put them on for her.
"We're going to get off before the mountains. I want to introduce you to a few friends of mine.."
She made her way up to the front of the bus to request the driver let them off early.
They probably weren't supposed to break the journey, but Bek had a nack for breaking rules....and influencing **others** to do so. Just the fact that Barb was heading to a *chilly, bitter zone,* in a *bus,* with *a lesbian* was proof enough - for there were 3 of her own personal rules abandoned right there!

The windy roads and hairpin turns made their stomachs flip a tad; they hid under the blanket entwined in embrace, until they finally arrived at destiny to alight the vehicle.
Barb had no notion of where she was or what was in store, but that was half the mystery and delight of her woman guide here. *It may be the only time I put myself this totally in someone else's control* she thought to herself....it was indeed out of character for her not to micro-manage situations.
It did however feel remarkably exhilarating......but of course the grey matter enhancements were an additional help in letting go so freely.
Initially. Then it became auto-pilot; and thats how new coupling occurs.

Barb caught a glimpse of their reflection in the bus window; like a **mirror**, with the dark lit night sky beyond, and realised how perfect they looked together.

They alighted the bus and it felt strange to move the legs after so long on the bus….like slow motion on rubber stilts. Barb felt light as a feather and fleetingly thought 'god I hope I never get back that 'life weight' sinking feeling again'…..it was preferable to feel floaty and vulnerable. A sensual holiday.
She had no idea where or to whom she was being taken, but she hardly cared. To take acid, you had to trust the person/company you are in implicitly, or it could lead to a paranoia mind-fuck disaster. (She had been there once before when someone had betrayed her trust. Visions of being attacked or murdered on side streets of Amsterdam had her in a terrible state for a few days).

However, if the company is well chosen it can be an adventure of a lifetime.
And entertaining to a monumental degree! The mind toy is at its best.

(Once, when she was in a more frivolous mood with 2 other lovely souls, she imagined herself as a Mars bar, and forced herself to try to squeeze into the hotel mini bar, so as 'not to melt'…..absolutely ridiculous to contemplate when sound of mind, but at the time it seemed perfectly valid and reasonable)
She had climbed up onto podiums at dance parties in the past too, and gone berserk for hours, in unison with the other folk. (Very out of usual character for her)
Another time, she got lost completely like something out of Alice in Wonderland, when in a french friends' huge chateau in France. A massive party was going on in the grounds with djs, staff, and a crowd of beautiful people all scantily dressed and speaking the language of love. It was like being trapped in a foreign movie being surrounded by such decadence and french verbal! She hadn't slept for literally days however, and wished to recline for a while. Christian had insisted 'choose any room you like, please be my guest'……
Being over 20 rooms on the top floor, she spent unknowingly hours on end wandering from one to the other trying to make a serious decision on which to elect as hers….darting in and out; jumping on beds, doing cartwheels down the huge ceilinged halls, and then forgetting which was which room and so forth…..in the end she slouched on the walls in the hall and slid to the floor, starfished on the carpet that at the time felt like a bed of candy floss, and slept the entire day…..
One other time she had gone to Madame Tussauds waxwork museum in london with a group of crazy friends. Decifering real life from dummy became almost impossible eventually and felt overwhelming and freaky. Like walking through halls of frankenstein creations trying to fool you as to their next move.

Once off the bus, with bags retrieved from the storage area below the vehicle, Barb followed Bek over the road, and down a tree lined drive that seemed to go on for ages. (You could never be sure of your perception when in that state though, as 5 mins can often seem like an eternity!…..all concept of time is washed away, along with logic and restraint.)
Finally they reached a clearing, and a huge looking country style estate emerged.

The smooth white pebbles in the circular driveway crunched underfoot; Barb always loved the look of them - so clean and white looking and indicative of a charmed life in her assessment.
Bek knocked on the door with the gold Italianate Versace-like knocker; no doubt European owned. It was reminiscent of a Tuscan villa, and seemed a strange juxtaposition to have such lush, european style surroundings when on a mission to the very nearby snow capped mountains. Barb guessed a private vineyard would be attached by the overall appearance of the place. And a long tree lined pool out back, that was rarely used. She could see it all in her minds' eye and was eager to see if she was right.

A stooped over little italian lady answered the door and without so much as a word, took Bek's bag and ushered them both inside. Obviously familiar, Bek enquired slowly "Mick home, Miss Sofia?" the woman shook her head with a look of concern and seemed relieved to have someone else's presence in the place now.
The confusion level was evident to Barb now......she remembered Bek mentioning something about a stop to a *girlfriends* place, but no word on this character.
As she ventured in though the large hallway towards the kitchen and dining quarters, the open terrace out back emerged with the pool exactly as she had envisaged in her minds' eye. Bingo!
This ain't half bad, Barb thought. Certainly her preferable scene to a chill-box with cumbersome clobber!

"Oh dear......looks like he's on the run again......the guy should have a collection of medals for his sprinting capabilities.....comes with the territory I know, but his life exhausts even me!" Bek said with rolled eyes. "Spare your energy gf, we may have interruptions by the uniformed hatred mob and have to run too"....
"I thought you said this was to be a 'rescue a girlfriend' stop....? Barb asked in confusion, and a mounting degree of concern.
"No, that's NEXT my love, the plot thickens here first....stay on track! Always a ride, this crazy life!".
It certainly was with her, Barb thought......god she knew how to pick them. Why couldn't she just be at peace with *normal* life and people, lol.

As it turns out, unravelling the threads of mystery surrounding 'Mick', he was obviously Italian mafia, and this was his hideout nest. Or one of them. Untraceable.
Kept in an alias name etc etc...but, being pursued by the authorities for illegal caper: (predictably prostitution rings; exotic dancer club; drugs, weapons etc - usual score)~ he had even had to flee here. Within the last 24 hours, from what Barb could gather, and the cops were probably hot on the trail right there and then....after him in force.
Barb felt vaguely weary, and went to sit near the tranquil pool; the gentle breeze rustling the leaves of the nearby pine trees. There was a distinct chill in the air; but she was in the throws of the chemical tingles anyway so it was an unavoidable sensation to be feeling the rush; -be it climactic or internal. It was a comfortable sensation all told.

In her peripheral, she heard Bek on the mobile phone to someone and obviously getting some more insider information as to her missing mystery mafia character. What he had to do with anything, god only knew, but Bek had an impressively colourful array of black book characters to call upon. They had that in common, thats for sure, Barb realised. And you could bet that likewise, they were all anomalies in society. Dangerous albeit wildly interesting.

Barb tossed her head back and closed her eyes a moment. Nothing could unnerve her now; she was impenetrably content. Whatever was going on around her, she was in for the ride. Regardless of company, destination or motive; so long as she was in Bek's *safe* hands...(or were they?...judging from her history to date of partner choice, she was no expert there....! It was always dangerous, risky and decadent). Regardless, she was on the ride, and not hopping off at any point.

Bek finally came out to join her and informed Barb that they would have a meal out near here soon, then crash before an early start to the next location.
"I really wanted to see Mick and check he was okay with a few overseas enterprises he had going on.....never mind. He shall re-emerge from his 'bunker' at some point....as he always does. Like a magician.....in any case we are always welcome to stay here. And its not too shabby a hotel to rest!"
Both the girls slowly showered in separate luxurious bathrooms, and got ready together in the master suite. Wow the Italians could be so ostentatious with their wealth and power Barb thought, looking at the ornate gold finishes and immense dimensions of everything. Big, bold, brassy and DEFINATELY mafia money.

Bek gathered keys, jacket and so forth and turned to Barb, grabbing both her hands:
"ill look after you, you know that right?" Barb had no idea what she was specifically referring to, or whether it was just in general, but she was hardly perturbed by anything or thought right now.... "Look I think we may have dodged a bullet with the authorities concerning Mick's whereabouts this time....they are evidently in hot pursuit as we speak. i made a couple of calls while you were showering to put them off the trail. In any case, if the shit hits the fan, ill just say I'm his niece, and have no idea of any of 'uncle mark's ventures'....as he always told me to say anyway. We're just visiting from outta town...."
Barb nodded. It somehow felt like de ja vu of sorts.....her ex used to say the same sort of things whenever they were immersed in dangerous shit. Which was all he knew, really. So constantly! The fact is he couldn't protect her. Or himself. It was just reassurance bullshit. Life was a hell ride. Its how you handled it that ultimately mattered. She'd learnt to stop fretting about the risks of illegality. It was just part of life in her history to date; something that was a mild mental hindrance but lets call it 'life tax'.
Barb nodded with an 'i understand; been here before' kinda grin.
They embraced, and Bek said "I'm so glad you're with me though. I really do feel like you're my girl. Its so......right...i hope you feel the same....!?!" - before Barb had the chance to offer a reply, Bek grabbed her hand and they hit the frosty night air.
 They walked up the long driveway to the main road, and then hand in hand to a nearby restaurant only 5 mins or so away - a cosy bistro type affair.
Sat in a booth, which Barb had instinctively chosen since it was akin to the 'gunfighter's seat'....easy to survey the whole restaurant from this vantage point undetected. Never turn your back!

It really was bitter and the warmth here was delicious; they were now quite famished from all the activity of the day. With polo necks high to quash the chill, they ordered red wine and a comforting dinner, rubbing their frozen hands together in anticipation.

Barb thought Bek looked 'handsome' all in black, and in evident control of where, who what and when. And she seemed delighted in the role of entertaining and spoiling her new beau. Such a contented partnering. They were all smiles and laughter.

The time had lapsed so seamlessly......they had now been awake and active for nearly 48 hours on the go. A day had gone without them realising.

And while on 'tour' with the photo shoot they had rarely shut-down either. Those ventures were always so damn exhausting; despite the fact there is so much time spent seated in hair, makeup, waiting, preparing etc. Waiting was the buzz-kill. Barb had never had the patience for it. Queues sent her packing for instance... she could never be a 'tourist'!

Both so exhausted and satiated from the food and wine, they eventually retreated back to the grand bedroom, and both cuddled up in the four poster bed that seemed the size of an olympic pool. With the drugs now tapering off, they wrapped themselves in the luxurious feather down duvet and floated off into dreamscape.

Spooned and swooned. That delicious feeling when you are that exhausted that a warm bed and cuddle is utter nirvana to the soul, and there's nowhere else you'd rather be.

An alarm sounded at 5am, and Bek jumped out of bed to get the caffeine kick under way. Where does she get that energy Barb wondered....she could have happily turned over for the rest of the day, she was that in the zed-zone now.

And then she remembered the skiing deal: it was part of the equation and why she would never fully embrace it.......obscenely early starts; teeth nattering conditions; heavy cumbersome clobber and the fear of god from the heights.....

Barb looked at the scant possessions she had brought, and realised that for the first time she was travelling light like a 'normal' person. She remembered that Bek had packed attire to adorn her with like a doll once there, but for now, she surveyed her minimal clothing to hand. There were no decisions to be made: it was jeans, jumper and trainers all the way.

She sauntered down the winding staircase, and they both sat on the porch to sip coffee and wake up. Their breath was like smoke in the chilly damp morning air, and Barb started to dread the destination afoot.

"So when we get to Nicole's chalet, we can unwind there until the morn and then we'll dive into the white powder action.....and I'm not talking up the nose!"

Barb squashed her negative perceptions, and braced herself for another joyride. So far so good so she shouldn't be concerned. In fact, to be fair, she felt she had enjoyed several wonderful meals, wine, company and the equivalent of a 5 star hotel standard accommodation. With someone so appealing to her it was uncanny. A holiday entree to entice further indulgence and luxury.

A wave of excitement now overwhelmed her as she realised how happy she felt. And how *rarely* one really feels that way; whether in company or the decadence of solitude.

Fully embrace every moment she reminded herself and felt proud that she had remembered to seize the moment. The mind can control the perception of life in all areas if you learn to guide it.

For later in her life, she would realise that her gut instincts were correct: life is tough and one-off times like this are sweet and precious. And not to be taken for granted.

The sound of gravel crunching heralded a car's approach. "It's the driver hon, not a raid alert, don't fret"….

Barb grabbed the few items she had packed for essentials for at whatever rest stop they would encounter, and went to sit in the car. The sun was starting to rise now……she realised that generally the only time she got to see this beauty was when she hadn't got to bed *at all* and was powering through a bender. A new experience to behold.

The coffee was doing its trick nicely and they chatted animatedly as they drove off towards the adventure zone.

Within the hour, they arrived at a rather grand looking wooden chalet - immense by any standards when you consider that it's a 'holiday abode'….

During the journey, Bek had given Barb the verbal synopsis on the next scene:

The occupant was an ex partner of a famous Australian rock star, and this was obviously part of the 'parting price' he was compelled to pay for being an abusive, cheating narcissist. She too had been hugely famous in her own right as an Italian model and budding singer, and he was reportedly smitten with this goddess, and only had eyes for her. However her bright future had been whisked away in a flash. A near tragedy left her scarred for life.

The saddest part of the story, was that the car accident she had been involved in, had pretty much decimated her gorgeous model face. Or at least rearranged it.

But upon meeting her in person, Barb felt that it was evident that beauty had once reigned on those high cheek bones. She was reminiscent of a gay friend who had surgery to remove cancer from one side of his face, leaving him with a hollow on one side. Impossible to mask though…..it was the ultimate price to pay for scars. Anywhere but the face, Barb thought in supreme sympathy.

Her speech had been impaired too as a result, so the fact that she had sunk into a deep depression and hermit state thereafter was far from surprising. And here she evidently felt at peace, and unnoticed by the critical public.

The most predictable outcome of all however:

When her looks had been cruelly stollen, the rocker took off repulsed, and pursued other young starlets on the scene. The ones he was subsequently seen with in the press thereafter had a remarkable resemblance to this woman's original flawless veneer. They were dead ringers for the original love of his life.

Upon opening the door, Nicole gave a genuine smile to Bek that said a million things. Even with her distorted features, you can tell they held some massive history, and that this woman held a candle for the beautiful 'boy' before her.

The rest of the gaps in the story were kind of filled in for Barb in body language alone: they had been an item in the past. No doubt Bek had been a 'saviour' to her in her

lowest hours and showed her love when she felt nobody could again. Not to say that she had 'jumped the fence' to become outright lesbian now, but it had certainly been an experience of uncontrollable passion she couldn't ignore or avoid. Barb now understood this implicitly. You can't control the urges of the soul.
They embraced for a long time; Nicole extending a hand to shake Barb's and then hugging her too as she welcomed her inside the jaw dropping interior to this wooden chalet retreat. Holy cow Barb thought in wonder…even the dogs water bowl was Versace!
She betted that choice few were privy to the whereabouts of Nicole these days, and the address of this hideout kept a top secret location.

No surprises that she spent her days writing a novel on her past exultations and nightmarish experiences. She explained over a wine later that day that it served to "purge her demons and her her soul…..the only possible therapy that would last"
Barb also understood this. Put it all to bed: let sleeping dogs lie and move on from the past stepping stones to the nirvana ahead..don't look down or behind. These were her personal rules too.

On giving the tour of the place, Nic had indicated the office area that she had just been disturbed from: a half drunk coffee mug sat on the gold coaster and the piles of sheets in neat trays showed a sense of order and chapter by chapter progress to her brainchild.
"i could never have babies now…..not after whats happened, so this is my family right here" Barb knew she wasn't referring to a problem with reproduction, but the fact that intimacy that may lead to such a fruitful outcome was impossible now. Her fame and subsequent appearance now rendered all the normal stuff nul and void. This was her life now : her dog and her writing.
Safe.
Speaking of sleeping dogs, Nicole also sought comfort in a large dog as partner these days. She hugged the beautiful pedigree labrador on the rug beside the open fire and kissed the languid creature. "They never, ever betray you" she smiled thankfully. "I never used to like dogs, or pets…or *animals* for that matter, but when my life took a dramatic turn, that all changed too….eliminating the *people* factor from your life can be so detoxifying and liberating. It works wonders in allowing you to harness your true spirit."
Barb's own brother had done the same thing. When in pain, he shunned folk and went down the canine route. A huge, painfully acquired namesake tattoo ran down his right quadricep of 'gypsy' the first dog he had loved and lost. Like he would never let her go; akin to 'the first lost love of his life'. Girlfriends would come and go for him, but in his books, fuck with his dog and you die..

They had settled in to the guest room upstairs in the loft, that was also plush, immense and homely. The girls had literally just dumped the bags and been shown around and then gone for a walk through the crunchy snow to indicate the local supply stops and so forth. The sound of the slush beneath their feet was soothing and the temperatures weren't as chilly with actual snow. It was the 'pre downfall' temps that were most punishing.

So here they now were now onto 'wine time'. It got dark earlier, so 4 pm didn't feel so crazily wrong to commence anyway! After all, early nights, early morns were the name of the game with this caper.
Although it didn't exactly turn out to be an early night anyway, as is the usual outcome when the company is right. The conversations went on till the early hours and when yawns by the fire all round indicated shut down time, Barb felt she could sleep forever. An open fire; a delicious home-cooked meal; several bottles of red and no angst were the tonics to render one ready for peaceful coma-ville.
Nicole proved a wiz in the kitchen too: tonights' menu had consisted of:
A fabulous and diverse antipasta platter to start (which in itself was a colourful work of art). The fresh meats, cheeses, oil soaked artichokes and olives, sun-dried tomatoes and the freshest bread.
To follow was a porcini mushroom and ragu fettuccini with a sumptuous butter cream sauce and more bread to mop it up. Plus of course a huge Italian salad bowl as side throughout. Even tiramisu to follow. Such decadence in chez chalet.
An open fire and red wine sealed the deal marvelously. This private Italian restaurant certainly served to provide 'insulation' for the chills ahead.

She had just waved a magic wand too, as there had been no mention of guests arriving. It was evident that the door was always open to Bek however and like all the other characters Barb had met with her, shone a torch for her.
And then there was the last stop at the mysterious 'Mick's'....she had just strolled on in like she owned the place; staff welcoming her in like family. And Steven just showed that his work was only at full potential when she was beside him as team. Now these 2 girls were like a comfortably married couple. You simply wanted her in your life. Regardless of capacity. She added a sense of quality.
What an intriguing character Bek was. You couldn't help but love her - she was just captivating when you had the luxury of her presence.
A shining example was right before her: for it was obvious that Bek was a 'past, jilted lover' herself of sorts - and yet she was still besotted with her and always would be.

Nicole hugged her from behind and kissed her cheek, while explaining to Barb :
"i love cooking - it became like healing therapy to me too, and I use it like my meditation time. Im constantly putting down a wooden spoon or moving a pan off the oven to quickly jot down a brainstorm writing idea to expand on, before it evaporates. The mind is so fruitful and idea rich when you just let it go in peace"...
Barb couldn't have said it better herself. She always respected loners and folk who had learnt to love their own company and time and weren't reliant on people, other agendas and so forth. It showed strength of character and was the most admirable and respectable trait in her view. They were more *evolved.*
This woman was evidently a shining example of that. Sadly, it usually takes a cataclysmic tragedy or disaster to get one to that stage of evolution.
Barb felt deeply saddened for her, but then realised there is always a silver lining to every horror story....and yes, the m*ind does* perform magic when it is allowed to roam free of it's own accord without white noise static. It entailed getting really acquainted with SELF.
(Most people have no concept of that; too absorbed in playing the acceptance ego game.) And it meant eliminating stress....and no men!

When everything is gone, you are exposed and vulnerable and a new phoenix rises. The **mask** is off.
But something told Barb that Bek held up the **mirror** for her……

They finally turned in, and Barb was a bit nervous for the next days' mystery line-up. She knew it meant action time. Bek was a 'no fear' girl, so it was bound to be a death-defying experience if she survived it!
But the satiating cuisine and beverages with scintillating conversation was having affect and she crashed within moments of hitting the pillow. She could have slept for days now, but knew it would be brief.
Sure enough, come 5am, lights were on: Bek was jumping up and down on the bed to serve as active alarm (!) and Nic was alighting the stairs with a tray of cups, plunger coffee, milk and toast.
She sat on the end of the bed and started to serve.
Oh boy, no rest for the wicked Barb thought; aware of the fact she hadn't even had the chance to wash her face before the human assault had commenced!…..her sleep time was sacred. But it would have to wait.
Coffee would assist she knew, so she freshened up her face, drank a glass of water and joined the breakfast brew crew.

Bek and Nic discussed 'runs and routes' and other boring ski deets while Barb tried on the clothes laid out for her by her stylist in the wee hours. She certainly LOOKED the part, and Bek was evidently excited to take her victim for the hell ride, so she reluctantly surrendered to the day ahead.
"My valley doll here will prove victorious too!"……Barb glanced meekly at the ski-bunnies huddled on the bed as she gathered her stuff to shower and prepare for the hell ahead.
She was evidently still deliriously weary so she knew she no doubt looked the part, and probably had Nicole wondering if her Pet name was true……

(valley doll *refers to the 60's movie based on a famous novel. The plot centres around 3 women who embark on their career and future, but one in particular falls victim to administering* 'dolls' *- (prescription drugs) - seconal, nembutal and various stimulants.)*

After the whole choosing ski boots and getting fully equipped pularva was ticked off, Bek and Barb alighted the lift, and soared along the the misty heights; the powder puff carpet below bringing a sense of calm. They chatted about Nic and her undeniably gorgeous persona; agreeing that the cliche of **'beauty is not skin-deep but deep within'** rocked solid and she was the ultimate model for the concept.
Barb had actually forgotten that she was heading for activity, and was just enjoying the serenity of the lift journey and ambience at these soaring heights, when Bek grabbed her hand, announcing 'ready?' and her peace was shattered. They hopped off - so lightening fast it snapped her back to reality. She nearly lost her footing in the snow -

but it was when she peered ahead into the sense of nothingness and mystery and was frighteningly aware of the steep slope below her feet, that she started to panic.

A clear picture was impossible in the mist and gentle snow and it was like being blind and expected to plummet on down an incline of madness!

Her natural inclination was to 'get low' and crouch to her feet, but Bek scolded her 'no, no rise up and get ready to conquer my love.....come!' she took her hand and Barb all but squeeled in panic. They were gaining momentum. Fast. And she felt so desperately out of control it was like nothing before. (Well, the closest for Barb was when she and her girlfriend used to go roller skating down the steepest street in the neighbourhood, and at times when she fully let go, she would take kilos of skin and flesh off when the harsh gravel finally won the score)

She did grasp the sense of exhileration and excitement, but it just wasn't her preferred skill for that. She always got enough of all that in her life chapters without having to succumb to the elements and gruelling aspects of this sport.

A difference they had: Bek was a veteran skier; obviously introduced to the caper as a tot, and Barb was a veteran in other real life hell experiences through simply jumping in the deep end and hoping for the best.

They had both evolved as a result.

Different tactics; same destination.

A few runs down together (at differing speeds and styles, obvs), and Barb was over the caper; leaving Bek to practice her magic footwork with rhythmic fancy while she sat in one of the ski bars to wait.

Sipping on a schnapps (not 'as <u>you</u> <u>do</u>' but in fact as she <u>craved</u> since sleep deprivation always left her craving sweet)...she had to admit that it had been worth the trip for so many other reasons than just the skiing part itself. She determined to catch up on sleep the following day while Bek had a day to herself in slope solitude, so they would both be in perfect 'balance' to enjoy their together time more.

Part of a good relationship, she realised, was recognising the differences and the beneficial needs of both parties, and being flexible enough to provide the space to perform those personal quests for serenity.

And at this point, nothing would be more serene to her than a proper nights' shut eye.

Sans the snow song-n-dance routine. She would be happy to *glimpse* the snowflakes from the bedroom window- (wherever they ended up tonight), vs actually frolicking in and falling all over it.

Oh boy...where would they end up tonight she wondered? Bek had mentioned just one 'quick stop' to Nic's chalet so ....?? Another schnapps helped her to resign herself to the fact that wherever it was, she was fine with it. Almost as uneasy on her feet as she was with skis on, she got up to leave when all of a sudden, she was whisked around in a waltz by Bek herself; obviously euphoric from the healing powers of the powder. They grinned and headed back to wherever Bek had in mind to haul them next.

Barb could already feel an early dinner and bottle of wine coming on, and suggesting as such, Bek concurred, and hurried them along to settle into new pad and prepare.

"We'll stay at hotel accomodation next my love, and head back tomorrow. I know a place with discount rates for me as I've known the owner for years, but one more day

of this for me, and it will have weaved its restorative magic and life goes on, eh! Yes….i know you want your beauty sleep and ye shall have it."
Brilliant, Barb thought. She had read her mind and instinctively understood her immediate needs. Without hinting or a mention…..Now what man does that?!

They slept like logs after the early start; brisk (read punishing) conditions, and a comfort meal and wine with cosy open-fire setting and each others' blissful company.
The hotel was perfect: snug and fitted with all essentials, and smack bang in the middle of all the action of the snow-covered land. A mere walk from the slopes, shops, bars and restaurants, it was like everything Bek had arranged: bang on target.
And she was evidently in her element - both here and as a tour guide, but not being selfish about it. She was still so understanding of Barb's distastes and respectful towards them.

As she left at 5am the next morn for the run-down, she left a note beside the hotel coffee maker for Barb: "Go get yourself pampered, princess - the spa here looks fine!"….along with a wad of notes to spend. Now that's a gentleman, Barb thought with a smirk, as she dragged her weary bones out of the comfy hotel bed and sidled up to a much needed caffeine-fix zone.
And not a bad idea either, she thought, feeling tension in her back neck and shoulders. As fit and exercise-diligent as she was, skiing used different muscles to what she was used to obviously.
Coffee, a few jumping jacks and in-room fitness and she went off to explore the village. So nice to have a day to herself - makes it a real holiday she thought happily. She hated the rigid agendas and 'programs' most people adhered to with 'holidays',…..you always needed one after them she thought! Holiday that is.
She knew she would return to the city in a much better mindset now……certainly with a whole new outlook. For who expected desire to hit her so suddenly out of the blue?!

The ride back was much easier than the one going - and seemed much faster too.
They had both dozed off in cuddle-mode for much of the journey this time; which was a relief to Barb. Those hair pin turns in a speeding bus always made her stomach flip with anxiety. (The past again of course: she had been in a few accidents, and the bus drivers to La Caleta where she lived a while in Tenerife were manic murderers! She often opted to walk the hour home, the drive was that terrifying down a steep slope.)

They alighted the bus with zealous anticipation now. Life didn't seem so bad compared to their dismal views on it a week ago.
Influence and hope.
" Do you want to come to my place for a drink? The place is tiny, but has a great harbour view! " Barb offered.
Bek smiled back. "Thought you'd never ask!….looks like I've passed the test then!"

They headed over to Barb's north-shore apartment by taxi, still sedated from the sheer pleasures of a spontaneous romantic escape. Like cheshire cats, they entered the building; Bek looking cute in denim overalls, cap and lycra t-shirt. She had that undeniable style with whatever she donned - often that would make most look ridiculous!

She took Barb's bags for her and entered the lift, putting her hand in the back pocket of Barb's jeans in a possessive fashion. The lift doors closed and she kissed her with all the expression of ownership she could muster. They were there for several moments in ecstatic embrace, when the doors opened and in walked an insanely handsome dark guy with a shocked expression on his face......not because it was 2 girls getting it on, but because it was the boy who was after Barb after their first encounter the week previously!
(They met when she worked on evening promotions at a city club that he frequented. The clientele here were upper echelon - in the finance stakes at least; mostly italians and mafia; druglords etc. Being a night owl, night work had always suited Barb. Normal hours were just too hazardous to maintain - she was like a white witch goth girl! A striking, glamorous crowd frequented, but when they met, the mutual attraction was instant)
They had subsequently done 2 dinners together, and were in talks of a trip to japan on modelling pursuits - he with a different agency to hers.
He was a possessive muslim, but she overlooked that fact when faced with his dark, gorgeous pristine veneer.
He had insisted she meet his mother and sister after one day, and picked her up to 'go shopping first'....she was in her signature midriff-baring crop top and mini skirt type affair; belly ring and tattoos on display. Somewhat excited to be on a potential fashion shopping binge with the new fan, she had started scanning the racks when she realised he was already paying at the front desk for an item, that he waved joyously at her to don later..
surprises!!
She curiously followed him back to to car, where he proudly presented her with the package, insisting it would suit her perfectly for the meeting. It turned out to be a grossly oversized shirt that he intended she cover with to be in presence of the family.....muslim rules do not extend to western ways. And certainly not to sex appeal or flesh-baring!
A kaftan with enough fabric to cover an elephant; - they could have pitched a tent with the damn thing. She felt like an utter frump, but he was beside himself with joy at the mask he had applied. A veil of secrecy and deceit.
 She thought nothing much of it at the time, but thinking back now, it was perhaps a warning sign to pay heed to.....
She was not a malleable woman....and did not wish to be a hidden possession at any time. However, the excitement of a business contract abroad was something they had in common and were excited about, so she discounted all as they had worked towards planning a future venture together. They certainly looked great together. And safety in numbers was often key.
 The agent managing the contract for japan modelling work had commented about them: '*Madonna and Prince* on tour to the elitist nation!'

Barb shouldn't have been shocked by his appearance; before she left they had planned to meet **'the following week on thursday'** - he was to pick her up.......oh my goodness, it must be Thursday she realised, cowering in the corner with an expression of 'oops, I think I fucked up!'

His jaw was still somewhat dropped as the lift ascended to the 3ʳᵈ floor, and finally offered "Ah, sorry, I didn't realise you had company, after the arrangements we had made".

"Who are you?" Bek asked like a jealous lover..(which, okay, **was** the true representation of who/what she was.)

"Im Luke. Who are YOU?" She held out her hand to shake his with a nod and a : "pleased to meet you. Take your time. I'll offload the bags"

The lift doors opened and Bek possessively grabbed the bags and headed to the door with a knowing nod after Barb handed her the keys.

Barb felt momentarily speechless. The whole state of affairs had hit her by surprise as much as him, she felt sure! "I'm so sorry, can we reschedule to next week? I had to go on a longer trip than anticipated on the photo shoot darling, it kind of took an..unexpected turn.."

He eyed her with suspicion, and was evidently deflated, but was so besotted he relented to accepting her feeble excuse.

"Okay. Next week it is. But if any day is free after today, let me know eh! You have my number. I have info to tell on our assignment plans".

Barb had actually set up a casting with an agent aligned with Japanese talent anyway, and had been eager to meet up with him. She knew the contract was hers; the agent in charge knew her in the industry for years. It had been forefront of her mind, and all she could think of a mere 5 days ago... Just went to show how the mind turns to mush when love strikes and everything peripheral to the target in question just flies out the window forgotten..

"Okay great. Well unless I suggest or advise or.....same time same place?!"

"Sure" he gently touched her chin, too scared to offer anything more intimate with the scary 'bloke' in the background waiting for her.

A pang of joy hit Barb as she realised that Bek was jealous and possessive after all and this may actually be the real deal. Not just a brief romantic encounter.

Only time would tell.

She had however, tasted the forbidden fruit now.

Jumped the fence. Sampled the same side.

And it was pure joy at this point.....

They parted company and Bek approached her apartment with a deep sigh and an anticipation of lust. Bek met her at the door and picked her up to 'walk over the threshold' as a lover does on entering the door after being united at last.

She laughed as she closed the door with a wink to an empty hallway.

And the rest, as they say, is history...or maybe you'll just have to wait till the door is reopened...or keep reading to find out.....

Chapter 3:

Sarah seduction.

She deliberately chose a common name that was easy to remember.
(Even in a state of inebriation, one can still remember some simple titles. That was key here, as the more tanked these folk became the more generous the offerings)…..
She didn't want to draw extra attention to herself. There was certainly enough to be had in the field. That was for sure. This game was not for the shy, reclusive wall-flower.

The industry was notorious, however, for stereo-typical titles: (Candy, Brandy, Angel, Anastasia, Destiny, Chastity, Diamond, Dallas….and so forth). She wanted to stand out from the crowd, and yet, remain discreetly aloof.
'Sarah' means lady, princess, noble woman…it made her laugh to think of the irony in semantics!

The ladder of the sex industry. This was one of the bottom rungs. Baby steps. One can't walk before they crawl…
 Just as socially unacceptable as the other more obvious and risqué avenues of the trade, but a vital step to build psychological strength for the higher stratospheres. For they could damage a weak-minded vulnerable soul irreparably…and so, her mental training had begun……

Sarah opened her diary to survey the weeks' lingerie waitressing forecast.
It covered such a vast distance of the city; - her travel time between events alone was often an opportunity to strategy plan all aspects of her secret life.
As the train disembarked the station, she settled in 'her office' : pencils, erasers, highlighters, phone, and diary. The essentials.

One might think that body flaunting was an enterprise that left the mind to wither and remain dormant…the absolute opposite rang true.
For one had to be on the ball and mindful 24/7…..
mind/body to the hilt.
Not only did it teach her to become an astute strategic planner, but it trained her to become a micro-managed business in the flesh. Her body was her business and her tool, and she had to manage it with particular caution.
To expand again on semantics:

'Exposure' itself was the game……but fear of exposure to those in one's life was the biggest risk……she learnt how to protect herself from that here, and it held her in good stead for the game of life to come. Her world from now on, was one of masks and mirrors..

Since her bookings extended way beyond the inner city circle, a certain degree of anonymity was thankfully maintained. She wasn't likely to bump the characters encountered on these missions in her day to day activities. Or so she hoped anyway.
The outskirts and further afield were the zones of a wilder caliber of subject matter however; one had to watch their tongue….and their back.
The less educated were way more liberal with their tokens of appreciation. Go figure. Income for the week was usually spent way before their next pay-packet arrived. She was often the recipient of this cash-flaunting play, for the venues she appeared in were their watering holes. And if she played it right, they tipped with animated lustful appreciation.
It was all fantasy. And she was a figment of that in the minds of these (often scary) varieties of species.
Admirable from afar but unaccessible.
Untouchable.
A theme to represent the basis for her existence, despite the perceived leagues she was playing in.

The train doors opened and Sarah alighted, weary from the journey so far out west on the public transport system, but determined to cash in for the night. Her motivational thoughts were: one day I will be able to afford a private driver everywhere…and it won't be to seedy bars in the middle of the sticks doing secret work.   More unspoken burden pursuits.
There was a certain mindset involved for sure, and sometimes as she was changing into the chosen costume to flaunt she would have to literally call in all her reserve energy to assume a mental 'transformation' and do the role-play to the standard that was eagerly anticipated.
Dig deeper..

They adored her. And the tips were indicative of that.
Some of the other lingerie-waitressing girls would eye her cattily as she took the full tip jar with abundant notes and coins, and tried to surreptitiously stash it in her bag pocket; for they often had but a few tokens of spare change to show for their nudity display.

The patrons would eagerly await the flesh-baring show-time presents
spectacle; the anticipation was palpable as the stage or podium set-up was
underway. This was where the main show-girls (usually 2 per evening), would
come out to 'dance' (read strip) ~ in choreographed fashion. They were only a
10 minute or so segment per show; a small time to dedicate to a night's work,
and part of the reason many of the lingerie waitresses became enticed to
'graduate' and proceed down the same path. For comparatively, 2 hours of the
said catering work; often in front of mongrel men was a much harder ordeal in
many respects. However the fact remains: not everyone is prepared to take it
ALL off. Even the flimsy token of fabric worn by the waitresses protected
modesty of sorts, and left a tad to the imagination. Although she was often
asked to, Sarah personally felt that to go to the next level would have to be more
of a 'private showing' for her, and pay considerably more than stripping work
would.

She refused to go completely topless either, which was often the role…and
yet still managed to pull in the same take-home earnings as those who did. A
certain degree of dignity must remain.

She needed that.

Sarah started lingerie waitressing in conjunction with modelling assignments
from her city agencies. Even when top of the books, it was always in dribs and
drabs; ~ you had to spread yourself like butter to accrue some sort of reliable
cash flow.
Another secret to hide however. Unacceptable behaviour.
Mask.
But……money talks and bullshit walks. Period.
The risks of detection were high, but the rewards were unchallenged with more
acceptable work.
Do the maths:
less time; more mulah
        = no brainer.

The smell of stale beer and cigarettes. Sometimes it made her want to heave,
and memory association would never leave her. But it was the signature smell of
this trade. For it was these creature comforts that were required for the
characters to get comfortable and sloppy. And thats when wallets were opened.

Nevertheless, she would go home repulsed, and scrub herself rigorously;
washing the stale odour from her hair and body; while the expensive lingerie
soaked in perfumed soapy water.

She was introduced to this socially unacceptable caper by a girlfriend, Lola who was an aficionado in the trade. Lola was the partner of a close associate drug-lord Sarah and her boyfriend Alex used to hang with at the time. (Sarah's partner Alex was in cahoots with him; their abode constantly filled with taboo 'business banter')

The girls forged a bond at a city dance-party one night.

Sarah surreptitiously yawned, hinting she longed to escape the scene for home and a movie - she gave Lola a coy look as the boys chatted animatedly.

"God, it's embarrassing to admit that I'm ready to sack the scene already…it's only 1am!!" she whispered. Sarah and Alex were veteran all-night party players. Alex used to supply 'party-fare' to a huge list of associates, and their humble flat with city views was generally a hive of activity. However, it was becoming apparent she was over the whole 'scene' now and focused on more rewarding pursuits than smashing herself.

Lola concurred- being several years older - and professed that she was wanting to get home to 'do more *sewing!!'*

They laughed at their 'nanna' attitudes in the current environment of debauchery and party-mania.

Although she was in a 'stereo-typical' dancer/druggie union, both Lola and her partner were serious and dedicated to their trades, not flippant and immature. It was a career/passion and money-making enterprise to them both, and in her unique case a gifted skill.

She was completely sober for a start, and not the slightest bit interested in the *candy* so readily available to her. Sarah respected that implicitly. It was a rare example in her crazy world.

Lola was a <u>professional</u> stripper, and I put much emphasis on the adjective here. When Sarah first saw one of her performances she was entranced. Much like the gaping, suited crowd in watch. She felt lured to follow.

It was like a finely choreographed appreciation of the female form. Not smut and vulgarity as one might presume. She was also a gifted seamstress and made all her own costumes and flaunt-ware. Unlike the others who were there for the high cash rewards, it was her forte, and she stood out from the crowd.

For her, it was portrayed as a demonstration of ART.

But she was an anomaly.

Her demeanour was soft and gentle; she was an almost angelic creature.

While many of the other girls would hang around after shows, drinking, flirting, smoking and so forth, she would head home to sew sequins and diamantes onto her creations, and devise the appropriate choreography to suit the display. Her craft….she made it and flaunted it with such style and grace. And dignity intact.

As a result, Sarah followed her into the vocation of shows and bare bodies with confidence.....it was a gentle introduction to a world of the unspoken.

Her very first booking was to waitress for Lola's show at a reputable city venue. Lola had chosen the location wisely...
By all accounts, it appeared a more 'graceful' environment to gain confidence in the business, when compared to the more seedy/dangerous outer-city venues to come; (watering holes to bikeys and villains etc). However, that was a most deceptive concept. It was entirely contrary to the natural opinion/expectation......as she was soon to discover.
For men in **suits** could prove far worse creatures than **leather and boots!**

'Oh boy'.... Sarah breathed in deeply to brace herself for the spectacle. She emerged from the toilet cubicle in the chosen attire for the day: a cute calvin klein 'boy style' briefs and bra set with long 'leg warmer' dancer socks and heels.; bracing herself for the feline contingency in attendance.
The female toilets were a hive of frenzied activity at these events; crammed with all the waitresses and strippers dressing, adjusting and embellishing at the mirrors; - reminiscent of backstage at the fashion shows Sarah had participated in. A frantic change-room scene. Only this time the girls were to exit in substantially less fabric!
Piles of lingerie; makeup bags; feather boas; full ash-trays and swearing abounded.....the frenetic time-limit factor was always paramount at these events. Palpable show-time stress. Diva central headquarters.

A hush wave came over the women; she felt all eyes scanning her veneer. Was there a ladder in her stocking? A label hanging out perhaps? It was not until later, after the show that her paranoia was put to rest.
"Let's go for a coffee and debrief honey" Lola suggested with a warming smile; hooking arms with Sarah and leading her away from the bitch-bonanza catty zone.
"You did so great...thank you for supporting my act....they loved you!!! " she indicated the substantial tip jar in Sarah's nervous grip. Her tally was payment for much derrière groping however, and cleavage perving. She had earnt the rewards.
It was far from glam.

Sarah was aware of the aura Lola projected. She was nothing like the other women; ~ they obviously respected her to the point of near fame; - all aspects of their behaviour changed markedly whenever in her presence.
"How did you find it then? Were they gentlemen?" Sarah's mind cast back to the last 2 hours of adrenalin-enduced activity.
"Ah"....she exhaled dramatically. *"I was a nervous wreck to begin, but my initial reaction to the men in the room was that at least they were a gentlemen crowd; -suited*

in Armani and Versace, and perhaps a nicer caliber of male viewers, so I relaxed a bit more".... She didn't have the heart to express her inner anguish and turmoil after all Lola had done for her.

Lola smiled protectively, as she sipped her cappuccino - *"you'll do really well ! Are you interested to continue?"*

Despite it all, Sarah had already calculated the days' takings in her head, and the rush of it all way superseded the nerve-quota.

"Yes! Absolutely! I am so thankful to you for your intro and all ! Can you help me get started... ? When and where is the next one?"

"We'll sort all your bookings out, trust me! You will be a busy girl indeed" Lola giggled...."*but first, shall we go and stock you up with lingerie my love? You have such a perfect figure, and I know a great store just up the road. I think I forgot to tell you: the men prefer a g-string to briefs; ~ as cute as yours were. And push-up booster bras. You can increase your 'cup-size' to monster proportions with some of the better models! The skimpier and more revealing the better "*

...Aha! Sarah thought with relief, and visibly relaxed at last; her self-consciousness starting to wane.

They had all been staring at her wondering why she was not in the expected attire! Hers was akin to cute sporty gear in comparison.

How embarrassing....but at least she knew the rules of play now. Although she personally preferred the cheeky boys-brief style to a g-string, the idea here was (not surprisingly) - the more available flesh to view the better.

Tomboy was not the theme du jour to adopt. It was 'think sex kitten' for max appeal now.

Motivation for mission *pert peach* at all times! Not that she needed prompting; she had always been disciplined in that area.

Sarah agreed to the shop-tour and off they went for a spot of purchasing~mania; the ultimate reward for the days' success!

Inside, it was a complete underwear palace - stocked to the max with eye-candy fashion for women.

Wonderland!

Sarah looked on in obvious raptures, and Lola laughed.

"Get used to this love - I shop here at least once every few weeks for bits and bobs. I chop straps off bras and attach more glitzy ones and so forth; - good range here and well priced. But I can give you a list of other stores too. I mostly shop online...."

Sarah's eyes glistened with excitement. It was akin to entering a candy store of delights; a rainbow of colours and accessories abounded throughout.

As far as 'tools of the trade' were concerned, it didn't get more motivating than this! And to try something on in the change-rooms, where you have the privacy to scan 'the whole effect' it was a rewarding moment of pride too. Gratification for all the hours spent slaving away on the body beautiful, while others were meanwhile indulging and living a less narcissistic regime. Was it worth it? In this game, absofuckinglutely!

And one was rewarded for it accordingly.

Sarah had always had a thing about collecting bikinis and dress-up attire, but now she was obsessed with lingerie. G-strings; lacy push-up bras; suspenders and stockings. There was a new purchase almost weekly, for she often returned to the same venues, and the idea was to be new and enticing every time. As a man would say: 'why eat mince when you can go home to filet'....the opposite equation rang true here for them: why stay home with hamburgers and tv, when you can go to your fave watering hole and ogle prime quality meat live!
It can't be fatty or flawed though - picture perfect was key. Strutting your stuff in heels and the skimpiest underwear was akin to bringing the boudoir to a local venue near you....and it didn't come cheap.

For each 'showtime' there were usually around 2 or 3 girls with segments of their dancing. A band of several other lingerie waitresses were employed to serve the crowd of men, as they ogled the beauty unveiled before them. The crowd received visual stimulation of both a performance and catering nature; ~ they were in their element in the realms of feminine appeal.
God for a day.....
 Even a normally tight, ungenerous male will open his wallet gladly to reward the waitresses, when in this testosterone-fuelled environment of lust and adrenalin. They often became flamboyant and competitive in their tokens of enticement to the girls of their dreams. Cash and gifts of varying sorts abounded in addition to the wage itself.

And Sarah cashed in.....

She had intended to 'dabble in the debauchery' and *test* the water.
But like many of the other sex-industry related forms of employment, the tips alone spoke for themselves.
Cash-counting frenzies grew to addictive proportions. She was actually good at saving vs spending: she loved the feeling of watching her own little 'bank' grow!

Control.

Her once attractive salary base was a mere percentage of the take-home tally she accrued from eyelash fluttering; coy smiling, cleavage flaunting and butt-baring.
Always a price to pay, no question, but it sure beat a 'normal' ***desk job*** 9-5 for a fraction of the fees. That was a much worse scenario and one she couldn't accommodate any more. The irony was, she found that somewhat more soul destroying than these risque alternatives.

As one would think, a certain calibre of 'gentleman' would be preferable to a black-leather clad rough-nut from the perimeters of address code. Inner city = better 'work' standard....right?

Not entirely.....

For the corporate 'suits' were a difficult lot….although Sarah had assumed she would feel <u>more self-confi</u>dent being in such skimpy attire around well presented men in label suits and with company accounts than the blue collar 'spare change' lot, the reverse actually rang true! They looked at women differently. They were more arrogant. It was all more a stage for them, in a way!

Often, they took their clients to these events, as a show of appreciation (yet translated as a display of prestige; power and so forth). A grand multitude of reasons really.
Men were showy beasts…..and competitive to the point of aggression at times. Women were, after all, another acquisition, and at this physical standard, the ultimate symbol of success! And the communal testosterone caused them to behave in ways that were out of character..think 'gang' mentality.
Ironic!
They would compete for attention but also make you feel 'cheap' by default. Sometimes you could hit it lucky though: the concept of flashy - fluttering big notes in your direction in a *'look at me and how top dog I am'* (wanker) fashion was sometimes part of *their* show, with the rewards coming your way in the process.

But the bikey/criminal types were more the gentlemen in attitude; go figure. They had seemingly nothing to prove, except a need for some female attention and appealing display. They were also the most generous in the take-home offerings, for the most part.

Lola was respected enormously in the trade, so her intro was vital to Sarah's success. Instantly, she was introduced to the right people; - (read booking agents) for the waitresses, and arranged their venues and time-slots all over town). Before she knew it, she was on the 'books' of all the women who literally ran the show and kept the diary full to bursting.

Lunch shows, but mainly late afternoon ones were the standard gameplay. Three hour segments each, generally - (with a complete costume change in between, to keep the visual factor stimulating.)
The alias remained: 'modelling promotion work'….(which was true; there just wasn't that much work in that arena as anyone on agency books knows too well. It's the 'hurry up and wait' scenario. Invariably, in the modelling caper you would be offered the best jobs or cattle-calls when away; already booked; sick

or ready to quit the caper!) One had to supplement their salary for self-support.

The venues and unsavoury locations weren't disclosed to others either, as this would have never been accepted on any 'homefront'. It was a secret other world to the majority of women involved.

One had to cover their arse; watch their back and be totally self-wary at all times…it was mentally as well as physically exhausting (the 'double life' scenario was in fact more taxing than the actual workload itself, to be fair and honest).

Her diary was a sacred tool….the 'map' to her earnings. Like all her diaries, it remained on her constantly (or under lock and key!)

It all picked up momentum and speed rapidly….. There were many novices out there, but the professional agencies Lola lead her to employed performers (strippers) and girls alike. Plus, Sarah met more as she went along; learning to decipher the genuine from the amateur.

Had to be careful for the bitchy component though; as in every avenue such as this, the comp was fierce and feisty. She knew several ex-(and current) models, and uni students embracing the financial gains. It was not just for the 'cliche' crowd of risqué femmes……the lucrative component here attracted a vast array of women from all spectrums of life. But one had to be vigilant in choosing who to trust/associate with. There were several she hoped to NEVER see again…..and were an embarrassing (read slutty) example of female form.

The pay itself was 'okay' - standard…but the TIPS more than doubled that, and made it worthwhile. It must be accentuated here that those 'serving' the patrons, (the lingerie waitresses) ; -as opposed to 'getting their kit off' had to interact on a <u>verbal</u> level so there was a large degree of psychological games and tricks involved. But it was a delicate issue: entice without allowing the man (or woman) to feel like they had been given any green flags on a 'conquest' rating….it could prove challenging.

Sometimes there was a fine line between expressing: 'bring it on, baby' and 'bitch from hell' - she had a few incidents that required bouncers and whatnot. The danger was: you were on THEIR turf, not your own. These were THEIR backyards and drinking holes, and more often than not, they were here daily….spent more time than in their own homes.

Many were gamblers.. But one can't bite the hand that feeds, as they say. (Sad, but they were also the more cash generous).

In a nutshell: entice but still be nice when they inevitably get amorous…..if you received any conflicts in this game, it was hardly likely to resolve amicably; and they could make your life hell!

Like anything worth doing she had undertaken, it was terrifying to begin with…..she was almost sick with nerves and fear. You had to simply wing it at some of the venues; ~ it was often crowded, noisy and overwhelming if you are self-conscious. She would feel nervous to the point of anxiety-attack at times as she donned the flimsy fantasy wear. It often felt like psyching yourself to be hurled at a pit of hungry vipers!
But it taught her to walk the stage of life…..for there are no rehearsals.
Being mentally equipped was key.
Mind over matter.
Like any show of exposure, there are always masks and mirrors involved….

And there were makeshift-'mirrors' everywhere….poker machine screens, chrome fixtures throughout; ~ the reflection that stared back reminded her of many factors:
~to straighten her posture, hold in the stomach; maintain composure; watch decorum (and occasionally stop grimacing!); walk in a seductive fashion/manner (often while balancing 20 kilos of froth-bobbing lager in stiletto heels); stay self-protective and aware….and above all, keep it together. Externally at least.
It was a summoning force of internal resources at times, and important for her to don the imaginary 'mask' to deal with all the exposure.
The maintenance factor was good grooming skills she knew of anyway, with modelling assignments and promotional experience for years. It's just that the lovely suits and competitive cattle calls don't reward with the same jackpots as getting your kit off! Shame but fact. The umbrella-termed sex industry rewarded the shame accordingly. And this was phase one.
Baby steps…
The biggest cost however was the mental conversion required to immerse yourself in taboo activity.
Mind games…..it would hold her in good stead for other industries to come however so it was a vital 'stepping stone' process to go the full throttle.
The unspoken, oldest occupation of all..but I digress..

..and back to Sarah and her drinks tray.

"Are you on next week love?" the pub manager Bruce inquired while polishing some glasses as the closing time approached. "They're always asking when Sarah will be back and a few have even offered to pay you a wage to stay full-time every night here!"

God, I can't think of anything worse she thought, while summoning a masking smile. They had been a groping mob tonight, and the burly bouncer had to step in several times. He was a familiar bodyguard though; ~ she had encountered him on other assignments in the far-reaching bars and pubs, so he was ever-watchful and protective of her.

On one evening, after a successful night's takings she was on a high and stopped to farewell him with a broad smile: "Bye Sam, thanks for saving my arse again tonight; I know you always have my back!"

-"Always a pleasure Miss Sarah. I wish there were more ladies like you on; we could do with a touch of glamour and refinery in these rough dens!"

They chatted a while and he relayed a few remarkable tales about his times at other venues. Then he confessed he used to be a jail warden. "The ultimate training wheels for security! Had to get out though, it was a real downer being surrounded by crims on a full-time basis….now I just prefer to ensure the streets and drinking-hole venues aren't crawling with the mongrels, and usher them in to where they belong. Call it service to the public of sorts…."

He proceeded to tell her of one such incident inside, many years ago, when he had been on watch of the likes of the notorious Anita Cobby murderers.

"You may think that justice is never served to folk who commit such heinous crimes, when they seemingly now live in a protected and provided-for environment - maximum security……that is the general consensus of the public. But rest assured that it most certainly is.

One night, a few of the wardens covered the security cameras, dressed in clown costumes, then entered the cells and well…..sort of rearranged the occupants' features somewhat. Not to mention their internal functioning"

Sarah shuddered at the horrific thought.

"When they reported that 'a clown had beaten the living shit out of them' we all shook our head emphatically. "No sir, we were on watch all night, and saw not a thing. The guy is an utter loony~tune"

He bowed his head in deep thought.

….. That sort of shit starts to play havoc with your head you know. You lose touch with humanity and normal codes of behaviour."

Sarah left considering how much mental strength was required for this caper and **all** it's aspects. It certainly wasn't for normal folk…but cash in hand payouts rarely are. She couldn't remember the last time she had paid taxes. To be avoided at all costs! (However, truth be known, THIS fall<u>out </u>was the tax. Psychological. Bottom line.)

There seemed to be an underlying theme with her chosen vocations in that regard.

The lingerie girls she encountered on the job were a cocktail of variety, as to be expected; thus allowing them to cater for the spectrum desires of the lusty audience:

~the *sex-kitten*, pro-plastic enhancement set, that weren't quite ready to take the<u> f</u>ull kit off yet;

~the *alpha intellectual* lot - (doing said work to pay for their studies and future vocations) - the natural progression of course being to go further with actual stripping, or escort capers.

~The *girl next-door* (read attention-seeking) lot. Sort of 'plain-jane' - but don't be fooled. guys seem to want that innocence too! Besides which after a few schooners perception is skewed and mediocre looks damn fine…..(i.e. non-threatening flirtation for tho not so-genetically-gifted out there in the jungle. For beauty is often far too scary a conquest to seek….best not to risk deflation; in all its terminology)

~The *nymphos* that just want constant attention for their body and hopefully lots of no-strings-attached action in the process….(admittedly a minority lot as it was generally more about the cash than the action, but nevertheless..)

In any case, it was all about making the crowd (of generally men) feel

appeased; boosted; non-threatened and fantasy-fulfilled…..king for a day, so to speak.

It was often a repulsive experience for the girls; who would de-brief with a fellow worker comrade to cope ~ either in the change-rooms or after work for a drink. But nevertheless all was generally forgotten when the cash-count for the day was tallied, and outbalanced the score of distaste. Nothing comes for free.. Life skills.

Although Sarah didn't realise it at the time, it was psychological training wheels for male ego-boosting in the future.

For there is no avoiding selling your soul on some level to get ahead in your life.

Along this journey, one required courage. It introduced Sarah to a whole spectrum of different walks of life, and one must learn not to judge any character prematurely.

Many that she initially wouldn't have given the time of day turned out to be influential in her lessons.

On one of her 'assignments' in the way outskirts of the city, she met a girl who was to become a bit of an extra chapter in her life. Cassandra was an attractive, flirtatious brunette with a bubbly veneer. Sarah could see that she was a case of the 'innocent girl turns bad'. In fact it was a turn on for her.

She relished the work! She had actively sought work pertaining to more risqué avenues of self-employment. Prior to this, she told Sarah she used to work as a masseuse. The 'happy ending' variety….so this was no doubt a more glamorous promotion! 'Give me the drinks tray over the member *any* day!' she would gladly say, as she started her shift. She also had seemingly more modest standards than Sarah, and would happily flirt crazily with bikey and monster alike. Self-confidence issues for sure..It was more of an ego-boosting enterprise on HER behalf; a win-win all round with audience and for self.

As they left the venue at the same time one evening, they walked to the station together to catch the late train home. It was an abandoned small platform; one that would be every mother's biggest nightmare for a daughter alone in the wee hours. They stuck together for safety, although Sarah was mostly on her own at all times and unbothered by the dangers.

"Where are you on for the rest of the week Sarah?" - they got out their diaries and compared dates and venues. "Ive got the businessman's luncheon on next Friday and then ah…." - "Oh brilliant, me too!!" squeeled Cassie. "Shall we go for a drink afterwards?! First round is on me!"

She loved a drink. Mostly lager or strong scotch in fact - a difference between them. Sarah was more the stylish wine-bar advocate as opposed to the smelly pub. But one had to be open to all walks of life - particularly in this game. Besides Cassie was a sweet girl who had obviously had a rough life and was doing all in her power to boost her living standards and future.

"After playing masseuse~madam, i became a flight attendant. I was happy to reduce salary somewhat; quit the 'rub'n'tug' routine and don a uniform. I wasn't aware of how taxing that can be on the body though…..Anyway, that's where I met my husband, who was also an air steward. Sort of 'mile-high' style. He needed a green card, and I needed a man, so it was a 2 way result. We got married in Vanuatu, which is not really legit, but the piece of paper means the same to me….whatever."

Her smile faded somewhat. She was visibly upset and a tad jaded by his choice of location for their nuptialls..it was obvious he hadn't wanted or needed a rock-solid entanglement the same way she had.

"We rarely see each other though, as he is usually flying all over and we occasionally meet up in somewhere exotic. I get 'spousal discount' rates to fly you see, so I still get to roam the world without the ordeal of the airline industry. Milk it I say. Shift-work pays well but it really is a killer on the body and I'm much happier to do what I am now. I never thought I would say this but I absolutely love collecting and flaunting the lingerie collection too"

Sarah was impressed with the union, but also aware of Cassie's sadness so displayed an enthusiastic response:

"Wow…that's awosome that you both support each other's 'careers'. And he doesn't mind you lingerie-waitressing either. He's obviously not a jealous warden like so many men. Gotta love the bonus breaks for you too girl! Like constant honeymoon meets in lovely hotels..sort of trumps the TV and pizza routine of most couples"

Cassie beamed. "Yeah I know…..He tells me he has lots of work coming up in Japan. The crew get a hotel stopover in Fukuoku. I'm hoping to meet up with him there sometime soon. Never been to Japan!"

Sarah pondered: all the male qantas staff she knew of were gay, or secretly so (with a false show of masculine bravado) - Cassie had obviously found a winner in this one... Or nabbed a serious con man…..

Sarah wondered if he had the feminine traits of the general steward (?) It was, by all accounts, an unexpected scenario, for Cassie seemed to obviously favour the brusque grunting bloke to the stylish gentleman she admired.

Physically they couldn't be more diverse either; ~Sarah was tall, slim;
athletically fit; blonde and blue eyes with abundant bust. Cass on the other hand
was medium height; voluptuous albeit stocky build; chunky strong physique;
small bust and bigger hips; long dark hair and brown eyes.
Sarah was more reserved, while Cass was ever-ready to please.

Their differences aside, they complemented each other well. They worked
together on many occasions; they were both professional about attendance to
events; never drank or did drugs on the job, and had respectably high
reputations in the world they inhabited. They would look out for each other - in
this world where a woman needed to be wary and safety conscious at all times.

[*The future would see them encounter other chapters together too on a
working basis; both overseas and here….and even shared residence at one
point; - but that's another life away, so for the moment we focus on Sarah's
lingerie cavalcades around *this* city…]

When she met Debbie, yet another door was opened…..
Deb was more androgynous and reserved. She wasn't about the frothy flirty
laughter and eyelid battering antics of the majority of the girls in the trade. What
you saw was what you got. No fake displays. Sarah respected her implicitly for
that. Her stage name became Maxine: 'Max'~ which was apt by all accounts.
They literally bumped into each other at the bar one day while serving; ~ jostled
by the throng of male patronage of the afternoon peak hour. A cascade of
foaming beer spray splashed the girls as the schooner glasses clashed. They
looked down at their soaking gear, that was now becoming decidedly see-
through. Off to the bathroom to stand under the drier they determined and
excused themselves briefly.

"So whats the deal with you Sarah - you don't strike me as a natural in this
game; …..well, what I mean is that my first impression of you is more of
a..thinker than an exposer….."
Sarah wasn't sure whether to take it as a complement or a mild criticism, but
judging from Max's facial expression and stance she realised it was the former.
Propped up against the drier with head tilted and seductive smirk on her face,
she oozed lust and intrigue. Sarah felt a shiver down her spine.
Tingly.

"Well, I guess its the old adage really for survival : money talks and bullshit walks...I've tried so many other 'socially acceptable' jobs, but this one trumps them all for take-home value. Besides, I'm not in an economic position at this point to be more choosy".

Max concurred. " Oh look honey I'm a physiotherapist by trade, and after trying this once and tallying up the rewards vs the smut, I changed avenues faster than you can say slut!"

The smell of drying sticky beer was wafting around them; drowning out their designer scents - it was the fragrance fairground of the trade.

"Here, let me adjust this for you - the girls are about to jump free".....she tightened and adjusted Sarah's bra strap for her. Sarah could feel Maxine's concentrating breath on the back of her neck like a warm breeze. The tickle shot down her body like an electric buzz. Sarah felt vulnerable but also protected in Max's presence. It was like being with an intuitive man. The work time was not nearly so tedious for her that night. They brushed by each other with a smile as they ferried the drink orders back and forth. Sarah noted the natural sexy swagger of her new comrade. Fearless facade.

She found herself hoping they would team up again, and would set off hopeful to every booking for some time after that.

Until she eventually gave up - assuming Max had decided to quit.

But then it happened: a private event with just the 2 of them as star attractions. As it turned out, Max had been visiting her sick father out of town. And the very first mission she had on return saw them combine forces once again: a bucks party no less. It soon became obvious though that she had a short fuse after much concern for her Dad.

Maxine gave her a peck on the cheek: " How goes it sexy ....are you ready for the animals to be let loose from the cage?!" Sarah rolled her eyes; - she knew she was in for one of those nights, but she was also secretly thrilled to be partnered with her ally. They set about catering to the gathering crowd of ogling men. Serving drinks at an alarming rate and witnessing the usual semi-meltdown occur in 'usual behaviour boundaries' and conversation by their audience.

Slippery, sloppy slope..

"God I hope they get the dinner done soon, or we are in for trouble..empty stomach imbibing is the one-way ticket to hell."

Sarah checked her watch and glanced at the closed kitchen doors.

The initial gentlemanly banter turned to inevitable groping and delirium. It was a transformation to repulse even the girls themselves; let alone their partners of union back in the home base. "Argh…..they are such pigs……their only saving grace is the generosity of their perversion" Max indicated the roll of notes she had shoved into her bra. She turned her face to the bar to display a facial grimace of assertion. They both braced themselves before turning with full trays to paint a fake smile on and adopt a slow hip-swaying walk to the groups of gang animals.   On a rating scale of revulsion, men on a bucks night would have to be top rung….funny, even the baseline pay rates of such assignments were higher to cater for the trauma.

If one was even slightly inclined to turn lesbian, this trade was the ultimate encouragement to jump the fence full throttle!

Albeit in opposing black (Max) and white (Sarah), both the showgirls were in suspenders, stockings, lace G, bustierre, and towering heels; - the quintessential Victoria's secret vision. Sans the wings (!) No amount of perceived innocence could render one an 'angel' in this trade. Halo's had well and truly fallen off. Or been snapped beyond repair.

They were objects of underworld desire…the unspoken terrain.

And every wife, girlfriend and partner's arch-enemy. It was a mental burden and the hefty price to pay for the free-flow cash that came with the free-flow service.

As the night wore on and the table was finally set with meals to soak up some of the fluid, the inebriated men got eager for 'entertainment' time….and one of them yelled " hey girls, where's the strip-show action?? Must be time for hunger games…..!" Max was at the point of snapping now. "It's just us I'm afraid so soak up the view while you can…..you're on the clock, beasts" As she said it she protectively placed her hand on Sarah's derrière and sidled in close to her, like a siamese twin. The men guffawed and roared with delight "Thats more like it, some girl-on-girl action!!"

Playing up to them, Sarah spontaneously played with Max's hair seductively and coyly kissed the side of her tilted neck. They embraced each other, standing close and cheek to cheek, and for a moment Sarah thought Maxine was going to kiss her on the lips. The attraction was undeniable, and although the performance was innocent, Sarah found herself mildly surprised by the reaction to any physical display between them. It was all just about confidence, even if it was complete role-play. And who cared- it was fantasy fare after all! As long as it was a convincing display they were smitten. The men's mouths were open; drooling and they were gob-smacked by it. A sad indictment on the worried 'other half' waiting in their bedrooms at home, however.

It kept them mesmerised and silent for a moment.
Peace!
The girls finished their shift and retreated to the toilets to change and 'debrief' while they rebriefed. As they gathered the bundles of money shoved in their undergarments, they laughed on reflection of the night's charades. A definite success finale.

Both concurred that it was so much easier to just appease with a bit of innocent lesbian flirting than to 'walk the walk and talk the talk'…half the expenditure! During their flirtatious antics, the notes had just kept coming; wallets were spilled out in front of them, and literally thrown at them. Quite profound.

It became Sarah's trade rule number one thereafter: as distasteful a concept as it may seem, innate bisexual power was the ultimate male seduction.

Gratification. A win-win for all.

She was learning fast on the job. The bookings had been gaining momentum, and one had to preserve as much energy as possible so as to be available for all the cash earnings. Fitness and discipline was key, as was not taxing the tedious social quota skills. The catering trade could be notoriously draining if one got caught up in the social trappings and requests. The bullshit banter; psychological ego-stroking and 'niceties' was exhausting. Learn to say NO when needed. For one must always have reserves.

A hint of risqué revelation on the other hand, was much more energy efficient! Ie: keep quiet, just reveal a little more flesh. Albeit a socially perceived disgrace, physical taxation was less damaging. And she had acquired a robust threshold in that regard.

She continually sculpted her body to fulfil the role accordingly. There are several methods for preserving the body beautiful, and everyone is aware of the paid shortcuts: plastic can provide body enhancement, but NOTHING beats damn hard work and discipline in all zones. She had seen some shameful knife-work in colleagues go horribly wrong, and did not wish to suffer the same fate! Nevertheless, veneer polishing was crucial. Always a price to pay; lots of hard work, like it or lump it.

For she wished to save, protect and preserve her subconscious mind, brain and soul for more important pursuits…

Chapter 4:

Gangsta girl games.

Perhaps the most influential character she met in this dynamic world of the undergarments and underworld was akin to something out of a *movieset.* The one that springs to mind instantaneously is the Sopranos.. ~for the attire; bling and lingo were all in complete synchronicity with the show. Not to mention the environment and attitude! But to set the scene, so to speak, we head to the suburb of Leichardt;- little italy.

Where you can find pasta, gelato and italian mob-central…..

Sarah had been working in the industry for some time now, and established herself a good well-known reputation. The agency bosses all knew she was the best booking bet, so the phone was pretty much off the hook……so much so, that she started to think she could self-graduate on some level. She had done the hard-yards of acclimatising to the brutal industry, and now she decided to utilise her knowledge and contact-base; recruiting her **own** army of reliable women, ~ (substantially more attractive specimens than the usual band of lingerie labour brigade might I add)

As a <u>manager</u>, she remained the ultimate professional: top notch standard and service were guaranteed. - Some of them (in fact most she selected) were new to the trade, and envious of her evident daily earnings. They were keen to watch in awe and adopt Sarah's learned methods of attack: maximum results for minimum outlay and trauma (!)

The bookings took them all over town, but the most regular venues happened to be here, in mob-town. The little Italy was, as expected, the area most endearing to all forms of bling and acquisition. Whether it be dramatic gold jewellery; girls of envy; or fast, kitted up cars with outstanding sound systems. *Prestige* was the order of presentation.
And everyone knows: sex = money = power.

So this caper was synonymous with such terrain.

The team were all like the sisterhood anyway; carefully chosen close girlfriends she had worked with in modelling fashion parades, promotions and so forth; no stranger to presenting the body beautiful. There were incentives to the labour too: they would crash together at Sarah's beachside hideaway on weekends after shifts, to debrief on the vulgarity and exposure, and unwind. They affectionately named it 'castle headquarters.'

Nothing like a cocktail by the beach to untangle the nerves; shake the trauma and reboot!

Her closest gang included a busty sex-kitten German, a gregarious and gorgeous Latvian, and an aloof feline french girl. Even if the night wore on slowly, and proved tedious and painstakingly unsavoury, the aftermath was always a celebration to aim for. The beachside palace was constant party central!

Sarah had attained several venues' approval for booking personally so she
would meet her group at the destination early and retreat to the change-room
to discuss any issues or questions before the floor work commenced. They
would often mix and match outfits, or swap if they realised something had
been showcased on them before. One had to keep the visual show different
and varied for maximum appeal.

One of her girls, Hannah had the confidence and aura of a veteran player
already. She had long been self employed in a world of 'men and facade
capers'..it was pretty much the theme of her life. And her car, fashion,
jewellery and lifestyle were always indicative of that. But she was the first to
admit: nothing came for free. She knew that it was labour no matter which
way you looked at it. The key was to make it short, sweet and victorious. And
get out fast. After any booking she was changed, out of the bar and with key
in the car ignition ready to bail at lightening speed.

She was sort of the 'mother hen' amongst the clan. Hannah would go
around adjusting bra-straps to ensure the bust was on maximum display;
tease and style hair; add extra makeup and generally do the final
embellishments before the 'show' began. She was obsessed with flaunting the
flawless female form, professing that *"a woman's body is divine and sacred and
should be worshipped! The male body is such an ugly thing……all dangly bits n
all"*….needless to say she <u>endured</u> men for their necessity in supplementing
her lifestyle, but was seduced by female beauty.

She could fill a tip jar quicker than you could say 'go girl' and was always
a fine example to have in any of the sessions they were assigned to. For she
managed to miraculously complete all sessions maintaining a *"you can't afford
me dreamer…..look, but don't touch!"* power.

It was enigmatic to behold.

And the crowd adored her.

[She also, would join Sarah in other chapters on future paths in her life.

But again, I digress and urge that we return to the drinks tray. And the
over-flowing tip jar..]

At the well-known watering hole on the main street of mafia central, Sarah
was a popular piece. For she was learning that the Italians and French
seemed to prefer her to the indigenous folk. She was obviously more

appealing in that category to the 'girl next door' variety and so forth.
Statuesque in heels, she often towered over the other girls and patrons alike.
She often got asked if she was Russian, Italian, or Greek

(A fact that had her in the plastic surgeons' chair requesting rhinoplasty at
more than one point! For they tend to have stronger features)....she aimed to
soften.

The industries she was embroiled in were a constant battle with self-
conscious perception. Any perceived flaw was a constant burden to bear.

A narcissists' breeding ground...

A girlfriend of hers, Princesca had some work done on the nose - (she *was
of* italian decent) and went from a huge beak to a teenie-tiny little turned up
cute one; shaving more than a decade off her appearance in the process.
Sarah felt compelled to follow, as she had a strong romanesque-style nose,
but the doctor dissuaded her from the scalpel capers, describing hers as
'striking and strong'.) In any case, her features were more prominent than on
the short, round, cupie-doll cupcakes that most local Australian guys
favoured. Maybe it was a feeling of dominance for them? Sarah was often
way too scary to approach for her comparative towering dimensions. She was
aware of that fact now, and at times it was a saving grace from groping
mongrels amongst the throng. She progressively learnt to use it as an effective
tool of self-protection. Heels became the accoutrement du jour. Imelda
Marcus knew the go.

When Arno walked in, it was like seeing a skinnier version of Tony
Soprano. The swagger, designer tracksuit; bling; obviously crafted and
displayed biceps and looks were all so incredibly cliche classic that Sarah had
to stifle a laugh.

By all accounts it looked like a tremendous show, but the more time she
spent around these gangster boys she realised that it really was just how they
naturally were and behaved. He had a look of power about him that she
found a tad arrogant until she realised that he owned the joint. And most of
the suburb itself. He was notorious mafia royalty in this town, and his word
was gospel. He too was feared and revered, albeit not of grandiose height
proportions. It gave an edge of excitement and attraction to a not-so-pretty
lad. He had an aura of 'don't fuck with me' that Sarah always found sexy as
hell. Power and money was her ultimate seductive lure.

There was one particular venue she was still working solo at, but had her eye on accruing as manager for bookings with her girls. There was something about this place that made her a tad anxious. It seemed different from the rest, and her shift times were entirely different to elsewhere too; often around lunch time through to early afternoon. Maybe its the 'pre-siesta' shift she thought. It surprised her how early some locals started on the amber fluid! The pool tables here were always busy with a hive of activity.

There were usually an impressive line of shiny Harley Davidson bikes propped out front, amidst the scattering of custom-designed cars so over the top it was bordering on hilarious. 'Practical' did not seem to be a necessary commodity.

She had asked to speak to the manager but was informed that he was never to be summoned unless it was an emergency or he would be furious! Then she started to learn of the infamy surrounding certain bigwigs of this parade and became obsessed with learning more..

One shift as she went to the bar for tray fuelling, the bargirl took it from her and passed it to another waitress. She looked up in shock. *"Forget that Sarah, you are needed in the office. Here"*….,she handed Sarah a gold-rimmed tray (that looked suspiciously like Christofle or Versace ware) ~ with a whisky shot; a cigar; a machiato coffee and a canolli on it. You couldn't get more of a classic array.

Sarah grasped the edges of the offering with a tad of fearful anticipation; not sure what the expected protocol was here. As she was ushered through the grandiose doors that looked like a 'fireplace' facade, it opened into the private den of the kingpin himself. So very eccentric Italian decor within (as should be expected, no less) : intense gold dramatic features and finishings throughout. It looked like Versace himself had arrived and waved the midus-touch wand on the scene. Bling-mania ornate show ground! She half expected to see a jacuzzi somewhere, with the classic gold design adorning the edges.

"Ciao, Sarah…..come in love. About time we made an acquaintance. I hear you are our most popular piece"

(the term 'piece' had her searching his desk for any visible signs of one there… no gun immediately evident, although she suspected it would be in the desk underneath. Ever ready for a showdown, no doubt. Particularly as his notoriety had it.)

Such a movie set - it felt like 'action, camera'….she thought as she became aware of the heat the gold lights above were casting upon them. She found herself surreptitiously scanning the room for any evidence of hidden cameras. *"Hi….sir…nice to meet you. They tell me you are a busy man and never to bother you, so I'm fascinated to be in the realms of your 'office' space….or 'second home' as they inform me"*, she nervously smiled and nodded.

He took off his glasses and observed her keenly: *"By 'they', I assume you are referring to the bar staff….did they tell you to call me Mr Esposito or Arno?…. The latter is fine for you, now that we are more familiar"*…glasses back on, he returned to his computer; meanwhile indicating a space on his huge desk for her to place his platter. Chunky fingers and the hugest gold bracelet tapped onto the space in front of him. His jewellery alone was kilos in weight she thought. The Italians really do love their gold. They were akin to naked without it. The cross adorning his neck was so majestic it literally cast holy beams like an aura.

Being in his presence made her a tad nervous; Sarah had heard some pretty heavy gangster stories about him involving raids with cops, dogs, guns and so forth, and even a few secret, albeit covered up fatalities and massacres. The rumour mill had it that he was literally an untouchable villain. He virtually laughed in the face of the law.

As she was leaving, he ushered her back. Stopping what he was focused on and giving her his undivided attention now, he said *" Sarah, I need you to do shifts for me in the games room. It is around the corner. I'll personally show you location later   ."*

He lowered his voice a notch: *"It is an illegal card game room. The guys are all like family though, and you are safe, but it must be completely confidential. They just want their macchiatos and sandwiches served with a smile basically."*

With that he looked back down and shifted the reading glasses back on his nose. *" Oh, ~ and wear stylish garb for that. Sexy, but covered. Think 'italian lady of leisure' style…."*

Sarah opened her mouth to speak but no words came out. He slipped out of his chair; grabbed his coat and walked to the door to let Sarah out; equipped with tray and a degree of confusion. What the hell was italian lady of leisure she wondered? As he turned the door handle he simultaneously placed a roll of fat notes down her bra. Oh my goodness..this must equate to a years' worth of tips she thought. Does this mean I'm 'owned' now?! Can I handle it??…as she retreated to the ladies' room to retrieve her winnings she sat on the toilet to count. Holy cow….. This must be what it feels like to win the lottery.

Later that afternoon during her shift, the bargirl ushered her over again. *"Listen Sarah, I just want you to know that you are always okay with Arno. He will protect you. He's a really rock-solid guy - forget the fact that he's mob-man and all the gang-warfare related stories, folklore and whatnot."*
Sarah wondered why she was telling her that.

It was obviously a cue leading to something more. Was she privy to the confidential information Arno had given her too, or was she being paranoid? She seemed to read Sarah's curious mind:

"He wants you to be reassured that you are safe <u>with</u> him is all. Don't be scared…. If anyone will look after you sweetheart, Mr A certainly will! I just think you should know. He wants you to join him after work today"

….there it was. My god, she thought - what for?

Was it just for the private bar address or **more**? Every possible scenario entered her mind for the duration of the shift thereafter and had her somewhat anxious by the time she was due to change and say ciao.

What was the modus operandi here? New terrain. Did she just hang around at the bar? Wait in the shadows for him to retrieve her? Go to him in person?

Just as she was thinking all this, she felt her arm being hooked, and being led away so swiftly she had no idea what happened. Back in the 'office' once again, she found herself alone with him, as he cut up a couple of fat lines of rock cocaine.

O-oh……

she knew this would be the real deal and she would be in for a ride.

"To calm the nerves miss Sarah. I would like you to relax and join my domain with some other lovely folk - it's the weekly soiree session with me and some select folk; I would truly love for you to join us if you may?!)"…..his arm pointed invitingly to the enormous powder trail. She noticed a tattoo on his forearm, which looked suspiciously Japanese inspired, but she couldn't be sure. He moved and

rolled up a hundred dollar bill deftly and smiled, again indicating the tempting offering before them. But her commitment to herself was to remain disciplined. For after this weeks' wages she would have reached her first financial savings' target! And that was more of an aphrodisiac and thrill to her than anything else fathomable.

"I'll graciously decline this time Mr Esposito if you don't mind…i sort of have a busy week ahead"….she detested the inevitable come-downs too. The last time she played in this cocaine candy caper she nearly tipped a drinks tray with several schooners over a guys' head. With intention I add, not accident!

It wasn't the best place to be when in the 'hospitality' industry. All accommodating traits fly out the window..

"Oh relax - you've earnt it. Take the rest of the week off! I will more than supplement your salary, don't worry about that my girl!" As if to justify his claim, he threw another massive wad of rolled up notes at her, which she luckily caught. Holy cow - must have been thousands there. Her skin tingled. She couldn't help herself: GAME ON!! Now we're talking…..

"Well maybe next time - a half a line sometime after a shift at the new venue or something….next week is not so frantic for me but this week is ballistic!" he looked at her with a smirk and obvious approval at her defiance and professional attitude.

Discipline in the face of such fun'n'games was rare. Especially in an industry such as this one.   *"Ah I knew you were different miss Sarah……i will hold you to that promise! The invitation to my abode with a select crew still stands….."*

It was a debt she would have to pay back in a **social** aspect she realised; - but hey…..wasn't that sort of the whole name and definition of the game here?!

"Come on then and I'll show you the other office. You can start tomorrow afternoon at 5. If you need me, I'll be on call for you 24/7" - he handed her a personal card with simply his name and number. Embossed in gold of course. *"I mean it Sarah"* he peered seriously over his glasses at her. *"If you need me don't hesitate"*..

Sarah's mind wandered: she had endured many 3-day epic events when under the influence of the powder puff. The clock hands just seem to whizz around manically of their own accord and before you know it, the next week is upon you! But it had been in a **true** social sense then. Party mode. This was different.

Sometimes it's welcome and at other stages in your life, its definitely counterproductive. Everything depends on the tax vs the bonus. Anyone who has partaken in the temptations of decadence becomes aware of that eventually.

In this case, it would be somewhat *necessary*, and when she eventually did comply, definitely a chapter worth recapping in her history library......episode *mafia mayhem mission.*

And it would prove to be the first taste of the underworld that would become a theme in her working life.

Arno was the first work-related character she encountered whereby the cocktail combination of RESPECT and FEAR rang solid. In some ways, she started to view the two traits as synonymously one and the same now. It was the standard combination as far as she had experienced; a very powerful force.

He was like her Sam Giancana - reverence tinged with dread.

And so she had accompanied Arno, somewhat reluctantly to the next work location tour. He showed her the tiny secret room of gaming he had referred to. One would never have encountered it without being shown; it certainly was at a most discreet address; hidden off the main drag down a private side-street; almost akin to a garage. The patrons were like something from *the godfather* too; hunched little old men clutching cards and sipping on scotch or short strong coffees. Their concentrating focus brought creases to their foreheads; all seemingly tanned and weather-beaten, in the traditional italian sun-seeker way. The room was generally silent compared to the pubs she was used to; more of a low octave mumble and serious discussion on strategy. An elderly woman behind the 'kitchen bar' was stooped, and busy making coffees; the constant whirr of the coffee machine was a signature part of the background din. She began placing typical Italian baguettes with what appeared to be cheese and salami on plates. All was being laid on a tray and ready for her to distribute among the focused folk.

The room was almost foggy with smoke; ashtrays full to the brim visible on every table, atop red and white checked tablecloths. So stereotypical;

Sarah looked on with wide eyes and curiosity. Count the crosses she thought as she noticed the signature chains around every neck in the room.

"So, this is the other office love", he indicated as he pushed a side panel in one of the walls and retreated to the secret cave within. Outstanding plush luxury lay hidden here behind the facade of smoke and mirrors. She gaped: A huge luxurious black lounge; glass coffee table and cinema dimensions TV were in one half of the room, and a massive black marble desk in the other half. Work and rest place were nestled together.

Sarah noticed that the men outside didn't bat an eyelid as he entered the secret chamber. *"This is the other place I tend to reside, if you need to find me"* -she wondered why that might ever be the case, but nevertheless, good to know!

"Okay great"….she smiled surveying the room carefully. The guy was obviously serious about the 'businesses' he was embroiled in; both his office sites catered for comfort means as well….tracking him down to where he was 'staying' between these 2 she had already seen and wherever he officially called 'home' would be a bit of a task. No doubt a deliberately savvy setup; masterminded to achieve his safety from detection with the law.

As she propped against a silver pillar, which she suddenly realised was a stripper pole, she felt a glow of excitement at the secret show before her with the good guy/bad guy character in her presence. Not your average adventure after a shift at a pub!

" I have several other offices too, but you don't need to concern yourself with those right now".

Good grief there were more! He was indeed a bit of a business baron.

Arno grabbed a coat from behind his desk chair, as there was a bit of a chill in the air now. His gentlemanly gesture of putting his jacket over her shoulder as he glided her back out to the games room was comforting….oops, or was it to cover her exposed midriff? she now wondered; a degree of paranoia setting in.   She hadn't come prepared to do a tour of duty with 'his majesty' today; her change of clothes was more 'sporty/sexy' variety. She had needed to catch a ferry and train from the beach address after all. He had changed from tracky into designer pants, crisp shirt and polished shoes, she noted self-consciously.

Her mind then drifted back to a muslim boyfriend who met her while working in a nightclub. He was a gentleman - despite some of the locations he frequented, and one day took her on a 'shopping' trip. As she was scouring the racks, he went up and bought her the largest 'shift' style shirt to don that she considered frumpy beyond belief; but it was evidently a must to introduce her to his mother. The exposed midriff and cleavage that he adored were NOT welcome in all circles.

As if he read her mind, Arno opened a cupboard door to a mini wardrobe, and grabbed a sparkly stylish black-silver dress. *"If you would rather change Sarah, be my guest. You can pop it into your bag in any case. Its yours. I'd love to see you in it."*

She excitedly accepted the stunning piece; draping it over her arm with obvious joy. The couture label was still intact and it was her exact size. She folded it neatly in her bag, as she put his jacket on properly and decided she should at least give him a catwalk show if nothing else at some stage, for his generosity.

His serious tone returned as he audibly entered the more modest games room once more. *"When I ask you to come here, you don't need to do much Sarah but look good and smile really. The men will ask for coffees, and sometimes a sandwich or a scotch but generally just cruise around and change ashtrays etc."* He showed her behind the modest 'kitchen' settings available. It looked more like a corner setting of a glorified 'Italian deli' really. The coffee smelled sensational she noted though and the olive bowls and baguettes were surprisingly inviting also; fresh and neat. The benches and prep area were outstandingly clean too; no cockroaches or rodents evident.

A pretty cushy job! - she ascertained as she nodded with approval. This would be a no-brainer after any local shift in the area and would supplement her earnings substantially, she calculated mentally. He put his hand on her lower back, and then she felt an object in her skirt pocket. She looked down and another roll of notes was visible. Yet again. If he kept this up, she would have a deposit on a property in no time! She was starting to like the **'gangster girl game'** and realised what was meant now by 'he'll look after you'. She had assumed that meant 'in trouble' but it equated to financially too. She smiled with glee despite herself.

He wasn't the most attractive specimen, it was true. And definitely height challenged. But this sort of caper tended to make him sexy as hell in her view.

For her german girlfriend Hannah had tutored her well in the art of appreciating the fugly financial winners versus the dead hot deadbeats of society.

Appeasing veneer or financial power. The general rule was that you couldn't have both.

Fact.

And so equipped with this knowledge, she was ready to play now..

When she showed for the first time, she had decided on dark navy chiffon pants; floor-length draping and flowy style. Paired with a silk shirt; ~ the hint of a lace bustierre top vaguely visible beneath the sheer fabric. It was a rather conservative albeit stylish look, with the hint of sexy thrown in. She added simple diamond stud earrings, and a gold and diamond cross around the neck for what she felt was the ultimately appropriate embellishment. It was a nice feeling to represent oneself this way in comparison to the usual tip-accruing facade. Didn't feel like work at all.   She found herself sashaying into the smoky den with a degree of excitement at the new venture; and yet still a tad reticent about the language barrier; illegal aspect and so forth. The usual mix of nerves, but on a much less punishing scale.

The men glanced up from their game momentarily and nodded in her direction. She hoped she was met with approval on their behalf. This project was outside her normal, familiar terrain parameters so like the focus of their attention, everything was a bit of a gamble! She wanted to play her cards right…

A tad self-consciously she started wandering around the room with a smile and gathered ashtrays for clearing. The woman at the bar had been replaced with a little old man this time. Busying himself with the snacks department and revving up the caffeine corner he peered over his specs with a toothless grin. He was stacking plates onto the tray and with her attention nodded to indicate her catering task. Coffees, baguettes and the odd scotch here and there, the tables were now housing happy patrons. They had a smug look of pampering about them now; she figured they weren't used to this much attention; particularly by a strange towering woman with no italian lingo flair as yet to speak of.

A few of them graciously kissed her hand in appreciation; a gentlemanly gesture that she found so refreshing. These mafioso crew had more style and finesse about them than any perceived 'gentleman' in the normal life here.

Irony…..

She felt like she had stepped back in time to another era. Being the nostalgic movie buff that she was, she imagined Bill Collins himself giving a passionate review of the whole affair, in his usual delightfully pedantic fashion.

It was like the scene of a *Marcel Marceau* movie. Aside from the red checkered tablecloths, mono or sepia tone prevailed….akin to a black and white silent movie, with a distinct smoky scene throughout.

Very gangster she surmised! A thrill coursed through her skin at the sheer madness of the experience. How many people ever got the chance to be in this scenario she wondered? For most it would probably be one of danger and avoidance, but for her it was the dance of dreams.

Although some might consider it unnecessary, in addition to the mafia men she attended to, she still continued with all other bookings as usual. For the more money she counted, the hungrier she became.

She was caught in the wake of the addictive money wave now. Best to ride it out as long as possible. She was bound to hit the shore at some stage. But for now, cash in while you can..

Carpe diem

Most of the venues Sarah worked in were far away from her beachside home which served well for her. It created a barrier for the homebound retreat from the frenetic pace of the work-life. It also offered her the anonymity she required to continue in this field without further torment. She felt safe to reside in privacy ~ far from the seedy sites she catered to.

The pub bookings were invariably scattered all over the city limits and beyond into the quieter suburbs; where the general vibe was more low-key than city slicker bars, and the style plus facade of the folk there more casual too.

She had become a master of the train and ferry system; albeit its frustratingly unreliable schedule which compelled her to resort to taxi transport means too. The hours spent in transit were time to transform the mental space to suit the strength of character required. Perhaps the most important part.

Amidst her lingerie-loving escapades, Sarah found herself oddly being required to buy lots of WHITE wear. Head to toe: suspenders stockings, G, bustierre etc. Sort of the 'angelic look'. It was the biggest request on the venue circuit, go figure. For every time she wore the virginal white costume, the tip jar would need changing several times! Hence, regardless of her preferences (who wants to wear white lingerie and pasty looking stockings when there is so much else sexier available?! She felt like an albino fairy in the frumpy garb. Nevertheless…..) - one had to follow the monetary victories. Must be due to the fact that it is the quintessential *fantasy* look she ascertained. For she indeed felt that she looked like an imaginary vision floating through the grotty watering hole. (Think apparition..) ~ Or just short of the wings and halo for the innocent appeal(!) For after all, that non-reality escapism mode was the ultimate name of this game for all concerned…

There was however one offer that come up on <u>the</u> local circuit. A venue literally minutes from her home in the mall area of the beach walk became an option. She initially shunned it for fear of detection, being literally on her doorstep. But one Saturday, in desperation one of the booking agents begged her to step in for a sick waitress. She agreed as a 'one off', but the minimal time spent getting back to her weekend capers made it too good to refuse: She was working there from 2 -4pm, and literally home in a bath by 4.20! Extra cash for the weekend luxuries. Forgo the cheap case wine and go the champagne!
Speaking of champagne, the show she found most outstanding here at the shed bar was a showgirl doing a dance routine incorporating a huge cocktail glass filled with bubbles. It was most unique - the patrons didn't mind the fact that they got somewhat splashed with all the action, and the room had become filled with floating fantasy bubbles. It certainly took the 'girl jumping out of a cake' image to a whole new level. It was sort of fun and innocent….brilliantly appropriate for a happy bar crowd.

So Sarah's 'time off' was now spent with a few hours of work close to home too, to further supplement the living standards. She worked hard and saved as much as possible. A trait that served her well in future avenues of employment too.

Before long her personal portfolio included fixed term deposits, and shares in banking corporations plus computer companies. She had property investments next in her sights; something grander to aim for. There is always a need for a goal or 'light at the end of the tunnel' in any work regime, she realised. Otherwise the score is unbalanced. In her world, the personal price was too high to not reap the profits in the best possible way. We've all heard of danger money. This was psychological testing money. Not for most..

It was a couple of weeks later that Sarah realised she still hadn't 'paid back her debt' to **the** man behind the money. When she finally saw him emerge from his den at the card bar one afternoon, she smiled and nodded; deciding if the offer arose it was time to accept. He hurried out of the place with phone to ear; obviously caught up in some drama. Then as if he instinctively knew her thoughts, he suddenly rushed back in and took her aside, whispering : *"i'll be back in an hour or so darling. Why don't you change into that dress I gave you and join me for a relaxing evening? Up to you.....you can finish early today."*

He raced back out and she glanced at the clock on the wall - she had only arrived 15 minutes earlier.

Hardly a heavy workload to speak of today.

It was about to start though....

For unlike most, Sarah generally found social painfully punishing for the most part. Who would believe she was the quintessential hermit loner? Her income base was almost entirely based on dealing with people, social and the public. Bane of her existence in some regards.

```
"I don't hate people. I just feel better when they
aren't around"
(quote Bukowski from 'barfly'.)
```

But it seemed that the more she put herself out there, the bigger the rewards. No pain, no gain.

She suddenly realised another bundle of cash had appeared in her pocket.....oh my.....she grinned impulsively. The other work was starting to feel like an 'alibi' to this more lucrative venture! (She could never speak of it, so according to the rest of the world the modelling and promotional bookings just kept coming).

Sarah was indeed collected within the hour, and quickly whisked off through a back door on the far side of Arno's office. *"We will just need to make a brief stop on the way"* he said as the limo driver opened the luxury car door open for her. Her nerves of anticipation were somewhat squashed by the glass of champagne he handed her as he answered another call *'Pronto.'*

As he spoke rapidly in italian; an authoritative tone attached, he rested his hand on her knee. The dress was utter luxury: both visually and texture-wise. Nothing beats quality and style she thought as she sipped and observed the rest of the world going by outside. She knew she could get used to this life, and by all accounts, play the role required well. At least her confidence started to gravitate in that direction as the bubbles proceeded to permeate her system.

Numbing peace.

More relaxed now, she took his hand as he ushered her out the door and off to another plush office entrance. Again, a secret address one would perhaps never find unless privy to the specific location. She sat on the huge black leather lounge to fix her lipstick while he busied himself gathering some files, notes, a briefcase and so forth. This man was so intriguing. And surprisingly not the slightest bit sleazy!

She looked up to find him standing before her with a tray outstretched for her to accept. There it was: the line she had promised she would partake in for party capers. On a gold rimmed gleaming platter no less. She knew she was committed so didn't give it a moments' notice as she took the straw, and the harsh white powder sting burst through her nasal wall to the mental toy room.

This would be grade A quality merchandise for sure. Games often ventured in her life, its true, but in this instance a totally *alternative* situation.

The next few days sort of got lost in oblivion…..well, clock-wise at least. Granted, it was a most entertaining time from start to finish. And one that was spontaneous and unexpected (albeit anticipated from declarations made)

Although not her preferred itinerary for the weeks' forecast (knowing the quantum physics of self-recalibration involved) - sometimes one just has to take the plunge and seize the moment….particularly in the mad luxury of youth.

Besides, this was **work after** all.

A brief knock at the door had him answering discreetly to a gruff looking man with a serious aire about him. He mumbled monotonally to Arno before taking the pile of documents handed to him and doing the customary hug, kiss and back slap that is their signature trade greeting.

Off he marched, and then was suddenly replaced by several other Italian characters, each nodding and proceeding with a sort of mental telepathy communication technique. From mere body language alone though, she could tell Arno was the boss. Sort of like one of those movies where you know the plot and circumstance, but can't access the volume control or subtitles capability.

Mirror to hand, she was pretending to be intensely embellishing her makeup as she surreptitiously observed the scene in her peripheral vision. Thank god she had the 'toolkit' for constant self-maintenance she thought with relief, feeling somewhat like a star in a show…the last thing she needed was to look and feel second hand.

Moments later, off they marched on duty while Arno gathered his coat, keys and some things from his desk drawer. It's the 'piece', I know it!

Sarah felt certain as the cocaine set in somewhat and gave her a warm glow of excitement. She simply couldn't help herself, this sort of experience always made her feel more alive.

The forbidden fruits of danger.

Way outside normal parameters, and definitely a chapter for the book of her life!

He held out his arm for her to grab and lead her off once again to the next entertainment zone. The limo took them to a street address this time, albeit at the back of a house;~ down a long driveway with grape vines hanging over the entrance, like an atrium to a vineyard. Again, very italianate she thought. She could be in Sicily!

They entered the home, but it was more humble and cosy than the more

austere offices he inhabited;~ evidently all over this suburb it seemed.
Looked like this must be his true haven of relaxation she thought as she
watched a more relaxed expression take hold of him too. *"Now, drinks..what can
I get you princess?"* he asked as he rubbed his hands together and happily took
on the more at ease role of host.

She didn't notice the karaoke machine in the corner until later, when some
of the other guests took to the mike and the stand. She was literally followed
in by a small group of others: all girls. Average appearance; albeit cutesy.
They were no more than 5 foot 5 or so high, and more stocky build. One was
a hopeful actor and another a singer/ dancer etc. The other two she saw as
simply 'party extras' - bubbly and fun-loving.

All said, there was no cattiness. Although she knew now that Arno
probably wouldn't stand for that. It became evident that the 2 with agencies
for bookings were here for the kudos (and no doubt funding) that came
attached with this man. It was a bit like watching Hugh Heff Sarah thought
with a smirk. They were all over him with affection 'daddy A' . She realised
he liked the pure innocent excitement of the girls and their ambitions of
stardom some day.

He probably fancied himself a dream-maker…..and she had begun to
realise why. He was god here! It was easy to see why he could be perceived
as the ultimate ticket to some young hopeful's fame and fortune……..
The godfather.
(Well, certainly for a small town like this one at least.)

He was surrounded by young groupies here, all pandering to him; and
flaunting their apparent 'talents'. He seemed to take it as entertainment and
'time out' from his usual grind. This whole suburb was his playground it was
becoming evident. She wondered what his real name was. Surely he must be
using a pseudonym on the streets for identity protection?!

The 'gangster gear' glow had set in somewhat (cocaine) - and she knew
from experience that it was definitely quality merchandise and not cut with
crap (as was often the case in this town)

Sarah had the familiar tingly sensations all over, and found herself
chatting animatedly with the team of 'wannabes' as they took turns singing on
the podium. Not her caper - the whole song and dance routine with an
audience. But she embraced their evident joy at the appeal of the show. There

was certainly an element of entertainment none the less, and it was no doubt a welcome distraction for mr A and his usual in-control demands and reputation. Seemingly constantly surrounded by a team of gruff looking possy, this must be a needed down-time touch. His facial expression was softer now and tension lifted.
So this was his idea of 'weekend relaxation'……..why watch tv when you can go live!

She had to admit, some of the girls had good pitch and a certain degree of potential; if only she could groom the veneer they might stand half a chance! She did take out her makeup purse and demonstrate on one girl at one point, who was delighted with the results of 5 mins' artistry know-how with the right tools. Transformation success of *face* at least! The body was a full-time job story; - to craft the body beautiful took much dedicated toil. Particularly at their more petite height-challenged range. She knew her towering dimensions were an advantage in that regard. But nevertheless she couldn't deny that it was a full time job for any soul, regardless of genetic dimensions; for to neglect the castle, one would watch the foundations start to decline..

Oddly coincidental, she realised she had a missed call from Sven, the booking agent at her modelling agency. She adored him - he was a lovely camp chap and definitely the life of every party (of which he was always top of every guest list in the swankest A-list functions and soirees all over town). True to his nordic roots, he was the embodiment of adonis: looks to die for. Blonde hair, blue sparkly eyes, golden skin and killer smile.
Alpha all the way. Almost Arian 'hail Hitler'…..
Sarah got on with him like a house on fire; he was a fabulous representation of the agency - particularly when compared to the more austere agency owner, Katrina. He did have to contend with a lot of her pedantic crap as her 2IC, but he seemingly handled it with aplomb, and kept the agency reputation glowing when she threw potential grenades in the works. (Sarah was actually convinced Kat had asbergers syndrome; - zero social skills, but an uber achiever who accepted nothing but her standard of excellence). His job description was to deliver the same messages (that she dictated); albeit translated with a gentler, more considerate edge. Ie: palatable as opposed to acidically toxic.

God knows how he did it though after non-stop partying and events attendance with no doubt many sleepless nights.

He was a walking miracle: always looked fresh and rested and patient beyond belief. Come weekend he was, himself, booked out relentlessly on the social circuit.

She had bumped him a few times at gay functions; both of them in a costume of sorts and inseparable when their worlds collide. They spoke animatedly on a few occasions of opening their own agency in competition to 'dragon lady', and rocking the modelling industry of this town! For he had everyone wrapped around his little finger (including boss Katrina evidently) and it was impossible not to be caught under his sparkly spell.

She excused herself and left the room; deciding to give him a quick call back. He would love this update! He answered almost immediately: *"Hello there honey bunch - are you power~pouting ?!"*

she laughed…..*"you know I can't talk much with the show in the background but suffice to say we need a long cafe sesh out to recap this one babe!"*

"….ooh goody; I wait with baited breath!! (Sounds of hands clapping while phone was rested under his chin)…*You are mine all next month though hon; I have bookings for you interstate….call me when you aren't prancing n dancing, you adventure-seeking-goddess, you….!! - toodles"*…..

Sarah returned to the scene of wannabe starlets and their gangsta target, and sat back to soak up the scene. She preferred to be a witness than to partake in many social scenes that weren't of personal preference and design.

This was an odd setup ! But a new experience nevertheless. (Forget the fact that she had no choice and it was essentially part of the work). Curiosity triggered at least. She was, after all attracted to any bizarre situation to add to the mental bookcase of life events. There was always something (read lesson) to be taken from it in a subconscious sense.

The podium had become something like a 'next best talent' event as the girls took turns to perform for the king who applauded and gave a scored review of their efforts. Sarah whispered a few suggestions to Arno from time to time, and he nodded thoughtfully with hand cupped to chin - evidently relishing his role of master opinion-maker in his throne.

As far as Sarah was concerned it was a hysterical case of fantasy dreamland for all the participants; no doubt enhanced by the primo supplements. But what the hell?! Let them go for it. Dull reality was bound to kick in soon enough.

A knock at the door had them hush for a moment. They all looked at each other. These events were strictly invite only, and Arno's expression indicated he hadn't been expecting anyone either. *"Shall I go answer for you?"* Sarah offered; breaking the silence and gesturing to move towards his door.

"If you wouldn't mind princess. Check the peep hole first. Safety control always".

Sarah walked solemnly back into the room; heels off and on her tiptoes. *"Its the law"* she whispered, wide-eyed, to which he simply rolled his eyes and started to go attend to the hinderance.

"Its that time again boys? Do you think you could give me a courtesy heads up next time you think?! Im not so keen on 'drop-ins' you see...."

The next scene happened so swiftly, it was a whirlwind intrusion that saw sniffer dogs and a band of around 20 uniformed armed cops raid the joint. They searched every square inch of property and pulled out boxes from cupboards; items from shelves; suitcases from under his bed etc.

Sarah felt a rush of adrenalin surge her veins. It was both scary and exciting at once. The magic mix that she adored. And blended with the addition of class A stimulants, she felt excited in spite of herself; making a radical decision to have a bit of fun with the scenario. Spontaneous delight. No harm in that surely..

The stage had been the scene of innocent entertainment before. Take it or leave it really. But *this* was more her cup of tea!

She moved into the kitchen, brushed past a few burly uniforms and flipped the kettle on. With a toss of her hair she flung around and announced gaily with audible volume above the barking and frantic din:

" Well now, since we have some extra guests in tow I've put the kettle on........tea or coffee anyone?!"

The ditzy girls were stunned to the point of visibly appearing shell-shocked. Guilt ridden all over their face with those dark, dilated pupils and wide eyes. Gone was the stardust in them, they were now mirrorballs of terror.

Arno himself was the epitome of cool; propped back in his armchair with his legs crossed and a calm smirk on his face as he surveyed the chaotic scene. He seemed to be enjoying it, and amused to the same degree Sarah was. His power was evident now more than ever. For he obviously felt no threat by the attack.

When Sarah witnessed his nonplussed veneer, her confidence was maintained and she started to mingle with the crew; offering beverages while trying to encourage them to retreat to the kitchen area away from possible evidence.

But of course the contraband was bound to be found or provided in this scene. It always was! If it wasn't a definite bust then it was always created by design, with evidence planted for retrieval. She knew that from experience with Danny and co. And Arno did too. It's how 'the system worked' here in crime-world.

He probably just prepared himself to write another cheque to 'send the hindrance away'…..temporarily, at least.

"Well, well….Whats this powder trail on the coffee table then"? one of the policeman exclaimed with an accusatory grin as he indicated his white forefinger proudly.

No doubt Arno had offered his 'hospitality' to the group on the glass top here, to eradicate showtime nerves and so forth.

It was only a hint of evidence to be sure but enough to cause alarm. The officer looked like the cat that got the cream, but Sarah longed to beat him at his game.

With super quick thinking, and her best sugar-coated Marilyn Monroe voice impression, she pointed to the terrified starlets and declared:

"Do you think these gorgeous faces get that way of their own accord?! Why it's my anti-shine foundation powder of course! Is it a crime that I took the role of makeup artist for these glamour girls?!" she opened her Versace makeup bag and took out a small plastic clip-bag with a compact tablet that tended to spill makeup powder dust in her bag. She had excitedly remembered that she had wanted a small covering for its' protection, so had seized one of Danny's cocaine bags to store it in. Brilliant!

As she indicated 'exhibit A' to the audience in the room she was aware of the surreptitious smirk of delight on Arno's face as he watched her play up to the mob.

"An artist needs a workspace after all ~ I improvised, using this table as my workbench, and enhanced the palettes you now see!"

She grabbed a small pinch of the powder which was thankfully very pale, and scattered it on the table in demonstration, indicating her large powder brush.

" Innocent private entertainment officers. A select group of budding performers united to practice their craft…..now what's the harm in that?!"

There was a silent delay in the room as she replaced her makeup items slowly but dramatically before the congregation with a look of *'and…. I rest my case'..*

Arno applauded while grinning: *'Encore miss S'.* I couldn't have said it better myself ! Now gentlemen… And token women in uniform. Time is of the essence…..i think you've seen enough for this episode. Shall I escort you to the exit?!" He was calmly enjoying himself and the scene played out before him in his private place of residence.

[In observation one would get the impression that this scene replayed almost weekly - it appeared to be a common practice intrusion in the home of the baron, and one he found tremendously amusing versus the slightest bit scary or risky.]

The team slowly started to merge in the hallway exit area; having completed their tour of duty attempts at scare tactics. But it was like a game to Arno; he wasn't perturbed in the least. If anything, just a mildly brief interruption to his down-time frivolity activities really. But one seemingly just as enjoyed.

Sarah decided her role had been fulfilled for the moment too, and started to gather up her belongings. She stifled a yawn. Sleep was needed soon to reboot for the week aheads' challenges. And her social graces were on their last legs now.

Slinging the large handbag over her shoulder, she realised one of the policeman was lingering; ~ he was right behind her and as she turned she realised he was one hell of a looker! It was rare she ever thought that of men; she seemed to spend her life appreciating the beauty in the women that surrounded her in every facet of her life.

"Miss Sarah, I believe you live in another area of this town; - you don't strike me as one from these parts".

She wasn't so sure what that meant but she replied *"I'm heading for home now, yes. Northshore way"*....her voice trailed off as she realised it was best to never supply personal information to anyone. Particularly with the leagues she was working/playing in.

"Could I be so bold as to offer you a lift home then?"

She was about to decline and graciously excuse herself and then she stopped in her tracks. If she gave a nearby street or something and not the exact address, it would certainly save her the hassle of heralding an alternative driver at this hour. She knew Arno would have his own private driver to hand, but she didn't want to be a known guest by them either. Retaining anonymity was always a challenge.

She put her dark sunglasses on and nodded with a smile. *"Okay then. If you don't mind! - just down at the Queenscliff road heading to further northern beaches is fine. Im visiting a friend there today."*

She said her goodbyes; hugged Arno in the hallway as he whispered in her ear *" thanks gorgeous, see you in a few days eh"* and passed a roll of money to her discreetly in her palm.

Victory again!! She couldn't wait to re-count the token 'earnings' of the time since encountering this powerful man.

She got into the police car, and actually felt a tingle of nerves; she was attracted to the tall, dark and handsome uniformed hunk in the driver seat! Something she hadn't felt in some time.

They chatted as he drove and before approaching the drop-off point, he asked: *"So…would it be inappropriate to invite you out for dinner sometime?!"*

Sarah smiled. Wouldn't Sven be impressively blown away by this finale to the story of the last 12 hours!!

" Um I guess so. Im free Thursday night if you can make it."

He smiled back. *"Let me check the roster. Im sure I could adjust the agenda to suit that for you!"* He handed her his card.

"Call me with details of your food preferences and so forth and we can reconvene for a date"

"Is that what this is?" Sarah retorted with a smirk of satisfaction.

He grinned and drove off.

Sarah walked the short distance to her discreet home address and opened the door. She dumped her bags and jumped straight in the shower. It was a warm summer day today; quite steamy.

Should she take advantage and prop on the beach for a while to dip in the ocean as a refreshing interlude to a bake-and-relax session?

No better way to spend a day off, surely! Days like this made her thrilled to be living merely a few seconds from a quiet beach corner.

She pondered the last 24 hours that had transpired while under the cooling, invigorating spray. What an epic event:

Karaoke at the drug lords' private den; a taste of primo class A stimulants with wannabe starlets; a somewhat daunting drug raid (dogs included); a lift home in a cop-car, and a dinner date proposal!

All in a days' work she thought as she dried off and reached for the wads of cash courtesy Arno that she had stowed in the bottom of her handbag. Who would believe the shit that went down in her world? Literally…

The 'home-bank' was rocking solid now. Impressive growth spurt in a matter of only a few days in fact. She must get the loot to the bank for smart stashing soon she reminded herself. A sock drawer is hardly secure! Locked safely away in the safety deposit box under lock and key..like most of the memories of her worklife to date.

Sarah closed the fascinating book she was engrossed in, and sipped on her cocktail while reflecting yet again on the previous weeks gone by since meeting the notorious Arno. Too recent to *reminisce*; ~ she was sort of bound up in it NOW, but nevertheless she still felt a distinct memory chapter evolving **as** she endured.

Never had her financial gains reached such stratospheric proportions so incredibly fast. It was unheard of! Such is the allure of crime-related illegal cash she thought. No wonder people continue to take such grandiose risks, despite every scary example of penalty hell that is projected at them from every media source. A few of her close allies were case in point.

She had often wondered if there was a mental/personality connection between those who commit heinous crimes and /OR take huge risks….a mental component that holds these individuals apart from the *rest* of society….ie: those deemed '*normal*'. It was a very vague term.

What the fuck is normal anyway??

It depends on who is the one is asking the question for a start.

We all differ in opinions one way or another.

Her mind wandered off. She found the world a petri dish of study creatures and was always drifting off into anthropology mode.

Re intrusive thoughts: the author of '*the psychopath test*' explains that:

*"(Intrusive thoughts' are all over DSM-IV by the way, as symptoms of Obsessive Compulsive Disorder and Generalised Anxiety Disorder etc; all the disorders characterised by an <u>overactive</u> **amygdala**. I used to see them as positive things: journalists should be quite obsessive and paranoid shouldn't we? But ever since I read about 'Intrusive thoughts' in DSM-IV I've found the idea a little scary, like they're something serious.*

I dont have them all the time, by the way. I wouldn't want you to think that. Just sometimes. Maybe once a week. Or less.)"

Sarah laughed. She had been captivated by a write-up about this author, Jon Ronson, who was studying the relationship between crime/risk-taking behaviour and perpetrator. The common denominators required, in essence.

She was enthralled and devouring one of his collections like a hungry wolf. For she had evidence all around her of his curiosity topic; - her world was full of crazy people after all. Normality was akin to the kiss of death in her company spectrum.

His book 'the psychopath test' was not surprisingly a best seller.

(Admittedly, his entire tome was written before 9/11, when the *whole world* went nuts. Literally.)

This man (the author) had even gone into prisons to interview a few characters as subject matter for his book.

She had been obsessed herself as to why perpetrators committed the same crime after rehabilitation and release from prison. And people took the same crazy risks even after punishment and torment.

Have you noticed that the same characters went in and out of jail repeatedly usually; often deliberately seeking re-institution? Its the modus operandi.

They re-enact the same behaviour out in the scary 'real world' - when released from their cages. Despite all the risks and heartache penalties that loomed in their future. Nothing could be scarier than a lifetime projection behind bars, surely..

Well, depends on the character it turns out. For *them*, the reverse was true. It was on 'the outside' that proved much harsher than the safety of the big house!

Ronson's conclusion was that there was a checklist of personality traits common to all these criminals that separated them from the rest of society, enabling them to fulfil the task with zero remorse.

It was of course to do with the grey-matter wiring. She had always been captivated by the 'unique' and, like the author himself, wondered if her obsession with the topic made her an eligible contender for the 'loony bin basket' herself (?)

He suffered acute anxiety issues himself, so his paranoia was on steroid levels. (Surrounding himself with hardened criminals, mass murderers and utter psychopaths as subject matter was not serving as a therapeutic means! Hardly conducive to alleviation of his symptoms)

Hence, did this preoccupation indeed translate to/suggest an addition of masochistic tendencies? To pursue situations that were obviously a danger zone to self ?

Sarah thought of all the characters she surrounded herself with; knowing full well they were counter-productive to 'mental stability'.

But that equated to BORING after all. And who wants that?!

The stand-out facts from his investigative thesis, if you will, was that besides the obvious fact that these folk possessed a serious lack of empathy, an evident resilience to torture and a high pain-tolerance threshold, the **amygdala** in their brains don't shoot the requisite signals of fear to their central nervous system. In other words they were 'numb'..oblivious to human emotion and suffering. (And hence, definitely classified as autistic too in that regard.)

"Which is perhaps why they are so successful and interested in the predatory spirit" he wrote.

It made them potentially dangerous.

But what explained it all the most regarding repeat offences in certain types, was the fact that after certain testing (brain MRI scans etc) it was discovered that these individuals were actually stimulated *excitedly* as opposed to upset, when shown images of grotesque torture, gore, terror and so forth. They <u>were turned</u> on! (Or, at least, euphorically fascinated)

The terms 'predator and victim' are thrown around airily by them; all is categorised by those 2 categories. One is either weak or strong. Period.

And the part of the brain governing MEMORY was compromised in them all too. Hence explaining why they literally *forgot* the incident, thrill, penalty etc and just proceeded to repeat/play out the whole same scenario time after time.

Like remedial zombies.

The term 'once bitten twice shy' does not refer to these people. It was akin to a dangerous form of early dementia, Sarah thought.

They were the no-fear 'go getters' of society. And not surprisingly the ones that reached the highest stratospheres in the corporate and power fields.

To translate: the world is pretty much run and dictated by psychopaths. They believe these traits are necessary to *'make a difference; get the job done'*. They had the guts to seek the glory.

They don't do failure.

They are in it to implement the 'seek and destroy' tactics they believe necessary for leadership.

They were held in esteem by people everywhere; idolised for their strength of character.

They were engagingly enigmatic too:…. *"a quality that flourishes in absence. We are dazzled by people who withhold something, and psychopaths always do because they are not all there. They are surely the most enigmatic of all the mentally disordered."*

They take no prisoners…..

Up the guts, plenty of smoke.

Boom!

No wonder they are so convincing at serving propaganda to the masses!

A scary concept for the 'normal layman' who believes in and relies on them as the powers that be.

The author of the psychopath test: concluded that

"its a frightening and huge thought that 99% of us wandering around down here are having our lives pushed and pulled around by that psychopathic fraction up there"

At one of the seminars he attended the conclusion was unanimous: everyone in the field regarded psychopaths in the same way-

Inhuman, relentlessly wicked forces, whirlwinds of malevolence, forever harming society but impossible to identify unless you are trained in the subtle art of detecting them.

A fascinating concept she thought. The personality traits required to get to the top of the game. It applied to those in a powerful position, and criminals alike.

Alpha monsters.

As further reinforcement to that concept, to quote Martha Stout, the author of *the sociopath next door:* (who verified that the terms psychopath and sociopath were in fact interchangeable):

"They are everywhere…..in the crowded restaurant where you have your lunch. They are in your open-plan office.

As a group they tend to be more charming than most people. They have no warm emotions of their own but will study the rest of us….."

"Which means you'll find a preponderance of them at the top of the tree?" she was asked by Ronson.

"Yes! The higher you go up the ladder the greater number of sociopaths you'll find there"…..

They are skilful imitators. They wear masks better than anyone!!

Sociopaths love power. They love winning. If you take loving kindness out of the human brain there's not much left except the will **to win.**

God I could write a thesis on this psychological mindfuck shit, Sarah thought. The umpteen paramount chapters of her life in association with psychopaths was evidence of that.

For these were always the characters she chose to love. And they were all raving lunatics!

It appears that to be capable of pursuing certain life paths, ventures and so forth, one must indeed be an authentic psychopath.

On that note, she picked up her phone to call Sven. He was due an update. And he had left her a curious message regarding an 'overseas proposition too tempting to refuse'

" It's a modelling contract in Japan sweetie. The agency is calling a casting. I want you at the helm!"

Oh god another time, energy and makeup-consuming cattle call she thought. They were generally disheartening. You were treated like a moron piece of prime meat. And most characters involved were narcissist nasties.

"I know what you're thinking honey, but I met the agent on Skype, and there is a more important pending aspect here; you and I could team up to 'recruit' more girls for regular new flesh. Its all safe. These guys don't fuck around! Anyway, anyway.....lets meet up soon to discuss the proposition. Ive done my usual spy search and there are no rats smelt here. Just oodles of moolah.....in the most financially powerful place to be in the world! If that doesn't get you, then nothing will..."

She hung up and let the concept dwell in her sub-conscience for a few days before she met up with Sven. It became irresistible after a while. She knew the number one place to be in this industry to really blitz it cash-wise was Japan. Impossible to ignore the potential golden egg.

They met the agency rep at a backstreet inner city office location. A rundown office space that appeared to be under current renovation.

"Please ignore the scenery darlings....it will be a pristine palace at some stage suitable for our agency headquarters"

The Spanish lothario flicked his mane seductively as he sidled up to Sarah. *"Oh gorgeous! I have fond memories of our mannequin parade days all over town. They were such a hoot! Fancy us being brought together again!"*

Sarah remembered Pedro and his octopus-style brotherly love when her and the girls were set off on locations all over the city to perform mannequin duties. Small world.

They had got on well, she just hadn't liked him 'like that'

Handsome, narcissistic and arrogant; he had mastered projecting the metrosexual image to aplomb, and managed to use gift of the gab in many avenues to get where he wanted to be. Actor extraoidinaire.

<u>"Wolf in sheep's clothing"</u> Hanna had described him when they all worked together. *"He plays gay to get into the girls' change room and have his wicked way"*

You had to hand it to him though. Master of disguise. When the corporate and business world didn't work for him, he went to the arts - took up acting, dancing modelling and anything else that took his fancy and managed to impress all and sundry.

Clever. Deceptive.

He was adept at the art of **reinvention** in other words, and despite his flaws, Sarah had to admit she respected that. The ultimate survival tool after all.

He was lovable in a protective way yet just slimy enough to keep at an arm's distance.

Having just got back from a modelling and dancing trip to Osaka himself, he was now professing to be an expert in the capers of glamour escapades in the Japanese underworld where cash flowed like sake.

"Did you bring your book?"

Sarah produced 2 portfolios for him to peruse while Sven stood and made for the balcony to light up a cigarette. *"You know those things will kill you. And they are a hazard to the complexion sweetie, didn't you know?!"* Pedro berated mockingly while he scrolled page by page tilting his head and sticking stickers on various shots that appealed for the Japanese market. They were into severe glamour and cutesy. Some of her 'creative' shots were a bit too tomboy for this crowd.

Each job was different.

Generally speaking the portfolio's contents needed to be so diverse that one is virtually unrecognisable from one page to the next. He was on the hunt for the ones adhering to japanese fetish.

Sven rolled his eyes skyward, tossed his head and ignored the advice thread. *"So Pedro......ðaaaarling, when ðo you think we coulð have a date with these slant-eyeð gun-wielðing bigwigs to send her abroad and into the lion's pit?!....Or should I say Sumo pit"*

"Well..there's some fabulous stuff here. I only need four but so many to select from; I'm just going to take copies of them all. Shoot them straight over and get back to you. I have other girls going too - some to Osaka and some to Nagoya where the yakuza master reigns. Only the ones I think can cope will go to him. And you will definitely be one, I can almost guarantee"

Sarah felt a mixture of excitement and nausea pervading her gut. The prospect was tantalising yet terrifying.

"I will arrange for the agent to come over and personally accompany the selected crew of models over, so I shall be in touch asap with all deets on that score. But in the meantime make sure your passport is ready for action and your diary cleared....it will be a contract for some time, so consider yourself missing in action from thereon in.."

The sounds of that were so enticing to Sarah that she felt tingly with anticipation and decided to go home and start fully preparing for departure mode. She had been living the life of secret seduction here in this town for some time now, but she felt the expiration date readily approaching and the desire to take it to the next level in exotic terrain was to be the start of a new chapter.

She was ready....

After the meeting Sven went to a bar with her to debrief. He also wanted to hatch a new plan with her that had been brewing in his grey matter for some time now.

"Listen Sah, I really think we could take advantage of this opp and start the 'agency faction' we always dreamt of."

Sarah wondered if he was being serious or it was just the long island ice tea taking effect. This drinking hole was notorious for making super strong power elixirs to knock your socks off. The gay squad seemed impervious to the strength of the inebriation!

He continued: *"Im talking send you off on a recky tour, and then flip a new fleet of fresh faces over for you to 'manage' offshore….. We share a cut of the action and build a mini empire…..think of it like a glamour export house!! Our girls are in huge demand on japanese soils and worth their weight in gold. (Light as that may be, we can grow it to statesferic proportions financially for US!!) They are in demand for an array of roles there from my investigations. Modelling, dancing, promotions and hostessing to name but a few. The options are endless - and its all there within our reach now to take advantage of"*

He was virtually drooling with greedy lust at the prospect of the Yen's power and Sarah had to admit she was kind of caught up in his spell.

She was the *victim* of seduction now!

She continued on with the lingerie waitressing work on the side to boost the 'pocket money' for the looming trip ahead. Or, perhaps it should be considered 'safety money' she considered.

Careful strategic planning was always paramount to success and survival in any pursuit undertaken.

A foreign land with a different language, culture and psychology demanded a certain degree of self-guarding mental peace of mind to be sure. And everyone in their right mind knows that means financial security.

Arno was helping fund that aim enormously also; the man was both a villain and saint to her! A seductive combination.

In her time off work she started studying the japanese language at an evening class, and commenced packing bags for the mission.

Weeks passed and she finally got the call from Pedro to meet the Japanese agent Akihiro. It was to move swiftly from the point of meeting the charismatic asian gent. In fact, after the meet and greet, she was advised that the flight was less than a week away. He seemed to think that was MORE than enough time to get fully prepared. (Hours away!)

Welcome to the Japanese way! Go, go, go..no rest for the wicked or the wise. Ever. Effective machinery never stops. It is infallible.

She had been selected with 3 other girls for the 'first round' of postage, so to speak. The mafia boss had been entranced with a photo of her taken with gold jewellery and a golden glow about it. (Ie 'expensive' veneer) - it was the ultimate glamour look in her collection of portfolio offerings. She was expected now to embody that image endlessly. She felt a degree of stress and high standard pressure looming in her vocation forecast.

But the monetary incentives were certainly there. The yen was at its strongest ever so now was going to be the time to cash in. She braced herself for a challenging ride.

The day finally arrived and, sleepless from nervous anticipation she met the girls, Pedro and Akihiro and dealt with the airport pularva. She thought it was such an ordeal.

[little did she know that travel ahead would be much more hell-bent and fraught with trauma as a result of terrorism; but indeed nobody did.]

She had always found company to be tedious. Particularly women. In this industry especially. So much artificial fairy floss bullshit. She much preferred the company of males.

She spent much of the flight talking to the japanese agent vs the frothy girls in tow, and was relieved when they finally touched down.

They were taken straight to the mafia boss for meet and greet, - then to their respective 'mansion' - at this stage an empty apartment to be refurbished with the individual requirements of the girls.

There was a futon on the floor for a 'nap' to rest up before having to doll up for the official dinner meeting with the big dude.

Hot saki drunk in sunken tables not an option but a necessity (!) - almost to 'keep face'.

Nishihara san was wildly fascinated by Sarah and told the agent as such. It was a great start to a journey like no other she would ever face..into the dark illegal underworld of japanese mafia playgrounds and gambling arenas.

When she was finally settled she called Sven to 'check in' on the situation and report back on progress thus far.

His phone was on message bank which was very out of character for the boy. He was generally the man who never ever turned his mobile off; it virtually had to be surgically removed from his tight grip at all times. It was his lifeline for both work and play and as such was akin to a vital limb.

A few days passed and she did the same to find the same result. Goodness maybe he had switched numbers or something and had no way of notifying her or something. (?)

She decided to call the modelling agency during work hours in the respective time zones to see if he could be located there as a last resort. The agency owner bitch from hell answered and when she realised Sarah was after Sven she audibly sighed with anger. *"I don't wish to hear his name muttered again EVER, do you hear me?!"*

Sarah retracted with shock. Katrina had been besotted with the man for as long as she had known them both which was several years now. And she had even admitted to Sarah that she had a secret crush on the boy; despite the fact that she was well aware his fancies lay in the opposite sex category.

"He has been arrested on embezzling charges Samara. I'm absolutely dumbfounded. It is a monumental mindfuck". She started to sniffle and Samara actually started to feel some compassion for the hard-nosed business baroness. She also realised suddenly that she had been addressed by her **real** name; she was so used to the Sarah alias title. It was kind of a double shock.

"He has stolen cash from the company.....MY COMPANY at astounding rates for several years now......it is the hugest slap in the face to me. I trusted him with my life......this agency is my baby and he has damaged it irreparably."

"Oh my god,..... I'm in shock.......are you sure?!" Samara asked with confusion.

"No question. I have all the proof. I will see him burn in hell for the way he has back-stabbed the hand that not only feeds but funds his stupendously decadent lifestyle.....he will do time now for many years. Deepest darkest cell. May he spend his hours repenting what he has done to me"...She started to sob with abandon now.

Sarah felt her pulse racing; she wondered if the woman had suspected his side-line business plans with her also although there was no indication at this point. She felt a tad guilty for the plans they had made. Even though now they were undeniably nul and void.

The woman signed off with a final warning:

"Don't fall for seduction Sarah.....it is an enigmatic trait that wins all sorts of hearts, but at the end of the day you think you know someone but you DON'T....trust only yourself. Period."

Sound advice that Sarah was already intrinsically aware of….but nevertheless this revelation about her former ally and comrade was a shock to behold.

My god what a rollercoaster Sarah pondered as she looked around at her foreign surroundings and thought about the loss of her rock back on familiar soil.

Where to from here?…..looks like she would learn to fly solo from now on. And as far as seduction was concerned, Sarah knew that would mean dedication to speaking in the foreign tongue.

Amazing how one deeply challenging chapter can actually prove to be a segueway to an even more impactful one to follow. As if the steps of courage must be taken in sequential order.

She breathed deeply to soften the nervous anxiety flooding her to the core, and to brace herself for the next ride.

And the most challenging new chapter hence commenced..

The Scarlet Woman

~

"*My show is not a conventional show…like theatre, it asks questions; provokes thoughts, and takes you on an emotional journey. Portraying good and bad; light and dark; joy and sorrow; redemption and salvation. I do not endorse a way of life, but describe one….and the audience is left to make its own decisions and judgements. Every night, before I go on stage, I say a prayer: that the audience will watch with an open heart, and an open mind..and see it as a celebration of love*" *and humanity. This is what I consider freedom of speech; freedom of expression, and freedom of thought"*

(Quote Madonna - from 'in bed with Madonna'.)

Chapter 5:

Part 1:

GIVE ME MOORE..........

Are you game to play the game?

She had been, and won. Plus lost too.

Now, in hindsight as she reflected on the chapter, it was almost surreal. She again felt relieved she had taken such risks in her youth, as the prospect now was beyond terrifying.

As were many of the crazy experiences she had endured. But being no stranger to danger, it had been like second nature to her. Extremes. Happy medium was not granted access.

The danger here was of a different kind though. It was soul stuff. Recesses of the grey matter. Locked into the memory vault forever; never to be erased.

A big price to pay.......

And again, she found herself reaffirming the fact that nothing came for free. There was always a debt to pay for any perceived gain. It took risk. And courage.
And often, a degree of youthful stupidity.

Still, no point pondering alternative paths now. In another life maybe. But she was stuck with this one so best to move forward and process the outcome with a positive spin, for sanity maintenance control.

She had a choice: release it from her heart somehow, or go nuts!

She of course chose the former, but somehow the two options still became intertwined.

Still, she reassured herself that in fact, real 'living' is often done by the crazy. The sane ones tend to just float in limbo-land existence.

So, she revealed her story in all its guts and glory. Glamour and filth. Prosperity and poison....

"   Hi. My name is Christie M.
I was christened that by the booker agent boss (for want of a better term)…….. when he hired me.

Darren was a natural in the industry after his previous years of service.
He was a somewhat mysterious character, but a father figure nevertheless. He had a nack for taking you under his paternal wing and reassuring that all would somehow work out well in the world.
His wife and daughters helped run the show; forever motivated by the enormous profits. As were we all. It engenders a degree of madness in one, this quest for big biccies.
Amazing what you become capable of when abnormal chunks of moolah are thrown into the oquation! And wo are talking chunks. Big fat banknotes of hungies. It was the definition of euphoria.

I loved to fondle them and count them. Watch them grow…………

"Christie, you're seriously insane to leave a treasure chest in your SOCK DRAWER! Bags and bags of cash girl……if someone breaks in, you're done!! Get your arse to the bank and put it safe, for god's sake!!"

It was in fact true. And she was right. The bedroom was at the front of the house, on the ground floor, so access was crazily attainable.
At the time I lived seaside, on the outer fringes; a more laid back retreat from the frenetic city action. It was a private haven to return to after the nocturnal battlefield.
The free life I led at home was a far cry from the paying one.

Hannah….. She was the protector. Arch nemesis. Doppelganger. She was all those things, and cunning as hell.
We were like Siamese twins. Almost inseperable; yet often opposed. In work and play.
A symbiotic relationship; it was a marriage of sorts. One that was destined to crumble with the castle for the sheer wildness & decadence of it all.
In fact, she had led me to the game in the first place when she realized my obsession with

cash counting and investing. She remained baffled by my need of tangibility though.
To use an analogy: I liked to nurture 'the sock drawer' like a thirsty plant; feed it and watch it grow.   She tended to throw the cash seeds to the wind contrastly, in a 'now you see it….now you don't!' fashion.
(Which is general human nature it seems.)
She expected replenishment in the cash stakes and took it for granted, whereas I was always living in the mode of 'damage protection control'.

Translation: *there is a crisis just around the corner that will smash your finances if you aren't prepared.* And that is the rule in life that was/is constantly reaffirmed! I'm an anomaly…(which is of course why I 'was what I was'.
'Normal' was not any part of THIS caper.)

My investment portfolio to this point was small, but not to be sneered at when compared to other peers my age. With several bank shares and fixed term deposits, I held grandiose fantasies of an empire someday. Always the dreamer…
Hannah on the other hand was like the red Ferrari she drove. Or the Bentley, Porsche, etc. Serious and high maintenance. A cash guzzler.
I made it; she ate it.

I had an intense aversion to watching people devoid of money management skills being in control of it. Hann was no exception. I tried to encourage her to save, but she felt no need, as the supply always seemed to meet the demand thus far! She had not yet encountered panic mode…(the code I lived by of 'save for the inevitable rainy day' – ie crisis, was a foreign concept to most. Always in survival mode..)
The 'pretend boyfriends' she acquired while with me were chosen solely on their ability to provide and donate. Cars, houses, jewellery,- you name it. She was a skillful collector. She would acquire her loot……and return to me and the nest. They would bore her endlessly however, and have her forever sighing and professing "if only you were a man, I'd marry you!"…

And for the record, she was was not only a german glamazon, but a testosterone-fuelled rev-head to boot. That coupled with her absolute incompetency in financial planning…..pure husband material!! Their opposite natures made them sublimely linked.
She could drive any car, at maximum speed, and pull it apart too. Mechanics, step aside!
This blonde, big boobed damsel in distress was not in need of assistance! She would change a tire in stilettos if necessary.

Are you confused at this point?

Okay, lets be straight up.

And start again. Right from the start…

Hi, my name is Christie Moore.
I work with my girlfriend Hannah.
We are high class escorts.
Our pimp is Darren. The booker and watchdog. Sort of .

He was a natural in the industry after his previous years serving as a cop on the seedy streets of the city's inner beat. There was doubtlessly little he hadn't seen, with the 'forces of corruption'. Everybody knows there are no all round good cops! It just doesn't pay..
A solid, stocky brut of a man. Who could be gruff as hell when provoked; but gentle and cuddly underneath. You felt safe with him, as in a protective security-guard sense.

After our former years dabbling in the industries of flashing the flesh, it was the natural progression for us too. The graduation into the 'big league', so to speak. But the initial phase of any daring undertaking is bound to ignite sheer terror at first.

'The game' is of course umbrella terminology. Hooker for example is less complimentary, as is harlot. Or whore. (That's definitely the worst, and ranks up there with the 'c' word.)
We were specialized creatures however. Polished performers. Hence the pricetag.

For each girl required, in addition to the physical attributes, certain specialties that set them apart and made them most desirable, ~ but unattainable.
This was the magic.
Addictive.
In that sense, Darren was the dealer to the multitude of addicts that joined the foe.
And we were the drug.

Once these victims had tasted the forbidden fruits, they nearly always came begging back.
My skilset was to fuck minds, not bodies. The lingering grey-matter orgasm that haunts.

And that, my friend, is what brought them back for Moore...... I will start now, in story fashion, to reveal the events as they unfolded
A brutally honest portrayal; using the third person becasue in a sense, it does feel like somebody else lived through this period as I observed from above.
for the mind has a way protecting the soul...

Chapter 5:

Part: 2

'No more ribs please!'

Criticism, like rain, should be gentle enough to nourish a man's growth without destroying his roots."
-- Frank A. Clark

When she entered the agency for the first time with her girlfriend, she was fear-less....(that feeling component proved to rapidly follow, however.)

The two had been to lunch; had the hair and nails done and were suited up to impress. Just like another go-see or 'cattle-call', only the rewards for this venture sounded way vaster and more lucrative.

She had nerves like butterflies with the adrenalin rush of anticipation. Nothing that rewarded grandly was without a pain tax. She knew that. She anxiously eyed the menu trying to ignore that nauseous gut feeling so familiar. However, Hannah convinced her to calm her nerves with memories of similar scenarios that had played out in her life:

*"God, Chris, you lost your virginity to the son of Harry M. Miller for heavens' sake! You spent a weekend with that megastar Harley actor....and **then** when I set you up with George, he introduced you to Renee Rivkin and his 'assistant' playboy chauffeur Gordon Wood. Big players....that get away with murder... literally! Caroline Byrne's 'leap' off the gap was not suicide - you know they're saying Gordon pushed her. Notorious party boy that one...hey - remember those mirror sided arm-chairs with a straw compartment?*
Power people....We're thick with this calibre of society already girl....it just makes sense to actually get PAID to be involved in social at this level as we are. 'Coz theres no denying it's hard work! A full time job."

So after a few glasses of wine, she was in the mood for a meeting. It was like a game to her. (To this point, she had excelled in the interview procedure when in the lubricated zone. Her confidence appeared, and along with it the convincing verbal. She nearly always got the job, but once the challenge had been won, she would resign. There was never enough cash incentive for her!)

This time however, it wasn't about gift of the gab. She could have kept her trap shut entirely while he scanned her body from head to toe for any perceivable flaws or problem areas.

After modelling this wasn't an issue. You get used to walking around in underwear or half naked while under scrutiny. The assessment was almost the complete opposite however. No jutting bones allowed here!

After the 'bodycheck' that was routine practice here, he smiled and gestured for them to sit at the desk with him. "Don't worry, you'll get used to this. We even check the regular girls on a weekly basis. Have to keep everyone in tip-top condition. My reputation is at stake here"

Darren slowly perused her portfolio with a smile and raised eyebrows. "Great photos. You're quite versatile. It almost looks like many different girls"

He closed the book and looked up with a more serious expression. "However, this is another world to fashion, and you need to understand that. The girls we recruit would never make it in the modelling game. Physically I mean. We don't want to starve you; we actually encourage you to eat!! I think you have much potential, but we need to fatten you up!"

He stood to retrieve some money from his jeans pocket, while waving to some other folk appearing in his doorway.

"Okay girls, that's enough for now. Hannah, you go sit in the waiting room, and darling here - take this and get us 3 serves of spareribs with fries will you".

"Huh?...Oh-Ive just had lunch!"

He stared at her sternly. "I DON'T CARE!!"
Hello………….the angry cop was making an appearance. Gone was the serene gentleman who ushered them into his room.
He pulled a massive pile of hundred dollar bills from his briefcase; fresh from the bank it seemed, and whacked them down hard on his desk. "Does THIS appeal to you ---?? Is this what you're here for? If so, then off you go on that little errand will you. Coz this lot ain't for the scrawny. Only the voluptuous need apply"…

He had hit the right note with her. The sight of that vast quantity of cash was the motivation to obey orders. For nothing else could have enticed her to even entertain the thought of such greasy takeaway food. But if that was what it took…

She was a mixture of emotions as she stood awaiting the artery-hardening order. What was she doing in a takeaway joint on this seedy street; wearing Chanel suit and towering heels? A wave of nausea overwhelmed the earlier wine-induced high. She sensed eyes on her as she took the 3 plastic bags of ribs n fries. It was a juxtaposition of images. Grease n glamour.

When she returned to the agency, Han was nowhere to be seen. This only served to add to her trauma. Oh god, had she stormed out or something and left her stranded with this brut?

She hesitated as she entered his office, for a moment not sure if she would cry or vomit. "Please sit love" he said gently with a warm smile, producing cutlery and napkins from his desk drawer. He took the bags and put one in front of her. "Two for the already fat guy and one for the princess!" The room stank like a greasy spoon now.

They chatted as she picked at the food self-consciously, wishing she had packed perfume as well as the toothpaste and brush she always carried. Mental note to put in handbag when home.

"Sorry for the tyrant before, but its for your own good. Hard love baby, hard love……..."

He took a book out from his desk, and passed it to her.
'Babies names'….??

She looked up with a confused expression as he answered the phone: "Yes love. No problem. Keep the phone on; Im right here. Get the cash straight up though. No money no

honey." He grinned at her as he hung up.
"That was 'Claudia' on her first job!" he announced proudly, referring to Hannah.
"She has the 2nd one lined up in an hour to follow. Laughing all the way to the bank, baby!
So, what name have YOU decided on, love? No time to waste here……….."

He gestured to the book while he ravenously polished off the second takeaway package.
"Not really sure what you mean - ?"
"…Well, its time to christen you. New identity"

Aha. She knew this scenario well from prior 'occupational exploits' that required a more
anonymous approach for self-protection.

"So……..i have the job then?"
" As long as you join me for dinner every evening before your shift, sure. I may blame you
later for MY skyrocketing cholesterol, but we should have some flesh on those bones pretty
soon"
The phone rang again, and this time he cleared his throat and assumed an authoritive tone
as he explained the system to the potential client on the other end.
"Don't worry about a thing. There's always a first time. Our girls are all exquisite and
        professional…..Yes……no problem whatsoever. Credit card is fine. Her name?....." he
hesitated and looked across at her, squinting as his mind ticked over.

"I think ill do you a massive first-time favour and send you the one and only Christie.
Christie…Moore. She is an angel. You will adore her, I assure you……okay. Expect her in
around twenty minutes."

He hung up as he scribbled details down on a note pad in front of him.

Well if she felt sick before, she felt positively panic-stricken now. The adrenalin was in
overdrive. She began "So, what's….?" he put his hand up to stop her as he again answered
the phone.
" Oh g'day mate. Yep. No, she's not on tonight. (laughter) Ha ha, glad you were impressed.
Always here to please, mate! Look, Im sending you a new one now. Test drive. She'll be
there in……." (he glanced at his watch)" around 2 hours- (pause).Sorry mate, no-can-do.
She's sprucing up for you as we speak; cant get her there any quicker". Laughing:…."Only
the best for you, right! Okay, okay. Yep. Let me know. Cheers mate."

He ripped off the first sheet and handed it to her as he started writing the second one.
"You're off, Christie! Here are the addresses of your first two 'assignments' love! I'll call your
first cab now. Don't worry, just be gracious and we can workshop the protocol procedure
with you tomorrow. Call me when you're done"
With that, she was whisked off in a taxi before she had time to process what on earth had
just happened in the last 30 mins. Hell, she had just stuffed herself like a goose; been re-
christened in haste, and was on her way now, (at lightening speed with this maniac driver),
to the most frightening mission of her life. Oh god…

She'd done some wild stuff in her time, but at this early point in the game, it felt pretty much
like the pinnacle. On the terror quota rating, it reached a solid 9. (And for her, that was

saying something)….
She would grow to love her later, but for now, her heartfelt sentiments were: SCREW Heidi
Fleiss!!!

As her heart beat so wildly in her chest, she felt almost certain that a heart-attack was highly
likely! Where was the paper bag to breathe into for hyperventilation? She tried desperately to
calm her nerves; repeating the self-mantra in her head: the greater the fear and risks; so
too the rewards…

Out with the mask for this performance. Perhaps even a bagful..
there always seemed to be the double-life scenario for her. She really should have been an
actress.

They arrived at the first destination. As luck would have it, the client was not a veteran
player; he was as new on the scene as she was. Phew! This served to unjangle her nerves
somewhat with the knowledge that he had nothing to compare her to. Fresh meat. A
rehearsal of sorts. By the time she hit the second one; having survived the first, she was
ready for the stage, with mask securely fitted.

 The review was obviously shining on this 'test run'. She certainly hadn't been eliminated
from the game. Darren exclaimed "two encores Christie! They both said they would be more
than pleased for round two"   It was not only a relief, but a bit of a buzz for the ego.
"Once we have you trained up on our signature protocol you'll be laughing! "
But what sealed the deal was the take home package, which she counted in the taxi on the
drive home in the early hours of the following morning Yes, laughing indeed. All the way to
the bank ..or at least the sock drawer for now. She had never imagined so much cash for
one 'shift'. That provided the ultimate high; and she was indeed hooked. Excuse the sort of
pun….

At the point of anti-climax though, one is susceptible to crumbling.
She still cried herself to eventual sleep after the first evening's encounters. How could she
not? It was a cocktail of emotions, sensations,
thoughts and actions that had bombarded her under pressure.
The most outstanding of course being the awareness of the stigma attached to the capers.
Not exactly pride inspiring stuff. And yet, she was strangely the most self-satisfied she had
been in so long. This had fulfilled her on a multitude of levels.

The irony.

And so began her foray into the dark world of secrets and sins behind closed doors.
Always a creature of the night in her occupational pursuits; - her bodyclock was set for
nocturnal, that's for sure. She had tried to deny it on several occasions, but it proved to be
fighting her natural biorhythms. [The only time she got to witness the 'crack of dawn' was if

she had never gone to sleep in the first place. (which was a lot! How she hadn't burnt out yet was a mystery)]

Likewise, she was wired differently. She envied those who mastered normality, but it just wasn't her game. She was incapable of 'regular, tax-paying' employment. She had dabbled here and there, but for brief periods only, as she felt the sanity guise rapidly slipping. It always left her defeated, depressed and penniless.

No, it took more than that to make **real** money, and she knew it.
From her own experience, and what she witnessed from others, the normal vocations, and the victims trapped within them bored her senseless!

It was as it sounds: 'The daily grind' only served to grind you down. She'd rather 'do time', frankly!   Was she an alien species?...... Her mind momentarily drifted back to her capers in youth:
the pretend friend she affectionately named 'Tankrid' – with the green hair.
~and the game of: 'lets do exorcism and murder scenes on the rooftop!' with her girlfriend, using tomato sauce for blood; - as her friends' father photographed them while hanging from a tree limb ......ahem .... WACKO.........!!

So there were no surprises really when she started to play the unmentionable game. The ultimate taboo. Talking about it with family and friends was of course akin to admitting you had contracted AIDS while at at the dinner table (!)......so it remained the secret game.
And like all things she undertook, she intended to excel at.

She knew there was still work to be done though. The veneer and game-plan needed crafting to perfection.

 She set forth on the quest to layer the hourglass that the sex industry demanded.
So the next week saw her forcing down all the culinary taboos; always under the observation of the boss: hamburgers; fries; pizzas, curries etc ~ but mostly spareribs. Darren always insisted on bloody ribs. Until she pleaded for some clean Japanese cuisine at the point where she could no longer do up the zipper on her skirt; busting at the seams.
It was intensely uncomfortable. Disgusting. This was the price she supposed, but enough ribs already. In this instance, it most certainly was NOT a case of you-are-what-you-eat!

There was always a challenge involved to acquire the ultimate rewards. As with anything in life.

This was the point where she COULD have turned around and closed the chapter, summarising it as an experiment, but not to be pursued further. However, the sensory perception took hold. She couldn't resist.
[They talk about the sense of smell being a forefront one in acts of intimacy;~ it can lead one

to the next base by sheer animal instincts alone].......well this is where she smelt the MONEY. And it was the biggest aphrodisiac possible.

No experience is a wasted one. Whatever doesn't kill you makes you stronger....right??

They wanted flesh, then she would give it. More ample by the minute it seemed.

Curvy Christie: enter the game. If you dare.

If the price was right, she would give them more Moore.........

PERHAPS YOU ARE FAMILIAR WITH THE MUSICAL MAN OF LA MANCHA. IT'S A
BEAUTIFUL STORY ABOUT A MEDIEVAL KNIGHT WHO MEETS A WOMAN OF THE
STREET, A PROSTITUTE. SHE'S BEING VALIDATED IN HER LIFE-STYLE BY ALL THE
PEOPLE IN HER LIFE.
BUT THE POET SEES SOMETHING ELSE IN HER, SOMETHING BEAUTIFUL AND LOVELY.
HE ALSO SEES A VIRTUE, AND HE AFFIRMS IT, OVER AND OVER AGAIN. HE GIVES
HER A NEW NAME - DULCINEA - A NEW NAME ASSOCIATED WITH A NEW PARADIGM.

AT FIRST SHE UTTERLY DENIES IT; HER OLD SCRIPTS ARE OVERPOWERING. SHE
WRITES HIM OFF AS WILD-EYED FANTASIA. BUT HE IS PERSISTENT. HE MAKES
CONTINUAL DEPOSITS OF UNCONDITIONAL LOVE AND GRADUALLY IT PENETRATES
HER SCRIPTING. IT GOES DOWN TO HER TRUE NATURE, HER POTENTIAL, AND SHE
STARTS TO RESPOND. LITTLE BY LITTLE, SHE BEGINS TO CHANGE HER LIFE-STYLE.
SHE BELIEVES IT AND SHE ACTS FROM HER NEW PARADIGM, TO THE INITIAL DISMAY
OF EVERYONE ELSE IN HER LIFE.

LATE, WHEN SHE BEGINS TO REVERT BACK TO HER OLD PARADIGM, HE CALLS HER
TO HIS DEATHBED AND SINGS HER THAT BEAUTIFUL SONG, "THE IMPOSSIBLE
DREAM", LOOKS HER IN THE EYES, AND WHISPERS: "NEVER FORGET, YOU'RE
DULCINEA"....

(QUOTED VERBATIM FROM 'THE 7 HABITS OF HIGHLY EFFECTIVE PEOPLE.')

Chapter 5:

Part 3:

Polishing the trophy.

Women wanted men who made money, women wanted men of mark. How many classy women were living with skid row bums?

Charles Bukowski. Ham on Rye.

**The sex industry at its' most elite is a fascinating world; inhabited by a vast array of exotic creatures who, contrary to the prevailing belief, are usually the higher echelon of intelligence. (One must stress 'usually' here; at the lower levels you still get the cliché characters of course)
From her experience at THIS level though, the irony was that they were predominantly the ALPHA league. They aspired for more out of life than the norm, and were prepared to take the daring steps to achieve that.
They are USUALLY well-educated, and often pursuing the elite categories of specialisation: medicine, law, etc, ~and this side was often their double life…(yes, smart girls use their body for money too)
Alternatively, they were seeking to snare the perfect, well-established, successful husband; while bypassing the usual methods of 'casting'.
Cut to the chase so to speak (and accrue funding in the process!) ~ Forget dating websites, this was the ultimate: 'try before you buy' ….(or in this case, ARE bought).
They had been sold the dream: they wanted in on the high life, and sourcing their own Richard Gere from *Pretty Woman* …a grey haired older gentleman with the bank accounts that knew no ends…
Some dreamt of being 'discovered' by Hef. (The Hugh Hefner-type is of course the cuddly older sugar daddy wanting a princess to spoil.)
[The third category is an obvious one; although it should probably be mentioned also: the chicks who are in it for the intimacy, attention and satisfaction in that regard (read insecure, &/or nimphos) ~they are less likely to contract the 'nasties' with this calabre of clientele.]

Intense discretion was mandatory here. With regards to the high class escort category at least. The hotel suite was like a doctor's surgery : all information and procedures remained closed behind that very door. These fees guaranteed ultimate privacy. (Don't get me wrong however, there are ALWAYS exceptions to every rule; that is life! But this was as safe as it got.)

They commanded payment on par with their future vocation or relationship; enabling them to afford the embellishments only the prosperous can maintain. (It should be pointed out here that 'gifts' also fell into this category as a sideline donational bi-product. They were usually of the lavish variety.)   It
served as a way to make ends meet in 'the real world' , and support their higher standard lifestyle while they attain their degrees. Or self-crafted perfect wife/partner material.
In that sense, this could be seen as training for their future too….

how else do they understand the art of:
~managing such phenomenal amounts of money?!.....
~and overtime sleep deprivation??........
~how to provide the two roles that every man requires: the wife AND the saucy mistress?!
An education of sorts……personal evolution.
Economy and seductress survival kit 101………

The high class escort is usually the admired polished showpiece that struts majestically through a hotel lobby with an aire of sophistication. She wears the labels one cannot afford; the jewellery one dreams of; the hair and makeup of a runway show…
and oh, the shoes…
She can converse knowledgeably on a vast array of topics; often speak a menu of languages, and once an expert in the field, is the quintessential actress. She can accompany one anywhere and remain undetected by other folk.
She stayed in 5-star establishments; travelled 1st or business class, and always received the quality 'extras' that wealth covers with additional fees.

She is ready for the world of EXCESS! In fact, it IS her world, in all senses of the term. It is all she knows. Sadly, the normal world is dismal in comparison. This was the evil flipside. She is an alien from another world now. Spoilt to the point of destruction. There's no turning back…

It all sounds relatively easy, and most women would announce : " Pah, I could do that in a heartbeat!"

Behind the scenes however, there is a huge amount of polishing that goes on. It is essential to provide the client with the tantalising trophy delivery that knocks on their hotel door; (while making it all appear natural and effortless), and thus commanding fees that are synonomous with extreme specialisation.
The package requires discipline, physical endurance, and mental control. (The psychological fallout can be life altering so 'mind gym' is something that needs constant monitoring for survival.)
This is of course in addition to the hours of sprucing; - diet, exercise, plucking, waxing, mani/pedi, facials, CONSTANT shopping for lingerie and accoutrement, and an intimate relationship to the king: her hairdresser.
She must have the fantasy wardrobe akin to a porno movie-set, and be able to fashion it with supreme confidence and flair (no easy feat!)

At the level Christie intended to reach, there were several other aspects involved.
She must be au fait with fine dining; display the etiquette required accordingly, and, if possible, capable of reading a menu in French.
She must be up to date on a variety of world issues, and do her 'homework' on each client: their areas of expertise, interest etc.
She can essentially blend seamlessly into an elite crowd, and appear by all accounts to be born into aristocracy.

But above all, she must be versatile to the point that she is capable of defining, and morphing into WHATEVER fantasy you so choose, instantaneously. (This is an incredibly tall order with computer access today! How does one compete with unrealistic graphic perfection?!)

This is what the package was all about. Where the specialties lay. And why the actual hours 'on the job' itself were a very small percentage of the overall expenditure.

Christie was put through the training paces with Darren (the pimp) in the, (as he liked to call it): 'recruiting the troops' technique. He was building himself the little 'army' of soldiers to send out into the field, where he always commanded them to 'TAKE NO PRISONERS'.
[The war-y terminology that was his signature means of expression was in fact not too far from the truth. It was a battle, and certainly not for the weak or fragile. It's a bloody jungle out there, after all!]   Another fave signature adjective of his, was 'GANGBUSTERS', which he

would frequently pepper his statements with. (Noting its' dual semantics, it was actually rendered most appropriate for the man)

1: slang: A policeman or law enforcement officer who works to break up organized criminal gangs.

2: A most successful, profitable business ; an experiment yielding gangbuster results.
Both applied to him: past and present.

Darren tried to cultivate a 'family rapor', or bond amongst the players (or his 'recruits'), but its WOMEN we're dealing with here! The girls displayed a degree of that, usually for his approval; (and due to the fact that they all fell into the united category of 'hated by other women' for various reasons); ~ but they remained ever- aware that bottom-line: it was dog-eat-dog.
The competition was fierce.
Survival of the fittest.......prosperity for the perfected.

"When you arrive, the very first thing you do is collect the cash. If its via credit card it will all have been pre-approved this end". Darren indicated the credit card swipe machine on his desk.

Although happy; as she was used to this form of transaction from past exploits of the similarly discreet (and non tax-paying) manner, she was at first surprised that there would ever be *cash* exchanged at such amounts...........but think about it. No evidence; no proof. Untraceable.The way everyone concerned liked it to be.

There was a degree of comfort too, in the knowledge that Darren had solid Interpol connections; and had utilized them on several occasions. He was extremely vigilant on the safety and protection of his crew. (This of course was vital with the inevitable exposure to drug barons and criminals in this game. Dare I say it, but some excitingly interesting characters reared their ugly heads; certainly far from dull or 'normal' types.
Big biccies baby; cash only. Kind of comes with the territory)

Darren continued : "If they offer a drink or room service, or better still, a meal out, always be obliging: there are at least 2-3 hours involved in that alone!"

Ha – I'm one step ahead of you, Christie thought.
She could already recommend all the best restaurants in town, and as far as occupying their attention for hours on end..she was a master of that, in verbal alone. She would prove that a client rarely got away with not appeasing her pleas of hunger over batted eyelids, and hence be in for the triple figures, were any FURTHER gameplan to proceed behind closed doors.
It was paid-by-the-hour work. The ultimate goal was to extend the booking while blindfolding them to the passing of time......

" Okay, now for the seduction routine"..... (this was the *work* bit. IF it had to come to that.
She intended them to be so engrossed and entertained by her company alone, that this was something they were happy to wait for. Her 'mind manipulation technique' was well honed.

Yes, it was…*SHE* was a sure thing. But just watch her attempt to defy that entirely…therein lay her challenge.)

"There will always be a luxury bathroom in the hotel suite. USE THE BATH. Take time to run it with bubbles; light candles, ensure music is playing if possible etc. Set the scene for the scene. It is recommended that you get into the tub with them, but at the very least, wash them down; slowly. Your entire focus is on the art of extending every single booking. The wash alone should take the better part of an hour if you play it right."
This was to prove a task with many a male who would profess to have 'just showered', but it was to be encouraged to 'play by the rules' with gentle reinforcement..(or insistence. The last thing one wants to contend with is poor hygiene. Hello…just not on).

"After this, a massage of some sort is in order, even if only de-stressing weary shoulders". Darren had recommended a massage course to the girls to heighten their repertoire, but it proved to be difficult time-wise. In any case, you kind of learn on the job anyway: what works, what doesn't. Like anything: practice makes perfect. (She would massage their grey matter and egos mostly; works wonders on almost every man, believe me!)

The extra details of the inevitable X-rated scenes to follow will be outlined in a more eye-opening chapter later. For now, all that is required to explain is the technique Darren sold his girls on:

"Fire and Ice. Save it for the grand finale. In the early stages, ensure to order room service ice. Use the ice cubes and the warm water from the tap for this procedure. Start with using the warm water in your mouth during oral performance, it is a most desirable temperature and will have him in the palm of your hand. Then, to bring on the jackpot, alternate with the ice cubes. Bingo, we have a winner……..every time!" Darren prided himself on the fact that: "there is rarely straight out sex involved. My girls actually have less sex than the average girl on a weekend out. They are tantalising temptresses that perform a manner of sensory delights, and leave a much more lasting effect on the satisfied customer. Who will inevitably return for more. My girls are like Velcro to the men…"

>He proved to be correct on these summations . For the ordinary vocations got people screwed far more than the escort industry did!

There are several other considerations too, which Darren outlined in the training, and is summarised as follows (not in order of priority):

1.**Transport.**

The girl must have a 'personal driver' that she trusts to ferry her all over town, and then home at crazy hours, with assured secrecy. Finding someone to fit the bill is not as easy as it sounds. (You know cab drivers: they are verbal overdrive in themselves and love a good story to relay!) Needless to say, monetary incentives were involved.
If she preferred to drive,(as was the case of a few of the tomboy crew, including Hannah,~

who had mastered the art of applying lipgloss at top speeds), their cars were of the 'turn heads' variety.

We're talking the envy of every vehicle-adoring man (which is-hello-the entire male population….and lets face it, the majority of women too.) Darren insisted on this, although persuasion was rarely necessary! He had established connections with car dealers to recommend to anyone requiring the wheels to their fortune. His wife and daughters seemed to change their cars like fashion. It was ego- boosting at its best.

2. Personal Veneer

Wow, this is a big one, and of course the most vital.

As mentioned before, every escort is subjected to the regular bodychecks by Darren and co. it had to be a brutal rating at this level.   (which sadly left a few of the girls compelled to smoking and drug habits in a bid to keep the weight down, and a seasonally fashionable addiction to the diet pill 'duramine'~which is essentially anxiety inducing speed.)
There had to be medical visits regularly, (to the Doctor Darren had empowered with the complete medical history reports of his entire brood) HIV results etc were of course mandatory, and could be produced to satisfy any concerned client.

Many of the girls had a background in dance of some description; or at least a dedication to fitness. This in turn may have awarded her the 'human pretzel' flexibility of a rubber band; an obvious advantage. She usually had a personal trainer at the best gym in town.

She can generally recommend the most prestigious plastic surgeon in town (as she usually knows first-hand, and has the purchase to prove it). Unless she was one of the miniscule percentage blessed with natural funbags having defied gravity, fake boobs are almost an essential. But the menu of alterations is endless; elective surgery in this industry is like a trip to the supermarket.

3.Self-promotion

Following on from the physical attributes sector, a range of visuals that enable the girl to be marketable to a broad range of clientele is necessary. Darren had an established photographer to hand (with experience in shooting the covers of the mens' magazines, so well up to speed in attaining the best 'vantage point' for the shot). Photos adorn the website, as well as being there for the booker to email to interested parties. A picture tends to speak louder than words. Especially for the visual creatures that men are. It was the best form of self advertisement.

4: Establishing the Vault

Having the cash (which lets face it, is tax-free and basically illegal) carefully hidden is essential. There were a few methods …..(sock drawer NOT recommended!):

~the casino (the playground of the mob; an obvious one);
~a bank account of some description (although it would raise suspicion with the frequent visits of cash deposits so vast that one is perceived as the secret assassin of the moment) Shares; stocks and fixed term deposits were also a sound option. (Bring on the actress tears here, and explanations of 'the death in the family' as you invest your new 'inheritance' wisely.)
Spread it like butter for less detection.
~The best, which Christie chose in addition to the above, was a safety deposit box.
The little key to the treasure chest. Added to constantly. Out of sight; out of mind and risk of theft. And about as rock solid safe as it gets.

The key here was obviously **savvy diversification**.....

She opened up a personal company with Shelfcom: 'Christie Moore Pty Ltd'. This stamped it official: it may appear, by all accounts to be a game, but it was actually a serious business.

5: Etiquette

Obvious. No swearing; chewing gum; drug-taking….(a seemingly flexible rule), or seeing clients on the side (ah, ditto). Fine-dining is offered to those in the know. Get with the table manners protocol and behavior of a queens' table please, quick smart. Read a menu in French; study your wines. Its like good grooming skills on the social level!
Learn to handle your liquor; or abstain. Imbibing is usually the road to the polished mask slipping somewhat. (Think slippery slope.)
Garlic, asparagus and curry are culinary taboos for obvious fragrant reasons.
And don't order anything requiring fingers. Avoid fish where possible, as he may not be offay with the Heimlich manouvre. Choking is rarely resolved in a glamorous fashion (!)

6. **Handbag candy** (we elaborate on this later), but the basics are:

Always carry toothbrush, paste, mouth freshener, tissues, spare underwear and perfume. An emergency number on speed dial, and some sort of weapon.

So…..essentially, she must embody the pure example of what ALL men admire; straight men desire; gay women revere, and straight women hate!

Chapter 6:

Part 4:

TRIPLE FIGURES......
wake up
and smell the money

"I have nothing against money; give me all the money you want. I will not refuse it. Because I've been dead broke so many times···.I've been so dead broke, starved so long, I realise the value of money. It's tremendous. Money is magic. I'll take all I can get. I hope I never miss a meal again."

(Bukowski on having no compunction about enjoying newfound wealth and lifestyle upgrades)

It became rapidly relentless.

Now familiar with the protocol, the girls were in constant motion; all over town, and interstate.
It was off the hook. Literally. The phone never stopped; Darren was ecstatic.
As for the girls, their desirability ratings soared sky high, as did their frequent flyer points.
And more importantly, financial forecasts.

There had been a few articles and press releases about the agency. Mostly done in a tasteful fashion thankfully. Having spread the word, the girls were not only in demand locally but interstate too.
It was both thrilling and terrifying, as exposure and detection was high on the risk radar.....

Christie had been sporting long, sleek, platinum hair for work to this point, but one day, in a spontaneous moment, she got it cropped short without bothering to seek agency approval. It was a bold move and a bit of a risk, but she sought a differential between herself and Hannah….(not to mention something a tad less high maintenance.)

Her hairdresser on the main gay drag had deliberately left the answering machine on for her appointment requests at nocturnal hours…(Who books an appointment for the *following* day at 3am??! He must have tweaked as to her secret game, although he never let on, and hence, had her constant business and *trust*).
She had selectively recruited him purely on his ability to transform the locks from drab to fab in lightening speed;~ although his effervescent personality was also endearing. His years of experience in New York salons had granted him the midas touch. (These were the good old days when he was establishing his business; as a relatively unknown, compared to the virtual celebrity status he has since acquired.)   No names mentioned here; therefore! His styling advice now graces the pages of every magazine in town. Suffice to say, taking a gamble on the crowning glory was something she pursued with confidence when in his control.

Christie and Hannah were like twin peas in a pod in many respects; she craved a defining feature to set them apart. Unique had to be the order of the day. Boredom avoidance......
Running late for a sudden booking, she arrived at the agency flustered, and with the new wavy curls. There had been no time to do the straightening iron routine, nor get to him for the magic finishing touch, so she had resorted to the mousse scrunch attempt in desperation. Tousled tresses it had to be.
Hannah rushed over and ran her hands adoringly through it. "I love it!! its goddess glory." Darren smiled and nodded with equal approval. Sometimes the risks do pay off. (Usually not with hair though, so it was a lucky result!)
He thus marketed them on the descriptions: "Claudia is just like the original Miss Schiffer of supermodel fame" and now that he had Christie plumped up to hourglass proportions, he would proclaim:
"and as for our Miss M, well Christie is Marilyn! Monroe that is."

 In the early stages of the game, while adapting to the new double identities, both girls almost let slip their real names during performances. "Hey Han…ah, HAND me my bag, please!"

Claudia was kept as busy as Christie ~ they remained tight though.
Even to the point that they always tried to involve each other in each of their bookings.

*Being bisexual was a definite advantage in the game. The magical threesome, or, more precisely, girl-on-girl action was, and always will be the number 1 request. (And it also remains one of the most civilized by all accounts!) In this regard, as a team, they had it in the bag.

Ask any male you know. Go on, I dare you! And just for the record, although sad but true, the fact remains: any man who denies some sort of exposure to, and participation in the sex industry (in one way, shape or form) is either lying through his teeth, or heavily into (read reliant on) cyber porn.

A woman needs to understand that a man will not be satisfied with the same dish every night of his life; regardless of how sumptuous it may be. Or how creatively flavoured it may become.
Save your soul: have no faith in monogamy; it will always be a myth..

 Hannah was a bitch by all accounts, but Christie had a soft spot for her; ~ only she got to see her authentic side, that could be most endearing. She had bestowed more genuine affection on Christie than any other of her vast portfolio of men.
And as far as sexy was concerned, she was an inspiration. Nevertheless, many men told Christie that they preferred her svelte physique, and found Hannah to be a bit on the 'well-covered' (read 'fat') side. Still, each to their own preference. That's precisely what this industry catered for at this level. Basic mathematics:
if you can afford the fees; specific orders = corresponding deliveries, guaranteed to please.

But Christie remained in awe of the round, feminine curves Claudia exhibited; while maintaining a controlling, dominant masculinity. Similarly, Hannah longed for the lean dancer/catwalk look of her counterpart. But her 'german big-boned structure' did not allow for the hungry look. Alas, the grass is always greener…
Thoy woro a good team. Doth possessing masculine and feminine attributes. That Is actually the definition of sexy. A bold statement I know. Glorious of body, yet strong of mind.
For there is no point having the hot veneer without the fire to ignite it.

Even Christies' ex boyfriend was aroused by her risqué vocational pursuits. She found it satisfying to watch him squirm…..   Their chemistry had inevitably culminated in bedroom nirvana; she would always hold a memory of their magic. He was like a stealthy jungle cat: strong, yet feminine and sexy. His flowing blonde 'lion' locks were the envy of many women! It was unlikely they would ever meet again without feeling a desperate animal urge to go to the place they knew best.

Again it should be pointed out: it is always an eye-opener to see the transition in one where big money is concerned. Amazing what former barriers can be broken down on the journey to financial freedom…
Christie's well-honed perfectionist training earlier in japan no doubt assisted with this level of supremecy…..on both a physical and mental front. For it takes strength of character; will and mind.

It was a Thursday afternoon, and the girls were getting ready at Hann's place for a change. Only because of the location of their evening destination.
She still lived with her folks part-time when not shacking up at Christie's beach hideaway. On the odd occasion that Christie had been compelled to stay at Hann's folks', they would sleep together in her huge four poster bed, and then spend the morning there with diaries and chocolates. Luxury.
In any case, it was always a bit of a slumber party.

The 'primping' procedure was always a lengthy pursuit for them; and in fact usually the highlight of the whole evening. It was never less than several hours for Hannah to get the mask in place. (She advised Darren that less than 3 hours notice for a booking was a 'frantic, drop everything and throw yourself together' stint, and to be avoided at all costs!) Christie would often have consumed at least one bottle of wine while Hann fussed over both their makeup; styled their hair, and dressed her up in a million different outfits like a doll. She was a brilliant self-taught stylist from years of daily practice, and was generally most disapproving of anyone else's attempts!
They would have a ball; giggling for hours on end, with colourful recitals unfolding of their encounters. Both had cunning senses of humour, so the verbal repertoire was priceless. Often times they were in no mood for the theatrics involved in the events to follow, and longed to just remain in their own perfect company. Take off all the putty; replace with a facemask; don sexy (albeit comfy) underwear and watch videos with popcorn and cocktails.

Still, no rewards without punishment.

On the odd occasion that they had a whole day together and weren't booked otherwise, they would go to the Korean bathhouse for a steam; scrub; & massage. Or a trip to the nail bar for the acrylic infills session, then out for lunch and a lingerie browse. All forms of grooming and pampering were top priority, and considered an investment in self.

To this point, Hannah had maintained that she was off on 'promotional work' or modelling assignments to her parents, and remained ever paranoid that they might suspect otherwise. Christie had lived on her own or with boyfriends, so no alibi was necessary. The life and facts she shared with family and others was a mere fantasy compared to her reality and always had been. She was a professional mask wearer.
Nevertheless, they both came from well to do families and protecting their loved ones from exposure was an exhausting escapade.

Mrs M appeared in the doorway, the pet poodle a permanent fixture under her arm as usual. She always liked to give the verdict on the showponies, before they headed off into the ring of fire.

"What about that gorgy little Chanel cropped jacket; Christie would look fab in that with her flat stomach"
Hannah rolled her eyes: "As opposed to my flabby gut you mean!"

A former model herself in her youth, Hann's mum had married young to an older man, and had trained Hann from birth to 'be well groomed to win the heart of some billionairre'. She was strict and critical in appearances to the point of obsessive. Christie often felt it was a bid to please her mother that Hannah endured the tedious affections of besotted, ageing fat old fools.   It had instilled in Hannah an insecurity at EVER being caught without the mask on perfectly. When in the boudoir, she would go so far as to pre-set a morning alarm, sneak to the bathroom and do full hair and makeup; then return to bed and act asleep. She would fake a yawn as she pretended to wake, with a 'this is how I look first thing in the morning, honestly!' girlie smile. There was to be no seeing her in a natural state. Everrr. She had always been like it. Christie had observed Han's shenanigans for years. Heaven forbid that someone witnessed the tiny spot on her forehead so masterfully disguised beneath the warpaint! No lover got to see her in her a-la-natural state except Christie.

The game was, in fact, one Hannah had been privy to her whole life! It was second nature to her now. Christie couldn't contemplate it herself without a massive cash-up-front incentive. Hence her tweaked interest now.

"Stop being defensive Hann. You know what I mean" her mother retorted.
" Where's your new watch?"

The most recent gift from a beau: a sleek Cartier Panthere; white gold and absolutely dripping diamonds. It screamed "Im expensive, so don't touch what you cant afford!" Hannah took it from her impressive jewellery box, and secured the clasp.
You could see the pride on her mother's face as she added the final touch to the masterpiece.

"What time will you be back love? Im not expecting it to be an early one. Let's hope not!"

Hannah opened her eyes wide with a stern expression as she glared at her mother. Christie was confused as to what sort of 'promotional' assignment her mother believed her to be engaged in, that went way past midnight.

 "Don't wait up, Ill be quiet when I get home".

The dog yapped with a 'who do you think you're kidding'-like air about it.

"Okay" her mother whispered now, creeping closer : "Well, don't worry; your secret's safe with me. I promise not to tell your father because it would kill him..... but just tiptoe to your bedroom please, so that this one doesn't go nuts and wake him!"

Christie looked at Hann questioningly and she returned a 'I had to tell her' look back, with apologetic shrugged shoulders. The mask had slipped...

Wow. Christie was mortified that Hann's own mother would cover her arse in such nocturnal taboos. And in fact ENCOURAGE them -no matter how desperately she wanted her married off to a filthy rich prick. I mean, hiding from the husband that their daughter was secretly a

highly paid prostitute….hello!
She couldn't imagine her own mother ever doing it, and nor would she do it for any daughter of her own. She found it disturbing to witness a somewhat sick relationship developing between them, and felt protective of her friend. Wasn't the term 'mother' supposed to signify ultimate protection from evil? Obviously not in Hannah's case. A sad state of affairs.
They were thick as thieves, those two. When all was said and done, no-one could compete with the mother. Mrs M had made sure of it. Hannah deserved all the trappings of wealth; for she had suffered for it all her life. Both on and off the field.

As India knight commented in a Sunday times newspaper article in June 2015 on sugar babies and sugar daddys:

"

The startling bit was the mother who said languidly: "I think all children are born with

certain assets. One of hers is that she is beautiful and has sexual allure, and that gives her erotic capital. Why shouldn't she use it? Its a supplement to getting on in life"

"

…It always irreparably hurts the womans' soul…

When Claudia called in Christie for a double; or vice versa, it was a victory. It wasn't like work at all!   In fact they had virtually perfected the scene.

The first incident however was of course terrifying. Like any new, unchartered territory. Until the mental safety mask is created and secured. Despite any previous relationships of the lesbian category, these were roads untraveled.
Something unsettling grabs you the first time you become the eye-candy of a voyeur while in the motions of a sensual interlock. A bit like the first time one fucks with wall to wall and roof mirrors. (As im sure we've all done! Well, if not, let the imagination go to work.)
There's no hiding from the critique. Its like allowing flaws to expand to magnification proportions.
Being self-conscious is inevitable until one learns to ignore the audience. Something like stage-fright I guess. Once that barrier is belted down though, it becomes intoxicating.For both the player and the viewer.

It was a power rush to behold.

The key was to maintain the sense of SELF, and not lose your identity despite the metamorphism that evolves. Remain the same inside. Like 'Hannah' when viewed in the mirror: spelt backwards, it still remains exactly the same…

The three of them were in the footballer's grand suite . He was on a high from the days sporting victories, so was in fine form to celebrate off-field with a gift to self. Darren had sent him Claudia, who, in turn, rapidly encouraged him to bring in Christie too because he 'was a star, and deserved it!'
One was a luxury, but two was a fantasy come true…..
Why not indulge? He had cash to burn, and an ego to ignite even further! It was a win-win, and everybody benefits from that.
Christie poured herself a glass from the champagne wine bucket beside the bed. The elixir of courage.
He was a well known sporting identity, so they would need to be wary of any lurking paps on their retreat.
But pay no heed…..let the show begin.

" I know I can get in the scrum at any time, but I want to see you guys do it!"

The girls looked at each other knowingly, and proceeded. Tentatively at first, then with confident momentum. They started with kneeling on the bed in a sensual embrace; alternately tongue-kissing and withdrawing in a slow, teasing fashion. Then some snarls and dominant hair-pulling in between the lip smacking. Sensual and rough play intertwined. More forcefully now: pushing, pulling, licking, sucking. They had read the client well; this is how he liked it played in the bedroom. Nipples were exposed, along with various ambitiously flexible poses and venturing tongue capers for the visual enjoyment of the master.
He lay in comfortable reclinement with glazed eyes and a smug expression on his face. Muscly arms were folded behind his head, and a vertical pole affixed between his chunky thighs.
"Ah, its good to be the king!" he drawled with a contented smirk, before entering the pack for the game to commence play.

LIVING THE DREAM. CHOOSE YOUR FANTASY······

" Fantasy is escapist, and that is it' s glory. If a soldier is imprisoned by the enemy, don' t we consider it his duty to escape?···if we value the freedom of mind and soul, if we' re partisans of liberty, then it' s our duty to escape, and to take as many people with us as we can!"

(J.R.R Tolkien)

The job requisite was immense. Particularly at the higher level that some of the girls reached; where the fees increased even further in accordance with their expected roles and status.
Contrary to his anticipation, the initial bookings inevitably culminated into something more for the client. Perhaps he should have been issued the following survey?.... :

Choose, and tick from any or ALL of the following list:

*partner (vague). Elaborate…..

*mistress

*'business associate/colleague' – (accompany on trips etc)

*showpony/ handbag – (ego booster)

*entertainer/dancer/stripper/seductress. (clarify)

*party girl / companion.

*dominatrix

* NOT SURE….. feel free to add any other description of your desired order here.

For that's what the eligible bachelor expects!
-Or the playboy about town……….or the couple seeking some spice………….or the married man buying the chosen double life…………(or any man really)
At these fees, he was granted more than a hooker.

He bought the dream. His dream. And the dream girl with it. She would embody the all encompassing fantasy. For he could afford it.

For a man to feel complete, it is a multi-faceted requirement. Its not just about the physical performance, (albeit the importance of that issue.)
In accordance with this, he was often a businessman who was seeking a solution to long lonely hours in transit and hotel rooms. Often people don't realize they crave mere companionship until the pleasure of it materializes in front of them.
Yes, there was literal dick stroking, but the EGO and masculinity perception needed stroking more. It was a subconscious need that he was unaware of. There was much psychology involved.
It's a fine calibration to achieve the equilibrium whereby all expectations were fulfilled; all categories acknowledged:

the strong, in control man/ the insatiable, yet vulnerable voyeur king / the lonely man. A tall order. Huge.

It was almost more than the role of a wife, and many 'relationships' were forged on these journeys. At least that was the case for the girls who graduated to the top price bracket.

In Christie's experience, most of the men wished to 'take off' the power mask, and pass it to someone else for a change. (This obviously became addictive to the girls too; particularly if they were control freaks!)

Christie was a pro at booking extension. She was all about DAYS (read nights), not HOURS. She had morphed into the masterful manipulator! The men found themselves caught up in an intoxicating mindplay whirlwind.   Labotomised to the passing of time.
They would abandon the business, assassinate the credit cards, and go missing in action under her **spell..**

*WHEN YOU ARE the salesperson AND the product, it is advisable to follow/apply the SS RULE……..
(Stimulatory seduction technique).

This is as it sounds; a stimulation of all the senses:

>visual (first impressions linger/taint)
>pheromonal (fragrance; body odour/scent)

>touch; taste (no elaboration required here)
>.....and not forgetting the grey matter; ~ which incorporates the sense of
sound....(intellectual stimulation; ~ ego-boosting. Psychological)
The combination of all initiates the hormonal response required.

A successful seduction essentially requires the stimulation of the brain's ventral tegmental
area and cardate nucleus; below conscious awareness. These areas are activated during
chemical attraction and are incidentally also involved in major purchasing decisions.
The routine of the professional temptress is hence like advertising. Of self. For the ultimate
goal is to create a method that causes any given person to fall hopelessly in love with any
given product.

The concept of sex is like food and a healthy diet: never rush, and always keep him hungry
for more. As with deprivation, creating a sense of longing is key. Always leave something to
the imagination. It will linger and torment......and create an insatiable desire.

The standard vegas striptease is 7 minutes long. After 1 minute, she removes her top, and
by 6 minutes, she is generally naked. The novice in this game could be forgiven for thinking
that this is the idea; - and gets naked too fast, as it is what the audience is there for. Its
not.....   *Sex is biology.*
Sex appeal is marketing.
Its not the naked body that's exciting, it's the possibility…

Like the stunning, majestic red-back spider she used to keep as a pet in a jar, Christie would
weave her magic spells on the victims as they were lured into, and then caught in her web of
sin.

****

The girls were figments of the erotic imagination that came to life.

The initial purchase however was always done via the powerful combination of internet
visuals, and Darrens' convincing verbal. Christie herself got an insight to his role intimately,
so to speak. She was in recuperation from a little 'enhancement', and Darren seized upon
the opportunity to take a much needed break. He had already confessed to Christie that
there was a degree of trouble in paradise:
" Love, I need you to man the phones while I take Rosa and the girls on a holiday. You are
the only one I trust enough to assume my role in my absence. You'll be doing me a favour,
and potentially saving a marriage".

She knew she was hopeless at 'kicking back and healing'; she could never do the bedrest
caper. Besides, she felt she owed it to Darren to support him in some way, as he had done
for her. He had voiced her suspicions on his home-life, and that in itself was a confidence
that should be respected. Not that she wanted to become involved in any way; perhaps this
would seal the wound for them.

So there she found herself in the **'big chair'.** The 'gatekeeper' booking seat; - calling the
shots and hearing all the.........phone filth.

God, it was WAY worse in his shoes than hers, go figure! Huge shoes to fill. Now she understood why he would answer the calls and often hang up within seconds, cussing expletives.
The girls were in hysterics watching her facial expressions as she received outlandish requests in rapid succession, and did her best to bring the eager caller back to a certain level of decorum.
It was an interesting experience, to say the least, but by the time Darren returned to resume the role of 'taming the wild beasts that tried entering the cage' - she virtually leapt into his arms with relief. Enough behind the scenes exposure; she needed to be out in the field. Collecting the dough.

It was a more difficult position to be in here, she thought. The gatekeeper got to 'see outside the square'; being not as close to the equation. It was from this vantage point that it became startlingly clear what a complete GAME this was about. It was make-believe; dress ups and role-plays and performances......it was another world to what most exist in.
All the sprucing and putty aside, Christie decided that one of her first missions was going to be to purchase an array of WIGS and hairpieces for the craft. She ascertained that this way, when you look in the mirror pre-event, you don't see *yourself* as such. This masking effect would definitely help sometimes. Its purpose mostly to serve as a reminder, and create the distinction between *their fantasy and your reality*......for its when the two collided that she saw problems occurring.

Being in the control seat *where it all happened* is where she had to be; but it had nevertheless opened her eyes to the other side though, that proved imperative to getting the girl maximum work:
The website.

Christie had eventually done the photo shoot for a collection of various promotional looks. This included sexy lingerie; fantasy dress-ups, and some tasteful beachside nudity. Initially hesitant about the exposure, she eventually succumbed, under the added persuasion of Darren's wife, Rosa:

"Oh Christie, your client-base will more than triple itself if you are on the website, love".
She had witnessed it with many a girl since her recruitment. And then she had realized it further as she constantly referred to the visual references for the 'stock, as she sold it' over the phone. ('refer to our catalogue range of model options!') It proved to seal the deal almost every time.

Yes, a picture speaks a thousand words.
Enticed by the further fees, she finally acquiesced.

It was easy with the chosen photographer (they were both pros! So to speak.)
She found it amazing how comfortable she actually felt in front of him with the kit off. The most highly exposed shots (literally speaking) were done on a cliff-face at the beach. The others were done mostly at Darren and Rosa's lavish abode; using various props (eg: masks and champagne), and even some changes initiated by the daughter's – who gave her some wild gear to don also.

Like her perception of Hannah's mother, she had a somewhat sickening feeling in the gut about Darren's entire family getting involved in the game. His wife and both daughters were actively involved in all proceedings; ~enticed, like her, with the prosperous gains. They were all genetically blessed and of the head-turning variety, which served of course to be a quality representation of the agency.

The girls were quite young, yet they were often involved in the booking procedures.(Hard to imagine allowing your teen daughter to do virtual phone-sex in a bid to book escorts for work??)

Greed.

Im sure it didn't start out that way for them, but it rapidly evolved. Well…its what granted them the enviable wheels and wardrobe they sported after all !

They welcomed her like part of the family, but she sensed a disease brewing in their 'once normal' family unit……there's always a price to pay.

Rosa was beyond thrilled with the photo results. " Oh Christie, they are superb. I want a copy of this one blown up!" she announced with pride.

She was the madam of the brood, and protective in a maternal-ish way. Christie had met up with her to select the best ones for the website. (The 'mother figures' in the game were a special species that were evidently most supportive of their girls being whored around town, it seems. Another world to the one she knew! Was she old-fashioned she wondered?)

Rosa drove them in her Bentley to a trendy café for a salad and some wine. They had connected on a friendly level; as mothers and daughters do I guess. She had even taken Christie into her confidence about marital problems surrounding suspected infidelity. Which was disturbing for Christie. A problem shared is a problem halved, but she wanted to turn a blind eye to the toxic fallout of this cash-cow venture they had built. Happy to participate for the wages as they were, but not keen for additional mind-scrambling. The threesomes she allowed herself to become entangled in were cash-driven, and not of the tug-of-war variety. She wanted no wars of loyalty.

Rosa stopped momentarily and implored: "Why didn't you do modelling properly? Seriously, girl"………

Christie responded emphatically: " Oh,I did! Mostly overseas. But I have the intelligence to realize that there are only two avenues of making big cash fast: sex and drugs".

As they were driving back to the agency, Christie thought: what a curious role-play interaction the day had held..   'Mother' tells daughter she loves the naked shot of her to promote for prostitution, and that her husband (daddy!) was fucking some of his staff on the side…And 'daughter' confessed to the mother that she knew vast, fast cash was only awarded to the perceived scum of society: drug barons and whores.

Delightful……

Christie and Hannah were legendary café queens. Their huge handbags were veritable mobile offices.

Strategically planning and scheduling the week's appointments was becoming a secretarial

duty of profound proportions!
They would sit for hours on end doing 'diary duties'; equipped with coloured pens, stickers, highlighters, calculators and mobile phones. Hannah in particular should have had shares in 'liquid paper'. The vast amount she used while making constant changes increased the weight of her diary to several kilos !
All the while they sat sipping on cappuccinos ; nibbling on some pastry or cake and intermittently laughing while they 'worked'. It was generally the fun bit. When it came to actually ticking off the weeks' appointments, some of the 'showtime presents' performances they gave were quite note-worthy.

In her first six months, Christie had cultivated a vast array of character portrayals. It was mask-mania! Nida would surely have opened its doors.

It was obviously not something she could ever dare *speak* of, so once again, the written word became her means of expression; ink her private voice.
And so she had secretly begun a diary of descriptive summaries and events.

She understood voyeurism, for she herself was a self-confessed anthropologist....(were not the two related somewhat?)
Needless to say, she had pretty much seen everything. And heard it too. There were the clients who just wanted someone to assume a 'psychologist' role; listen to their problems and stroke their egos mostly.
For others, in providing their fantasy expectations, 'twisted kinky' didn't even BEGIN to cut it. We're talking triple X rated. Disturbing even.
She had her boundarles and 'no-go zones' of course, but It had opened her eyes to (excuse the French), what a *fucked up* world of individuals we live in!

 Ooh one needs a healthy sense of humour...

Part six

ENCORE,

MISS MOORE!!

One has to wonder:
If you can tell a girl by the depths of her handbag, what are the contents a CALL girl carries?

Well, firstly, (certainly in Christie's case), there was more than one. Bag that is. For it was essential to have a bag of tricks when 'turning tricks'!

There were the necessary items, and then fallback-plan options. One was powerless without the toolkit. (Or maybe this was equal parts true and psycho-somatic?) Whatever. Every vocation needs SOME sort of tools of the trade. These were the general items; ~ categorised by the absolutely essential;

and the *occasional* selected additional accoutrement. Prevailing to the object in question:

*ALWAYS:

- Toothbrush/paste/floss/breath-spray (food and sex go hand in hand, hello)

- Perfume; mini hairbrush

- Spare underwear

- Spare stay-up stockings

- Makeup bag (for touchups mostly; lipgloss essential for the pout)

- Weapon (?) a Swiss army knife usually. Also comes in handy as a bottle opener; scissors for tags off new clothing items etc.

- Defence item (mace?)

- At least 3 lingerie changes

- Fantasy costume (clients' choice if specific request)

- Condoms/lube

- Cash (for quick getaway)

- 2 lots of personal cards: 1 being correct deets, the other not…(hand out the latter liberally if necessary to appease the ugly; drooling)..

- Phone with speed dial safety numbers

And last but not least: - a notepad to jot down any quirky aspects on the client to elaborate on later.

SOMETIMES:

- Massage oil

- Snack (bloodsugar); - be prepared for a marathon.

- Bikini (jacuzzi foreplay?)

- Spare shoes (the 'cfm' category for bedroom only)

- Hairpiece/ wigs ? (nothing says seductress like the surprise change. Also for eg: he may prefer a brunette so cater for his whims accordingly)

- Mask/ whip/ dildo/ handcuffs (some of the girls had of course much scarier items added here, but this is Christie's permissible list.)

- Passport (if confident in convincing the smitten that more exotic locations may be the go)

- Anything else pertaining to the client's fantasy ~ description if specified….(nb: a wig may be required for some of the purchases!)

They say that men initially scan and classify a woman in a categorical fashion:
mothers; virgins; sluts and bitches. Sad, but true!
(They also say that a man knows in the first 15 minutes whether he would be willing to marry
you!)

Christie would confuse them through the art of morphing into any of these if necessary. It
was a case of first classifying the MAN and defining his wants/needs. A psychological task.
It was mind-games at its best.
She would often confuse them, so they *couldn't* classify her…..and were forced to take her
seriously. Thus the intrigue and addiction.
The irony was that in Christie's experience, men respected her MORE in this vocation than
in the *normal* fashion. Strange but true.
High-class escorts represent prizes of prestige; - they gave men a superiority complex!
Bingo. Winning result all round.

JULY, 24th, 4.30am.

Time to start a diary I feel. The mind is bursting at the seams with memory imagery, and the
only way to stop the mind chatter is to share it in the customary Christie ceremonial fashion.
With the ink routine. I'm a better writer than talker anyhow. This world I am exploring is an
anthropologist's playground! The immense cross-section of clientele provides such a vast
wonderland of characters to explore.
After each shift is the best time to debrief, while all data fresh at the fore, and ready to
divulge.   For example, it is now 4.30 am.

[I guess its best to jot that with the date; it usually clarifies the success of the evening.]
So if several days lapse with no entry, it is hence a good sign, as I have secured the long
haul event!

*Note to self: after each diary entry, tear off notes from handbag notebook. Any evidence
could be damning..

--- **

An interesting evening tonight…to use a cuisine-based analogy: lets call it 'entrée' for this
hungry client.
Nice guy; from out of town. Seemingly straight-laced; no repulsive aspects detected in phase
one. He's here for another week or so, so we shall see if his hunger extends to 'main
course'…and then 'dessert'.
Always listen to the gut: mine tells me he's in it for the degustation.
(summing up in advance: that's 3 stints with him; minimal 4 hours each. $4,800. Hmmm…

Don't like those numbers. Prefer to bypass the $500 mark, so shoot for an extra hour at least. Obsessive compulsive? Moi?)
Im confident it will be a satisfying 'meal' in all!   The proof is in the pudding after all; always aim to get to dessert. The final course. The sweet climax.

Tonight served to whet his appetite, let's say.

The other one scheduled for tonight is now tomorrow, as I extended the above (as I do)..... gracious of him to be patient for the prize. Might take him a little token 'im sorry' gift or something. Maintain the quality standard.

A tiring day at 'the office'.......being social can be a drainer. My cheeks are sore from smiling.

July 30th, 4am.

Ok, time to crank up the volume here. Block your ears (and eyes!) if you cant take the heat...

No use giving a summary/rendition on the life if not completely honestly, or else, what's the point, right? Its sort of the definition of 'diary'. All secrets divulged.

I have by now encountered a vast and wild array of requests, and have managed to totally decimate any pre-conceived judgements on folk for mere sanity control!
I have however culled the acceptable 'personal menu list' somewhat. There has to be limits after all.
(Lets call it self-respect maintenance. For which without, we might as well top ourselves..)

So, call me fickle, but I have declined several clients on the following personal criterion:

*no fisting. (Women pay for the tight-lipped aspect of a non-child bearing physique. Why rip and tear the prized item?)

*no golden showers or the worse # 2 variety...(elaborated on later in this list). Im BEYOND hygeinic. Perhaps obsessive-compulsively so.
Degradation is not on my degustation. It's a cringe course, not worth considering.

*no animals involved. Leave the more civilized living creatures at peace, for heavens sake! If you choose to house them, then good and well for you; just don't get intimate with other species. Its criminal. Even the term alone: 'bestiality' is shudder inducing.

*no butt plugs. (On me that is. If the client is into the rear-ripping-routine then that's their proverbial, perverted prerogative) Quite happy with the backdoor closed other than for the purpose intended, thankyou very *much.* Again, each to their own. My select social crew are homosexual, so let it be known: no insults intended..

*no anal sex (read above)

*certain roleplay restrictions…..(eg: the 'grown baby' thing. What is that about?? Would YOU change the diaper of a thumb-sucking 45-year old man on a business class flight? I mean really. Grow up.)
Three words only: not-going-there………

*and finally, as for the faeces fetish…having someone shit on you?? I'd just go get a regular job for that sensation! You simply couldn't pay me enough..

Does **DEPRIVED** in the primary years equate to **DEPRAVED** in adulthood, I wonder??

I mean, this list will doubtlessly grow as I venture further into the wild whims of the nocturnal hunting ground, so stay tuned…

However, these are the current no-go-zones. Im generally pretty out there by all accounts, but reading these restrictions, am I an old-fashioned, straight-laced BEIGE victim?! …..In a sea of exotic flavours, am I a *vanilla* virtuoso?!
Certainly, when compared with some of the other girls in the game it would appear so.
But THEY are the 1 or 2 hour crew; they fit the definition of the trade. Yes, they are a sure thing.   I haven't yet been labotomised to allow for such capers……and never will be. There is an enormous difference.
Im the **'nights+'** variety. The never to be forgotten. [(ooh, arrogant much?!) To clarify: this statement is made based on Darren's feedback; requests, and repeat bookings only ~ not personal opinion.]

The former puts out with no remorse; whereas I with the conscience and soul has a code of ethics to be obeyed.
Hmm…….the 'wholesome' whore (!)
Play the game by MY rules, and it will be the guaranteed pleasure of your life. Yes, I play the dominant role with aplomb. PVC not overruled.
Still, each to their own. One man's fantasy could be another man's nightmare. And vice versa.   Desire and repulsion can intertwine here; in a dreamscape aspect…
A necessity for the working girl is to realize that she is forbidden the luxury of assuming shock factor.
It is at times hard not to judge, but the human race is worse than animals, truth be known.
(They are way more civilized, as pointed out in the aforementioned menu.)
I guess we just need to gently educate some people that it doesn't have to be a putrid state of affairs to result in the memory of your life……

August 1st, 6am.

Okay, im starting to realize after tonight, that there is a general (albeit profound) pattern emerging here.
Not THE golden rule, but a more likely prediction, pour moi. The animal farm.
A potentially sore topic for some.

I had one of the rarer HOUSE calls tonight, and although it was an utterly divine abode, it was run rampant with dogs. Big and small.
Never been a dog person myself, must confess. All the slobbering and mess and ripped stockings and all. And then there's those filthy fleas…Prefer cats, but not a pro-pet person at all really.
(They say that means you have a selfish nature. Perhaps 'tis true).

The dog-versus-cat people debate…

You know, its actually true: people tend to emulate the characterisitics of the animals that inhabit their domain. Determining if a pet is in possession, can enable me to write a virtual character reference!   Always exceptions to every rule of course, but one can make a pre-conceived 'assessment' based on the domestic inhabitants of the non- human kind. (for one needs to be quick to 'read' people in this game.) I focus here on the 2 most prevalent beasts.
On this basis, and personal encounters, here is Christie's thesis:

On an anthropological level, I have observed that **cat** people tend to be more independent folk.

The alpha; 'leave-me-alone-im-fine' variety. A tad arrogant perhaps. Well groomed; and higher standards. Cat owners, like their pets, are more self-sufficient.
They are more into the stream-lined, modern, low maintenance approach, in all aspects of their life. They are methodical; neat-freaks. Generally disciplinarians (a bit like myself)
Usually unattached. Prefer to buy on demand.
(Also read clean cut; perfectionistic, highly professional, fit, & generally slim build.) Think Christian Bale in 'American Psycho'; -delicious!
Sex-wise we're talking straight-laced…..(in this game)> Missionary + short 'n'sharp menu. Occasionally rough, but never a problem with erection. Programmed; timed; scheduled.
(Cats are definitely sexier; their counterparts possessing sleek, smooth-talking boudoir finesse….like my ex. He was a slinky jungle cat for sure. Purrrrr.)
Usually most hygeinic. Generally into voyeurism and supreme quality lingerie admiration. A seductive dance routine or strip tease usually high on the list. Can often be found with wall to wall (and ceiling) mirrors. Narcissistic tendencies.
Loves a shower. Bathroom immaculate.
For me? This equates to easy bookings. Love them. Respect them.

As for the **dog** owners, this can be seen as a warning sign : "Beware the owner"
~Has self-worth issues. Needs 'man's best friend' to compensate for inability to tolerate oneself, and craves the unconditional love aspect. Needy. Is no doubt more into the perverse; masochistic; abstract or downright disgusting as a result. Not that fussed with appearance or health. Often lazy. And fat. Slobbish. Quite literally, their lives are a complete dogs breakfast in entirety. These are the people who need CONSTANT companionship and reassurance (read hero-worshipping). Hard work. They are, quite simply, not happy with their own company. Incomplete souls. As a working girl, this has a profound effect on the night's menu…Dogs are draining. And dirty. Fleas are bad enough, but fear the ticks more…(Lyme disease renders you paralysed. NOT on the wish list)
Not to mention unco-ordinated and clumsy. (I was at an outdoor cocktail function once and witnessed a slobbering dog jump up and lick the contact lense right out of a guy's eye! Socially uncouth behaviour, to be sure.)
Somewhat later on, I experienced the sad lifestyle of a mangy mutt owner first-hand when I took on a 'dog-sit' assignment in the UK. It entailed house-minding and walking the creature. The owners initially seemed okay; simple but 'nice'……however the 'rule book' for this flea-infested example of germ-ridden fur feature was like a biblical horror story. Case example: "at 4pm he has his 'crudite hour'….just dice up small cubes of carrot and cucumber - he loves that. For dessert, the same style with apples. Aside from that he is on a yeast, wheat, dairy, protein-free diet so please adhere strictly to our guidelines"….One would think they were referring to a pedigree, prize-winning poodle, housed in an outstanding plush palace, not some horrific restrictive dog box way out in the depressing burbs of outer london…..and lets not go into the deets of the mindset required to scoop up steaming turds of dogshit thrice daily with a plastic bag. I felt my whole persona and self-respect plummet to an all-time low…..The owners perceived the whole picture as wondrously fulfilling, conversely. Either their imagination was on fire (and good for them if so) - or I'm an utter alien species that doesn't grasp the whole 'adorable beast' concept…..but the overflowing 'toy basket', treats jars; dietary rules and 'baby wipes'…..we're talking psychological substitution for inability to conceive…… more fodder for a psychiatrists convention to be sure.

[Oh boy, I can see it now: the wannabe celebs with their 'handbag accessories' , and the croquet-playing teaparty-set with their prancing poodles - in UPROAR over my claims…..]

*Yes, like every rule there are exceptions..
[I have known some pretty obese cat people for instance (fat cat). I have befriended several ultra stylish, glam women who love dogs also. This scenario does not apply to them in the slightest!
I have encountered some pretty pedantically obsessive dog owners too (usually the small to medium variety; - ie rodent proportions to heavy handfuls. The *big* dogs are generally attended to by fellow slobbering messes!)
~ It is all merely a ***general*** observation, let it be known!]

Not that I wish to own one myself, but personally, if a choice is to be made, I go the cat person any day. (Perhaps that should be added to the client's preliminary survey?:
*choose your pet of preference: feline or mongrel)

This of course compels me to massive limitations; as men are generally like dogs aren't they! (unless extremely alpha, as is my desire): faithful guardians; jealous mongrels or needy puppies…

In any case however, on the domestic front, I can't help my belief that all animals belong OUT and the humans IN. Germs. Hello……….
Certainly none of this welcome-at-the-table; or heaven forbid, IN the bed business…
a ridiculous notion.

I once had a tattooist who was into pet ferrits. I was relieved to see her wash her hands and don gloves before ink-scarring my arm. I think I might draw the line myself there. Domestic pets are one thing, but this is bordering on vermin.
Verboten…!

***POST SCRIPT (in reflection, during self editing)**…

In fact, SCRAP THAT….I've made a tremendous faux pas in those outlandish claims - so it must be recognised that it was indicative of the held perception at that particular time. It was a prodigal period of narcissism and flamboyant decadence, and with big money comes minds of madness! These statements reflect this episode of extremes.

FACT: I can now determine that dog lovers (particularly the small-medium variety) are the more considerate and compassionate souls on the planet. And can be all the traits described for the cat owners written here too! (Including those to follow that have remained as additional opinions of the time).
Ive even succumbed to an affection for the furry friends in several circumstances myself.

Never owned one, but respect from the sidelines, so to speak.

So there. I take responsibility for opinionated mistakes and bury them with lament. xx

August 1st, 5pm…..

Cont'

Just getting ready for the nights capers, and was thinking: being the extremist that I am, I will take the thesis deets that one step further on the domestic pets issue..

(Warning: a potential health-hazard)

It can furthermore be predicted as to the preferred **poison** of choice, too.

-assumption chemical wise:

*CAT (owners) :

sometimes, class A involved. White-powdered paws…

Loves the upper echelon party scene with the beautiful players of society, and can often accommodate accordingly…..(certainly fund-wise, with my contacts).

Result: 2-3 day bookings. Paid to party! Grey-matter dancing………Cool cat.

Sunglasses an absolute necessity.

*DOG (owners) :

I suspect he is a fan of cannabis. (and the resultant curries, beer and pizza)

Mutts = mull. Dark n dirty.

There are bound to be hard-on hard-ships.

Result = mental abyss. Verbal void.

All over, red rover……….

HOWEVER, with all that said, to hit the WOW mark on the Christie meter, one has to be complete <u>within themselves;</u> needing of absolutely nothing. Including pets.

Like myself.

Does this person actually exist outside the realms of my imagination??.....

Ooh, gotta fly.

Time waits not for those with the towering heels to heaven..

Ps: Oh, forgot to mention yesterday that the entrée inevitably led to the main and dessert for the 'meal master'…(3 bookings all up; exceeding the predicted fees !!) ~ PLUS promises of a rekindling when he is back in town.

I rather enjoy David's comical chants of '**Encore, Miss Moore!**'

August 3rd, 2pm

Well, that was a rather spontaneous state of affairs last night.. I actually only got in a couple of hours ago. I shall elaborate in a min, but first, credit where credit's due:

I honestly don't know where id be without my personal taxi 'chauffeur'…any tick of the clock, day or night, he's there at my beck and call, girl!…does the man EVER sleep? Im usually flaked out in the back seat, so I hope he's fully awake as he powers through the city tunnel at lightening speeds!)
He never asks a thing but 'how are you this fine night/day/morn Miss Christie??' No explanations or justifications ever necessary.
I mean, its got to be a tad obvious that a girl needing a transfer home in the wee hours or late morn from top hotel entrances; in towering heels, tired makeup and often clubbing attire has to ring a few alarm bells. Surely! He knows the full caper, so he is paid well to just arrive, deposit ….(location wise, get your mind out of the gutter) - and shut the fuck up. He's a gem!

Anyway, back to the nights' performance.

This one deserved a grammy. I was 'roped in' to a booking with 4 other girls,.....(more like lassooed!) who are relatively new to the game. Darren had held off sending me in case one of my regulars called, but after his anguished incoming call from one of the girls who 'didn't know how to take it from here' he urged me to intervene. Even if only for an hour or two. "They've never done a double, other than Sage love. The guy wants a harem, and they have no idea how to appease him other than one-on-one. They need your expertise, Christie. Go take the control seat..."
So, there I was, in the midst of a jam-packed king-size bed, commencing the orchestration of an orgy. And by orgy, I mean *mental fantasy orgy.*
(Im going to do my best here to recap the events as they occurred while still vivid in the memory bank.)

(I refer once again to the fact that the vocational requisites of this escort role are almost unfathomable at various points. Flexible is such an understatement, its laughable)

I must admit, doubles are a breeze for me. Girl on girl is second nature. The fact remains: men are visual creatures; and women are SENSUAL beings. (Satisfying these needs in both is vital for climactic results to occur) Hence this vocation enabled the means of expression in those avenues to freely flow. It is a win-win all round.
Besides which, I preferred to be more of a 'fantasy showgirl' with partner assistance, than have the extensive 'one-on-one ANYTHING goes' repertoire of the standard girl for hire.
(my personal menu for solo action is extremely limited, as you know. Standards, baby, standards)   The twosome-tango-show with fem colleaugues is kinda my signature thang I guess.
But people managing en-masse is another state of affairs entirely ~ Especially where an ego-inflated ethnic guy; blinged to the max and thinking he's some sort of hip-hop demi-god or something, is concerned! At least the backdrop music was kickarse.

"Well, lets appease the beast then girls; ~he's a brazen prick to be sure, but he's the one with the dough, so we have to give what we know......" I was in the lavish hotel bathroom with the 4 others, trying to mindstorm the choreography for the absurd scene. I mean, I fully understand the concept of extras for spice, but FIVE??   What is a word stronger than challenge (?)

"Okay, so are you cool if I sort of manage this thing? I don't want to overstep the mark, but SOMEBODY has drive this vehicle home......" They all nodded; ~ a sight to behold however. Oh boy: one biting her fingernail; one was nearly crying; one with her head bowed, pouting, and the other sat in resignation on the toilet seat. What we needed here was humour. It always saved the day.
I even introduced some smuggled contraband: a bottle of champagne. "For stage-nerves, lovely ones. Our little secret". It always assisted massively in times of crisis too. (In empathy, i was reminded here of the lingerie catwalk modelling I had to do in Japan, where the choreography was all terrifyingly in Japanese..I was actually issued more than a glass of the sparkly stuff then by my agent to cope!..but back to the scene at hand.......)

"Okay then, show me everything you have in fantasy attire. I want the lot. Empty your bags." I wished I had the camera for that scene. It was priceless! The combination of wardrobes and accoutrement was an eclectic collection that Warhol would have been compelled to abstractly capture.

"Okay, we need different looks and personas to boot." I looked around at them and decided on their best showcased veneer.

"Here Angel. You are playing babydoll tonight. "I put her blonde tresses into pigtails and handed her the tiny pink sugary attire. She WAS the most angelic looking amongst us for sure. And totally inexperienced, so lets ham that up to the hilt with innocence play. "Cutesy, but caboodle- cleavage capers. Now stop biting your nail, and suck on your finger instead!"

" Augustina, its bitch patrol for you. Go the domination appeal. Do us proud; don't be shy!" she sported the snarl better than any of us, so the black PVC bodysuit with cutouts for exposure of main 'features' was hers; plus a whip to brandish. I threw her my black kohl eyeliner too, and said "get drawing. Think gothic"

"Okay, now Brandy, you need to attend to his ailments….and fuck knows they are mostly in his head!" they laughed in agreement with me on that fact. She was issued the micro-mini nurse's outfit, with stethoscope and dinky toy emergency kit box (containing lube, massage oil and condoms.)

" God, see if you can downsize that ego somewhat by *sedating* him or something…… oh, for reference, I'M JOKING….!!" (the last thing we needed was her taking me literally, and then having to ('escort him to') -manage a discreet hospital stomach-pumping)…

"Sage, you're with me hon. We take the lead." We had done several doubles together, so she was easy to gameplan. Darren loved our complementary combo, and would recommend us to all and sundry:

"Ah, but Christie comes with added spice!" he would profess to to the eager caller. He knew her name (sage) was a herb, but he continued to say it anyway. She was almost the antithesis of me: brunette; dark olive skin; brown eyes; mid-height; ample build. She was also a lesbian, so her natural lippy fem antics were an immense turn on for the voyeur. He had even used us in a seductive magazine photo shoot together, with eyes and privates covered.

" Choose whatever you want and do your thing". She used her thigh high boots to full effect; with cheeky shorts for that award-worthy 'nigger-booty' bum of hers, and uplifting lace-up bustierre top.

"So guys, I want you to watch us start the engine and then integrate where you can, and following our prompts. Spend some time here looking in the mirror and visualizing the character that is suitable to your look. Think of it like a mask you have to wear for a theatre performance. Its all an act, so have FUN with it!" I watched them smile, relax and even start giggling, so I knew it would somehow be okay and we would laugh more about it later.

"You need to wear your own cfm heels ~ or swap. But max heel mandatory. If the shoe fits wear it!"

I got out mine that were so scandalously high that they made me almost tip forwards and would be too risky to assume without health insurance. (Such lavish foot coverage is usually best found at tranny costume stores!)

"Brandy has the essentials in her 'medical box', so make sure you retrieve them as needed. But GO SLOW with the show…if you do it my way, the actual action will be wham-bam, was that it, mam? the intention is to get him off on what he *sees*, not *does*"

"We cant judge a book by its cover, as you know. It is impossible to know exactly his spot-on tastes, so we need to be flexible. The deal is: if he looks the slightest bit disinterested or bored in any way, you come straight back in here and select something else from the dress up pile and change immediately. Take the initiative; be creative! We can return everything to its rightful owner later but for now we have to cooperate and share". The looks amongst us all were perfectly varied, so there was limited chance he would not be appeased with SOMETHING here.

Sage and I commenced the 'foreplay' scene; kneeling at the foot of his bed in sensual embrace. The kissing was slow and natural, the caresses a visual delight. In the peripheral, we could see the cock rise, like a morning alarm. 'Its time'…
At my breathy cue of " Well, do we fancy a FANTASY Mr Man? Where does your mind take you on the exotica erotica?"…
Enter stage left and right, in an almost synchronized, choreographed fashion the confident sexy temptresses. Dancing, and moving in the seductive way that best suited their respective looks. My words had hit the high notes: they were in their element, and giving him maximum show expertise – even I was impressed!
I watched his eyes dart hungrily from one to the other as he reclined in awe. His diamond earring was enormous and sparkling, and the ridiculously oversized bling cross necklace rested on a mass of black chest hair. (Im SO not into body hair…its one of my major turn OFFS actually. Maybe why I prefer the smooth-operator lippy-fem appeal? Brazil is a place I would probably enjoy…)
Still one must turn a blind eye to the features of repulsion……he was a wog after all!)
The girls were aware that the idea was to stretch out the booking as always, so the show went on in blind ignorance of his attempts to get 'his show' happening. In an 'upmarket' porno fashion, they would occasionally come close and tease him: Angel would brush a pink feather gently over his zones of effect; Sage and I would showcase bends and hair-flicking stripper manouvres, Brandy would take his pulse, and rake her fingers thru the chest forest etc. I would indicate who needed to 'take centre stage' at various intervals, so he was constantly aroused. He was gagging and begging for us all to join him, but this is where I signalled Augustina to step in, with light but sternly administered whippings through clenched teeth: "Down boy, you do as I SAY……its not YOUR turn"…
By the time we actually got INTO the bed with the man he was set to shoot. The final harrah of having the entire harem swamp him in sensual contact with teeth and touch was too much for him to bear. So, as usual, the seconds of penetration were almost non mention-worthy.
As we left with bundles of cash, it was smiles all round. I felt most self righteous to witness the understudies embrace the craft of Christie:
"Encore gang! A happy man, a well paid show; no fucking needed, and time to go"….

Never a dull moment in the stage life of an escort…………..

Part seven:

Being ac**count**able

for your actions....

August 15th, 7am.

There's a new boy in town to add to my regular clientele. So, if I was to **COUNT**, that would make it 4 reliable participants that pretty much keep my diary complete.
I have of course encountered MANY cU*ts in this trade (as you can imagine), but let's add the additional *vowel* here…. This lad is in fact a **COUNT.**
For real!
He is descended from northern Italian nobility, with the bottom-less bank account to prove it.
Wow - an Italian Count no less…it is akin to royalty!!
I think he is actually the youngest millionaire I have ever met; let alone 'dated'. (I mean, one can expect such wealth at the more ancient end of the scale, but at 23??) He was born into it, (as opposed to acquiring it), and like all the other European boys of such stature I have met, it proved to be more of a curse than a blessing. The irony.

In any case, it's a refreshing change to see such a young, handsome man with the gold cards 'n red carpet capers,~ as opposed to the ageing; well-established; typical millionaire ~ who uses it like a power to compensate for his deteriorated; mid-life (and beyond)-crisis state.

[And yes, far be it for me to deny that there is an instant 'blinding' effect that occurs when a fat, ugly, (or crinkly 'n decrepid); most UNdesirable man has access to the high life that immense wealth can afford. And they of course know it and possess the arrogance to boot! Power tool. They don't have to WORK for the killer physique and pristine veneer; their acquisitions account for that in substitution. Cash speaks louder volumes.
It roars.

Absolutely absurd, yet true: money grants one the perception of sexy too…think for example oh, let me see…Mick Jagger! Struck with the ugly stick BIGTIME. Hello…]

It is for the same reason, that if you have been to Asia for any period of time, you will be shocked by the prevalence of western men/Asian girl combos. How many times have you seen a most unattractive (read repulsive/grotesque) fat old white fool with an exquisitely immaculate little Asian doll?! Nobody would bat an eyelid at him in western countries, but the unspoken rule of thumb applies: Money grants one access to the forbidden fruits. However, once the cash has gone……….off with the mask! There he is in all his non-glory hideousness. Stripped bare of the armour and banished from the castle……….

Anyway, I digress. In discussion, he speaks limited English too, which adds a tad of heightened sexual appeal. (Hit me with an accent and it usually gets the heartbeat rockin'!) He has cute mannerisms;~ my favourite being when he passes me the credit card and declares "you know 'ow to sign my name, so you can shout tonight, ja!"…..
If I showed interest in, or admired anything he would declare: 'don't look at me- you have the money! Buy what you like!" (Could I be falling in love with this one???!!)
So many important boxes ticked…… ✓ ✓
Everything is always a case of 'only the finest will do', as he was no doubt accustomed. He automatically bought the most expensive of anything and everything, simply 'because he can'.   Example: last night at around 6pm: 'come on, you want to eat dinner at the casino restaurant? Then we can play some roulette downstairs!'……I of course agreed to whatever he suggested (albeit my distaste for the 'gambling seat' at the casino)….but was concerned about my bags and where to leave them etc.

'don't worry, we find a place to keep them safe'……….this actually translated to 'show me the MOST EXPENSIVE SUITE YOU HAVE IN THIS ESTABLISHMENT and book it for the next 2 nights'……..
Can you believe, in all that time, we spent a grand total of ONE HOUR in the grandiose ballroom-sized top floor facility; - simply to shower and spruce up for the next adventure on the town. (oh, he lovingly shaved my legs in the massive spa bath, that's right!) Bath in its decadence for a spell, if you will.
A glorified 'change-room' in other words……. at higher daily fees than a round the world flight…   oh i love this job!!!

August 18th 2pm.

Just spent 2 very prosperous evenings on 'count-caper' patrol, so have been granted the night off by Darren!

Have spent a few hours with Hann to debrief on various encounters; both been so busy we've hardly seen each other in a week. Had a good laugh over coffee and cheesecake. She of course considers my interludes with the count 'cradle snatching' as she is more

familiar with the other end of the evolutionary scale, age-wise. The usual demographic where wealth is concerned. Anything under 55 is virtual cougar territory in her opinion! Ive often wondered what they discuss, or have in common?!
(I have to say between you and me dear diary, it is indeed a blessing that she is so street savvy and well endowed…for it compensates for the occasional verbal faux pas on her behalf. A few eyebrows must be raised, no doubt)

*example: " oh god I wish you'd been there Christie. I tried several times to rope you in, but Darren just kept answering with 'she's still visiting Italy – and looks like she may stay longer in the castle. 48 hours and COUNT-ing ha ha ha' – like I had any idea what THAT meant. I knew you'd never left the country! At least not without trying to take me with you…."
I attempted to reply but she rushed in: " Anyway, this guy was amazing. He's 'only' 64, and he's promised to take me skiing (!!) overseas, and has already bought me SO many gifts, (waving the flamboyant gold bracelet in my face)… AND he's eager to meet you too!!………BUT he's got a head like a twisted sandwich". At that point I lost it of course, and between the hysterics managed to cough out: " I think you mean twisted sandSHOE hon"…as the saying goes…

August 19th 4.30am.

Well, here's another thing…..

Ive never seen so many men fall so rapidly in love; never mind smitten! These evenings are often viewed as more like DATES than client bookings.

Gina was proposed to today! The Spanish sweetheart was flaunting the rock like some trophy prize, and it was a sizeable gem, I might add. Of course this was in confidence amongst the girls, although I suspect she couldn't care less now about the inevitable sacking for having broken rule #1. She certainly didn't need to work now; ~ the sugar daddy had landed and she was set to….. **be** set.

I couldn't help laughing either; her English is so minimal. Verbal comms were obviously not the priority manner of the union in her case. In fact, ive never really seen her talk at all. She always appeared to be on a rohypnol whenever I did a double with her! Even her client bathing technique was so slow, it was almost hypnotic to behold.
Perhaps he was seeking a 'mother figure' – you know, to nurture and rock him into a demented lullaby after a hard day at the office or something?
Ha, or maybe he was sick of demanding, nagging women, and just wanted someone who would shut the fuck up!

IN ANY CASE, I wish her well. She was a very gentle soul…(read a tad on the weak side), and is one of those 'needing husband' types. And with that characteristically Spanish pear-shaped, fertile physique, she was no doubt ready to produce en masse. She had navigated her way to the bank: both sperm and finance-wise. While bypassing the normal social labyrinth.
                                        So bravo girl. Mission
accomplished!

[Im not advocating this method as a way to get hitched; merely pointing out that the success rate is seemingly high. I wouldn't say that it was the SOLE purpose, but the priority goal, certainly, of this job was to avoid struggle-street later on....men were subconsciously preferred on their ability rating to provide this future comfort-zone. One doesn't take on such secretive, anti-social vocational exploits without such grandiose rewards! (And lets face facts: any client that won over his maiden knew these were the unspoken rules of the game. Never to be broken)...]

As far as a screening process goes, it doesn't get more thorough than this, certainly.
For the term: 'know each other inside and out' rings true after a relatively short period of time (read bookings). The men are often investing in their future too, therefore.
One that satisfies their preferred human list.

So......it's a win-win all round.

August 20th, 6am.

Well the night was slow for all concerned tonight; it was the first time all the girls were congregated in the agency. (We all hate that. Would rather endure the company of an unsavoury client than be compelled to experience bitch-mania in a group situation.)
Lets face it: women are never friends; they are by nature way too competitive and jealous. It just-doesn't-work. Darren was even having a tough time convincing the callers to secure a booking. Even in times of financial crisis, business in this industry always remained what it sold: a sure thing. So, what was it: full moon or something?!
Well, at one point he called me in and handed me the phone while he was scribbling something down, and sending a text at the same time. He stopped briefly to put his hand over the receiver and said in frustrated resignation " they want to speak to the girl in question direct. Just handle it like an interview! The guy wants to buy Christie as a present for his partner....."

All very vague.More clarity required for the script........
Well...i may not have a client update from 'in the field' to report tonight, but this phone conversation was certainly note-worthy! I took the phone in hand with a tad of trepidation, as I closed the office door to segregate myself from the jealous snarling lions in the pit. (I mean, I don't mind being in the 'throws of three' if it is managed under my selection or preference, and is an act, but when I am called in to perform magic spells on trouble in paradise...that's actually when it's a mind-fuck.)
" Hey Christie. We think you look and sound amazing, but we just wanted to talk to you first! Darren has assured us that you are the one we want, and we looked at your picture and are both besotted!" the guy had an American accent, and was soft spoken; rather sexy. Then the woman jumped in " Oh honey, we would love to have you join us, and I think im already in love with you before I meet you!"
okay..........I realized that getting the full picture of this booking's mission would indeed take more than the preliminary call. It was a tad confusing.

He continued: "You see, we haven't been together for 5 years while ive…been away, so now I want to give a special gift to my loved one. Will you join us on celebrating my release?" I was momentarily silent; they actually sounded so dead-set genuine that I felt compelled to join them and discover more of 'their story'. I was fascinated.. besides which, my gut is rarely wrong, and with these two it already told me that they were really good, spiritual people, (regardless of prior convictions) – and that it would be a union to remember.

I meet them tomorrow evening at the casino. He said he would collect me from the furthest roulette table, and would be wearing dark sunnies.
Mass intrigue.
The suspense is palpable…
I'm there with bells on!

August 25th, 5pm.

Holy cow. I just got in! how many days have lapsed since we last spoke dear diary? Been missing in action with the two new REMARKABLE people in my life. I honestly can't remember the last time I had so much fun; nor connected so strongly with someone. Solid soul-food stuff. (Never mind the fact that it was chemically enhanced)……this was a quality chapter from beginning to end……and the best thing? Its only just begun! Every once in a while, you meet someone who enhances your life in some way; makes a real difference to your world. You experience extreme gratitude. It has only just begun with this pair. They will be with me for life. I know it deep in my heart. But back to reality……mine is so golden now that I have them in it!!

Must crash now…way too long no shut-eye. Shall elaborate anon.

August 28th, 4pm.

STILL haven't had a chance to elaborate on the magic triangle capers as yet, so hold that thought…

In the meantime, ive been kept amused by my other lad……..how do I enjoy his decadent antics? Let me count the ways!! Its like being/playing tinkerbell………I just flit around in sexy garb and keep the affectionate Peter Pan happy. Welcome to the land of the ever young………that's what being a millionaire is all about. Almost by definition. He milks it for all its worth. And I'm there to be his plaything in the 'city playground'. It's a tough job, but apparently I do it well. Fun fact: I can't believe he loves the album ive listened to for years

and nobody has ever heard of !   *Sigue Sigue Sputnik!*
My music tastes have always been somewhat non-mainstream so this was a surprise.
We played it for hours singing and dancing like lunatics for *hours* while we both got into the

spirit… (me- with the music and he… with the liquor) It was like the hotel scene of a hedonistic bad boy band. He was spraying vodka around the room like it was water.
My concern **is** for his liver however. Ive known some hardcore drinkers in my time but this guy lives *inside* a vodka bottle. Straight up on the rox. If I wasn't here and ever keen to do meals at all the best restaurants in town, he simply wouldn't eat at all. " My veins have no blood; they pump with Stolichnaya vodka." Hes a walking miracle…or maybe its just the endurance of youth. But can money buy you the extra life when this one expires through abuse? Apparently so, if his claims are true: he intends to (wait for it) – CLONE HIS LIVER!! Im not joking; he's deadly serious. He certainly has the funds to afford the appropriate specialists. But moving right along……
I'd been at the bar with the awesome city views for hours after dinner, before I realized Darren had left an urgent message. A radio station was set to interview Christie. Oh my goodness……he had explained that I was 'detained' (as is my professional want), and they were hence compelled to 'phone me bedside from the plush harbor hotel suite'. I was in deep slumber typically, (what do you expect at 8am in MY world?!) ~ so the responses were no doubt husky and soft. But who knows, maybe that added a sexy flavour to it; one can only hope….!
The usual array of questions, prying for deets on notable figures I have encountered in my trade. Details were craftily danced around on my behalf, with a sense of humour. Apparently the response has nevertheless been great; im sure Darren will debrief me later.
I must confess, at this point though, that I am so painfully tired……after the interview, count Dracula stayed cuddling me under the sheets till we decided the next venue to infiltrate.
Been a long innings, but the princess seriously needs the luxury of some cloudy soft pillows and solitude to 'reboot'.
Note to self: ask the count crazy lad – if he loves me (as he professes), then while he's getting the liver cloned with these super scientists of his imagination, could they possibly design that pill that supplies one with the benefits of 8 hours straight sleep? Forget the jewellery etc, this is the gift request for me! If I ever GOT any sleep, I would dream about this wish…

That was 2 days ago…..
We are now INTERSTATE in Melbourne…..it was so spontaneously wild, I LOVE it!! While having aperitifs at the swanky hotel piano bar, we started on the topic of great restaurants and shops in this state vs Sydney and before we knew it were on a first class flight here!
We are calling it a 'reci-tour' before we land here for the races soon. Need to be in the know of what's the best of the best here for ensuing verbal banter with the aristocracy and that calibre of society, right?! Professionalism calls on homework to be done. I am studying the top-notch dining establishments over a coffee…

Grandiose suite again; 5 star studded ~ and I'm loved-up to the max with all the bags of shopping delight he insisted I pursue. Luxury prevails as always. Oh the fabulous fur coat; miow……..

The excess baggage fee wont be a bother for him either, so don't fret, I have to keep reminding myself! I even called my sister and mother to double check their shoe size so I have gifts to share the love..
The bar tab here is reaching profound proportions on the count......priority we investigate his liver cloning mission he speaks of soon I think......

September 1st, 4am.

Well I really have to give the report on the days/nights spent with Jay and Maz. It was one of the most extraordinary events in my life to date, and worth a special mention before the pace of my work world just pushes me on...

After the initial 'phone interview', we had set a date to meet at the furthest roulette table in the casino. All rather undercover; gangsta style.....Well, there he was, handsome guy. Even with the shades on, I just knew there was a cheeky sparkle in his eyes!! (and when he took them off, he looked like David Bowie! Same mouth; eyes and aura).
He hugged me and threw a few chips on the table for a spin before taking my hand and leading me to his hotel suite, within the actual casino complex. Immense; glorious. As I had expected. There was no shortage of funds here! I felt so comfortable with him already; I kind of instinctively knew I was going to be in it for the long haul.

He introduced me to Maz; his girlfriend of several years. A tall, exotic creature with an ebony glow, and long flowing black hair. Majestic, like a mane. It gave her a degree of wild, carefree madness. There was no denying her beauty however. She was of aboriginal decent, and he was American Indian. It was a combination of extreme forces! Their little daughter was bound to be a special gift.
As he refreshed our champagne flutes from the icebucket, he explained that this was a 'special celebration' ~ think 'welcome to freedom ceremony'. He had done time for 5 years; during which Chaylie was born. So not only was he incarcerated for her birth, but had missed the initial years of her life. To meet his 'newborn' at age 5 was a gift but also no doubt, an emotional ache.

Jay was joyous in the fact that Maz and I connected so easily, and naturally in an instant; it was the most important aspect of this mission. He needed his girl to be pampered; for they had both done their time. He stood at a distance; with his head tilted, and his hand under his chin – observing our mutual adoration from afar.
I was entranced by her aura. She was like a chocolate fairy goddess with a soft heart, and a volcanic side to boot. You could see it come and go in her eyes; dark and deep like a shark. There were no apparent irises at all; just black, fathomless pupils. She was captivating, to say the least. And a little scary too. There was no denying, she ignited carnal passion. Her allure was part gentle, sensual goddess and part free-spirited wild creature. Impossible to tame. Hot mamma...
And she seemed content with my presence and similar vitality. It was exciting to be with them both; they were like enigmas to behold. The sort you meet once in a lifetime.

She confessed that she adored my soft lips, and being the sensual kisser that she was I didn't mind!

It is perhaps the most important aspect of all carnal capers for me. Nothing else rates on the radar; nor eventuates to the next level without this vital foreplay role. All culmination and climax is a direct result of the kiss rating.

(As Hann had explained on several occasions: "I am German, obviously, and Christie here is an albino nigger; as you can see by her lips!")

Although not directly involved, Jay was observing approvingly from his vantage point, and his presence was felt.

He offered a straw for the generous lines he had cut on the huge, ornate table in the dining room. It was an almost sacred sight; with the chandelier above; offering a soft, ethereal glow. The table hence served as a religious-like oracle, and we took grateful *communion*.....

(The semantics of which, after all are: shared beliefs, thoughts, feelings and practices.)

(I sensed this was as close to anything ingestible to be obtained from the intended dining structure.)

No *grace* at this table, but ritual offerings, yes! Let the four day party begin..

[Anyone who has experienced the higher end of accommodation and associated lifestyle antics understands what im talking about. Yes? *If I had a dollar for every time I was offered Coke....* (and I'm not referring to the fizzy sugar fuel liquid here; though perhaps equally as venomous); *I wouldn't have to work at all!* I had partied ridiculously madly in my youth, but after doing it at this standard, the retrospective fashion seemed like a travesty of justice. It is without doubt, the cashed up man's enhancer of choice.]

There were frequent 'magical deliveries' made to the hotel by an anonomous source during the ensuing four day period; during which Christie was somewhat 'missing in mindless action'...much to Darren's joy no doubt. I mean, 96 hours...

The festivities revolved around sensual spa baths, and wardrobe changes from glam to lingerie to party to bathrobe to naked.......and repeat etc. And heart to heart conversations throughout, in every room of the suite to the point that, I feel I know these two more than myself now! Talk about fast~tracking a friendship. But this is *more*; I know it. I love these people. Genuine; unconditional love.

And they reciprocated the sentiment wholeheartedly. It kind of spoilt me for 'normal' human interaction I think. It was the most intense, REAL bond I've ever had in my life. They were not only the most beautiful people, but BEYOND fascinating. Oh the stories...and all deadset honest accounts of life experiences to date. It takes a lot to shock me, but they certainly ticked off that aspect. It kind of got a little silly after consecutive days of sleep deprivation though......that is when the laughing started, and the witty banter. Intense, gut wrenching belly laughs that left me gasping for breath. You know the type; the ones you so rarely get and crave evermore.....

Sigh....

September 2nd (?)

Ooh play misty for me……..

The country girl has certainly gone wild!! When 'Misty' arrived for her interview at the agency several weeks ago, Darren sent her to me for the standard body check. (good grief, im certainly clocking up the hours of 'training for management' for any future venture in madame-ville…..if I decide to run my own agency now, it will be a walk in the park!….)

She was easy to approve. Flawless really. She certainly needed some 'polishing' in several areas, but the basic canvas was good. Terrific tall and lean physique; silky sleek chestnut hair; milky smooth skin….. literally brought up on a farm, she had the innocent angelic 'untouched' quality about her. Organic. (Hmm…not for long.)

So after I had given the report to Darren he christened her. Misty. (sort of sounds like the name for a horse, so being the country gal n all……!!)
Hard to describe her appeal; she's not exactly beautiful, its more her 'girl next door' attraction which apparently has the lads in raptures. This was proven by the photoshoot she had done the following day. For amongst those fabulous professional shots that were selected for the website, a snapshot of hers was thrown in with them. It had her with no makeup; a simple singlet and cutoff denims, holding a mug of hot chocolate on a country porch. Ironically, this has proven to be her calling card; the one that sold her time and time again…..go figure.

She was contrastive to me in many ways, but the same height, so we worked well in the 'doubles' stakes……and contrary to the initial impression, she was FAR from shy! Oh good grief can this girl work a BEDroom…i've never seen anyone enjoy this job so much.
She's beyond hooked (!) it all comes so naturally for us in the performance stakes. In fact, she is a breeze (not to mention a great kisser) – so we are officially a 'twin-team' now, and it is almost a given that for every booking we get, the other gets too. Double trouble. And now that she has the makeup and 'self masking' tactics well under way she is a knockout….and almost a far cry from the doe-eyed youth that first arrived.
Likes the candy that goes with the territory a bit much which concerns me……(don't get me wrong, we've had some fabulous blow-outs, but she's new to the game, and I can see it getting out of control)…..there are some hints of come-down agro occurring that could be her downfall..
In any case, she is quite worthy of a diary entry now, as I reflect on the weekend, and how it evolved………

I now have an obsessed lover on my hands!!!

Sept 3ʳᵈ

Well what got off to a slow and uncomfortable start at the agency tonight ended up being an absolute ball. ___

Its rare we are all huddled in waiting for a job to materialise so a room full of competitive women vying for Darren's favouritism as first cab off the rank reminded me of the traumas of catwalk claws out. Not a pleasant environment. You could cut the air with a knife. All the girls, to be fair are gorgeous and lovely *individually* but we all know what happens when a group gets together.

 In any case I was finally summoned in to the room with 2 other of the more…shall we say offbeat girls in the clan. I could see the other girls folding their arms in contempt with looks of "why not **me**?!" As reluctant as I felt being grouped up with these 2, I was indeed relieved to be exiting the office of oestrogen hell.

Both were kind of plain, but Darren had taken them in and moulded them somewhat into the vixens he now sold them on. They started off as plump girls on the street, struggling to pay their rent and their study tuition fees. The before photos are unrecognisable to the women that now prevailed. He got them both gym memberships and a 'skilset' each and now they're earning more than the average doctor or lawyer! Rebranded christening of course.

Alexa is a tall gangly strawberry blonde (that looks very much to me like a drag queen), and *Chanel* is a petite, albeit voluptuous curvy doll. Rumour has it that Alexa has a flexible skill with juggling balls, and ballbearings or something….(details of which I have no desire to discover), and Chanel's specialty is absolute costume and role-play. Tonight she was sporting her French maids outfit. Feather duster to hand….also an accoutrement that is of obvs advantage.

Tonight he sent all 3 of us to a single guy's place….I thought: oh dear. I could be in for a bit of a weird ride here. Well I have to say it was hysterical and bordering on vaudeville routine. Hey ha hoopla, the circus is in town! Thankfully the ballbearings didn't make an appearance but the juggling act ensued with Alexa (along with several very flexible poses in the routine), while Chanel energetically dusted everything in sight….balls n all. (No explanation required there.) Not sure where she gets her energy from….. but she's a bit of an energizer bunny with a wide-eyed permagrin permanently attached to her heavily made up face. Its most theatrical to witness. Plus Alexa even got out the fluro hoola hoop and did a showstopping gyration in it.

I simply couldn't stop laughing. Like im talking doubled over. And it was infectious to the guy too - we both sat in the audience in hysterics. I basically poured the nerdy guy his beer; acted as his viewing buddy and watched him shreik with delight as he applauded them and repeated 'encore, encore'…..the poor guy was just lonely basically, and wanted company and someone to engage his interest and ease his nerves. I could just imagine him being bullied, so tonights' task in addition to the entertainment was one of a mothering nature. Give him back his carefree innocence, so to speak. Freely and without reprisal.

He was easy to typecast into what he really wanted. Comfort! And company.

We stayed for 4 hours and he loved every innocent minute of the fun. Darren got a glowing report from him, and we headed back to the agency in fits of laughter. It felt therapeutic to us too, go figure! A 2 way street. Tit for tat. No puns intended…

There really are some very lonely, sad and forlorn victims out there in the dark of night who are willing to pay big money for safe escapism. I feel like im qualified to be a psychologist. And im sure im earning way more…..

Sept 4th

Roll up, roll up….Darren was about to partner me with Alexa and her bags of tricks, but she called in sick last minute. (Phew, just quietly. Not sure we would be a match made in heaven somehow. I find her quirky but not the *slightest* bit double material. It would be a circus freak show I feel!)
So he sent me with Chanel. Who at this point was skipping around the agency like a fairy with huge eyes, so it might have been just to get her out of his hair!

Hmm…..energy provider? The verdict is not yet out….
(The night had started off somewhat slow, but it rapidly got radical and racy.)
In any case I was exhausted by her enthusiasm and felt cortisol overdrive in her presence. The job time flew thankfully as she was so eager to please, and took command and centre stage. She was a sensual one though, ill give her that much. And we doubled easily and naturally. I had brought matching lingerie: black leotard for her and white fringed bikini for me. It was like Snow White and rose red; Disneyland viewing for the bloke in his head. We did this spontaneously choreographed erotic show in the huge window panes of the hotel; like jewellery box ballerinas in a frame with harbour backdrop. It was really clever, we both admitted after as we counted the wads of cash he had popped down our tops. A private show and rep intact. Another happy customer. When Darren says he sells his girls as 'entertainers' he really ain't joking!

Meanwhile, back at the ranch, all was quiet on the western front. We were lucky to have nabbed what appeared to be the only job of the evening. He'd already sent most of the girls home.
Regardless though, Darren was obvs angry at Hannah as he saw some photos in the press of her away skiing with one of her clients…oh dear. Sprung…..

The thing was though, when you reach the standards we were at it took a LOT to be kicked out. A stern warning is most likely all she'll get. Celebrity status will award you that grace. He asked Chanel and I to stay on just in case one more request came in. Having broken the ice on matchmaking endeavours together, we felt at ease and most comfortable. And she kind of intrigued me; as exhausting as she was. I couldn't quite pinpoint it.
When it was almost sure that we should call it a night, we heard Darren arguing on the phone to his wife, so we left him and sat in one of the other rooms. "You have such lovely eyes Christie!" Chanel got out her makeup and started defining them further. Serious black eyeliner. And lashes. It was nice to have someone else play with makeup games so I just relaxed with it, accepting the fact that tonights' face wash would be more robust.
She started to talk about her sad past. I felt like crying but didn't want the black ink to run down my face; god knew I must have looked gothic enough already.
Then while she chatted she started doing a very elaborate 'tattoo' design all over my face. Heaven help us if a job came in…..Darren would fume! His mood tonight was already grim. I would never normally allow it, but I knew that every artistic stroke on the face symbolised a confession for her as she released her demons…..and turned me into one (!), so I allowed her freedom of expression complete. Therapy for her. And interesting and most relaxing for me. Except for the content of her words. It went a bit like this in summary:

~abandoned by original mother; adopted by a horror pair; ran away and lived with hippies and in homeless shelters; got hooked on drugs and booze from the age of 12; went into

rehab; got engaged to a wife basher; ate through her emotions to the point of behemouth proportions; met Darren and begged for cash in the hand work; went away to halve her size for eligibility; and he virtually 'adopted' her after that. She even calls him Daddy sometimes and sits on his lap. The diff is, now I understand that it is _innocent_. And she really considers him her father.
And so here she was now. "I don't go to the gym at all; hate it!" ~ So, how did she lose all the weight one has to wonder….

"I have a dirty little secret. It's my best friend and got me into this shape fast. My lover. My **Duramine.** Shhh…don't tell Darren or the girls or my slimmer arse is grass!"

By this time I knew my face had been a blank canvas for her scary craftwork and wondered how I would get home looking this way.

Aha I thought. She lives on speed! The girl basically functions on amphetamines. No wonder she's got the energy of a hyperactive child and keeps off the pounds! (Anyone who's done a weekend bender on class A drugs knows its a sure-fire way to shed kilos like crazy. The metabolism goes into overdrive burnout. Or should I say burn off…) How they get away with marketing legal speed as a 'diet pill' is bordering on criminal.
She got out a photo of herself 6 months before starting her daily dosages and I gasped. Morbidly obese! She was lucky she didn't have stretch marks. I'm not making excuses for her, but her personal journey kind of led to here naturally. I didn't blame her but I did feel a bit responsible now. I made a note to self to try to persuade her to join me in workouts etc instead as she was headed for a body meltdown car crash. You could see it a mile off…

"Girls it's time to scoot. Ive already lined up….what the FK??｣｣ Are you kidding me? Kids indeed. You're fn lucky the agency is closed for the day. Kindergarten is over. Go home. Play with crayons or something….Christie ill have to drive you personally; you can't go out the door looking like that. You'll get locked up. And tonight, scrub your face….tomorrow I want no trace of craft time. Chanel - you **should** be on probation….Go, before I change my mind"

Daddy wasn't happy with the kids tonight. But tomorrow it will all be alright. Goodnight.

Sept 7th:

An interesting few days…I found myself doing something radical I haven't done in ages: clubbing after work last night. Decision entirely made on the company I was in. Rare I ever rate it as worthy of my time if not paid by the hour!

Darren had me paired up with someone I have rarely spoken a word to ever. We smile, but she's always buried in a book or writing notes for her studies. "Oh she's an intellectual nerd and built like a stork!" Hann would profess regularly.

Turns out, miss studious, conservative bookworm with the giraffe dimensions proved to be a somewhat exotic bird who loved to dance and and really let her hair down. And by hair I mean mane. Chestnut and usually up in a bun; the gangly shy secretary look is her everyday image. On appearance alone, you would never imagine in a million years she was a callgirl…..but I guess that is her charm in essence. Rule number one: never ever judge a book by it's cover….sometimes what lays beneath the veneer is a total contradiction to ones' perception.

(A bit like the fact that most of the famous top models confess that their youth was one of ostracization by all peers, and an often studious outcast education. They are teased for their towering height and picked on for their braces, hair colour and glasses. And the 'cool chicks' will classify them as ugly ducklings and geeks that will never get a boyfriend interested, let alone a female friendship. But these unique creatures are the ones head-hunted by agencies for their differences and sophisticated aire of unique beauty. Their quirky 'faults' are perceived as a standout eye-catching feature. Eg: tooth gap; eyes far apart; moles on face etc. 'Ugly is the new beautiful' kind of took over the industry and has continued to supersede the likes of Christie Brinkley and perfect beauties that had once reigned supreme. Ironically, the 'super cute, most popular **IN**' girls often end up in a drab future when these 'uglies' bloom.)

She would sit in a corner alone in the agency with some intellectual tome, and quietly study for hours. Reading glasses on; hair in a French twist or bun; legs folded, tres conservative suit and court shoes. A misfit for sure, but there was a sensual charm about her that obviously captivated her clients. She was one of the girls who got requested again by nearly every man she met. 100% satisfaction rating. The quiet achiever. Even Darren was careful not to interfere with her intellectual train of thought. If a booking came in for her, he would send her a message on her phone…from his office next door to where she sat! The other girls would got heralded with a shout from his chair.

She looked up as she got the text, and quietly packed up her mobile 'office'. Then she walked silently over to me and hooked arms as we left to enter the waiting merc downstairs. I thought : 'this will be akin to being on a meditation retreat where words are forbidden and all is tranquil and calm'….I even felt really peaceful in her presence. Just before we arrived at destination : the conservative but prestigious Raddison, she held out her hand and said 'Audrey. Pleased to meet you'…and that was it! We were off to a show of what would be spontaneous choreography and I silently hoped the chap was a shy non-chatty type. Darren was generally pretty good at type casting though, and luckily he hit the mark in this case again.

Enter the room we did, to find the guy hiding behind the door for sometime until he felt ready to approach us and take off his specs. Still in full suit, tie and shiny shoes he held out his hand meagrely and said "hi im Alistair…I know this isn't your first time but it is mine so im sorry….Im so nervous I feel positively sick"….Audrey gently started massaging his shoulders while I went to the mini bar and suggested some elixir of courage. He nodded and said "ill have whatever you guys are having…or suggest…..I ah don't normally drink or go out so ill let you decide"….

Anyhoo, as the night wore on it became easier and he was a canvas to model any way we wanted to fashion so it was like being an artist in a sense. Like an alien had landed on the planet with zero notion of human protocol; interaction or communication. An easy assignment to master! And after 4 hours he was indeed a smiling happy customer.

Audrey sent a message to Darren saying "all okay but I've just got my period and an intense migraine and Christie is exhausted, so can we be permitted to go home now?"

With that done, she hooked arms once more as we bid Alistair the great farewell and headed off to the foyer downstairs. Bypassing the staff she stood in the taxi rank and wolf whistled to herald down a premier car. "Come on Chris. We're off to let off some steam"....

As curious as hell, I acquiesced and let her silently take the lead. One must seize new life opportunities when they land on your suspendered lap. You never know where they may take you. An adventure worth taking for the sheer mystery of it all!...

September 8th:

Well its damn lucky that my booking tonight is not till late, as I didn't finally get to bed until dawn after the Audrey adventure; with sore feet from dancing and a croaky voice from yelling to be heard in the loud venues. Its now 5pm and I only just got up! Though weary as hell, im still kind of in a fuzz of contentment at having such a fantastic time and taken quite by surprise in all regards.
My body clock is used to topsy-turvy conditions with nocturnal rendezvous almost daily. Like they say, milk it while you can... burnout is imminent someday but for now im still alive.

Carpe diem and all that jazz....

Audrey had taken us to a few amazing venues, and knew the doormen and security at most. Some were very private/underground dens of darkness in candlelight; bathed in mystery and secret. Extremely interesting and mostly alternative occupants who were quite obviously of a caliber of society that preferred the lure of *safety* in these sanctuaries of seduction and sin. Irony at its best. No doubt plenty of stimulants abound, as the places rocked on till nearly 10am at some. Audrey was a misfit too, so it was obvious she was in her element. She dragged me onto the dance floor, as exhausted as I felt, but after a while, I also found it liberating and quite therapeutic to just let loose. Her hair was still up, but partly gliding free, and she was sidling up VERY close to me, almost raunchy but devoid of care or conscience. We danced on for hours, and on a few DJ shift changes, would move on to the next location in her map of the city nightlife. It was nice to have someone else take the lead for a change and just follow along!
(It should be stressed that clubbing is by *no* means my thing anymore...I got that caper out of my system when VERY young; still at school. My girlfriend Mel and I used to say we were at each others' place for a sleepover and hit the city and 'the Cross', knowing well, like Audrey, all the doormen, bouncers and staff. They all took me under their wing like a 'wild child of the night'. Some of those haunts were like a second home to me! Once I fell asleep in one and the bouncer had to pick me up and deposit me in a cafe while the cleaner did the morning rounds of vacuuming. Another time I met the son of one of Sydneys most famous

sports commentators, and spent the night dancing and laughing with him - much to the ultimate pride of my brothers' later!)

In any case, this was a rare circumstance I now found myself - back in the nocturnal venues of rebellion, and having a surprisingly great time! I put that down to the company though mostly as Audrey was lovely and so stylish and unique that we didn't look like crazy dance floor sluts in the slightest. We got lots of compliments on our sensual freeflow display. And it was natural, given that it was sort of the nature of the beast in our secret industry, and practice makes perfect in that regard.
At some point we went to a funky cafe for a caffeine hit to energise us further, and she started to talk free flow as well. With much confidence, she spoke on many intellectual topics, which was hardly surprising considering she was sitting the bar in law in her 'real life'. And criminal law at that! Now there was a revelation to report....I thought mentally: I may need her someday....

It was a great night all told and we planned to do it again sometime. I could see why she found it a stress release from our challenging role-play nocturnal tasks for cash; coupled with her relentless studies and discipline. So again, I refer to the old adage -
never judge a book by it's cover.... And by the same token, never judge a person by their vocation either.
this was a true case of masks and mirrors right here.....

Always beware the silent types....there's a different animal lurking within!

Date: Sept 9th.

Well, today Hann came over to the place Ive been hanging at in my free time (a client's actually.....shhhh!!)
Yes, you guessed it. '***The boy's***' again.

He's a workaholic; I think he just likes to know that I come and go like a cat! He's in the inner city so super convenient for after work. (the other day, when I arrived, he had hung up all my clothes from my bags; costumes; outfits etc on a sliding hanger! But not in a possessive, freaky way or anything. It was actually quite nice. "So they don't get crumpled". Considerate, no!)

We spent the weekend on his Halvison cruiser. It's his oceanic getaway; ~ his go-to retreat/escape. I think he values time on board here more than in his terrace. I get that.......
He made us a wonderful light seafood meal (oysters; lobster and salad) with marvelous wine and for the dessert to follow......that was *my* role. I announced I would serve his, while seductively pouring it down my thighs for him to lick off from there. I think the kid in the candy store was jolly....(!)
As much as I am a huge fan of the ocean however (it has always held a massively important 'saviour' theme in my life) ....i am not that thrilled with the nauseating rocking after an

evening of indulgence and imbibing…..i think I awoke positively green. Contrastly, he awoke with a massive grin.
A crazy associate of his joined us on the boat and insisted I get straight with the hair-of-the-dog ritual, and I surprisingly admit that the breakfast of baileys on ice worked wonders to settle the insides.

He's great company too; fab sense of humour and skilful in the kitchen. A massive foodie and into travel. Desperate to take me to the south of France; wine territory! (I sort of don't need the 'other' boxes ticked at this stage, as the job allows me those 'pleasures') – which is lucky, 'coz **business** is orgasmic for this one. He is seemingly disinterested in bedroom capers. I've never encountered one like this before; he's a strange cat in that regard. Sexless I mean. Never known a man like it. Or woman.
Libido has left the building….
Perhaps concerning, but a refreshing break for me though. Its like I'm 'on holiday' here. He likes to spoil me rotten too, so bring it on I say! Almost tempting to marry one who likes the finer things…BUT/AND doesn't require marathons in the bedroom. (Will the holiday last?? Will I still enjoy it later on?)..

He is the first to admit that his business is 'his mistress' and describes sealing the sales deal as 'orgasmic'…..sexual terminology relating to work only….maybe we are more similar than I thought (!)

Which prompts me to consider some of the revelations of this profession……for my role is one of psychologist and psychiatrist in some regards, and that is no exaggeration.
With male sexual performance: Alas……its always a case of **all** or **nothing.**
Literally……seriously!! Doesn't' the happy medium exist??!

 [I've had enough experience with men in this caper to comment with utter sincerity:
its either a:

~ libido-revved hard-drive grunt that is seemingly insatiable, (and at times needs taming) or :

 ~ a *blah,* barren, non-existent state that requires nurturing and repair……
One does tend to naturally waver to the 'other side' when the quota dose of each is fulfilled….

Where to be in natural harmony, fulfilment and balance, pray tell? the lost paradise..
I am convinced the middle-ground is a foreign land one will never arrive on]
All or nothing.
Such are the hormonal havocs that be I guess…..

Anyway, Hann settled right in here and started doing our pedis and face masks, and then she got out the fabric for the costumes she is making us. Luscious of course. She's brilliant with a sewing machine.
"Chrissie hon, we're going to Mardi Gras next year as the best looking couple, im determined!!"   Its only September for Christ's
sake; 5 months in advance?! " Yeah, but we're always so fricken busy now, I have to just do

it when I can grab a spare minute, so best to start early!" She is right of course. The time flies so fast its terrifying…
"We're going as the "VERSACE URBAN COWGIRL BARBIE TWINS!!" she showed me the sketches as we sipped on some wine that the boy had left for us.
They were sensational; I was way excited!

Cowgirl hats; sexy PVC black mini skirts with Versace ribbon trim; serious push-up bustierre bras with gold detailing and pins (as is Jianni Versace's signature embellishment); Elvis style sunnies (!), divine tiny handbags (for makeup and gum only of course) and even a fancy Versace water bottle holder. There wasn't a chance we wouldn't hit the gay mag social pages with this getup!   "We are going to need a tonne of fake tan, and for me, water only the day before. Flat abs a must! You need to put me through your fitness paces, Christie!"
The sound of the front door opening had her tilting her head and scowling……We were in not much more than underwear, and she stood with her arms folded. (He had caught me off for a walk once in his boxer shorts, so was used to the fact that there was no shyness regarding exposure with me and my crew.)
I introduced her to him, and she looked him up and down in a territorial fashion, as if to say 'a rooster in the henhouse?? Whats *HE* doing here?!'

He was back from a few days on his lavish boat, and looking tanned and windswept. "Oh, sorry, don't mind me, I'm just returning to MY house…..pretend I'm not here"
I smiled apologetically, and he winked at me as if to say 'I understand. If you want to elaborate later, no prob'. It was such a comfort zone here; even his two cats brushed up against us as they strolled off to bask in the spot of sunlight on the bbq terrace. 'The feline palaco'…..i think he liked it that way!

Wherever I lay my……mask, that's my home…..

September 10th:

I awoke to the wafting smells of fresh croissants, bacon, egg and toast. And up it came on a gold tray no less, with freshly squeezed orange juice and a perfect cappuccino. I can't say im not loving the room service here! Cant say I haven't comfortably part moved in either.

(I may not be *on the books*, but the perks just keep increasing in volume and standard…along with my booty)

And as if to reinforce the above statement, you won't believe the events that followed to the brunch in bed….

Clapping his hands, he re-emerged from clearing up the kitchen with:
"Okay, quick shower and get ready, we're heading out shopping today princess"….well no further prompting required there, obvs. This is something I do really well, and I have the profound instinct that he will try to match me, as we know he loves a challenge!
Cue drive on into a prestigious…..**car yard**?! A suited man approached, obvs a buddy of his

and they shook hands and had a big hug.
Beware the car salesman I thought! (having gone out with one in my past. They are qualified to be politicians they are so adept at distorting the facts. Read lying bastards! And they're often irresistibly well groomed and sexy so you tend to be transfixed by that as they swindle you into a bargain you didn't need. In my case, my ex had me at hello with his Harley Davidson and cute butt in leather….much to the concern of my mother as we got matching leather getups and cruised around town together like something out of sons of anarchy. Windswept, interesting and caught up in the fantasy danger drama)….
But back to reality, next thing I know im modelling the drivers seat of a cute BMW Z3….white exterior; red interior. Very Duran Duran I thought….hmm I could rock this number with hair blowing and shades to mask. And oh how I adore the heated carseats! Utter bliss on the booty.

As I sat in it fantasising about being as savvy as Hann when it came to the wonders of wheels, I heard the lads talking faintly in the shadows. "Oh you've *got* to get it for her mate, look at her! Seriously…..and snap it up while you can! I have others keen to collect it this afternoon if you don't…..incidentally, she's got very nice legs!" The boy chuckled " oh mate you have no idea. She's got great everything!"

Enough said… im now nervous as hell about pursuing a license to drive the new toy gift. Barbie mobile is selected and now mine. Holy cow.

I pretty much know how to drive perfectly as my dad taught me ages ago, and the only reason I didn't get my license there and then was because I broke my elbow on a run (fence in the way!) - and had it set in plaster. The incentive to power on with it now has just landed but when will I find time to study the book and get lessons?!….dont panic. One milestone at a time on the barbie barometer…..

Date: not sure………..

F&*$!!!!!!!!!!!!!!!!!!!!!!!! Christie is temporarily rendered out of action. As a result of her own rash actions……now the tedious waiting game commences. Punishment of sorts, I guess.

You know those times when its just mass bombardment? One thing after another; tested beyond the parameters of patience?! Well this was a classic case here. I must surmise: when one is in a state of advanced sleep depravation, they are not sanely accountable for their actions.

I have seriously low tolerance bandwidth at present, obviously…(more depleted than usual)…
The evidence is all around me ~ the wind is blowing in off the street and the ocean through

the broken front window, where a trail of blood leads from there to the bathroom! I now have
to sit and wait for the repair guy to come and replace the window frame, and god knows how
long that will take. Backtracking……explanation to follow…..

Well 'tis rare, but horror episodes **do** occur in the seemingly sublime world of the scarlet
woman…   its not all prance, dance, cash and dash
ALL the time.

So, after a somewhat delayed getaway from tonight's lunatic client…….(bordering on
restraining-order tactics required) – short of me giving him a taste of honest Christie verbal, I
managed to pry myself away, and into the safety of my driver's vehicle at last. 'Directly to the
QC, James, pronto!' ~where I crashed in exhaustion in the back seat. (NB: the QC is of
course the 'queen's castle'…although I am far from queenly at this point. More like a
venomous black witch. And the castle is now in a state of semi-ruins)
Upon arrival here, I could not for the life of me find my house keys. Spent ages rummaging
through my bag; squinting in the dim 3.30am light until I gave up in defeated resignation, and
did what any crazy, over-tired wench would do…..i took off 'the shoe' (weaponly features on
MY slippers, as you know. Heels of destruction) – and HURLED it at the window in audio-
enhanced anger, so I could climb inside and into bed.
As soon as I was safely inside, (after carving up my limbs from the serrated glass edges), I
emptied my handbag on the bed and bingo – there they were. The keys were just hiding
below the mass of other paraphernalia I am compelled to lug around. Naturally! So after
attempting to clean up the blood bath from my wounds, and finally crawling under the
sheets, I am now freezing my tits off with the new ventilation of a smashed window pane,
and cant sleep a wink. Tears are a waste of energy, so ill exert frustrations out on page
instoad. Oh hello, here comes the rain.Of course!! What is this day about? Im done being
tortured. My penance for services rendered perhaps??...

Sept 14th.

Two days later……

The windows have been repaired back at the seaside castle. I did feel like a caged animal as
I remained dormant while waiting for security to be established once more
though……tradesman are hardly accountable for punctuality, and all time is money for
me….(I don't know how women handle the prison of 'housewifely duties' stationed to a
house with no freedom or interaction..it's a sentence to insanity surely…)

Anyway, speaking of restricted liberation…… I'm into a glass of Dom at "**the boys**" right
now, celebrating my ticket to enhanced freedom furthermore…I GOT MY LICENSE TODAY!!
Yes, belated of course, but done in the fashion I prefer. When right; and to the supreme
level…(he did after all buy me a *sports' car* to learn on ~ hello; the incentive is right there).
'twas however a tad IMPOSSIBLE to remain inconspicuous as one learns the road ropes in
such a showy beast. My nerves were somewhat shot before I even got to the test. It was like
'presenting to the stage'….as I cruised around hoping for a quiet neighbourhood to harness
my skills in private. Forever on show..

Anyway…..word travels like wildfire in this game. Im already being hounded by Jade….who
has had her car repossessed, and like myself, is an absolute basket case without the
freedom to move n groove.
A petite little Asian goddess this one. Actually, Eurasian looking. That finesse-filled blend of
exotic imagery. European and Asian parents no doubt. She is requested like there's no
tomorrow at the agency, and don't she know it! There is certainly a thing among men for
Asian chicks; its high up there on the fantasy wish list for most. Must be the underlying
assumption that she will be somewhat submissive…well, that was certainly not the case with
miss Jade. Their expectations are always JADEd on that score, as she becomes the
dominant whore. And she is 100% obsessed with nothing but the finest things in life. And
expects no less. The arrogance is bound to bite her in the arse eventually though. Always
does….

She came around yesterday to request 'borrowing' my fine wheels for a while, with promises
to 'fill the tank' and return in pristine condition and whatnot……thankfully the boy stepped in
and put his foot down (god, excuse all the rev-head terminology flying thick n fast here…sort
of the theme at hand though) – he gave her a "No sweetheart, you go ask YOUR boy for a
loan of *his* wheels; this is the baby I bought for Christie". (Nice! After all, I don't need the
angst in the 'office' – if he isn't top of her fave list now, its no biggie to me. She pretty much
hates everyone. White-powdered nose freak issues don't help. You know; paranoia…bouts
of rage and whatnot. Im sure she was way more placid before she became tainted with the
game appeal and its related poisons.)

Loving the lads' 'brotherly support'…..regardless, it is a tad puzzling….for one paid highly to
be an exceptional (but nevertheless, a SURE) thing….is it :

~something I should be concerned with, and take on as a challenge?……

OR

~a damn fine compliment that someone would pay such grandiose fees for my 'company
and conversation' alone…?!   I prefer the latter obviously, for the
relaxation and ego component to it, but a psychologist would beg to differ…

Back to the Jaded one…..Her latest wildboy beau is certainly a looker himself. A tall, super
fit Adonis type; somewhat Scandinavian 'golden boy' looking; ~ ex-personal trainer in fact -
(you get the picture). He has been working part-time as 'security' for the agency, and none of
the girls mind one iota…..he was missed last week though. Evidently in action. We all
thought he was working elsewhere for a spell, but it turns out he was in battle mode. Not
sure of the full story but one of his 'enemy territory' took to avenging him and there was
some violent sessions that ensued. He has been in hospital for 4 days now, with a patched
eye and fear of lost eyesight for good. Jade tells me he was blinded by a surprise run-in with
C4 explosives…..(this is the sort of gangsta shit we are talking about.) Not pretty. And now
pretty boy ain't so pretty either, no more.. I suspect that the car may have been needed as a
tool for revenge and quick getaway…. 'eye for an eye' so to speak.
Well, I certainly don't want *my* shiny new acquisition playing host to such games of gangsta

warfare!! I also wonder how long the magic will last for those two…Jade is not likely to suffer a physical scar in her lover. I'ts always either looks or cash. Bigtime on both. And you know the pretty ones…gobsmacking in the physical arena, but mummy is generally obliged to pay…zero cash nor financial nouce. So now he potentially has none of either…..i'm betting she will split the scene.

But as for my four-wheeled beauty: she is to remain safe and sound in the garage here for now, until we can give her the appropriate debut. Put the top down; out on the open road and let her go ballistic! Blonde hair flying; great music pumping; anticipation mounting… She yearns to be far from the city and the madding crowd…..i'm thinking the vineyards way out, for some wine tasting in the countryside?! Maybe this is even the foreplay **the boy** needs too…?

September 15ᵗʰ:

A slow start to the evening tonight. I had sushi in at the agency with Darren and the phone just didn't ring. For hours. Ho hum….So he sent all of the girls home and I was just about to leave when Brandy arrived. And the phone rang! (Damn! I was hoping to get an early night, bath and vid in)….in any case it was such a cruisy night after all that I now have all this energy to devote to you dear diary and have some fun with literary leisure time….luxury! Darren was so relieved that the entire night wasn't wasted that he gave the 'twice the fun' spiel and had us both out the door in 5 mins and on the way for showtime. Double trouble. Ivo novor partnered with her before so was thinking : who knows where the night will take us. (As it turned out, my summary alliteration is '***bandanas and bananas'*** *!*)
Brandy is an older woman but has maintained herself super well and hence gets the sell. (A lot of the men out there prefer older womon thooo dayo, go figure….she is one of the most popular girls on the books.) She's not as old as Melody though. She's the eldest by far. (And also requested often!) - but Brandy is definitely a bit of a mother figure amongst our clan. She is a personal trainer with her husband ~(who she tells me totally approves of the work that she does…and loves the extra cash she earns….sounds like a match made in hell to me! I doubt any man who allowed their wife to work in this caper could be decent and trustworthy. Especially at her age. Heaven forbid….in my view this is a short lived 'when you're young and wild and stupid' exploit - get in and out fast….stash the cash and dash!!) Nevertheless, I must admit she does look amaze for the extra history up her sleeve. The gym dedication has earnt her the prizeworthy super fit physique (muscles and curves. And no gravity curses). She is an inspiration for the future. And with a face reminiscent of Christie Brinkley she has the full package eye candy doll gig going on.

She grabbed my hand : "Come on Chris ill drive us; the wait for a taxi will be too long!…." Always sceptical of driving and parking when you're headed to the likes of the Grand Hyatt, as we were. [Hann was always an exception though; - valet parking of the Bentley, Ferrari or whatever wonder wheels were her current toy was easy and prestigious and added to the rep appeal. But this was a 'normal' car…(I have no idea what. Im not a motor fanatic. I leave that to Han!) so I felt a bit anxious.]

She took off her bandana and let her golden mane cascade down her shoulders. "Hubby
and I've been house-painting today. Im so absorbed in the home decorating antics I was
reluctant to work at all tonight". She would look good in overalls. And tight Tee. Buffed
shoulders and all. I think that might be more of an image for her to rock than anything X
rated….. She was
famous for not taking a bag with her to bookings so god knows what she did to
entertain….where was the lingerie and extra heels?? Cute dress and all. But you know…

Parking wasn't too tedious; we didn't have to walk far and she paid the meter up for 4 hours.
Which was a bit optimistic, but better to be safe than sorry.
We got to the room and the guy was so casual it felt like being invited to watch a footy match
on telly or something. "You girls want a beer?…or whats your poison?…" I actually laughed
at the suggestion of beer. Literally! I hadn't ever been offered anything but champagne or
wine ever. He was a young bloke though. Evidently successful and cashed up. Money lying
around; a Rolex on the table etc. It was a grand larger suite for one guy too - kitchenette,
fridge etc.
The tv was playing in the background and then he took a phonecall for some time! Brandy
whispered "Cool - that takes care of half an hour! We should have this guy in for a few hours
at least at this rate."
He was sitting on the couch and turned to say "help yourself to anything ladies. The fridge is
stocked. Sorry - have to take this call"   "Oh take your time sweetie - don't mind us!"
Brandy said sweetly. After over an hour of us chatting away amongst ourselves I was
thinking it was the easiest booking EVER…obvs the guy was an egomaniac and just the
'concept' of buying 2 of the most expensive girls in the city was a rush for him. Suited us just
fine! Wish there were more like him…cheers to the narcissistic male specimens!
Then Brandy said in a responsible tone "oh look we'll have to do *something* for the poor
guy.. A show at least!" She was about to burst into laughter. The music on the tv in the
background was pretty cool and we were both kind of grooving as we spoke. I took a half
bottle of champers out of the fridge and she chose an apple juice.
I got my bag of tricks out and said " I've brought matching black pvc numbers we could don?!
Im sure we could role-play these out."
She raised an eyebrow. "Why not!….makes a change from gym lycra after all! Let's see
when he gets off the line…we don't want to rush a thing…he's already up for a grand in ca$h
and all we've done is get to know each other and chat!"
Eventually he came over and apologised. Then the phone rang again! But this time he took
the call with his eyes glued on us both and just watched. Brandy propped herself up on the
bench and lingered her fingers over the fruit bowl. I went over to massage his shoulders
while she seductively took a banana from the bowl and slowly peeled it in front of him. You
get the picture! By this stage we were up to over 2 hours and I was almost elated how
relaxing it had all been. The Moet had soothed the mind somewhat too. He simply watched
us prance around the place dancing, giggling and flirting and so forth and then we thought
we should go change into the more visually appeasing numbers. He smiled approvingly and
nodded his head as we gestured towards the bathroom to change. And the guy carried on
with his business calls! We took AGES to get changed which didn't bother him at all. 3 hours
had swiftly passed and there was only one more left on the car meter!
As if fate had blessed us, when we emerged he whistled and said "Girls, I'm **so** sorry to be a

killjoy but I have a conference call with New York shortly so I'm going to have to cut this short"….(oh and we were having such fun!!) He got out his wallet and paid us up in cash for **5** hours. Then took four extra hundreds out for us both as well. Love this guy! "Maybe we should come visit you again at a not so busy time?! You've been such a gentleman!" He grinned. "I tell you what, as soon as I'm back in town, ill take you up on that!"..he pondered for a moment.."I tell you what: you've gone to so much trouble to look so lavish, why don't you do me a little show! I haven't got long, so as you leave, just crawl along the floor to the lifts like cats!" We both had to suppress laughter with serious focus….

The scene was reminiscent of "91/2 weeks", where Kim Basinger crawls along the floor towards him while he places down notes for her to collect….only we had wads of it up front, so no grovelling required! Funny - the guy did look a shade like Mickey Rourke too….(those were the gorgeous boy days before he got his face pummelled boxing)…

We slinked along the floor super slowly and as I pressed the elevator button, she purred like a cat sexily and waved a 'paw' in his direction. The guy was simply hiding behind the corner watching. And evidently impressed enough to call it 'a night'. Voyeurism at its best. Catwalk indeed.

Brandy and I laughed all the way to her car. I was going to get a taxi or call my driver but we were having so much fun I let her drive me home and change out of the catsuit here. Wait till Darren hears about this episode!

Im still laughing as I write all this. The job *can* be tedious sure, but nights like this make it all worthwhile. Now for the most fun bit of all: time to COUNT the cash!

date: Sept 16th.

Some ponderings; concerns…..a personal aside……

Hmm,…...always swore I wouldn't' get cosy with a client….but he is slowly coercing me into part residence. And spoils me rotten on the gastronomy front.

This is concerning '**the boy**'….(I don't know why I call him that - he's a decade older than me!)

But he's old school. Has style. And money- and knows how to use it. Bit of a Bond. Likes a blonde (!) Chivalry ain't dead with this one. Subconsciously I guess he could be serving as a 'safety net' from continuing with the traumas of the trade….but am I blocking my ears to whether he would CONTINUE to deliver all those things for me down the line?

He says he's okay with what I do…(for now)…but we've all heard that before, right? How long 'till he serves the suicide sentence for anyone who's worked-it-girl: HOUSEWIFE-ville…??
(of course one never realises that until its too late, and they write about it later, ahem)…

I know he likes collecting 'nice' things…watches, artwork, cars, suits, shoes….women? He doesn't want the usual from me so I'm not sure what the future would hold…would it be barren without intimacy? Would the female need for some sort of desire from partner strike *me* as the years went on if we ended up a couple? For **now** its glorious, - (as reinforced by last nights' booking….the guy just worked the entire time; mobile phone permanently affixed to ear, and was content just to have 'pretty background viewing')....it was bordering on euphorically easy! Just make sure you look good! I can do that....where do I sign up ?! Discipline is my middle name!   Bottom line: anyone who is prepared to pay $400+ hour for company alone has high standards! But....am I just a handbag? Does he see me as a human or an acquisition?

We have so much in common: travel, fine dining, the best haute couture....our standards are def not in the normal range. Am I his mutual muse?

He doesn't want kids, but he loves cats! When we spoke of our shared passion for the south of France, he professed: "Oh well will you just marry me **now**!" - (and I don't think he was joking.) He has already said "you are the one" on more than one occasion....is it all part of the role-play fantasy scene or is he for real? I really can't tell....he's got me stumped this guy. Fantasy and reality intertwine somewhat. What's real deal and whats make believe? In some ways, on observation, it appears by all accounts that he even convinces *himself* of things that he presents. Strange cat. I'm sort of intrigued....always attracted to the ones that confound....(is it because I like a mental challenge?)

But anyway...to resign and do that protocol-ridden walk down the aisle thing that the rest of humanity seems to somehow find dreamy... This situation says: "I hereby hand over the power to you....my maintained lifestyle and future are in your hands now"....

Plus another issue is that I've caught him out on a few little lies...nothing *serious*, but a lie is a lie; regardless of intensity. If you can lie small, you can tell a whopper! He's a salesman so it comes easy. Rolls off the tongue. But **my** he's convincing. He should be a politician! And he wears designer suits so well! Sigh... (Hopefully it is not a character trait to continue as I really like him! Must gently raise that topic soon. Honesty is absolutely crucial....)   Am I ignoring sound reasoning because I *want* to believe him? Or is it just his gifted, well honed sales verbal craft that is so convincing it seduces you?

Am I falling for him, despite the internal voice in my head and my heart? Decisions made when in the depths of desire are often much regretted later....as they say, love is blind! Am I scared? Terrified more like! I'm shaking to admit it though....I think he's won the bid to my heart. Applause... Where this will go? To be continued I guess....

One thing is for certain, any man I choose to abandon **this** standard of lifestyle and cashflow for, not to mention COMPLETE INDEPENDENCE will have to give absolute assurances that it will all continue in the future at the expected standard. It's all destined to doom otherwise. That's a no brainer, surely....if the said marriage were to end, one would have to be **set** *for life*, no question. If one is bought in this caper, one's future is assured, no?!! It is the silent contract code of engagement.

But should this be in a *written* contract format so there are no 'misunderstandings later'.......or a memory loss of how all this started...and should continue accordingly..........??

I feel I can trust him enough to know he realises all this. He's not a fool… and I'm strongly considering his 'offers'

i'll write that contract at some point for him to sign.
You know, keep it in a safe or something so I'm protected. Note to self…

For one doesn't sell ones' soul to be doomed with a life containing no fine future after all!!......

September 17th - 20th:

Awesome. A besotted client from weeks ago has paid Darren in advance for 4 days away interstate to accompany him on business travel! Job description is just gold: 'play convincing role of partner, to convince colleagues of '*stable, settled down*' status for better business deals'.

"Christie, Pierre said, quote: he finds you most *beguiling*. Said in a complimentary way obviously, not nefarious. I need you to play 'executive wife' and leave the saucy mistress games behind. Pack designer label power suits and I'll give you the wedding ring from my wife to wear the entire trip. But guard the gold or you will incur the wrath of the missus!"

Everyone knows that a married man is considered more bankable in the field and less likely to be devious with company budgets. Playboys are notorious expenses; both monetarily and productively.
This is the ideal role for me!! Good practice for the future someday too I guess…..my mind wanders to 'the boy' and how cosy we are becoming. He's starting to give hints that I have limited time in this caper if there is to be a more permanent union in the future. A **scarlet woman** does not have a 'marriage material' resume to flaunt!

But for now I'm in a fluster trying to pack the correct attire and race to a hair appointment for the classic (read conservative) stylish hairdo. And squeeze in nail infills if I can….they always fit me in without an appointment but fingers crossed its not busy like the other day.

The guy is French and we spoke for hours on the differences between countries. (Thankfully my experiences there with wealthy French lads had me well versed on all things pertaining to 'the good life'.) His melodious accent is utterly delightful - I can listen to him for hours…I've also noticed a pattern: French and European guys all seem to favour me more than local men. I am apparently more to their taste. Which is an obvious advantage when it comes to globetrotting.

This afternoons' flight is to Perth for 2 days, and then Melbourne for 2. Business class. Hotels yet to be revealed but knowing this guy they will be the best. He'll be busy during the days so plenty of time for me to pamper, shop, and generally relax before showtime at dinner. I love the fact that so much business is done over Michelin star cuisine! Mercifully, I can decipher menus in French and am quite wine savvy. Just quietly: here's hoping I can enchant him in a more *nefarious* fashion so that longer airmiles can be clocked abroad!

He's an utter workaholic and all over the world so this could be the start of adventures far and wide. And the more I do it, the more I realise I was BORN to travel! (Part of that is no doubt genetic; my viking father is an avid traveller and endlessly dreaming of new terrain to investigate. He always wanted to be a pilot and the closest he can get to the cockpit is being on a flight as often as possible!) Im a bit the same. I'm an archer after all. Saggitarians need to roam and conquer the universe! A lack of flight forecast at all times can be a health hazard of profound proportions……

Sept 21ˢᵗ…..

Okay, getting back to the topic of WHEELS that seems to be the continuing theme of the week….

'**Count** car-crazy' has enlisted my support in purchasing a new set of wheels! He booked me of course, so I'm paid to shop again……must be getting good at this (!) I knew it would be an experience to remember; ~he will go for something in the realms of top-notch for his top-gear fetishes no doubt. Meeting tomorrow to satisfy his need for speed..

Sept 22ⁿᵈ….

Holy cow…….i'm still trying to get my pulse rate back to a normal level. There is no other way to describe today's shopping spree other than a combination of exultation and sheer terror (!)

He is hilarious though……he had to get all the professional getup to go with the machine; the full lycra racing car suit etc. (This should have perhaps been a hintful indicator that he would not be shy.)

A shiny black Porsche …..and he even said "I will *start* with this one, and work my way up"……oh well *naturally,* because I guess a porshe is only for the common people really… I replied: "you fn cheapsgate! – why not go for the *lambourgini* if you mean business!"…..in hindsite, I shouldn't encourage him if I value my life!

I don't know what I was thinking but I was eager to take off in the new shiny showpiece, until
he started the engine roaring and took off. As then I endured 20 mins of perhaps the most
gut-wrenching fear of my life. I mean…the rare sobriety issue is always one with this boy to
begin with; but then his daredevil grin was in keeping with his fearless attitude and confident
control of the wheel. I quite literally screamed. No shit. It was a knee-jerk reaction. I was
paralysed…I may still need therapy.
Suffice to say that there was an audience apparent EVERYWHERE with the lunatic rally king
and the hysterical blonde; - he quite literally didn't care about the speed limit; the risks
involved or anything at all. My god…….kamikaze……..ive been in cars with mad guys before
and even been in an accident or two, but this was in another league of almost suicidal
seeking danger.   When I could actually talk, I had to
interrupt his fantasy momentarily with "sweetie, this is not the *autobarn*…..traffic lights are
there to be obeyed, or your precious license will be confiscated! Sorry to be a killjoy, but I
would like to see tomorrow…." He snickered, and then he did slow down…..partly because
we were luckily near the hotel, and partly because there were cops in sight. (usually I hate
them, but their appearance was a godsend today). Ooh but I live to tell the tale…..encore
miss moore…..

Well, it was fun n all, and when I've recovered I will shop with him again….but im thinking of
suggesting something in a more life-*enhancing* than potentially fatal category….like a spa
retreat overseas or something (!)

About to leave the suite for dinner. Gobsmacking view of the harbour……just sipping on
some Cristal before takeoff. Palette cleanser if you will. We don't have to book at the best
establishments with him these days. They have a radar for the platinum card, (despite the
fact he is often dressed down) and they manage to provide the best table every time……joy.
He's wearing his Armani tonight though!……oh how I love a man in a suit with money to
boot. Sigh…

After today's 'workload' I will be needing a stiff drink though……..

Sept 23rd:

Well dinner was a delight last night, and did serve to soften the blow of the day's *Porsche
panic.*

Had oysters; lobster and dessert….not to mention the finest wines and liquers. This fine
dining lifestyle requires a well-used gym membership, I tell you! Heading in today for a big
kick-butt sesh.

We discussed the option of going interstate for the races last night! He let me manage it all
booking-wise, so I love taking the 'driving seat' this time..plenty of time to plan too so
relishing in the delights that a card of substance (his) and computer access (his) has to

offer…..   Call it roleplay fun; ~ me donning the secretary
garb so to speak.
He is playing boss…

Hmm…..need to be in the know of what's the best of the best in Melbourne for ensuring
verbal banter with the aristocracy and that calibre of society right?! Professionalism calls on
homework to be done….I am studying the top-notch dining establishments over a coffee….

LATER - SAME DAY…..

Okay… secretarial duties accomplished. I cover many guises in this line of work!
Top hotel; top suite; first class travel etc. Tick ~
His insistence. Usual menu. How can one resist? Plus he has the etiquette and grace of a
count…the agency has been pre-informed and im booked up for 4 days. Gentleman.
(Another man would try to scam the system, but when cash is not an issue, I guess the
courtesy-rating booms louder.)

He knows ive had a few run-ins with Darren of late, so this should help to soften the blow in
that regard.
The early start will be a killer for me, but im sure the hotel spa will manage to balance the
score on that issue. No doubt a spot of shopping will serve as therapy too; all in a day's work
really.
The fashion there is more on par with Europe so best to take advantage. The couture and
accoutrement selection in this town is pretty drab, conservative and dull, so it will be a
refreshing change.
Tables at the best restaurants for 3 dinners; a lunch at the races in the VIP box and a
booked hair; nail and makeup artist to the room prior to the proceedings. Sorted. Love it.
Anticipation palpable.
Several bottles of Cristal and Krug to be provided in the suite, and Stolichnaya vodka on
demand for the boy. Priority check.
The 'work' part will be when contending with some of the social elite comes into
play…..totally dull……mask on for that show. Comes with the territory, alas. However, the
rewards outweigh the 'taxes' in my view, so well worthwhile.
It's a *whole two months* away (sigh), but time does fly when you are having fun, so keep the
good times & the gold cards rolling I say. May the days and nights beforehand fly swiftly…..

Sept 26th.

Missing in action again…..

A curiously intertwined state of affairs…and a smorgasbord of taste differences..

Had another booking with the boy on Friday too……(that kind of extended to the whole weekend thereafter…..shhhh!)   I hate to lie to the agency, but most of his payments have bounced; he's a bit of a 'cash juggler'……you know, shifts money around from account to account. Hey, I've encountered so many shady dudes in my time and he's not one of them, so I don't ask any questions about the apparent shuffling scenario….there's a lot going on but I have enough on my own agenda to bother worry about his.
It's his company and sense of *humour* that gets me every time. Fine food, wine, venues etc
     he loves to spoil and excite a girl, and all he wants in return is your genuine expression of joy and laughter. Who am I to complain?! It's a bit too cosy really…i tend to completely forget my role in the 'workplace' when im by his side. Anyway, enough JUSTIFYING my sneaky interludes with relationships of substance, I will recount (excuse the pun) how the time evolved:

Friday night **my count** had tried to call me in, but I was already committed to **the boy.** I felt a tad torn obviously…..i don't like to let my team down! He extended the invitation to my 'plus one' but that just felt a bit weird.
He'd booked 'dinner and show out'……but if **he** had reserved the venue, and it involved entertainment, you can pretty much bet it will be on the seedy side (!)
Bingo – his fave **strip club**…..which as it happens is a stone-throw's from the boy's. I mentioned it and the boy said ' Well I'm happy to accompany you no problem'……very chivalrous of him. (And frankly, just plain uncomfortable for me!) Especially considering he was paying me for the night out.
In any case, we went. They got on really well…which shocked the hell out of me. Both a tad possessive of me in their own subtle ways, but it didn't become nasty thank god.

I left for a loo stop at one point and bumped into Lila – of course! I was bound to know the star stripper from the former days of lingerie waitressing. Oh boy…
She is actually one I respect enormously – with her its more a form of ART than pornography.   I'm all for dining out in a fun environment; however having nudity in my face as I commence the main course is not my idea of haute cuisine (!) Even if it is by someone I know well, and she gives a most tasteful and professional rendition of her craft compared to others.   Each to their own obviously, but it wasn't for the boy either. He had his eyes averted the entire time. Cast down, every time a girl took the catwalk of derobe-ville. So cute! Very gentlemanly of him indeed. He didn't even flinch when count grabbed me to sit on his lap, and fed me baileys icecream for dessert (like a lap dance in reverse)
It's got me totally sideswiped. Chances are he's putting on a good show himself to win me over.   He's a salesman of an award-worthy stature so who knows how much is genuine…He is a **man** after all…but then, he's not a sex fiend in the slightest so…(??)
In any case, as if trying to express his version of 'entertainment' vs count-cutie's, he suggested a trip to the vineyards in the sportscar. How can I resist? I reciprocated the generosity and 'clocked out' after the Friday night, telling Darren I felt sick with cramps and headache. (forgive me)..so time from then on was 'donated in goodwill and genuine desire to be with him'.   I hope he saw it that way, I think so.

The next morn we packed up a 'hamper' of pate; cheese, croissants, French baguettes and real butter, chocolates etc (all the good 'contraband stuff' for a girl's working waist!) and headed off for 3 days of imbibing brilliance.

My god we are still here…its just too good. I don't want to leave! Today he booked a horse-drawn carriage to transport us to a private banquet table in a remote hinterland setting, with delectable cuisine and primo wines….sigh. It's picture-book perfect. Will the dream end? The princess doesn't wish to wake up……but alas she must if she doesn't want to reach bohemeth proportions!

Part 8A:

diva antics

Sept 28th…..

Oh my goodness…..the unthinkable…..
It was bound to happen in a city that I am nocturnally navigating however.
Sitting at dinner with one client, over candlelight no less, and a shadow appears at the table as another client approaches to greet you…..(with pained jealousy in his eyes). Oh my. It would be easy for one to develop a SERIOUS case of paranoia in this game. It sort of feels like sitting in a bubble;~a goldfish bowl…where you are being potentially spied on by others who have dabbled in your diary.
When you are playing the girlfriend role for so many, and you are GOOD at what you do, they fully believe that they are your one and only..they have actually created a monogamous fantasy from your convincing play. If this is what they want to believe.
At Chicane with…(client A), listening intently to a rendition of the day's business, and a rant about the political state of affairs, (over a dozen oysters and a crisp Riesling, while mind drifts to other weekly engagements to attend)…
~And: (client B) interrupts our rendezvous. And the worst part?....i had said I was *unavailable* tonight….sick I think it was…oh god..
Tried not to slink back into my chair; -put on the well crafted **mask** of *'sheer delight to see you – what a surprise!'* and stood to introduce the two (cringe)…
Welcome to the wonderful world of indigestion and potentially lost lovers…..

Sept 29th….

I nearly didn't go in tonight.
Just wanted to curl up in a ball in bed all day and eat chocolate, frankly.
Sweet solitude….oh how I crave thee….
But..we feline creatures of the dark have to roam and conquer regardless of weakness…..for it serves the financial demons well.

Sept 30th.

Good grief…sometimes its like being an extra on a segment for the jerry springer show. The mind boggles….
I've delved into a world where the reality is way more freaky than any fiction or sci-fi.
What's the deal with the *foot* fetish? (Not as extreme as the man in nappys, mind, but still worth a mention)…
Strange instructions from darling Darren today: 'get ye to a footspa, pronto'. I glanced at my feet and they looked fine to me! Well groomed and all. (Well, aside from a blister or 2 on the heels from accoutremental induced wear and tear. Sadly, the most glamorous pins are the most tortured ones.)
"A new client in the ring. He's already seen 3 other girls, but so far none have reached the 'tootsie triumph'…your turn girl" well what the…??
"We have a foot fetish guy. He's not interested in you; your skillset or anything else but the fabulous **feet**. They must be meticulous. Get a luxury pedicure; wear your best heels, and have a bag of changes. Forget the lingerie; I'm talking SHOES. Go walk all over him!"
Oh my….we had hit 'rock bottom' with this one! Was it an excuse (read REQUIREMENT)….to purchase a new set of my favourite accoutremental embelishments?? Me thinx so!…
Right then, surmising the situation, I realize that this calls for 'mission Imelda Marcos' channeling….and I happen to be just the girl for the challenge, as it happens.
It's not 'till tomorrow night so I might grab me those absolutely dynamite darlings I window spotted the other day. They just hollered 'these heels were made for walking'..!!
Let the foot foray begin.
Stay tuned…..ahem, footnotes coming (!) lol

Nov 1st….

OH THEY LIED, THEY LIED….they weren't meant for walking but FLAUNTING? Oh my, yes indeed! I think I may have turned *myself* on more than the client with these beauties!! (~he insisted on a mirror aside the feet for max perve spectrum. You know, like the kinky guys put mirrors on the walls and ceilings surrounding the master bed. Every angle covered…) so I got to see the full glory of my well spent purchase. Downside? I may need foot reconstruction if I walk any further than around a carpeted lounge room, so they are not in the 'practical' category. But as I said, beauty never is.
Sensationally perfect for pole-dancing and tricks, if you've got the core strength for it…(ie with feet in the air mostly, while upside down.)
No these are for 'carpeted stomping ground' only.
I went to the said suite of Mr (toe-tally smitten)….and upon opening the door, I can quite honestly say, that he never looked me in the eye once! No problem in the usual chest-height vision with this one, he was way way below the uniform male vision zone.
He pounced on them like a tiger and fondled them; kissed them and oozed lust over them (my feet that is). I can handle the kissing of every toe routine okay, but I must admit, I'm not the hugest fan of the toe *sucking* capers (how does he know for sure where they've been? It's a jungle out there..)

I actually insisted on a seductive bubble-bath soak while I sat on the edge of the bathtub; just to reaffirm the hygiene component. You know. Stay pro-fessional and all.

He was literally frothing at the mouth when I dried them off and blindfolded him while I 'redressed' them for his satisfaction. It evidently ignited sheer passion in the anticipation. And when I announced there was a whole bag of other 'dress-ups surprises'- so he should extend the booking fast, - he nearly came on the spot!

"Oh Christie, your CRYSTALS are driving me wild".....(I had put diamante embellishments on each toe, and the new shoes were adorned with Swarovski diamonds and crystals too, so it was a sparkly attention-grabbing spectacle. Sunglasses needed perhaps?!)

"Now come to papa....walk over to me, slowly....oh yeah, oh fuck.."

I promised to bring out the Versaces; Ferragamos; and Dolces tonight **if** he extended the booking…and if he was a good boy, next session would be an encore of any faves; ~plus Chanels; Guccis; Pradas; and so forth.

As a final note, I excited him further by entrusting him with my foot size, so that if he was out and fancied the urge to purchase some other fabulous numbers for his private display only, (as other men would kinky underwear; lingerie or dressup gear for instance) - I would comply with his wishes too…

A satisfactory night all told. A few blisters, but a delighted customer. After the encore, envisage this sight:

He crawls aside me all the way to the lift (oblivious to the witness of some other horrified hotel patrons) and gently caressed and kissed each foot 'adieus'….as a lover would kiss another in the usual fashion while the lift doors are closing.

I keep breaking out into laughter just recapping the evening to be honest.

Hell, who needs TV?!

Nov 2ⁿᵈ:

Call from Daz:

"Well……bingo. You have him toe-tally smitten. Well done tiger!

Polish the bag of tricks and keep them ready for next week. He's interstate on a business convention for the next 3 days, but as soon as he touches back down, he wants the catwalk company of yours truly again."

More tip toeing ahead. Notice is always good to prepare.

As one usually does for a fashion parade: water-based meals for the days prior to give the svelte physique, so too must one consider the prepping for the prancing. There is to be no barefoot grinding on gravel; no sweaty trainers or restrictive footware for the time-being. Ugly homipeds or slippers while behind closed doors….(nobody knows the efforts one goes to for client appeasement….at times it ain't pretty!)

I have the night off.

Forget the facemask, its ointment massaging the feet for me..

LATER THAT NIGHT....

Goodness....I got an invitation to spend the night with my admirer girlfriend, since she had a night off up her sleeve too!

We've both been run ragged of late; constantly on the books and Darren allowed us a night of grace. (I get the sneaky feeling it won't happen again though as we all know that time is money in this world....a luxury evening comes at the price of potentially thousands! For **all** concerned....) ~ must consider this the only 'holiday' in a while then....for unlike other professions, one simply can't relax with free time when so much money could be being made and in my case lovingly counted.
So when the husky voice over the line seductively suggested *'champagne; sushi and luxury chocolates in bed with facemask and girly videos'* it really did sound like an offer too good to refuse! To say that I am MYSTYfied would be a gross understatement.
She is indeed smitten and so lovey-dovey.....The evening felt like being with a 'boyfriend' of sorts. So seemingly natural and relaxing; entwined in bed together with Calvin Klein lingerie; facemask and flutes of bubbles and banter over a frothy movie.
Then the next morn we decided over coffee to go lingerie shopping since that's what one in this game considers the most fun and fruitful way to invest some pocket change. And it brings back rewards from admirers every time. And low and behold, Hann called asking where I was....(cue jealousy 2 ways ~ from both the phonecall and present company).
"Ive been waiting for you!! What are you doing out with plain bloody Jane? That one'll never make our grade girl! Stick with your own standard....Reputation. Hello! When will you be home? I want to make you dinner! I went shopping and filled the fridge"...
Oh dear....meanwhile Mysty sulked and pouted in my peripheral before literally dragging me into the bathroom to put on a spot of mascara blush and gloss to go to Oxford street. Her cheeks were already glowing mind. She's got that....sort of obsessed look in her eye. Oh dear. Seen that one before. And it never ends well! Will go with the flow for now though...maybe ill suggest a lunch out soon to gently explain that 'platonic princess' games are the go but romance ain't on the cards....?! (Note to self: consider overnight.) God knows when that opp will arise though since we never stop bookings and days are sacred for *pull-yourself-together-and-reboot* duties.

Anyway, we went to one of my fave stores that caters to gay guys; party girls and drag queens alike. It's dress up mania here and we are like kids in a candy store at such venues. It trumps 'normal clothes shopping' tenfold. Fantasy all the way....
We couldn't resist matching fairy outfits....micro mini baby pink and white flare skirt dresses like I used to wear for tap dancing and jazz ballet concerts (!) with wings, and a wand....hysterical.   Darren   will   adore   it   for   doubles   bookings!!
Then we cast our eyes on sparkly disco pants in pink and blue, with matching feather boah 'boudoir' style coats. That with a genie/madonna style hairpiece; a cute bustierre and platform pins and another theme team getup is decided.

Then I get another call from a girlfriend I knew in Tenerife days! (Min was a very close girlfriend I worked with in promo modelling and she hooked Danny and I up with contacts for work on the island. She was always a pro on the sales front. Gift of the gab that girl. And stunning to boot. A wild mane of thick chestnut hair framed the pinnacle of the 6 foot giraffe!) Well cue invitation to her *"birthday party which this year will be at Sleazeball. Please come! Bring Danny….and a girlfriend if you want!"*

Cue an urgent desire to immediately seek some fabulous costume to flaunt while in the perfect palace to purchase. Timing tick!

Well **country girl** then well and truly goes **goth**.

Misty?….more like Morticia!

Laughter intense. Sublime to the ridiculous reigns supreme here.. Couldn't resist also getting matching black PVC numbers (hers a catsuit, mine a mini dress ~ so tight you could asphyxiate in them) With spiky headgear like a tiara of thorns, and sky high heels of torture. Must do a photoshoot together in these for the agency for sure! The phone will be off the hook…we compell ourselves to perpetual client control…suckers for punishment! Masochistic behaviour…

My mind is whirling….Not sure what Danny will think of this getup…we split a while ago but he is still most protective. And its best to stay apart as we can't help reuniting if we see each other….its a magnetic mayhem zone! But…if I have a 'plus one' I could do the event without the danger of his sex appeal….maybe.

Looks like she will be my partner for the party night then. A team effort mandatory as they need to be worn together to stick to the theme:

<u>**Sadomasichist sista bondage twins!**</u>

Nov 3ʳᵈ…..

Wow; welcome to the wonderful world of WANKERS. (Yep…..figuratively *and* literally speaking).

I got a booking with an alpha male merchant banker/wanker tonight, who just wanted to watch himself reach ecstacy while directing me to perform visual encouragement…..that's a nice <u>way</u> of putting it. It reminded me of the scene in American psycho where Christian Bale observes himself fucking 2 women while running his hand lovingly through his hair; sucking in his cheeks narcissistic-style, and flexing his biceps.

He was playing 'director' and asking me to display my flexible Barbie skills; to full visual advantage. Meanwhile he wanked over me while watching himself in the mirror. The satisfied look of completion was directed lovingly to himself as he virtually blew a kiss to self, and dashed off to shower and spruce up for the next meeting.

An appeased customer……with himself evidently. I'm glad I assisted him to reach such a glorified state of self-satisfaction. (No problem whatsoever when you are paying me barrister-equivalent rates; no drama, my friend.) After all…..if he doesn't love himself with such intensity, nobody else will (!)

'Don't mind me' I said, showing myself out as he pouted in the bathroom mirror.

Nov 4th:

Its show time again…
I'm exhausted after a long set with Hannah over at a beachside mansion.
She roped me into a booking with a team of lads……it had a daunting flavour about it to begin, but as it turned out it was just another show-set. No action. Just the boys wanting some private entertainment.
No public; no press; no repercussions. Win-win.
Again, a select crowd of gents, the identity to which I cannot reveal for obvious reasons. (I won't even write it down for you dear diary…when it comes to having your privacy invaded on the written score, I've been there before!)
I'm sure that the lads that we speak of would never acquiesce to viewing girl-on-girl action to the ultimate degree when in the company of their girlfriends etc. it was a male-bonding ritual display that I've seen oh so many times before…
I'm sure everybody else has too ~ the combined forces of testosterone overdrive in one room. And how different one performs when 'let loose' from the usual relationship scenario, and encouraged by peers!
Hann and I are fine with what transpired; a natural show to be fair. We are totally at ease with each other and our bodies in their full glory, so once the 'stage nerves' dissipate, it's just a case of give us a great DJ and we are good to go.

We had selected matching lingerie sets and she had done her usual bathroom magic with makeup and hair for us both. Barbie twin entwining at its best. Sensual intimacy that is never reached with man and woman….they understood this as they looked on. You could see it in their eyes…they would never have this. They could only ever envy it from afar.
Encores; extended booking; a happy crowd and a code of silence forever more all round…done.

Nov 5th…

Got a booking for Jay and Maz tonight!! Paid to party again. Joy.

They invited me over early, to get ready and enjoy aperitifs with them before the soiree commenced. It was Maz' birthday and she looked stunning, as always. A vibrant red dress offset her exotic dark features and flowing jet mane perfectly, and with her marvelous physique and towering height in heels she was a showstopper.
It was to be a huge party of the most eclectic crowd I think I've ever seen! There was no classifying these two – they were evidently adored by *all* walks of life! And understandably so. They did the courtesy of booking me too, (although I would have happily gone after work for free, had it still been kicking on!)

To set the scene: a packed house and outdoor terrace area, with pool pretty saturated with energetic occupants too. Much singing, dancing, laughter, and affection all round – a joyous scene.

It had apparently been orchestrated by jay's brother Dean; a king of co-ordination and flair for detail. His demeanour was in keeping with his talents: flawless. I chatted with him briefly and in those few moments surmised that his sense of humour was addictive too– he had me in hysterics! His evident energy and enthusiasm was unrelenting; - (how he had this zest when in his tenth year of HIV + was a marvelous mystery….but then, much about this family was.)

Jay was perched on a table inside, surrounded by chatting guests all around him, displaying a mixed-bag fashion stirfry…

(there were tomboy dykes; pouting lippy fems; herbal hippys, corporate suits, Adonis queens, trannys, musos, nerds, arty folk, goths…you name it. They were there, in almost cliché visual form.)

So rare to **see** them all grouped together and blending seamlessly. Like magic. (I never have to that degree since, by the way)

No doubt Dean was part the puppeteer.

Amidst the garrulous chaos, Jay had his beloved guitar on his lap and started strumming…'driiiiiing…honey, I want to sing you a tune'…and off he went.

Naturally gifted. A true performer. And from the heart too. We all loved him.

A petite angel appeared on the stairway with her hands on her ears: their little daughter Chayley. Cute as a button. I went upstairs to give her the gift I had brought her (as I felt I already knew her after much time discussing her with her mother). It was a mermaid Barbie doll. She loved it, and held it in bed as she asked: 'Can you read to me?'. I happily obliged, and was there for some time until her eyelids started to droop and she was off to the la-la land we all love to reach…(but eludes us somewhat the older we get).

'Can you please tell mum and dad to keep the noise down a bit? And don't stay up too late. They will regret it tomorrow!'……..words of wisdom from the mature little missy. She reminded me of Saffron out of the comedy series 'Abfab'-parenting her partying diva mother.

Maz was meanwhile flitting around laughing loudly and chatting with guests, and when she saw me return to the scene, she called me over to introduce me to a group perched on the edge of the pool. 'We thought you had gone! Were you upstairs chatting to the 'boss'?!' Me: 'yes, she's out for the count, but has issued instructions for you to adhere to a curfew!'

Maz saluted to attention as she lit up another joint. It was soon afterwards that she took to the 'podium' for her party trick of dancing on tables, with hair flying wildly like whips.

One of the guys near the pool was a bit of a wanker, and evidently thought he stood a chance for gaining my attention/admiration. I gave him the look. The 'what part of fuck off don't you understand' glare, to which he responded by lifting me up and throwing me in the pool…shoes and all. Big mistake.

Huge.

Maz came flying over in a protective rage, and gave him a seriously uncensored verbal serving while rescuing me with my sodden hair and clothes. The locks *had* been done, and I was in one of my favourite dresses. Now I was very drowned-rat un~glam, and somewhat irate.

'Not with the Armani on you *arsehole*; what were you **thinking?'**….she slapped him on the head, and ushered me upstairs to a warm shower, towel, and change of clothes.

All I kept thinking was: I don't allow top-notch paying clients to do that and get away with it. They wouldn't dare! Hell, they're lucky to touch me at all half the time….What a rip-off !

Thank god Maz was like a viscous watchdog, and she would make him pay in humiliation at least! She took me by the hand downstairs with a 'touch her and you're dead' look.

She is quite a rare creature, the birthday girl. Like part deep ocean predator, and part free-spirited fairy…..both sides came out in equal proportion, yet unpredictably.

Black / White. Good witch / Bad witch. Manic magic in my view…

Nov 6th:

Had an eye-opening double session with mayhem mistress **Melody** tonight. Actually, it was quite an early start for nocturnal behaviour; 5pm – so lets call it late *afternoon*. I wouldn't call it 'delight'….more 'dreaded fright'…that this case was into. We ventured well into the hours of dense darkness though.

(After which I had_to_ bolt to meet Mysty to get ready for the party…god grant me energy…I fear some enhancements will be in order….who am I kidding; look at the company…we're going to Dannys' to collect him so….'battery' assured!)

Melody is older than me (nearly 15 years in fact) so she kind of suits her dominatrix role. It's quite amazing how constantly she is in demand; - there are obviously many men out there that need to be beaten into submission by an older woman. A scary number in fact……the 'don't love me, abuse me' following is immense….her disciples' demand and fan club was now reaching profound proportions.

I can kind of appreciate the *kicks* she gets as she *lays in the heel* as I myself am a self-confessed control freak! There is always a touch of masochism in perfection-seeking types.

I've been a bit hesitant to join her in forces though; I know she breaks many_of_ my rules….she goes places I fear to tread….takes it to another dimension entirely. Her domain is her chamber. Their desire is the dungeon. Enter at your own peril; with pain threshold at its peak.

In any case, she brandishes the whip with commanding authority, and I'm sort of the sultry 'assistant' to her beatings…..

She has a killer bod; the black PVC looks hot I must admit. Many dedicated hours of maintenance I'm sure….but then its obvious. She is disciplined beyond the call of justice…

Gotta love those scary boots and hell-bent heels too (and yep she knows how to use 'em) She'll walk all over you and kick you when you're down…

she'll pull your hair and yell commands at you. She'll scream abuse and call you disgusting names.
…She'll nearly choke you; push you and punish you with whips on raw skin; leaving souvenir scars of her wrath….
Force you to wear a 'gas mask' and cut off your oxygen till your face turns shades of blue….(must admit, the face suffocation bit is a bit high on my panic radar…even to witness).
She'll make you crawl along the floor 'till your knees bleed, and perform revolting acts…..like cleaning toilet bowls for instance. With a *toothbrush*.
(Oh despair….and the lack of hygiene!)
play us a *melody*, and scream evermore….

She is a great kisser however. Brilliant in fact. Most sensual and oozing sex appeal when in the throes of passion avec moi…such a contrast. Me the feminine feline and she the wild dark wicked one stalking me like a panther.
And he loved to see that between his intermittent sentences of grief and torment.
Pain and pleasure. He needed them both. To the extreme.
Welcome to the chamber of hell…..for one man's hell is another mans heaven….

In this vocation, the sexual deviants that hid behind <u>closed doors</u>, opened them to **us** only.
It was the recipe for success for this insatiable freak. And he's not alone.

There is someone just like him living right next door to you…….

Global touring

"The world is a **book,** and those who do not travel read only one page"…

St Augustine - Philosopher and Theologian

Ah travel travel travel…..how I love thee. How I NEED thee…Interstate good; overseas BETTER! im an archer. I live to roam and conquer…(for health!)
I am a free spirit and a global gladiator. And I respect, and gravitate towards the same in other folk.
Speaking of archer antics, I am reminded of a photo shoot weekend away I did for the agency. It's where I met my beautiful Bekky. She was shot with a bow and arrow in a dewy morning forest, donning nout but birthday suit and brilliant bod….Wild. Carefree. Urge to seek and destroy. Lust-worthy.
Oh reminiscing must cease..
Back to the here and now.

And since we are on the subject of gender jumping femme fatales…..

~ its obviously the week for black leather!
(Having just had a dose of the **melody** tunes, the black theme lives on further)

I had a scheduled photo shoot for a sports mag with Augustina, and she turns up on the bike in the standard uniform as such. Mind you, she does make it look HOT!! For a dyke she is definitely of the lippy fem variety; ~ she's obviously the 'wife' to her partner, but in the case of doubling with other women she takes on the dominant role.
Darren thinks we compliment each other: she olive skinned; dark hair; masculine and athletic, and moi more the blonde, sensual vixen type.
The article accompanying our images exposed sportsman celebrities as among the highest paying clients for the sex industry; since discretion is absolutely mandatory to keep reputations intact. No specific names were mentioned, but its not rocket science to assume the identites of such gents…(!)

We had to emulate various sports participation in the sexiest version possible.

(think :
~naked behind *cricket* pads and with face mask on as a *wicky*
~long sox and micro mini *football* shorts;
~getting ready to serve in *tennis* with streamlined tiny dress;
~skimpy lycra *swim*suits (say no more)
etc.
The exposure was a risk, so sunglasses were donned for identity protection.
Still a nerve racking one though. Darren tells me it will be issued on the flights next month, and my brother is scheduled to be on tour then. Even if he remains oblivious, a fellow team member is quite likely to recognize me or see an 'uncanny resemblance'. Hmm…
One has to take on the promotional aspects of the field for max appeal, (esp considering the high incentive rates of this shoot!) - but let's hope the risks bear no humiliating repercussions…

Nov 7ᵗʰ:

Sipping on some Chardonnay while I get ready for a lunch out with Miss Mysty….its time to have 'the talk' I feel….if I don't set her straight on the platonic parameters pronto, things could get a bit bunny boiler rather rapidly. (Fatal attraction….single white female….get the picture peeps?!)
I kind of need a drink to deal with potential fallout from the obsessed one I'm now burdened with. Dutch courage so to speak. I'm nervous….she is a force to be reckoned with! (Men can be possessive but I've found women to trump them all!)

She's virtually inferring that we are 'a couple/an item'….which has raised more than a few carefully plucked eyebrows.

Last night (6ᵗʰ) we went to Min's birthday bash at Sleazeball in the matching black PVC numbers we bought shopping together. A hit all round….but she wouldn't let me so much as chat with anyone without coming and protectively sidling up with arm around me etc. Mind you I think I classified her wrong….the innocent Mysty likes to be the bloke in the equation. Im usually bang on track with people assessments but last night has curbed my confidence somewhat!
She came across all innocent country girl initially and has displayed that soft side in doubles antics too, but the alter ego is another story. A fear inducing feline has emerged.

Interludes of brief rage became rapidly apparent, like a surge of testosterone needing to release. Eg: regarding the spiky tiara gear:
"**If** you poke me in the eye **one** more time with those thorns bitch…."
- Cue snarl and face of fury. Oh dear…the beast has surfaced. Im sure the class A capers had something to do with it….certain warts appear after snorting and cavorting. As we all know. I've personally seen it a million times before. Not for anyone with fragile personas. (We had stopped off at Danny's apartment (my old address) north of the city to purchase party sachets for birthday girl and ourselves. As you do. Always handy having a plethora of

druglord contacts.)
But even Danny was a bit taken aback by her masculine behaviour….evidently a bit nervous to say anything wrong or get too close to the fire. I could tell he was hoping for some one on one time alone with me as we usually would at these dance parties. Natural instinct. But she had well and truly prevented that event. The kissing display was where I realised I have to light the stop sign asap!
After the party, back at her place she confessed being sexually abused as a child by her uncle. Ah….bingo. Therein lies the germ….

I booked my fave table at a fine restaurant on the water northern beaches, away from the city crowds. I also know all the staff well. (Safety security net!)
A 'lovers tiff' (which is how she will view it) needs to be had in a private, safe haven, no….?!

November 8th:

Ah… thousand thread hotel sheets….how I adore thee!…
A much needed luxury slumber after flight here to Melbourne last night, for the races on the 10th. It was a mad panic pack as usual, but as the count said 'I don't know why you bother! I buy what I want and need when im there!' So I won't have any prob doing some retail therapy in addition if needs be. He always tosses me his platinum card to play with anyway.   At last! I can down tools (except makeup of course) till flight back on the morn of the 12th. (However, makeup artist and hair stylist are booked to come to room for the event so I have time to rest up and be in party form for then, and they can do the magic.) Time out for me….Heaven knows, dealing with equestrian egos and god complexes will be work enough at the racetrack!

And gosh don't I need this respite after the Mysty mayhem scene yesterday. Oh dear the tears…she didn't take the discussion content well. It was very much akin to 'telling someone the relationship is over'…which is <u>nuts</u> of course as there never was one! She is delusional. I had to call Darren afterwards and warn him she was fragile and may do

something radical….he is making sure she is kept busy and no time to reminisce and miss.
And im pretty sure the future forecast work schedule will not involve us united together for some time till she gets her emotions in check. Oh god the female blues! Men can be so much easier sometimes….

And count crazy one here is easy: case in point. He just wants to spend as much time blowing cash at the casino as possible!….not my joy obvs after being a pro on the *other* side of the table and knowing the stats on house vs patron…so I will accompany him at some stage for mere fun and cocktails but the rest of the time he can hurl chips to his hearts' content..(conversely I prefer to pile mine and cash them in)

So now as I sip on room service coffee and nibble on half a pastry (which is actually contraband I know)....I get some lovely **me** time to write, have a bubble bath in the palatial bathroom with Salvatore Ferragamo amenities, and then meet him at the happy hour downstairs before dinner. (Just quietly, I may well get 'happy' a few hours in advance though...the luxury private bar downstairs is beckoning me wildly!) Besides, we have 24 hour butler service here and the hugest dining table (think boardroom dimensions)...which I know he loves as a dramatic 'I am the king' performance of his manhood on....I can get a massage tomorrow if back issues arrive, but in any case all poss on this luxury doorstep. If we outstay our welcome at happy hour ? As we normally do when together..~we can always herald the chef delivery at will.

Besides, these bathrobes and slippers are almost catwalk worthy! Oh the texture. Princess muck indeed.

We're at the Crown Towers. The **Crystal villa** no less. (He asked me to book it on the name alone, crazy bugger. "I want Christie and Cristal at the Crystal." As you do! Never mind the fact that its one of the most expensive establishments stay in this city, but hey im not going to complain my friend. I am willing to count the virtues of keeping a smile plastered on, while collecting the cash to <u>count</u> anon....

Nov 11th:

The theme of yesterday was of course PRANCING....the horses pranced (not that I bothered to watch much); I pranced (princess fashion~ having prepared myself for no eye rolling or smart arse remarks); the count pranced *on tables* (!)...as is royalty's want; and the other occupants in the tent did their posh prance performance. (A voice inside me was saying 'someone tell them to get off their high-horse'... *Off* the field, not on it!) Yes, the show was very much IN the tent as opposed to outside it. And by <u>tent,</u> I mean the premium birdcage marquee. (So very UNcontrite in so many ways, but hey that's the wondrous world of the upper **crust** and their superior aired **toast** to society.) Jolly good and all that fluff. Toasting was of course top notch champagne with canapés and the like. As one does.

The thing that amuses me the most is that my count trumps them all on status, title and worth and yet he takes the piss with more sheer abandon and joy than anyone Ive seen! Beyond larrikin...there were more wide eyes and dropped jaws in one room than you can imagine. Hilarious! But no laughing....you know, smile lines and all. (And speaking of which, lets talk about the bottoxed faces, pumped lips, stretched jaws and lipo'd middles, to name but a few enhancements in the doll tent. This lot doesn't need to work on veneer and slave for it as some of us do. No, their prestige or pay packets award them the cheats' retreat; with paid 'artists' on hand frivolously to scrape, cut, inject, mould, tighten and melt any perceivable flaws at whim. Fake rocks in this domain.

As previously mentioned dear diary, my aversion to all things pertaining to the world of gambling is one resulting from experience in the croupier stakes... but the count can bet all he likes. Bless him. Its all loose change for him in any case. He won; he lost; he broke even….before heading off afterwards to the casino, having 'warmed up' with all the gamble ramble here. **Horses for courses** indeed. Lots of people big noting themselves (with big notes) and reacting blasé to any outcome. We eventually headed off arm in arm to the waiting limo and hightailed it to the blackjack table. The Crown Casino is better than Sydney in my view. I've stayed there with him also but from a familiarity perspective, being interstate is definitely preferable to not being recognised. He played while I perused the restaurant menu and booked the best window table for dinner.

Nightcaps at the bar downstairs before it closed, and then we cuddled up for a great sleep. (He normally cuddles up with a vodka bottle so this was a bit of a treat for him)
Theres nothing like a day in the high life to inspire some retail therapy, so we headed out to Bourke Street to get the excess baggage tally up to a better ratio. Oh how he loves to spoil! And how I let him….Designer sunnies, handbags, shoes, coats, (including for mum and my sis) and a vintage collectors' barbie doll! Hence, new Louis Vuitton suitcase required to transport said loot home. It's the most fun way *'to put on weight'!!*
So all told, well worth the trip away, I must say.

Horses….what horses?!

Nov 12th:

Now having established that I'm far from an equestrian, I'm not a 'boaty' person either per se….(despite the fact that I *play the role* when on **the boys'** boat….far be it for me to be ungracious on his aquatic 'workspace'
I say that because, frankly, boats when you **own** them are nothing but work, problems, huge expenses and nausea. I even got sunstroke helping him paint the deck with varnish….cue green gills and shaky chills…..)

No, The ONLY way to enjoy them is to hire or, better still, be invited on a super luxury yacht. (I know that for SURE, as I went to the boat show with the boy one day. The utter decadence on some decks is beyond imagination unless you've been on one first hand)
~it is indeed the playground to the rich and famous and up there with the private jet toys.

So the invitation tonight to play with playboys on a luxury liner with 4 other exquisites was met with no aggravation to say the least! Last minute panic call aside and all…
Darren called in a fluster : "Chrissie I need you there **now** to secure the booking ….the other girls will follow but I need you to man the ship up front. Its an easy one veneer-wise, just wear something glam and suggestive"
Glory be….cue mad panic rush to primp and princess up. Bit of a broad job description but nonetheless…
One of the gowns from a catwalk I did for a designer was the chosen wrapping. Mildly see-through in the sun; a sleek silk number with delicate floral design….stylish but

coyishly sexy with the very best lingerie beneath. (The sort of attire you thank yourself for working your butt off in the gym - literally)

Hair up in a chignon, Dolce and Gabbana shades, and Versace pink diamond toe candy....stiletto height, but since they are coming off on board anyway, they hang nicely off the handbag like rich bitch bling. Grab spare gloss, mobile, cash and dash..

Wow...yes a glass of Cristal for Christie on arrival will suffice adequately thank you very much!.....toss the nerves overboard with glee, and join the throng of suited adonises.

And much to my surprise, they were indeed a gentleman bunch. None of the usual competitive male ego shit. (Albeit a display of vying for my attention, and many complimenting which does a girl no harm)

Lots of merchant wankers (no surprises there) and captains of industry in general. And me the only female in sight...(until the other 3 were to arrive....asap I was hoping before the vessel moved on.)

Meanwhile, here in the hull, hors d'eurves were divine and the champagne kept flowing.....gotta love this hard days' yakka....oh the stress...to select the oyster or the sushi ...?! Never mind the mini quiches, truffle bites and caviar blinis....the waistline whittling will have to wait today!

Besides, im going back to 'the boys' after and the gym will be in order while he works tomorrow...(he's getting used to calling the exclusive Hyde park club when he can't reach me these days... "christie, line 2....you're being paged..." at least he knows where to find me. My trainer Kent is a nazi but he *does* get results. He'll be a famous football coach one day for sure...)

Admiration for the suits that abound I must admit. Def an array of Armani, Prada, Ferragamo, Ermenegildo Zegna and so forth.... A few double-cuffs and punchy cufflinks too ~ which is an etiquette bravo....like a men's catwalk strut...and a tad cute and humorous without the shiny shoes~pertaining to deck etiquette.

Oh and note the arm bling....I spy with my little eye (and counting) the Rolexes; Tag Heuers; Jaeger-LeCoultre; Breitling and so on.

Forget the salty sea aroma, I can quite literally smell money...and I DO love it! Sigh...how do the mainstream cope? Elite standards once tasted are indeed a permanent tattoo on the *want* radar, and will cause one to be forever seeking....

At long last the girls arrived; flustered but fancy.

The guys all gave visual approval thankfully; so the arduous 40 minute wait was worth it. Obviously there was no specific curfew. And price was not an issue; - (I'd already clocked up nearly 2 hours pay myself and every sip of glorious top-notch champagne was tough work indeed...)

As a team we didn't disappoint:

Jade was in a frothy little cocktail number in ... you guessed it :jade green;

Gina was in an aquatic blue skintight satin gown that, with fishtail base made her look very much the highseas mermaid;

and Principia was in a baby pink hourglass frock that showed her curves to their ultimate glory. Think Sofia Loren, with blonde hair.

With Jade a petite brunette Eurasian; Gina a ginger German glamazon; Principia a giraffe Italian with the cutest button nose and signature Italian platinum do; and little old me.....the combined group allure provided max appeal.

We were like a getup from Charlie's angels...(Darrens' angels do the boat biz)
But the question on everyone's lips no doubt was: did suspenders beneath the glamour hold the guns?! And who would be the first to draw?....watch out gentlemen.
We may appear innocent but don't try any chauvinistic male stunts!
As the night wore on, and we maintained our sense of style and dignity (and all couture strategically intact and left as per arrival, thank you very much)...the lads on the other hand progressed and partied themselves to a somewhat dishevelled state. Shirt buttons loosened; ties flung over shoulders; eyes glazed and stances swaying - (and not from the rock of the vessel.) They were the epitome of lads loving lager. Swill and swagger...

When we *finally* got back to shore at 11pm we alighted with much relief; reattached the heels, and wandered off into the dark waving before we turned into pumpkins.
Quite simply:

Paid to party

 Jade Kindly drove us all back to the city in the latest wheels of glory gift she was sporting. A tangerine Ferrari! Got to love her work....that was fast. Car-less Jade doesn't last. She's a determined one....I imagine she will take great risks in the future to get what she goddamn wants. A busted childhood will instill nerves of steel in one.
So yes.....another long and arduous job complete.
Marine mission accomplished.

Back at **'the boys'** now as I write; showered, changed into cosy lounge attire, and awaiting the late supper he is lovingly preparing. He really is getting rather serious. Its almost a 'good to be home' sensation now.....I feel like one of his lazy, pampered cats. He does seem to collect strays (!) Is it a 'rescue with kindness' role he likes to play out? I'm not allowed in the kitchen as he invents his masterpieces. The look of horror on my face as I witness the butter and cream that is liberally loaded is taboo in the domain of the chef.
And the wafting aromas abound: of clandestine comfort calories, and tonight? I don't give a hoot; I'm giving conscience the boot....The last one he whipped up was a chicken and mushroom in decadent cream sauce number, so goodness knows whats on the imbibing menu tonight. Every mouthful is marvellous, but you know what they say: a moment on the lips; a lifetime on the hips.
The things one does for love, sigh....sacrifices must be made.
the clothes may get tighter as the future looks brighter....

Nov 13th:

Oh my god...I cant believe JS was in town.

Holy cow; - he asked for Christie and Claudia but we were both booked so he had to go with the new Swedish girl Alesha.
She is still far from being polished; ~ body way not up to par, and very limited skillset other than an exotic accent really. Apparently Darren had no choice as the phone was off the hook all night and this was his only option!
He was most reluctant, but the feedback was brilliant; - he loved her! Go figure......being the comedy king of our times, maybe he just saw the humorous side of paying those fees for someone so new to the game. Who knows? Maybe it was the shy innocence and awkwardness that rocked his boat.
We shall never know.
He was only in overnight, so it was a case of: wrong place at the wrong time…
(Hann and I are devastated. He is a legend. My god, what a page for the 'resume' that would have been)
We were both with regulars. I hope they realize how privelidged they are to have kept us from the all-time booking high.
Sigh. Craving comic relief..

Date: ?Nov 14ᵗʰ I think

I'm not lazy, I'm just tired! I had a good heart to heart to Darren the other day about really wanting to 'just appease my regular partners'…I had a few to sustain me, and its comfortable and easy…
He understood but still tilted his head with "Christie you can't ignore the requests that come in either, as amongst them all might be *another* fine prince to add to your current crew! Plus, its professionalism love, you need to constantly 'get out there' so to speak. Milk it while you can."
Okay, granted. On all scores. But how many do I need? Funny, I changed my tune soon after that convo.

Darren is now talking relentlessly about sending girls over to Dubai to entertain the sheiks..that whole prospect is masked in mystery and danger I think…(Summary: it excites me senseless!)
Hard to ignore all the stories you hear though. You know: white, blonde-haired; blue-eyed women being sought; captured; tortured and abused. Even having limbs amputated so that they can't escape.
The risks are a tad high……a little daunting……stepping into unkown territory to the extreme.
 The middle east does have me totally intrigued however. Eyes are the mirror to the soul, but what else is behind the dark drapes of fabric? Cloaked in mystery..
Quite seductive really.
I guess the men are all intimately familiar with the *eyes* of their women…..not a lot else to visually set them apart.
Eye-catching gloves though. The women use their henna hand tattoos as the only form of permissible 'exposed jewellery' so to speak. If they disobey, they have been known to have acid thrown on their faces.

Ink and mascara…black ink and barbaric behavior.
Like all risky things though, the payout is immense. The rates these oil barons would be prepared to pay women are beyond the realms of the imagination. Kind of supersedes the risk component when you are seduced with ridiculous sums of flamboyant flying notes…
I'm staying tuned to the feedback further. Plus im DESPERATE to fly Emirates first class. Oh luxury joy..

Nov 15th:

Now when it comes to British nobility, one would choose a Duke to be shackled with, surely….the only prob of course being the press attention that comes with the grandiose aristocratic inheritance and entitlement.
Theres a price for all that jazz…
But on a slightly lesser rung, in the meantime, an earl would suffice.

So as I arrived at the Park Hyatt with the paper from Darren's notepad of notoriety, it was only after I got swarmed by a group of photographers for some crazy reason (obvs because I was mistaken for someone else)…that I noticed the name above
'room 707, 7pm'….

Lord Aaron…!

Considering the fuss in the foyer, I'm assuming that the title is indeed correct. Gosh….this is all a bit intriguing. I was thankful for the Chanel handbag shield I hid my face behind when surrounded by paps. It *could* have been exposure danger but a girls' accoutrement can indeed come in handy in other ways when needed…(incidentally handbags when loaded the way I fill mine are viable swinging weapons of attack if required! Amnesia not ruled out)

Knocking on the door, I wasn't the least surprised to be greeted by a young, handsome, clean cut gent with a wonderful aftershave scent. Exquisite suit and tailoring; shiny shoes, watch and cufflinks….tick tick tick. He had however loosened his tie and the top button of shirt undone, so im guessing the most tedious meetings of sir sexy's agenda for the day were done and dusted.
He grabbed my wrist for a dainty kiss, and stepped aside for me to enter his version of 'castle substitute' abroad. The most amazing suite; ~one of the best id cast eyes on to be fair. It was like a ballroom! Chandeliers; gold gild framed paintings; beautiful decor, and look at the size of the rosewood table alone..
So very, very English.
And tonight I felt very much the English rose…
Such a gentleman. In appearance and behaviour, and not the slightest arrogant. The proper English accent and etiquette is definitely a desirable trait to boot. All class. (Literally in his case!)
On my request, he gave me some family history while pouring my Krug champagne. All nobility aside however, (as im paid for discretion at all costs, and cannot divulge

anything further than that to y'all)~ he was the most delightful company and suggested some room service from the menu too, to avoid the animal in the zoo antics that would no doubt play out in the restaurant downstairs.
Oysters, beluga caviar, and lobster tails ensued - oh and some dainty golden Phoenix cupcakes to follow, that were indeed gold dusted : -im guessing the menu alone would render a 4 digit figure for our little evening supper 'snack'.
Got to love the life of the uber rich (and famous)…sigh.
We managed to talk and laugh freely for 4 hours (!) and not so much as a hint of any action otherwise. So regal. This was fairytale fodder.
Total respect from countess Christie.
With a stifled yawn at midnight, he excused himself to retire before the gym and meetings first thing in the morn. I left as respectable as I arrived, and very much satiated and elated. And yippee….
He has booked me again tomorrow for lunch! - so im assuming an all-nighter will result..
Wave the flag for Great Britain and its aristocracy elite.
Darren will be my biggest fan.

16th:
As per predicted above….divine

Nov 17th:

Back on stage. Costume change.
I was booked for a session with a high-flyer corporate king of sorts. Yes he is somewhat well known. Notorious in some circles….
Loves playing power monger evidently. (Doesn't he get enough at work?)

He's sitting at his computer tonight the entire time I am there; STILL WORKING ..occasionally glancing over his specs to inspect my *progress.*
He wanted me in French maids outfit. Yes, to **clean**, and talk French (when permitted to talk – and yes where possible…I am seriously limited at this point! Note to self: up the French repertoire somewhat, in your spare time…or better still, negotiate an all expenses trip to Paris or something. Now we're talking!)
Outfit is so hot. He approved of my work attire: White stay-ups and white apron over black micro mini skirt; tiny little 'uniform' top with push up bra overflowing; black patent stilettos and pink feather duster to hand. Cliché as crazy, but timelessly requested.

His instructions of "dust this; polish that…is my maiden succumbing to LAZINESS??" etc were pushing the boundaries. (I'm a control freak. Always struggle with authority in case you hadn't surmised this by now).
A bit of spanking here and there and flirty suggestive looks. But that's it! No other interaction as such – on a more intimate level at least.
But he's like others I have encountered…the **_business_** gives him the ultimate orgasm essentially. Just a bit of 'sideline encouragement' is all that is desired. Married to and

forever more in love with the work.....so, I guess, he just wanted to have some 'company while working'....another visual freak.

My god, he would be wanting to pay me those rates to do **housework** though.....in a sexy manner no less.....in ankle-crippling shoes......
PLUS, having to obey instructions without backchat...oh boy ive earnt the fees for this role! My patience has been beyond tested.
How do normal women cope? My back is aching from all the bending over... And they do it daily FOR FREE.
Its torture unthinkable...!

Ps: Darren just called me to say he wants me to accompany him to France on business! I do love travel, but I hate housework.
It's a conundrum of profound proportions!....but, I guess, huge money talks and foreign language bullshit walks (in hell-bent heels), so...
what work woes we must endure to profit and gain...sigh.

its day 3 and **count**ing......
yes, he's got me in for the long-haul again! I had mentioned feeling weary from all the 'external requests from fetish fellas' and he got protective and all. Bless him! Booked me with Darren for Friday night, then just called him back and said literally 'she's mine and on the clock from now until I say stop'
Cue elated text messages from the agency of bravo; encore; milk-it baby etc.
The cashflow of this boy just has me in raptures I have to say...it really is 'easy come easy go'...hereditary hedonism.
We started at the best suite in town. LOVE this hotel....he knows it!
The bathtub even has heels on.... Quite respectful of the finer sex that respects hygiene and high fashion!
Crystal champagne and lines of top-shelf Charlie to kick off proceedings. Followed by a good bout of carnal chaos on the immense banquet table as he swiped everything off it to the floor and devoured me on it. The chandelier above his head kept clinking and threatening to come unhinged.
Then it was off to the 'change-room' for me to play diva and dance on window sills. As I was prepping the canvas in the huge ornate mirror, he got onto some bizarre lines of conversation......as you tend to under the influence of the double C. I mean I know we have it locationally to thank for the white wonder but, how we got onto the topic of 'kidneys being stolen from people while asleep under the stars in **brazil**' though, I will NEVER know!
He has an uncle there, who had fed him abundant stories of horror, evidently. He tuts while shaking his head 'He tell me it is the most dangerous game, the organ theft racquet'..well hello. No shit, Sherlock.
I was starting to feel kind of crampy in the guts with all this talk (!) and was relieved when Celia arrived for a double act for a few hours. He wanted to watch me with a brunette. It was our first interlude together, and her first ever girl-on-girl booking.

(Darren always puts them with me on their debut, as they return to him keen for the next one, whereas they had started somewhat terrified.
I know that feeling intimately, so im sympathetic to their initial stage-fright.)
It went well, and we kind of put on a good show I felt. I was in white lingerie and she in matching black. Count belted out some awesome tunes while we seductively danced in the huge window frame overlooking the vast harbour behind us.
The count was happy looking on from his 'throne' with a bottle of stoli vodka and a contented smile on his face. Good to be the king again.

That was 2 days ago.....
We are now INTERSTATE in Melbourne yet <u>again</u>.....

Gosh im loving the luxury of spontaneity that wealth affords you with my cuddly Count!
We decided to take advantage of the prior 'reci-tour' we endured for the races. Plus I'd done pretty thorough research when I played secretary booking our Melbourne Cup escapade, so we are kind of veteran players in this address.

However, I am continuing *'work studying'* the top-notch dining establishments over a coffee...one must remain perfectionistic in play at this league, so I've acquired a bit of a skill in keeping up to speed on what's on trend in cuisine magic...for the world of the imbibing and gourmandising elite is ever evolving and a full time job! Not one to be scoffed at.   Don't say I don't take pride in my job....
... (and let's be honest, just quietly, its a bit of a hoboneby for me to be fair)
The caveat is of course is that the chosen accommodation of splendour and secrecy MUST include an ample sized gym. And be utilised daily, at that!
Always a tarif for luxuries in life, but it is what it is. And knowing that the rewards ever await is the biggest motivator of all.

One of the other aspects of travel I have found - (even just baby trips on the doorstep of your own country) is that it whets the appetite for grander escapades abroad.
The happy hour Krug session here last night in the bar had us embroiled in a solemn meeting on **where** exactly we should focus our horizons on next. Serious work indeed!
The list of options is vast and naturally favouring <u>one</u> incorporates several others *also* by default in the more exciting vicinities on the *other* side of the globe....
for there is no point going *that far* without truly absorbing a plethora of nations to explore and compare.
So inevitably, a discussion on a '5 day sojourn to Europe' evolves into a
'3 month strategically researched, planned and booked' affair....as it does!
If he's game, im in!
To be discussed further regarding specific dates etc;- its a tricky enterprise with current 'agency commitments' to adhere to...must be most savvy and strategic.
Lucky I'm good at tap dancing....

Christie had a 3 week hiatus from her diary debriefs, as time did not permit her 'this' luxury....a new 'project' she undertook required constant travel, packing and maintaining the veneer (in between the bouts of shopping; pampering; dining; and......occasional 'action'; _though, concerted efforts at avoiding this were generally successful₁).

One of the clients she saw after her 'chat' with David (to continue allowing new ones into the field), turned into a rapidly regular one. So Darren had proved right.

The guy became smitten overnight. She was his complete fantasy.

So much so that he based his entire business itinerary around her; and ensuring she was included in the long haul aspects as well as the local and interstate ones.

Again it should be reiterated on her behalf that it is amazing how forgiving one becomes for human flaws when they are masked behind immense generosity, wealth and prestige.

Men who aspire to 'gain access' to women of this caliber understand the unspoken mathematics. It was simple:

physical condition vs financial outlay

...if the latter bears more weight, then he stands half a chance.

Luckily, to maintain such levels of financial victory, they are work Trojans, so the time expected to be administering seduction was minimal at most₁....somewhat of a saving grace.

" Oh.....Christie honey you've had to see Mr dark horse....i don't envy you₁₁" Hann said with a smirk.

"I hear he's not the most handsome lad on the block....but he certainly has the 5_star hotel circuit as his home_base. If you can handle it, lap it up, I say...."

They both understood that this game required one to turn a blind eye to many unfavourable human aspects: old age; physical flaws of all kinds ~ (like excess body hair for instance); kinky quirks that evolve into repulsion, etc.

 Mason fell into the 'forgiven' category....due to the seemingly hefty budget that knew no bounds.

His lifestyle incorporated first and business class travel globally; dining out at any venue he chose; 5_star hotels; and limited time off in his hectic business agenda; ie a workaholic while his arm candy shopped and pampered.

On paper, for Christie, that was her dream Prince to the rescue!!

(One can then turn a blind eye to the vulgarities of the male body. For instance: the excess body hair that is such a turn off when the back particularly resembles Chewbacca, as this poor sods' did). In any case she had totally mastered the art of avoiding physical contact by psychologically massaging the ego and providing verbal company on an intellectual scale instead. It was a skill that baffled the men but had them addicted to her presence and attention in other ways so their original intentions were turned upside down.

In Mason's case, he found her company much more entertaining and refreshing compared to the majority of time he spent dealing in business with boring–as–batshit types. The contrast was huge, so she had that aspect in her favour.

There's no denying: she had made enormous personal sacrifices to acquire access to life in this standard. And she wanted it to remain that way; whatever the cost. If it meant contending with characters that were far from tantalizing and playing the game then so be it.

Hanna squinted her eyes as if studying her soul:

"There's something you aren't telling me......so come on. Deets on the enticements if you will! Come on, Darren already told me about your 4 days away in Hong Kong on the budget of a celebrity...."

Christie sensed a tad of jealousy in her ally so she downplayed the facts somewhat. Difficult to do so under the circumstances...

" Well,..... the packing is pissing me off, let me tell you! Kind of over the living out of the Louis Vuitton for the moment. We just got back last night from 3 days away, and we are off to L.A tomorrow morning. Early. I insisted on the Grand Hyatt like before, but he hasn't reported back yet. His secretary is booking it all as we speak apparently." Sigh...

Hanna noticed her fondling the chunky diamond encrusted chain on her neck , so she quickly continued:

"Then, he has already organized tickets to San Fran in a fortnight, and speaks of NYC to follow. First class Singapore Airlines. I need an extra suitcase for that one.... and 2 days worth of packing and primping prep for sure. So..."

She had stopped listening and her eyes had lit up:

"Oh, and you'll be overweight with that beauty – are you kidding me? It must be 8 kilos at least! Did he rob a Tiffany's store or is he really that shop–savvy??!!"

Han's in–built radar system was always on auto pilot.

She was a scanner for shoes, watches and jewellery of notable standard, and she could sum up a person's credit rating in seconds.

"Oh bravo girlfriend, he's a catch then!"

Oh how she could change her tune about a person in a flash when blinded by the bling! Her tolerance for vulgarity was second to none when it came to money.

She clapped in approval " I tell you what, I'll bring over some magazine and catalogue tear-outs of the 'shopping list' you need before you go, so you don't waste time with pesky salesfolk and can cut to the diamond chase......you have weeks to work the registers. Im talking bags, shoes, jewellery, and classic timeless fashion....." She felt she had a valid a role in the missions ahead, so Christie granted her that and just shook her head with a grin while resuming her unpacking.

December 8th:

Hello my dear friend....my darling diary I have neglected for so long. Oh how I have missed thee!

We're at a stopover in Singapore currently, before heading over to the states.

He's off at meetings all day (yippee!) and im left in this uber luxury suite with a side of smoked salmon on a platter to dip into as I please....trying to keep the svelte physique while galavanting around the globe is a full time job. This was the healthiest option and im not complaining. The fridge is also filled with champagne obvs, so im one happy traveller. As long as I hit the gym hard daily I stand half a chance when the American menu takes terrifying hold of my waistline…

Anyhoo, having done my sweat sesh and written postcards to the folks, im now going to take a bubble bath by candlelight and relax before primping for dinner. We're of to Spago's so I need to look my best.

Having recovered from last nights' glorious dinner and ahem cocktails (classified as the 'work' bit for *me)*....he had a request which I permitted. Reluctantly. Sigh. Room service cocktails...(I don't even like cocktails! Im a champagne girl)...so yes I made sacrifices didn't I........he wanted to *pour his over me*, which is filth and disgust in my books obvs. But it gave me the excuse for a bit of an animated tantrum and rushing retreat to the bathroom for an hour to wash off the sticky goo....by which time he was sound asleep snoring, so it turned out to be a blessing in disguise! Bravo. Job done. A naughty confession: this morning I told him more happened than it did, and got annoyed that he couldn't remember...(praising the 2nd bottle of wine we had at dinner that rendered him somewhat giddy and brain dead!) oh you wicked bitch....

December 10th:

Love this time of year! Beautiful gold trees adorn the drive to, and in Changi airport. Festive music abounds everywhere; even the airport lounges. First class travel is def the way to go. Service of high standard starts from the moment you are checked in.

God help me if I ever have to downgrade to cattle class. I wont be equipped to cope! Id rather not fly…

About to board the plane for **San Diego,** where he has some meetings before San Fran and L.A. Not the world's most exciting locales, but im sure ill work it. As usual I've packed like Liz Taylor, so thankfully this standard of travel allows a *freight* amount!….I noticed other travellers looking on in shock at the 9 suitcases and bags. I reiterate: I would never cope with economy. Not a way to slink gracefully around the globe. How do the poor folk pack? 20 kilos? My handbag alone weighs more, surely.

Last nights' dinner was sublime. I had chicken with truffle mash and the most divine sauce. I literally cried it was that good! The wine was off the radar. Like euphorically lush. Satiated and excited for further excursions to come, I went home (to hotel suite) to finish some last min packing while Mason made some final calls. I was clad in my leopard print mini dress and matching lingerie and at one point Mason stopped; hand resting under his chin as he gazed on with adoration. After a while he confessed: "You know, from the day I met you I've thought of you as a wondrous GAZELLE….~its a thin, graceful antelope."   Wtf…?! Well now, thats the first time I've ever been described like THAT! Maybe he means im a wild woman, always running away from any form of attack?!…which be true..

Anyway, I shall report more later after the next 20 odd hours. Looking forward to champagne, some girly flicks and some beauty sleep….in a proper bed up in the pointy end of the plane! Only place to be…..

December 12th:

Okay, at LAST….showered, unpacked and ready to partay. I feel SO refreshed after the long flight go figure. The full horizontal bed I guess. I got 7 hours sleep straight. Pink satin eye mask in place and earplugs in and I was in the clouds…..

We are at the Hotel Del Coronado which looks like a movie setting from the 50's and 60's….and indeed, I chose it on the fact that it was where Marilyn Monroe filmed 'Some like it hot'! That was 1958.
The poolside setting in particular is SO that era. The umbrellas above the deckchairs looked authentically 'as was' back in the day, and I could just imagine women in the high waisted bikinis and caps doing graceful dives into the crystal blue shimmering pool. Attendants walked around in full white suit and ties with trays of cocktails, cigars and burgers/fries. It seems to have modelled itself entirely on retro memorabilia. Love it. The weather on arrival was glorious too, the huge swaying palm trees creating a private canopy from paps and public.
I stood there in hotel robe and slippers and mentally planned to get here with a good mag, sunnies and the drinks menu to hand. I need this! A tan will be welcome thankyou. Casper be gone.

We are dining downstairs and of course there really is no option but for me to wear my white dress and heels and platinum bob wig a-la-marilyn! A dalmation style black and white fur coat (as there is a slight breeze in the air); diamond jewellery and a dainty white clutch for spare lippy and camera and im good to go. Breathy laughter, lots of photos, a 3 course cuisine sesh and a sashay back to the suite before midnight to truly wrap myself in luxury hotel sheets before tomorrows facial and massage commitment. Life's tough, but bring it on…

Dec 15ᵗʰ:

NOTE TO SELF: NEVER, EVER EVER ORDER FRESH OYSTERS BEFORE A FLIGHT…..

Even the first class toilet room (which was virtually all mine with the meagre amount of travellers in this section) was not the antidote to extreme, violent offerings from both ends.
Ahhhhhh…..hell. Food poisoning! What a loss of some fab first class flying miles. Missing in torturous action….

Oh well at least its **L.A** in the forecast, as the loss of 4 kilos will be welcome there for sure so there's a positive. A bit like Miami I guess: you can never be too rich or TOO SKINNY! My stomach muscles are in agony….oh bring on the 6-pack.
In any case, the curves are easy to remould when in constant travel decadence, lets be fair. And lets call it a detox as the healthy vegan fare in the self-conscious capital will be abundant and easily accessible for a while. And there is so much indulgence and glamour ahead to be had, and shopping, hello….so a few days respite now will equip me for (better) action.
But for now, time out…..im on slow mo survival mode….

Part 9

The **Madonna** Syndrome.

Reinvention.

" Dad, you don't understand. It's cathartic. You can't get to one place, without going through another place"........

Christie was told she looked like Madonna constantly. She had a similar face, fit body shape; and she certainly had the costume change/ Diva antics down pat.
In her youth, Madonna was her idol.

She was a mirror........

She respected her strength of character. Madonna admits her flaws, and states her aim:
"I know I'm not the best singer or dancer; what I'm interested in is pushing buttons; being provocative and political"
They were both huge advocates of supreme body conditioning. This was partly accredited to the worship of intense fitness training, and ashtanga style yoga. It was all about discipline. Madonna has never denied working damn hard for the assets she possesses. After all, it is only awarded to those willing to sacrifice the time, energy and devotion to body crafting.

Despite her wildness, Madonna Louise Ciccone cultivated a maternal love for her enterage of dancers. Christie similarly had a caring, mothering way with her clients; male friends; brothers and lovers. Madonna gained creative inspiration from the pain and loss in her life. It was Christie's motivation for everything too. All the choices she had made in her life.
For it is unfortunate but true: from great sorrow and loneliness, true brilliance is born.

The wording from her song: family:

"When I get lonely and I need to be.....love for who I am, not what they want to see.......brothers and sisters, they've always been there for me........we have a connection, home is where the heart should be. Keep it together in the family; they remind you of your history..brothers and sisters, they hold the key to your heart and your soul don't forget that your family is gold.......the family that plays together stays together.....keep keep it together keep keep it together forever and ever......when I look back on all the misery, and all the heartbreak that they brought to me....i wouldn't change it for another chance, 'coz blood is thicker than any other circumstance"...

Christie couldn't have worded it better herself. When her close-knit family unit was decimated, her life directions took a dramatic turn too.

In the movie : "In bed with Madonna" (the title alone of which was bound to spark criticism!), her eunterage of dancers were interviewed and quoted as saying:

"Madonna does feel more in control when she doesn't extend her personal emotion, her love, her exposure to sensitivity too much.

She has many barriers….

There's not that many people she can trust and get close to, because everyone wants something from her.

*She's fishing for affection. I suppose she's testing for who can be REAL with her; be **honest.** I don't think that anyone is honest with her…….*

She has trouble connecting or giving herself away to one person. I feel that she's very in the moment. She's impatient, 'cause she wants things done. She has a lot to do….busy life……definitely in a race against time. Everything is subject to her approval. She's a perfectionist.

There's a whole world of things going on around her all the time, and sometimes she gets caught up in it.

Its very tense. She's unhappy a lot of the time.
I just feel like she's a little girl lost in a storm sometimes…"

Her never-say-die attitude was synonomous . She was determined and disciplined to the point of torture. They were both fearless…except where failure was concerned. They repelled all forms of *external* discipline however; (read authority) ~ theirs was a personally driven one.

When Madonna was warned not to 'crutch touch' or she would be arrested, she failed to comply. (It was in reference to the simulated orgasm antics during 'like a virgin' in her tour shows; - she stood her ground and refused to compromise her artistic integrity.)
A rebel by nature, she adhered to her convictions; impervious to public criticism. Religiously speaking, **she was labeled a whore**……

the tirade that followed much of her choreographed expression was akin to public stoning. But as we all know, negative press is in fact, ironically, perhaps the hugest victory…

In her 'truth or dare' capers, in another time, she would have been burnt at the stake. But hey – it's Madonna! Fame permits unlimited revulsion..

She will remain, with Jackson, one of the best performers of all times. There is no denying though: those with superior talent possess a common characteristic: they are *control freaks* to a frightening degree. The perfected magic by design cannot occur otherwise.

The roleplay Madonna performs and the costumes she dons are an expression of her devised artistry. However she seems to be most adept at reading an audience; knowing what the world embraces to see…she gives them what they want and hence her continued survival. The public and press are cruel – yes they have criticized her many times but the fact remains: she is still alive and going strong, so the formula works.

For the high class hooker, the room becomes a private stage. She accepts the requests, and plays out the fantasy accordingly. She becomes the object of the desired dream, and reality becomes a world outside the confines of the walls she is within. For at the end of the day, *escapism* is the theme and driving force of most people's search for peace…she gives them want they want and need, and they reward her equally. A symbiotic relationship of sorts.

For both, it required quintessential versatility expertise. The eclectic menu for both was most extensive; the array of **'masks'** to be worn extraordinary.

Christie had 'catered to' doctors, surgeons, lawyers, merchant bankers, celebrities, sportsmen, drug barons, ex-convicts, and even tradesmen.
Women, men, gay, bisexual, straight, confused..

Dressed up, dressed down, fed fetishes, choreographed shows…
and played a multitude of partner roles, the likes of which your imagination couldn't even fathom.

Fact is most definitely stranger than fiction in this case!

Yes, the menu of roles she had provided was indeed vast; part of the lure of this game was the psychology involved. She was ever amazed at the bizarre and shocking desires of people in high-powered positions; does it go with the territory? Power = perversion?? The upper echelon were apparently so far removed from the socially acceptable norm, it was almost frightening! Sometimes, the mere intrigue for Christie was indeed more rewarding than the fees.

One of the prices to pay for this standard of existence however, was the difficulty in **natural,** *normal family propogation.* Madonna was ever aware of her biological clock ticking; and though she represented the world of extreme fantasy, the whole 'immaculate conception of the madonna' idea was one that required a painful reality check.
And so she pursued an appropriate 'sperm donor' to amend the situation, and complete the

missing aspects of her life…..(the fact that the man in question was the spitting image of Jesus was in no way by conscious design of course). What do **you** think…..?
It's Madonna, hello!
Its difficult not to assume therefore, that like all other aspects of her life, this component had been carefully monitored with precision also. (I again refer to the emphasis on the operative word 'natural' above)…And so her choreography evolved, and offspring followed on to carry the legacy.
Christie similarly anguished over the fact that she may remain childless and regretful later in her life. But it wasn't something she wished to concern herself with now. The question was…..*when* ??
Unquestionably the biggest price to pay of all….future loneliness and sadness was her destined tarif.

So Madonna had been crucified on several occasions for her risqué attitude, & the lewd content of her performances. Particularly with regards to the prudish catholic faith. Even the bold cross bling she fashioned as ironic accoutrement was almost a slap in the face to the Italian faith, considering the daring content and lyrics of her craft. The press had a field day…..she was a genius (!)
There is always a price for standing your ground on certain beliefs. Mankind loves to attack anyone who dares to tread outside the square……but in Madonna's case of course it was a double edged sword. For she benefited further from the uproar and abuse. It was irony at its best. For her notoriety was also her salvation.

And to describe a high class escort in one simple adjective: **is not '*MATERIAL* GIRL' the ultimate summary?!**

Christie was similarly aware that she was compelled to face criticism for her words; revelations and opinions. Her loss of loved ones was to be imminent, as she sold her soul. Again.
But she certainly wasn't afraid of being alone now. She had suffered it for longer than she remembered. And she welcomed it now. Like her closest comrade after his periods of incarceration; once you have faced death and your demons head-on, there is no fear left. All that remains is pure love…

I am blessed.

So in this line of work, Christie played the roles of an insurmountable catalogue of characters. Versatility was key. After all, the ultimate ticket to success (and continued survival) is **Reinvention**.

Chapter 7:
Part 10:

As good as it gets....

"I want a guy..........that loves me for who I am; - aside from all that.......lovin' stuff."   Marilyn Monroe.

The peak. The Summit.

She had no doubt reached top of her game. In the game.
'On' the game........
Of, at, in, on,~ (this game has been referred to in all these formats) -
WHATEVER, she had blitzed it.

So naturally, she had to wonder: was this as good as it gets??

A few press articles had been written about her and her selective peers. Their contents spoke volumes, and did the description more justice than can be explained here, so it is perhaps best to quote from them:

*newspaper article extracts:

Under the title: **Will that be on Amex, Sir??**

And following the caption:
*In a twist to Linda Evangelista's quote: Christie won't get **into** bed for less than $10,000.....*

" Working for ......, they are part of an elite group of 10 women billed as the most expensive in town. Their clients are wealthy, mainly married, businessmen.
They have each been selected for their perfect bodies, polite manners and communication skills.   To assist their conversation skills, they are required to read the 'financial review' every day, so as to discuss business and political issues with their clients. They're taught how to order wine, appreciate fine cuisine, and dress like a Chanel model. They must have their hair done twice a week and their nails done once a week. They are expected to wear the most expensive labels. And they must be experts in the bedroom. They earn upwards of $400- an hour, and average a yearly salary to rival the

Prime Minister's. For them, having sex with a stranger is a business.

The agency is a franchise inspired by the former madam to the stars, (He*$* Fl%*^s)

Some of the girls have been asked to get nose jobs, breast enlargements, liposuction and facelifts. With more than a thousand girls having applied and only 10 on the books, its one of the most coveted agencies in ………Augustina is planning on taking out a loan to have her boobs done later this year. She speaks about it as if it were as simple as changing her hair colour.

Armed with a bag filled with lingerie, fantasy outfits and sex toys, the girls' evening follows a predictable path. The aim is to receive the maximum reward for the least possible outlay.

The agency also caters to a lot of married couples in threesome situations. But the girls are also employed to simply keep men company. Famous men at that. "We do a lot of sporting celebrities and a few Hollywood big names" says Madame………, the figurehead of ………, an agency she runs with her husband. Nothing more is revealed – absolute confidentiality is their trademark.

"Its all an act" says Christie, one of the highest paid girls in the agency. Christie is revered by newcomers: "any advice Christie gives, I listen to".

A leggy blonde with large breasts and high cheekbones, Christie stands out from the crowd. She's polished – the ultimate professional. As she strides into Madame……'s home, a large pink mansion on the side of a hill, the first thing that hits you is her height. Towering more than 1.8 m in stilettos, yet weighing around the 60 kilo mark, she is in the supermodel mould. But with her face done up and hair dyed a white blonde, she comes across as more Barbie doll than sex symbol.

You get the feeling she's a woman terribly lonely in a world full of men and French champagne.   But without doubt she's making money. She has earned up to $10,000 a day, and has a yearly income in the hundreds of thousands. She presents another twist to Linda Evangelista's notorious: " I don't get out of bed for less than $10,000." Christie wont get **into bed** for less than the same amount.

She has mastered the art of extending each booking. Rather than demand oysters room service, she'll suggest dining out. "I always order three courses- it takes longer".

Able to muse on current affairs, suggest things to do in ……..(most of her clients are from interstate or overseas), and make gaga eyes over the dessert wine, Christie will rarely have a booking for less than six hours. "And you'd be amazed how rarely I have sex. Most of the men just want companionship- and maybe a bit of oral".

But she's had her fair share of kinky requests. "One guy asked for two girls to come to his room dressed in skintight black PVC. He then asked us to go into the hotel corridor and slink along the floor like cats" The bloke simply hid behind a pillar and watched. Others have asked for the 'secretary'. After noting all the details of their fantasy woman, Christie falls into character from the minute she enters the room. "But most men just want you to turn up nicely dressed with some fancy lingerie"

When she says nicely dressed, she means more than a sun frock. "I have to wear designer labels. Ive had men ask to check the label in my suit jacket. They argue that their wives and mistresses wear Chanel, and they don't want to lower their standards…..this is a high maintenance job."

Not only do the girls have to pay for their own clothes, beauticians, accountants,

hairdressers and transport, they also give 50% of their earnings to the agency.
Madame......admits: " Ive had girls begging to be on the books, but I need to have the pick of the bunch. My clients are very particular. The preferred girl is a size six with large breasts and blonde hair....We've even sent girls to work for certain middle eastern Sheiks. They become their full-time girlfriend for a year, and get paid".

Unlike the stereotype, Christie wasn't forced into prostitution because of economic necessity. Nor was she addicted to drugs. "I saw it as a way to make a lot of money" she says. "I plan to retire in the next few years. By which stage I will have a nice investment portfolio"
For others in the agency, says Madame......, the dream of Prince Charming is still alive and well, and does happen. "Last year I had an American billionaire contact me – he wanted me to find him a wife! And one of the girls from the agency married her client, and by all accounts is living a fairytale existence".

*sports magazine article:

Turning Pro

Cashed up stars hooked on ......Girls.

" Christie is laying back on a lounge, one elbow propped up on a lip-shaped satin cushion at ......headquarters in the inner city. She is dripping gold, and suave as you like in a black Armani power suit. Christie's Mercedes is parked downstairs from the office, which has a quality address at the big end of town. Sharing the same floor of this office building are a law firm and an investment advisor. Matter-of –factly, she says: "on the average week, I make about $12,000".
The lawyers and investment advisor should be so lucky. They do the same to THEIR clients as Christie does to hers, and don't get a quarter of that! The wages of sin are all around the ......office walls – erotic paintings that would do justice to a prominent, if slightly off-centre art gallery.

...from all accounts, she is a beautiful woman, worth every cent of her $500-an-hour as a call girl for (the country)'s most exclusive escort agency, ...

So what's a detailed description of an escort agency and the lifestyle of its high-priced hookers doing in the pages of Sports ......, you might ask? Simple really. These days when a girl says "hey big spender", chances are most of the biggest spenders are sports stars.

Today, there are probably 300 home-grown sportsmen whose annual income tops $500,000. In many cases these are blokes too young for a wife and family to spend it on, and too well known to walk into a nightclub and just pick up a girl.

All the champ wants is a few drinks and sex with the best sort going. Says a prominent rugby league player: "Of course I use the escort girls. Why would I bother putting up with all the idiots in nightclubs, when I can make a phone call, charge it to my credit card and spend a few hours with a woman who looks like Elle Macpherson?"

….late at night, when it's a big lonely place, and there's ample left on the credit card, the temptation for a costly shag is an overpowering one.

"They've bought flash houses, the best cars, all the latest electronic toys…why not the best women?"

(Darren) is a fast-talking big bear of a man. He hates the word "prostitute" and won't hear of his girls being called "sex workers" either. Says (Darren): "that's construction site mentality. Our girls are not hookers in our minds. They are entertainers…executives getting ahead. Sex is just a by-product".

The girls are contracted and provided with a personal accountant, physician, fitness trainer, make-up artist and hair stylist. Their clothes are Versace or Armani. The motor cars equally European and expensive.

…..there are four stages of eroticism. The first is called "voyeurism"………strips seductively.

The …………coach rarely gets past stage three, Christie says. He likes the Japanese geisha treatment.

…She doesn't understand a thing about (the sport), but as long as she looks interested, that seems to satisfy him. She hugs him and kisses him. It's the intimacy that our girls provide that makes them so expensive. She just kind of turns a deaf ear, compliments him on his body and that perks him up. Most clients of that age want to talk about what they did, and have someone nice to listen to them.

Bondage is a surprisingly common thing with sports people. They have high-powered lives. They don't want to dominate you, they do quite enough of that on the sports field. They want someone else to be in control.

….the two biggest spenders are a Sheffield Shield cricketer and an Olympic swimmer.

………Track and field athletes have a reputation for lustiness. Five – yes FIVE………ladies were called to the exclusive ………hotel suite of a world-class sprinter……………in town to attend a corporate launch……………Says Madam…………: "He spent almost $20,000. I don't know how much he got for coming out here, but I'm delighted to say he turned over a fair bit of it with us"

Equally undemanding is the racing car driver………and the jockey: "He's a bit of a fantasy man. Every time, it's a different fantasy. Not whips and spurs and stuff. I suppose he gets enough of that on the track. Its just that he likes me in a nurse's outfit one day, sometimes a maid's outfit the next.
It's like being an actress. You have to become the woman they want."

"I know my jockey will call in. he spends big on me - $1,000 or more every time. He told me he and his fellow jockeys were negotiating for a bigger riding fee. I told him I should do the same"

Accompanying the magazine spread were seductive shots of Christie in lingerie and skimpy outfits, donning props of champagne and fur coats etc; and in various bisexual poses with the other model, Sage, in sports attire. Sage permitted her face to be shown, but Christie insisted that her eyes were to be covered (masked) for identity protection purposes. They were all touching on risqué; yet tasteful.
The main photo, was her sitting on a bench in a designer bikini, with head tossed back, suggestively pouring condensed milk into her mouth from a can…

There were doubtlessly others, but these were the articles Christie and co were privy to.

Once, a girlfriend called up Christie and warned her about a major article that had just gone to press. She noticed the mag on her international flight for modelling parades abroad and instantly thought of Christie's brotherhood. Both keen sportsmen in their own right…….her fear of detection was omnipresent.

Truth be known, her most influential and heartfelt associations were crafted through this trade. Lifetime associations had been forged. *Not* in real life.
It was one of the risk-rewards. And she had earnt them.

Of course it can be seen how it became addictive to all concerned: the agency owners, the clients and the girls themselves. The extroidinary funds involved, and the power rush of it all was an aphrodisiac in itself!

The men received the best of both world's: both dual and private.
Being able to 'have your cake and eat it too' – but **only when** the craving arose was hassle-free, convenient, and preferable to a *full-time* relationship scenario. [The cake was also 'gourmet-plus' standard ~ fit for the table of a king (!) Ego-boosting for sure.]
Time **alone** is absolutely crucial for personal satisfaction, too.
To have both was nirvana!

(It should also be added that he was more than happy to surrender the fees that qualified him as safe from the stalking, insecure, possessive attacks he had no doubt experienced in prior relationships. No bunny boilers here…)

Some of the girls were also control freak perfectionists, so naturally assuming that role was one they relished; ~ relinquishing the customer of their usual duties. Having someone else 'take the control seat for a change' was akin to intoxicating for the man, too.

There was often a 'father figure' connection between client and escort. Probably due to the massive age-gaps that were often apparent, and their desire to 'spoil a younger princess'; (who in addition, made them look good of course). Made them feel manly, I guess. Which is really what every man needs: Verification of their testosterone quota; even if it is only an illusion (!)
Besides which, it is rare for a successful, cashed-up man to even LOOK at a woman his own age.
Let's face facts…
(for example, Christie had even been taken to international zoos and funparks for god's sake!)

For the **object** of their desire, it is suitable also. The girls are not engaged in these capers to score a lad with the arse hanging out of his pants! This calabre of women doesn't tolerate cheapsgate fools, regardless of genetic blessings.

A match made in heaven then?
In many cases, yes!

but in life, there is always a price to pay…

Christie also figured: it was a question of how much you valued your worth, essentially.   So in distinct irony; to turn the pre-conceived notion of escort work on the head, a simple question:

Would you rather:
a.) Go out and 'pick up' some normal 'bloke' for free, in some scungy joint, club or bar, as the majority do,

OR

b.) Have an arranged dinner date at a top restaurant with someone eligible & having a degree of prestige…who is also willing to pay handsomely.

????

The category of partner, and outcome of each is *vastly* different, and the ironic undertones are astronomical.

Lets consider…

* *THE MEN:*

The former (a) is essentially 'in for the kill', and there will be no enticements forthcoming. It is a natural (and mutual) assumption that the pursuit of (a) climax is imminent. The very nature of their meeting ground establishes this. (No assurances that he won't be a psychopath or murderer either!)
And certainly no pre-approval for safety, nor bodyguard antics on hand.

The latter (b) knows instinctively the nature of the woman; nothing but the best will do. He has had to pass the 'gatekeeper' to get to her. She emulates power, seduction, style and quality; an aphrodisiac in itself. He is most accommodating generally. After all……she gives what she gets !

* *THE WOMEN:*

The former (a) will no doubt wake *somewhere* disheveled; feeling like crap and ashamed. They have scant, if any knowledge about the partner they had apparently snared, and attempt to exit the scene unnoticed. (Cue panda-eyed walk of shame…..the paranoia will set in the next day too, as they scan the internet wildly for any devastating visual reminders that may have resulted during her inebriated bed-binge.)

The latter (b) will have discussed much over their dinner 'date' and feel well acquainted. They have usually *slept* in a luxury hotel suite; wake feeling refreshed and pampered, and leave with promises of other rendezvous; gifts and bundles of cash.

Humiliation.
Exultation.….

Kind of makes the non-escorts appear like the cheap and trashy ones, no?!

Chapter 7
Part 11:

Always a price to pay.

Stigmata.........

Quantum physics teaches that the pendulum forever swings: the positive; the negative. Happiness; distress. Health; disease. Up, down. You can never rest on your laurels when at a high or positive point, as the low plummet is hence inevitably just around the corner. And vice versa. The ebb and flow ......forever changing, ever evolving. Never constant.

Like all aspects of life.

Including the joys of it unfortunately. Maybe this is where the term was coined: Nothing in life is free. There is always a price to pay. No joy without hardship. Nor bliss without disappointment. Abundance without massive loss.

For all the noteworthy aspects of this game, the downside was perhaps moreso severe. It appears by all accounts that this was a glamorous period for Christie, and that she had reached a status akin to fame. However, the fallout was bound to be devastating. To make real money in life, the price is high. For what is left when you've sold your soul?

Firstly, and most obviously, the stigma attached is reprehensible.
Not only is it a social taboo, but anyone engaged in it is compelled to a life of deception. Not dishonesty as such, but their **entire** existence is masked in dark secrecy. Never to be spoken about. It was a heavy mask to bear. Once the mask is taken off, it keeps coming back to haunt the mind too......you imagine you can still see it in the mirror. And all the characteristics that go with it. It was like a grey-matter tattoo.

The mental library has so much backup data; the virus is forever virulent.

Article quotes to support this:

The girls aren't proud of what they do. They are petrified their
families will find out.

"ive been having nightmares" says one. "Everyone thinks I'm still an
au pair. I purposely keep a high chair at home and always have toys
floating around the car - they're my props. It's hard always living
a lie."

Relationships are forever strained; a boyfriend is rare. "It's so
hard to trust them. And its hard to be natural with them because
when you're with them it feels like work."

"there are times when I've got to close my eyes because it's so
unbearable. I wouldn't want my sister to have to go through that."

Hannah and Christie's friendship eventually dwindled. Only a bomb could have blown them
apart. The fallout of their chapter in escort-ville was irrepairable. This was a devastating
price to pay for their actions.
Darren's failing marriage was to be a result of his 'kid in a candy store' attitude to his girls.
The inevitable eventually occurred, and he embarked on a dangerous liason affair with one
of the escorts. She played him like a puppet, and had him eating candy out of her palm. The
disease spread like wildfire however, on *so* many levels. Countless days/nights were spent
with Christie consoling his teary, heartbroken wife and daughters, or, conversely covering his
tracks. She became a spy and a tool. It was like being the victim of divorce, and she was the
apparent weapon of attack.
The final collapse occurred when Darren urged Christie to coordinate **a threesome with him
and his wife** in an effort to rebuild the marital destruction. That was Christies' cue to do her
bows and exit the stage. There was no other choice for her. Way too heavy. It would have
been like *incest.*
There was no fee that would possibly compensate for the mental toxicity resulting from that.

Hannah's father eventually discovered the truth behind his daughter's nocturnal enterprise.
He was of course mortified. Although a robust and fit man, it was shortly after that he
suffered his first heart-attack, and multiple triple-bypass surgeries ensued. Hannah suffered
a near nervous breakdown, and was compelled to endure a lifelong suffering of extreme guilt
and causation of his fragile condition.

Similarly, Christie was paranoid evermore. Her exposure to high profile sportsmen and the
like made exposure within her *family unit* (particularly her brothers) on the highly likely list
too. Family was her *backbone*. She felt like she was to be a victim of vertebral damage.

In addition to these personal heartaches, it was difficult turning a blind eye to all the infidelity
that goes on. It sort of instills a lifelong trust issue. Coupled with that is the guilt of being the
source (or obsession) behind these betrayals.

(The fact is that if it wasn't one woman for the client, it would surely be another. This doesn't make the burden any easier to bear, or process though).
Christie was perceived a social butterfly, but was actually a loner. She had crafted, and worn the party hat well and it proved magnetic. But it was exhausting. And she earnt every cent that she ear   nt.

For she couldn't just 'go through the motions' like other girls. No, it took virtual metamorphism on her part. (If witnessed, NIDA would have no doubt opened its' doors to her)

Many of the girls that left the industry to attempt a 'normal' existence failed dismally. To go from such extreme payments to a regular salary was, quite frankly, a mindfuck!

Christie for one, found that she was forever 'looking over her shoulder'. The distinction between fantasy role-play and reality can become blurred and misconstrued for some. When would some deranged obsessor come up and tap her on the shoulder, or hold a gun against her head for 'unrequited love' ? It ignited additional paranoia.

To maintain a sense of **self** was the biggest challenge. It took a tremendously strong mind, and was draining. To live dual lives in an almost 'scitzofrenic'-like existence is *many*
masks and mirrors   .
Clear vision and optical illusion must be finely tuned and managed.
The problem was, her expertise became her curse…..Christie was so adept at morphing into whatever the client desired……so convincing at the craft, that she no longer knew who she really was herself.

She had heard, seen, and pretty much done it all. No innocence left. Some of the disturbing requests would never leave her either. She was having to play nurse (often literally) to a severe sickness in the system. Was the world really so full of such broken characters? Does a child *deprived = depraved* in adulthood, she wondered?

Yes, there was a great opportunity to meet a potential partner; the princess fairytale rang true for a few…but the downside was that the clients wore masks too! Where does make believe end, and reality exist? How could any candidate she encountered in *this* world ever be trusted in the *real* world? The cliché: *a leopard never changes its spots* is engrained in us all….the awareness of 'prior convictions' in *both* parties is a tainting aspect for any future, trusting relationship.

Sadly, after this chapter, try as they might, the girls involved were generally somewhat damaged from ever performing the role of a perfect wife.
Saucy mistress, and almost everything else, yes. But perfect wife material, no.

They were furthermore compelled to feeling that any form of social should be a paid event/action…..it was like brainwashing. There was a circumstantial association thing going on. Social/intimacy = count the cash.
(A bit like when smokers have a coffee or a drink….they feel naked/vulnerable without the other part of the equation. And lets face it: money IS power. I don't care what anyone says)

It rendered them tainted socially essentially ~ it was all work!! Destined to be loners/recluses/hermits??   For you can never erase the history you carry in your head and your heart from such exposure. You have sold your soul…..and you may have been paid handsomely for it, but nevertheless. There it is.

It is like living a lie…. Denying the truth only leads to psychological, (and eventual physical) torment and destruction. A plastic surgeon would understand this; allow me to use an analogy here:
~the resculpting; shifting; enhancing; adding; eliminating processes that occur only act as a mask for the decay that lay beneath.   The rest of the world, and the mirror now see a perfect picture, but both parties know the underlying truth…..it may lay dormant in the grey matter, but the original data information remains. And never leaves.

You can run, but you can never really hide…

The 'we met on a blind date' explanation (read fabrication….) begins to rapidly wear thin…..lies have a snowballing effect. Beware the massive boulder of deception that amasses from such verbal violation.

On a personal level for Christie: in jealous rages, her lavish jewellery gifts from *other* clients had been seized and thrown away by one, in a petty act of demonstrative possession. During arguments in that ensuing relationship, Christie had received satanic spats of "once a whore, always a whore".
There were always apologies of course, but the scars remained.
In retrospect, she really should have responded (equally sardonically) in parrot fashion, with just an extra word added to his <u>little</u> 'mantra'; and applicable to <u>him:</u>
"*once a whore* **SHOPPER**, *always a whore shopper*"…
Physical attacks (or *stigmata*) would actually be more preferable to this degree of psychological torment.
Besides which, his dalliances with working girls would render him forever more on the suspect list.

The stigma never leaves. For either parties concerned.
Following a tirade as such, she would have been inclined, and indeed *entitled* to end the relationship, or have an affair…(even professional folk had verified this fact for her), but alas, her mental concept now was that it was a paid act. It was work.
How to just do the human integration thing without exchange of fees was a foreign concept to her now. It was akin to being a victim of brainwashing. Forever stigmatized.

And then the *new* reality becomes an illusion; but the rose coloured glasses have to come off eventually. ***Everybody*** knows that a millionaire's bank account makes amends for his ageing, vulgur, fat, (or hideously scrawny) ugly façade. The aura of sexiness is apparent. But when all the money is lost and embellishments are stripped; what are you left with?? When the mask of disguise is removed, the true image appears in the mirror. It is far from the glorious splendour that once stood.

When one has been exposed to this extreme standard of lifestyle and free-flow cash, it is like a curse. For without its continuation, there is a sensation of immense depravation and sorrow….
It was like the antithesis of 'royalties'*:*
in a permanent state of immense contrition, **she** would continue to
pay for the profits earnt…

<u>Masked Misery</u>

If only you could truly see

behind my mask the real me

but time has glued it to my face,

and a frightened phoney takes my place

For the world it seems is harsh and cruel.

I relish in knowledge but act a fool

and to save my heart from being torn,

my mask smiles while I cry forlorn

It saves me like a mad cocoon

but judgement day is coming soon

The damage done-

true identity lost

the inner me must pay the cost….

~Christie.

Chapter 8, 9and 10

FAITH, IRONY, PERCEPTION, BIRTH.... AND DEATH

A trilogy series

****

The first Act - **1,2,3....**

Chapter 8 Part 1:
Labrats, Scarred for life.

The couple sat in the waiting room of the tattoo parlour. The third party was yet to arrive. He was a # 27 too (birthdate) ; they were self-destructive by nature! She had found her kindred spirit. He was part of her now......
It was no surprise that he was late.

They had all agreed on a tattoo design during one of their epic indulgent weekends at the party castle. Trio trouble!!
They often say that 'three's a crowd' or refer to one as the 'third wheel'.......Crystal had found that conversely, there was more of an issue with *two*. Three was a balancing agent for her. Always had been. And being a similar anomaly, Jay completed the equation for her perfectly.

They would gather over a meal and some wine at the enormous table in the couple's big home: always fish rice and salad. And chilli. Tonnes of it.
Similar to the way he lived his life: he loved to burn like crazy......like a candle. The ensuing 2-3 days would entail immense heart-to heart connection on a soul-level. It was like a doctors' surgery: all topics were open and sacred. And the only rule here was: stay hydrated!

They shunned all other forms of social interaction in preference to this comfortable private gathering.
The friendship level was beyond a gift. Most people only just touch on the surface of soul connection, but these three were in a symbiotic zone of blending. It was a love that was so rare.....she was painfully aware that it had a used-by date. Sure, they were completely in the moment every time, but she wished she could freeze these occasions, so that they, too, wouldn't melt....or be stolen/seized.

The tattooist donned his gloves and got busy with the pain administration. Anyone who says a tattoo doesn't hurt is lying, but it's a pain that one endures (and usually repeats) knowing that there is a lifelong gift that awaits...[whether it is to be a meaningful gift that remains a pleasure is up to the individual however]
(The general public consensus is that quite frankly, 90% of tattoo victims were utter imbeciles, and this process was done during a period   of   inebriation.)
No, for these 3 folk it was _body art._

The selected icon was the Egyptian eye of Horus. They were to get it on the shoulder of their arm, for protection. It was to be a safety device symbol, for both within the confines of prison walls, and the real world alike.....as in: _always looking over my shoulder_...i've got your back.
Twenty-sevens were no stranger to danger. They needed to self-bodyguard...

He was out from a chemical-related stint in the big house for 5 years. Originally, he was to be _'doin' a deuce'_ but through good behaviour and whatnot, slashed the sentence by half. He was a generous and trusting soul....to his detriment. One of his supposed allies had turned rat.
There are no such things as 'partners in crime'!

It was during his incarceration that he had developed a friendship with an ex-university lecturer on 'psychotropic drugs'.
With their unified power of lab know-how and street savvy genius, (not to mention the advantage of hours on end to focus on a project to perfection, devoid of 'real world' distractions); they gave birth to the syndicate of elite poisons:
the grandest racketering 'franchise' in the country.
They had masterminded the operation that was to further grant him the nororious title of perpetrator

'A1'.

This of course refers to 'class A', - (of which he had managed the largest; most successful interstate ring to date.) He had been the brains behind the operation that originally got him to the clink. (through those various rats). It was seamless, but you know...trust nobody...

Now, in the new improved venture he was the strategy puppeteer. There was an extra stand-out element too....this was like *nothing before*.

He described the operation framework and the chance of it unraveling if adhered to, was nil. Yes, of course it was an unsavoury issue, but the fact remains, he was a genius. Bravo.

To say he was struggling in 'the real world' was an understatement. However he felt he had a safety net with these two. He called them all a 'tribe', reflecting somewhat on his American Indian heritage. And so the ceremonial scarring was to be a reminder of the loyalty to the gang too.

He was a complete free spirit. She wondered how he coped when in isolation and cement walls. A weaker soul would perish. With part Indian heritage, his confinement would have been on another level.

On one occasion, in the customary relaxed zone of the party castle, he opened up about some of the turmoil that was day to day routine behind bars. The sensation of unrelenting; 24-7 fear rocked her to the core.

Some of his haunting stories moved her to tears, and would never leave her. It remained her biggest fear of all time: incarceration. The stealing of chapters of one's life. There was no worse punishment known to man.

Life is short.

Every year, day, hour is precious......at least that's how it *should* be viewed. Sadly, we usually lose sight of that fact until something fatal snaps us into proper perspective.

It was ALL about perception...the way one views any situation; and indeed reacts to it, culminates in the grand total of a life.....2 people could have identical lives; and one basks in the glory of his fortune while the other perishes and rots in the mask of martyrdom. It is survival of the fittest. Well, on that score Jay was as robust as they come. Was he unbreakable??

She admired and respected him. For despite his perported sins on this earth, his strength of character, mind and complete loyalty to

those he loved held far more weight.   The irony: her most trusted, valued comrade was a repeated felon, who spent chunks of his life in the slammer. (!)
He had proven repeatedly to be a better soul than those who played by the rules; lived boring lives and had pristine reputations. She despised weakness. And she saw it in everyone. (Including herself evidently, as those traits in others you repel are often the dormant unsavoury aspects of your *own* being/psychi)

Mirror .....

The eye of horus became 'the eye of perception'. The all-seeing eye. It not only served as a protective emblem for them all now after personal traumas, but it was a REMINDER to always watch your back too.
Look over your shoulder.
Never trust anyone but yourself.
This was vital for continued survival; they all knew that. But part of the battle for mere mortals with emotions is that they let the guard down in moments of empathy and whatnot. And this was where the shield was dropped and one got injured.
They had all been scarred for life.
This symbolic scarring reminded them of the battlefields of the past. And not to return.
but sometimes, life has cruel twists and turns...

It is a sad fact that those with the most potential to succeed often sabotage their future in self-destructive ways. People wonder why they turn to forms of release that render them scarred in some way. It is because they are misfits.
And to find a sense of peace, they alter their perception...... it allows them to _be_ without feeling like a freak.

They belong...
This generally involves a bit of science. Some lab magic.
Mind-altering medication...

Chapter 8 Part 2:

CRYSTAL'S METHOD OF PERCEPTION......

"When a person has access to both the intuitive, creative and visual right brain, and the analytical, logical, verbal left brain, then the whole brain is working. In other words, there is psychic energy taking place in our own head. And this tool is best suited to the reality of what life is, because life is not just logical, it is also emotional"

Steven R Covey. The 7 habits of highly effective people.

In the league of class A illegal substances, we all know what the main offenders are. Even if we haven't dabbled personally, we all know of various contenders. If not personally, then certainly through the media; celebrity and rockstar faculties.
There is of course the paramount players: heroin; cocaine; ecstacy and hallucinogens, namely LSD.
Or more informally: Smack, Charlie, Eccies (or E) and Acid.
Class B consists of amphetamines (speed), barbiturates and cannabis, and C is the steroids, valium etc.
They are all illegal, and classified loosely according to the supposed harms they cause, and the subsequent penalties they carry.

Crystal considered it a bit of a wacky way of categorising them. From her experience personally, and what she had witnessed, alcohol and most certainly _cannabis_ (with it's multitude of more familiar aliases: pot, weed, black, hydro, grass, ganja, hash, herb, reefer, joint, stick, cone, etc) ~ was **way** more irreparably destructive to lives and brains! She wondered if the _'minds behind the classification acts'_ had actually partaken on a _personal_ level....

In any case, they were all mind blasts in their own fashion; with inevitable after-effects. Undeniably addictive, they possess the power to send one down a slippery slope of diminishing returns.

But there was a question: which category did **crystal methamphetamine** fall into?
Answ: It was a B! Obtainable only by a doctor's script, apparently.
(however if anyone has witnessed a partaker of crystal meth in full flight, it is doubtful they would deem it less damaging than one on an E for instance!)

The most common in the social circuit, and the one that Crystal and Jay in particular had been familiar with in the past was Charlie (most know that is cocaine.) Many times were spent chatting over lines of 'joe blow' but it didn't satisfy completely. There was always that underlying (...read urgent/ insatiable) need for <u>more</u>. It was uncomfortable and tainted. Left you somewhat scattered and on the edge of your seat, like a cat on a hot tin roof.
The rest of the list was circulating and available also.

The last one is a bit of a scratchy one though. Moreso than rough speed.
I have seen documents on hospital cases of violence and episodes of terrifying mania that have resulted in victims.
Crystal meth. Ice.
It is usually smoked in a pipe; pretty damn hazardous on nasal cavity.
Its harsh; rough; robust and undefeatable....one can develop the super-human strength of a fantasy hero on such chemicals! Complete personality and normal temperament overhaul. Manic madness essentially. How it didn't reach class A stature I'll never know....
However the ENERGY AND STRENGTH it provides is apparently addicitive...and the MOTIVATION to endure beyond the body's limits is what creates the following. It is however a notorious life-wrecker...(and 'meth mouth' is nothing to mouth off about, either)

BUT, escaping to our imaginative garden for a moment....
 what if one could soften the blow somewhat (forgive the pun); ~ take away the anger component and just focus on the intense energy and euphoric metamorphism that it provides ~ minus the tendency for homicide?
What if it was a heavenly hybrid of :

-a high-note methamphetamine component for crisp clear, motivated focus ~
-coupled with the smooth loving glide of top-grade MDMA ecstacy relief...
thereby encompassing a winning edge for mass diversified appeal? (there's no denying: some like to soar **high** and crystal **clear**, while others crave the **relief** of **physical** ecstacy; forcing them to get out of their mind and into their body).

Is this possible? Does chemistry allow for such a miracle? Dream on.
The pulse races just thinking about it...

So......what **if** you could alter one's perception to a height of confident mind clarity and courage to pursue impossible feats in a state of immense joy;
~ defying the bodies' usual stamina restrictions?
What if a complete, instantaneous PARADIGMATIC SHIFT was indeed a possibility ?!
What if, not only enhancing the *brain* receptor sites to an optimal height of clarity potential, it had underlying currents of ecstacy for the *physical* body too?
The creation pays homage to the mind and body simultaneously.

Not only that, what if it was a **less toxic** concoction formulae; using more pure, organic methods of creation......Utilizing water vs the usual chemicals to achieve this better result, and thereby not damaging the body to the same extent? This 'gentler' result allows one to administer in the more socially acceptable manner: (*snorting* through hundred dollar bills etc)...
What if it allowed you to go for 3 days, and achieve more in that timeframe than an average two months or more - (when usually relying on increased caffeine dependancy)?
What if, what if, what if......**are** we dreaming?
This fell into the too-good-to-be-true category.....pure fantasy surely.
I mean.....hello, we are talking bestseller list now baby.....bring it on I say, and don't be shy...

So then let's refer back momentarily to the game of 'classify the poison' devised by the pesky powers that be.....
Forget the old A,B, C......we now add a new category.
This was HOLY!
And we all know that religion is a crutch.
As such, it held tremendous power over humans. Don't get too close to the ceremonial fires.

One would have to NAME the ultimate drug, obviously. The new hybrid would need a christening....a private classification amongst its select participants.

Considering that life is what you make of it.....(one can sink or swim etc blah blah blah)- :
Two people could have identical lives, and one would be content as hell while the other would rot in black dog gloom.....wouldn't it be fair to say that it is all about PERCEPTION in a nutshell? How one perceives life..

Then '***perception***' it is!
For whatever your mindset before commencing communion with this substance, it is inevitably sent to stratosferic glory. Positivity rating to the max.
All is great; life is fucking amazing...

You could rule the world....(!)

And to give historical backbone to that claim: one man did.....
For did you know that **Hitler** himself was psychologically dependant on _Crystal Meth and barbiturates?_
In fact, it was the core of his private life behind closed doors!
When off the pedestal of reign, and within the confines of his hidden underground bunkers at his private mountain retreat. It was here that a vast array of evidence pertaining to his drug-fuelled tirades was discovered after his demise. He was an injector.
 It is no wonder his Doctor Theodore Morel had his own room there.
For progressively, Hitler was showing signs of disillusionment and disdain.
It was around the time of 1944.
He had difficulty sleeping and profound anxiety. His PERCEPTION was shifting. Increasingly detached from reality, he was talking jibberish.
He received paranoia and betrayal among his enterage, for irrational decisions made while in the crystal meth zone.
The man was no longer immortal; and aged overnight.
He had developed coronary artery disease. Footage also showed a left hand tremor as evidence of Parkinson's disease.
This should all be no surprise for the man responsible for the death of millions of people during the phase of his insane dictatorship commands; including the gas chambers. It is astounding to note that the public too, became addicted to the aura projected by a man so clearly deranged.....
When Dr Morel left him, he announced suicide.

Crystal was waiting at the usual spot to pick up her comrade. She always drove over to the university where he taught, and collected him after his shift, to do the weekend ritual. The 'teacher' role was his alias. (The real work was in the lab, - and with strategically planning production, execution and distribution.)
She knew the 'alias caper' routine firsthand, and was a veteran player herself, in fact. She realized that the majority of her jobs had been in the 'under the table, cash-only' department. Read illiegal. She had choice few legitimate forms of employment to speak of!
People must assume that her whole life was as a 'kept woman'.....if only they knew the truth.

This time he presented her with a gift.
"What on earth is that Jay? Good grief, 10 kilos of rice?" she laughed quizzically at the apparent luggage he had in tow today.
He placed the massive pillow at his feet and turned to kiss her.

"Oh, honey its our *jasmine* rice –so fragrant and divine" he held his hands together in prayer.   "We can have it with the glorious kingfish I caught on my boat this morning". Curiously, Crystal couldn't detect the usual aroma of the fragrant grain she realized distractedly, as she embraced her most precious comrade.

They adored the smell, especially as it would waft throughout the terrace from the rice-cooker while preparing the fish, fresh chopped herbs and salad together. In fact anything to do with *'jasmine'* was synonomous with him.

She would burn essential oils of jasmine when he arrived. It evolved into their bouquet of blessing.

Psychosomatic of these occasions……their sacred ceremonial scent.

She knew he was probably on his 3rd day or so of sleepless existence. He didn't rate sleep much. Bit of an unnecessary hindrance really. He would deny himself the need as 'best left for prison or when dead!'

It was a gloriously warm spring day. A rare chance to go sleeveless; they had their matching tattoos on display. These were the best times to congregate, with the temps so comfortable. The rains had stopped; the clouds had cleared, and people were smiling everywhere. It was good to be alive!

While she cruised on down the highway, they laughed and chatted as they recounted the 2 weeks between their sessions together. His eloquence and intellect always enhanced her mental acuity. Such stimulating and *genuine* folk were so very rare, she had found.

 It always astounded her how he had managed to maintain such refinement after years of incarceration, that usually chisel away at, and roughen one.

They arrived shortly thereafter to the greeting of Crystal's husband, Hunter, doing his paces with the usual grin on his face and mobile phone in his hand. He had to be surgically removed from it at times she felt; the business never stopped….it wasn't healthy. Robotron…

These times they shared enforced 'time-out' of the usual patterns. Got him connected to a human being on a 'soul level' vs a selling-hype rendition.

It was akin to his therapy session.

'I'll be with you in a moment' he exclaimed as he strutted off to complete the deal at hand.

Meanwhile Crystal busied herself at the extensive open bar; pouring them both an aperitif, while Jay placed the massive rice sack up on it to open.

She assumed he was about to start prepping the dinner. For he loved getting hands-on in their kitchen! It was all part of the festive journey. Especially with the fresh fish he had caught that day, coupled with chopped coriander and his extroidinary tolerance for chilli. He often preached its benefits in keeping with a natural high.

 And of course, his jasmine rice…

She dropped her glass to the floor as she turned around.

He revealed instead the largest lump of solid white mass she had ever laid her eyes on.

Atop the black granite bar, it contrastly glistened like a huge arctic structure. She quite

literally grabbed for the sunglasses on her head. There was no doubting what it was, and it certainly didn't classify as grain!
Volume-wise? Well it was a 5 kilo Hessian rice bag that held the contents to capacity, so...
Let's just say: enough to threaten the future freedom of any participants. For life.
No risk; no gain. It was terrain already travelled.
'Here we go again' she thought...

He chiseled a tiny corner off to sample. It was microscopic in comparison to the mass total that gleamed before them. She knew it was enough to last them days....
and it was, literally, just the tip of the iceberg....

"I drove from one side of the harbour to here with **that** in my car?" her jaw dropped as she recalled the number of policemen she had encountered on the drive home, being weekend traffic. Her skin _crawled_......but she knew that shortly therafter, would tingle.....
Hunter simply laughed: "fuck me brother, talk about bringing the goods"....

On a few revealing verbal sessions over their regular meetings, Jay would mention various tidbits of information regarding the actual procedure behind his well-crafted enterprise. It was evidently structured with complete focus and an eye for detail as to any potential 'loose threads'. Time behind bars obviously allowed for this constant contemplation. Virtual obsessive compulsive rechecking and perfecting, one would assume, no?.....
 Crystal concurred: to be totally focused, one needs to be in some form of isolation or segregation. Regardless of how much you consider yourself a 'multi-tasker'; alpha intellect and so forth, the distractions of day to day general life (in the 'real' world) allow for accidental error.

One of the facts that arose was that transportation for illegal matter was always best via his favourite ally : **the ocean**. A no-brainer, obviously.....and yet, when you hear these facts it sometimes still triggers elements of surprise and intrigue. It was best not to venture too far into attaining details further; although it was often so tantalizing to behold that inquiry was unavoidable! But never forget, as they say: what you don't know can't hurt you......curiosity killed the cat.
Nowadays they have even seized incognito vessels (like submarines) shipping tones of cocaine etc; particularly over (read under) the carribean).

Like any professionally masterminded drug cartel, the strategy he'd devised was seamless.
As analogy: it involved a flawless _relay-_ by the time you reach (or catch) one participant, the baton had already moved on with another. None of the players knew the identity of the others. One major drug deal involves a series of people to deter detection and confound cops. An octopus of arms...
The 'catch me if you can' theme was one he had excelled at, and why his notoriety was elite status.

Crystal and Jay's domain was like a 'doctor's surgery' of confidential information to an array of characters, who felt comfort in it's welcoming confines, but Jay was, by far, the top of the list.

At these proceedings, they would commence a fabulous slow lunch at the long pew-like banquet table, spanning several hours of witty banter and laughter; always a sustenance sensation. It was meticulously prepared and devoured; ~ generous and nutritious to sustain the hours ahead.
 Hunter would always be the eager one to start the next course.
"You guys have done enough chopping in the kitchen. I'll take over now" he would rub his hands in joyous preparation.
As he set to work with tray and razor, Crystal and Jay would clear up all evidence of the fine feast.
Straws were laid out, and one by one they would take turns in communion. The lines were robust and lengthy. Crystal generally preferred to go last. She always felt the initial rush of nervous anticipation, and would have to brace herself for the ride. For it was never half-hearted. It was total dedication to the force.

*(The usual, and most rapid methods for straight crystal meth 'administration' as aforementioned were via injection and smoking from a pipe. They preferred to **snort** this more 'graceful' version....salvaging the teeth, and avoiding track marks was a major bonus of this style;~ not to mention a similarly rapid result.)*

[*the fact that her nasal cavity would be singed forever more was a meagre price to pay comparatively..]

By this stage the boys were perched at the bar stools leading onto the terrace, with the afternoon sun providing a backdrop halo for their expressions of peace.
She knew the initial price: no pain = no gain.
Her nose would sting like crazy as the poison rushed into the millions of sensitive receptors of the nasal lining. No doubting, it hurt! It was rapid to hit the brain-barrier however, and the intense rush was like nothing on earth.
Waves would permeate the entire body; a tingling awakening of **all** the senses.....she would almost sigh with relief at the sense of homeostasis; 'coming home'.....
(it was often commented to her that she was way more *normal* when on a chemical boost than without.)

and she was fearfully aware of this fact.

Chapter 8 Part 3:

* A STAR IS BORN⋯.

The ensuing hours were spent with in depth conversations on a vast array of topics. All the players were gifted raconteurs; ~ had amazing life stories to tell. And the memory banks were literally so full of them that they would astound even *themselves* as they would :

'reach for book chapters from this enormous library' in the grey matter.

In a sense, it was akin to therapy: coming to terms with many of the experiences that life throws at you…..or you throw yourself at.

Could it be considered *rebirthing* in a sense?? Like insects in a crysalis, they would shed the old skin, with all its scars, to make way for the new.

"It's somewhat frightening how much courage Dean and I used to have in the early heyday…..

God, the stuff we used to get up to; - super crazy shit!! I mean we had legendary parties all through our youth. He brought me up when mum died, and he was mad as a cut snake, so it was a fun way to grow up I guess….!"

Crystal and Hunter were privy to Dean's exceptional character traits; ~ it kind of went hand in hand with his brilliance and creative finesse. "We used to take international or interstate trips faking a broken bone of some sort, and even go so far as to caster-plast it beforehand! The walking frame contained ahem…contraband narcotics…..and we did it so many times without a hitch, I've lost count. It would be madness to consider such flying risks now, with airport security the way it has evolved……i mean it was insane back then, but smuggling them so blatantly now…..i shudder to think….."

One of the stand-out stories was Jay's rendition of the birth of his gorgeous daughter Chayley. A fellow 27/11 like Jay and Crystal were themselves – it was bound to be far from regular!

It entailed the description of his beautiful, albeit volatile wife Maz; who reacted adversely to painkiller drugs administered (as is the case with certain native races; whose tolerance level is somewhat more compromised. eg: American Indians; Aboriginals, etc…. categories to which they both fell into!)

She quite literally became satanic; long black hair flying like whips as she ran naked through the hospital, and started swiping at staff with the power of a gladiator. "Somebody has stolen my baby!!!" she boomed with huge black eyes of murder……(this is all *pre*-birth mind you.) Jay had tried to calm and restrain her, but it was like confronting a giant. She virtually broke his ribs; winding him as she landed with her bulk weight and girth atop him on the hospital floor, beating him repeatedly in rage.

So there they were; hospital beds side by side.....in a private ward, no doubt only entered into by staff of extreme strength and courage.

Hunter and Crystal could hardly breathe; they were so doubled over in hysterics. It was stomach cramp material! The sort of precious, therapeutic laughter you experience regulary in <u>extreme youth</u>......... and then only crave, seek and dream of for the rest of your life.....
Laughter is without doubt, the BEST medicine on earth!! It is perhaps the part of childhood that is gold most of all.

So many humorous renditions.....it was like stand-up comedy at its best!
Isn't life stranger than fiction though. Who needed TV if you chose your comrades wisely ?
His raconteur tales were impromptu and unpredictable...the surprise element each time was like a gift.
So many great times shared....if only one could freeze those moments. Seemed a shame to shove them into the memory banks thereafter, and sigh with nostalgia as they are recollected from the library collection. It is not healthy to dwell on the past though.....moving forward is the key. Savour every moment NOW.....one hour at a time.....one hour at a time.

And then there was the more dramatic confessions.
Jay's time behind bars.
He didn't speak of it much; just mentioned crazy characters from time to time with details to make your jaw drop.
Ironically, some of the 'nicest blokes' were the most hardened criminals. But then, the entire story of Jay was a lesson in irony to be fair.
For instance:
*" All the **Milat** gang were there (as in Ivan). Quite a strong family unit; - you wouldn't pick them for the atrocities they are responsible for! Actually decent guys. And not imbecilic in the slightest. But when you hear the 'campfire stories'......oh god. I tell you, one doesn't need books or TV behind bars. If you're into horror, its quite entertaining really! The real-life stuff is, well hard to hear obviously, but much more compelling than fiction"*

Crystal and Hunter knew that the stories that unraveled were the sort that never leave you, but, as he described them, they too were compelled to hear them:
"So what **are** some of their deets of bar-banter?" they would insist, as they huddled at the bar. He would give them the look as if: 'are you sure you want me to continue?' before he indulged details further. They eagerly leaned in:
"Well, they were comparing notes for instance of what its like when a human skull explodes: for eg: 'Yeah man, that sound as it splats against a wall and the blood n brain are all over you like they've been in a blender'...
Jay would have a glazed look as he recalled the verbal horror:
"..... or the gut-wrenching sound of flesh as it is being carved up by a knife.....or of bones cracking as they are broken....." he laughed, somewhat sardonically.
"I didn't want to get on their wrong side, put it that way!"
Play the game....

He had learnt to master the skill of <u>wearing the mask</u> for survival.

There were little tidbits of torture tales he would pepper conversations with from time to time when in the mood. Always with humour, but the undertone was far from funny.
  "All those things you hear about it?....it's that plus.... plus, much more. Your imagination could not conjur"......

There was one time though. He opened up. The one and only time.
The three of them were on chairs inside. It was raining outside. A storm for memory. He was always so hell-bent on inspiring humour and positivity into everyone's life; it was the only time she could recall that he spoke *solemnly* from experience.
He started to talk openly about some of the deeper, disturbing stuff. The unrelenting fear. The atrocities witnessed......it was a miracle he had not been a victim of sodomy or physical mutilation like so many others had. He avoided conflict and got on the wrong side of nobody. Kept to himself mostly. Invisible. But what he saw...these are the horrors that would never leave him. And the stories would haunt Crystal forever more too....she couldn't contemplate the concept of 5 years in such an environment. It was the equivalent of pure hell. Didn't get worse.
It was not the <u>deprivation</u> fact that was the issue; ~ he, like Crystal was a master of discipline and abstinence; -they were no strangers to pushing themselves beyond the normal limits!
No, it was the *exposure* to what goes on behind bars. Being compelled to see, hear, smell, live in the same vicinity as such barbaric human suffering. It was a
'5 year nightmare, that you just don't wake up from'.....
No escape.
'Prison' is a state of mind.
But **this** was hell and damnation....

Due to his advanced intellect to these stereotypical 'types', he was usefully employed by the wardens as 'the psychological voice of reason'. This supposed privelidge was actually a brutal burden for him to bear.
Beyond all the other stuff.
 For they would deliberately situate him in close proximity to the characters on suicide watch. He was a non-threat guy...one that seems to fade in the background. A life-saving characteristic.

"Unremarkable...forgettable...aren't they the best qualities in a spy?"

Quote from the series 'the Crown' (S3, ep1)

He would endeavor to talk them down from the ledge.....he had about a 50% success rate. The rest were scars he had to carry for life. The sounds. The screams. The gruesome finales.
Five years of unrelenting psychological terror. It was a lifetime really.

"…..but then, you reach a point when you are finally <u>desensitized</u>….you break through the human barrier…..nobody can touch you now. You have witnessed and endured the worst it could get. Fear leaves the building…..
that's freedom in a sense I guess"
He was right of course. Fear is what keeps us from living life. We all have it.
So to take a Buddhist twist on the scenario, he was *privelidged*.

Perception…

And his beloved Maz……ever supportive and faithful. He could never thank her enough for that. All he could do was make 'an honest woman of her' when he got out. He would give her the most magical wedding ceremony to confirm his love.
And Chayley……his total purpose. His life. His baby. The motivational force for survival when most others would have rotted. He missed the first 5 years of her life. Precious times.
He had to be there for every step of her life from his moment of release. This was his future.

Hearing all this just reinforced how precious every second was. If anyone understood that Jay did. He had done his time. He had been put on 'freeze-frame'. Now he had to live a fulfilled life. Digest every moment fully. Completely. Doesn't get much more Buddhist than that. He noticed every tiny detail; expressed joy at the most basic, simplest pleasures. He taught everyone in his path so much.
How to live.

So…back from the reverie, and at the 'party palace', a change of mood and stimulus was often required.
They would take turns playing DJ for whatever audio enhancement took their fantasy-fancy during the phases of flight. Crystal would do many a 'diva costume change' for dancing on tables; and the guys would potter about and discuss all manner of 'lucrative business ventures' among other things.

The place was vast so it was easy to change environment when required, without even leaving the confines.
And to reach the pinnacle (like their physical states) they would climb the mountain…
-venture to the top; the fourth floor of the London-style residence. There were 94 stairs to climb….
Jay would often exclaim *"there <u>must</u> be local restaurants and bars that are closer, surely!!"*
On the roof terrace with its' stunning city-scape views, they would dip in the warm spa; sip on cocktails; and blare the music out to the world – with a sound system and complex remote designed by gay club technicians….Say no more.
 Their private nightclub under the stars……

The floor below held the guest-room, which Crystal would always have prepared for Jay. Needless to say it generally remained untouched, but was nevertheless there on standby, in case he decided to do something radical and rare, like grab some shut-eye or something.

It was a unique combination of time spent alone *and* in company. As and when desired. Perfect!
 The complete terrace layout had, by progressive design, been created specifically to cater for this private, VIP form of entertainment it seems.
The decadence that remains behind closed doors is often astounding.

There were a few times the cops arrived. On one such occasion (that to relay, had some of her gay friends in hysterics)- Crystal answered in her silver party dress and sky-high heels with cocktail in hand. The boys in blue instructed her: *"its time to close down your party and send all those guests home immediately– there have been several local complaints"*.....
Trying to tell them it was only her with friend and husband for a casual dinner night sounded so far fetched...there were strobe-lights; smoke machines; and glitter balls dancing in the background, which they had hired for a recent 80's themed party.
They entered the property to survey the scene closer and upon realizing she was correct, left with a confused smirk on their faces, and a final word of "volume down!"
Apparently the music had accidentally been left on way upstairs via the remote; blaring out to the streets for the world to hear. It sounded like it was huge private dance party that just kept going.....their notoriety for decadent home entertaining was being established (!)

Trips were made back down to the ground floor bar for another small 'top-up' line from time to time, as the hours passed and the body gave signals of approaching fatigue.

The legs on this substance though were mind-boggling. One could literally last for days, even when weary at the onset. Therein lay the danger...

On a few occasions that Jay had been detained with family matters his end, and was unable to attend, Crystal and Hunter had partaken themselves when lacking motivation to complete arduous tasks involving many hours.....for there was always a supply available at 'the bar', courtesy Jay.
The outstanding amount they would achieve in a fraction of the time while under the influence of perceptive power, was proof enough of its oligopoly potential.
For example: a four storey english style terrace with mountains of stairs is no mean feat to *de*feat in a cleaning endeavour. They would often go about it in a frenzied; military precision manner and achieve a day's work in under 2 hours. Result! It was all about the **clean lines**.....literally!

"Tell me <u>again</u> about the organic ketone production!!!" she would implore Jay; .....as if to reinforce (read justify) her participation as holy, healthy and good.
-it was <u>natural </u>after all! The body and mind love it right?.........(!)

Fresh fish caught from the ocean less than 8 hours beforehand; steamed rice, biodynamic crisp salad with her homemade dressing, lots of purified water with the wine......and *organic* lines for dessert.....how healthy were they??..........

Perception....

Deception?

Jay's flamboyantly gay brother Dean had given his nod of approval, not surprisingly. In the recreational enhancement arena, he was a hard marker.......and a die-hard partaker!
For the most part they were keeping it a private, sacred concoction; not for circulation. Nor distribution as yet. It had to be very carefully introduced and monitored.....way too valuable and potentially dangerous to just throw out there to the fragile world....Jay was still in the *'testing the waters'* phase and observing what transpired.

The trilogy labrat sanction.

Dean had introduced a sample *taste* to a few hardcore players in the scene; ~
the consequential response and demand for it was so overwhelming; - it was the definite template marker for success. (for in the social sector, it is somewhat well known that the gay community take the cake & all the icing when it comes to volume indugence ; both in tolerance of, and survival rates!)
He had described it initially, and they had laughed at his 'diva' rendition.....however his perceived hyperbole became HYPE for them. Instantly.
They knew they had struck a gold mine.

It was terrifying......

A star is born...***the only way to kill it, was to destroy the parents.***

Religion is a crutch; - the ultimate *mask* of internal turmoil...hold onto the faith.

Well, we all know of religious freaks:
born again Christians...rabid Jews; devout Hindus; manic Muslims; Buddhist devotees...
This was *their* private religion, and they simply couldn't wait to start the ceremony, and worship the god of perception!
The best way to describe the spiritual adoration, was like how the African Americans perform their gospel gatherings......it is one hell of a joyous, colourful party! Embrace the spirit and joy with your brotherhood! It is a gift to be alive!

Hallelujah......cartwheel down the church aisle; sing and dance to the concert of the lord. Rejoice, rejoice....
Completion. Fulfillment.
Love...

So now, let's sidestep for a moment and consider then the BIRTH of the perfect miracle, were it to exist.
For the 'parents', like the chemical aspects, it was a formula of sorts:
The equation of science with objectivity.
It could be proposed that:

~to devise the production of this alien substance would require a stringently <u>controlled environment</u> for the *panel responsible themselves*, thereby yielding optimal results.

~It would take a certain type of character/s perhaps forced into making it their entire purpose; ~ reason for being. Obsessively, compulsively so.
The all-consuming pursuit of excellence.

~It was essential the creators be as natural, pure and toxin-free as possible, to dedicate complete, clear focus to the holy creation. It must be Alpha.

A1......

~These 'scientists' would need to incorporate regular, (enforced?) rest, exercise and nutrition. Peak conditioning for maximum performance.
In other words: Near-superhuman status creates/promotes corresponding productive effects!
Simple mathematics: the grand sum total of the output is/would be in direct correlation with the quality of input.
And so forth.
You get the picture.

~It would take hour upon hour of sacrifice to the cause; involving complete, undevided attention, devoid of 'real world' distractions. Allowing them to live in that very moment and execute all actions with controlled precision.

~It demanded discipline, abstinence and wholehearted dedication.

A strict, regular, unbreakable routine.
The likes of which are near impossible to manage and maintain with the distractions and deterrents of life in general.
This was quintessential science after all!

~The unique project required the epitome of high achievers.. (literally!)
No room for error here……
But was this 'formula' not a true *mirror* reflection of ultimate productivity in **all** aspects of life too?
Perfectionism breeds brilliance, after all.

~So for the makers, it required a period of restrictive isolation.

Incarceration.

For to reach the promised land…

you must first

do the time.

The 2nd Act - 4,5,6,7,8.

Chapter 9 Part 4:

and

down

came

the castle......

- *"if you're going to try, go all the way. Otherwise, don't even start. This could mean losing girlfriends, wives, relatives, and maybe even your mind. It could mean not eating for three or four days. It could mean freezing on a park bench. It could mean jail. It could mean derision. It could mean mockery – isolation. Isolation is the gift. All the others are a test of your endurance, of how much you really want to do it. And, you'll do it, despite rejection and the worst odds. And it will be better than anything else you can imagine. If you're going to try, go all the way. There is no other feeling like that. You will be alone with the gods, and the nights will flame with fire. You will ride life straight to perfect laughter. It's the only good fight there is."*

(Charles Bukowski – Factotum)

The drinking demons had started to take hold for him.

It was finally becoming apparent that he could no longer dictate his own routine while maintaining a life-enhancing existence….'on the outside'.
For in this 'line of business' it is not exactly by-the-clock routine.
It is a dynamic, volatile concept…like managing a dangerous beast. When HE was reinforced in capture, he excelled. He was like her; ~ addictive personality disorder. It is why he soared to the levels he did after all!
But now for his own wellbeing, his wings needed to be clipped. For he was reaching out of control status. Like the success of his product would be.
The slope was slippery. He was sliding fast……

The stress of a role such as the one he had masterminded is one that the general public has no possible clue of, unless they have been privy to such underground antics, or indeed participated themselves in some capacity.
They just label the likes of Jay to be 'gangsta villain' material; ~ to be avoided and not trusted one iota. Judgement making without firsthand knowledge.
They know nothing, these ignorant folk…..but people will form their own opinions, won't they. Let the mere mortals assume and label to their hearts' content then…
Whatever.

Her duty was to protect her closest people and the place she was trying to desperately hold onto.
Hunter had 'rolled the dice one too many times' in business, and it was a slippery slope for him too. Only the stuff sliding down was the financial future along with all the foundations. They were on the brink of losing the house.
The grand, unique 'box' that had housed so many memories, and for some reason Crystal felt that her future livelihood was tied up in its structure.
It was quite an investment; they had made it together. And she had supported him wholeheartedly right from the onset. But she begged him not to trust certain folk, or proceed with wild schemes.
But he was akin to a gambler and he had no plan B. Entrepreneurs assume the privelidged role of impulsivity as part of the **'craft'** !
Had it paid out as was intended, all would have been rosy and sweet! She could start a 'normal' life. But it was far from rosy….it was rank now. The way he juggled funds like a 'magicians' illusion'; making miraculous cash supply appear at the eleventh hour (as was his pattern) ~ had all been a well-worn mask of *SMOKE AND MIRRORS…*
and the inevitable exposure occurred.
Literally.

They couldn't afford the proper repairs required for water-leak damage; the faint smell of mould was evident. Termites had started to nest happily on the rotting rafters, and the pest control gang were having a field day on the premises.

The deterioration was evident everywhere you looked. The torrential rains of late had proven too much for the heritage structure; it was seemingly on its last legs. Big pockets were required to fund the maintenance and repair now.....

A huge bubbled pool of water adjacent to the rooftop jaccuzzi looked set to burst into the foundations below. She had nightmare visions of the walls caving in and collapsing around her. What a way to go she thought.....smothered by 'the roof over your head' !
Oh the appalling irony...
It was almost a race against time now. Either find the funds to hold onto the stakes NOW, or sell up and out fast and start a new life. Somewhere. Somehow...

The now ominous-looking gargoyles had been strategically placed like 'security guardians' on the highest point of the roof terrace; their intention to ward off potential danger and evil. Not unlike the matching scarred badges of honour they all wore on their arms; - like dedication to the tribe, and protection from villains.
Both had seemingly failed...

It all looked hopeless.
She was frantically searching for a solution. But it was out of her control.
And being a self-confessed control freak it was torture...

Jay meanwhile was out of control himself. To be the kingpin required precision beyond infiltration. But he was weary, and vulnerable. And sleep deprived to the point of mania. He turned to *spirits* to awaken his spirits; - to the contrary this only served to cause his focus to fade out of vision. The carefully seamed fabric of his fortunes was starting to come undone. Unraveling inevitable....

Time was ticking and her desperation increased. The sleepless nights spent pondering her options were fraught with anxiety and panic that weakened her to the core. She felt trapped with no way out.
This dilemma was engulfing her and could only be addressed through external intervention.
From where......with whom.....and how, without repercussions?

It was a private issue that she felt unable to discuss.
There had to be a solution somehow...
She had an inherent need to salvage the house, for it represented almost a decade of her life assuming that it was a rock solid safety net. Her plan B.
She had forgone a normal life of 'the family building years' to attain this advantage. Played the good wife. The hostess, the support system.
But it was out of her control, so she felt doomed to failure.
It needed a big cash injection. And no doubt a degree of desperate begging.
The 'plans of attack' that she conjured during the early, distorted hours of morning seemed logical, but upon waking to the harsh light of day proved to be wild notions beyond contemplation.

The forces of corruption had to entwine at some point.

For albeit diverse directions, their battles were on congruous paths.

Like Crystal, Jay's marital woes were becoming heavier day by day. What had happened to the happy ever after? What utter bulllshit that is!
Her mind drifted back to both their weddings, that seemed only yesterday, in all their glorious promise and hope.
Chayley had been their tiny flower girl, dancing around on twinkle toes like a fairy; ~ dimpled cheeks; sparkley eyes and petals in her shiny hair. Her innocence was gold. It was Autumn and a slight chill was in the air, but she kept prancing about unphased.
At one point in the proceedings Crystal had sat between the bride and groom at their table. It was a true portrait of contrasts: Aboriginal goddess, American Indian 'David Bowie' lookalike, and her in her towering heels, cleavage and blonde hair out. In her white fur with black dots she looked like their pet snow leopard as they huddled in harmonious union.

As to her own lavish affair, they had employed the expertise and finesse of Jay's gay brother Dean at the helm as wedding planner…(say no more!).
She wanted unique, and was guaranteed it with him. He fulfilled all her wild requests with constant feedback, as he reported daily into her lavish suite at a city hotel, where she was residing in the follow up to events. She sighed now, as she realized how far they seemed to have fallen since the halcyon days of *hang the expense; go hard'….*
The guest list was a stirfry of family, friends, captains of industry, 'A' crowd socialites and even politicians. One of her bridesmaids was announcing to all and sundry that she was *"involved in the wedding of the year!"*

Crystal frowned as she realised how very few they still actually continued contact with after such a generous spray for all concerned.
After the church ceremony, the bridal party had photos on the open roof terrace while the crowd gathered below for the champagne, canapés, and ensuing reception entertainment. The free flow bubbly and open bar with several staff on hand ensured that the guests were in fine form for the consecutive drag shows that followed.
A famous drag-queen friend shared Crystal's second floor changeroom and they chatted in between acts; comparing notes on shoes and various fashion accoutrements. She was over the top; embellished to the max and adored by the inebriated fans that celebrated her accentuated glide down the staircase to the 'podium stage'.
By all accounts the function was far from the heartfelt, speech-saturated event most experience; ~ it turned into a veritable nightclub, spanning several hours……and for a few, several days.

Now in retrospect, it became apparent that it was tainted from the onset however…..for the one person she wanted more than anybody to be there was unable to attend.
Jay and Maz had called from the hospital, dressed in their formal attire to apologetically report that Chayley had fallen and broken her arm badly so they were detained. Crystal

had kept checking outside for a sign of their arrival, but the security guards positioned on the red carpet entrance shook their head every time.
They never arrived.
Crystal was crestfallen at the news. The whole night was a bit of a blur after that incident really. Certainly not the Cinderella affair that most women wish for on the one significant day. Even her mother in law commented *"Your eyes were glazed as you walked down the aisle as if you didn't know where you were! We worried for you in those heels…."*. Luckily the attention of the bride's despondency was perhaps grabbed by the dancing sex-kitten bridesmaids, that didn't walk, so much as *grooved* down the red carpet in her wake.
She now realized with shock that the perfect ceremony for her if there was ever a next time would be just the 2 to be married and Jay as bridesmaid AND best man….
how one learns to streamline and prioritise when life provides reality checks.

So Jay committed to assisting financially to get Hunter out of his slump. A double-edged sword…..Crystal felt her skin prickle with warning. Yet another loan….Hunter was digging himself a grave that would render him an irreparable reputation.
The once impressive resume, or 'CV' was now a case of 'collapsing victim'.

As to Jay's insistence of *'financially backing him in brotherhood goodwill'*….This *may* have been a solution…but her gut told her it was only another temporary 'bandaid' and the sinking ships would inevitable still go down.
-only the guilt of enrolling the support of her ally could be a burden she would carry forever….
But desperate times call for desperate measures.
And it didn't get much more desperate than this.
It was no time to be humble or proud.

So Jay was trying to protect his family and future from exposure, and support Hunter's crisis simultaneously, and Crystal was I guess on the same journey; albeit a different strategical route obviously.
But one must eventually recognize that risk-taking in itself (of which they were all guilty); with the associated adrenalin rush, can become a dangerous obsession.
But the bond between Crystal and Jay was too strong.
It was like dual suicide, and they held hands as they were submersed…

"That's the problem with drinking, I thought, as I poured myself a drink. If something bad happens you drink in an attempt to forget; if something good happens you drink in order to celebrate; and if nothing happens you drink to make something happen…"
~Charles Bukowski.

"Hey Hunter, how's the business going?" Jay enquired; bleary-eyed at the bar.
For perhaps the first time, Crystal opened her eyes – out of concern mostly – to see his withered veneer. He looked old and tired; bloodshot eyes and slumped stature.
Beaten.

She observed from the kitchen while she laid out the plates and cutlery.
He was drinking…..but the liquid was clear.
How stupid; she had assumed on many occasions it was just water, as she was in fact consuming herself.
It was the week before, after their soiree session that she noticed the breeding bottles in the garbage. Empty vodka. My god – so many…..
It explained a lot.
His creative vision was usually so flawless, and yet only last week, the photos he had taken of her were blurred out of focus and useless. It looked like the man behind the lense was in a state of delirium. A picture does speak a thousand words. Volumes in this case.
(Rule numero uno: never partake in the goods for sale.
Don't bite into the fruits of your labour, or they will indeed become poisonous…)

Charles bukowski quote from 'tales of ordinary madness':

"I had come off a long drinking bout during which time I had lost my petty job, my room, and (perhaps) my mind. After sleeping the night in an alley I vomited in the sunlight, waited five minutes, then finished the remainder of the wine bottle that I found in my coat pocket"

The concept of him managing the complex enterprise efficiently, to attain rewards fast, & rescue his mate while in THIS condition was more than concerning to her. She was growing increasingly anxious.
Alcohol should only be used in moderation as a 'digestive aid', after all…..(yeah, who follows THAT rule?!).
And being the addictive personality that he was, bless him, it was all or nothing. They say moderation is key…well, 27's will always be locked out in that case.
Jay and Crystal were normally very strategically precise in all their undertakings. (Operative word here, being *normally*)…but now he was showing signs of defying his usual persona.

Sleep and peace was not on the radar for <u>any</u> of them. Dire despair.
And they were increasingly relying on *Perception* to pull them through……

But you know how it goes….the mind is such a unique toy! It performs incredible duties of 'protection' when sanity is threatened. And things are shoved to the subconscience, as they are too difficult to process at this time. Marvelous!
But it all has to come out someday. What goes up must come down, and what is there, albeit masked, can't hide forever…..

Jay hugged Hunter at the bar as they said their 'cheers' yet again.
"Look mate, I'm prepared to back you 100% - you know that brother. I'll give you my available fund resources now, as I know there is more to come on the horizon. Get you out of the jam at least"….
Now there was a glimmer of faint hope at least, and she embraced it. For she had to.

There were a stream of ensuing phonecalls at length thereafter between them as they offered each other support. Almost daily. She hated phonecalls in general, but like everything, with him it was different. They spoke openly about all the secrets they shared. The sacred information that was never to be revealed to others, particularly concerning his 'vocation'.
 For the trio only…'Tribal rites' so to speak.
He still managed to maintain a positive tone and make her laugh; it was becoming the thing that got her through the day.

Hunter was meanwhile missing in action much of the time. Sometimes he wouldn't get home till way after midnight, and retreat to the spare dark room with a 'pounding migraine'. Days would pass when they wouldn't talk at all.
It was becoming evident that he couldn't face her. She was his truth.
The truth hurt…
"Men also pay a price for their superiority. A woman with tired legs and a migraine stands behind every successful man…..And a divorce is behind every successful woman"

(So wrote Maria Sveland in her book 'Bitter Bitch')

Crystal was not blameless. She had broken her most important rule: exhibiting full trust.
She had let down her guard and put full faith in his business acumen.
All the global trips 1st class; the shopping; the 5-star existence…..she had assumed he was steering the ship according to prevailing conditions and granted him the control seat – there was no foreboding indication from him that it would suddenly cease and disappear forever! Wasn't the lavish lifestyle part of the original contract….?
Never wise to proceed unless a safety net or plan B is in order…..in a perfect world at least.
Her perfect world was shattering before her eyes.

She knew she would, in time, learn to mend the bitterness she felt, and the sense of subterfuge. She had hoped to find someone with financial prowess on par with her own. For now though, it was at the point of panic stations.

So Jay became her voice of reason, and reassured her all would be okay, just keep the faith that the tough times would end. She knew he was sacrificing his own welfare to assist them in this crisis. And taking further risks to do so.
"Oh my darling sister girl, I would do anything to protect you, you know that"…….

Life chisels away at the soul, and it had awarded them their 'armour'.
For albeit both extreme loners, Jay and Crystal found peace when together. But all other human intervention was deemed their idea of hell.

In the 2015 book Chasing the Scream (collectively known as "the War on drugs"), author Johann Hari argues that it is not the chemical that causes addiction so much as a sense of disconnection with others.

**"So the opposite of addiction is not sobriety. It is human connection," Hari says.
"The primary problems of alcoholics are defective relationships with fellows," Peter Lawford agrees.**

They met in a park one day and sat together on a bench, basking in the glorious afternoon sun. It cast a magical glow on everything at this time in spring. They were observing the children at play, when Jay commented: *"wow – look at the halo around that girl's head – it's surreal!"* as always, he was first to notice the marvelous minutiae of life.
He would have done anything to make her happy. Her American Indian was as faithful to the tribe as they come. Such a selfless, but enormously giving soul.

But one tends to forget: he was a gangster villain after all. And he was forgetting to polish his weapons.

And to trust no one..........

Chapter 9 Part 5:

Paps 'n' taps...

She instantly felt it in her gut.
He called one day and it was different. He was spent.

"Oh you know, its all just crazy.....Maz has moved out, she's had enough. My daughter hasn't been home in days....I'm just so tired Crys......I just don't want this anymore"......
His voice crackled over the line; a bad connection. She could vaguely hear him.
"Mohammad is coming over for the pill-press soon, so we can start production. Maz begged me not to keep it on the premesis. My own fault I guess...this is my punishment"
Crystal felt sick. It was insane talk.
*"Oh god Jay, **I** begged you to have no evidence anywhere near your home or mine!!".*
Usually he would have been ten steps ahead of **everyone**, but he wasn't thinking straight. He couldn't think at all. The guard and shield were down; it was obvious he was done fighting.

"Yeah I know.....we're moving it to the warehouse later. It's out back in the garage at the moment. I've been meaning to move it for weeks, but then there was all this shit going down on the homefront so it kind of hasn't happened. Plus I've been out on the boat most nights"......

She knew through all her favoured encounters that witty, gifted, creative types always seem to be owls vs larks. Their fires burn at night. Unfortunately, they tend to burn out too... they are prone to depression and radical mood swings, plus addiction.
Essentially: troubled souls.
Stating the bleeding obvious, their perception of life is different.

She knew his escape was the ocean. It represented peace and equilibrium for him on all levels; he gravitated towards its magnetic pull when he needed to reboot. He would battle the high seas on dangerous waves in a flimsy dinghy sometimes, to challenge his mortality. It was an intrinsic need.
He would fish while the rest of normality slept; and bring home his victorious catch. As if it represented his right to continue existence in this dismal world.

" I got into bed, opened the bottle, worked the pillow into a hard knot behind my back, took a deep breath, and sat in the dark looking out of the window. It was the first time I had been alone for five days. I was a man who thrived on solitude; without it I was like another man without food or water. Each day without solitude weakened me. I took no pride in my solitude; but I was dependent on it. The darkness of the room was like sunlight to me. I took a drink of wine."

Charles Bukowski, from FACTOTUM.

Jay was slurring his words.
*And mentioning top-secret apparatus without **code**!*
 It just wasn't him at all. It indicated an almost surrender-type suicide.
Forget Russian roulette; this was akin to tap-dancing on land-mines.

The nausea swept over Crystal.
"I just don't' care you know, I'm just so…tired"…
The phone crackled again.
"Jay it's a really bad line honey; - go and have a rest and call me back later this afternoon, do you promise me?"
They hung up.
And she threw up.

That was the last conversation before the tragedy.
And you know this tale is about things happening in threes….

" A MAN charged with the death of 18 year-old cyclist *Jacinta Bromley has pleaded not guilty to all charges.
Jay (surname) 48, faced the court yesterday on charges of negligent driving occasioning death and not stopping after an accident.

The charges both relate to (location) at 4.45am on November 6.

The case has been adjourned until January 25."

She heard the news via the press.
The media and paparazzi would have a field day with this shit, distorting the public's perception to fantasy. Especially considering his past convictions and 'nicknames'.
The notorious 'A1….Druglord….villain…murderer…..
Fact and fiction……who can tell.

The truth remains though, he was on the road to the boat as usual.
3am, and god knows what number of consecutive sleepless nights he was at.
And there was a near-empty vodka bottle in the car.
Death sentence.

She would have to talk to him for the full fact sheet though. She knew better than to trust what she read or heard – other than straight from the horse's mouth.

but alas this horse was hellbent on *shooting himself* in the broken leg…

The phone was their lifeline. After repeated efforts he finally answered. Without even talking yet, she could feel him slipping; his demise becoming more rapid. She intended to comfort and council him with words. For what more could she do?

You can't escape the past. The sentence would be his daily conscience. That's the worst there is…….

" I take full responsibility Crystal, - I'm going to change my plea to guilty. They have me pinned for a hit-n-run anyway, and someone has to do the time for the trauma to the parents…..i know what that must feel like "

Ever selfless, he was already walking with his hands up.
It was breaking her heart.

Mr Irony…..he had more admirable character traits than she had ever encountered in someone before, and he didn't deserve such repeated hardship.
But who would read this and understand…..still grant her sane judgement?
Especially now…..

What then is to be said for the power of karma?
Kismet?
It sux…….

" Was there any other evidence on you, or in your car, or home at the time of the incident? "

The phone kept breaking in and out, and crackling; like it was long-distance. She could feel the distance between them, and she longed to bridge the gap; desperate to protect him from further accusations.

" No....i tossed the bottle, but when I got home to Maz, I just told her what I had to do. I went to the police station and confessed that I was the driver that killed the girl"
*" **She** was inebriated though right? Completely off her face.....swerving all over the road on her bike?"* Crystal urged, expressing the complete injustice of the matter.

"Maybe....i think so. Not sure. I can't be sure of anything"
He was in shock, for sure.
"Hang on Crys it's Mohammad at the door. Business as usual. Gotta get this stuff underway; we are already behind schedule"

It sounded like he was knocking or tapping on something. Bizarre.
"Is that your phone or mine hon? It's that.....tapping sound again! Every time we speak ....for a few weeks now"....

Then upon suspicion......or maybe it was realisation, she hung up and slumped to the floor. She was still sitting there motionless when Hunter got in. Oh the exposing details discussed between them daily.....
Nausea swept. Vertigo struck.

Holy fuck,
the walls have ears.....

Chapter 9 Part 6:

Buckle up....

He was at home when they arrived.
They waited for his daughter Chayley to leave for school and they swooped.
A swat team of 15 raided his premises and found the incriminating evidence they were looking for.

Crystal remembered the day of his capture vividly.
The memory was like a recurring nightmare, that she felt she had played a significant role in. For they were all perpetrators of sorts.
Despite who took the rap, this sentence would be served by more than one.

She had felt it instinctively even before the news hit.
She had collapsed in bed; too ill to move.
Even the most basic tasks seemed insurmountable.
And she did what she often did in times of despair:
She called her mum.
She didn't give specifics. She just said: *" Something terrible has happened. I'm completely broken".....*
Her mother was well trained in her art of *cryptographic* messaging; prior incidents had trained her to be somewhat of a 'code-cracker' to protect the safety of her wayward daughter....so she gave the response she knew was best:
"Don't waste your energy on talking. Sleep. Just stay there darling, I'm coming straight over now"...

For 6 weeks, they (the Feds) had been tapping the phones of him (Jay), his accomplice, and any close, regularly contacted acquaintances.....(hello)
Someone had it in for Mohommad, apparently; - his partner in the operation, and had informed the police.
He too went down. A single parent supporting his 8 year old son; he had a masters degree in chemistry.
His backyard experiments had backfired.
It was like groundhog day for them both.

Meanwhile, in a paranoid frenzy, Crystal ran around frantically hiding all forms of evidence. Powder, pills, straws, razors from the bar ...all were flushed or tossed in garbage bags in backstreet alleys.
She never left the house without cap, sunnies and head down and never for long. This is what agoraphobia must feel like, she thought.
Whenever the phone rang, she jumped and hit panic patrol. Terrified she eventually pulled the cord from the wall.

Whenever a car drove past or pulled up she hid behind the curtain and spied on the prevailing street activity.

Once the postman knocked to deliver some mail and she dived to the floor; heart thumping, and hid behind the lounge!

She ran from room to room searching for bugs and hidden cameras.

She felt she was in a fishbowl.....her perception was blurred to a surreal state.

At the American Indian's residence, a pill-press and a kilo of powder believed to be MDMA were seized.

Police will allege that the paraphernalia was to be used for the manufacture of ecstacy tablets.

It indicated a potentially large-scale operation, and the law would not be kind.

As the second, and much larger offence of this nature, the outcome looked grim.

He was arrested and charged and that was that.

Life was cruel.

Crystal wallowed in self-pity initially....he was her only true friend.

Now he had been stolen from her too.

Recurrent nightmares of their conversation played out in her head, like on repeat. The truth he had confessed about the reality of what *really does* go on behind bars. In the big house of horrors.

At one point she held her hands to her ears to try to 'make it stop'.

There were spirits swooping on her; causing compression to her whole head, like in occult horror movies. She had been visited by spirits before.

She knew that and felt their presence once more.

In times of immense emotional turmoil, one is opened up and vulnerable to spiritual guidance. Or intervention.... Psychic powers too are enhanced.

Once her deceased grandfather came when she was terribly ill. He had told her 'she must be strong and endure'....he knew she had it in her.

They come to assist at times, but for now it felt more like a foreboding warning of hell.

Her mind told her to face the reality of the situation however.

There was no point in hiding and facing the music later.

She pronounced Jay dead to herself, and lapsed into the deepest grief she had ever felt.

During a harrowing four days, she contacted his family and discussed the legal action to be sought with her and Hunter.

Maz was obviously distraught; the weary look she carried now represented her extended period of hardship. And it wasn't over yet. She knew that.

His brother Dean was ever-ready and suited up for all legal activities and interactions. No doubt it was killing him inside too.

He was a staunch supporter of his younger sibling Jay; their brotherly connection held years of history together, and books worth of war stories and hysterical incidents.

Just to listen to them recite snippets of their past was the most fascinating insight to a unique pair. Closer than most brothers I have seen.
Crystal and Hunter would have selected their company over anyone else's at any given time – given the sheer entertainment of it all!
Through all their hardship, their perception and recital of it all was beyond inspirational and magnetic.

Though in many regards, they were actually like chalk and cheese.
Dean was so pristine and strategic in all undertakings (a generally typical gay trait); whereas Jay was contrastly more haphazard in all his undertakings. And risk-taking.
There was no other word to describe them both than BRILLIANT however; both individually and collectively.

Little Chayley was a precious, gifted little specimen. Stunning, intelligent and street savvy, she had adopted a stir~fry of traits from all the elder generation. More the quiet, observer type though.
She was currently undergoing a phase of rebellion; seeking body embellishments and adopting the physical expressions of a goth.
Dark n gloomy. But who could blame her really…..
She had found a father figure in her uncle Dean through all the years without her own father. That grounding was established, and set to be relied on further now.
She had witnessed more that any other child of her age; that much is pretty much guaranteed.
She was an old soul in an angel's body…

To bring a modern day; relatable analogy to the equation: Chayley was almost the identical double of <u>Kylie Kardashian,</u> of reality tv fame - ('the youngest self-made billionaire').
Chay's future potential was stratospheric, and witnessing her blossom to supreme success would be a joy to behold.

Crystal's mind cast back now to the number of times she had driven while loaded. Feeling in complete, ultimate control.
Was it an illusion of perception at the time? For she had certainly lost all her confidence now.
She usually loved to drive. Most others can relate to that too, no doubt.
During uncertain times, sometimes its best to just take off somewhere in cruise control, with some music to soothe the soul. Or some hardcore hiphop to thrash out the angst…….wherever your mood takes you, or wants you to be.
But not today. Her hands were shaking as she took to the wheel for the arduous journey out west. Braced herself for the highway to hell.

Destination unthinkable….

She stopped outside Dean's place and he came out to embrace her and Hunter. He handed them some documents to read, and a book with some cash in the sleeve cover to try to smuggle in to Jay.
"Hunter, thanks for the brilliant character reference on his behalf; it means a lot. He needs all the help he can get".
The book he had given them to pass on was the one from Jay's time in rehab with Maz. They had done the 12-step program together. AA, NA….they were veterans. The daily mantra taught there of 'one day at a time….one hour at a time'..etc would perhaps stand him in good stead for the ensuing battle ahead.
For it all seemed way too overwhelming to comprehend at this point. God knows how many steps were in this but it was more than a dozen….

"Guys, just to give you some mental prep info: he's looking at minimum 10 years; maximum life. Don't mention around Chay though; best he delivers that piece of news himself"
Crystal and Hunter visibly braced themselves for the emotional ordeal ahead.
*"Oh, can you hold on a moment though, Chayley wants to see you"…..*he rolled his eyes. *"She's just grabbing her ventilen puffer. We spent the night in at the hospital last night, with her severe asthma and anxiety, poor love. I suspect the first of many."* He shook his head in resignation and concern. *"It's going to be a long journey to wherever this will lead…..i can only support her to try to focus on her studies. Though at this point that seems like mission impossible…"*

Fleetingly, Crystal realized that his little girl would be 26 by the time she saw her father 'back on the outside'
How the hell could she possible comprehend that and succeed with her law degree? Although…..chances are, considering she had opted for CRIMINAL LAW, she would now have a real-life training advantage.
But how does one comfort and support someone through that terrifying prospect? Another decade of fatherless years….it was unpalatable.

Chay came running out, and gave her usual dimpled smile, which was like a mask from which she hid behind in terror.
*"I'm okay, um….guys can I **please** come? I really want to see my Dad. I have to see him…."* she begged.
Crystal had enormous trouble holding back tears as she stepped out of the car and hugged her.
They were in the sports car so she looked at Hunter questioningly as to where she would sit. With only two belts, it was really best for two.
"You better ask uncle Hunter, hon!"
"Of course, sweetheart. We'll take you to your Dad."
He stood to get in the back as she dived in front, hugging them both as she buckled her seat as co-pilot.
"Let's go. This car rocks" she had a newly pierced nose and tongue, which she kept clicking nervously.
 Perhaps the wind in her hair will be a bit of a tonic and help open her lungs? Crystal thought hopefully, desperately looking for a positive excuse for the request.

They took off down the highway, her foot to the pedal on the open road. The wind and gentle sunshine was refreshing, and like relief. But dark clouds loomed in the yonder sky.
Beyond the long gloomy road to nowhere…

Chapter 9 Part 7:

Charlottes' Web.

" When I was little, I had to read a book for school about a spider and a pig.

Its main character, the spider, was portrayed as sweet and gentle....nothing like the object of my arachnaphobic mothers' nightmares!

Later, in one of my attempted forms of employment, (that involved the dreaded desk-job; a 9-5 structure; and a far-from-social computer nerd crowd), I adopted a pet spider for company on my chaotic desk.

She was shiny; smooth and beautiful; not hairy and ugly like the general run of the mill mini monster pest. For she was the redback! She wore the beauty pageant sash like a goddess. Sleek, jet and majestic......

I would pick the wings off pesky flies, then throw her their bodies as her lunch-hour treat. A tad dark, yes.....but its in keeping with the topic at hand really, isn't it!

I kept her in a jar, but, beautiful creatures are often opposed to feeling trapped.....they are bound to retaliate in some way if unsettled.....

One day, I discovered that the jar was empty. Someone had left it open, and she had made her escape from the containment. I was so sad. I took it as a sign, and I resigned from employment myself. Fled the confinement. For it was impossible to endure without her.

I never missed that job, but I missed her.

I had done my best to keep her safe; happy and comfortable, but some creatures will never really feel that way. They weren't

meant to exist with us. They will inevitably stop spinning a web
of attempted integration, and leave the nest......"

Crystal read over this writing she had kept from years ago.
Once again, she realized how often **life imitates art**…
Osar Wilde had it in the bag.

*Children's stories and imaginative fantasy reads are a way people can deal with trauma.
Often, these stories are written by people finding a way to deal with their own personal
crisis. A therapy of sorts. It brings enjoyment to others, and a sense of peace to the author.
Translation: the pain of turmoil is not a wasted woe.....Crystal x*

On the very first painful prison visit, not only was Jay surprised to see his daughter, he
was shocked that they were admitted at all. The prison was in a state of 'lock down',
and had been for 2 days.
The day before no-one had been permitted entry except for coroners.
There had been a riot a few nights beforehand, and 2 men had been killed right near
his cell.
The hell had well and truly begun.

He had held Crystal's hand as he had delivered the potential verdict to his daughter.
Chayley was too intelligent to talk gently to. She saw through any 'sugar-coating'. He
gave it to her straight.
*"It's going to be 10 years Chay. I need you to be prepared for that. And I want you to
be strong and make me proud. We both know what your future holds and it is gold.
Don't be deterred"*.......
She sat back, arms folded and squinted her eyes as though in interrogation telepathy
that read 'there's something you're not telling me'....
He continued, reading her mind *"okay, so there is a SLIGHT chance I could be in for
life, considering I have manslaughter charges compounding also, but this is worst case
scenario"*
*"We're going to do all we can to make sure he gets the best representation, hon – and
your uncle is on the case right now, even as we speak"* Crystal interjected.

Chayley clicked her tongue again. *"They told me it might get infected, but I'm scared to
take it out in case it closes over"* she said, referring to her tongue mutilation
embellishment.

(translation: can't process this information…. quickly change the subject….)

"Hey dad, do you know him?" she pointed to a beastly looking character at a nearby table.
She was obviously in denial. As was Crystal.
But would they ever accept the truth?…….maybe the mind just simply won't allow it to. For survival.
Chayley took the coins Hunter handed her and they went over to the vending machines together.
Jay apologized as he held Crystal's hand and asked how she was coping with it all.
She looked down as she tried for his sake to stop the tears.
She would never come to terms with this. Like Chayley, she was just investigating strategies of mental survival as they occurred to her.
Images of torture constantly loomed, particularly during the stillness of night.
Darkness.
This was like dejavu; - memories of stories of his previous ordeal and the horror it entailed were permanent fixtures in her mind.
She remembered what she had learnt from her mother about *putting trauma aside until the strength was mustered to tackle it.* When might that be?
Would she ever climb out of denial?

She looked into his eyes and saw that his soul had died along with hers.
Yes- their sentence had well and truly begun.

Catastrophe lurks around every corner…..life comes at you hard, to hit you in the face. Life is full of surprises, some of them good but most of them…catastrophic. That is what my mother asked me…has no one ever told you that life is catastrophic? Well I know now that it is. That is the way it has always been…and that what matters most is the way one handles catastrophes and heartaches, the pain of it all….

From Barbara Taylor Bradford:
The Ravenscar Dynasty

Jay's trial date finally arrived. Crystal and Hunter walked from their inner-city home to the courthouse. City traffic was a nightmare.

The air was crisp and chilly and there was a hazy grey fog around......a bit like how their minds felt, trying to comprehend the magnitude of the occasion.

To see him on that box, where they felt he DIDN'T belong, and to know that his daughter was there in witness too was painful to anticipate.

She was in the middle of exams, so not sure it was the ideal break between study......or maybe it was, considering the topic at hand (?)

Chayley arrived with her new beau in tow. A fellow goth-looking guy; his lips were visibly almost blue! Crystal thought : gee, I must be getting old.....all I can think of that relates to this form of perceived beauty is 'the cure' and its appeal in the 80's! The whole *emo – goth* craze....it eluded the elder generation. The 'fashion palour' of this crew was not dissimilar to the vampire fetish: avoid sun at all costs, encourage anaemia and don't display anything colourful on self. The closer to appearing like you had just woken from the dead and escaped a morgue, the better. Chay's natural olive glow didn't allow for this obviously, but she was giving it her best shot!

She had also adopted the associated fashionable veneer: long sleek jet hair; purple/crimson matte lipstick, sombre attire; -not an inch of them aside from their skin was anything but black. It was like she was doing her best to look ugly.....but she would never achieve that goal! More like underground vamp goddess. A far cry from the little tinker-bell dimpled cherub that Crystal witnessed grow up, though.

Both had downturned mouths (<u>don't</u> WHATEVER YOU DO smile) and a special lingo of sorts. *If* talking was indeed necessary.

She still gave a huge genuine hug to them both though, so deep down her heart remained; albeit encased in gloom.

Maz just looked the picture of mourning. Sorrowfully beautiful.....Morticia. The scene was very *Adams Family does the legal system*.

All told, it was like attending a funeral ceremony......

Even Dan was in a crisp grey suit with dark grey tie. Pristine, but serious.

The following six hours was surreal; the majority of which was spent waiting for proceedings to commence. The waiting was of course the torture.

They all just wanted it to be over with; whatever the prevailing outcome.

As far as Crystal was concerned, she's had several encounters in the law arena. She'd also done work experience at the law courts in her teens, and the intellectual supremacy of the barristers was almost seductively enticing to her!

It was like witnessing a show of convincing verbal vitriol really – like a *game* to them. All they knew was they had to **win**...(how much actual TRUTH was in their award winning performance, one would never really know.....)

*(*In hindsight she saw the parallel between this opinion and her attraction to her husband Hunter.)*

So as the appealing formula goes for her, they were black and white......a necessary evil. Courthouses fascinated her but were up there with HOSPITALS on her terror radar! They represented grim forecasts mostly.....one generally tries to avoid them in life.

As the defendant arrived from the docks to take his stand on the witness box, he got eye contact with them all individually; a visibly emotional exercise for him.

Dean whispered to Maz, Hunter and Crystal: '*Oh*.......not the ideal outcome I must say'.....as the grey-wigged magistrate surveyed the room. 'Her reputation preceeds her as the most ruthless in sentencing criminals. I was hoping for a different judge'. The prosecution was at an advantage from the onset it seemed. This fact was felt by all in waiting.
With several articles in local rags insinuating that he was the murderous villain, and the compounding charge of drug-related crimes after prior convictions, the verdict was not in his favour at this point. Destined for damnation.
Manslaughter; 2nd offence arrest for drug possession on a grand scale, and evidence/seizure of apparatus for the intent to manufacture and supply illegal substances......what hope did he have??
God help him if the jury were not open-minded.

Ever the good soul, he pleaded guilty as he said he would. No retreat.
His honest and remorseful portrayal of events was extremely painful to bear witness to. It was almost like surrendering to the advantaged enemy; watching a good ship go down.......

Luckily it was not a long-winded affair. The actual in-court-time was done and dusted in under two hours.
The uncomfortable seats were worse than Crystal's memory of wooden church pews. He'd done his confession and admitted guilt. Let the hell be over......

The judge issued him with another 'deuce duty'.......but as Dean reassured us later, it was potentially a 15 year sentence.
If his confession had done the same for the judge as it did for everyone else in the room, it would have warmed her heart.....the only hope now was that there would be a retrial and she would slash the initial punishment.
As they sighed that it was over, they realized that it had only just begun.
Jay's fate *for now* had been sealed, and was out of anyone's control.

Crystal mentally heard the clanging of gates as Jay turned to bid farewell with his eyes, and left the sad courtroom.

Chapter 9 Part 8:
@ Return to sender....

The ensuing 18 months were spent visiting Jay and writing him heart-felt mail.
It was difficult to 'put it out of your mind' and continue life; he was such a huge part of their lives and there were reminders; evidence of him everywhere.
Art he had done for them adorned their walls; so much music brought memories of him to them, and even the smell of jasmine now made Crystal cry.
It was indeed a sad state of affairs.

Crystal's entire 'social life' had been reduced to prison visitations, along with all the glory that entailed: ~ the tedious 2 hour journeys; intense humidity of the cement jungle jail ; body checks and searches, interrogations; sniffer dogs.
And an exposure to the scariest slice of the public than she had ever encountered....(more from the **families on the outside _visiting_** than the scary perps inside themselves, go figure!!)....
In the 'meeting room' that consisted of bare basics: plastic chairs at numbered tables and a vending machine for sugary drinks and crap, was where they would congregate in waiting, for the boys in their standard greens. Many of them were like swaying gorillas, no question; a step above primates. Freak show.
Totally cliché-image crooks.
Then there were the occasional nerdy geeks that you wouldn't expect. The ones that looked like targets for torture. The super-brainy – crossing that fine line into degrees of gifted insanity.
It goes without saying that there were an abundance of 'terrorist' types. The middle-eastern dark _mono-brow_ set; ~ that we have been in the last decade conditioned into feeling we could trust as far as we could throw.....
 And finally, the 'invisible lot', like Jay. The ones that seem to slip through the cracks and not grab your attention in any specific way. This fact, coupled with his 'life-learnt degree in human psychology' had perhaps kept him alive.....

So this environment was what Crystal seemed immersed in now. The influence of which sealed the sentence: this conviction was done by more than Jay.
Is this what her life had been reduced to? Talk about riches to rags.......halcyon to hell story.....
She retracted even further from normal life as it was. And the people in it.
Lockdown.

They were both on a congruous journey. His isolation, though enforced was not dissimilar to Crystal's existence on 'the outside'.

She had always been a misfit, but now, more than ever, any type of social gathering or situation was particularly difficult; be it friends, family or otherwise.

Crystal - thinking aloud when in a social situation:

As the conversation bounced along, she found herself drift into the familiar state of 'white noise' conversion. It was her way of mentally transforming unsavoury or foreign topics into a more palatable, almost meditative drone format.

Call it sanity maintenance I guess.

Who *are* these people? (In essence, referring to <u>anyone</u> she had any social interaction with during these dark times). Are they the crazy ones, or is it me? None of it made sense to her. She was wired differently, that much was for sure.

This constant need in others for attention, company, 'hand-holding' etc.....it was the antithesis of who she was. She didn't understand it or respect it. Even in her *darkest* hours, she had hid alone to lick her wounds and heal in private. Not turn to (read 'lean') on others for strength and emotional support. Not <u>their</u> problem!

She had always cherished her solitude; It was not only a luxury, but an *essential*. In fact it was paramount to self-progression and enhancement on all levels, she had learnt. She knew her limitations though: she had never been a multi-tasker. Everything in her world took complete focus and dedication to be executed to the standard she required. The distractions, therefore, had to be eliminated. And **people** were, the biggest distraction of all.

She had spent more time alone than in the company of others and she preferred it that way. It was like the sigh of relief to be left in peace to be, not only a self-critic, but a *pro-active* one in bringing about the changes that were required.

After all, people always dreamed and talked...blah blah, blah....but talk was cheap. She blocked her ears to the relentless fantasy psycho-babble of others.

To be totally alone and hence face the personal demons head-on was the only way to move forward.

Those inured from certain life exposures must experience miraculous survival techniques. Or die.....

But had she known ANYONE in the course of her life, other than Jay who actually felt the same??

Maybe others were capable of multi-level activity, and were therefore more perfect specimens than she? Who knew.

If their lives weren't such an apparent dogs' breakfast, she could have accepted that fact quite easily! She would observe and maintain the opinion that it was a sign of weakness, and that they perhaps needed to be left in enforced solitary confinement to sort their shit out!!

As the night wore on, it became evident to her, that this person now talking,(like ALL of them), was akin to an alien.

For here was a man who had **never** been alone in his entire life…. and it terrified him.

For her, the reverse concept rang true: *NOT* being alone affected her the same.

Jay was the only person who had ever really understood who she was…

- " Yes, I hated to get out of bed in the mornings. That meant starting life again and after you've been in bed all night you've built a special kind of privacy that is very difficult to surrender. I was always a loner. Forgive me, I guess I am off in the head, but I mean, except for a quickie peace of ass it wouldn't matter to me if all the people in the world died. Yes, I know it's not nice. But I'd be as contented as a snail; it was, after all, the people who had made me unhappy. "

- (Charles Bukowski – **tales of ordinary madness**).

To cut a long, sick, sad story short….
Crystal became ill. She was heart-broken mostly, and felt lonely.
Empty.
Her health plummeted and she was told by a live-blood analysis healer that she was 'a ticking time bomb'. She knew that instinctively. Death was imminent.
She was rotting here.
She knew she had to be radical.
So…she left the country and started a completely new life.

Again.
New country; new terrain; new language; new environment. Salvation.
For the phoenix cannot rise without complete change of existence. On every level.

The one *constant* was the contact she maintained with Jay.
She couldn't run; she couldn't hide. But she could learn to live again.

They continued to write. It transcended the enormous distance between them through the art of 'speaking on page'…
But they were connected by another force….for they were both 'holding hands' in spirit while they instrospectively emersed themselves in a life-saving process of *rescripting their own paradigms*….

It is not often that someone comes along who is a true friend and a good writer. Charlotte was both.
(E.B White~ the last line of 'Charlotte's Web')

*December, 22 '08

My gorgeous sister girl,
Thankyou so much for your beautiful letters. Its wonderful to hear your voice in my head as I read them. I miss you! Especially at this time of year.
………
I will soon be able to go out on day leave/works release/education leave. Strangely though, I was quite content without being allowed to go outside of the gaol (hopping on buses and trains dealing with the world again…….)
I was quite happy in my little world of walking, reading, training, eating and sleeping. The simple life…..
From your letters, I sense that you are making major decisions in your life (again!)
What a life you have had! Just like me, you are not shy of an adventure! I adore your bravery and commitment. Listen to your spirit and follow your beautiful heart.
Im pretty happy in the thought of a new year. Have definitely done '08. This coming year I want to strip away the little collisions that steal my focus. I want to find strength and consistency in breath…embrace the big picture – feel alive every day!

I loved reading in your letter about swimming at night and
cartwheels on the beach!
I find myself desperate for smells: jasmine; gardenia; the
ocean; incense and perfume; coconut suntan oil. Please put a
few drops of perfume in a letter and send it to me. That would
be dreamy........

You are in my heart always. All my love,
xoxoxoxxoxoxxoxoxoxoxoxoxoxoxoxoxoox

*January 30, '09.   #211842. H
BLOCK.

It's been really hot this summer. Almost unbearable here
amongst the concrete.
I would consider doing unspeakable things for an extended
swim in the ocean; its probably the thing I miss the most. Please
dive in it for me when you get the chance.
.....i study for 3 hours, then go back to my cell; change (more
greens!) and go to the gym until 6.30pm. Lately I have been
doing an all-over, body weight workout. Pushups; situps; chin-
ups; step-ups and lunges every day. The low intensity and
variety seems to suit training in the heat. I think if more
intense, I would give up after a while; there is no way to cool
down when you are finished.

[* It was on both the envelope and the letter, along with his identity number, but
Crystal pondered: is he really at that cliché address?? Cell block H....
seriously ??]

*April 26, 2009.

Sorry I haven't written for the past few months. Actually, you are the only person I write to except for a few friends in other gaols. Anyway, I hope this finds my sister-girl happy and healthy in the land of the endless horizon.
All is well here in the land of the endless day.....
There are only 95 of us at the moment which, as a group of misfits, is quite manageable. We have palm trees (yum); a good gym; work is great (computers) and all-in-all my time is flying.
I have already started my final year routine of training, studying, and getting closer to my spirit, so without distractions, I have no excuses to be anything but very well. I envy you for your discipline; its something I have trouble maintaining on the outside. I hope that this journey will imprint the importance of taking care of myself and those I love – its hard to do one without the other.
I really do hope you come for a visit – I miss you terribly.
I often think back to when we first met, and _______ and I fell so in love with you. You were so dreamy and funny and mean to the "help". I also think back to the love you have shown me since. Soft lips. Kind heart. 27/11. Forever....

Thankyou too for describing your time/day to me, so I can sense how and where you are – like my twin. You write beautifully about Bali. It all comes back to me....
'Saya mau pergi kesana sekarang'.
I used to dream in Indonesian. In west Irion, no one spoke English. It really takes hold of you (the country/culture) when the language saturates your dreams....

....i should be able to get work release and day leave soon. Well, nothing has happened as yet.....
if nothing else, gaol has taught me patience. Once I am approved, they will insist that I stay in the country for at least a year to satisfy my parole. Of course, if they deport me, I am free to roam the planet. (funny how that works!)
You asked if there were any funny characters I share my living space with. I think I have been here for too long, because everyone seems really normal to me now. I don't really have very much to gauge people with because the baseline here is dysfunctional.
_______, who I have lived with now for 14 months is a handsome, black, muscled, scary armed robber who is hard on the outside and soft on the inside. (he likes chocolate too). He is really protective of me because he says I've taught him more

about negotiation and kindness and forgiveness than the other people in his violent life (he is 28 and has spent the last 7 years in gaol).
He is bald and trains 3-4 hours a day. He loves martial arts and he is a really gifted painter. People are terrified of him even though he is nice to everyone. He puts people to sleep by cutting the oxygen to their brain; then ties them up - only when they piss him off. (quite funny).
He is incredibly tidy; cooks dinner for me every night (with hot chilli!) and he doesn't snore. I really like him.

....im going to leave this letter at that and send it on its long journey across the oceans. ....i love you with all my heart. Please write to me and send me a perfumed letter (+ photo??) so that I can make _______jealous! (all he gets are letters from his family).
Time is going quickly. Soon I will get to spend some time with you in the real world. You are in my heart always.....

Xoxoxoxoxox

Crystal recognized the profound healing this land had provided her with. On all levels: physical, emotional, spiritual, and mental. She decided to permanently honour the people with a sign of respect in the form of some additional *body art.* The hindu religion specific to this region was a blend of Buddhism and hindu darma. It was unique, and entailed never-ending colourful ceremonies and communal gatherings. It infiltrated your being on a soul-level.

On one of her adventure trips to Ubud, she had learnt that the hindu 'ohm' symbol must only be displayed above the waist. Otherwise, it is actually more of an insult! (this lesson was learnt through the reaction she got in flaunting an ohm symbol on her belly ring. You live and you learn when it comes to alternative cultures, beliefs and religions!)

The higher the better so she got the ohm specific to bali inscribed on the back of her neck, with rays emanating from it as a sense of surreal highlight or glow.   Underneath, in ancient sanscrit it was adorned with 'lahir pertama' – first born. This too, was a unique aspect of the people, who were named according to their number in the order process. (first, second, third born etc. after fourth it reverted back to one in the naming procedure)
They say that the soft flesh on the inner arm is a painful region for tattoos, but after this episode Crystal reckoned the neck would HAVE to be the area one suffers most for their art….it is a nerve location that seems to feel the pain to a greater intensity. Not recommended for the faint of heart, or those not fully committed!

This action represented an aligning with the land. It was her home now.
Her chosen address.
Like a *'return to sender'* barcode……

No date:

Darling ……
Your location sounds as divine as ever. Thankyou for transporting my spirit!
All here in the 'land that time forgot' is marching on.
I was going to write you sooner, but they are closing down here and im not sure where I will be going! They have already moved out half of the inmates, and because of my immigration concerns, it's a miracle that im still here.

They only have me for another 18 months today!!
I cant wait to see you again and walk on a beach together in paradise.
I should start practicing my bahasa Indonesia:
'Saya sudah telalu lament dari desana' ; – I am already too long from there.

Its fantastic you are using your time so well – I really like your ideas.
Mind – body– spirit……you got it goin' on girl!

So, I still have no word on my immigration status.
At this point, I am still an American refugee……

I have been taking great care of myself of late. I am going to live to be 1000!
(we are already old souls)…..
with spring I have picked up my training (weights) and am feeling all aligned.
I love spring……feel like I should be breeding ! two years without sex is not natural. Still, there is, as you say, a spiritual strength and growth that seems to come with abstinence.
If that is the case, I will either be enlightened or extremely horny when I finally leave here….

All told, my time seems to be going quickly in here as I am studying and training – and I don't really feel as though I am missing out on too much.

I wouldn't mind walking out of gaol for the first time on the day of my release; much better impact……

Ps: I just realized that I hadn't mentioned Maz and Chaylie throughout this letter; – a bit selfish and remiss of me! They are both doing well and ask about you often.
Chay is sitting for her HSC soon (she finishes the day before our birthday) and she has already been accepted to study law on a full scholarship (a saving of $140,000 !!) She is healthy and focused……
I speak to her every day on the phone, and I am so pleased at how wonderfully she has grown up. Under the circumstances, it amazes me she hasn't played the 'victim' card; – dropped out of school and gotten into drugs etc.
good girl (27/11).

Maz is doing well at work and goes to the gym 3 days a week. She still doesn't drink/smoke/do drugs. We still love each other in our limited way (me being in gaol!) Actually we are probably closer than we have been in years – she loves to see me clean and sober………

Well that's it from me. Please find me in my dreams.
Its almost our birthday again. I hope this letter finds you across the oceans.
All my love always,
J xoxoxoxoxoxo

Note: the prison mail provides a distinct lesson in **irony**. The letters deliver a true sense of the isolation and deprivation of incarceration. However, one can sense that when coupled with the healthy aspects of minimalism, it is conversely quite *liberating.* At the time of these exchanges, she was on a similar journey herself. Her living conditions were meagre; her possessions few, and the cleansing aspects she felt that resulted were *peace* at its most profound. The more she simplified, the more she felt relief.

It is also evident how much better they flourished respectively when adhering to a <u>disciplined routine</u> lifestyle. Without external distractions.

She also found that when she interacted only with the local people it was far more rewarding. They derived pleasure from the simplest things in life. Their Hindu culture instilled this in them. She envied the joy and wanted in too!

The western complex ways of life are toxicity to the max.

They both concurred that abstinence of any kind was a key disciplinary measure; the personal rewards of which were inner strength and fortitude.

Grand total summary: SURVIVAL....

Not that she had been there personally, but she assumed this situation was mildly similar to pregnancy......(ie: a mother 'forgets' the turmoil endured in the past, and the vows to 'never again'......and yet repeats the performance!)

After the ohm-adorning episode, one would have assumed Crystal would abstain from more pain induction for the moment.....but being the masochist that she is, she couldn't resist the urge to symbolically recognize another important phase of her life. Not one that was pleasant in any regard, but one she vowed not to forget, nevertheless.

Her celibacy.

She decided to place a red rose on a heart encased in stems of thorns.
She figured the emotion of the ordeal was adequately displayed by this image. Extending out from that she honoured the two places that had 'touched her heart' most in her life to date; where her personal growth had been accelerated. japan and bali.
Her eastern enlightenment.
The former was represented by a branch of the 'sakura' tree. Cherry blossoms. The latter was a row of the kamboja native to here and the tropics in general: the frangipani.

Spring 2009.

My beautiful sistergirl,

I hope this letter finds you happy and well. I just received your wonderful letter, a miracle in itself having navigated the labyrinth between us – and it delivered such wonderful gifts! Exotic tales from afar of lilies and laps in moonlit pools; meals of coloured rice and fragrant spice; warm oceans with endless horizons.......days filled with drums, music and dance, and of course, sweet solitude. Through your beautiful words and wisdom, I was/am transported across the distance that separates us.
Oh the tattoos! I must see them soon. Chayley has been asking me to get a 'sleave' when I get out – I don't think I will go

that far, but like yourself, I will get something to honour the solitude and celibacy.

You asked me to tell you about my time at home on 'day release'. Well, it had bits of everything I guess. Just being in the car, on the roads, getting to 'home' was pretty intense. After three years of travelling at walking pace, I was quite sure we were going to die. ....is a really safe driver but I spent the entire trip holding onto my safety belt; eyes forward unable to speak. Nice. Our first (and only) stop was the beach and it was beautiful – amazing surf, crystal water, just perfect. When we got home it was really strange seeing all of my own things which I had left so suddenly a lifetime ago. I must have spent an hour looking at paintings, opening little boxes, staring at photos. I felt a stranger in familiar surroundings.

The daughter wasn't due back for a few hours yet, so we had sex. It is great – you have to try it! I think for 27/11's no sex for too long is unhealthy, ya?

After Chayley came home we had a great lunch (basmati rice; kingfish with thai spices; broccoli, salad, and of course CHILLI). We then got really comfortable and watched a few DVDs. At this point of course I was feeling pretty relaxed/sleepy and it was time to go back to the Big House. Awful feeling....

I have been doing work as a logistics co-ordinator for the corrective services. I love the feeling of putting on the suit and tie; all 'pumped up' with my 'felon melon' (gaol haircut). The meeting of two worlds. Actually, it's just nice to get out of my 'greens'.

A change of pen. That ink was too intense. I think it was affecting my brain! Anyway it feels great to be writing to you now, so close to the end of my sentence.

What a journey – over a thousand days and nights to get to where I find myself now. Mentally, physically, and spiritually it has been a test, but now I recognize it as having been a gift. I've never felt so clear and alive. Maybe spring has something to do with it – I've always felt my heart swell at this time of year.

What I would give to lie on the sand with you and watch the stars, the gentle sound of waves and a warm scented breeze. It seems forever since I've had a swim. Actually, it's been a long time since I lay under the stars. Please save me a spot on a moonlit night......

Now that I am allowed to stay in the country, I am concerned about them letting me leave in 2 years. Will you visit me? It's all too far away at the moment and time has a strange way of sorting through the impossible – "the future's not ours to see – ke sara sara"......your husband tells me you are considering a move to Europe? I know you have both grown tired of this town.....

Maz and Chayley are both well. Chay is almost finished her first year at uni, and seems to be enjoying it. She is talking of moving out of home and living in a shared house with friends closer to where she studies. She is looking beautiful with her dark eyes, honey skin, large breasts (can I say that?) and she is that magical age – 19, on November 27.
Ahh....what a life she has in front of her...

Marvelous Maz too is travelling well, and has stopped smoking. Brother Dean has been in and out of hospital a bit lately. The HIV is starting to take its toll. His liver is giving him lots of grief and they are talking about a transplant. He is still positive within himself – amazing man – and I hope he hangs in there until well after I am released.......

Well that's enough about the rest of the world. ....,I miss you and think of you every day. Where will you be on our birthday? Let me wish you a happy birthday in advance and say 'I love you'. I hope and pray that the gods are kind and they watch over my beautiful sister girl always. Its strange how you and I find our lives so often in sync. No one in this day and age writes letters to each other. I smiled to myself when I read that you are enjoying life without your computer. In the same way, a part of me has enjoyed being uncontactable for the past few years. Simple life.
I feel the planets are shifting though and an old cycle of transition is about to end. Bring on the new day!

I love you dearly, my 27/11...
Oxxoxoxoxoxoxooxoxoxoxoxoxo

'The bums lived down there by the hundreds in little cement alcoves under the bridges and overpasses. Some of them even had potted plants in front of their places. All they needed to live like kings was canned heat (sterno) and what they picked out of the nearby garbage dump. They were tan and relaxed and most of them looked a hell of a lot healthier than the average Los Angeles business man. Those guys down there had no problem with women, income tax, landlords, burial expenses, dentists, time payments, car repairs, or with climbing into a voting booth and pulling the curtain closed.'

Charles Bukowski - Factotum

Crystal had read about the autobiography of Anwar Sadat, past president of Egypt. She recognized the parallels:

" So he rescripted himself.....it was a process he had learned when he was a young man imprisoned in Cell 54, a solitary cell in Cairo Central Prison.....
He learned to withdraw from his own mind and look at it to see if the scripts were appropriate and wise. He learned how to vacate his own mind and, through a deep personal process of meditation, to work with his own scriptures, his own form of prayer, and rescript himself.
He records that he was almost loathe to leave his prison cell because it was there that he realized that real success is success with self. It's not having things, but in having mastery, having victory over self. ....

Sadat was able to use his self-awareness, his imagination and his conscience to exercise personal leadership, to change an essential paradigm, to change the way he saw the situation. .....from that rescripting, that change in paradigm, flowed changes in behavior and attitude that affected millions of lives in the wider Circle of Concern"
This was an exerpt form 'the seven habits of highly effective people' by Stephen Covey that Crystal found profoundly enlightening. It reinforced the importance of the journey they had been on while 'in prison'. For it was more than simply self-improvement.
It was survival.

Crystal remembered, and took solace in Jay's mantra from one of their many precious times together 'on the outside' :
" if you're a victim of fear and torture, it will engulf and destroy you. If you <u>surrender</u> to it, you will be free. Strength lies in retreat. After all, ***prison is a state of mind"*****…..**

This is the lesson.

The Final Act
- 9,10,11.

Chapter 10 Part 9:

CRYSTALISING CHAOS.

And so we continue on with lessons…..life throws them at you. You have no choice! Sometimes, however it is beyond a challenge to ascertain exactly what the hell you are supposed to have learnt, beyond the hardship. Sadly, It Is never without pains and lifelong scars that the biggest lessons of all are learnt…

Life went on…….for Jay with his prison routine; Chayley with her studies and spending time with her supportive 'paternal figure' Uncle Dean; Hunter with trying to rebuild a business; and Crystal ?..... with a new life entirely to navigate.
The whole aspect of personal healing was energy consuming enough, let alone the additional duties of studying a new language and establishing a lifestyle routine in another place that suited her needs and sentiments adequately.
Strangely, it was not so dissimilar to Jay's journey. Both were personal ones. Absolute privacy was mandatory. His went without saying, and hers was <u>by design.</u>
Her only communication for the most part continued to be the letters to Jay.
He would keep her informed of news on the family; snippets of info on the curious characters he encountered, and updates on his sentence situation.
It finally reached the stage of his release; - 2 weeks to go, and it was time for him to make up for the *lost time* with his wife, daughter and brother.

Just as Crystal was starting to feel energized and renewed for the first time in so long, he hit her with the first bout of depressing news. And although it shouldn't have been, it was a shock.
Brother Dean had taken seriously ill. He had proven to be, by all accounts a walking miracle; a freak for one with HIV+ for over a decade. And let's not forget his tolerance for indulgence beyond all others! Due to this, coupled with the fact he had the undeniable endurance of an Ox, Scientists had not surprisingly used him as a 'lab rat' since he seemed to be defying the normal processes of decay. They were bewildered by his apparent absence of any signs of illness whatsoever!
However, it was finally starting to take its toll. Symptoms were emerging, and as life is often cruel, they were rapidly increasing day by day.
He was suffering liver problems. He was in for testing and treatments daily and the prognosis was disturbing. It looked like he was finally giving up the fight. The beast he had defied for so many years now had the upper edge. Aids was targeting the primary organ. The liver masterminds immunity and detoxification. You can't fuck with the king….it orchestrates the whole performance, after all. His demise was imminent.
Eventually, Hunter contacted Crystal to announce the news that he was given 'a month at the most'. So Jay would have a week or two only with his brother by the time he was released. Better that than nothing, but it seemed a harsh way to be introduced back to the 'reality of life' on the outside……'welcome home'.
No wonder felons actively seek recapture when they are finally released. The grass ain't exactly greener!!

Good old Dean was true to himself till the end though. Not surprisingly, he had pre-devised his bucket list….crazy and courageous, in keeping with his vibrant nature! And knowing him, he would be actively ticking them all off until the ability to do so was finally stripped from him entirely. Although years of carrying 'dormant' HIV should surprise nobody that it finally won the war, it is always a shock where death is concerned. It would have torn yet another hole in Jay's bleeding heart.

She called him on the day after Dean's passing. As ever Jay was at peace with another shitty situation in life, and most grateful that he had the final days with his bother, even though it was mostly at bedside vigil with his sister.
The three of them had held hands as Dean gracefully moved on to the other side…well, that was Jay's verbal rendition of it. Always one to create some sort of peaceful, fantasy scene to protect those he cherished.
No doubt it was a most cathartic exercise for the 2 remaining siblings.
" It was beautiful hon….he had us both by his side, and he felt he could finally let go as the 'circle' was complete. There was a light afternoon glow of sunlight hitting his bed; it was surreal and perfect!"……
Crystal was weeping as he continued: *"Chay wanted to be there too, but she hadn't slept in 4 days from nursing him 24/7 so she had sadly been issued 'doctors orders' to seek some shut-eye herself at home. Her asthma symptoms are pretty intense. It has destroyed her to think she missed it, poor love"…..*
What a deeply disturbing way to be reunited with his family after another bout of sheer hell. Could luck be any worse for darling Jay?

Crystal desperately tried to offer some words of condolence, and comfort:

*" I'm so so sorry darling, and I feel so incredibly disappointed I am so far from you at this horrific time. You know you are in my heart always however. I am with you in spirit. And thank god you still have beautiful Maz and your little angel.....your baby. **Chayley** is your world now"...*

" I follow your bare footsteps..
Past the ancient sandstone rocks.
We skip down the slippery slopes to the cold river.
Our hearts pounding in time "

Abbie Paterson, 2016.

The weeks passed, and life went on.
But they were painful. Sad.
Crystal felt the deep sorrow and loss of her friend.
He had served so many sentences already......death seemed to compound them further.
Life was so damn cruel.

She became more of a hermit than usual. She simply couldn't be bothered with people, and idle small talk. Waste of life.
Yoga,   yoga,   serenity.......
Avoid the foreigners; stick to the spiritual natives. They will guide you home....

"He was a professional alien, a person who liked to be alienated, and I think he played that to the hilt"
The poet Lesley Woolf Hedley - referring to Bukowski.

*She got another email from Jay, :

'the girls are okay. Chayley in particular seemed to be making great progress in her therapy sessions. The doctor said that it was like she had made some serious life decisions and was finally at peace! It had been a fortnight of silence for her and deep introspection that had us really concerned, but she is finally breaking through with these newfound conclusions. And she smiles again! And has clarity and satisfaction because of them. Maz and I are so relieved'....

Well at least someone is faring positively from this, Crystal thought. She knew that Jay and Maz would be very concerned and protective of their daughters' welfare after such an emotional blow.
The loss of Dean would have hit her the hardest.
But her apparent strength was a relief. Evidentally she had reached a cathartic phase.
She is stronger than we give her credit for Crystal thought. Children often are.
We should learn from them. They provide the greatest lessons of all.
The goal is to stay young.

Life is even shorter than we think.....

Chapter 10 Part 10:

Fallen Angels.

Crystal found a poem she had written in her youth. Generally perceived as a social flamboyant person the irony was fierce...

On the verge of release,

what veiled insanity lies

and no-one can detect

though some suspect The Hurting cries.

Its dormancy frustrates the mind

and coiling and twisting, cannot unwind.

Panic-stricken, the facade pursues

a phoney demon

~I stand accused.

For two is one,

but only one you see···

and this moulded vision

replaces the real me.

*('The Hurting' was the most impactful album in her audio spectrum of the time)

"The boundaries which divide life from death are at best shadowy and vague. Who shall say where the one ends, and where the other begins?"

Edgar Allan Poe.

No, no no no......no.......

She couldn't believe what she was reading. Was this a cruel joke? A computer virus or something? It was like waking up to a nightmare as Crystal read morning emails with her coffee. She felt the room spinning.
Delirious.
Almost out of body.
She ventured out on the porch and stared at the duck pond, where her balinese sister had 'seen angels in it' for some sort of peace from this mental hell. But no escape was forthcoming. She had to slay the dragon direct.
My god....my hands are shaking....she thought as she picked up her phone to make contact and put some sort of perspective on the situation.

The usual international delay in connection.

Finally.

" Hi hon its me......Jay, I don't know what im reading; some sort of sick, twisted joke.....this email says its from you. Tell me you didn't send me an email 2 hours ago. Please...."
Incredibly, he greeted her like nothing had happened.
" Oh hey Crys!! How are you honey? We miss you so much!.....
Ah, yeah, I wrote that this morning. This news is as of today. Yeah....it's not an easy one. I just......."
His voice trailed off for a moment.
Shock.
" I just really thought you would want to be the first to know. Despite the fact it is ....bad news.......i ah... have so much to do but.....i keep thinking I might be dreaming this day up!! I'm sorry to share Crystal......Oh I hope you don't mind me informing you this way with no warning. I'm not thinking very clearly.....
Everything is a bit surreal right now. I'm just......
doing what needs to be done".......
Crystal felt her heart beating so loudly in her chest. It was like fight or flight; being cornered by some monster that you don't know how to escape.

Her adrenalin was in overdrive as she paced the porch while he continued:

" Yeah it was around 7 am this morning. Maz and I were just leaving with Dean's ashes – today was the day to scatter them for my beloved brother...."
(now that's enough hardship for one year right there, surely, Crystal thought. For they weren't just brothers. They were best mates too; albeit their contrastive natures).
So sad....

"It was on the porch as Maz was locking the door that we noticed her"...
he was referring to Chayley. The apple of her dad's eye. Both her dads'. Jay and Dean were both paternal figures.   She loved her own father so desperately, but when he was stolen from her (for most of her life in fact) she seeked solace, guidance and grounding in the arms of Uncle Dean.
Crystal suddenly became aware of another characteristic trait that she and Jay shared. When life and it's reality became too harsh, one reverts to ***fantasy*** *land.* Was it a 27/11 thing? These dates tend to indicate someone non-mortal.
Alien.

Survival...

"She was in front of us.
In suspension" (like time, for them both at this point)
"She did it beautifully, though! With a simple satin scarf. Oh, it was almost an ethereal sunrise this morning! The birds were all chirping in joy-song...
She had made this decision weeks ago. It had brought her the peace that we'd witnessed.

She had lit a candle, and written us the most beautiful note before she did her final ceremony...

and hung herself"...

Chapter 10 Part 11 of little 27:

Crystal's lament.....

The next few weeks were like suspended in time. Crystal walked the beaches at sunset, sobbing uncontrollably, and sometimes had to sit on the sand as the emotion hit her so hard in the gut she could hardly breathe. It was like a seed of disease that was growing – and she needed to get it out somehow, for she knew she would be sick otherwise.
She would wait till dark, when she was spent. Numb. Nothing left to sob out. And when one is in such a weakened state they know they just have to go on instinctive autopilot. For the mind melts down, and the body shuts down, and you are like a fading shadow.
Grief.
She almost hypnotically got her pen and slowly.....started to write.
Purge herself of the germ.
And in doing so, she started to breathe a bit less shallowly.
And sleep returned. Albeit sporadic.
She had been here before, and she would heal again.

But for now, she created a new reality for what the facts were.
This is how she would remember this time. It was to be locked in the vault and sealed forever.
Her creation came to life on paper.

Chayley had been a gift to the world.
She needed to be immortalized in prose.
So she created her vision

And she offered it to Jay and Maz to hold onto to…

My darling, darling Jay,

I'm sending you some words tonight

I found so difficult to write…..

Please keep them always;

They're from deep in my heart.

It's time for you now
To make a new start.

Stay strong & go forth

Knowing others are there too

And for each painful step,

We'll walk them with you.

You're never alone
In times of depair

For you and Maz,

I will always be there.

And during the times that are unbearably dark,

Call me & I'll light a spark

You are like family to me;

This is the way it will always be………

IN LOVING MEMORY OF LITTLE GODDESS #27.

November 27 1992 – 7/11/2010

I walked down to the beach
and as I sat on the sand,
I felt a presence:
little sister holding my hand

She looked so serene
as she whispered to me:

"It's so calming, -
& safe,
down here by the sea"

A gifted misfit
who felt she didn't belong;
-knew she was cherished & loved,
but somehow.....life just felt wrong

She'd inherited the virtues
of this unique family way;
there was nobody like them:
Maz, Cass, Dean and Jay.

Bright as a button;
sharp as a tack
-& like her Mum, exotically beautiful~

What did she lack?

In Bali Hindu there are many gods,
but the 3 main ones ARE:
Wisnu, Brahma & Siwa

Siwa was present,
and was making Char sad.
He needed to go,
as his powers were bad.

We offered a prayer
& asked Wisnu to appear.
His role is the Guardian;
he protects us from fear

I laid the Chanang offering,
as I had learnt
Then 2 sticks of incense
we solemnly burnt

We prayed for divine guidance,
as smoke wafted through the air:
How to protect ourselves
from internal despair

A ceremony we held,
and with 27 chants,
she stood with her aura
& started to dance

She was so truly special,

words couldn't express,

how much she was loved,

 & wished happiness

Breathtakingly gorgeous;
a few stopped to stare
as I placed frangipanis
in her sleek, stunning hair

Then as we watched the sunset
we began to tire
Tonight's was spectacular;
A huge ball of fire !

She smiled & said
"tell Mum & Dad now I'm free"
as we sat in the moonlight,
down by the sea

I understood now
she felt no longer sad;
Men fishing on the shoreline
reminded her of her dad

He used to retreat here too,
he told me
On his boat in the ocean
he found harmony

We stayed through the night,
'till the sun rose again
and her face now looked calm
where before there was pain

Then a bright ethereal vision
with halo appeared
Like a symbol to vanquish
all that we'd feared

He hypnotically proceeded
towards Chay and me
then began wading slowly
back into the sea

A true free spirit,
she longed to take flight
To the beckoning call
of the yonder white light

She squinted, then gasped

with joyous surprise;

A look of recognition appeared
in her beautiful eyes

She blew me a kiss
as she ran off into the blue, yelling:

"Wait for me Uncle Dean,

I'm coming too!".......

Chapters 11 - 18:

TRAVEL TALE TITBITS AND RACONTEUR RAMBLINGS....

Chapter 11

Technical travel traumas.....

One might expect that a plane would have passed a few tests BEFORE all the passengers have boarded and are ready for takeoff...but one might also be forgiven for forgetting, once again, where one was. Ah my beloved bali.....

I was set to takeoff for London yesterday at 4pm, and here I sit now, 6.30pm the following day, balancing my pc on my lap as I recap the last 24 hours' events.....

So as we slowly proceeded along the tarmac, an hour after schedule yesterday, it was realized/determined by the pilot that oh no – there was a technical hitch that might need repair...don't go anywhere. Stay tuned...
One hour later, as I realize my connecting flight in hong kong is slipping away, it is announced that 'this may take 4 hours'......15 minutes later: 'we are calling hong kong for advice'.......which had me stomping off to the supplies area requesting a glass of wine ('or a bottle will do!')....with a stewardess returning to my seat to deliver the news that 'no beverages are to be served until in the air'......BANGSAT!! (I say this because you don't speak bahasa, so no apologies for my swearing tirade required)
 30 mins later:

'we have to offload you all, and get back to you'

Queue pandemonium; bag frenzy; plummeting blood sugar and mini bouts of aggression and violence...
So back out to the terminal, to sit in a pack and wait for SOMEONE to give us info of the plan.......what plan?!?!
The cathay staff were as confused and solution-less as we mere passengers!
The stories unfold: a myriad of menus destination-wise (and languages to boot) that that were to connect from the first flight: LA, Dubai, Athens, Amsterdam, Australia, Japan, London (ahem) etc.....that all needed to be compensated for by the responsible airline: monumental chaos and missed business; meetings; family arrangements etc etc.
And one little lonesome cathay rep; sweating profusely and trying to calm the angry herd....

There's me, sitting and thinking: 'there HAS to be a sitcom in this madness!'
Cut a very long-winded description of the mass swearing in a million languages going on short, 5.5 hours later, they start to bring

out our check-in bags for collection.....one by one......(**so** bali!).
but, oh gosh oh no.....they have lost my bag!! Wait another
hour.......finally it arrived, and I watched the group left scratching
their heads as they were told 'we aren't sure' as to the
whereabouts of their belongings....(?!)
(this is perhaps where I started to laugh hysterically as I realized
that the situation was beyond belief on all scores possible. Im
talking collapse on my bag with tears running down my face in
lunatic-like resignation)

And so the night wore on...shuttle buses were finally booked to
escort all to a designated mystery hotel. People queing and
fainting from dehydration and starvation etc.
I meet another lady from London, and her balibot daughter (*a
stuuuuuuning* duo), who coerse me into jumping a taxi instead to
bypass the mob and beat them to a room and complimentary
meal somewhere.....hopefully before midnight.
The Ramada hotel (a relief: much better than expected) was
arranged, and we swiftly checked in, and had the bellboy bring
our bags.
But oh no, ive run out of pulsa for my bali phone so I have no way
of contacting the husband and driver waiting for me at the other
end!
What to do? Mind a haze as its now 24 hours since ive eaten, and
im ready to murder someone.....i explain to the bellboy and he
exclaims proudly: 'I tell my wife, she give you topup!'
me (in bahasa) : 'what, she comes here NOW, or I must go to
her?....i will miss dinner. Already 10pm!!'. His reply: 'I call
her!'......oh boy.....
There must be the gods, as he managed, miraculously to do it for
me over the phone; have me ready for comms; give me the room
rundown etc in under 10 mins. Massive amazement from me, to
say the least!

Off I go to the complimentary buffet to eat something before my
vision goes blurry and I blackout. But ooh, not much left, as the
buffet was supposed to close at 10pm, and its after that
now.....and the kitchen has run out of food for the night. (!) I meet
up with my vanilla and mini-choc comrades: Karen and Mia. (the

beautiful blue-eyed glamour single-mum with the dark exotic junior _surprise_...perfect pairing; you've gotta love it)
We fared better than the rest food-wise however, (albeit somewhat cold by this stage)~ who were compelled to fill up on white rice, noodles and doughy buns (no problem; many were chinese – they were happy, as it is their food of choice).
I resort to paying $35 (£20) for a _sip_ of wine that I was NEEDING at this stage, more than the food. Rumours spread like wildfire that the next flight will be the 6am one, so I calculate in my head that there is no point actually going to bed at all really, as I have to leave soon. Brilliant!

Back in the room: I go to send email with the free wifi but oh no, pc battery too low, so must wait till tomorrow....
I'm excited to note there's one of those 'hotel beds' I love: like clouds of bliss with big fluffy pillows and doona to cuddle up in while cool aircon allows one to actually _desire_ covers....(ive been sleeping without but a thread for 6 months in tropical delight)
I shuffle around in the complimentary THONGS / flipflops provided (bali's answer to slippers I guess)....ooh but forgetting my aversion to cheap rubber.....hail the ALERGY ALERT....(i break out in an inflamed angry rash, and proceed to scratch feet frantically for the entire night......the antithesis of comfort.....so scratch too the blissful slumber rendition. Cloudy pillows and cosy duvet don't cut it when the feet are on fire.)

I call reception to ask: "what time is the re-scheduled cathay flight tomorrow?"(as of course it is impossible pour moi to relax till I know what the f^±...the gameplan is.) "I'm sorry miss lisa, we will inform you as soon as we know"
 Me: _"how?_ Note under door? Sms? Email? Phonecall? Knock??".....
answer: "Ah.......belum tahu pasti sekarang, tapi aku akan kasih anda tahu segara'...(they speak native tongue when stressed and confused....translation: "**N.F.I**'!")

So I repacked; showered; and laid down with one eye open waiting for....something.....
Next thing I know, its 7am, and my alarm clock is in the form of intense drilling on room next door...I phone reception and am told

"ah yes, it must be our maintenance *'friend'*!".....to which I (yes actually) reply: "Well! let me get hold of this bloody friend of yours and **strangle** the f^&*er!"
I *could* sleep all day but don't of course. The battle continues. I get up to see if msg under door; on phone; on email etc.....message pigeon on balcony maybe....
No joy.

I go downstairs to crowds of arguing people, to get shown a 'list' of all the personalized rescheduled flights....oh boy, this must have cost cathay BIGTIME!! Ages pass as we all await viewing the ONE AVAILABLE LIST to be passed around. I suggest a photocopy might be in order...'ah! Photocopier. yes we have! Can do!'.......great guys; - logic, ya.... lets go!
I get my verdict: Singapore airlines flight for me later tonight. Hours to kill though. What to do to stay awake....

I go down to breakfast but.... oh no....they are closing now, so throw down a triple-coffee; grab a handful of papaya and head back to room once again.
There is a fab pool and gym here but.....you guessed it.....no cossies or gym gear on me. I head to the gym anyway; workout in my underwear (!) and jump in a sauna tor an hour to sweat out the cortisol overload.
Ooh....dizzy now. Maybe not a good idea. Lets hope it helps me sleep later...when plane takes off......if I get on one etc...oh, and it actually DOES take off...

I get to the airport 4 hours early; queue for an hour; speak in bahasa; tell everyone I love them, and get issued my exit-row seats that were pre-paid for at last. Sigh. With assurances that the adjacent seat was free and would be blocked off (most important, otherwise no benefits for vitally needed solitude and peace!)
So now I wait.....as to whether I ever *leave* denpasar is yet to be determined, but stay tuned for more entertainment.

And the moral of the story is....(drumroll)....
Ah.....there isn't one really. Except perhaps: NO morals or expectations must apply/should be had here on my island of the

gods. For they rule the land, and if they want to play (read reak havoc)....don't get in the way!
Just laugh and play along.....ho hum, ho hum....
Yes, ONE flew over the cuckoo's nest.....but some wings were clipped, so cannot fly!!
Bring back the halcyon days of business class travel she sighs; on planes that left the ground. with style on board....

Yours truly, a shattered-beyond-belief balibot. Xoxoxooxoxoo

Part two..war and peace on flight #1:

On board at last....time to relax!!
Ooh...NO YOU DON'T...there'll be none of that girl! Conflict costume time.....prepare for massive disputes with fellow passenger....(who, as it turns out, is as wrecked and ready to commit homicide as myself....if only she had mentioned that earlier!)

It goes like this: arrive at designated pre-paid extra room seat; spread out gear to luxuriate in private peace; get told takeoff is imminent, and find a woman approach and start moving my stuff off adjacent chair. [at that point, I would describe her as pear-shaped, sour-mouthed; middle-aged (as of course I am a wishful thinking youngster, me, ya..) flabby-limbed Australian (or is it South African?]

I note a souvenir bali kite in her original seat stow-pouch. Need I say more?
Anyhoo, she assumes the right to take a throne next to moi, and the ensuing tirade goes something as such:
"is this your stuff?" ...me; in shock my eyes like saucers: "yes, of course! Why?"
"well move it, coz I wanna sit here"
me: "what, for takeoff?"
it: "no for the entire flight"…..
"Well, im sorry to inform you that I paid for the privelidge of 'space' without other people, so there will be none of that!

"what you paid for is LEGROOM only; I know my rights, so I shall be sitting here end of story"....
"What is wrong with your original perfectly good chair?" I enquired ? She:"I have my reasons, and I don't need to be explaining them to the likes of you....."
(ooh, you wanna **play** beeeatch??!! Me thinx......if anyone fancies a showdown when I am in a sleep-deprived; plummeting blood sugar state, watch this space I say....)- with SPACE being the operative word.
I proceeded to lay out all my stuff on the floor in her way; stretched out my legs etc while she put an eye mask on; now cramped in the corner seat, to pretend slumber. When she awoke and told me to 'stow it all above', we broke out into a massive verbal performance that lasted the better part of an hour; entertained the entire cabin; and ended with us both LAUGHING at the end and chatting in a friendly fashion. The full 360 degree scenario...I really didn't need the FIGHT OR FLIGHT sensation triggered, but to see the positive side, I knew it would ensure a come-down sleep on the connecting flight.
(The woman had actually simply moved to an exit row seat she hadn't paid for, and id been promised would remain free. With prior experience as a trolley dolly, she knew she could take such liberties without repercussions...(oh but I ensured it came far from free for her. Much stress and anxiety fees incurred!)

Then: the lesson learnt here:...
 it is very windy in capetown; ~ known for it in fact...~a kite makes the perfect souvenir indeed(!)
THE END....

Well, as I sign off now, im about to board the A380-800 (superjumbo); the largest passenger aircraft....deets for your thrills dearest travel-junkie father, as I know how it turns you on....
xoxoxoxoxoox

Chapter 12

~QUEEN B…..
The princess and the Bee.

*Warning: narcissistic content!

Samara was barely herself these days. She was dancing on the brink of sanity and teetering on self destruction. For she had been completely alone for months;(albeit giddyingly happily so)…yet dreading what lay ahead in her life, and was *now* attempting the marital role yet again…

but, in a state of enforced limbo felt the mask slipping…

It was exhausting.

"Meek wifehood is no part of my profession. I am your friend, but never your possession"

Vera Brittain, first world war nurse, writer and pacifist, *Married Love* (1926)

In both her countries of residence (she would flirt simultaneously between the two) she went through distinct phases of preferred, recluse behaviour, alternated with attempts at 'normal integration' into society and its associated protocol palarva.

The fact is, she wasn't good at it! She often thought she would be better off just to remain permanently alone…..or with a baby to nurture for company.

Summary: a messy state of affairs.

She sought a crystal-clear mindset and conscience; devoid of the 'normal people-factor'.

Always selective of her candidates for *shared* time, she was still much more content with her own company.

Alien.

Cue the timely **re**-emergence of <u>Bill, like a white knight in shining armour</u> [Or '*William*' to be more precise (and appropriate to his prevailing nature)……*and black leather*, more likely (!)]

He had done a fabulously convincing disappearing act for well over a year…much to the distress and concern of Samara. They had forged a unique friendship bond; one that entertained and intrigued her. And then, he quite literally went off the radar; uncontactable by any means.

(By that stage she had been convinced that she was not *meant* to have friends, as she had always suspected….for they either vanished (evidently); back-stabbed her; betrayed her trust, or simply got sick and died!) She couldn't help but ponder therefore: was SHE the comradeship kiss of death ?

She had thus began to suffer paranoia, ~ sensing that indeed SHE was the culprit; akin to a monster…perhaps the curse was from *her* after all…

….had they unwittingly walked into the web of the ….<u>black widow….?</u>   *Similar to a redback spider she would flaunt the scarlet sash like a beauty pageant queen*

(To define : a black widow spider is sleek yet venomous….her ploy is to seduce, conquer and devour ….poison and eat her mates!)

Samara would have preferred reference to a regal *queen bee* than a deadly spider, obviously; but sometimes one has to face facts. For the truth will always bite you in the arse eventually.

She quite simply fell in love with the special ones: gifted albeit tortured souls…(but there was always a lot of fine print that went with these unions).

So it was a shock and a half to receive the email in her inbox that he was back and apologetic.. and eager to meet up. Just as if nothing had happened. Such was the story of her life. Much, or indeed MOST of it was unexplainable.

She had made a vow to quiz him as to the reasons for his 'sojourn to outer space' for nearly 18 months….and then decided that the mystery component was perhaps more suitable. For it had been a diversion of sorts to her daily woes for some time. So let's just leave it at that then. It had, in addition provided her a certain degree of curious entertainment and wild scenario~provoking:

had he been **arrested**? Been **murdered**? Died of an **over-dose??**?….her mind was frantic with ideas and notions. Any grey-matter dancing for her was met with welcome approval - for she despised anything or anyone boring….it really was a waste of valuable time!

She had toyed with the idea of going to his abode to investigate…and possibly rescue his adorably plush pedigree cat from abandonment. She figured: if murder or death had in any way been involved, the smell would be a sure detector by this stage. His blind next-door neighbour would have been alerted to the stench of rigour-mortis though, surely?! Or perhaps he was too afraid to investigate further. The mind boggled with analogies. It was better than scrabble or chirades. Fact always trumped fiction in her view!

One solid fact remained though. She was definitely a **fag hag!** The tally of 'girlfriends' that she had accrued throughout her life that were, by definition, GAY MEN way outnumbered the actual female ones. It had always been her thing. The magnetism of alpha gay men. The unattainable..

When it came to masks and mirrors, these beautiful boys ruled the roost to be sure!

She had been to William's pristine flat in the past, and, with respect, ascertained that he was clearly the queen of minimalism;- clean lines and obsessive compulsive hygiene. Alpha to be sure, there was no detectable flaws in this gent she had acquired on a quest for dinner-party ingredients one day.

(Samara and Bill had met outside a favourite London store when the fire alarm had signalled and were consequently locked out with a mass of other disgruntled folk.) Announcing (with some unladylike accentual cussing) that she was off on a walking mission to another Waitrose venue, he hastily agreed to join her on the quest. A brief intro, then it was arm in arm comrades - with free-flowing convo like they had been friends forever. Such was the camp appeal that worked in her favour and suited her partner preferences.

He had quirky, often odd mannerisms that intrigued her. The way he signed off emails as 'your waitrose friend' in the beginning, and when re-announcing his existence ('hi girlfriend, sorry for the time lapse but I'm back…)was a key to further unravelling of his bizarre ways.

Likewise, William physically maintained the aire of narcissistic supremacy he embodied, (and she hoped she upheld herself) - that was both relatable and irresistible to her.

In general, their intellect was superior to the hetero crowd; not to mention sense of humour and quick witted banter. Time spent with the carefully chosen ones was always fulfilled with much hysterics on her behalf…..(the old adage : 'don't smile or laugh if you don't want wrinkes' went well and truly out the window with these lads.. So if the price to pay would be buckets of botox down the track to compensate for the laugh lines then so be it - the cost was worth it for the quality comradeship and entertainment factor they never failed to deliver!)   Her laboured time on self-preservation lifestyle, grooming and 'veneer' presentation never went unnoticed by them either. It went without saying that a gay man's attention to detail was on another level. One she understood. And respected. When she had enhanced her lips mildly for instance, he was the first to zone in and notice. Immediately - and grant praise: "ooh loving the kissers babe; subtle but out there and pouty perfect!!" Comparatively, others who saw her daily hadn't noticed a difference in the slightest.
Attention to detail.

And contrary to their '*physical* preferences' let's call it, they were the antithesis of mysogony…(the title of which was often awarded to the unsavoury <u>straight </u>men.)   Such is the irony of life….*they* tended to put women on a pedestal of sorts; honoured them and

gave more satisfaction and self-esteem. Gratification. (Always exceptions to
the rule mind; they could also be the bitchiest witches too! ~ the idea was to
be a judge of character when selecting these specimen acquaintances.) She
sought only the *genuine* queens of glory. Not the ones that stung with
poison….(but one can never be TOTALLY sure in life, right?!)

Samara and Bill met for lunch twice at a local eatery of favour. It tended
to be their little routine: do a venue twice, and then proceed to the next. Once
was never enough…..and twice whet the appetite for new, unchartered
culinary terrain. They were insatiable…

She was thrilled beyond belief to have discovered someone to do a
leisurely lunch with. So far, she had failed in finding anyone to fit the *bill* (no
pun intended) in years. And as such, had represented a lonely soul in choice
venues, with computer as her token partner. (The device also helped to deter
the inevitable *'oh she needs to be saved, poor lonely girl'* interpretation by many. In
fact the complete contrary was true. She relished her solo status as she
savoured her menu choices.)

The first chosen address with Bill was moroccan inspired - he shared her
love of cumin and fragrant fare. bravo! Conversations of culinary
compatibility ensued, and then after perhaps one wine too many….a taboo
topic inevitably arose. One which she almost fell off her chair with a cocktail
of shock and relief. His 'alias' as a nurse and vet and whatnot was where his
initial training lay, yes. But the REAL money he made was in the avenue of
the other world she had been exposed to.

Their little secret.

He was a male escort !

No wonder he had such style and desire for (read NEED) 'the good life'
and all that that title entailed.

Low and behold…..Of *all* the fabulous and flamboyant lads she had
adopted, this one was such a kindred spirit of like-minded pursuits and
preferences, it was indeed like peering into a mirror. And seeing oneself as
the opposite gender. Coupled with that, he was the most unpredictable guy
ever….she never really knew what verbal she would be in for at any given
time.

Moody. Changeable.

Familiar turf for sure

They were like a married couple in many ways…without the
'intrusion'(read penetration). But she wasn't getting any of that in her regular
marriage anyway, so celibacy (sadly) continued.

"I have too many fantasies to be a housewife. I guess I am a fantasy"..

Marilyn Monroe.

But I digress. Back to the here and now. When she had lost her lad (so she
thought at the time) she left back to the island retreat home in the tropics;
forlorn and confused as to the mystery back in London.

It was just before her return to their communal British soil that he
reappeared, so a timely performance to be sure.

Anyway, as the story unfolds itself, the plot thickened even further on the
case of the curious queen. For he made an announcement - (via the medium
of internet since she was on the other side of the globe at the time of contact;
abiding in her beloved non-reality island.)

He animatedly wrote that not only was he back; well; alive; kicking; and
apologetic for vanishing, but he was the happiest he had ever been in his life.
His tall-order life partner had finally arrived ! Joy to behold. He couldn't
wait to introduce Samara to his new beau.

She couldn't help but disregard the annoyance of his former bizarre
behaviour, and feel thrilled for the guy. It was evidently serious, as they had
been together for a year now; - this wasn't just one of those fleeting flings one
usually hears of with the homo lads. No. This was like marriage material. He
had admitted he had done threesomes with male partners *involving* a woman,
but other than that his loyalty remained with the male sector. He had always
envied her ability to maintain faithful behaviour to a marriage despite years of
isolation and celibacy. It wasn't healthy, but she had remained loyal
regardless. She often pondered though: what would the difference be then?
Would **they** perhaps make an ideal couple…??there was no action to speak
of in her homelife anyway! How she had remained loyally faithful for so long
was a mystery even more to others than herself.

He respected that and told her as such; even though he expressed the fact that he believed she deserved much more…her denial of rights was somewhat of a virtue in others' eyes. And perhaps that had sent him on his own personal journey for a more permanent union with a man worthy of his attributes.

She was thrilled for him that he had won the lover lottery…. for not many of us do.   She wondered with curiosity whether he had found his prince via their familiar 'cut to the chase' method of escort introduction. She would have placed bets on it, for there is no surer way to get to know someone than via this nifty method of 'casting'.

Coincidentally, one of the papers at the time defined a few prevailing attitudes:

"Transphobic means prejudice against transgender people; whorephobic describes similar attitudes to sex workers."

As she was set to be returning to the great Britain 'other home' shortly, she became excited at the luring prospect of meeting up with a joyful couple who suited her social 'ticklist'; ….choice few did to be fair and honest, so she spent the majority of her time solo. Which was fine!

But now the fun new concept of actually sharing a glass of wine and a laugh with someone *else* brought her some comfort and 'warmth'. Especially considering the other hemisphere was the temperature anti-christ when it came to her bodies' calefaction needs. Going from the tropics to northern european chill-zone was a body shocker.

The fact that they were in raptures and beyond happy was the most enticing factor. (Other people's woes and dramas weren't something she wanted to allocate time for these days; for god knows she had enough of her own to contend with)

Two weeks later as her open suitcase was being stuffed to completion, like a french goose and she was swearing profusely (also in french)~ the familiar sound of her arriving emails heralded again. Ping!

She didn't check it until later that day however as the mission at hand had her complete attention. Packing was the bane of her existence, but a burden she had to endure being a resident in 2 different countries on opposing sides of the globe. And she was in no way a multi-tasker!

Often, the whole computer issue was a hindrance to her on her buddhist-minded island existence of minimal clear-thinking and lifestyle pursuits. It often brought with it bad news...and on occassion horrific announcements. Mind-fuck material. Particularly from family or close associates. It was love/hate with her adorable apple; an often detested device.

But with the stresses of travel and whatnot, it is an inevitable evil, so she knew she had to cop it sweet for now.

Her fear at *this* point was an alert of another airline calamity that would hinder her journey - like so often in the past. Stress levels were always high as the due date of departure loomed....not to mention timely distractions here in the crazy 'land of the lost'.

The duck squawks heralded feeding time at the pond beyond her porch. 5pm. She realised she still hadn't attended to the MAC duties so she hastily turned on the computer to refer to the dreaded in-tray.

There it was.

Another tale of tragedy and woe. She couldn't fathom what she was reading......it was beyond disturbing.

Harsh reality trumps imagination every time, she realised yet again, as she shook her head in disbelief. Bill's hopes and dreams had been decimated in one foul swoop. Or should I say flush. His beloved beau had suffered a sudden heart-attack and died.

On the toilet!

It was devastation and she could feel it in his written 'voice'.

He was lost and needed her for support...how long until she was back? She sadly began a reply of sympathy; reinforcing his suggestion of grief-counseling, and urging him to seek buddhist input somewhere local to himself.

Survival.

A day later, to put icing on the chaos cake, he further informed her that now there were mysterious allegations surrounding the demise of a perfectly fit and healthy man; whose family now placed blame <u>entirely</u> on Bill. He must be the culprit they thought! How else could one in perfect health cark it while having a crap?

So now not only was he grief-stricken and ostracised, but also *framed for murder!* She was returning to another land-mine....

She assured him of her imminent arrival soon, and told him to only surround himself with uplifting, positive people in the meantime~(i.e. His mum and Jake his cat)

But Ooh…..The concept of foul-play added that element of intrigue to the whole scenario: she knew him to be innocent no question - but the allegations assisted in fashioning the fatality further.

So:

The vanished man reappears out of nowhere, and ends up embroiled in a murder scene of which he is the star suspect.
Fodder for story-matter perhaps?
Absofuckinglutely my friend!

[As already stated, leave the imagination at the door, since reality serves much more interesting subject matter. And twisted reality always seemed to end up in her lap]

So when the next segment of his sordid story was revealed, she decided to make some reference notes of the tragic tale.

Sadness was a repetitive theme of late; ~ she had witnessed many people fall ill and die that year. Particularly with regards to the big C. It was definitely the chapter of 'LIFE SUX' in many aspects of existence.
Very hard to stay positive and unaffected. Everybody can relate to that in these troubled times. However being nearly October, it (the horrid year) was nearly at completion so she hoped the new year brought more health and vitality to all those she knew. Enough hurdles already. It filled her with dread wondering what the next upsetting scene might be.

So, on an absolutely bitter morning when they met for lunch one day, she had a feeling something was awry. Her instincts rarely betrayed her, so she felt the familiar tightening in her gut.

He had recently cancelled on meeting her for a birthday lunch; much to her distress as it was to be something she had looked forward to, like a gift to unwrap. He hinted at health issues but she was not in the mood to ponder them further. Just get the tainted year over with, she thought with disdain.

And so here it was : the first social meet in the *new* year, and she was not geared up for any more grief.

As the conversation started over the first wine, she asked his feeling towards children….would he ever consider donating sperm or something to father a child? His genes would evidently be welcomed! (tall, slim, devilishly handsome, **intelligent** etc.) Ticks ahoy.

The answer was hesitant. He loved kids but he shook his head adamantly : "my sperm is not ideal, oh no."..

At first she translated this as meaning: " *too costly, a hindrance to my particular lifestyle - not ready to reduce my personal standards for such* an *imposition*".

For thus was a general attitude among many of these lads…..and why their appearance, lifestyle and living standards by all accounts was top notch when compared to the family-pursuing lot (!)

Then here it came…."I didn't want to tell you till I saw you in person….but that's why I couldn't make the last rendezvous my love.

I received the dreaded news that I am officially HIV positive."

…BOOM. Another bomb.

She felt her eyes well up and her skin prickle, and the familiar knowledge that she may well have to farewell yet another close comrade sometime down the track. My she sure knew how to pick 'em. WHY were the extraordinary characters she was attracted to all tainted in some way that was only revealed later? They only seemed to own a small allotment of time on this earth - perhaps they belonged somewhere else all along.

But god she was done with the goodbyes…..it was like abandonment issues for her now. She just wanted someone to stick around long enough to share the journey of her life with - for she worked HARD at preserving her own. And it it was by no way easy; - took a tonne of discipline, abstinence and denial.

Her face fell. Forlorn. Sorrow. Familiar sensations and turf.

He grabbed her hand " oh don't worry about me hon - god it's NOTHING like it used to be regarding this issue….medical advancement has

come through with the goods." He retrieved a pillbox from his pocket with 3
huge white pellets like horse capsules.

"I just have to take 3 pills a day and I honestly feel fine. Even on an empty
stomach, no problem! Look - watch" he tossed them back and downed with a
glass of chardonnay. She doubted it was an ideal method of dosage but
encouraged his positive outlook nevertheless.
Nodding with staged reassurance, her mind drifted back to her other friend
who had been inflicted similarly years ago…and only showed symptoms
much later. (However, when he <u>did,</u> his decline was lightening speed. And
then *poof*….just like that he was gone.)

For she cherished the company of William - and besides, she had already
experienced losing him once already!…..life has a way of sending
messages/protecting you at times. Maybe this first round of his absence had
been training for when she would officially lose him completely. Who knows.

He had changed his Facebook photo to the one of them together at one of
their lunch sessions; - she in her classic madonna leather jacket (*'looking fierce'*
as he described her)- and he in his Prada sports jacket that was a gift from an
ex-client (and although a casual look, was probably worth the cost of a small
car!)

She had shared some photos of her in her 'dress-up mode' on some of the
gourmet home meals….one of which was with a mini dress; high boots, and
gun - doing the 'charlies angel' pose. He posted it on his page with the caption
'*my bond girl*' in action'.

It was a fabulous union of cliche proportions - they complemented each
other well in many respects, (read diva)….and despite their differences, 'got'
each other. Something we tend to take for granted but actually a rare find in
life….

He was also quite perceptive as to her home-life hell of the moment. She
hadn't given much detail, preferring to try to relax and escape her woes when
they met; the whole point of the friendship enterprise after all. She was
touched by the fact that he jumped to her rescue (verbally at least): " You
know you always have a home babe, no matter what happens. Don't forget
that…don't hesitate to come stay with Jake and I - we would love to have
you with us; a perfect family trio"…. He indicated the convertible lounge that

folded out into a bed for one. Very sweet and thoughtful. It was lovely mental ammunition to keep on board even if it was only ever a fantasy placebo.

They met up again at a later stage at one of her favourite venues. It was affordable to her in the current financial crisis her husband had them swamped in.

On a Monday, the prices on main dishes were half-price, so she spoilt him with champagne and wine in addition to that. He wasn't a beer-drinker per-ce (and neither was she - too bloaty) - but from time to time she would indulge in a cider for the sugar energy kick if required.

On this day she had no sleep under her belt from the night before; a pattern adopted from the stressful household she was trapped in. These outings were like an opportunity to 'escape from the fortress' for a spell….in the name of sanity maintenance control!

All things considered, he looked rather well, but she could sense the underlying sensation of grief, loss and heartache. He had put on the mask for the day; she knew that tactic well. It was the survival mechanism mandatory to face society on any level. Others perhaps might consider it an issue for a psychiatrists' chair, but she understood it implicitly!

He was still suffering from the loss of his lover in addition to the news that his life span would now be compromised.

When he admitted to her that he had been HIV positive just before Blue's demise, she was in utter shock. "You mean you contracted it from HIM ?" He bowed his head as he replied: " You can't dwell on the past hon, must let bygones be bygones; life is from present time forward - you know that even better than me. Its buddhist basics!"

He told her she was the only one who knew this - their secret…..a sorrowful one for anyone to carry in their heart. She wasn't good at this.

She felt suddenly sad once more. He had loved this man so much that he had been prepared to die for him also…contracting AIDS was not something you could take lightly in any circumstance. She guessed he figured that life without the full joy of him was not an option, so he had risked the grim reaper too, and been struck.

Tears welled in her eyes, but he interjected wildly :"Oh don't panic hon- its no drama - modern medicine has come a long way! I just have to take 3 pills a day - even on an empty stomach is fine. I am taking care of the situation"~

repeating almost verbatim his former remedy explanation. As far as she was concerned he was a ticking time-bomb. All she knew was that it was a death sentence. Somewhere down the line….date T.B.A so to speak…how one lived with that subliminal knowledge was anyone's guess but it was most certainly a monumental mind-fuck.

He showed her some photos of Blue from his phone. At this point she was further dumbfounded. It proved an amazing revelation: He was an identikit replica of her past lesbian lover, Rebekah, all those years ago. And when he said "do you remember the singer from the 80's- Sinead O'Connor? He looked exactly like her!"…she sensed a sense of pride in his voice. He thought the black and white photo he displayed was the utter vision of beauty and perfection. She concurred: she thought she was looking at her Bekky, who she too had shared intense intimacy with, and taken tremendous risks with. That was the likeness she referred to above all other descriptions: 'her Sinead O'Connor'.

So his Blue and her Beck were identical; - they shared the same taste even. They could have been twins for sure…it was like the model of the <u>perfect</u> androgyny.

He had set up a 'Blue memorial page' on Facebook, which heralded a mass of heartfelt sympathy messages from all his crew; far and wide. Suicidal thoughts were broadcast aside the picture of his loverboy. It became a regular event whenever he was experiencing a low swing. He felt compelled to share his grief with as many as possible….it was his way of dealing with it. Evidently those who knew him also excused his somewhat twisted tactics of pain management, and thoroughly supported him through messages on his 'lifeline forum'.

There were moments in their initial session meetings together whereby she sensed a hint of <u>**Asberger's syndrome**</u> in her comrade…(his foibles later grew in magnitude to profound proportions, ~ to the extent that she felt qualified to write a thesis on the condition!….but more on that later.)

She was bewildered to the point of classifying him a study subject now. He was unknowingly becoming a source of scrutiny and research. Her immediate notes from all their rendezvous ensued….Post meeting she would pour herself a wine at home; reflect and scribble notes while still crisp in her mind. No shared time was wasteful; she maximised on the drama and detail!

An article by dr Marcola caught her eye:
'vitamin D regulates a gene responsible for the conversion of tryptophan into serotonin…..when this vitamin is lacking so too is serotonin, which can produce neurological defects'.
To her knowledge he had rarely left his UK soil at all in the history of his life; it may go partly towards explaining his apparent psychological deficits. (And no doubt that of millions of others here, Scotland and much of Europe!)
Coupled with the knowledge that intense trauma brings forth OCD traits, his case was therefore no surprise.

He tended to have suspect (read scant) social skills in a few (most) regards; none of which bothered her however. It actually added to his unique appeal in her eyes in fact. She always went for the weirdos in society. Fiction fodder; an author's playground… Normal bored her senseless as indicated prior.
She pondered: perhaps people considered her somewhat in the same boat herself? She had always been perceived as somewhat of a diva; - albeit solo-player…..it was now evident: they both loved their little 'stage' in life. A most select (or solo usually) audience in tow….not a crowd….yet another similarity between them. It made them anxious. They preferred intimacy.
All his little quirks and social faux pas….she started to realised she was looking in the mirror in a sense after all. It (he) might be considered another chapter from fifty shades of *autism*…
Samara had acquired a slight fascination for the affliction after witnessing British shows such as 'too ugly for love' and 'the undatables' that highlighted the social condition. The fact that these seemingly insane individuals were bordering on genius intrigued her immensely. She recognised it in so many people….

She would give him token gifts, ~ as was her little tradition with all her closest comrades on their 'lunch/dinner rendezvous'. It was designed as a gift of love of course, but alas with him it backfired; - and proved akin to poking him with a sharp instrument, like torturing a laboratory pet!

Some egs: The bottle of balsamic she gave him for his salads was deemed 'too big - will clutter my kitchen'....(?!) Another bottle of tequila she gave him, since she knew he enjoyed shots, was also 'too cumbersome'. He passed it onto his neighbour like a hot potato. All items rejected to maintain 'clean lines'.....hmm......my token gifts were nought but a hindrance, in effect, she thought.

The birthday card he had intended to give her at the time was delivered in person in a belated fashion, that had him somewhat flustered: a stream of texts and emails urging her to reply: 'do you want me to still give you the card? It is here, shall I bring it? Or no?'.....she responded in the affirmative, which had him scripting on Facebook that 'i will turn up to meet you then with a red card in hand as you wish'... it lead Sam to ponder: was she out of line to profess this as *far from normal* behaviour?...

His devotion to Facebook was bordering on obsessive; it was akin to a lifeline crutch. His habit was increasing.

He later announced on the same forum that "I bought Samara an aesop lip gloss token gift today and shall present it to her when next we meet." However, when he saw her he showed it to her; half used and said 'so do <u>you</u> want one?' Her eyes widened in disbelief.
He was flippant, fickle and unpredictable.

Forgive the brutal analogy, but he was also tighter than a fish's bum! On a bitter London morning for example, having prized herself away from the home heater; and her boots were skidding in snow on the journey to meet him, he insisted she come in to see his 'baby -*Jake*'. Indeed, the little cat had turned the colour blue in the chill....as she rapidly was too. "Is it just me, or is it colder inside here than out?!" He agreed. "Yes perhaps babe, but I only use the heater once every quarter; saves money on power you see."

He would often interrupt others, or her conversation with comments or admissions on self - in an almost 'attention seeking' manner. This of course was not the intention, but it is the way anyone else would surely perceive it. But the feelings evoked by his increasingly erratic behaviour concerned Sam. In spite of this, she tried to salvage the date; again cutting him some slack due to his state of emotional turmoil. But with his ensuing comments, Samara's blood pressure soared once again.

Likewise, as she started to explain her union with Bekky in support of his own crisis, he jumped in with a random, unrelated (albeit enthusiastic) comment of :

"You know what I watched last night ?? - can you guess?"…..she stopped in her tracks; mildly annoyed that he had broken her thought pattern once again, especially while in her currently weary state.

"Pretty Woman!" - I love that movie…..i re-watch it all the time. " You know where Julia Roberts is in the glamorous hotel bubble-bath and Richard Gere asks her if she would be with him for a *whole week* and she replies : " You couldn't afford me!" and he names the price and she submerses herself in the bubbles with bliss?! That's me!! It's us!! We have done that babe…..

Its our life hon….its the story of our life!!"

As they walked home from the lunch venue, he got out his earphones and put them on his head. He said " Oh hon these quotes are great!" - he was on one of his favourite topics again: ~his addiction to the British series: 'Downton Abbey'.

He also had a cute habit of, when referring to any show, asking "which character do you most relate to? Which one <u>are you</u>?" - he had already pronounced her Patsy from AbFab on a few occasions. He could quote any show and character he favoured verbatim. It was an impressive, but also obvious obsessive trait.

So when it came to Downton, she said "Oh…..and laughed: "must be lady Elizabeth….at least thats who I would LIKE to be; such style, grace and oh that accent. Proper english!"

He immediately shoved a huge set of earphones on her head, and let her listen to several quotes from Elizabeth herself.

She couldn't help but laugh - it was the only item in his bag; and she had felt weird for bringing the usual pepper grinder to lunch! Then he asked: "come on now, which one am I??" - she had no idea and he jumped in with his usual fashion of *'listen to me'* with: "why the Dowager Countess of course!" to which he thrust the headphones at her once more to hear quotes from the majestic dame herself.

It was a punishing walk home, albeit only 15 minutes or so, as is often the case in this city; always grey clouds and a gush of shock-factor wind around any given corner, waiting to torture and chill you to the bone. In this instance it had only been made bearable to her with the belly full of food and wine she had as insulation from lunch, and the lure of a heater and more wine awaiting at home.

They played text-tag for a while that evening and she sensed a state of depression emerging in her boy. Not surprisingly under the circumstances to be fair; especially with the often distorting aspect of alcohol in the mix. However, she expressed her concern and empathy. His Facebook page suddenly alerted a 'ping' message, and she noticed his announcement that he'd *just been to the doctor and have contracted a throat infection and the flu….brilliant…back on antibiotics again*'….wow.

His immune system really was becoming fragile. Even a walk like that in the elements can render him malady-ridden. It saddened her to consider his potential plight. Why did she always choose partners with a limited time-line for her to enjoy? They always seemed to leave (or she did), get arrested; die…a rolling stone gathers no moss as they say. She had spent her life pretty much moss-free then, with fleeting episodes of close comradeship for the memory library. It dated back as far as early childhood, and changing schools every two years.

Paradigm.

It should have come as no surprise when a week later, he pronounced himself 'the irish guy' now - out of Downton Abbey! Schitsofrenic character traits is something she was familiar with..(didn't she herself do a bit of that already, to be fair? Ie : 'who am I TODAY?!'…for it was always changeable and unpredictable).

Bill also uploaded a photo of the royal family to his Facebook page, posing the question: which royal family member are YOU?! His choice was of course, her majesty: the queen (!)….queen B indeed..

His close association with his Mum, Jan had been evident from day 1 : even when they met for the very first time at the store, he showed her the ring "from my mum - we are inseparable"

He proceeded to put her on the phone to Jan every time they met up - (usually as Samara was in mid conversation, or perusing a menu or something)…so she felt like she knew 'mum' (albeit often under duress) ~ even thought they had never met in person.

Estranged from the rest of his siblings (no doubt his idiosyncrasies had pissed them off at some point!) - he remained a faithful son and mummy's boy.

She was a typical Brit; ~ a committed home-body; seemingly averse to travel beyond Great Britain's shores. Samara had found the pomms to be most traditional in that sense. In general at least. Jan must have thought grey clouds were normal, and sunshine was an 'island postcard concept' only.

'Serotonin is crucial during fetal brain development'

- as stated by the Dr in the fascinating articles she had read on how Autism has risen in tandem with vitamin D deficiency.

His mother had never left the UK either, so it stood to reason in her view!
And further:

"If a mother is deficient in vitamin D, this may have severe consequences in the developing fetal brain of her child, because maybe that gene that needs vitamin D to get activated is not getting activated. As a consequence there's not enough serotonin being made in the fetal brain, which possibly could affect the way that brain develops....

Vitamin D and low serotonin have been linked to autism by many different researchers. But no one has put the two together as a mechanism going 'Look, maybe the low vitamin D leads to low serotonin in the developing brain. This may be part of the reason why there's an increase in autism, and maybe part of the way why low vitamin D leads to autism'"

There was one occasion that was mildly perturbing and one she would prefer to avoid in the future: he attended one of the lunches under the influence of 'the battery'.

Class A.

An alpha's stimulant of choice.

She found it no surprise that he had succumbed to the powers of crystal meth to combat the immense grief over his lost lover; coupled with the hardcore truths about his health forecast now.

He had turned up post- client session that had obviously included partaking of the pipe and was a mile a minute....(as one is when fired up on the racy toxin). He had admitted to resorting to its powers as a stimulant to enhance his 'work'….the escorting opportunities had been okay, but sporadic, and he worked from home. She assumed he had some on hand to assist in sudden bookings as such. She understood that. But the timing….

She had started to lose the thread of the conversation; it was fragmented and scattered and with the background drone of the gastropub too it was a bombardment - not conducive to relaxing indulgence.

But then, his whole situation was a shambles to deal with so this scattered mind-scape made sense of sorts. Apt. She knew from experience that the altered state made one super productive, and allowed no time for focused thought. A diversion of sorts to life's woes. For a moment.

Reality will kick in soon enough, but for now, just 'get active; go hard and fast and power on'….no time to think….

Brain Bandaid.

She herself had accomplished monumental task lists while under the influence of it's powers; blocking out the existing daily worries,~ but sitting down to a relaxing chatty lunch was not what it was intended to assist. The complete reverse! To be in the presence of one afflicted also tends to induce anxiety and paranoia in the company too.

He ate frantically, at a rate of knots, like a chipmunk on speed, and had finished before she had even put down the pepper grinder. She felt indigestion welling even before she began.

The conversation had shifted to assassinating the menu vs the update of their realities; certainly more entertaining with the mental take of someone in the 'quick, witty zone'-he reaffirmed the classic example of alpha homo humour even moreso than usual:

"Argh! - You can't be eating that fish!! How DARE they serve it with *tail* intact n all"… Horror….his face displayed the disgust of someone who had never seen a whole fish with its tail before…as it **is** generally served! She glanced down at his plate of bratwurst, mash and gravy with eyebrows raised. "I think it might be preferable to a *floating turd* somehow!"

By all accounts, however, it must have appeared they were having a ball; not squirming inside…as was the case. She felt out of her depth here; helpless and not the slightest bit relaxed, and he found any social situation excruciating. She was relieved to get home; exhale and decompress from the event.

Over several wines and some mindless girly TV viewing, which she stared at blankly while her mind wandered back to the frantic affair at midday. It was actually immensely sad.

Smiles and laughter in the face of the social mirror often mask the truth that tortures at the core…

On another of their rendezvous, he got her to meet him at his humble apartment beforehand for a sip of champagne before proceeding to the venue. Nothing beats the palette cleanser of choice she thought, so she agreed to the bubbles beginning to their day.

He said he had to wait for 'a delivery' meanwhile….obviously of the pharmaceutical nature (!) That translated of course to 'i have a client booking here tonight'

She watched him thoughtfully as he crouched down in his kitchen so as not to be detected; head darting back and forth in a somewhat manic fashion. He was so interesting to observe she thought. Certainly far from stable, but it (he) was better than watching dull UK tv- go live!

It disturbed her to think that he relied on the powers of assistance for his work….but hadn't she used alcohol in the same way before?! The calibre of vocation tends to call for some form of courage assistance. Don't throw stones, she reminded herself…

The next time she saw him he was thankfully much calmer and easier to chat to but she could see him slowly sinking into the depths of depression over his reality. Manic swings of elation…and complete decimation.

He would gravitate from being very upbeat and humorous, to dark and (literally) suicidal within a short time-frame. Sometimes, minutes even.

For instance, they would have fabulous lunch session catch up together, with much laughter and witty banter….and within an hour or 2 she would receive a suicidal text that would plummet her into corresponding despair on how she could assist his ailing pain.

It was like dual personality; scitsofrenia of sorts.

They had shared a most memorable, fun time together; it was evident alcohol was not conducive to prolonged health….depression really hits hard when under the influence of the relaxing elixir.

He was cultivating a somewhat hurtful habit of just withdrawing from scheduled lunch bookings at the 11· hour too. It was a protocol assassination.

But did he *realise* he was offending people she wondered?…she felt it was a fundamental component of the affliction: zero conscience.

For he didn't seem to be the slightest bit aware that he was socially dysfunctional in every area.

She normally gave no second chances with people. She could take them or leave them. Solitude always welcome! Now he was skating on thin ice in her books. Which was sad, as she felt she had connected with someone rather special and hopefully long-term.

His Facebook messages too bore a grim reality: he was on the edge. One morning she joined the crew of a notable number of supportive allies that responded to his days' report:

" I'm done…there is no reason for me to be here anymore. I don't want this any longer. I want to be with my soulmate"…well, if that wasn't a cry for help online, it was certainly a grim forecast of his psychological demise.

However it issued the required result: a plethora of respondents had come to the rescue. I guess it (the communication medium) was akin to his rock: knowing that others cared and as I put it: '*needed him*' to stick around- she typed a reply: ….'life sux and tests us but you have to be stronger than that'…

In times of acute stress and/or extreme trauma, little idiosyncrasies or traits of off-kilter behaviour become more prominent.

He was a classic case.

After their meetings, she had started to jot down some notes as they occurred to her, in recollection of the day spent with this intriguing specimen.

Until this point, she realised in hindsight, the shades of Asberger's syndrome were only vaguely evident. Now, it was on steroids. Stark, obvious proportions. However, she realised with vague concern that this was true about herself too. Mirror mirror on the wall…

The monsters rear their ugly heads; for they flourish under the influence of threat and cortisol fire…

She noted how much better he looked physically however and told him as such. "Yes, that's because I've been taking better care of myself hon; avoiding the fast zone and so forth…..trying to nurture the immune system. Oh, and I only use Aesop skincare; I have that to thank for my youthful face!" All things considered he actually looked the figure of health.

But life can mask inner truths with an appealing veneer. (Or, as Shakespeare put it: *'the devil hath the power to assume a pleasing shape')*…..

Masks and mirrors.

As time wore on, he evolved further. It was on one of the ensuing lunches that his autistic quirks became *outstandingly* evident. As they walked to the venue together chatting, he rushed ahead in a panicked fashion; alternately pointing to the cafe and looking back at her : " there babe - THAT'S where we are going" .. The statement was urgent, not a mere informational aside. He did it not once, but <u>several</u> times. As if he had no recollection of moments before.

It was, by all accounts, a rather anxious and weird display.

They had a nice time together; mingling with the staff and soaking in the unique splendour of the venue. A recording studio outback; photos of famous memorabilia adorned the walls of the cafe interior. Rocker royalty. It was a cheerful, upbeat location, that with the hearty homestyle fare and bon vivant crowd served to put a smile on his face momentarily.

But as they left, the London grey clouds and threat of rain in the distance was a reflection of his rapidly darkening mood too.

At his place for another wine to follow, as was their customary 'debriefing' system; they would summarise the venue and cuisine and so forth and access its scoring factor. If it hit the high note, then they would return at a later stage. If not, then it was on to the next one, and they would both prowl the streets for that, eager to meet again for the ceremonial lovers' lunch.

However, it was at this point Samara realised that there was a finite timeframe for their union. She felt him slipping, and his idiosyncrasies and paranoid paradigms were becoming even too much for her to bear.

There was certainly enough going on in her own world; she didn't need the extra burden of someone else in the quest for a friendship…if it wasn't a win-win then…well, to be brutal, what was the point?

She did adore him however, so allowed the rest of the day to unfold.

A gracious exit was never on the cards with ANY relationship, but she could do her best. She stood in the pristine kitchen with him; so clean you could eat off the floor. Handing him a container of her homemade salad to have with his dinner, she said: "there's some dressing here I made too". His eyes widened in horror: "yes, I love your dressing…but don't put it in the **same** container as the salad; even unopened! It must be separate….far away until I use it!!" he was becoming manic again.

He continued attending to some washing up in the sink, in a frantic fashion; rewashing each item repeatedly.

His cat meanwhile sauntered innocently along the clean granite bench and he freaked: "AH - I told you, dirty paws!!….contaminated…must be cleaned!!"…(was he referring to the bench or the paws she wondered?) He proceeded to wash the paws of the stunned pet over and over again in a flustered panic.

Samara stood back observing. He was bordering on hysteria now whilst displaying this intense obsessive compulsive behaviour. It was disturbing. Certainly not a relaxing finale to the day.

She gathered up her stuff in a motion to leave, while downing the rest of the wineglass.

He noticed out of the corner of his eye and then a different personality suddenly flashed in. "Oh I need to show you family photos babe! Don't go yet!" He guided her to the hallway, where 2 lines of portraits hung. He took pride in explaining the 'hall of family fame'…20 years of framed feline memorabilia! Each cat he had ever owned and its timeframe spent with him.

O..kay…

His father had died of an overdose, but she knew he had siblings that he preferred to stay well away from. He was still a mumma's boy, as earlier outlined, but his cats gained precedence over all else in his esteem. He treated them all like little humans. Even the latest one, Jake, had, as announced on his Facebook page, received "full back n crack pampering session - clean as a whistle and now a plush, pampered pussy".

The photo attached showed a stunned, disoriented little furball; - frozen with shock and no doubt trauma. (We all know pussy-waxing is far from painless!)

She left that date feeling scattered and mildly depressed herself. He was a handful, there was no doubt. And her hands were already full enough. What had started out as a chance to unwind in some interesting company, and share fabulous food and wine while outside the realms of her usual chaos had backfired. She was far from relaxed; she always got indigestion in his presence, and there was no relief from personal woes; it proved to be adding to them. Comedy relief had turned to masked misery. The joy was gone.

Tick, tick tick…

A new Facebook update finally came from him - one Samara had predicted for some time now.

The photo of newly acquired ink: " Blue" scribed along his arm above his wrist. She knew oh too well the personal power of permanent reminder scars.

She felt tempted to post a comment:

" So when you're feeling lonely, sans Blue,

glance at your forearm and bolster strength anew…"

She managed to refrain herself however, for their connection was proving strained now, at least to her. Sometimes the power lies in silence…

She had left to her other warmer home for a spell, but they maintained contact via email. He had expressed interest on several occasions that he was super keen to visit her island retreat himself: "being buddhist and all as I am!" he would say…..god, she thought, I think he needs a hell of a lot more than vitamin D dosage…

It was a prevalent condition in the UK that deprivation of sunshine benefits and the constant grey cloud coverage produced depressive behaviour in folk, but Seasonal Affective Disorder didn't even begin to cut it with this one! Her investigations into the link between that and behavioural afflictions was supported intensely by her pet lab rat.

Another date was set and she specified that it was to be a very quick trip to London only this time, so better to prioritise diary dates in advance to avoid disappointment.

Could he confirm?

He agreed, and reported back that the venue had been booked and it was all concrete planning. She continued to remind him however: emails, texts and so forth.

So the day arrived and there it was. The trifecta. Literally just as she was exiting her apartment to leave for the venue, a text came. He couldn't make it. Not even the courtesy of a damn call. Watching his sacred Tennis with a wine no doubt she thought. Was Wimbledon worth more to him than what they had, or was he unaware of the audacity of such an insult?
It was in fact the third time he had done the very same thing.

Last minute let-down.

In fact, the first time, she was actually sitting at the restaurant waiting and had the embarrassment of excusing herself - stood-up with sympathetic staff in tow.
Paradigm.

Normally this would be perceived as the height of rudeness, but his 'affliction' had granted him pardon on social taboos time and time again. But not now.

You know that fine line between brilliance and disaster area? He had jumped the line into the dark territory. She realised she was done. With it all. With him.

Her tolerance quota had exploded.   Expired….

Empty now.

She sadly trudged to a local restaurant/bar and ordered a glass of champagne. Cheers to the queen…

Raising a toast to his demise, she took out paper and pen and added to her notes on his frustrating foibles and faux pas. He had introduced her to some moments of complete bliss and enjoyment, but the pain was just as intense now.

Familiar territory she realised.

A leopard doesn't change its spots she kept berating herself…..it was a paradigm on her behalf to not pay heed to this fact.

She recognised it as a major personality flaw to repeat the same mistakes with folk; - she wished she could change that about herself!

Tears began to well in her eyes as she surveyed the busy London street below; she wiped them away and took a deep breath.

The venue section she had chosen was very quiet for the moment. A welcome environment when the emotions started to rear their ugly heads. Death always brought grief..

In his case, there was zero contrition after each episode; ~ he remained blissfully unaware of the damage he was causing.

The hard fact remained that though~ in life: **hurt people hurt people.**

And since interesting characters are a product of some degree of pain, what does it say for humanity?

She was saddened further by the fact that he had promised her unequivocally that he would proof-read some of her X-rated chapter material since he was the only one who was a veteran in the terrain himself. It's okay she thought. Talk is cheap.

Perhaps better to just keep it confidential for safety after all; who can you trust out there anyway?! Soldier on solo as always.

Another side to her appeared and she took up her pen once more to scribe the toxins out of her heart.

The amber fluid had started to filtrate her bloodstream and she felt a warm glow of painkiller

Queen B….the alpha had turned beta on her. As many before him had.
Stung by the bee…
He would have to be gracefully laid down in the box of misfit memories she kept in her heart…

RIP my friend….

<h1 style="text-align:center">Chapter 13</h1>

PACKING HUMOUR CHALLENGE....

Some trips are destined to be a disaster right from the onset.....but frustratingly, one can **never** be sure....😐

Its like gambling: all can go your way, and you win a smooth, relaxing journey, or it can be a <u>total</u> loss of time, cash and sanity.

These days, one tends to have nervous anticipation prior to any journey. Will it be turbulent or triumphant? One can have no expectations....for sanity maintenance mostly.

For there are no guarantees!

Travel certainly ain't what it used to be.

Gone are the days of glamour and luxury....

The one thing I <u>have </u>learnt through all my travel tyrant pursuits over the years in varying class standards (ie: from the *front* to the *back* of the plane) is that a **sense of humour** is mandatory....and paramount to success. Make it *top* of your packing list, and take it with you. (Patience is an added bonus, but sadly I have none of that)...

For without it? The experience will be doomed, and you're better off staying put at home!

And while we're on the topic of PACKING, you should know....im an utter lost cause! I should, by all rights and experiences have a <u>degree</u> in the art by now, but alas, no. I tend to give the late Liz Taylor (with her legendary 9 suitcases for the general trip abroad) a run for her money.

Condensing belongings?…. Foreign language….and I'm a linguist (!)

So when I was hit with the ultimate challenge of a strict carry-on limit policy for a 'cheap and cheerful' escape to Marrakech, I took it on as one would an olympic challenge. I'd had years of training, and had thus far failed. Abysmally.

It was time to rise to the occasion; shine in glorious victory, and do my reputation proud at last.

10 KILOS ONLY!! Are you fn kidding me?!

I get anxiety just thinking about it. Adrenalin overload even. But I thrive on that scary shit, so bring it on, I said….with the courage of a cowboy. Or cowgirl even.

Considering that my handbag contents weighed around 15 kilos on the *average* day without going anywhere at all, this was going to be tough. But nothing worth doing is easy, so…

This was the first stressful phase of the potential trip from hell. (IF id let it win, but I don't do failure well).

Secondly, the fact that I'd paid for partner to accompany me also, but on the day of said flight, he was still devoid of passport (being in the visa processing queue) - should have been a warning sign. For Marrakech is not exactly the ideal location for a woman to go alone. [The local men win the groping award - (no further elaboration required) -so safety in numbers is particularly code here]…

Thirdly, the train time I'd paid for did not even exist; contrary to the internet-informed timetable, so I had to forfeit that cost and herald an emergency car instead, at 3am in the morning, with a Peter Brock wannabe at the wheel; - to make the obscenely early flight time.

At this point, having paid the equivalent of two people's trips AND lost the train ticket, the cheap holiday was clocking up £ mileage. Even before arrival, holiday cash was spent; blood pressure was through the roof (thanks to the cocktail of sleep deprivation curdled with 'backseat driver tension') and with the French strikes still in action, the act of plane leaving the tarmac at ALL was looking doubtful.

Grim.

And yes, the flight was indeed, typically delayed.

Over 2 hours.

No service allowed…

Therein lay phase one of 'what the f…does someone have to do to get a damn drink?' Charles Bukowski would have had a fit.

Tantrum maybe….no, guaranteed!

Not that I'm complaining, but *when oh when* does 'holiday' start?

On arrival, I race out to see if the paid-for transit still exists, and have to wait in desert heat for over an hour for the rest of the car occupants to get their shit together (ie: collect bags; exit airport etc).

At this point, I'm gritting teeth with bitterness at the memory of the good old days of 1· class or worst-case-scenario business class travel. But survival calls for zen patience…i think.

In the car at last. And being the final stop of the coach, it is now over 9 hours since leaving the house in London. 11 since rising. Hmm…..

At hotel check-in, I remind them of my 3 emails and phonecalls in person requesting early check-in, and they look at me like I'm talking swahili.

'Yes, we try…please wait'.

An hour later, ready to commit homicide, I do finally get a room. Initial summary: doors don't lock; fridge is broken and safe has no key!

Great start…..

I report this promptly but have to wait 40 mins to move room.

Me: 'Look, I'll just have a drink at the bar while I wait'.

Vacant look. Silence. 'No madam' - (said with a fullstop!)

… 'Excuse me?' ….

'No drinking now. Cannot.'…I start to laugh but realise she's bang-on serious.

Meanwhile, I have to pay extra for a safe key as well as *taxes of the land* (whatever that fancy designed tariff means), so I have to withdraw cash from a local ATM. After finally locating one, two attempts fail. I anxiously inform hubby to report to bank, as I suspect we've been 'done over'…try another machine a considerable walk away and am successful, but am now hopelessly lost, and still think it cost us triple the actual amount received….sleep-deprived head now spinning with concern and anguish.

Another hour later, I move room at <u>last,</u> to discover that the sink doesn't drain; the toilet rarely flushes, and the safe was a challenge to open and close without breaking the key. Hmmm….

Oh stuff it, ill cope.

I head off on the wild goose chase for a damn drink now. ….thankfully, reception recommends a shopping centre which, after getting lost several times, and having walked in desert heat for yet another hour I arrive at. And realise it has a Carrefour store. Hallelujah!

Perfect. I know it well from Bali; -it's my home base restock venue so familiar terrain. And it always stocks import wine.

But…alas, not today.

Nor beer, spirits, or <u>any</u> alcohol to speak of.

"Its *Ramadan* madam. In a few weeks, no problem!" - this news was delivered patiently with a smile that I was so ready to smash off his face…

I mean, are you fn kidding me??? Do you want tourist financial support or not? At least Bali caters for the westerners' needs at all times; regardless of the ceremonial lunar calendar!

Hail the home benefits….

In desperation, I stop a blonde woman in the street to ask for advice (carefully selecting a victim that I think will understand my dilemma). Ie: translation: veneer = somewhat glam and ready for social antics)

She laughs: 'Yes, I speak English'… she gives me the name of a place not too far that she assures me will know the best advice.

"Im going there now, come - I take you!"….We end up at an Italian cafe I saw on my disastrous shopping attempt before, and I race in and scan the shelves for even a bottle there I could buy. Only salad bar and patisserie section evident to the eye. "I really need to buy some wine! Most places won't sell it to me for Ramadan, but there must be somewhere I can go….can you tell me?!"

Arms folded and a disgruntled look was returned my way.

Obviously even advice doesn't come for free these days.

I hastily seized an overpriced croissant and said "Look, I'll buy this now while you tell me!"with a desperate plea smile painted on my exhausted face.

Another store name is offered….

I wearily leave, tearing corners off the pastry to avoid fainting, and flag down a 'small taxi', and within minutes, arrive to the destination, and alas, the same fate.

"Usually wine , but <u>not now</u>"….

In utter frustration I grab a French man and virtually get down on hands and knees to beg for his assistance…he's french for gods' sake, SURELY he drinks…..

"It is difficult, no….its Ramadan now you see. I have stocked up on water…." His trolley I now notice contains about 45 bottles of Evian. Turns out he's a converted muslim!

"It's not a problem, really! Ramadan and no drinking while fasting. No problem for us at all!"

[Nobody gets the fact I've been T-totalling for a week now in preparation for a 2 day relaxing break which in my books requires a well-earnt drink….so far my reputation here is one of a desperate alcoholic on a reckless frenzy for a fix.]

I'm literally starting to cry, and he offers me a lift to a place he thinks might have some wine. Its *another* Carrefour.

I explain I've already been to one. He stops the car and speaks to one of the store guys in French.

Gets directions and sent on his merry way to another destination. I frown and realise I'm being driven all over town with a complete stranger in a foreign country that is predominantly French speaking and *yet* they allow a

wine ban for a religious phase…..(??) its the antithesis of logic, surely!! It
flows like water in France; can't there at least be a *dribble* here??

We arrive at destination, and I thank him profusely with minimal hope left
in me now…..the general consensus thus far is that it will be a liver detox
holiday, as opposed to the me-time indulgence treat I had in mind.
A holiday without a cheeky tipple is a health retreat….not something I was
needing at this point. In fact probably a hindrance to my health; particularly
psychological!
My mind cast back to the plane where for a second or two I contemplated
buying a few mini bottles of wine on board to take 'just in case'…..and also
the glimpse of the duty-free wine section that I sailed past, after having read
the internet advice that 'it is easy and cheap to buy when there so don't
bother!'……damn the computer crap!
Sigh….always better to go with the gut.
They didn't mention the significance of religious dates and abstinence
rules. I hate to deviate from a country's beliefs and rules but considering this
was a much required mini break for me from London, I had massive
intentions of luxury pursuits. Religious apologies and whatnot but the facts
remain….

Inside this store which is so incredibly small its like a local convenience
venue, my hope flounders and I sink with disappointment. I glance around
slowly and then, out of the corner of my eye I see a woman mopping a floor
behind a glass door. It's a second room beyond the store and…no
wait…..there are bottles behind her. I run to the glass, peer through and then
quickly try to open the sliding door. It's a cellar room! Well, there are spirits
on this floor but on closer inspection, a sign indicates that wine is housed
upstairs!! I feel for a second like I've won the lottery or stumbled upon
Aladdin's cave of gold - until I realise the door is locked and I can't get in.
Don't panic….(!!)

Virtually hyperventilating I ask the check-out chick if I can get in..
"Sorry miss. Cannot." The look on my face must have shocked her as she
tilts her head and says "if you have passport for I.D I can let you in"….

Knowing that my passport is locked in the dodgy hotel safe, and I had no photocopy sheets on me, my mind ticks over frantically for a solution.

"You can call the hotel - they have my passport info!"
She shakes her head adamantly. "No, I have to **see** it"…
I realise that by the time I return to the hotel and back the store will be closed, and the **whole** day wasted. So I resort to calling the husband internationally; (no doubt a substantial extra expense) in virtual hysterics; *pleading* him to send me an urgent image of the document immediately by email….my iPhone displaying the dangerously low zone of around 10% battery remaining.

He replies "No problem; I'm onto it now!"

He's great like that; springs to action in a dilemma. I sigh with relief but after 15 mins call him back to hear him say in frustration:

"I don't think I have any here! I didn't copy your new one yet." I tell him in a whispered, albeit exaggerated tone to 'send any of the 4 passport documents I've had over the years~ regardless of expiry just anything, SOMETHING to prove who I am'…
As to why I need it in the first place, I can't answer that for you as their logic eludes me, but I have to play ball or my holiday will never start at all.
So when the image finally arrives, I present it to the girl who says
"I just needed the number"….👓(translation : I could have given any passport number off the top of my head with confidence, and it probably would have sufficed)
She jots it down, 🖊 slowly ambles over, and slides open the glass door for me at last.
The ample wine selection is such a relieving sight to me I'm in an almost fit of excitement. Nirvana. I greedily grab a bottle of French Chardonnay and a fine red; wanting more but knowing my time limits…. so exercising restraint.
On descent down the stairs, I glance at them to realise that they are with cork. As in ALL the stock in store. And having carry-on luggage only, I couldn't pack the usual bottle <u>opener.</u>
"Can I buy an opener for these bottles please?"

The look alone made me realise it was a negative request, and I wondered what the hell to do next.

She gives me directions to yet another store. I walk another 20 mins; blood sugar now plummeting dramatically and energy waning.

I ask the store boy if they sell them and he escorts me down the elevator to the kitchen-ware section. Bingo!! Im in luck ! Its one of the screws you have to pull out yourself, but at least its something.

I'm so shattered that I make the sudden decision to buy a bowl, cutlery and a knife to cut a salad and grab a tin of tuna. Lame as it may sound and pitiful for a holiday evening, but nothing would relax me more than to sit on my porch in the hotel with my drink finally in hand and no more galavanting, public; pleading requests and missions but to unwind and catch up on sleep! A cold salad will be fine. Easy. No drama.

But could I find a knife ? Hell no……packets of plastic picnic-style ones only.

This is becoming like a sitcom. I virtually sit on the shop floor and laugh now - I'm deliriously beyond it all. I decide to shred the salad with my fingers. DON'T CARE!

Head off for small taxi and proceed to be ripped off blind by 2 guys wanting 5 x the usual going fare. Looking around and seeing no other taxis or cars for miles I count my losses, jump in and resign myself to their greedy tarif…something I very rarely do.

Finally back at the hotel I decide to at least do SOMETHING on the first day. The pool is looking packed and I'm so frazzled so I head to the front desk to request the complimentary hammam.

"We close the spa at 4pm madam"…..'Only if you go right now".

I bolt up the stairs; ~ stuff waiting for the lift, race inside, throw on my bikini.

Then head back down pronto for a spot of much needed pampering…..heart-rate racing; - but consoling myself with the concept that the holiday must be about to start any tick of the clock now…

As I'm in the spa, (sensing from the therapist's demeanour that she's tired and done for the day) - I join a throng of girls in the steam room. They are a group, and gorgeously black. (Ive always admired their gene lottery in the booty department - well pronounced and peachy without having to do a single squat or lunge!).

"Whatchya doin'?"one of them asks as I enter in bright pink bikini while they are all glowing in birthday suit alone.

Me: 'Oh, its my first time - I'm a hammam virgin. Wasn't sure if costumes were required….'

"Get your goddamn gear off girl! There ain't no point doing a hammam scrub down with clothes on! Mmm,mmmm'- head shaking; sing-song voice and signature jiggy moves they do with aplomb.

"We all gotta own our own skin girl!"

I take it off and sit in the corner; - a somewhat petite white figure amongst the robust crew. Tits a bouncing' booties a bobbin' - I'm thinking : amazing who you meet while naked in a steam room..

We chat away and become instant friends. I learn that they live not too far from me in London so we exchange deets and plan a girly lunch too. "Deffo girlfriend - you are on….." -accentuated with defiant booty wiggle.

Me and ma crib….yo…
I enjoyed the banter immensely! Expecially the lingo. Hail the hood…

The scrub itself was mediocre - like all aspects of this hotel establishment it seems. But nevertheless, I got some grand advice for other venues and plan to make a point of seeking a proper one the next day. We plan to meet up back in london and afterwards I head up to my room with glee to open the wines. Never have I looked forward to a quiet, well deserved sip so much before in my life. Would have to be in the bathroom rinse glasses though, or plastic cups, I just realised….Bukowski eat your heart out! Definately not Raffles now sweetie….

By this stage the blood sugar is starting to plummet at an alarming rate..and time is of the essence.

I hastily showered; freshened up; and set about the task of pouring a relaxing sunset drink for on the balcony.

The corkscrew was dodgy…definitely cheap and flimsy but I was determined.

The Chardonnay cork was beyond a challenge. It simply wouldn't budge. The next 40 mins saw me sitting at the desk in a pool of sweat and frustration screwing the stubborn thing up and down trying to get some leverage and a pull-force;- but no joy. So I started desperately digging with forks, and decided that if I could push the damn thing in I could strain off the cork bits somehow. It was to be the only way. I glanced around at the floor that looked like termites had raided the joint; - cork dust everywhere and now drips of blood as I had cut my hand in the process…(I couldn't help laughing at what the cleaners might think of the scene. Especially when later coupled with a dustbin full of food scraps and salad dregs when signs abound *'no food or drink allowed in hotel rooms'.)*

Be sure to deposit the rubbish I added to my following day's list.

The wine wouldn't go beyond a drilled hole that slowly dripped out of the top - it would take 10 mins to pour a glass but at least it was something. I rummaged through by bag and clapped at my 'hoarding' skills for once. A coffee cup from the plane had a corner with strainer at the top of the lid. Hallelejah! It was perfect for the task of straining the cork-flooded brew. And it worked a treat.

After pouring; accidentally breaking one of the glasses and then grabbing a plastic cup, I **finally** got outside before the sunset to take a few 'look-at-me-having-a ball-on-holiday' selfies and then sunk it as the sun did the same.

The world seemed better now.

So in I went to open the Red wine as well and make a salad to eat watching netflix on my iPhone. <u>If</u> I could get wifi connection….

The red wine glided out within seconds; it was a plastic style cork!

Well thank heaven for small mercies I thought.

Broke up bits of salad with my hands as no knife now; threw it into a bowl and ring-pulled some tuna into it with some leftover bread from the plane.

Relax….. 🍷

The alarm didn't work the next morning. I was so utterly exhausted that I slept in - only minutes before breakfast was to end....but I awoke feeling fantastic. (Besides, the spa girls had warned that the breakfast was far from 4-star, and perhaps best avoided anyway unless you wanted to feast on cold coffee and a plate of pastries.)

So no great loss there I surmised. But I raced down for a caffeine fix anyway before an invigorating swim to get the workout done for the day.

I must have struck it lucky as the coffee was hot! (Or maybe it had taken the whole 4 hours of breakfast time prior for it to actually heat up properly)....in any case, it went down a treat.

While standing there I caught a glimpse of 2 black girls at a table behind me, and mistaking them for the crew I met in the spa the night before, I turned to say hello. They looked up and replied back.

"Didn't I meet you last night in the hammam?" I asked meekly.

"No!" was replied with a smile....

"We're off to a Hammam today though. It's supposed to be the best venue for them here. It's called bain du Marrakech I think"

Literally, '*the baths* of marrakech..how bad could it be?! ....

My mind ticks over not only the prospect of potential pampering at last, but the concept of strength in numbers to avoid excess torment on route to the quest.

"Oh! That sounds *great* - where is it?"
We get chatting etc, and to cut a long story short, decide to all go together that afternoon for a girly indulgence sesh.

At this point I'm over the fight of avoiding driver ripoffs; man harassment and general turmoil, so although I usually fly solo for peace, I figure joining a group a wise option this time.

They head back to their room to relax for a few hours and I do the same to pack and sort before the swim. Coffee is kicking nicely; buzz going on. And feeling fine as sleep which normally eludes me came deep and solid last night.

The phone rings: its one of the girls I just met. "Look, we have been *trying* to chill out here but its not working. We're thinking of leaving early, and going to the market before the spa. You want to come?!"

Thrilled at the prospect of being taken out without having to plan and think myself I say "Oh god yes! In an hour or so…?" silence the other end. "Well, we were actually going to leave now."

"Can you give me one hour?" I beg - mentally tallying up the time to race down to the pool and thrash out some laps before getting ready to go.

Brief hesitation then "Okay….we'll wait"

I vow to buy them a gift of gratitude while out, and head off for a swim. Lift too slow - stuff it : run down the stairs as warm-up, throw my towel on a nearby chair and jump into the pool.

Being in the shadows not warmed yet by the sun, it was equivalent to jumping into an ice bath.

It took around 12 laps before I started to go into shock….(unintentional Cryogenics session!)

so I got out; raced back upstairs; showered and did some star jumps and pushups instead (!) ~ **improvise** is evidently the key word of this entire adventure, and the means to cope.

I head down to the lobby to meet them but no sign. My mood sinks as I feel I've lost out on the day's adventures now. I figure they've gone off without me, but get the staff to call their room just in case - to no answer …but then I see them amble down the stairs at last. I almost bowl them over with excitement and gratitude, and we all head off with a driver they know and trust and chat on the way to the markets. Which is actually the souks I realise now. Hell, I'm ticking off that *and* 2 hammams; besides all the drama….it was all that was on my want list to start! Double ticks. Miraculous amidst the mayhem…

It's a beautiful day; the sun is so alarmingly warming that I'm almost ecstatically bathing in the glory of vitamin D at last! Even if I buy nothing it is still worth the mission out.

But buy nothing I did NOT, - I went berserk as usual! But light stuff to ensure I didn't surpass the measly 10kilo weight limit home. Fabric coin

purses; essential oils; cooking spices; moroccan bling slippers; and various
jewellery bits'n'pieces. Equating to less than 2 kilos in all, so fine to add to the
minuscule luggage restrictions.

The open square branched off into a plethora of corridors; catering for all
manner of wares - like teapots (for the traditional mint tea and so forth); food,
clothing, accessories - it was a wonderland of browsing time that anyone on a
casual holiday/ break in the colourful land of Morocco could embrace/ absorb
themselves in. Usually for several days, as so much to digest, admire and
purchase.

The light streaming through the colourful corridors of wares and casually
browsing shoppers was ethereal - in streams like in a religious sense. It gave a
golden glow to the spectacle, and created a quintessential Moroccan vision. A
fully village-feel abounded. Stray cats wandered around everywhere;
particularly the side alleys off the shopping stretch; with hanging washing;
bikes, and young children playing and laughing in the streets. And where the
locals obviously resided in between their daily trade time.

The traditional muslim garb was evident from all vantage points, and
stereo-typical local types- particularly the older men; perched casually by
mounds of local dates, spices, etc, or wheeling carts or wagons of produce
through the roads in their signature heavy starched white linen attire.

After extricating ourselves from the labyrinth of winding and connecting
corridors we finally see the full light of day and exit through a passage back
to the square and beyond.

I stop to photo a group of Muslim men sitting on a mat with a PET python
to be met with outstretched hands insisting on payment. I know this well
from Bali, - the usual. If I had to pay for every photo I've ever taken in my
life, I wouldn't be able to afford to live! I tell them 'phone broken! Can't take
picture anyway!' and as I turn around see that the younger girl has stopped
to pat a pet monkey, but has had it thrust into her hands and is looking
terribly uncomfortable with the pesky creature and its' scratchy nails. She is
met with the same fate of insistent outstretched palms. I take several pictures
of her and explain that we are now utterly devoid of cash; dragging the girls
away from the insistent locals.

The girls get their bearings and after a few more scenic shots we head off to the Hammam spa to unwind from the days' shopping toil and torment.

They locate it swiftly and as we peruse the menu of luxurious pampering options, the woman tells me of this amazing anti-aging face cream that she bought nearby for a steal. I'm always sceptical of any tub professing those claims, but she added: "i never believe all the hype, but they did a demonstration on my hand and the results were astronomical! Thats what convinced me". They tell me the store is nearby, so we explain to the spa that we will be 'back in 5' and head off to try locating the magic vendor address. Alas, they can't find it and time is ticking. But suffice to say it is in the area, so I thought if I had time after my session on the massage table, I may feel inspired to investigate the neighbourhood further later.

Back at the bathhouse, the woman suddenly realises she has spent all her cash for the day and left her credit card in the hotel room!

A disastrous state of affairs; ~ for the concept of flagging down another taxi and dealing with the groping men (who, if they don't abuse you or torment you relentlessly will undeniably rip you off); returning to the hotel to retrieve and then back again is too much for her. And I'm certainly not about to do it after yesterday's traumas on the streets!

We swap contact details and bid each other farewell for the time being. I head in for my hammam and massage at last. And solo as usual after all.

The concept of lying down on a massage table and 'relaxing' eludes me at this point....for after the last 48 hours of unabating stress and challenges it would take one helluva treatment session to alleviate. Certainly no mean feat!

Here, they do alternate mini sessions of 'treating' and then disappearing. Mostly the latter. The temperature is too mild to be considered sauna or steam conditions.

I'm given a loofah scrub down; am left for half an hour; then have mud applied and the same applies. The sound of the dripping tap at the faucet behind me is like water torture. By this stage I'm so cold I feel goosebumps and shivers instead of that calming comfort one presumes a treatment brings.

Finally, she washes me down; puts a robe and slippers on me and ushers me into a waiting room where I am given a mint tea with WAY too much sugar in it. I decline; send it back asking for another - sans the toxic crap. Half an hour later it appears. I'm cold now so take my tea outside and sit in the sun by the pool for the next 20 mins waiting. This is the most relaxing; comforting part!

At the massage it is too soft for my liking. I mention I like a firm massage but she replies in half french '_relaxing_ massage madam'

I know I'm beyond spoilt back in my Bali home. I'm such a hard marker in this avenue of pleasure; best to never compare!

I realise at this point that it would have been far better to remain in the hotel and simply have a sauna - craving the benefits of an intense steam and detox. I know I always feel so clean and renewed after those. (Sideline note to self: Add **'infared' sauna box** to personal london want-list)

After treatment I head off to change a note to have the exact amount ready for the driver so he doesn't proceed to rip me off as they do here.

The vendor grabs my arm and ushers me down a corridor. 'Where the hell are we going?' I whine in resignation.

He insists: "you must see the '_women's cooperative_' at work; with special herbs and magic tinctures!"

I'm annoyed but once inside a huge shop site I realise, low and behold, that it must be the skincare nirvana terrain.

The woman is dressed somewhat akin to a pharmacist ; all in white and peers over her specs as she tries to entice me to purchase a multitude of wondrous cream concoctions. I mention the cream: 'my friend told me of an anti-aging cream'.....'Ah, of course'.....she brings a tub and demonstrates on my hand and sure enough, the results are there. I seize one and before I leave she convinces me to buy a few other items, one of which is an effective anti-snore powder 'how did you know I need this for my partner?'.....she replies with a laugh '"oh goodness darling, EVERY man snores!"

I finally retreat from the hectic square/market area; herald a taxi (showing only the amount I intend to pay) and head back to the hotel to unwind with a much needed glass of the remaining wine, and head down to the buffet dinner downstairs. The theme is local moroccan and it will trump running around the streets in a sweat, ~whatever it's like.

It is quite tasty but the convenience factor probably makes it even moreso. More wine in the room after cleansing face, with netflix movie channel on the phone is a tragic admission, but definitely the most relaxing option to complete the days' adventures and achievements.

After thinking the whole trip was to be declared an utter waste of time, I had actually managed to cram a whole lot into the one full day I had access to.

So a reliable *recky tour* it was.

Next time, I vowed to stay in one of the beautiful private Riads, with an endless budget; -a larger travel limit so I could shop without abandon, and much more time and patience....

God I'm a dreamer...but one has to hold onto the dreams!!

For without them we would never explore the wondrous playgrounds everywhere out there...

xxxxxxx

Chapter 14

Rain, Resourcefulness and Rosemary.

* Fag Hag in the Bag 

Well, it has begun. The rains are here with a vengeance. 💦
Inconvenient? Understatement.

Glamorous? Not in the slightest!......except for this *one special occasion*......

A fabulous fable of fashion forward fairies and floozies. Last night saw me caught in a torrential downpour on my way down Melasti Street.In a nutshell, all Sapphire *really* wanted, was a brief reprise from her room, and to get to desired location quickly as it was late…

['Rosemary' warung is my latest 'office' hang. Minutes away. Great food; gorgeous staff and very quiet. No Australians. Left in peace… = Bliss. Herb heaven.]
However, after being 'roped' into doing the dog rounds of panorama with Jodie; talking to **all** the staff from room to gate, and then the following interlude, the 5 min walk took 90…
(as it often does when Sapphire is on a time limit)……..

Bare-footed, (flip-flops are a health hazard on the slippery sidewalks) and drenched from head to toe, I was a sight to behold as I stopped at my local café to request borrowing a *'payung'* (umbrella). But alas, none to be found.

(When its *not* rainy season however, be sure that there are hundreds.)

As I stood waiting for it all to subside a fraction, I was aware of a bright light in my peripheral. Squinting towards the source, I was offered a mode of cover from two 'cuddly bear', debonair looking men.

The jewellery they fashioned was eye-catching; I found myself compelled to approach for a closer look, and naturally, a million photos! (Yes, im still part Japanese)….

Though past 9pm, I almost reached for my sunnies 🕶 to shield the glare emanating off all the sparkling jewels. (They say the way to a man's heart is to provide food fit for a king, but for a woman of substance, its bring-on-the-bling!) 💎
Was I in the company of pirates?? They certainly appeared as though they had tried on absolutely every item from a luxury high-end jewellery store, and done a runner with the loot.

As it turns out, this majestic married couple are eccentric jewellery-queen designers who frequent the island, and its not hard to see why they have accrued multiple awards for their

craft. I mean, talk about '***Midas Touch***'….holy cow……
(semantically, those two word descriptions of folk I now respect and indeed *seek* more than
ever, after past history…but that's another story…)
Naturally, they were happy to pose for the visuals, and, typically, their company name was
camp-spectacular as one would expect: '**Golddigger Enterprises**'. *Faaaabulous!*
I gaped wide-eyed as a special story was regaled as design inspiration behind each piece in
the gallery of spectacular accoutrement. And YET, they described this as their more
slapdash '*gardening collection'*. Heaven forbid the dress-up-set!
It was a bling bunnies' dream fantasy. There were more carrots at this table than a whole
carrot patch.

I felt my pulse racing with sheer excitement.   They obviously relished their trade with a
passion too. Kudos to them. Massive pedestal in my view.

One must bow (or is it curtsie?) to the Queen in respect…

So there I was, with the blinged-to-the-max-men, and before too long in hysterics to boot.
The sense of humour was on par with their designer skills (think the 'modern family' sitcom
couple).

So, how *exactly* did we meet in the first instance you ask? Well, they kindly offered me an
empty red plastic bag to cover my sodden bonce. Needless to say, they relished the role of
'knights in shining <u>armour</u>'(literally!) to my dripping 'damsel in distress' with aplomb.

Their prior resume naturally included the fashion industry, as evident by the certain je-ne-ce-
quoir flair they possessed.
"Please, accept our offering! My name is Matt" said one. "Hi Matt. I'm
drowned rat" said I.

 Matt and his partner Mick then proceeded to style me with the plastic accessory. Suavely
tied under the chin in a…not so much *cape* as **bonnet** fashion, they craftily took this stretch
of bright plastic and transformed it into an alluring fashion accessory to be flaunted.
Nat withdrew in a dramatic, gasping gesture (hands to mouth):
"Oh, so VERY Audrey Hepburn!!"

Yes, we were in my favourite café, <u>and</u> they were obviously fellow caffeine-queens, but I
fantasized momentarily about the what a fabulous (and apt) breakfast at Tiffanys the three of
us would have..

So then it was *my* turn to model for *their* visual collection.
"The stylish bag lady!" Mick declared, snapping away my bold embellishment with his phone.

And as we exchanged contact details, he announced: "Perfect, when we write you, we shall put:

       'hello lovely lady, is everything BAGus(good) in bali'??!!" Cue delighted laughter.

*(**Bag**us literally means 'good' in Bahasa Indonesia)

The captivating conversation ensued; I was furthermore intrigued, and had to enquire: "Goodness, aren't you afraid of being MUGGED"?!
Evidently, theirs was a multi-faceted profession. Intense self-defence training was an obvious pre-requisite in order to brandish the fruits of their labour, which was confirmed.

Mick: "Of course! Matt is a martial artist" he declared with pride.
A demonstration was in order, with Mick leaping (crouching-tiger-hidden-dragon style) behind his warrior shield: Matt the Ninja.

Meanwhile, the staff looked on in confusion at our animated exchanges.

These were regal gents; I also wondered how they travelled (which they had confessed was often).

In current packing pandemonium mode myself for the next trans-migrational fling, it remained a quandary and the bane of my existence, and I had to ask:

" So do tell, HOW exactly does one travel abroad with a mere 20kgs??
I have more on me right now; ~ my handbag alone is usually over 30!!
I mean, it's ludicrous. I struggle every trip, as I tend to travel like Elizabeth Taylor..

At Denpasar airport, I usually have a 100,000 bill I put in my passport for the check-in boy. You know how money talks and bullshit walks here more than *anywhere*......it usually allows him to turn a blind eye to my excess baggage tally. Last trip, I hit 9kgs over!! (Easy to do, believe me.)"

(Other countries are a different story of course. Try bribing elsewhere, and you render yourself potentially held captive with a wild toothless character in a deep dark cell)......call it the perks of corruption sweetie.

"So how do you manage with the jewellery?? The rings alone are more than 20kgs, surely, with those BOULDERS ; never mind rocks!!......"

These brilliant boys had taken James Bond *GOLDFINGER* to a whole new league. (Diamonds are a girl's best friend, but THESE beauties could be her secret lover.)

Mick offered the following advice:

" Well, all I can say is thank god they don't weigh **us**. And then there are Matt's bracelets, heavens to betsy how he even keeps his arm in the air. But it does make for a strong forearm if you know what I mean….nudge nudge wink wink.

Matt normally just pushes all the horrible people out of our way. It's called the 'Matt attack' rather like a dog barking on command.

Oh, and then there's always BUSINESS class which is one's preferred mode of slinking around the world with sufficient allowance for one's ball balls and sequins.

If one is forced to travel steerage then one must book three seats in a row. With AirAsia you can book up to 40kgs each ,which is ample if not much takes your eyes in the shops, oh and it leaves room to smuggle a 30 kilo house boy, young enough to be trained out of being stupid.

Do what Matt does, he flaps about … one half kilo bracelet comes off, flies through the air hits the vile little creature in the head, knocks them unconscious….and by the time they come to, the conveyer belt has taken over and your bags are on their way. If not already issued, you steal a business class voucher and make your way hastily to the lounge.

Our advice is: spend the dosh and go posh. "

Ah memories………..the halcyon days of travel.

(How's my progress? Having gone from red carpet to red plastic, Im a work in reverse)…

They also confessed that they are desperate to be 'Guncles' (gay uncles) to any available child, so on my dramatic exit, I made a solemn promise that they **would** be, to the one I elect to buy; steal; whatever… to deprive a couple like this of relative duties to some blessed, blinged babe would be an utter travesty of justice……Oh to be such a spoilt tot! 'Carrot patch kid' indeed.

From now on, as my coffee kicks in this regular establishment, I shall reminisce fondly of my two new golddigger gents.

Sigh…..Too many epic episodes in daily dalliances for the island girl. Just not enough hours in the day, nor printer ink to give each one the justice it deserves!

Ah yes, Aunty's been off with the fairies again……some things never change……

More camp spectacular vernacular…..

With love as ever,

Balibot. L xoxoxoxoxoxoxoxo

('B.L'…bag lady…bling luster)…

Chapter 15A

Arachnid curse

So here's a thing…and a question to a crowd…

When you're at your wits' end and in a state of fight or flight survival terror; feeling attacked from all corners…why does the universe send you something so mighty and **worse** that you feel like a wimp thinking that way (?)

Here's a ditty to make you pity…

So there I was, fearing eviction…being hounded by bailiffs and left bereft by the so called staunch husband type. Living in a castle that was about to seized, and on the eve of the 'escape plan' overseas to start a new life. Ticket was booked; bags were packed; all evidence absent. Nerves were on edge; raw and brittle. Hyper sensitivity prevails to kick in the autonomous survival bodily functions. (Reminder: fear is stored in the kidneys)…

So anyway, I'd rented and watched a movie from a local *video store* (yes this was another era indeed)..to try to quell the anxiety. Sleep was an impossible option so this was a time killer leading up to departure and check in. In a bid to not face a 'late fee penalty' (as no evidence of my name or address must be left in the country) - I knew it had to be returned to the store. It had a slot like a mail box to return the videos after hours. So at some ungodly hour of the morn, I got in my car and drove down to the store. (Pretty disappointed with viewing content fyi. But the mind chatters dunnit..so one is sometimes compelled to utilise any source to halt it.)

Sleep deprivation was starting to torment and the eyelids were wanting closure. The brain was exhausted from the final packing, sorting, booking etc. The roads were empty in the dark, still night. After depositing the vid I arrived home, parked the car and then hit ultimate panic mode…realising that in my haze of lethargy id locked the house keys **inside!** Everything was

in there: suitcase, passport, wallet, ticket…and a flight looming in a few
hours…

Somewhere in the recesses of my manic mind I remembered a discussion
at the bar with husband and co YEARS ago about the 'spare house key'
hidden in an obscure part of the roof out the back. To get to it however,
involved scaling the back fence; avoiding the thorned wire ; climbing up onto
a ledge in the garage, balancing with trepidation and reaching into a crevice.
In short, something out of mission impossible. On a good day. Of which this
was not. The desperation to use the toilet quickly had me scrambling to my
feet, with heart pounding in my chest. So finally, after climbing the fence and
ignoring the streaming blood down my arm and leg from the thorny trespass
wire; balancing precariously on a rail, I reached my hand up to the point
where said prize was hidden. But omg…the huge spider that crawled up my
arm and nearly knocked me backwards off my perch. (Like, you know those
bird-eating spiders that are the size of your hand?!..that's maybe a slight
exaggeration but you know what I mean.) I bashed the thing off and no
doubt infuriated the beast, wanting to protect whatever horrid little legged
offspring were lurking in the depths of darkness. And then I saw the hidey-
hole…absolutely **covered** with spider webs. Of course!!!!I have to reach into
THAT? Seriously? Why is my life so hard?????

So crying (literally) I reached my shaking hand in and pulled out the well
mummified key…wrapped up in so much plaster tape that it was virtually
impossible to find the object within. Frantically swiping the sticky web matter
off me and my hair and whatnot I'm now literally doing a tap-dance by this
stage after scaling the fence again and the bladder *bellowing* for relief. God -
how do I get this thing out?…so there's me walking around the backstreets
looking for a long sharp stick or something…ANYTHING to retrieve the key
to…what felt like the continuation of my life (!) Eventually I did and after
picking away at the encasing frantically with a pointy stick I finally got it free
and ran around to the front of the terrace; managing to open the door <u>at last</u>.
This is now nearly 2 hours since leaving the house for the store mind you, so
it was a race against time to shower and race to airport. But oh the relief!
Literally laughing (after finally having a pee) I felt like id won the absolute
fricken lottery….when the day had started with me feeling suicidal about
where my life had compelled me to be at the point in my life where I should
be free as a bird. But hey !- throw a monster beast and a fight for survival

obstacle course challenge into the equation and everything seems heavenly by comparison.

So keep that one on board next time you have a life situation of terror and panic....it could always be worse! There's an arachnid lurking somewhere that could put your life into sudden perspective. Or jeopardy.

True story. The end.

Chapter 15B

The planet at the pool.
A panoramic peculiarity…

Yesterday was a weird old day. Funny how events unfold here in Bali and the day evolves into something totally unexpected and fascinating…
(I live in a gated community of villa owners called 'PANORAMA'; - the semantics of which played out on an animated daily basis)

The traumas of *'mati lampu'*…
The power was off (again) for 8 hours; ~ along with all water supply.
You don't realise how much you take these for granted but they were TRULY missed yesterday morning, during the most humid one to date.
Such are the patience-promoting joys of the third world…

Mine was wearing thin (patience, that is), so I headed to the pool to thrash my frustration out with laps.
Panorama pool is kind of the 'crisis meeting point' here;~ be it the regular power cuts, or earthquakes etc.
I figured if I gave it a good hour there, I could :
get the 50 laps done;   do some bahasa study;   fill in some time [while the gods of electricity and water got over their tantrum(!)] ; AND soak up some vitamin D to boot. All good.

Well, it turned into a social extravaganza that lasted 6 hours!

Firstly, I was chatting to Jose (silent 'J') and his Spanish mate Pedro about the virtues of free-spirit existence. It got onto a whole range of other hilarious topics; wonderfully peppered by the humorous articulation of accent.
Including: the 'cockradeels' in the waters of outback Australia…..and the 'squirross' in the trees here…
Rain finally came so they headed off for their siesta nap ritual.
(Always admired that. Realise it's a talent I will never acquire, even if exhausted to the point of tears)

Then when I had reached lap # 7, up waddles prince Paulo. This adorable, cuddly camp Swiss character has lived here, on and off for 20 years, completely alone, and we only just met!

Turns out he is an ex-chef (and obviously gay), and had me in awe of the descriptions of the professional kitchen renovations he had pursued here.
Spent the next hour discussing restaurants in Bali ,(and all the chefs he knows/has worked with etc) and the difference in price……and then came the promise to have me over for a dinner party one night. Very sweet !

After he left, as I hit lap # 9, he returned with a tray for me of the most AMAZING home-baked goods; (like we're talking Michelin- star standard petit fours.) Holy cow. I'll be there for that dinner offer with bells on!

Lap # 14:- in prances Felipe; proudly flaunting his operation scars.
He just had his entire spleen extracted in Denpasar - (because he would: *rather die than go back to a Holland hospital*)
The op was supposed to be a 4 hour exercise, but ended up nearly 10, after which he promptly stood up and left.
"I should rest for today, but maybe we go for a drink to celebrate tomorrow"…………..
unbelievable.
[I am reluctant to ever step foot in his huge pad here, despite his invitations, as he houses his (ex)Balinese girlfriend, who refuses to take her meds. I went once and had nightmares for days. It was like seeing the girl from the Exorcist movie; the image never left me. No cleaners are game to enter the place; fearing the 'black magic'…….He's too scared to let her go; and sleeps with a chair propped against his bedroom door; a huge stick and a knife under his bed (!)]

Then prim n proper Josie came to walk Millie around the pool (her little 'rat'-like handbag accessory dog), and announced that the power was back on. Yay!
This English lady, I'll have you know, is the queen of the social set; and head of the entire bali gay community it seems.
She perched on the pool bar stool, and updated me on her latest round of relentless parties, dinners, trips, guests etc.
She is 62; looks late 40's, and out every-single-night. Without fail. Her idea of a night off is one where she gets home before 2am.
Her classic quote: "If I die on a dance-floor, I'll be happy"………
Made a date to do lunch with her next week before she gets hauled into her social regalia 24/7 over the new year. Crown for her. Diamond encrusted tiara even…

Lap # 20: A strange looking guy I have seen on and off here for years came to the baby pool with his 2 multi-lingual young boys.
He is very dark and sinister; I never knew what to make of him.
I told him that the power was back on, and for the first time, heard him speak English (he is French; they do not like to do so!)
Wo – out comes the life story:
His name is "Pitt" – the nickname from his days as a sniper in the special services.
Looked like a relief for him to finally talk of his dark secrets.

Turns out he was gunned down on a top secret murder mission;

nearly died; lost half his body weight and memory; contracted malaria, hepatitis and various other souvenirs;
and then fled to the tropics to marry a Balinese woman and start a family at 55.
" I am somethink…what you say : '*depressed*' now I sink. I had top peripheral vision before and could wipe out an enemy in an instant, POW…….but now I have lost 'arf my mind."………

Who knew such a vast array fascinating creatures hid dormant in the confines of my neighbourhood surrounds; waiting for a crisis to emerge. All with a story to tell.
 It was the most entertainment I've had in some time. (Thought I was the most private soul here.)

Oh but wait, - as the daylight starts to edge towards sunset- the gloriously worshipped golden hour here,
the 2 (I won't say fat)…'jovial' French madames treat those that are left of us here with their presence.
(They are the proud owners of a household of cats, and I do not exaggerate…its the feline palace at their domain and the recruits keep coming. They are renowned rescuers constantly on cat patrol…no stray hungry street kitten will be homeless if they encounter them.)
They abandon their army momentarily to visit the 'kolam renang' (pool) section for a bit of a social check-in.
Sweet as ever. Melodious accent. Super private.
Totes respect avec moi….

Ok, I finally reached lap number 50 at 5.45pm, by which stage I was a seriously wrinkled prune, AND…………..
the power and water was back off **again** for 4 hours!!!

So while folk here relished that sacred 6pm bevvy by the beach, I was a step ahead; - having indulged in the company of a COCKTAIL of characters all afternoon right here in my hood.
I encountered a *panoramic spectrum* of the residents.
The address lives up to it's title indeed.

So…
sending love from the Cuckoos' nest.
Some flew over, and some never returned………

Sapphire-sans-sanity
xoxoxoxoxoxo

Chapter 16

Ceremonial Circus Scenario.

So here it finally was........ the day devoted to the ceremonial blessing of the new villas. And we were profoundly aware that chaos would reign supreme.....
As I opened the door to my den, and peered out at the prevailing activity, I knew it was going to be a circus worth recapping.

The team of workers on contract to complete the construction had dwindled dramatically from 15 to 2, so it was far from complete! (Deadlines here mean nothing with the constant Hindu ceremonies taking precedence. I was told August......it was now October).

It was only 11am, and already there was a team of Panorama staff busily preparing the ceremony site, on the villa porches.
 The pillars were being adorned with fabric; the offering box erected; the table cluttered with the array of usual fruit, eggs and dried crap that symbolized gifts for the gods etc.
The prince himself, Krishna was already enthusiastically prancing around in full ceremonial garb. God, it could all begin any MINUTE now.......
I still had around 4 hours catering to attend to, and in my usual military~precision fashion, had devised the days' schedule planned to the minute......(perhaps in my lethargy I had forgotten where I was!) This land was, after all, an OCD strategic planners' equivalent to diving into the depths of hell. Rubber time (*'jam karet'*) prevailed as usual........as did the absence of specific data or information of *any* kind.
To give a brief outline here:
The basic questions, (over the course of a 3 day period):
"what time will the ceremony commence?"

the answer   "4pm".......
the next day: "5pm".........
today ? "3pm" and "oh.....i don't know, we wait for instruction from the royal family!"............
and*: "how many people will be in attendance?"* (read: WILL WE BE EXPECTED TO CATER FOR).........
the answer/s: "maybe 8"....... "oh, no more than 40!"........
a day later: "I think 30; maybe 35!".......
today: "not sure, but don't worry! Everything okay, just coming and have some food and beer and happy to bless new house!"........ its only bali royalty in attendance.......
"Fu%$!!"...don't panic......
I smiled through gritted teeth as I thought: sure! Why not relax.......
it could be 10, it could be **100** that we are expected to provide full catering (etc) for!!!......
lets just ask the gods to:
~   bring the food; softdrink; beer; wine; cake; etc......(fit for a king....LITERALLY),
~plus dress us in the kabaya with the deft hand of an origami specialist;
-and have all ready for action with a massive smile and an aire of nonchalance at WHATEVER time they decide to get the ball rolling.......no worries. Chill out!

I retreated to my room in despair and called mum to join me for a coffee on my porch; where I proceeded to vent to her and chuck a monumental teared-tanny at what awaited us in the day ahead.......meanwhile time was ticking.
Poor mum hadn't slept a wink as usual...(it had been what – 35 years of no slumber for her now?? I've lost count.....)
She wearily attempted to calm my frazzled nerves, before I retreated to my room to go into intense disaster management control and frantically get ready for action. But oh god.......what was that smell? It was like something had died in my kitchen. No time for the cleaner as usual, so grab the rubbish bins to empty myself again. As I tied the bag from the bin and lifted it to put in the disposal unit, it appeared: bingo! There was a death.....i had murdered once more. A rigor-mortised mouse....or was it a rat?! Hard to tell here; the size being somewhere between a large

rodent and a small cat. Beneath the rubbish bag! What the hell?....

So there I was doing a special sort of ceremonial scream dance and gag in the panorama gardens, (dressed in virtual underwear as usual mind you),....and urging mum and the boss man to witness the vermin violation I had endured.... "Look! I was right! The stench was a dead animal!!!"

How it got trapped in there is, like all things here, an utter mystery. However, it appears my ambrosia addiction proved to be my savior: death by smothering. For it was trapped under several kilos of papaya seeds.

Meanwhile, the poor manager Ketut had the gastro virus bug that was going around, so he joined me in gagging, and then hurried off to find a loo.

I go to mums room to see how Garry is going. Oh! Wow, he is already in the sarong, separi and headgear and looks fantastic! But..... what's with the bursted artery and blood spurting from his hand?......

so off I scurry to fetch bandaids and antiseptic. While I simultaneously fumigate my abode from the stench of rotting vermin.

Meanwhile, apparently the gods had sent some sort of sign to Mum: her bathroom was literally a pool~ flooded from a leaking toilet. The cleaner was busy mopping up the torrents with the wooden stick and cloth they like to call a mop. Fingers crossed the gastro didn't hit Mum and Garry before the day was done too....

I had planned to go and collect the order of abundant nasi campur (rice mix) for all the guests, but no time for that now. The mangku (priest) had already arrived, so proceedings were imminent. I hurriedly squeezed myself into the sarong and ceremony shirt that was now 3 sizes too small; tying the selandang around my waist to seal the discomfort in place. How many hours must I endure this garb? It felt like a hot and heavy corset in intense tropical heat: a new kind of physical hell.

Hearing the bell toll, we went to join the growing throng of tamu (guests) as the god games began. I spotted Bilot, the designated driver I had chosen to collect the food, and beseeched him to

assist. But it appeared Bilot was BLOTTO; eyes glazed in delirium from already raiding Garry's beer supply.
Oh boy.....plan B. I recruited another staff member and did my best to explain the address etc; hoping he could manage the task instead. Fingers crossed, as there was no plan C........

The ceremony was a multi-facited event as usual, which entailed several stages, in the presence of the royal family, who were seated majestically on the porch on their personal 'thrones' (chairs seized from my porch and others nearby).
It started with a mini bonfire (which of course the boys loved, since the Balinese are all arsenists at heart); followed by the burying of some 'lucky coins' in the dirt below the villa porch (which we had to assist in by seizing handfuls of dirt 3 times....always good in a white shirt)......and then all the table rituals with the mangku chanting at the fore.
Bits of feathers, strings, dried crap etc was placed on the offering ledge above by a woman assisting, and the priest continued ringing the bell and droning on as all sorts of activity continued at the table 'tipsite'.
Finally, Ketut urged us to join him on the 'podium' for blessings of self with the holy water, and prayers to the gods for protection. Several flower petals were taken from our individual canangs many times, and held between our hands as we joined in prayer.
Eventually, after a long-winded proceedings, it was time to do the 'catering' for the chaotic crowd.
The builders were all Muslim, so crouched sideline by the pond, eagerly awaiting the provisions – (especially the enibriation material apparently). They came first with feeding, as another ceremony was at another temple on the grounds, so the royals followed the mangku to continue events. (At this point it is perhaps stating the obvious to say that Mum and Garry were most bewildered by the itinerary...or lack thereof.) This was quintessential ad-hoc bedlam to the max. The way of the land.....
With enormous relief, I saw Nenga return with the box of makanan, so I began placing on trays to cater.
Nasi campur for the builder boys and a beer each.
We would have to do the royals next and ketut had suggested that the on-site café would be the best venue for them in privacy.

Alas no, it then became rapidly apparent that it was to be where we were, so let's hunt down plates to serve their meal on, and grab some tables etc to bring to their 'thrones'.....
Meanwhile JJ.....(jovial Josie for sure!) had popped in for a drink with Millie, her pet pooch, and sat on the step with wine in hand. "Oh, its always an f'n shitfight don't you know! They bring their whole extended families, friends etc, and YOU are expected to just keep the hospitality flowing – they will suck you dry for everything they can take. It's a nightmare! I warn you - watch your fridge, - half your alcohol supply is already gone!" she pointed to the staff congregated at the pond table with around 25 empty beer bottles already. Oh my god.........
Cheeky buggers.
(She then said her farewells and proceeded to disappear; MIA for 24 hours....... but still maintaining an aire of dignity during doggy walkies time the next day, while in the familiar state of inebriation.)

Back to the present dramas at hand though. The case of the missing beer cases......

(It should be pointed out: I write in a <u>dogs'breakfast</u> fashion dear reader, but you have to keep up......as I am permitted to under the circumstances.... for it is indicative of my state of mind don't you see....an organized thought process in such conditions is an impossibility to be sure!) .... Think wheeling dervish.....

"Guys we have coke and cordial here for you now" I said in bahasa, to which we received the delirious reply from Nyoman of (perhaps the only English word he knew):
"oh **bullshit!**"...(ie keep the beers coming).
So there was Garry's role ordained for the next 6 hours: the gatemaster: fridge security patrol.
But oops! There was some PORK in the meal!!! With them being Muslims, I guessed it was a compensation for their greediness, of sorts.

Meanwhile, Mum and I served the royal family their meals, plus their staff; panorama staff, and a few floating extras. "We need to present the cake next before they take off, or do another ceremony, or the gods know what else!" I announced to Mum who was not relishing our 'puppets on strings' role......

So, out came the cake. And talk about having it but NOT eating it. We didn't have time to stop for air let alone consider sustenance ourselves! For the fun and games was to get better still.

The huge box was around 5 kilos, which I had lugged home from a Kuta cakeshop after walking the hour to get there with Mum. Along that 'follow the yellow brick road' journey, we were greeted by several kneehigh mini folk with an animated "Hi!!!!" (at the decibal of a lungfull of helium gas) and a high-five which we had to bend down to greet. (I think it was the season for dwarf-throwing here at the moment or something (?!) In any case, I felt somewhat huger than normal here.)

Anyway, after a mini hernia to get the damn thing home, and backstrain extreme, we were now finally placing candles on it for Sugi and Nyoman to blow out. It had *'Terima kasih'* scrolled in icing, and it was a symbol of our appreciation for months of stress, anguish, cash loss and insomnia.

Photos all round, smiles etc blah blah blah.....

It was off to Mum's room to cut into 40 slices and distribute.

I was chief cutter (always a risk with my accident-prone knife skills!) – for on little gold plates, while Mum was to take on the trays for the guests. I noticed a few of my acrylic nails were missing.....oh god I hope they hadn't landed in the kings' slice of cake........(?!!) ~but alas no time to ponder the mayhem further. They are all awaiting more honouring.

Mum took an insurmountable amount of time to distribute the first lot of cake which had me thinking 'does she expect me to follow her with the next tray, or do I wait, or what?'.

I finally heard panting; a door creaking open and a sweating, pissed off mother emerged with the explanation of "Ive had to walk **all over** the grounds backwards and forewards; finding & following them to hand these out. They are scattered far and wide"........cue a look of fury I knew oh too well myself.......welcome to the whimsical wonders of *WHERE THE F^€£ AM I...??!!*

Garry emerges to announce that the royalty is departing and beckons us to follow them to the gate. "get back to the fridge Garry.....it takes seconds for them to empty supplies!!" we urged him.

Mum and I hurriedly scurry up to the front and do the animated thankyous, hugs etc etc before heading back wearily to tidy up; change out of the intolerable threads, and sit for a well earnt drink or 10 ourselves.

Another day in paradise **lost**.......like our sanity I suppose....

Chapter 17A

VIRULENT PSYCHOSTIMULANT….

In la de da London……….

It was her favourite time of the day.

That first smack in the head of caffeine. The initial mathematics of bodily functioning. Ah but beware…for it was a delicate equation.

If you got the mix right, it was like inserting grey matter electrodes.

The key was in the milk quotient, she felt.
Enough to stop gut rot, but not to hide, or mask the coffee taste. Many a time she had fallen victim to that danger when out. "There's no coffee in this!" she would declare, as the potent triple shot lay undetected to the eager tastebuds, hidden underneath a tank of hot frothy milk.

They were addicts, and they knew it. It was a vice that neither were prepared to sacrifice however. They had developed an increasing dependency on it over the years that now classified them as virtual connoisseurs, and they were beyond hard markers. He had impressed the socks off her by putting himself through something akin to barista school while trapped working in a chilly London pad over the past few years, and now greeted her with a flawless cup of heaven every morning. Euphoria.

She in particular was most disciplined in so many other ways pertaining to health and fitness of body and mind. Her controlled abstinence from all the other devils she had danced with in the past gave her a sense of grace in allowing this legal high to continue to add meaning to her life. In a survival-like addict manner, they read only the positive blurb on caffeine: (*'prevents altzheimers'* for example and 'a tonic for the liver')…..and they continued to *enable* each other with such encouragement. She had given up once for nearly 6 months, but the will to continue living had dwindled somewhat so she hopped back on the brew for sanity maintenance control.

The Pomms loved a cup of tea most of all. It was part of their heritage it seems. And in a 'when in Rome'-like manner, she too had succumbed to the comforting, warm, pick-me-up brew of the land, with the 'hobnob dunk' (biscuit) ritual on many a chilly afternoon.

But don't be fooled: it too, required vital precision. If the concoction was too potent, it could be a lethal brew. She was still wary and terrified after one experience several years earlier, which saw her over-indulging in the nation's beverage of choice the way they were accustomed......

She had attended 'high tea' with her husband at the Savoy, back in the halcyon days of no reserve. They had their *'bring it on'* hats on, so with the continually replenished tea pots and dainty gold stands of cucumber sandwiches and cakes, the finest champagne would arrive in flutes as a fashion-like accessory to the proceedings.

They had observed in wonderment as couples took to the dance floor in displays of statuesque tango, and as the champagne danced merrily on the tastebuds, notions of *'that will be us one day!'* fleeted across their mind in merriment.
But alas, like the milk, the champagne had been a mask to the powers of the pot, and after guzzling with gusto for several refills, the fear of death suddenly struck.

She started to panic, and felt her lungs seizing up, as her heart pounded wildly in her chest. She had gone into stimulation-overdrive, and was convinced a heart-attack was imminent. He felt similar sensations, so they fled the scene in a flustered; insane-like manner, much to the concern of the regal hotel staff. The rest of the afternoon saw her crying in a bath while trying desperately to breathe and calm her tortured soul, while he lay in bed at the Bond street hotel channel-flicking the TV remote like a speed junkie.

Thereafter had seen several years elapse with complete abstinence of the terrors of tea. It was a phobia to her now; almost to the degree that spiders were to her mother. Gradually, with decaf as training wheels, she had allowed it to re-enter her beverage menu list, but only if she was in complete control of the brew-strength. (Almost 'why bother?' level really, but she had conquered her fears at last, so it was a mild victory of sorts).

She always remained faithful to the stimulant of choice however, and worshipped her morning caffeine god religiously. She had also noticed with delight that since her last visit from Bali, London had lifted its game in the café stakes exponentially.

Her previous stints here had seen many a hopeful café visit turn into a bitter disappointment; literally. Somehow the word had travelled that this stuff was the legal equivalent of morning cocaine, and being the drug pigs that they tend to be, the English had caught on fast.
Those qualified to be real baristas were put on such a pedestal in her view, and she respected their craft with more than admiration.
If the coffee 'kicked' the way she adored, the man behind the machine (or dealer) had changed her life for the better! It was like Cinderella awakening from a coma.........they had found her 'on' button.

The breath of life. Ahhh........

Chapter 17B

The traumas of tradies.......
Jack to the sound of the underground....

okay, seriously.....
WHY is it that tradesmen always HAVE to do the noisiest stuff at the earliest hours??
Hammers, nails, JACKHAMMERS, drills.......it's audio warfare gone ballistic.
Is it their version of COFFEE or something?
Once one has been completely woken from the cacophony of headache material, its smoko time!!
For the better part of the day really.

They tend to resume in the afternoon, but not to anywhere near the din level as the vital 'final sleep hours' of the morn.
I have found this to be the case in both London and Indonesia.
Its like a right of passage to enter the tradie workplace:
MUST BE ABLE TO WAKE A NATION AS EARLY AS POSSIBLE DAILY, SO AS TO ANNOUNCE YOUR PRESENCE, and then just slacken off as the day progresses.

And is the passing of time a concept that they cannot grasp, or adequately express?
Ie: when asked the question: 'how long will it take' it is recognized as a game to them!
They love to play with your mind on a grand scale.
'oh a coupla days really'..........
(Note the diary date of that reply several **months** later).....

Also: a day of work with *your presence on the scene* to oversee...(task at hand) is equivalent to *a fortnight* if you are absent and they are left to their own devices.......
Do the maths!

You are still usually paying **by the hour,** mind.
Hourly rates are a constant, not to be tampered with.
All else is a playground to 'the guy with the exposed butt-crack'
(to use a cliché image yet again)

Oh, and while we are on the topic of all things to do with TIME,
who else has experienced a <u>week</u> (at least) of being stationed to
the house ...
– since the booked **8am Monday morning** allocation of their
arrival... (?)   the diary is full of liquid
paper, and it is now *Sunday* morning....(one has given up entirely,
and is looking forward to the Sunday sleep in when low and
behold)......bingo! Today is the day they decided it to
commence; never mind the pre-ordained booking of a week
ago.
And do you have a leg to stand on?
Well, yes! If you are prepared to do the bloody job yourself....
Otherwise you are at their mercy.

These guys are up there with dentists as the most detested people
we must include in our lives at various stages. They flip your life
upside down; make promises they cant deliver; go disappearing in
action......or appear unannounced like magic (always during a
really inconvenient time); render you sleep-deprived beyond
belief, **and** drain your bank balance.

The villains of modern existence......
Is it not more civilized to live a life in a village, with dogs and
chickens running around, and grass huts perhaps......(?!)

Chapter 18

In the name of health, ~ a healthy **sense of _humour_** is of paramount importance!

*<u>Self-diagnostic searching:</u>

<u>Wellness on the Web.</u>

Where 'health and wellness' is concerned, 'GP' stands for greatest propaganda.........
It's a conspiracy. Keeping us sick provides their income base! Its really best to avoid ill health at all costs, obviously, but if one **does** fall victim, they stand for a better survival rate through personal research.
So what chance do we have? Well, there is a wealth of information available to one online for free! Consult the good old web, my friend.......

It has become apparent to me of late, that there are a few disturbingly notable characteristics on self:

—pale skin (I am anaemic. I melt like a candle without the bi-monthly vitamin B injections) When not in tropical environs, I rapidly lose healthy glow (nickname: 'casper')

—visual sensitivity to light source (have you *ever* seen me without sunnies before 6pm??)
– eye colour changing with mood; surroundings, or for no apparent reason (blue; green and
often red)

–heightened senses (esp after caffeine!)

—unaccounted for strength and quick reflexes

– often hungry and/or thirsty
– extreme cravings for certain types of foods (or ones that can't be satisfied)
– often feel rundown; fatigued; tired, despite an adequate food diet and activity level.

Mental characteristics: 

—strong-willed; independent nature; confident
– intellectual/highly intelligent (though many would no doubt dispute this)…
—well-learned/educated; although not necessarily school educated (!)
– dark nature
– prefers nighttime over daytime; ie nocturnal nature
– moodiness/mood swings/quick tempered
– mental and/or personality disorders.

Psychic characteristics:  
Empathy

– mind reading….(yes, yes, I know what you're thinking: she's full of it)……..
– Clairvoyance (being able to mentally see things from a distance)
– Clairsentience (having knowledge that one cannot explain)
– past life memories (or are they acid flashbacks?)
– immortal soul, and a belief in reincarnation (with all the past lives I've been told I've had, it
makes me……around 540 yrs old!!) Incidentally, I also live in the land where reincarnation is
the basis of all spiritual beliefs.
– experience frequent dejavu
– involved in 'alternative' religions, or have 'alternative' spiritual beliefs….(I have the Hindu
Om from the island of the gods tattooed on the back of my neck. Enough said.)

Additional related concerns:
—unable to fall into normal sleeping patterns : sleep by day; live by night ~

[(the term 'morning' is not part of my daily vocabulary; unless I haven't gone to bed *at all*) In fact, when most say 'goodnight' before retreating with a yawn, I should really say 'good morning']
                                                                        – cold hands and feet (if not in the tropics, my circulation is suspect)
– thought of as a hermit, who tends to appear after sundown
– chronological age competes with the 'imagined' one; refuses to age [Im ancient, (see past-life history) but I think I'm 25]….
– my first impression of folk is based strongly on the 'pearly whites'. One must have good teeth!   And I myself have spent much money (against recommendations, mind) in opting for longer front teeth. I love a good fang (!) and when I recently nearly lost one in an accident, it was beyond devastation……

Oh

my

god………

I'M ..

A FUCKING VAMPIRE!

Chapter 19

Broken Shell

The boy and girl had walked the shoreline for hours, collecting unusual and unique shell specimens. Nature's wonders. These were visually eye-catching, with years of secret stories to tell, and they were most proud of their findings.

The spectacular sunset was occurring, a huge ball of fire behind them; but they trudged the sand to the pavement for the home-stretch before the final light of the day was replaced by the veil of darkness. They were stooped over, cradling the delicate trophies in their shirts.

A light sprinkling of rain began, and they shuffled faster to avoid the inevitable downpour. The boy's shells slipped from his grasp, and tumbled to the bitumen.

He gasped as one of them cracked, broken, as it came in contact with the harsh surface. He sat down to retrieve the pieces, and tried desperately to save them for fixing back home.

"Leave it, come on let's go!" the girl urged. He was panic-stricken. "That was my FAVOURITE one!" he declared…"You have plenty, and we can come back for others tomorrow"..

They both knew that they had selected the best of the best to be found, and there would be no turning back, nor settling for less interesting specimens, but she tried to calm his agitated condition and get to dry safety.

"Come on. You'll find some other nice normal ones later, I promise!" He was totally deflated.

Keeping it would mean a constant reminder of his loss, and every time he saw it his sadness would return, but he was determined to give it his best shot:

"I'm going to <u>try</u> to fix it, because it was the one I loved the most…the others are normal and boring. I don't want any other ones", his bottom lip trembling.

She understood. 'No, me either' she thought, in utter empathy……

It is sad but true that human nature is try to fix what cannot be repaired. When passion is ignited, one is all forgiving and ever confident of a victory……

Alas….it only leads to
the destruction of self.

Nature will do what nature does; one can't intervene. Survival of the fittest reigns........

I sat on her porch, watching the birds and butterflies fluttering around the fountain joyously, as her background music played. The gardens here were so soothing and medicinal. It was a calm haven, and a lovely chosen spot for her to reside. In the most private corner of the premisis, staff would sneak past in fear; only entering the adjacent room for cleaning when _absolutely_ necessary. As Hindus, their belief system does not allow for such anomolies ~ after all, she was both the devil and goddess incarnate.

Her once sleek hair was now a mangled mass of knots; like wild snakes entwining at the base of her neck. Her princess aura had turned positively _medusa_-like. She also had what appeared to be a contact lense in one eye only; crystal blue. The other was deep brown/black. This may have been the result of medication? – unsure. The eyes, as they say, are the mirror to the soul......It gave her the David Bowie allure, and added to her freakish veneer.

Aware of her glare in my peripheral as she chain-smoked, she was placid and lovely for the moment, but I was nervously anticipating the inevitable 'switch' in her nature. My cue to exit, and retreat to safety from the beast.

I had taken some photos of her when she called me over to visit. It was always an event to remember ....or fear. She posed seductively; showing off her assets in a skimpy 'pokahontas'-like outfit, her long, now mangled mane like a big shield behind her. "Were you ever a model?" I asked, her beauty even now, was evident, beneath the veil of madness. "Seven hundred years ago, yes" she confirmed. "But now, I am sent from the gods to rid the people of she" (showing passport photo of herself).

I often had to stifle a laugh at her incoherent ramblings; making a mental note to jot them down in my room immediately after the episode. She had the mind now of a child; was bereft of morals.

Often, in the early evenings, I would hear joyful music emanating from her room, and witness her singing and frolicking naked in the garden; her fairy-floss hair flying gaily.......

"Some people never go crazy. What truly horrible lives they must lead" .....
(quote by Charles Bukowski)

Shelley was originally from Java, Jakarta and is an _estimated_ 32 years old now. I say that because the Indonesians rarely know their actual birthdate or year! If I was to ask her every time I would no doubt receive a different reply: fifteen one day; forty the next.........eight hundred (!) and so on.

When I asked her if she had siblings she had replied 'several brothers' – but it was later confirmed she had one estranged sister only. Fact vs fiction......this too was a game to her.

(still, I have known a few so called SANE folk who are pathological liars to a greater degree! Hers was more cheeky immaturity. Innocent and inoffensive)

The rumour mill had her prior occupation as *prostitute*, but when I enquired further, her dalliances with older, wealthy foreigners and their resultant housing and gifts was no different to most other girls here. Or anywhere for that matter! Her history on that score was most impressive though. She was definitely one of those stand-out beauties that captivate and taint peoples' lives. Like the island she inhabited, she too was somewhat magnetic. It is through her most recent beau, and a dear friend of mine, that I acquired most information about her past life to date. For I, like he, and apparently many others, was somewhat caught in her spell.

Felipe met her at a club called 'Betty's'; where one of the notorious bomb attacks had occurred. He had adopted her like a stray cat during a breakup phase with one of her other suitors. She rolled from one to the next in rapid sucession; never alone for more than a very brief interval between the besotted partners she enticed.
She was somewhat like a redback spider! Sleek and glamorous. Dark and mystical. Desirable and dangerous.
(I used to keep one as a pet years ago; housed in a glass jar on the desk of a job I worked. I hate spiders persee; as do most folk no doubt, but the *Redback* is of an elitist category and belongs on the arachnid catwalk for sure. Like the sash worn in beauty pageants: ~ that contrastive streak of vibrant red.   I would watch the sleek legged black beauty attack flies and other insects I would toss within her reach.)   The fear/desire concept mirrored life; for the two are synonomous in the game of attraction. Beauty usually also came with its own dangerous price, in some way, shape or form.

In a similar fashion, Shelley would lure and snare the chosen victim of the moment in her web of seduction; and their inevitable attraction to her aura would always be to their peril...

I was at first bewildered as to his continued support of her as she slowly decayed before his eyes.

The very first thing I heard him say at the pool when asked how he was: "Oh.......my life is something like a **living hell**"..........

I was confused; it took some time for me to unravel the background story to which he was referring.
A handsome man, with a cheeky boyish aspect about him, and humerous personality to boot, the Dutchman had himself lived a somewhat charmed life chapter in Holland prior to now. His ex-wife was an apparent power-hungry alpha fem, who demanded respect and perfection. One of those who glow, but sadly will never be able to hold down a relationship.

The expectations of others were simply too high. He showed me pictures. She was a knockout: blonde, blue-eyed exquisite creature – the complete antithesis of his current love.

By all accounts he had it all: a glamorous social lifestyle; ample cash flow, and a stunning wife – the arm candy that all dream of acquiring. Nevertheless, he was unhappy with his life. Bitterly so.
He had eventually fled the marriage and country in search of a more peaceful, laid-back existence with an exotic bird of paradise. The only problem was that Felipe was, bless his soul, one of those fellow 'shit-magnets' that always attracts the rare, but *dangerous* birds. The ones that bite the hand that feeds…….or in his case, attempts to medicate.
Karma had obviously been at play when he left his unhappy marriage for yonder sunsets and a less cerebral beauty in partnership. As humans, we have to occasionally throw caution to the wind and take a gamble. But sadly, often when one feels they have won the *jackpot* in life and *people,* they come to realize that *the devil hath the power to assume a pleasing shape* ~ (thank you, Shakespeare), and the lottery was one big scam.

When he found Shelley in the new terrain, he thought he had reached true nirvana. It was all that he had lacked in his other life, and he carried on with the new relationship; blissfully unaware of the horror story to unfold.

Everybody else in our gated community knew her also, and was fond of her happy, sociable nature, and undeniable, genuine beauty. A lot of the Asian girls were 'cutesy' and like magnets to the western men, but she had something else; she was of another league. You couldn't quite put your finger on it…… part of her magic I guess.

He showed me several framed pictures of her, and some albums he had lovingly compiled during their halcyon days. Her face was fuller; the eyes gleamed and she was the pioturo of natural, healthy, glowing beauty. But there was some sort of mystical feel to her too. I could understand his attraction, and all others for that matter.
Now, there were hints of the original girl and her aura still there, but only vaguely. The gentle package had turned positively poisonous.
There were shots of them together by the pool at the stunning ocean-front view villa he had purchased in Candidasa, the quiet diving town as their lovenest/holiday home in the early days. They looked so content and worry-free. Like honeymooners, before the meteors of reality start to fly.

One of my girlfriends had known her the entire time; from arrival to now. She always stood by the fact that she was 'adored by everyone; ~ a most beautiful girl, whose vivacious aura was infectious!'……but what was most endearing to her was the absolute honesty she expressed. She was an open book in all regards, and made no attempts to mask that in any way. It was of course refreshing and rare.

When she offered to help her construct a CV to present for prospective employers, Shelley replied with wide-eyed pure innocence: "Ooh, the only job I have ever done is be a prostitute!"

As the story goes, she quite literally woke up one morning and turned

stark raving mad.

Simple as that! Not so much in gradual degrees as one might imagine….sanity apparently just left the building completely! Whooshka.
The mystery was unfathomable.

It was a cruel situation that life had presented: to destroy such a wonderful specimen.

Felipe; horrified, tried desperately to mend the mayhem; through every means possible. It was like having everything he valued stolen in one foul swoop.
Devastation didn't even begin to cut it. His heaven turned to hell. All attempts at medical assistance and treatment were aborted by her; the prevailing paranoia had her imagining that he was out to poison and kill her. *The redback wont be poisoned*!! Fangs, claws, you name it, they were out, and the once beautiful almond eyes turned matte black and murky, like a shark's. His lover became the enemy. Her beauty turned to grotesque; and she started to wither and age before his eyes, refusing to eat or leave the house at all.

*[in Indonesia, (well – certainly bali), *I was told* / folklore has it that the insane, or mentally-challenged are chained up like dogs. The Hindu belief of course is that they are possessed by evil, so they must be restrained for the safety of others. This is unfathomable in other cultures, but here it has been common, accepted practice for some time.]
Felipe was oh so aware of this locational scenario, and felt compelled to protect her from this fate.

Her prior adoration for him turned to utter repulsion. Despite all he desperately did to support and mend her, she absolutely loathed and distrusted him. How could she imagine he would harm her? He had done nothing but love her unconditionally, despite all her history scars.

As it turned out when I proceeded to investigate with some knowing neighbours, he was described a bit of a 'scoundrel, and a sexual deviant' – who would bring home 'extras' as souvenirs from clubbing pursuits for threesomes and so on; of every sex and description possible….(straight, bi, unsure; trans etc). Yes, there were several stories of 'ladyboys' entering their zone, and she being 'forced to partake in lurid activity'……this was shocking information which I had trouble believing; especially since it was relayed by some drama-queen types in their own right (!) I can only go on the facts as they are presented. As with life however, what truly does go on behind closed doors generally remains there…

He took her to several doctors; all of which pronounced a different verdict to her decline.
One said she was 'pretending' to be insane; another just insisted that he pray a lot, and seek the assistance of a *paranormal.*
She was prescribed a cocktail of various drugs; rispadol; serotonin; dopamine; - some of which assisted, but most just rendering her further labotomised. In any case, it was impossible to know if the solution was amongst them; ~ she would hide the pills under her mattress until he found handfuls and gave up prompting further.
He was eventually compelled to have her admitted to a psychiatric ward for a spell; hoping

that the intervention and enforced medication may have a chance to take hold. Apparently that too ended badly; she was abused further by the nursing staff, and left alone without food, water OR meds. He became riddled with guilt, and took her home once more.

He even contacted her birth mother, and urged her to assist in saving her rotting offspring. She did move in for a while, but alas, had alterior motives. She stole all Shelley's money; a bunch of her jewellery, abandoned her once again, and fled the scene.

[Not surprisingly perhaps, considering she had her daughter married off at 12 years of age to a violent, adulterous rapist. He would lock her up in the house with the pembantu (help) on guard, and visit her a couple of hours a day simply for sex and self-gratification. Meanwhile, his OTHER wife was pregnant.

Shelley eventually got divorced from the monster, but that very same evening, her mother arranged the next marriage to a similar beast.
And so the sick story continues.....]

It also should come as no surprise that she rebuffed men for a spell, and one chapter even had her embarking on a lesbian affair....with a (so im told) 120 kg chinese woman ! She was obviously jaded by the prior treatment from the menu of men, so this was a 180 degree spin in the other direction. As one does.
Alas, it too didn't end well, and had an intensely messy finale; culminating with a big scary stalker on her hands, that kind of made the men appear lame in comparison (!)

It was like pass the parcel....if she felt inclined to play the game with certain participants, she became their trophy and proceeded for a period. It was basically like high class escort work: she would pursue the best offer or proposal, with the best conditions. She became accustomed to top notch: 5-star existence; massive private villas here, beachfront with gazebos and the like…

Hours turned into days; weeks went by. She became progressively more and more twisted and psychotic. Officially deranged.
She would dance and sing in front of a mirror by candlelight for hours on end like an innocent fairy; smiling and beckoning to her pictures of Antonio Banderas adorning the walls. Her world was complete make-believe and fantasy. It was pure innocence and joy….but do not be fooled; she would snarl and hiss like Lucifer should anyone *dare* to enter her zone. She seized the knife block from the kitchen and locked herself inside her room with them.

Her hatred towards him had already figuratively cut his heart like a knife; this was like a symbolic culmination of her desire to attack him. The grand finale if you will.

After months trapped in the nightmare, Felipe was forced to hide in his room with fear, with a weapon to hand to defend himself from the evil monster should she attack. Nobody would enter his house for fear of the inhabitant; and all the Hindus were naturally terrified of her. There was amongst them the implication of *'ilmu hitam'* ~ the dreaded curse that pervaded the island.

Black Magic.

These people believed her to be a victim of it, and it was easy to follow suit in that mindset; it explained the sudden metamorphosis rather well after all…

I was absolutely gob-smacked by the story; and intrigued immensely. I found it one of life's mysteries as to how he managed to maintain his own sanity in such an environment. (or did he??)

What a battle. He was obviously a broken man in this cruel unraveling of events. Such immense sadness must have bestowed itself on him, and the will to continue must have been a daily trial.

I pried for details: " So what actually attracted you to her in the first place?" He replied without hesitation, and a broad smile: "she was beautiful….funny……sad…….and she had a fighter spirit."

A winning combination. There was the Shelley *cocktail*: ~ delicious but dangerous.

One can understand why the classic response to such an offer would be: "I'll have one of those!"

As my mateship to the poor guy became more comfortable, I was compelled to enquire: "Ok, Felipe, I have known several people who have done a 180 degree turn as a result of *chemical cocktails.* Some even killed their partners in car accidents; ended up in prison and / or a psychiatric ward themselves. As they say, what goes up, must come down. Quantum physics. There is always a downside to the magical forays into illegal high playgrounds. Be honest – what drugs was she on/ did you do in the early happy 'party' days??"………
I felt by this stage that he might feel comfortable enough with me to relay such private information; and it would definitely have been a missing piece to the puzzle. It would explain everything really.

If I had to guess myself, I would have assumed a long history of pot-smoking. This was the worst in my opinion. The hydro of today is nothing like the home-grown weed of the past. It was mind-fuck material now, and the outcome of abuse is irreparable.

Shockingly, he shook his head. " Na, she wasn't really into it like me. We occasionally had some ecstacy and she tried Ritalin once, but never Charlie or pot. It just wasn't her thing. It just made her paranoid"……. Her suspect track marks down the arm told a different story however……perhaps there was in fact a history of heroin abuse? Scarred forearms/wrists and smack tend to go hand in hand. it is quite a common thing in Indonesia to 'cut' the arms to absorb drugs through the slash vs using needles. Obviously a game of <u>Russian roulette</u>, but we're talking about class A and beyond here, so that's kind of the *theme of* this game……

He did enlighten me to the fact that she was most affected by outsider comments on her 'childless-ness'. He was sad as he confessed " It made her so upset when people would imply she should be married and with kids by now. They were all looking at me, of course! I don't want them. Never have. They would constantly harass her: 'he will leave you for

someone else younger if you aren't careful.'
I think she felt she had no future. She needed something more secure that I couldn't offer
her.."

Again, his guilt was evident; compensation his obvious intention now.

I had spent many an afternoon chatting with him by the pool about the situation. We called it
our 'office', and would meet at our two deck chairs around 3pm most days.
"Felipe, you've done all you can; let it go!! Its irreparable; she is beyond return
now"......words he had heard repeatedly, and was painfully offended by. Perhaps the guilt
of abandoning his former marriage had overwhelmed him or something, but he refused to
deny his apparent responsibility for her. Her gave her money; fed her, and finally convinced
her to stay in another quiet room on-site that he rented – (the one I spoke of earlier, where I
sat on her porch). So that he could protect her and support her, but from a safe distance.
Perhaps also regain *some* sort of life.
And he did start a new relationship, rather rapidly, with a girl from Jakarta who he met on the
internet (as is the dating venue of choice these days)..... her words were few; in fact to my
knowledge, her entire vocabulary spectrum didn't extend far beyond: " I am from Jakarta!"
like a wind-up doll.

She moved in within days, and bingo, he was co-habitating once again. She never left the
house much; just hung around him with whatever he was doing.

"Forgive me for asking this hon, but aren't you somewhat BORED ?? .....And do you not
crave some time just *alone*?!" I enquired over coffee one day.
He was an intelligent guy, and his wife had been supremely alpha; what was this caper
about?

"Ya, but really......this is no different! She doesn't talk, which is perfect for me! And if I ignore
her she just plays video games until I suggest wo do comothing or eat or whatever. She
does whatever I want to do, whenever I want. And when im sick of her I ignore her. I am still
alone really,......but not lon*ely*!!"

Well...most would say 'fair call'...but I assessed that it was nothing more than a mere stepup
from a blow-up doll.

When he himself started getting seriously sick, he began sorting his affairs, as one does,
including the will.
He had confessed to me that his entire life savings and inheritance was to be divided
between the *strays:* this new girl he had adopted and Shelley; - the house here in paradise,
was to go straight to Shelley!
I considered it an unthinkable proposal. Money and *PROPERTY?*? How could she possibly
know how to manage that? She couldn't even maintain personal hygeine! Brushing your own
hair was kind of basics 101, no?!!!......... – it made him appear madder than she was.
" You are *enabling* her Felipe, you have to cut the tie.....sometimes you have to be cruel to
be kind. You are actually not helping her, and CERTAINLY not yourself.."
He was so intent on trying to mend her, like a broken shell, that he didn't realize the bigger
task would be healing *himself* as the resultant fallout of the trauma.

Felipe was determined to try to retrieve Shelley's once crowning beauty. It was how he remembered her the best perhaps, and he wanted to keep her dignity intact. As one knows, HAIR for a woman is more than just a feature; it represents so much more…

As a last resort, the three of us had headed off in a taxi to my hair salon, where, in a desperate attempt to salvage part of her once marvelous mane, Felipe had tried to convince her to cut the knotted mass that now hung angrily from her head. " Shelley, you will look so much more fashionable with a short crop; see – even Livia has cut out a magazine picture of sexy Rihanna at the music awards last week!!!"   -he indicated the image I had brought to attempt inspiration using an icon.

We had premeditated the intervention; hoping that Senna could convince her with his professional advice, since her ears were blocked to anything either of us had said. *Everything* was perceived as a conspiracy towards her; her paranoia in all aspects of life now was so out of control after years of resisting any medication or help for the scitsofrenia that was taking hold like <u>wildfire.</u>

I had known Senna for several years; he was a dear soul, and had given me several mind-boggling predictions in the past, where he had been the 'messenger' from the higher beings. I knew that if ANYONE could convince her to take action, or Felipe to 'let it go', it was him.

I myself had tried to gently convince her that her hair couldn't be saved now, after I had sat on the edge of her bath for hours on end the evening before, and used bottle after bottle of product to try to comb out the birds-nest. All the while she played naked; - sang and splashed around like a joyous infant, oblivious to the world and life in general. She was singing at the top of her voice at times, and would break into intermittent giggles, which was very sweet really. The adjacent guests must have thought I was bathing a vocal child. Then all of a sudden she would become silent, tilt her head and express the scary serious look; channeling satan once again. I felt like an extra on a horror movie set!

Felipe was meanwhile running back and forth buying stores out of babyoil…..the only product she could stand to be anywhere near her rotting locks. He was so excited that she had permitted me to touch her – nobody else was allowed within a miles' radius of her! As it was, we were in an empty hotel room's bathroom, as she had no hot water in her own. (It was a relatively simple plumbing situation to rectify, but alas required someone **to enter** her room to repair, so it hadn't been done). To this point, the only person she had permitted within her zone was Felipe……and now myself.

[I became somewhat concerned at the facts that now occurred to me: I was hardly in a position to throw stones…..**my** fantasy world was perhaps just as profound as hers was! And when it came to requiring ultimate privacy and solidarity to remain calm and 'safe', I had definitely met my match! I always knew I was of a different caliber of society; ~ witnessing the antics of this lunatic and being able to *relate* was more than a perplexing concept. The madness and yet familiarity of it all was disturbing, to say the least!..]

She would from time to time gaze up at me with her sparkly blue and black eyes; grinning with contentment, until the transformation returned, along with the indicative 'shark eyes'. I would again retreat back to my room in resignation from the evil nymph. It was like in the movies of possession; eg the exorcist. There were flashes of the original 'occupant' but these disappeared as the other beast reared its ugly head.

The hair was way beyond repair, and a result of personal neglect. Perhaps weeks had gone by with no shower or hair washing; maybe months, who knows.?!
In any case, it was a health hazard to keep it on her head now. God knows what occupants might be nesting in there; it was like an external 5kg tumour. It is true in life, the external façade is often a reflection of what is going on internally. Like a map to the contents. This symbolized disease, that much was obvious. A form of amputation was in order.
She again refused adamantly however; rhetorting in a satanic spat: No, no – you are all just JEEEEEAAAALOUS of me……you, you and YOU.
She pointed at the three of us in turn: Senna, me, and Felipe last, with: "I mean, look at the man with no hair!!!!! Its pathetic. "

Poor Felipe. I sympathized with the way his ecstacy of finding a unique pet that *worshipped* him had turned to fear of her apparent *repulsion.* He just couldn't seem to sever the bond. It was strangling him. And it was doing her no favours; neither of us were qualified to handle scitsofrenia ~ she needed serious professional help!
He was apparently addicted to the 'rescuer' role……it was becoming increasingly evident. I had seen it in others before. Nothing I or anyone else could say would deter his involvement. He was masochistically adamant.
It must have felt like a broken record on repeat in his head, for EVERYONE relayed the same messages to him……no wonder he stayed locked away in his home for the most part, and rarely seen. A prisoner. [There wasn't even a number outside his place, just a bolted gate; like the fortress of madness. The huge golden "F" letter I gave him to nail on his front door, actually referred less to 'F' for 'Felipe' and more for 'FU*% OFF ! ' (!!)]

Shelley could not be dissuaded from her quest to keep the medusa crown. I watched wise Senna, who was quite the mystic himself. His reaction confirmed my fears: she was best left to her own devices for the health of all concerned.

He took me aside and explained: " It would be very painful for her to fix this problem. Many, many hours and staff. Maybe many days too. She wouldn't be able to stand it. You must be telling your friend to stop worrying now, because it will make him <u>very sick</u>". I nodded with agreement, but replied " I know darling but he won't listen, and neither will she!"

He continued: "There is a monster now – you can see it in the EYES…..She really needs a ceremony for take out the evil spirits; it is a sign. There is someone else inside now; inhabiting her body. If I touch her hair, it will make me weak and sick too……you must stay away to be safe and well"……….

My heart started racing with concern : I had spent hours trying to detangle the mass; would this make <u>**me**</u> sick now too?? My stomach felt acidic and queezie; I knew it was over.

As we left the salon once again in a taxi, I shared the backseat, somewhat hesitantly, with Shelley, while Felipe sat in the front. His sense of deflation and extreme disappointment was obvious. He had lost the battle. It was as if, by fixing her hair, he could perhaps 'bring her

back'…. Twisted logic tends to reign in the minds of those desperate for peace……
He was speechless the whole journey, while Shelley held my hand, grinning like a Cheshire
cat; loving the scenery and the the sense of being comfortable in the presence of others for
a change, I guess. What a bizarre state of affairs I thought. And how TYPICAL that I should
be caught up in it. (!)

On arrival, she bounced out of the car with a 'come, let's go to my place'! and skipped off
with us in tow; me urgently searching Felipe's downcast face for some sort of exit
permission. He resignedly answered "Ok Shelley, we come to your place…..but I can't buy
you the dress I promised you now. That was only the deal if you got your hair cut"……
She turned to face us with obvious alarm: " BUT WHAT WILL I WEAR WHEN WE GO OUT
TONIGHT??" ~she was indicating me as her partner. Oh god…

After only a few moments in her room, which were somewhat nerve-racking to me to say the
least, Felipe just up and left! "Okay, I leave you girls now. I need to be alone" ….wait
WAIT??……….

His head was hung low, and his eyes averted, so though I tried desperately to get his
attention it was to no avail, and he swiftly disappeared, leaving me on my own with her.
INSIDE her room.

" Yes, you must GO, but she can stay as long as she likes!" she turned to me as she shut
the door behind him. I could handle the porch; huge scope for escape. But this was another
level of terror entirely. " You wanna drink?" she enquired, opening a completely empty fridge,
and tilting her head for my selection. "Ah…..no thanks Shelley. You're very kind, but I had
lots of water at the salon."

Here was a curiously scary domain; like an old antique, bric-a-brac shop. And here too, was
her psychosis – expressed in her immediate surroundings.
There were all manner of things laid out on her table, like displaying her wares: jewellery,
clothes, shoes, masks, hats, scarves, candles, mirrors…. *lots o*f mirrors everywhere, devices
etc.

Amongst them were the earrings and chocolate I had given her; both still in their packets;
pristine condition.

Like trophies.

Though innocent symbols of childhood, the numerous teddy-bears and dolls she had strewn
from one end of the room to the other had an ominous, frightening feel to them. I half
expected them to come to life, with flashing eyes and flying limbs, as her army of
brainwashed attackers.
A collection of new mobile phones, mini computers etc were still in their boxes, untouched
too.

 (I remembered Felipe telling me how on several occasions he had bought the latest device
she had requested simply because…..well, she **had** to have it!) She couldn't master a basic
mobile phone, let alone any of this swanky equipment. The only one she used, apparently,

was the vibrator, left quite obviously in the middle of her un-slept-in bed (!) God knows where she did sleep….

the floor? the bathtub? The garden?......
(I scanned the room for any knives or versions of a weapon, but the kitchen was obviously null and void, and the most dangerous looking tool was the spike heels of some of her shoes. So unless she did a dramatic costume change, I was safe for the moment I figured. Who knew when the psychosis could turn psychotic? One had to cover their bases in such company!....)

There were various framed photos of Antonio Banderas, and Jesus, and a bible was perched on a shelf in obvious display. Yes, well, she was obviously not of the Hindu or Buddhist category any more, that much was for sure!
The silence had to be broken, so I blurted out: "So, what will you do for Christmas this year?"
She was chain-smoking as usual to the point where I felt like I was trapped in a dark nightclub; struggling to breathe. She thought for a moment and then shot back :

" I will make a movie of Jesus Christ Superstar, with Silvester Stallone! He has the body for the cross " she determined.   " Oh! I thought you would have Antonia Banderas in it?" I indicated her collection of prints.

 "NO, we had an affair before. He *still* loves me......" she sighed.
"So, ah.....will YOU act in the movie too?"

"No, this time I will do the dubbing into bahasa Ingris"

It was no secret that Felipe's health had been rapidly declining….(is it any wonder?) and I found myself concerned for my own wellbeing with such toxic exposure. He had been issued some concerning blood-test results; a quite mysterious blood disorder was apparent, but it had culminated predominantly in the SPLEEN, where the blood is recycled. (In chinese medicine, ill heath in this organ refers to 'excess mind activity' or quite simply: indicates too much thinking going on. Well…..hello. it doesn't take a medical expert to explain the reasons for this outcome! My gut was cramping on me now too - psycho-somatically, no doubt.)

Shelley became suddenly animated, and announced " Hey, let's make a deal!…….we go out jalan-jalan *(walking)* to pick up a handsome man……..like *SAMPSON* from the bible, but he is a REAL man!! But first, we go to my favourite restaurant. You will LOOOOVE it. We dress up, very sexy"…..

" Oh! Tell me about this restaurant! What is the food – Indonesian? "
" No, it is very expensive of course. I will have the oysters and lobster – VERY big lobster and caviar and champagne"……..

Ah the world of excess never leaves the memory of one. It is buried DEEP in the recesses of grey matter. Even after lobotomy…
Once bitten, forever shy….and wanting more.

Earlier on, I had relayed, in condensed version, the general message/warning from hairdresser Senna, and Felipe became angry: " Have you **really** been here that long that you believe in their black magic bullshit?! Are you western, or f@$%^ng Indonesian??" I ceased to press further, as it would only make him sicker. Nevertheless, Shelley was still somewhat of a mystery that required an explanation of sorts. And at this stage, that answer was as good as any!

Crazy too, as it may sound (forgive the pun), but it all reminded me of a deranged, luntatic lady I encountered at a café here once. I found my mind drifting back to replay the incident in my head….

 This character was in a party of 3; another woman and a man, and **they** were both ignoring her *outlandish* antics.
Food was thrown around; swearing was to be heard, amidst the high-pitched screaming, and she even lashed out a couple of times at passing staff. I think I sat there with my mouth open through 2 coffees; too enthralled by the entertainment to leave. It was surreal.
I was terrified to walk past her to the toilet after my 2 coffees in case she lashed out, but it became necessary. I tried to smile as I moved past and she eyeballed me like a tiger ready to pounce. As I was returning from the bathroom, the other woman said 'sorry if we disturbed you'….(was it any wonder I was the only other person in this usually busy café?!)"Its my mother you see, I had to bring her while I consult with her doctor, as she cant be left alone, or with anyone else"…..No shit, Sherlock.

"You are doing a good thing for your Mum" I replied. She softened, and to my astonishment started to cry. "She is such a lovely soul….its so sad to watch someone so healthy for their entire life suddenly lose the plot. Its mercury poisoning, you see……we had the most natural, healthy existence. We ate organic, and lived off a farm! There were, to our knowledge no toxins in our way of life as with city dwellers. Country air; wholesome simple lifestyle. This is beyond heartbreaking, but I remain my mothers' carer for the rest of her life now." All I could put it down to was aluminium cookware.
I was affected for days by the encounter, and found it terrifying to think that you can live the most pristine existence, and yet still be stung by life's cruel occurrences; deep within the biochemistry. It was out of our control, and fate often holds a surprisingly fatal twist that's unexpected……. Reminds us to value every healthy, (sane) moment we have……

*Exerpt from 'Ham on Rye', by Charles Bukowski:

I had made practice runs down to skid row to get ready for my future. I didn't like what I saw down there. Those men and women had no special daring or brilliance. They wanted what everybody else wanted. There were also some obvious mental cases down there who were allowed to walk the streets undisturbed. I had noticed that both in the very poor and very rich extremes of society the mad were often allowed to mingle freely. I knew that I wasn't entirely sane. I still knew, as I had as a child, that there was something strange about myself. I felt as if I were destined to be a murderer, a bank robber, a saint, a rapist, a monk, a hermit. I needed an isolated place to hide. Skid row was disgusting. The life of the sane, average man was dull, worse than death. There seemed to be no possible alternative. Education also

Meanwhile, Felipe was experiencing disturbing health issues. He had sadly been forced to
sell the dreamy seaside property in order to afford the increasing medical fees he now faced.
He had already invested a fortune into attempts to medicate Shelley and support her to date.
Something obviously had to give......
He showed me some of his blood-test results and explained that 'there are white; red cells,
and platelets. They have to watch my platelets as they are fatally low......'
The mystery of the blood is always one that I cannot fathom as I myself have always been a
dynamic anomaly in that regard. Doctors have always scratched their heads at my results;
they are a puzzle to all concerned.
In any case, I ascertained that his problem was focused on the SPLEEN. An excess of
particular emotions affect the internal organs. Mentally overthinking can damage the spleen
qi....(the kidney is damaged by fear; the liver by anger and resentment; the heart by sadness
or grief. Well, the spleen rules THOUGHT.) According to TCI (traditional chinese medicine)
the spleen is probably the most important strategy for healing, as it affects the body's
immunity and capacity to maintain and heal itself. His mind must have been so constantly
busy looking for the Shelley solution; its no wonder the organ was suffering.

It was after one of my trips away for visa renewal, that I returned to see Felipe bandaged
around the stomach. He had his spleen removed!! He was marching along, and proudly
flaunting his operation scars; 'it's a little sore, but Im fine......we go out for a drink
tomorrow?!' ......seriously?? If his spleen was gone, what did that say for his immune
system, I wondered. It made him sound like a ticking time-bomb. The whole sordid situation
had festered inside him like a germ that was bound to have dire consequences. Sure
enough, months later, he hijacked me at the pool to relay the latest news (or drop a bomb as
it were):
" I don't want to worry you, or to talk about this again.........but I have cancer. And I am not
going for treatment. I don't want to change my life! Im not going through that hassle and
discomfort. Life is too short anyway..."
It was like living a nightmare. I was engulfed with sympathy for him; it broke my heart. For
as we all know, once the health is gone, there is just no point. It is EVERYTHING.
The part I have never been able to work out though, is why it always happened to the *nicest*
people. I tried to support him through this dark period. But it was obviously looking grim. I
brought him around various healthy supplements; vitamins; a DVD on yoga for cancer etc.
He was most grateful, but here was nevertheless a broken man. There was no mask to
disguise the fact. I guess we are all like mirrors: we are a reflection of the influences and
people that surround us...

8 months later…

AIN'T LIFE STRANGE, THOUGH

The dynamics of body health are ever a mystery……
Upon my return after time away : (during which I was most concerned for his wellbeing. He was a dead man walking surely, with no spleen and a far from healthy lifestyle), he looked the best I have ever seen the man; by all accounts he appeared fit as a fiddle!!
There were circulating rumours that he had completely quit smoking at last, and was abstaining from alcohol. He confirmed it to be true, and added that he had started a new fitness regime. Swimming, training, long walks (flaunting his expensive new sports shoes.)
I was most impressed. And then the shocker:
"last trip for tests, I got a clear bill of health, - no cancer detected whatsoever!!!"
Wow…..it is *so*, so true: Fact is stranger than fiction, don't you find?!

Sadly, just as quickly as health returns however, it is often stolen once again in an instant. The dynamic eb and flow….

Time passed and he ended up deteriorating and requiring the chemo treatment after all. The last I saw of him was on his daily walking rounds of the property; the quest for circulation was vital to him at this stage. It sounded like emphysymia had struck and had virtually lost his voice. He had a shaved head, and a labored gait. The man was visibly less comfortable. Quality of life was null and void.

I hoped with all my heart that a miracle occurred and he would acquire symptom-free status once more.

He died on a Friday morning.
I was informed that his lungs got him in the end.

The cremation ceremony would see only a handful of witnesses. Such is the expected final scenario for hermits, lost souls and misfits…

AS FOR SHELLEY………as it turns out, she found the fighter spirit from within.
While I was away, she had been forced to move while renovations were underway on all the rooms. God knows how they moved all the stuff; not to mention her!!……what a drama.
Felipe had found her a lovely private spot some distance away; and would visit her frequently to give money and supplies etc. She had started to slowly resume medication on her own too, and was becoming amazingly lucid and 'sane' !!. One day, she was sporting a

cute little hat, and had strands of braids apparent. Her skin was glowing, and her eyes crystal clear and sparkling. He thought she looked lovely! It seemed to disguise the former alien at the back of her head well. But upon closer inspection, low and behold, it was completely gone! Her long fairy mane was again soft, smooth, and utterly knot free. He was gobsmacked. She must have done it herself. As to how.....i guess we will never know.

Summary : one of the biggest blessings life bestows upon us, are the miraculous little surprises that can come out of the blue. Never lose faith or hope, and keep dreaming.......life is amazing! *Nature* surprises us constantly. For every apparent loss, there is a balancing agent of gain.

Somewhere.

Equilibrium.

What appears broken, can be reborn in an instant……….

And then, just as instantly be seized and destroyed……

A year later, and a close girlfriend gave an admission in tears. She had

recently discovered that the man had been coveting an even **darker** secret for the last decade….

"He didn't have cancer at all!"..

the truth was, he had, and was fully aware of the **AIDS** virus.
She was devastated; he had sobbed on her shoulder so many times, and yet never once confessed the truth. But even more importantly, that he had the audacity to blatantly spread it afield to all his partners and encounter culprits. All those swinger parties and orgies too……it was a stirfry of doom.
Shame.
It makes one do dark things.

This was the reason he had prevented her from seeing him in hospital on the final weeks of decline. He had in fact been shielding her from the truth. He was in the dreaded AIDS WARD. Perhaps hospital's most sinister corner.

So like a deck of cards, all other associates in his physical history field were destined to drop like flies too. All oblivious zombies on death row.

Both his last girlfriends had it too..Shelley included.

It begs the disturbing question then: what is fact and what is fiction?

For you think you know someone, and their life story…and then it turns out you had no fucking idea…

Sanity is not guaranteed to last....nothing is!!

There is only **<u>one thing</u>** you can be certain of.

Death gets us all in the end.
And down with it one takes all the secrets, lies and subterfuge
too.   Pandora's box of shattered shells......open it at
your peril.

For the truth sux...........its a killer.

Chapter 20

BEAUTIFUL
KHANA
THE HAPPY MEDIUM

Once upon a time, in a paradise land: 'the island of the gods',

a flower bloomed with special powers............

When Sapphire first met Khana, their similarities united them in an instant sister bond.

Both intensely private, they would perform their daily rituals religiously; forever careful to remain close-guarded from external influences and evil.

They lived in the same complex; literally doors apart, and yet didn't officially meet for over a year due to their reclusive ways.

Khana was a crowd stopper.

 Blessed with a beautiful face, sparkly eyes, smooth skin, long glossy jet black hair and huge ever-smiling lips, she was the epitome of stunning sensuality.

Having modelled in several plus-size catalogues, she was unusually tall for an Indonesian, and seductively voluptuous.

She positively glowed.

Sapphire was envious, as she struggled to obtain a healthier physique after a somewhat turbulent chapter in her life.

In Khana, there was none of the usual associated arrogance with such attributes however, so Sapphire let her guard down, and the friendship blossomed.

Sapphire was forging through a phase of temporary separation from her marriage, and semi-detachment from life in general. She had burnt out, and was shutting down to rebuild.

Having left her country and years of limbo-land existence, she felt as though she had escaped prison!

She was shunning human interaction for protection, as it was toxic to her condition.

Khana was a refreshing influence however. Healthy, happy and safe.

A rebalancing agent.

Both creatures of habit, and painfully disciplined in certain areas of duty; they were however free spirits, and most averse to stringent, dictated routine. On this they held a unified stance. Sapphire had spent her entire life avoiding it, often taking risks to do so. Sadly, Khana was still compelled to comply. It was the inner conflict that pervaded her soul.
With natures that tended to act on impulse for a sense of freedom, this trait was appealing to others, but often to their own detriment. Sapphires' multi-faceted personality in particular always attracted crazy, dangerous or criminal people. They were fascinating, it was true, but she often felt that it was welcoming drama just leaving her room! For Khana it meant deviating from the responsibilities awarded her, and would result in incompetence, and hence not worth the aftermath.

It was safer to avoid the inevitable repercussions of a gregarious nature, and so administered privacy was the tactic they had both adopted. A constant struggle however.
They both longed for the apparent contentment of a **happy medium** existence that they saw in others. But was it all a clever masquerade?

Khana was perpetually working on being in, and appreciating every single moment, and Sapphire was soon to understand why. In her case though, the multitude of duties that manifested her existence had taken over. When the two girls met, it was like opening a door of perception into another world they both craved.
Spontainaeity was something Sapphire had denied herself for some time now, and she slowly allowed herself to indulge in the desired luxury, with the gentle encouragement of her new comrade.

Being a mother to two children, Khana's caring maternal instincts shone through.

She was extremely genuine and affectionate.

Her life was a struggle too however. It was a tug-of war between Hindu and western ways; and she raised her offspring accordingly.

Their naming was evidence of this; awarding them foreign titles in addition to the regulation Bali ones. ('Angie' was named after the Eagles song by the same name, and 'Dion', her son after Celine Dion.) They had 2 names, and even 2 birthdays! (their 'hari lahir' was their actual birth date, and another they celebrated 'western style')
It was a rebellious touch. Having divorced from a violent husband, she was a single mother – who stood her ground, and unashamedly sought the attention of foreign men to escape the chauvinistic Indonesian male mindset.

In Bali, men have first rights over children. Khana had obviously struggled to maintain an amicable stance with the father of her children in order to keep the babies.

She was envious of the apparent liberties of a western life; devoid of adamant responsibilities.   Like in Japan, it was freedom to Sapphire, but not so to the natives themselves.

But behind this polished mask there was another life.

Both Khana's parents had died shortly after her birth, and she was raised by her Aunt and Uncle.

By Balinese standards, they were extremely wealthy folk; they loved her like their own, and her upbringing was fortunate.

She knew instinctively however that she was a misfit; struggling for years with feeling 'detached from her own body'.

She thought perhaps it was due to the loss of her real parents; she spent years endlessly searching for answers to the discomfort.

She would wake up utterly exhausted and sleep-deprived, and felt constantly drained as if something was sucking the life-force out of her.

She craved peace but it was not forthcoming.

For she had been chosen, and her future role ordained......

As Sapphire strolled past Khana's villa one day, she noticed her talking to another woman she knew.

They were introduced, and Khana ushered her in the gate. "Come in, please!"

She was leaning against the door in a turquoise chiffon pool kaftan, smiling warmly.

"Ooh, sexeeeeee!! I like your style. We must go out together!!"

Sapphire felt self-conscious in her scant beach attire, and laughed nervously.

"Oh, im just going for a walk to the pantai before sunset; too much time in my room!"

A robust little dark haired girl emerged from the doorway and wandered over to her, staring up at the comparatively fair stranger.

"Angie, say hello" Khana instructed. The girl took Sapphire's hand and put it to her forehead, with the gesture of 'salim'; -a greeting kiss .
"We have never seen you here before. You must come over to visit sometime!" her mother insisted.

The mutual acquaintance smirked: "Ah yes, Sapphire is the worlds' most private person. She has to be literally dragged from her room!"

"Ooh, like me" Khana determined with an intense glare.

Sapphire turned to leave, and responded in defense :"Oh, I do get out a lot; I just don't make a scene about it, and im always happier on my own"….

Khana watched her knowingly.

"Well please don't be a stranger, neighbour! I feel good connection to you. Strong….."

"Ive never been lonely….loneliness is something ive never been bothered with because ive always had this terrible itch for solitude…ill quote Ibsen: 'the strongest men are the most alone' sorry for the millions, but ive never been lonely. I like myself. Im the best form of entertainment I have. Let's drink more wine!"

Charles bukowski.

Thereafter they became more familiar.

Sapphire had made it quite clear that she was here to experience 'the life', not party and partake in the nocturnal temptations up for grabs. "Kamu anak kemarin sore"…….been there, done that.   On any evening invitation she would dismiss herself early, and disappear alone. Khana quickly realized that Sapphire was not like other buleh (foreigners). She was different, with an air of mystery. She liked it and felt comfortable to express the spectrum of her life freely.

Like piecing together a puzzle, Sapphire gradually learnt more about her fascinating new comrade. She knew there was a story…..she could sense it.

The authentic spelling of her name was Kana; which meant 'flower' in bahasa Indonesia. In fact, her full name was 'Kana indah ~ beautiful flower. Sapphire mispelt it one day, and since then it evolved into the Indian version, which also meant flower.

"I prefer the way you write it! We write it this way now". So 'Khana' it became, or simply 'K'.

K went on to explain though that : "In bali Hindu, we have names for the order you are born with"

1st born is Putu , Illu or Wayan (- or Gede if male)

2nd born is Made or Kadek

3rd is Nyoman or Komang

and 4th is Ketut, after which the cycle repeats itself. These were the only choices.

"We are named one, but we have ALL FOUR sisters inside us, and they are there for confidence, protection etc."

Apparently, as far as Sapphire could ascertain, one represented the placenta; one the blood; one the amniotic fluid etc…..it was all somewhat confusing!

In any case, both of them were first borns; so Khana was actually 'Putu' in Bali, or in it's entirety: 'Ni Putu Juli Kana Indah'.   Sapphire opted for simply 'Illu'.

"Do you know, the name of my villa: SAMARA also means: 'protected by god'?! I guess I must be in the right place!"

It was true.
She recalled an incident in 'musim hujan' (rainy season) the year before. In addition to the deplorable state of the roads, this four month period was the only hindrance to an otherwise sublime existence here.
At its best, the rains were just an unpredictable near-daily occurrence that prevented any form of glamour. At worst, they were torrential and potentially dangerous - not only for the motorcyclists, but for anyone out and about. The roads and footpaths became hazardously 'licen' – (slippery).
This was on one such evening; it was an intense downpour, and she was trapped in a warung after dinner. She had been listening to the hammering sound of it, and wondering when it would cease; the road now appearing more like a gushing river with fewer cars and

motorbikes daring to proceed through the chaos. PATIENCE my dear.. ('harus sabar')…one cannot fight nature to satisfy the desires.
While practicing this skill, she observed the little 'cacak' gekkos scattered about the walls. From the peripheral vision they often scared you half to death; just darting around. Ha! That's what I need at times like these she thought: specialized, anti-slip toepads! They were supposed to bring good luck ~('bawa keberuntungan'); like many things here. [She pondered whether karma would come back to bite her in the bum for all the little ones she had accidentally frozen, toasted, microwaved etc, for they were utterly everwhere!]

 She opened her pc and looked up some deets to fill the time. They certainly had advantages. For a start, there were no eyelids; so insomnia-induced eyestrain was not an issue! The larger, noisier variety that often kept her awake: 'tokay' were nocturnal. It sounded like they were chanting their own name: "to-kay!" with enthusiastic volume. Fascinating little creatures: 'some species are pathenogenic, which means that the female is capable of reproducing without copulating with a male. This improves the geckos ability to spread to new islands'……. Brilliant!

At some point she impatiently left, umbrella in hand, but she knew it was a serious challenge to get to the taxi rank down the road. The street was like a swimming pool; she was wading knee deep in the torrents, and couldn't see a thing. There were no cars visible either at this point, it was impossible to drive through such conditions, but she knew she had to make it to the main road and attempt to flag one down.
On the footpath she realized that there were huge gaping manholes at various points, but it was difficult to detect them with the rapid waves rushing over them. To plummet down one would be tragic; people could quite literally disappear undetected down one of those things! She was absolutely drenched, but kept her eyes down, with each slow sodden step. Then the strangest thing happened.
She realized that she had indeed stepped right in the centre of one of the huge holes; one foot after the other, but miraculously, didn't fall in. It was literally like she had 'walked on water'.   She gasped in shock; her heart pounding wildly in her chest. Had she just escaped the most profound near death experience?? As she looked up, she heard a gasp of horror by another woman, staring at her who had witnessed the incident. Her mouth and eyes were wide open; it confirmed that Sapphire was not imagining what she had experienced. She did eventually make it to a point of transport back home, but she knew she was beyond lucky that night. Her time wasn't up yet…..
So, 'protected by god' was the most likely explanation, and a comforting one! Regardless of what 'god' that may be…

From her porch, Sapphire would often witness the offerings Khana would make to the temple on the bridge over the pond opposite. Khana said she saw good spirits and angels around it; felt good energy, and a great sense of safety.

As she felt more comfortable, Sapphire would visit K at her place (something out of her nature ordinarily; she only ever mixed with her blood sister, cousin and mother prior to that, who she respected and adored dearly. Females were never her comrades of choice. Too complicated, deceptive and exhausting!)

The grounds that they lived in were like a nature forest and wildlife park rolled into one, and were apparently owned by a most prominent and respected Indonesian family, directly descended from kings. The gardens were spectacular, and constantly maintained by staff. Sapphire would often take a long stick to retrieve the fat ripe avocadoes and mangoes from high in the trees. She discovered a kaffir lime leaf tree in the garden too, which she would 'prune daily' and incorporate in her healthy menus.
The massive lily pond with weighbridge and temple in the midst was a natural haven for wildlife. Ducks would flap their wings vigorously in the water; squarking noisily for breadcrumb offerings here, and in the afternoon would waddle around the grounds in their gaggle as if on parade. Tiny frogs would hop around the outskirts of the pond, and another nearby fountain. Sometimes they were daring enough to splash about in the muddy puddles that collected in rainy season, and one had to be wary not to tread on them!

Khanas' place was in close proximity to the pond, and she said she "saw angels in it. Very safe". Although they were in the busy 'city' region of Legian, this sanctuary was a truly unusual find. Within minutes walk away from the oasis was the hustle and bustle of hawkers; street activity and noisy traffic. Sapphire's place here was most humble in every respect internally, but the vista from her porch where she spent much of her time was a gift, and escalated the quality of her existence dramatically. It was paradise to the senses, and food for the soul. There was always the sounds of the fountain, ducks, frogs, birds, gentle rains, and emanating ceremonial background chantings The luschious garden colours that abound, the butterflies, clear blue skies, smiling faces….
Nature. Peace.

One time, Sapphire popped in late afternoon to a small gathering. This was 'luar biasa' (unusual) for Khana. She hesitantly turned to retreat, but was ushered in for a quick introduction. It was a spiritual looking crowd; a long haired hippy yoga-type male started conversing with her amongst the background chatter. "So, don't you get lonely? You live all alone with no family here?" A huge bellow responded from behind: " NOOOOOOO! She has me of course! We are sisters!!!" Khana retorted in an animated fashion. The guy tilted his head quizzically, responding "Oh, yeah, I guess you do look a little similar"………they both laughed.

There was a lot going on here. With Moslem Ramadan and so forth; the countless Hindu ceremonies based on the lunar calendar; and recognition of western events, at least 3 calendars were needed for referral. It was potentially chaotic; the task of running a business here was more than a challenge!

Khana took Sapphire under her wing; always explaining the often confusing Hindu ways and beliefs. Sapphire was studying bahasa Indonesia, but Khana translated on many occasions where 'bahasa bali' - their own private language was used.
Sapphire was fascinated, and fully absorbed herself in the education. It provided a healthy diversion from her other preoccupations and concerns. As a result, she slowly gained a greater understanding of the land and it's people. Their notion on things was often bizarre and bordering on comical. She was most amused by the concept that :

"the earth is a big ball resting on a huge turtle called Bedawang. Around its feet are coiled two large guardian snakes – the Nagas.

Way above the earth, atop the Agung volcano, the Gods and the ancestors dwell. We humans only occupy the part that they lent us, where demons are free to come and do damage. Sometimes when everything is going wrong, the turtle wakes up and starts moving , which causes earthquakes. To make them stop asap, we must make a lot of noise to wake the 2 guardian snakes" ....

This was her favourite. From her life thus far, she thought it was typical she should arrive at a land dominated by such mystical principles!

Then there was the amazing 'Nyepi' holiday that is governed by the Hindu Saka calendar (as opposed to the Balinese calendar), and occurs annually between March and April.
Essentially, the evil of the underworld is lured with feast offerings, then escorted away with a rowdy procession.   On the
day before Nyepi, Yama, the master of hell opens the doors wide to unleash a horde of demons over Bali!
A few weeks before the proposed event, the various banjars (community groups) participate in the huge task to construct giant statues of the 'Ogoh-ogoh' -made from a bamboo framework; covered in papier-mache and painted. They are huge monsters; sometimes towering over 4 mtrs tall.   At
nightfall on that evening, as much noise is made as possible, with firecrackers; gongs; cymbals etc and the procession of monsters parade noisily through the streets to meet at the major crossroad – where ferocious battles are simulated. It is a sight to behold, and definitely camera-worthy!   All the fighting
and noisy calamity is designed to terrify the demons that have been attracted there, and chase them off the island by showing them who's boss!
The next day is Nyepi, ~ the first day of the new Saka cycle. Everyone is required to stay at home; meditate, pray, fast, and abstain from any noise or use of electricity. It is a challenge to which there is a unique purpose: The intense silence of the deserted streets is such a contrast to normal that the demons think everybody has deserted the island, and they leave too, as there is nobody left to bother!! Nyepi is considered like a New Year.
Every 210 days there is also 'Galungan dan Kuningan' which actually comes from Balinese mythology..... Suffice to say, that there was never a dull moment here! People were often concerned that Sapphire must be 'lonely and bored'......the truth couldn't be further removed.

The Hindu system alone was bizarre enough: then there were the other religions thrown into the equation.
Khana went on to explain that half the population here was Moslem, and therefore dominant. The other 50% comprised Hindu/ Buddhist/ Catholic etc.

She professed that 'doolo'(many years ago): "the country was originally HINDUnesia before the Moslems changed it to Indonesia!"
She then relayed a prediction: " In 2012, Jawa (Java) will be 40% gone. There were Hindu temples there you see, but the Moslems destroyed them, so the Gods are most angry". Sapphire listened on in fascination.

"There has been much trouble here. You see sister, tourists went on holiday to the place where the king of terrorists is, Malaysia, wearing "I LOVE BALI' t-shirts. The Muslims were VEEERY jealous, and that is why the terrorist attacks happened"

Amazing……

She was also a wealth of additional information concerning the tropics' naturally healing benefits.   For instance, one time when Sapphire cut her hand deeply, she lost so much blood she nearly passed out. (She was of course most stubborn when it came to medical assistance, so avoided hospital and doctors entirely.) When Khana saw her bandage and heard the story, she exclaimed "Why you not call me sister?? It is easy to fix!" She walked to the end of Sapphire's footpath and plucked a handful of frangipani leaves from the nearest tree there. " The sap juice from the 'bunga kamboja' leaf stops bleeding, and disinfects the wound!"   Fascinating, and so simple and accessible. The answer was literally on her doorstep; under her nose all along!
She also learned through the local people of the power of fresh kunyit (turmeric) as a natural disinfectant and wound healer.
When someone she knew was warned of extreme high blood pressure, she followed the local advice of : "*minum dua jus mentimun, setiap hari!*" - drink two glasses of fresh CUCUMBER juice daily. It was a preferable (albeit risky) process to treat naturally vs the western toxic pill method. Low and behold, a week later, the reading miraculously plummeted from a dangerous 190 to the standard 120. (*NB: it is not recommended for one in similar threat to rely on this method entirely – this example merely serves to illustrate nature's gift to us for longevity and healing assistance*).

The aloe vera leaf is of course great for hair restoration and regrowth, and when ingested works well for calming the digestive tract. As a soothing agent, it enhances the functioning of the whole digestive tract and all organs concerned; plus relieves minor stomach infections. The plant is most prolific here.   Pepaya was
the best thing possible for the stomach, as a digestive assistant. Ingesting a spoonful of the

seeds daily was also an anti-parasitic measure.

Avocado provides nourishment for dry hair.

The virgin coconut oil native to here was a functional food for both its immunity-enhancing and beautifying properties. Enriched with lauric acid, when converted in the body it serves as an antiviral, antibacterial and antifungal treatment, and natural probiotic. Lauric acid also has the unique ability to fight lipid-coated viruses such as herpes and influenza and further studies have shown it to even crank up metabolic rate. As a treatment/mask for hair, and as a skin moisturizer or soother, it was also fabulous.

Sapphire was constantly introduced to intriguing new lotions and potions made purely with what nature had to offer; referred to as 'jamu'. If you opened your eyes; listened and learned, 'living off the land' for wellness was certainly attainable, and preferable to toxic modern treatment conveniences.

Even the 'Apotek' (pharmacist) she knew here, Ketut, would offer a choice of natural vs mainstream medication, according to your preference. (He himself, like her, always selected the former)   Just for example, when she had an upset stomach, he advised her to go to the traditional pasar and buy a 'kelapa gading' or 'kelapa mudah' (young green coconut). They usually presented these among the sacred gifts to the gods, but they also swear by them for internal maintenance purposes. He explained that : "It provides the good bacteria required inside. I always drink first thing every morning!" Natures' probiotics. They literally lop the top off the coconut with a sword-like knife and stick a straw in it. Cant get much closer to natural than that!

He also agreed with her general rule of keeping a bottle of colloidal silver on hand for its natural antibiotic properties, and to drink liquid chlorophyll daily for its neutralizing and cleansing properties.

Sapphire would take interest in what the Balinese believed in and did, and would learn something new every day. For she felt it was always worth exploring the alternatives to what the 'real world' prescribed.

"But the most important thing to remember is family" K announced over coffee one day. "Here in Bali, you don't have just the relatives. Noooo! You can CHOOSE your family, sister!"   It was a most satisfying concept to Sapphire; she thoroughly approved.

When Sapphire's mother Joslyn came to visit, she was immediately pronounced simply 'Mum' by Khana; who insisted on taking her on an a tour to see the real bali scenery by car. She was whisked off early one morning; the itinerary a total mystery.

After witnessing the colourful Barong and Kecak dance performances, K dressed her in the traditional kabaya to visit temples; showed her the spectacularly lush rice fields on the approach to majestic Mount Agung, and presented her with constant samples of Balinese delights to eat on the way. Joslyn had mentioned a sore hip earlier, so a stop during the journey was in order to see a special balian healer. "He is a prince, Mum. He will help you....." After the initial blessing ritual, Jos writhed in pain as he stuck a long curved bone

into her heel and twisted it. Sapphire looked on in concern. It reminded her of some of the authentic reflexology she had endured here; the most painful 'treatments' she had ever experienced.
Jos was in shock by the ordeal, but it did indeed bring her some relief, thank the gods! Khana had also wanted to take her to Lake Bratan in Bedugal, where the strawberries grow all year long, but time didn't permit. Sapphire considered these strawberries every bit as flavoursome as the true British ones.   It was a whirlwind all day excursion which exhausted Mum for a few days thereafter, and to process all that she had done and witnessed. However she felt honoured by the experience, and her insight to the Balinese sense of close community, and loved her new 'daughter'.

Thereafter, Khana would always enquire: " how is Mum, sis? Why she not come here to live and buy a big villa at Canngu? She has 2 daughters here. I would cook and clean for her; massage her and make her relax. It is what we must do for the mother. It is the bali way sis! Why she not come?"   As Sapphire relayed this information to Mum, she laughed. "Ah paradise. In my dreams!"…

"You have family here now too sis; I take you to meet Bali Mum and Dad at the temple, ya!"

After accompanying K to a cremation ceremony one day, she had been advised to keep the kebaya K had fitted her with. It was like donning a suit; tight-fitting and restrictive…and oh so hot in the tropical climate. She wondered how the women coped; especially on and off bikes and balancing the 'keranjang' (god offering boxes) side-saddle with extroidinary ease. It was a relief to derobe , but in it she felt very united with the people; it was all part of the community experience. "No, please keep this! You will need it for all our ceremonies, Sister"

The huge ornate abode and private temple of the bali parents was splendid, and obviously not of peasant standards.

There were gold embellishment touches as far as the eye could see throughout the vast property, and several grand rooms with huge gilded entrances. They were externally adorned with a large Swastika symbol . Although similar to the Nazi version, it was vertical as opposed to slanted. It was explained to her that "it is ancient Sanskrit, and means wellbeing! It is for protection".

Their private temple was represented by the Barong; a huge monster-like structure, that is reminiscent of a Chinese lion. She was captivated by the painstaking process of repainting all the intricate temple adornments for the beast; there were a group at work with fine brushes in one huge workroom. Mum explained that "it is all real gold. Nothing but the best for the gods. Our Barong is old, and needs to be renovated". The huge barong is the most sacred mask, and one of the most familiar, and this one remained here at the family temple. The room dedicated to the gamelan orchestra too, was a mass of gold; all the instruments shiny and extremely ornate. It all looked fit for a king.

Sapphire accompanied Khana on several occasions to the family in Ubud, and likewise, it was 'Mum and Dad' to her too. They were most welcoming, and hospitable. On arrival after the greetings, Sapphire would retreat to one of the many gilded entry rooms, to change into the kebaya. There was always the mandatory blessings and ceremony at the outdoor temple; usually with the huge extended family.

Dad -'bapak', conducted the proceedings in his white robe and turban; he was a 'Pemangku' (high priest)

The holy water was collected out back in big plastic buckets, with much of the family assisting.

'Neneh' (grandma) was a most intriguing feature. She looked about 120; was tiny and had obviously not cut her nails or hair....EVER. She got involved, and would hand out an array of offerings to outstretched hands as part of the ceremony. " She cannot cut the hair Sis, she get VERY sick if she does; all power gone." Her gray notted mass of hair was entwined into a massive bun atop her head; carrying it around was an impressive dispay of balance and deportment!
Like most Balinese, the elderly in particular, she had absolutely no idea what her age was. It was always guess-work. To make matters dramatically more confusing, their calendar, the 'Pawukon' has a cycle of 210 days, which corresponds to one year. This Balinese year is comprised of 6 months only, with 35 days each. With those calculations in mind, this would make her potentially centuries old!

Mum ran a restaurant in Ubud, so the grand spread to follow was always a feast. The succulent 'ayam betutu' was a 12-hour cooking exercise; and Mum's was the best Sapphire had ever tasted. The waft of lemongrass and fragrant herbed stuffing in the slow-cooked chicken permeated the ceremonial proceedings, and hungers elevated. It was the bali equivalent of a roast dinner! The buffet also comprised sate Lilit (compressed seafood on wooden sticks); regular satays; sop babi; sometimes babi guling (roast pork); the traditional lawar (like stuffing); tum; nasi (rice) etc . Sapphire ascertained that it was indeed far tastier to eat the cuisine the traditional style, with 'tangan manis', the sweet right hand; - as opposed to cutlery. The rice needed finger 'blending' with all the tasty accompaniments.

 The 'Rujak' sometimes followed for dessert, a special favourite. It was like a spicy salad, consisting of shaved pineapple, young green mango, cucumber, bengkoang (like potato), and kedongdong (sweet and sour asian fruit). The dressing was a mix of palm sugar, salt and tamarind, which was poured over. At its traditional best, it included lots of chilli for the 'padas' hot hit. It was surprisingly good as a digestive finale to the meal.
One time, Khana stopped the car down at Legian pantai, where a rujak stand was set up on the sand. "it is the best here, sister. You must try". The unusual combination of sweet and spicy reminded her of Japan, where often opposing sweet and salty sensations lingered in unison on the palate from many snacks.

Sapphire loved sampling all the flavoursome food. It was an occasional treat for her however, as incredibly rich, and contrastive to her usual pristine diet, which utilized the fantastic organic local vegetables; tofu and tempeh. She also adored all the tropical fruits; particularly the papaya, exotic durian and jackfruit.

Sapphire had previously attended a traditional wedding and a cremation, - both of which were fascinating spectacles to witness; but being part of a family environment gave her a true sense of feeling what their real life was like – behind the social mask.

Ibu (Mum) had labored in the kitchen for days to prepare all family feasts, and Khana would do the 'daughter duty' and commence massaging her weary shoulders. Once she asked " Do you have uang kecil (small change) sister?" Sapphire gave her a 500 rupiah coin and she commenced rubbing it vigorously on Mum's shoulders till they became red raw; virtually bleeding. Mum moaned in agony as Sapphire opened her mouth in mock horror. "Sakit! Too much air." Khana determined. " If there is gas in the body, the skin turns red. We must take this out!" Mum continued writhing until the redness vanished and the skin returned to normal colour. She smiled with relief, as did Sapphire!

Another time, Khana's sister in law handed her the new-born infant to nurse. There was a slice of onion stuck on its head. Sapphire wasn't sure whether it was meant to be there, and pointed with interest. "It protects the baby from evil" she said nodding. "I had to go into the kitchen first before I hold baby, sis. The kitchen is sacred. The place of fire. Brahma. For this reason, the baby and the parents cannot enter the kitchen or the the temple until the baby is 3 months old. The mother is considered dirty. For some of the big temples you must wait 6 months. A woman is not permitted to pray when she has the menstruasi, either"
She remembered Khanas' confusing explanation earlier about the placing of the placenta in the home after birth. It was apparently kept there, in a jar or something, and Khana had summarized with: "You see this is why the Balinese rarely travel, and stay close to the home and the placenta!"

After a long lazy afternoon indulging at the banquet table, a refreshing breeze would soften the heat before the long journey back from Ubud. Khana would play indonesian music and sing along happily during the drive, stopping at intervals to translate the lyrics for her student.

Sometimes, she would break the journey with a warung stop for a snack and some icecreams for the kids. She loved a green glossy plastic looking salad, which was, as it looked, slippery chewy. "Its called 'buloong. It's seaweed and veeery good for your complexion" she explained. Being the queen of green, this was a new one for Sapphire, and again, reminiscent of Japan. She loved seaweed, and while at the Tokyo fishmarkets, her best friend there had ordered absolutely everything green on the menu. It was a hilarious sight; a table full of green bowls!

Sapphire was invited to all family based occasions, and attended as many as possible.

But it was evident to her the double life Khana was living. It reminded her of her 'tomadachi' ; -closest comrade in Japan.
Ever faithful to the traditional ways, and yet hugely involved in a western life too.

Sapphire learnt that Khana had yet another set of parents in Perth (the 'elected' category). After adopting them on a holiday they spent in bali, she had spent much time there with them, and blended seamlessly into a foreign lifestyle too.

Hers had been a charmed life; a far-cry from the village mentality of these people. She was often presumed the partner of some wealthy foreigner, with her polished, 'expensive,designer- like' appearance. Sapphire recognized that she shared her passion for the finer things in life; and was no stranger to it. In fact, her first impression of Khana was high class escort. Her grooming was impeccable, and she stood out from the crowd wherever she went. To accentuate it further, she'd had a long-term relationship with a French gentleman, and as a result had acquired a unique French accent! She had referred to Sapphire as a 'beautiful Barbie doll' in a complimentary fashion on several occasions, but Sapphire longed for the curvy feminine veneer of her comrade.
Khana was devoutly patriotic to her roots however, and would adamantly defend the Balinese people – sometimes inviting hostility amongst uncouth, disrespectful foreigners. She was no wallflower; her strength of character was a virtue. She preferred her solidarity to company for the most part, that was evident. However she was always most gracious and tolerant of 'good' people, and would endure even the most boring company with a smile out of respect.

And yet Sapphire detected an underlying sadness too. Another trait she could relate to.

"Hey K, how do you say 'Masks and Mirrors' in bahasa?".

"Topeng dan Cermin.........Why do you ask this?" she gave a puzzled expression. It was indeed a somewhat random enquiry. "Oh no special reason. Just to put into my diary so I don't forget. You know I like to write".........

She worked in a boutique on the Seminyak shopping strip, and Sapphire would often pop in to visit, and take Khana to a café for her break.
Alternately, they would perch on stools in her shop, and she would sometimes wave her hand to the passing bike vendor selling makanan. This was a common sight here; they were like little mobile warungs, that delivered tasty meals, coffee, fruit or snacks to your doorstep or shopfront. She loved the bakso, or meatball soup. The boy would serve and bring her a piping hot bowl to the desk to devour. "President Obama is visiting here now Sis. He spent some years here in his childhood, and he loves the Balinese cuisine – the nasi goring and all

lokal food. His favourite is the bakso too!"   On several past
occasions here, Sapphire had been warned of the threat of potential terrorism with high
profile people, or certain religious occasions; plus the dangers of natural disasters from
earthquakes or tsunamis. The expats and locals remained pretty unphased by all the
concern, and carried on with life as usual. In fact they were usually totally oblivious to the
information. It was always a storm in a teacup, but the Australian press loved it. It was only
through contact with the outside world; Australia in particular, that matters were negatively
exaggerated.   She sent a text to Khana
asking : "Should we be concerned if we go out tonight? There are terrorism warnings for
popular places with Obama in town".........
The reply came: "Don't worrie sister. I'm not scared. I have my god! Xoxoxoxxoxoxo"

They would sit for hours and discuss all manner of things, but always with a deeply spiritual
tone. Nothing was off limits with Khana though; she seemed to be able to maintain her faith
amidst a personality that was eager to devour all that life had to offer. Her graphic
descriptions of intimate encounters with men were risque and entertaining; bordering on
pornographic – albeit so innocent and seemingly permissible.
She was always the life of the party. Her smile so constant and heartwarming; she was like a
magnet to both sexes. When out for a drink, she would toss her glossy mane around and
shake her ample bosom; singing loudly in her own world of bliss. She had no tattoos, but
nature had provided her with a sensual beauty spot on her right breast, which she kept on
show, and it served as the only jewellery required!
She would order a strawberry shisha pipe 'for desert', and hand it around generously with a
Buddha-like grin; attracting an eclectic crowd.
Khana was forever falling in and out of love; -Sapphire had trouble keeping up! Her
blackberry was the constant companion, for the sole purpose of receiving the constant
stream of love-letter messages from her beaus. As with all true Balinese, she was in tune
with matters of the heart, and hence powerfully passionate. She was unphased by
appearances; it was how someone made her feel 'in her heart'. Listening to her regale her
encounters with full accentuation, made one crave the 'magic' she found in people; it was
something the modern world had definitely lost touch with.

She was as highly skilled as Sapphire at dealing with the fleeting sensation of most
relationships. For some dalliances it was a bitter pill to swallow, but practice made perfect. It
was actually a good lesson. Like here on the island, in life people come and go......better
one gets with the program!.   The
constant influx was something they preferred. A degree of detachment was always reserved
no matter how much the heart fluttered.
K was like witnessing two people who were poles apart, but had merged into one being. She
had an inner core strength that Sapphire had never seen in someone before; particularly
female. She had always respected that trait, and gravitated towards folk of that calibre. And
yet, despite this, she was a most serene, calming and positive influence. Therapeautic.

The themes she seemed to highlight about the life here were RESPECT and PROTECTION.

Sapphire remembered her pranic guru instructing her to: 'get out of your head, and into your body', when she had been at her weakest point. Putting it into practice was something that required meditational assistance. In fact, the two processes were one and the same.

K was obviously extremely intelligent. But this skill of switching off the mind chatter ~ was it something attributed naturally to her entire race, or was work needed to master it for them too? They were so placid and happy for no apparent reason; appearing almost labotomised at times. Or like sheep on 'soma' , as in Aldous Huxley's "A Brave New World".

She was forever chiding Sapphire: " You must not be thinking too much! Just listen, and do from your heart….. Not thinking!"

One day, she spontaneously delved into a Hindu background lesson, but Sapphire sensed it was leading to something more profound.

"there are three gods Sis.

WISNU is the guardian. He is the water, and his wife is Dewi Sri, the goddess of rice.

SIWA is the destructor. He is the wind, and his wife is Laksmi; the god of cemeteries. She is the 'security' of death.

BRAHMA is the creator. He is the fire, and his wife Sarasvati is the goddess of books and study."

Sapphire noted with amusement the inclusion of the wives, with equal emphasis.

"In our Canang offerings, you see different coloured rice. Yellow is for Wisnu, black is for Siwa, and red is for Brahma.

Every 15 days, we also give offering to the demons; Bhuta and Kala. Black rice, and rotten food"

Sapphire had wondered about the Canangs for some time. They were left outside shops, warungs and restaurants, and at every temple. The patrons would present them in the traditional attire, and perform 'ayab', where the incense is lit in the most sensual manner. The fingers are held in a special fashion and the smoke gently wafted in the breeze, usually with a frangipani held between the fingers. This gesture was to entice the gods and was like saying "silahkan!' – please accept" It was the most gorgeous display, and Sapphire longed to learn the skill.
"it is in the fingers. We learn from very young at school. It is also important to train the fingers and toes for our traditional dances. It is a skill we must practice as we grow". She did a demonstration, holding up her hand.

It was true. The way they held their digits always looked so painful and double-jointed,- yet seductive.

"the canang sari must contain flower petals; some sweets ; be sprinkled with holy water and have a dupa (insence stick) so that the smoke allows the essence to reach the gods or demons."

Sapphire was also amazed, and often amused by the additional items left as offerings to the gods. They were accompanied by fruit, eggs, biscuits, bits of cake, lollies, money, cigarettes – you name it! Just one of the time-consuming tasks that filled their lives. Obviously hours were dedicated to laboring over these intricate displays, that would later be trashed; walked on; rained on; eaten by stray dogs etc…before it was all repeated the next day. 'Selarlu sibuk'……these people were always busy.

Sapphire was busily scribbling notes of all Ks verbal offerings; there was always so much to absorb. She often had to go home and decipher her own scrawl.

" You must come to a 'hari pernama' (full moon) ceremony with me sister, ………….. I think you are ready"………

She gave Sapphire a look that, if she read it correctly, meant "don't say I didn't warn you"…

With that, she took a sample of Sapphire's food and tossed it on the floor. "this is called 'mejotan' sis. It keeps the spirits happy, and balance in the universe"……

Although she was eager to live in the Hindu manner, Sapphire didn't adopt this ritual.
She learnt that if you performed mejotan even once, the spirits would recognize it and expect it to continue; demanding it with every meal. If you ignored them, (or in her most likely case, simply forgot!), they would classify you as an enemy and cause you an unbalanced life - frequented by horrible occasions, accidents or death.
It all sounded quite superstitious which she was averse to, but being a single white woman who lived alone here, she felt it best not to take the chance.

Khana did it religiously on behalf of both of them, but Sapphire would often grab her glass and declare: " they are welcome to anything but my wine!! "

There were of course, temples everywhere. In homes, they were kept in the back for security.   Khana went out to hers often when Sapphire arrived, and one day she asked her why. " I must announce to the gods if you stay here a while sister, for your safety."

In her 'dapur' (kitchen), Khana kept a special stand, which was basically a multi-tiered canang. This one was dedicated to her dead parents, and she would do a ritual ceremony for them every morning. It would contain the usual ornate display, plus fresh flowers, coffee, fruit and rice. It looked like a tray with breakfast order! She also kept a small plate of whatever meal she ate at the table for them, and the usual piece for the gods too. It was like leaving the sample of Christmas cake out for Santa on xmas eve…

One day, dressed in a green kabaya, she ushered Sapphire to follow her upstairs to bless the offering. Sapphire was inquisitive as to the above loft. The entire family resided completely downstairs; the two children sleeping with her in the one bed. With the obvious space available it did appear somewhat cramped. On the ascent, to Sapphire's amazement she announced "I am a balian healer, and can bless you sister, like Bapak did in Ubud". One of the Mangku's functions is to prepare and bless the holy water as Sapphire had witnessed at the family temple, and Khana also did this in her own home.

On arrival, the upstairs section was 2 enormous rooms, one of which was totally empty except for a mattress on the floor. "If you need massage for healing, you can come here" The second room was completely green; including the walls, curtains and floors, and contained the most amazing display. It held a king size bed with green satin cover; atop which was a huge bunch of fresh flowers, and scattered petals. It looked like a hotel wedding suite! At the head of the bed was a framed picture of what appeared to be a goddess of some sort, adjacent to which was a mini temple, and another tiered canang stand, with the same contents as her parents' one below. At the foot of the bed was a bowl to soak the feet.

" You see sister, I have my own goddess. This room is to honour her, and she sleeps here. She is called 'Nyi Ro Ro Kidul' – you can look her up on the internet! Please, sit down. I bless you"

Sapphire kneeled down and cupped her hands for the 3 holy water sips she was to take. It was 'kelapa gading'; young coconut juice, which Khana, had done the blessing ritual on first. It tasted delightful, and was one of the medicinal gifts of the tropics; being fabulous for the internal environment. "sometimes it is just water from the earth or fresh from the mountain, as long as it is blessed. I use the coconut juice because it is special and I prefer to do it this way".   She performed 'bija', sticking the wet rice on her forehead. "If it stays here a long time, it means you are a good person" . She then handed her 3 grains of the nasi, instructing "eat one for each of the gods, Wisnu, Siwa and Brahma".
She placed a fragrant frangipani in her hair, and sprinkled her with the holy water.

" Nyi ro ro Kidul loves flowers and to dress up. Her colour is green". It sounded like a fantasy story from a childrens' storybook, but went part way to explain Khanas' preference for all things green; including fashion, and her love of nature. She looked identical to the framed picture above the bed. "I too cannot cut my hair; must keep long" she explained as she deftly coiled her magnificent mane into a twisted bun, and secured it in place miraculously with no apparent aid.

"When I am confused, and am thinking 'kenapa begitu?' ~why like that? – I come here to her and she guide me what to do." Khana smiled serenely, adjusting the flowers splayed out on the bed.   Fancy that. On the island of the gods, this girl even had her own private goddess, who lived with her and she consulted with in her upstairs room!

"She is also protection from **black magic** sis, very important. Many people come here from the curse of 'Ilmu Hitam' , and I save them, with her help. She protect me too! It follow me because of my powers; I am always the target for Ilmu Hitam."

"Really? Why?"
"Yes, because I am HAPPY! People can see, and get jealous of that"..... No further

explanation required on that, Sapphire thought. A genuine smile is often a cursed accessory to bear.
It certainly gave the term 'divine intervention' a whole new depth, though.

Sapphire investigated the background of this mystical goddess, Nyi ro ro Kidul. There was abundant folklore surrounding her. In Javanese and Sudanese mythology, she is legendary, and known as the Queen of the southern sea in Java, where she is in control of the violent waves of the Indian ocean.   She was
often illustrated in mermaid form, with a tail, and the lower part of the body a snake. The mythical creature is claimed to take the soul of anyone she wished, and changed shape several times a day!

One Sudanese folktale is about Dewi Kadita of the Pajajaran kingdom, in west Java, who desperately fled to the southern sea after black magic had hit her. She jumped into the violent waves of the ocean where the spirits and demons crowned the girl as the legendary Spirit-Queen of the south sea.

Black magic spells were usually cast for jealousy purposes here, just as in Khana's case, and there were countless stories of evidence to this practice.

Once, during her time in Seminyak, Sapphire had listened in mock horror as one of the staff, Ketut, relayed an incident with his brother. " You can choose to believe or not believe up to you. He have a good job, make good money, have beautiful wife and children. But many people jealous you know. He was very healthy and fit; and not smoking. One day, when he was watching television, he just collapse from a heart attack and die. He was only 30 years old."   If there was anything to
be scared of, Sapphire thought, this would surely be it. There would always be jealousy and envy, it was inevitable ~ hence one could be a victim to this curse and not know it. She could see why the Balinese were so preoccupied with 'protection'.

Ketut continued in a warning tone, shaking his head with emphasis "but you can choose to believe or not believe; its up to you."
Apparently if you believed in black magic, you were more susceptible to it, so she did her best to dismiss the notion. However any time a problem arose or a health incident occurred, her thoughts naturally gravitated towards the dreaded Ilmu Hitam that pervaded the island.

"Next time I go to the Grand Bali Beach Hotel in Sanur, you must come too! There is a room there, all green, especially for goddess Nyi Roro Kidul. We go to visit and pray"
As the legend goes, there was a massive fire on January 20th 1993, where all the rooms in the hotel were destroyed except for one. It remained completely intact. Inside this room there were no signs of fire or or damage; it was like a miracle.
Room # 327.
A number that actually had relevance for Sapphire too.
She felt it would be appropriate to pray for the loss of her other little soulmate sister here.
For she had been one of the threesome - that shared the birth date 27.
All people who come here to meditate and pray must be accompanied by security. They all claim to have witnessed the presence of the Indonesian president Soekarno and goddess Nyi Roro Kidul.

"I have dreamt I made love to president Suekarno! If you dream of things like this; with famous people, or a president, it is like a special omen".

"Most important to bali Hindu is the REINKARNASI." Khana was growing used to Sapphire's constant note-taking in her presence. She had taken to getting pen and paper prepared ready before she even commenced speaking after a while.

"Its about Karma. Must be a good person, for the next life. But there will always be DHARMA and ADHARMA; good and bad people " - the black and white checked sarongs they wrapped around the statues at temples and so forth were representative of the good vs evil in mankind. There was a system here and everyone played their role. If you adhered to the plan you were an example of dharma, and as such, your chances of a good chapter (life) next time round were elevated.

"Heaven and hell is right here and now sister. There is not another place, no! – it is all HERE. If you want your next life here to be a good one, you must obey the system of karma"

It sort of explained why they went about their laborious duties with a smile on their face. Like in Japan, where her tomadachi kept instructing her: " this is the system and the rules; the way we do it! You must stop asking 'why', and just DO!!"

The notion of 'recycling' back into the same place was synonomous with Buddhism. Both recognized the potential fate man was subject to, and were about ways to ease that suffering.

"All newborns are possessed by a past life. My son Dion is 'buyut', his great grandfather". She was satisfied with that outcome, it seemed. " I was lucky I had my son first, because reinkarnasi can only happen within the same family if there is a boy! The Balinese see the daughters as like bad luck, and are constantly praying to the gods for a son. My daughter Angie is someone distant called Renuk."
"So, how do you know all this?" Sapphire asked. "Because there are special healers who can tell you the spirit. A paranormal. They start to talk in the tongue of the person who has reinkarnasi the baby, and become them so you see, and then you know. It is like meeting the person."

Sapphire had read plenty of blurb on reincarnation. Stories such as: 'if you have a contorted hand, you were a thief in a past life.' Or , 'if you lose your voice, you were a liar or a cheat'- are rife.

"Only if you marry a WESTERN man, then you can keep the reinkarnasi in the family. This is why we want foreign husbands!" Sapphire's eyes widened. This certainly explained a hell of a lot here. She had previously thought they were sought only for the money but she was realizing more and more that there were alternative motives. To take the tremendous pressure off the women to produce sons, this scenario would provide immense liberty. It was their dream life.

That evening, she read up further.

Reincarnation: 'one of the consequences of the principle of karma phala (belief in the fruition of one's deeds) and samsara (belief in the process of birth and death) is that the individual inherits his status as a result of the past lives……only those who have reached supreme serenity and liberation (or moksa) can have access to paradise (nirwana) – and be exempted from returning to this earth'……
God only knows what was involved to reach that status, Sapphire thought. Their entire lives were totally geared towards appeasing the gods.

"Important to understand that Bali is the most sacred place on earth. So many spirits and gods"………… When a friend of Sapphire's opened up a new café on the main street in Seminyak, it was at a T junction. She invited Khana to meet her there. David was keen for any feedback and advice, but was unaware of of the review to come. She was of course most respectful and courteous towards the man but insisted that a few changes be made. She surveyed the premesis and then hooked right in:
"You must be telling staff to make offerings to the big main temple outside every day to respect the gods! If not, all bad spirits come straight up this Jalan (street), because it is a 3-way junction, and is very bad luck for your business! The demons love crossroads as they can easily harm humans and provoke accidents here"
She also pointed to the offering box in the front of the café. " This must be higher than the head for respect. The demons are low and on the floor; the gods are high. And there is no offering in it! How can you be doing good business? You must move it up quickly, and tell staff to put offering here too. Every day. Give them money to provide for the gods."
With that she sipped on her coffee, and selected another decadent pastry. "If you want your business to succeed, you must be honouring the gods the Balinese way for protection! Your staff can guide you but you must provide for them to do so"
She went around to each staff member and had a little discussion with them all, adjusting their uniforms and adding a managerial touch to proceedings. The owner virtually scratched his head, but assured her he would comply.
Sapphire loved these insights, but they were exhausting. It seemed the more you learnt about the hindu dharma system, the more there was to learn…

There came yet another bout of 'gumpa' –(earthquakes); this one being the strongest on the island in 30 years; ~the intensity far greater than the frequent tremours experienced in Japan. Sapphire clung to her bedframe, imagining the roof caving in from above. It was like the shaking bed scene from the movie 'the exorcist'; which had haunted Sapphire in her childhood, and caused extreme anxiety and insomnia. The foundations of buildings rocked and in places cracked, items crashed off shelves onto the floor.
Khana later reassured her sister: "Jangan tekanan batin!…..Don't worry, the Balinese people have done many BIG ceremonies, especially for the 'earthworks'!"

She then added detail to the importance of ceremonies for so many purposes. Both natural and created by man, any disaster was amendable in their eyes with the assistance of the gods.   "Can you imagine if we not do many

many ceremonies for the victims of the terrorist bombings? How SCARY for those poor spirits left on that street! It is the island of the gods, you know. So many good and bad gods prowling around...........
We must say : Please, go to the ocean. If not do the ceremonies, the souls are not released and are trapped. Cannot move!"

Later, as they were discussing natural healing , and Sapphire's preference for the balian healer method to western style, Khana exclaimed: "the Balinese people cannot afford expensive hospitals – NOOO! But they are scary places anyway. All the spirits of the dead western people, and no ceremonies to release them and set them free! Here, when somebody Hindu die in the family, we do ceremony to bring the spirit home to rest. Not leave it floating around, stuck and lost! This is why we are very scared of the hospital!" Ha! Another thing they had in common, Sapphire thought.

Khana was always up at the crack of dawn to hit the pasar (markets) for offerings to the gods, and preparing food for a ceremony of some sort. Perpetually busy, she still remained patient and always appeared fresh and well presented. How she never looked the slightest sleep deprived was a mystery.
At night, people would just appear to talk to her in the safety of her home, and visit the goddess upstairs for assistance, advice, healing or protection. They weren't invited, and came unannounced; it was obviously some sort of 'safe house', or haven, which seemingly never closed!   The room adjacent to the god room upstairs was assigned a 'rumah sakit' role. Like a hospital bed, the massage mattress there was often used to treat sick folk with the healing hands.   As
already established, Khana was a private soul and happiest alone; this constant influx of people was something out of her control.

One time, Sapphire felt all choked up from the pollution and fumes on her walk, and could hardly breathe. It created a sense of anxiety so she too stopped at K's place on the way to her room. Always airy and fresh, she felt invigorated after her sessions there. Khana took her upstairs and instructed her to pray to goddess Nyi ro ro Kidul for the problem; after which she gave her the holy water, blessed a large mandarin, and instructed her to eat it. As she left, Sapphire did indeed feel tranquil and calm, as though she had been given a dose of oxygen. The very next day, low and behold, the most extroidinary winds came. The powerful gusts blew away the pollution and circulated fresh, clean air all around.

With all these evening 'patient consults', Khana admitted she hardly slept a wink. Perhaps a couple of hours if she was lucky. But she never turned a soul away. "I must help them sister. It is my duty". She also explained that deep sleep was a danger for black magic, as you were off guard, so if awake you remain protected. With her own nocturnal bodyclock, Sapphire wondered whether this was part of her own problem!

With all this going on 24/7 in Khana's world, Sapphire wondered how she managed to be a mother as well. There were also seemingly endless rituals and ceremonies which occurred for every purpose and reason. There was even one to thank the gods for the motorbikes, the primary mode of transport here!   The ceremony timetable was another mystery to Sapphire. It was based on the lunar calendar and changed annually. Sapphire herself was pedantic to the point of obsessive compulsive at times; it was no wonder she blended with a culture that was replete with ritualistic behaviour! Nevertheless, getting a grip on the dynamic Balinese calendar system; coupled with the belief and ritual system was akin to mastering an extreme sport!

One day, as they were involved in an in depth conversation over lunch, Khana announced: " The dragon in the ocean is for protection, sister. You must understand, I am the dragon." She nodded her head emphatically. Sapphire had no idea what she was talking about! "If you come for 'hari pernama' ceremony, you will see how the gods talk through me." These ceremonies occurred regularly to acknowledge the full moon.

Finally, the revelation was announced. "All my life I am questioning why I feel so confused, like I don't understand what happens in my head. Then I am told that the gods have chosen me. I cannot help it. When I was born, they give me this power, and I have to be their voice. They control my body sister. I know not what I do; people tell me"

With a confused expression, Sapphire listened on as she spoke of these evening ceremonies, often occurring at Canngu. "Sometimes they are good spirits that come to me, and sometimes bad too sister. But you mustn't be afraid. When they possess my body, I dance in a crazy fashion, and loud singing, sometimes in different language. I don't know Im doing it. My transport is the horse, and the dragon is the bodyguard. I grow long long nails, and hands like this……. then I eat many many telur bebek, sometimes still with skin and with milk and honey. I shake my head wildly like this. You know I hate duck eggs sister. When people tell me how many I grab and eat, I cannot believe. Yuck!"

Sapphire mentally translated the scene :

She became possessed by spirits ; danced and chanted like a banshee, often talking in foreign tongues. Then, becoming the horse that draws the chariot for transport, or the dragon that protects her, she would take on their characteristics. She grows clawed, monster-like hands, and feasts ravenously on duck eggs, (which she despises!) - often with shells still on; while moving frantically like a wild beast………with no apparent recollection of the activity.

Unlike other examples of Muslim messengers she had encountered, Khana actually became fully possessed by the god or devil; becoming them completely, and could not remember a thing afterwards.

Sapphire had heard countless stories of witnessed possessions here; predominantly beach-side, where the victim/medium would get 'crazy, scary eyes' and run wildly into the ocean. This story of K's seemed a little far-fetched, but now she suddenly remembered Khana's other 'mum' from Perth describing exactly such a scene with Khana, in a freaked-out fashion. However the woman was on meds at the time, and Sapphire had just dismissed the rendition as a hallucination!

As this realization struck Sapphire, she noticed a swarm of tiny insects directly above K's head. A shiver ran down her spine. This paranormal indication confirmed to her that her friend was most unique, that's for sure.

Good grief…. She was a MEDIUM.

It struck her that it was both a gift and a curse for Khana. She had been bundled with enormous responsibilities, and performed all her duties with acquiescence, but she longed to be free of the role, and do as she pleased.
This was the mask she had to wear. 'Topeng'. Here, just like there are sacred dances, both theatre and actors' masks were charged with magic. The power ascribed to masks was very strong. ' they are sacred since they serve to tell the story of gods or kings, who also had divine origin. As soon as the actor wears the mask, he becomes the incarnation of the character – he doesn't just play him, but becomes him.'
It was as though she was a puppet, and the performance was controlled by the gods in the upstairs loft. Sapphire also learnt that apparently every fifteen days, offerings are even made to the masks and puppets! They named this day 'kajeng keliwon'.

A local rag, under the title: **Spiritual possession** professed:
" Balinese religion is an integration of Hindu-Buddhist and shamanist beliefs, characterized by a regular cycle of temple festivals – featuring elaborate food offerings and other ceremonies as needed for rites of passage, healing, or crisis situations. Music and dance play a major role in Balinese religion, as does trance. Trance dance is practiced as a way of being in the world and serves as a medium to satisfy the supernatural beings.
Trance is a culturally valuable trait in Bali, and is an important shamanistic virtue. Once possessed by a spirit the entranced medium speaks with the spirit's voice, giving instructions for ceremonies, finding lost objects or helping the body to heal
(courtesy the bali advertiser, 2012.)

Her sense of confusion was something Sapphire could empathise with.

So many roles. Who was she really??
It was true that Bali harmonises the world of man with the cosmic world of the gods, but in K's case there was a little too much going on!

She explained later, as if to seal her fate:

"I am 31 now sister. I have 4 years left only." She dropped her head in sadness.
" I try to do as much as I can; live like normal until then. Every day is special; I just want to have fun! Must be thinking positive like that. Or else you go crazy!"

Sapphire grabbed her hand with concern "what do you mean four years left?"

"from the age of 35, I will be in the hands of the gods completely, to offer service as mangku , healer etc. They have chosen me. They will dictate my life then, and *become* me. I will communicate on their behalf. At that time I will be happy though, because I am not Khana any more, I will be exactly as they want me to be! I know it is an honour, and I must be grateful for the privelidge……but sometimes its so hard you know, and I am so tired"……

" I thought you were already doing *all that*!!" Sapphire retorted emphatically. She was in shock; trying to grasp the full concept of the situation.
Who made these rules? She wondered.

"NOOOOOO!! This is just taste of what is to come sister. Prepare me for my duties. For my life ahead – in THIS life. But it will be for them, and AS them, not as ME right now."

She shook her head with teary eyes, then suddenly smiled as if another personality had taken hold.

"Anyway, today is special. We are together. It is a beautiful day.
Not thinking too much sister….
Not thinking too much"…

THE END.

Chapter 21

The Gamemasters

She found that she just couldn't help but smile……and sometimes even laugh out loud spontaneously.

Uptight aliens were frustrated madly by it all, but if you maintained a sense of humour, it was actually amusing and refreshing; contrastive to elsewhere.

 She wondered whether any other location on the planet had the same entertainment factor as this place? Not in her experience.

It was occupied by Gamemasters.

 There was always time for a game, a performance, a dance, a chat, a song……

Everywhere you look, near the beach or streetside~ scenes of chess or card games; guitar or bongo-drum playing; vibrant ceremonies and rituals.

Even the 'makanan' was like a pre-school party of a time long past. Forbidden 'non' foods : Always fried and with sauce; vibrantly wrapped. Lots of sugar………and no alcohol please!

The sounds of the past emanating from every venue, shop, pub. Music with lyrics, from the 80's and beyond; transporting one back to fond memories of simpler times.

Enter the regression timewharp: old-fashioned cash-registers; archaic weighing devices; calculators, pens & paper for the simplest of arithmetic…..

It was like the land of eternal youth. Peter Pan.

They were always eager to play; dress up in vibrant colours, wear makeup, costumes and masks.

And always looking in the mirror!

Even as adults, these folk had a childlike innocence about them….. and yet a degree of cunning too.

They could feign ignorance, but would often beat you at any game. Applause!

And yet, when it comes to serious dedication to a faith, these people are second to none.

It was serene, and yet evil.

White and Black.

Dharma dan Adharma.

Unlike with material waste, they are totally preoccupied by personal recycling.

When you die, there is reincarnation, or 'reinkarnasi'.

This philosophy is the backbone of their existence.

Every move they make is for the next 'game' of life.   (She was onto her 9th one, for sure)…

For heaven and hell is not a separate place. It is here and now!

God and the devil both reside within. Which one you bring to life is up to you.

Black magic was the fear; protection the priority.

How you play now, determines whether the next game will be Nirvana or Hell , when you return to the gameboard. Play by 'the rules' or face damnation!

For many moves in the game of life, there are risks involved.

Topeng dan Cermin ~ **Masks and Mirrors.**

They wore masks frequently; both literally and figuratively.

Yet they served as mirrors to the rest of us; they showed us our flaws.

In the game of life there are no rehearsals.

As a 'visitor', whatever moves were a mistake in your past lives, you were reminded of them here, yet, in a way, forgiven.

For it is about the right here, right now that counts.

They have mastered the art of being in the moment. We were all novices; our lives way too complex.

Play this game right and there is always reinkarnasi as reward. This was the goal.

The quality of your life to come was how you played the game **now**.

Like chess, one wrong move and you could lose.

Big time.

Chapter 22

SIDDHARTA AND THE PHOENIX

a Riches to Rags Rising tale…

"You forget that the fruits belong to all and that the land belongs to no one" – jean Jacques Rousseau

What does one do when all their worldly possessions and everything they value are taken? We're talking all but the tattered shirt on one's back remaining……

Game over. Love, set and match.

Marriage, the halcyon years, the abundant wealth, the lavish lifestyle, the looks, the health.

All gone; nothing but sweet and sour memories remain.

And down came the castle……

How does one pick up the pieces that are left, and carry the eroding carcass to the mirage of peace?

Carrion.

Carry on? ……or not.

 Rot.

Some people are control freaks on all levels, but survival is an autonomic response mechanism.

Depending on the individual, sometimes the phoenix rises of its own accord….

She took down the mirror in the bathroom. And then the one on the wall.
The withered reflection that stared back was too much to bear.
The icing on the chaos cake.
The sunken cheeks; sallow skin; dead, vacant eyes; grotesque collar bones and stick-like limbs. It was as far in the opposite direction to attractive that was attainable.
She had always prided herself on grooming know-how, but this project was impossible to resurrect. The canvas was way past its use-by-date. No amount of magic putty could re-mask this tragedy of appearances.
The only salvation was sleep it seemed. Escape the whole existence experience, for the value was gone. Being a part of it- and conscious- was a living nightmare.

Coma.

Lethargy and no motivation were the mainstay. She felt acidic, and suffered a constant 'skin crawling' sensation. Even music was too much for the emotions.

Anything that had the potential to stimulate an emotional response (which in her case was virtually every waking moment) was painful; exhausting. The nerves were raw; exposed; vulnerable.

She always stood by the fact that if you found yourself incapable of reading or listening then it was an indication that severe imbalance had occurred. Even the senses were shutting down and closing shop.   But when it was unbearable to even contemplate enduring any form of human interaction or company, it was dire. She was there. Extremist. As always.

Charles Bukowski from 'tales of ordinary madness':

"I was vaguely considering the fascination of starving to death. I only wanted a place to lie down and wait. I didn't feel any rancour against society because I didn't belong in it. I had long ago adjusted to that fact"

As she lethargically unpacked the suitcase with the few clothing items she could stand to be seen in, she surveyed the villa and its open-aired loneliness. This was like a friend to her. Hibernation. And here, for the most part, complete anonymity. A degree of peace.

Step one was to soak up some of the vitamin D that was on offer. Bask in it. Slowly cook. For she was so very fragile, raw and cold…

She wandered out to the communal pool and sat on the edge; mentally devising how she could derobe and slide smoothly into the water unnoticed. Others were in the peripheral vision, on their porches, and lounging on deckchairs. She felt their gaze on her. Their language was foreign, so of course she naturally assumed they were gasping in horror at her and commenting on the freak show. Her journal notes of the time profess *'my external body is a reflection of my internal scream'*
After a while, being self-conscious was just part of the equation, and she learnt to just let it be. For she was in it. No escape for now. Complete discomfort on all levels; in the soul.

Whatever, let them stare, she thought as she immersed herself in the pool water, warmed to a tepid level from the tropical midday sun. It felt like fluid homeostasis. Here and the ocean would be her water beds of rest. The body beseeched her to go embryonic. Back to the source. Rebirth. That was real, uninvasive healing.

A package arrived, containing various vitamins and household supplies. Her husband had included several copies of a photo collage he had made of every family member with her on numerous occasions. The backdrop was the huge unique terrace they had owned. "to put up on your fridge, to make family feel closer   xoxo" he had written on an attached note.

It was visual hell on all levels; ~the most prominent being how far she had decayed since these shots of former health and vigour. And the absence of her family backbone was another cross to bear. Back in the box with these posters of torture, she thought; ~nowhere near ready for that emotional reminder. There was to be no maudlin behaviour!
The ego would keep her in the past, and she had to move forward for survival. All memories were toxic at this point, she must detach herself from those completely now. Cut the umbilical cord……

The lost house too; her baby. Much had been sacrificed to hold on to this acquisition and the associated lifestyle, but it had amounted to a wasted decade of anguish. The family building years. She had lost them all. The siblings had meanwhile expanded their familial unit for her observation, as in contrast she had held onto the goal of protecting her entire future financially. Or so she had thought. The sins of money and its eternal quest. Nothing but doom.

She had watched the castle crumble; brick by brick it seemed; amidst the lies and deception that she had contracted herself to. Every waking moment had been inspired by building an empire; the grandiose stories supplied to her had been SO convincing! Bravo on the sales pitch. But the rubble that remained was the ultimate slap in the face that reminded her of the mantra: trust nobody but yourself.
All efforts had been for the purpose of moving forward; but she had instead fallen backwards in a heap.

Lock down.

He had made many big mistakes, but at least she could say on his behalf: 'strong is a man who realizes that his love alone is not enough, and sets free the bird to paradise'........for those who really knew her understood that she couldn't be caged. She needed to be a free spirit; like a bird......

And she had earnt her time in the sun.....

So here she was with nothing but her own trust and intuition remaining. And scant at that. Somewhat swamped and hidden, but fighting to climb out. For the body was so far out of balance from the burn out; she was only just above water in a drowning sensation. Fighting for air and hope.

It is said that the stomach is like a 'little other brain'. She had been neglecting hers. She knew now with intent conviction that she must listen only to her gut, for it had far greater knowledge than the head.

She started to visualise 'white light' encasing her for protection, and would burn a white candle every evening during her yoga dedication time.

Some days she was so lackluste she just couldn't get out of bed, or, if she did, it was only to the other daybed outside. At least the glorious colours all around from the splendid gardens and clear blue skies with birds and butterflies served to medicinally soothe her senses. A far cry from the dungeon in the previous abode of the other life.
As immense as it was, the interior had been dark and evil there, like a dormitory of punishment. The rooftop terrace was spectacular, but the gale force winds at that height, (four stories up 45 stairs) made it too much of an effort. She had to grab a fur coat and brace herself. Utter discomfort.

The glory of near nakedness here was a relief. The temperature was 'home' to the body; carefree and unrestrictive. That sensation alone made one feel wealthy and abundant! She was not designed for the punishment of cold climates.
As with all locations in Asia she had visited or resided in, she got frequent waves of intense *dejavu*; particularly where there were palm trees and huts. She must have lived a past life in a village somewhere. She felt like an example of anachronism.

It was becoming apparent that when she came undone, she fled to Asia. It was where she mended and eventually became whole again. It welcomed her being on so many levels; felt familiar.   Grounding. Rebalancing.
Preserving. Nurturing. Restoring.
Equalizing.
Whether deliberately or subconsciously, she always ended up in the East.
The West destroyed; the East rebuilt.

Yes, she tended to adopt an anthropological role, but situations often somehow felt like roads once travelled......she had been there, done that before. In another life.

At the core, she was a free spirit. But when she denied herself that aspect of her being it had dire circumstances, as she had proven on more than one occasion. For the real world masked what was truly within. She knew she didn't belong in that game.
It felt right to be here at this time. Part of her destiny.
It was such a transient place, creating a true sense of liberty in the individual.

Her circulation and adrenals had been bombed, along with her immune system, so she started regular hot stone massage to try to reboot the system. Along with that came the acupuncture, reflexology, and the other menu of treatments on offer at affordable prices compared to the previous location she had dwelled in.

Even when the cash was flowing like water, the lifestyle had never reached the comfort standard that was attainable here on a mere few dollars a day. She planned to soak herself in it completely. Batho in it.

The quest to build a bright future had failed, and was no longer the aim. It was just survival now. One day at a time Moment by moment..........live each day like it's the last.
Dwell, and get well.
She sought to saturate herself in the very core basic, simple joys of nature and freedom.

Always the extremist, she had endured wealth and loss accordingly. Having experienced both she felt eligible to comment: In some ways, having surplus cash created more problems than the reverse ~ poverty.   Conversely though, it bought one TIME which is really the essence of freedom, and a most vital factor. [How ironic then that the term 'doing time' was supposed to be a punishment. She understood why the institutionalized found the reverse to be true. The real world was where the suffering lay....]

On a certain level of perception (only attainable by those left devoid) ~ with nothing comes abundance.....freedom is the ultimate goal. It is usual that people only get to experience this state when it is enforced.

She had been to both places; in the reverse order to usual. As she enforced the positive aspects of a life made simple, her mind would swing uncontrollably however. For she was aware, with a degree of disdain that the high life was like a drug to her. She would always crave the 5-star existence. It was why she had walked the steps others would fear to tread to get there……for nothing was free. Only risk-takers reached the promised land….

Once she had got there she fought passionately to hold onto it, but the control was not in her hands and she felt it slip through her fingers, like a tissue in space………

Such was the conundrum of the mind. It was a full-time internal debate; ~ the 'monkey on her back' she did yoga and meditation to try and tame.

The balance **between the two** was terrain untraveled. A foreign land.
For both are equivalently required. It was a mystery place. Perhaps it was indeed nirvana……

So…..she surmised, destitution and/or prison GAVE you time, but enforced restrictions and limitations.

WEALTH brought much extra burden associated with all the embelishments, but BOUGHT you the luxury of time. If you can afford to pay for assistance; shortcuts or alternatives to any arising situation, then this is a sense of freedom. You can buy time that others would be restricted from due to financial boundaries.

…And with extra time comes the ability to think properly………. And with the thinking, one can avoid mistakes. For when the mind is allowed the grace of time to ponder certain concepts in the subconscience, the truth is revealed in all its splendour.

Rushing procures the answers on demand and under the pressure of time-constaints, with no allowance for contemplation. With this usual method, the most likely outcome results in mistakes, or in the least : uncertainty.   She had found this to be the bane of her existence, and now saw the errors of her past. Too complex. Simplification required.
It is in the recesses of the subconscience mind where the truth lies. We only reach this place through a relaxed meditative state and letting go……one needs time to do that; coupled with the mindset that stress doesn't allow.

Remove the burdens………..slow down………..think………..be.

In the modern hectic world, we power on thinking we are invincible; with the courage of a cowboy!   Its like being on a treadmill, only the speed is usually amped in increments and the limits pushed further. Must keep going……..must push ourselves harder and achieve MORE; do BETTER………the sad reality is that it is actually self-destructive.
It often (read USUALLY) takes illness to strike as a warning and remind us as humans, how fragile we actually really are. How valuable true health really is. Unless we pay heed and slow down our pace, the consequences can be dire and/or irreversible.

*Poem to the alter-ego self to relent to being in the very moment:

If only I could help you to see

that all it takes to be happy and free

is to recognise pleasure as well as the pain

a challenge we must take to keep our lives sane

'Cause amidst all life's chaos that we are thrown

it's nearly impossible to fight when alone

but when you have someone who really does care,

a problem to you is one that you share

The antithesis of happy is 'fear'

when we lock all inside and hide every tear

and we think that loneliness is the cure

for it often hurts more to watch than endure

But fear is an evil that permeates our lives

it festers - and on deep depression it thrives

but once we realise what we have here and now

things always get better and work out somehow....

Albeit not religious per se, she had increasingly felt an affinity to Buddhism over all others. As she delved further, she realized why she had always been like a fish out of water in her Christian upbringing.

Had she indeed been an example, to date, of asceticism; albeit unknowingly?? This spiritual
practice involves punishing the body as a way to attain serenity and wisdom.

In **Buddhist** teachings, enlightenment is there in all of us to harness; the skill lies in the
power of perception. There is always suffering – our mind causes it. But you can be free of it
if you understand it.
It was a realistic approach she believed. The background behind it was that in life, this
suffering is endless. Fact. Buddha just tries to come to terms with reality; -life and death are
inseperable!   All things change. It hurts. This is
life. Our relation to life is losing it too…   Siddharta
therefore, had merely sought a coping mechanism. If there was a possible way out of the
mortal suffering ~ a way to become enlightened; become a Buddha.
The reason we have interest in Buddha, is because we ARE Buddha! He is there in us all,
we just have to find him. "Remember me as the one who woke up"…

[**Hindu dharma** was very similar, in its notion of (albeit preoccupation with) reincarnation.
Death leads to rebirth. Humans are suffering beings; bound to the wheel of death and
rebirth.]   However, whereas Hindu dharma was
based on karma of actions, and subsequent rewards in the 'afterlife'; Buddhism was simply
about the *very moment we are in*, nothing more.

Buddhism encourages all emotion; how we live in our own hearts.
It is not about being special; it is about being NORMAL.
Caste was irrelevant to the Buddha. His teachings focused on the universe *within*.
One could be from any caste; what makes you noble is if you understand reality. If you're a
good, wise person, then you are noble!
What she found gave it the greater impact for her, was that Siddharta spoke from his **own**
experience; from his own heart. He had discovered a new way: the middle way. Balancing
between the excesses on both sides. The problem, Buddha taught, is desire……
Siddharta had resisted the evil 'Mara', who represented desire, lust and temptation, and in
so doing, all the demons waned.

He had joined thousands of <u>renunciants</u> ; - who embraced poverty and celibacy; ~
renounced the world and lived on the very edge…abstinence and celibacy was mandatory to
reach the promised land of enlightenment. The ascetic pursues the truth by taking the
requirements of survival down to the absolute minimum possible; barely enough food to
survive; subjected to the elements; meditate fiercely for all the hours of awakening. The
sensation of feeling like one is dying in comparison to one's life as it was is essential to
being reborn as someone who sees……

Spiritual-seeking ascetics in India still believe that by subduing the flesh they can gain
spiritual power. For more than 16 centuries, throngs of pilgrims have gone to *Bodh Gaya*, a
small town in N.E India. For Buddhists this is the most sacred holy place. It is their mecca
and Jerusalem.

Siddharta was starving himself in the quest for enlightenment, but he couldn't sustain his
pursuits without food. A village maiden had appeared with a bowl of rice porridge which she
offered the withered man. That moment of generosity and release; when he accepted the

rice was a decision towards *life*. It was akin to 'grace' in Christianity. However in Christianity the grace comes from the divine. In Buddhism it comes from the _ordinary_ – eg a kindhearted girl who sees someone in pain and reaches out.

So like all the 'books' of religion, there was a story. This one made more sense to her however; ~ she felt so many parallels to Siddharta. One of the quotes was disturbing, and when she read it she began to cry:

"My body slowly became extremely emaciated" Siddharta said. "My limbs became like the jointed segments of vine, or bamboo stems; my spine stood out like a string of beads; my ribs jutted out like the jutting rafters of an old abandoned building. The gleam of my eyes appeared to be sunk deep in my eye sockets like the gleam of water deep in a well."……

"emaciated, exhausted, Siddharta punished himself for 6 years, trying to put an end to the cravings that beset him". He tortures himself, trying to destroy anything within that he sees as bad; the spiritual traditions of that era. He said that you can be liberated if you eliminate everything that's human – coarse, vulgur; anger, desire. If you can wipe that out with force of will, you can go into some kind of transcendental state."

Siddharta had surrendered himself completely to the hard training that he was given; in an extreme- like fashion. He discovered however that after many years of pushing his body to the extreme, he had not answered his question. It hadn't worked. He was on the verge of death. Then he remembered a day in his youth, at a spring planting festival with his father…. She concurred: ones mind generally drifts back to any happy times from their youth when coming undone.
Siddharta had put his faith in 2 gurus. They hadn't helped him. He had punished his mind and body. That had almost killed him. Now, he knew what he must do. To find the answers to his questions, he would look within and trust **himself**……

You will keep strong, you will fight on.

Even when all you love is gone.

It must be intrinsic in your soul. It lights your fire; it keeps you whole.

Power lies deep with the Phoenix within, that rises to eradicate every 'sin'.

Don't look back; power march ahead. Forget what's ensued; …evolved;…been said.

Hope remains within your heart. You can rebuild; you can restart.

Never lose the will to proceed. Forget every fault; embrace every deed.

Fight the demons of your own accord~

CHAPTER 23:

She had arrived in a land of unrestrained expression. The creative juices of these people flowed, they were artistic masters. Unlike the other world, one was not constricted by societies' doctorines; ~ (at least not for her as an 'alien'.) Yes, of course they had an expected order of performance (adharma), but it was nothing like the ridiculous protocol of the west.

Temporary residence; the perpetual 'visitor'. A liberty state.
It was the only way to reside and heal when in such a depleted state of health.
The 'fly on the wall' concept. Be in it and participate, but don't get too close.

This period of her life proved to be a tremendous learning curve in so many ways. Predominantly about herself. People are complex beings, ~ she started to realize that most people didn't know themselves at all! The vast majority exist in a disembodied state. She sympathized, and understood the feeling.
To use the term 'alien' in an alternative sense, these folk must feel as though an alien had invaded their body…

Devoid of the balls and chains of commitment and possession, (and mostly, human company) …one was free to float inwards and mend. She was aware of how luxurious and rare her situation was, and reminded herself daily to be grateful.

Health is a dynamic state; dependant on a multitude of factors, predominantly environmental. It is not a condition that remains once acquired. Maintenance takes work. It is a full time job. It is a lifestyle choice. The mind/body connection is inseperable. Perception of self is a most vital force.

She was also a firm believer that for healing to occur at all, one must remove themselves
from a particular location, company and environment entirely. Very few actually do. She had
come a very long way……(figuratively speaking as well as literally!). So much time is wasted
on others and their psychobabble…
Confrontation with self is terrifying for most folk, and why they don't/never evolve.

For one must close their door and exist completely alone.

Excerpt from Bukowski's 'tales of ordinary madness - notes on the pest':

"the pest, in a sense, is a very superior being to us: he knows where to find us and how..

unlike you, the pest has hours of time to shoot through the head. and all his ideas are contrary to
yours but he never knows this because he is continually talking and even when you get a chance to
disagree, the pest does not hear. he really never hears your voice, it is just a vague area of break to
him, then he continues with his dialogue...

these destroyers, although they have no idea of your thought process, they do sense your dislike for
them, yet in another way this only encourages them. also they realise that you are a certain type of
person - that is, given a choice of hurting or being hurt, you will accept the latter. pests thrive on
the best slices of humanity; they know where the good meat is...

...so then. well, this pest need not be a person who knows you by name or location. the pest is
everywhere, always ready to attach his poisoned deathray onto you.

...I am pest-meat."

Some of the stuff sold in the 3rd world stalls on the local village streets here reminded her of
her early childhood. She would hold a weekend 'stall' outside the family house; selling
homemade bookmarks, cards, lavender bags, bags of birdseed(!)……much to the
amusement of her parents and neighbours no doubt!

They good-naturedly bought the useless crap amidst exclamations of delight; ~ encouraging
her creative vision. Even at that tender age, she would put herself in a position of potential
criticism; if the dollars were there. As one gets older, this natural confidence and enthusiasm
for such pursuits is pummeled out via society's judgement.
Here however, they were untainted by the prison walls. The childlike innocence remained
and it was refreshing to view. A vast comparison. Healthy vista.

On the good days, she would venture out for a walk; always an adventure. Glorious
surroundings and happy faces.
Mood food.

She would often sit on a crate at the traditional pasar (fruit and vegetable vendor) with pen and paper for the daily lesson in bahasa Indonesia. The only way to learn a language was to get native; she knew this to be true. Reading all the books in the world will not give you the sense of circumstance to use the knowledge; nor the unique pronunciation.
For example, when she had slipped over on the pavement in rainy season, she got them to teach her those words:
'slippery' =' licen'. And 'to fall down'……well, there were 4 ways to say that; ~ 3 in bahasa Indonesia, and 1 in bahasa bali! So therein lay the lesson of that day. Needless to say that it was like chirades, and always a theatrical endeavour that entertained her ~ and them, immensely.

At other times, it was all too much and she would trudge wearily to the café opposite to sit quietly and soak up the atmosphere; sip on a coffee; maybe send an email message or write a postcard.

Slowly, the energy levels became balanced more frequently, and she felt the lifeforce starting to re-appear. Like a dying plant that finally acquires the water and sunlight it requires for photosynthesis.

Maybe it wasn't too late after all. It was still a long slow journey though. She had no choice but to be patient. The healing time required was in direct correlation to the degree of destruction. Substantial.

The philosophy of the natives here was that the universe contained negative (demons headquarters); neutral (mankind), and positive/high/sacred (the gods). Man was not just part of the macrocosmos, but was himself a microcosmos : 'the negative shows itself in him too, through his angers, his passions, or through illness………and it is therefore necessary for him to work on maintaining the balance in himself.'   It was comforting to acknowledge this mindset; she felt she was surrounded by a community that would be sympathetic to her plight.

It would take some rather radical lifestyle changes to reach her goal.
It was time for rebirth. New life. Next chapter……
She did some research on the internet, and began with the christening.

'Letha' ~ pronounced like 'Lisa' with a lisp made her laugh! But the depth of its meaning was appealing, so that would do for now. In Greek mythology, Letha was the name of a river in Hades that causes the dead to forget their lives on earth.

No past. Only here and now.

For those who experience, or escape a near death experience, they vow to never forget it. To put a positive spin on it and see the silver lining in the clouds of doom, these priveliged few gain a new appreciation for all life has to offer – an insight that others will never experience. It is like a superpower for survival…

You stop wanting, and learn to just be. Desire-less; just dwelling.

Buddhism teaches: Nirvana is this moment seen directly. There is nowhere else than here. the only gate is now; the only doorway is your own body and mind. There's nowhere else to go; nothing else to be. There's no destination. Its not something to aim for in the afterlife, its simply the quality of this moment.

Just this.
Here. Now.

Pay attention……

She had become more acquainted with the woman who owned the set of villas at this place. Rose lived out the back, and would invite her in for a tea or snack from time to time. Letha was courteous, but would never stay long; preferring to remain private and alone.
An explanation for her condition was unnecessary; one only had to look at her to see the suffering.   It was a private hell, and would remain so. Talking about it required way too much energy and emotion. In any case, the woman and her family seemed friendly enough, and they were most encouraging that she rest up and restore her strength and vigour.   One early evening, as
Rose finished watering her garden, she urged her to sit on her porch step for a moment, and look up into the sky. "Come, join me! I always sit here at the end of the day and count the stars in the sky. It calms my nerves and puts things in perspective." Her husband joined her, and together they pointed and counted. It was a ritual they had come to obey and it was comforting to witness.
Every evening, same time, Letha would peek her head around the corner and see them perched there, doing the evening roll-call of the heavens.

Another time, she watched from her porch as their young son sat on the grass near the pool concentrating on a project. He had a plastic 'bintang' supermarket bag and a few sticks, and was busily crafting a home-made kite. He took a short break to devour a plate of mango and various chopped tropical fruit the family staff delivered for his afternoon tea. When the project was completed, it was brilliant. Flew like a dream, and entertained him for hours. Such a simple, yet innovative exercise. The womans' husband exclaimed: "We encourage him to do this. Keeps him out of trouble, and this toy costs us nothing!"
Children actually using their imagination actively outdoors; so much healthier than in the *other world* with the toxic video games, phones, iPads and junk food. Refreshing. Rare!

These sort of surroundings, in conjunction with nature in all its rainbow splendour were conducive to a sense of calmness and natural healing. Soul nutrients that would no doubt benefit her plight. She would witness the plants flourish majestically, and imagine herself doing the same.

They were similarly abundant, but unlike those in her stomach, the butterflies in the splendid gardens here represented her newfound freedom as they fluttered in the breeze.

Like with everywhere she went, she had taken to long walks here, to soak in the different
neighbourhood and scenery. The camera always accompanied her on these exploritary
pursuits. Her passion for the unusual minutiae of life abroad was something she loved to
share. In the past, the repeated photo shots of fine dining restaurants and top hotels must
have aggravated and been a bore to those she inflicted; now, her vision was on a completely
new level. She was opening her eyes.
She found herself captivated by the children and immersed herself in a project of
photography with them as subjects. She had always adored Asian and black children ~they
were beautiful, gentle and natural. In their traditional garb, they were little dolls. Her visual
collection was growing and extremely unique. She would patiently await the perfect
expression or pose for these postcard memorabilia. She soon gained a somewhat
impressive photographic collection on her pc. Incredible, she thought, how all those huge,
space-hogging photo albums of the past were now stored on such a small item.

Similarly, the street ceremonies here were frequent and amazing to capture on film.
The women in the variously coloured, snug-fitting 'kabaya' and neatly pinned up hair, had a
polished, sensual air about them. They managed to maintain this while patiently on and off
bikes side-saddle, balancing god boxes.
The men would sit gang-like in rows, perched on steps, chatting amongst themselves.
Dressed in the sapari, with the turban-like hat and sarong; they remained super cool. The
mob. They donned black sunnies, were usually smoking, and adjacent to motorbikes. She
found this gangster-like veneer seriously seductive!
As with all of Asia, they loved a uniform! The Banjar in their groups with the black and white
sarongs often had the weapons to boot. Even shop security wore crisp, heavy fabric attire.
How they coped with the tropical humidity was a mystery, but it didn't seem to bother them.
It was a culture of dramatic expression, fashion, and community bonding.
She was proud of the fabulous array of pictures she had collected; it was truly calendar
material.

A few weeks before, she had captured an amazing traditional ceremony event, where she
felt almost VIP as the token buleh present.
One day, while at the well known 'Warung Made', one of the waitresses she had befriended
handed her an envelope. "Please, can you come to my wedding? I would be very happy if
you say yes!"   The 'bernikahan' (wedding) invitation
was extended to 'Letha and friend', but of course, she attended alone.

On the day, she had met up with the excited couple: the 'Mempelai Wanita dan Pria' at a
location nearby. After the initial greetings, she had ridden in the car with the bride and groom
to the family residence for the multitude of ceremonies to commence. It was a fair drive, at
least 30 minutes, with the bride handing out bright pink cupcakes during the journey. "These
are my favourite cakes. I love them!"
She was heavily pregnant, and it all looked exhausting for her; ~ the least of which was
enduring the splendidly ornate, yet heavy and uncomfortable bridal adornment. Solid gold,

the headgear alone must have weighed a stone! A balancing act; she had to stoop to fit into the car. The husband on the other hand, sported a plush purple velvet vest, dramatic makeup and eyeliner, (in fact, more than the bride), and a huge sword....
She found her mind drifting back to her own unusual wedding, where 90% of the invitees were gay, and the entertainment was an outrageous drag show!

On arrival, the 3 of them were welcomed with an entry ceremony of sorts, which involved some chants; a cracked egg on the footpath, and some incense. (!) The bride was still holding her hand when she was greeted by the throngs of attendants, it was a bit of an honour.
Plastic chair seating had been laid out in rows for the event, amidst several roaming dogs; the family pets. There was a central pedestal, like a four poster bedstand up on the stage podium, with the usual vast array of offerings atop. It was called 'sarana upacara' in bahasa. This receptacle apparently cost a fortune to erect; - often the entire life savings were poured into the ceremonial stand, and to be brutally honest, it looked like a tip-site full of all manner of trash!
The ceremony here was to be the first of many, it seemed. She was ushered to a front row chair, where the children kept her amused, as she awaited the performance.

On commencement, the Mangku (Hindu priest) went through a series of lengthy ceremony rituals; which involved placing objects in their hands and their hair, tying bits of string on their wrists, waving feathers over them, blessing them repeatedly etc. It was totally bizarre and captivating; she took over a hundred photos of the show, and the spectators alike, who were equally amusing. It was to be a souvenir of the memory she wished to share with the bride as a special gift. There appeared to be no other photographer on site, so she she took on the role, with serious commitment.
They were then moved to various other locations outside the family home for continued rituals; some of which the guests were eligible to witness; some not.
After about the 10th location and ceremony change, and several hours later, she wondered : will they be officially married by the end of THIS day??

A lunch buffet was finally offered, during which her exclamation of "phew – lead me to the wine or beer!" was met with stares of puzzlement and misunderstanding.
She perched on the stairs with the others; eating the rice and accompaniments with her hands as they did; while under their constant observation.
After the exhausting experience here, she said her farewells to the parents of the bride and groom, and was whisked back into the car to a mystery location for the reception party. Holy cow, the show went on!
Luckily it was in Seminyak, and close to her villa, so she left for a spell to shower, change and exhale without the audience's glare, before heading back for more of the same.
The camera was almost full to capacity; the guests WERE actually convinced she was the official wedding photographer! There were many questions asked of the strange, tall, skinny blonde visitor. As always she felt like a bit of a spectacle herself.
She took advantage and practiced her bahasa with these lovely people, who were only too keen to assist, and scribbling down translations frantically. She knew full well that it would be a most exhausting day when done. She was already feeling somewhat drained, especially in the heat, but chided herself: spare a thought for the guest of honour; the 8 month pregnant

bride!

She had thought that would be it for the little old camera, but as she entered the brightly coloured 'party room', she couldn't resist snapping away again. It reminded her of something out of 'play school'! The candy, cakes and sugary drinks kept coming, but still no evidence of the forbidden elixir: alcohol.   It was all about the sugar high it seemed; her arch enemy. These smiling faces were buzzing on the effects of $C_6H_{12}O_6$!!

She found herself feeding off their vibe, and the warm glow of community bonding gave her an almost emotional sense of glory.

A few hours later, an impressive dinner buffet was offered for yet more feasting; with the traditional babi guling, satay lilit, tum, lawar, sayur etc. Great pride had obviously gone into this offering, and the presentation and aromas of the display were sensational.

Letha had already exposed herself to all the traditional fare on several occasions. As you do when in a different terrain. For you have to walk in the shoes of the people to get a real feel for their life and culture, even if it is at times hard to swallow!

She had travelled to Ubud to the famous 'Warung Ibu Ocha' to sample the roast pig, crackling and lawar there. It was considered to be the best in bali; several cooking shows had filmed it overseas.   (Personally, she had tried better here, when recommended by a knowing local; - even including the delicacy 'lawar' with pigs' blood, no less.....she hadn't been shy! One has to taste all life has to offer after all.....)

The venue overlooked a river, but the meal was somewhat tainted by the faint sounds of pigs squeeling in the slaughterhouse below…

She also loved the sapi(beef) rendang and sop buntut (beef stew) that was a local fave. The ayam (chicken) betutu and bebek (duck) betutu was hard for her to resist on menus of local fare. She never understood how foreigners would come to this fascinating land from far and wide, and sample none of the local cuisine.

As she served herself a generous portion, Letha retreated to the back room near the kitchen with the bride to sit and chat for a while. She had thankfully replaced the heavy headgear and marital garb with a more comfortable outfit. The tedious mask had been marvelous, and she had worn it well, without complaints.

The now finally married woman pointed out another now familiar 'sarana upacara'; the huge 'bank-breaking' stand filled with offerings. She proceeded to explain that "it is so expensive to do wedding in bali! It is why I have to wait so long to get married, and now nearly baby! We must keep working, working, saving to afford"……

That single stand alone was worth somewhere in the vicinity of a years' rent.

"How are you feeling?" she sympathetically asked the weary girl; balancing her huge internal miracle on her lap.

"I am so happy, happy!" she replied, with the plastered serene smile these people mastered at displaying. Whether genuine or not, it was so convincing, you found yourself believing them.   " I am so lucky.

Handsome husband, baby soon. Very happy!" she had served herself some of the delicious savoury makanan, but the pink cakes took precedence. She kept picking away at these as she chatted with a Cheshire-cat-like grin of contentment.

It almost looked tiring for her to speak at all, but she continued; zombie-like to Letha and others, out of respect to her guests.

Letha finally did her farewells to all; hugging the bride and promising to bring her copies of the photos as soon as possible. "I will come to see you with the new baby and bring you a wedding album gift!"

Back at her villa, she poured herself a glass of wine, and eagerly loaded the pictures onto her computer to view. Looking over them felt like seeing illustrations for a childrens' book of mythology! It was fascinating and splendid, and the participants were so joyously happy. She would cherish these pictures always. What an honour to have been such an integral part of a most amazing day; ~ a traditional Hindu wedding. She had even lost all self consciousness, and had just emersed herself in the experience whole-heartedly. Completely IN each moment.
Blessed beyond belief, she started to cry as she felt happiness appear like a light.

The days turned into weeks and slowly the clouds of doom lifted. She got back into the daily yoga and even bought some calming CDs as background music to her candle-lit baths.
Her place became like a full-time home spa. Masseuses were available on call at all hours, and she took advantage; still too self-conscious to reveal flesh in a more public domain.

She met a vast array of European guests as they congregated at the central pool, or waved from their nearby porch.
One guy who was staying in the villa next door to hers was always seen in lycra cycling gear. It gave him the appearance of a circus performer; she could visualise him on the trapeze! He really just needed the 'stuck on mustache' to complete the look….
The German Adonis introduced himself as 'Vitty' as he offered her some of his Durian fruit, and explained that "It is my favourite food on erse, and better in Bali zan anyvere!"
He cycled 2 hours to Denpasar and back every day, to attain his supply from the traditional pasar there. "Surely you could find it locally, as it's native to here; that's one hell of a distance!" Letha offered in amazement.
" Ja, but ze lokally sold variety are imported from Thailand or Singapore; I vant only the Bali one! It is more 'ard to find;- I 'ave to travel far, but no problem; it is my fitness anyway!"
Letha tried not to laugh as she imagined him waking every morning for a hundred pushups and situps with chants of " you vill cycle like a maniac till your eyeballs bleed from their sockets, and it nearly KILLS you viz heat exhaustion if you vant to feast on ze king of fruits!!"
As it turned out, this guy came to Bali every year on a fruit-fest sabbatical, it was his ONLY intake! Even the staff were intrigued by the 3 huge garbage bins they had to empty from his room daily; full to the brim with fruit skins and empty spiky durian cases, like a nest of porcupines. Usually, 'orang asing' (foreigners) were most offended by their unique aroma. In certain hotels, there were signs in lifts with the image of the fruit and a huge red cross through it; 'no durian permitted' on the premisis. It had been referred to as the 'vomit fruit' or

'shit-smelling fruit' (!)   She found
out Vitty had previously been obese, then undertook a radical fruit-only-diet to lose a mass of
weight and become super fit......and has never eaten cooked or savoury food since! It was
an example of supreme discipline, but how incredibly 'langweilig'(boring in German) -she
thought.

 Letha was fascinated though; with a Gym-comp worthy physique like that, the amino acids
must be present in the Durian. How else does he acquire the required protein to sustain
muscle mass??   She did some
research.
Well! The overall benefits are manifold; the fruit nutrition benefits are infinite.
In particular, they assist in removing free radicals from the body with their high antioxidant
value (which is measured by their 'oxygen radical absorbent capacity', or ORAC.) They also
offer protection from wrinkles, hair fall, memory loss, macular degeneration, Alzeimers, colon
cancers, osteoporosis etc etc and so on. Amazing.
It was a most acquired taste. The local Balinese loved it, and during durian season would
crouch streetside to indulge with fingers.
Personally, she loved it but in moderation as it was very rich and creamy; she could see it
being a distinct flavour ingredient in desserts too. She felt it was rather decadent, and lent
itself to an accompaniment of a rich buttery chardonnay for digestive and palate
enhancement. Bliss! Funnily, she didn't even notice the 'unbearable stench' that people
associated with it.......(another example of most things Asian feeling natural to her.)
Ambrosia indeed!!

*(Malaysia is like a 'sister' to Indonesia with regards to the language: by all accounts you can
be understood there when equipped with Bahasa Indonesia; albeit a mildly different idiolect.
Hence it was an easy transition for her; - a break whereby she could express herself almost
as freely as home. The food is similar too - and the fruit/veg almost identical so papaya and
durian are an intrinsic part of the terrain.
On one of her trips there for visa renewal she discovered from one of the locals that
combining the fruit with alcohol could be lethal! The native people were well aware of the fact
and yet she had only just encountered the truth behind the chemical reaction that
ensued....ingestion of the two simultaneously literally exploded the stomach ! Like a
bomb.....   She had been lucky to escape this fate as she
had enjoyed it on many occasion with a punchy, dynamite chardonnay!)*

She also loved the Jackfruit, which was similarly high in protein and nutrients. It is the largest
treeborn fruit in the world, and native to India. She learnt that the seeds from both the durian
and jackfruit were boiled and used in various recipes, having an almond-like taste and
texture, and she began to do the same. However, she remained ever- faithful to her
absolute favourite tropical fruit of all: the papaya.

The vegetables too were much closer to how nature intended; the colours vibrant and
flavours more intense. She would buy fresh daily direct from the local traditional pasar;
(market). She felt a slow return to health through living off nature's gifts on this sacred land.

All matters of the heart aside, it is a fact that whatever state one is in, having the hair done elevates a womans' view of life in general, even if only for the day!! It is pampering that is akin to a drug for the majority of females, and finding a good hairdresser is top of the essentials list. The best hair maintenance experts are generally gay, and the relationship one establishes with him is often more intimate than marriage! For the salon chair is not only the throne of pampering; but often the psychiatrists' lounge too,~ from which the personal secrets shared are a sacred monthly ritual. One should remain faithful, but of course they generally don't. (She herself was guilty of being a 'salon slut' in the past.)
She had found an amazing one here and he was located literally at the end of her villa driveway. Way too convenient. The cost here was of course a fraction of elsewhere, so it was a luxury she could afford as often as necessary. She relished the joy, albeit the fleeting glamorous results;~ the prevailing wind, surf, rain, or 'bike helmet head' here would surely kill the crowning glory quite rapidly.

She also knew from past experience with both herself and others, that radical changes in HAIRSTYLE represented more than just external appearances......there was much deeper-rooted significance to this visual indicator. It was a sign of the times.....what was going on in the life (and health) of the individual.

Senna was a gentle soul, and an absolute perfectionist. She adored him; he had given her the best colour of her life! In addition, he was somewhat of a mystic....
One day much earlier on, during one of her very first visits, he had advised her to 'get out of the house in your other country'......this was at the stage where her husband was still there, just prior to the sale of their old house. It had drained them on every level. Not that they needed much prompting to initiate the final stages of detachment, but the message he conveyed this day was so profound that the very next day, all buttons were pushed.
As she looked at his reflection in the mirror while he tended to her locks, she was utterly dumbfounded. His eyes had become watery crystal blue, like aqua-marine-man....it was like watching someone possessed! He was trance-like; moving like a mannequin.
Out of the blue, he started to explain " this place you were in, it is evil........all good that went in there goes immediately out. It goes up the stairway, and out the door at the top. The door is facing the wrong way too. Bad chi. Very, very bad energy. Evil. It will take your relationships; your health; your money and destroy it all...it is dangerous. You need to get out and away – fast. Im sorry, this is not me, but the god, Allah has told me to send this message to you and I speak on his behalf. You must tell your husband to get out. He is in danger. You are lucky to be here and safe"......
In complete shock she sat there, open-mouthed; trying to fathom how the hell this was happening. She had told him absolutely nothing about the place whatsoever. All he knew was that her husband was there and she was here, and in a weakened state.

Senna continued her hair after this spiel; his eyes finally returning to normal again.
"Wow".........she exclaimed; her skin still tingling somewhat. "That was amazing Senna. You looked like you turned into somebody else when you delivered that message to me! Does

this happen a lot to you?"   He tilted his head, and with a gentle
expression began: "I must be working together with my god, yes. Only some people have
this assigned power. Allah chose me to be the messenger. I can do the evil too, like voodoo.
Black magic. Some other people who use the evil tool become like a genie; like a sort of
madness. If somebody want a person to suffer sickness or to die, I can make this happen.
For sure. But I don't want to Letha! I prefer to do only the good work for my god. If a
message come and I choose to help somebody, I do for him. I don't want to be black magic
master! You put out good, it comes back to you in return"   "IN SHAA ALLAH".....god willing.
So, she surmised, the Muslims, like the Hindus had a strong belief system in a type of
karma; used black magic as a weapon, and apparently, believed in a correct manner of
performance. Like dharma.   "You want something good for
yourself, you must be not just praying to Allah, but working for him too! On Fridays, all men
must pray to Allah."
She knew she could never catch him on a Friday before 2pm, so that explained why.

She called her husband immediately afterwards, and he was equally mystified.
The very next day he emailed her that the house was going on the market asap, and he had
meetings lined up overseas for complete migration.

In any case, back to the present........ she had excitedly left for a salon session, as the hair
was in dire need of attendance. She was loving the swimming as therapeautic exercise, and
had increased her sessions to a hundred laps on some days! However the chlorine was not
loving her back; she looked like a swamp monster. The hair was now decidedly blue/green.
To the point where she had actually been asked where she went to dye it this hue!
(Embarrassment city)
It had finally reached the desirable length for her now, and she was enjoying the versatility of
it. Just needed radical colour correction.
She wanted to go to café Moka for a cappuccino beforehand, but she popped into the salon
to let Senna know first. (Booking here was generally not essential like elsewhere; life was
designed around spur-of- the- moment behaviour. Something she was trying to get used to
after years of scheduled life.)   The other
staff welcomed her warmly, but apologized, explaining that he was away for Moslem
Ramadan and Idul Fitri; plus nursing his sick mother. " He is away until next month, his
mother is very sick with cancer ". She hoped he could perform the good kind of intervention
in this sad instance.
She had no plan B, but decided there was no other option but to try somewhere else in his
absence.

After coffee, she went for a walk to find another salon. She actually wandered quite far, and
ended up in the edge of Legian Kelod, just before Kuta.

One salon down a side-alley was ridiculously cheap, and she found herself stopping to
consider. It looked fine internally; basic, but by no means decrepid, and the woman was
most warm, gentle and inviting. She was in the perfect mindset to sit, relax and receive some
TLC, so she thought: what the heck, here is probably as good as anywhere......if it proved to
be great at that price, she would return, as it was beyond a bargain.

She observed the colour chart and selected the farthest on the 'pirang' (blonde) category. It was with a product brand she was unfamiliar with, but she didn't register that fact. Instead she sat back with a pile of magazines and let herself go to that sacred place of salon bliss. She often did that; meditatively,- so engrossed in relaxation and magazine reading that she wouldn't even look up in the mirror until the job was complete: dada!

This time however, she was forced to. The woman had wrapped foil around her head to 'seal in' the colour apparently; and was fanning her head as she sat; something she had never had done before. An instant burning sensation arose, and she felt her heart beating rapidly and alarm setting in. After a short while, it was literally to the point of unbearable: " Ooh not good. Too hot!! I think we need to wash out now!"
The woman replied " No, must be waiting. Soon, soon. Don't worry" she continued fanning more vigorously, and got other staff to assist and do the same. Letha tried to stop the panic but it was rising like fire from her gut just like the furnace on her head.
She couldn't stand it a second more, and got up to go to the basin; shaking her head with distrust and fear. Relaxing? This was utter torture!
They washed it out in cold water and her scalp continued to throb with the shock.
She returned to the chair with towel-wrapped wet hair and resumed reading while practicing deep breathing. The hairdresser started to comb through the hair, and Letha felt a fluttering of hair, like snowflakes emerge on the magazine she was engrossed in. She looked up, and ran her fingers through the decidedly blonde tresses now. It had the appearance of 'pot noodle' ; the super soft corkscrew-like pasta in a cup;- fake food that you add hot water to. Apparently the texture was now the same as it looked. Like watching a horror movie she felt entire tufts from the roots bounce and spring off in her hands. " OH MY GOD, WHAT HAVE YOU DONE???"..............the woman was trying to massage a treatment through rapidly now with her hands. It was most evident that she was in as much shock as her crying victim, and was at a loss of how to rectify the damage. " Don't worry, it need moisture, its okay, its okay"...
The other staff rallied around with wide-eyed horror; the hair still cascading down onto her lap and the floor, as if being chopped off with scissors.
Letha realized it was as bad an outcome as was possible. She was to be near bald. To the point where not even a huge hat would disguise the look. Amazing where the mind takes you on the survival tour when things are quite frankly too much to bear, isn't it!
So this is what it looks like to be a chemotherapy patient she thought. Silver lining: where art thou?   And then it came: the voice in her head: "You don't have cancer bitch; its just a chapter in your life. Its only hair for gods' sake. It will grow out. You are lucky! Snap out of it. Get over it"......

With that she just resumed reading with almost a calmness about her. The adrenalin high and low had occurred. Fight and flight. So draining. Just let it be. Out of your control now. The woman had started to attach extensions in an attempt to rebuild the destruction, but the results of this too were utterly disastrous. The roots of the blonde extensions were black for gods sake; it was almost a joke! It would serve to look like there was some hair emerging from beneath the caps and hats she was to wear for the next few months at least.
Who would have thought the day of pamper she had anticipated would evolve into the 'lab rat torture-chamber experience from hell'?

If it was indeed true, as some said, that 'long hair = long life' then this life was destined to be brief for her! Let the new one begin she thought with calmness.

They had the audacity to charge her **full price** for the procedure, and for some ridiculous reason she couldn't fathom, she did! (Dumbfounded with shock no doubt). An acquaintance of hers explained on inspection that her scalp at the back was red raw with third degree burns; and the matted hair was blood-stained. She was flabbergasted: " You PAID them to do that?? Anywhere else, one would have the pants sued off them!!"

She wasn't imagining the extent of appalling the results had turned out. She went to another salon the next day to enquire about possibly head-shaving. Back to the source. There really was no other option. The woman in the salon explained that the hairdresser would return the next day and could attend to her then, but she was most sympathetic and concerned. She saw the distress it had caused Letha and felt so sorry for her she handed her 2 pots with plants in them. "Please, I want you have these. It is aloe vera; very good for make grow!!" She demonstrated as she snapped the end off one of the leaves and showed the emergent clear sap that she then rubbed onto Letha's head.

Such a kind gesture, she thought as she took home her medicine garden. She knew the benefits of aloe vera for a host of other issues too; including ingestion for digestive complaints, so it was a useful plant to have on hand. It was not only regenerative for the hair, but within itself : if you replant a clipping from the leaf it will reappear; like a lizard's tail!

In any case, she returned to the location of hair murder again the next day. This time to declare that she 'needed more treatments!!' The woman and her staff were naturally surprised to see her, and were all very nervous. Her nerves were raw and she was emotionally drained from the experience. Justice needed to be served. She confidently selected utterly everything on the menu and spent virtually the entire day there as they massaged; waxed; pedicured; face masked; and pampered her butt off! At completion, she withdrew her wallet and shook her head. "Sorry, I have to go to the bank and get some cash out"……after which she never returned.

Why hadn't she retained the lifelong lesson she knew so well: YOU GET WHAT YOU PAY FOR!!   Had this knowledge been temporarily removed from her conscience like a lobotomy? Perhaps she was so engrossed in living complete antithesis of her indulgent past life; who knows. Or perhaps she was just meant to make this mistake and evolve from it as part of the regrowth process……(in all forms of the term!)

When Senna returned, she saw the horror in his expression as he enquired " what did you do??" she virtually collapsed into his arms, laughing and crying at the same time. As already established, the state of a womans' crowning glory is literally life-changing. To have endured this experience, and come through with a positive edge was gound-breaking stuff indeed!

He agreed. Shave and start again. Virgin hair. What a blessing!!
She declaired with utmost sincerity: "I will NEVER leave you again Senna, I swear!!"

(Sadly, this gorgeous gent has since passed away from cancer in his Javanese village, rest his soul. His demise will affect many a bad-hair-day….)

One day when she woke up, she felt a slight wave of excitement for no apparent reason.
She was still drastically weak, but there was a sense of hope. She thought she saw her
cheeks rounding somewhat; not as concave and cadaver-like.
How she yearned for the chipmunk look! You could always hide the body, but never the face.
She actually dreamt of being fat!
In any case, despite probably imagined, she was going with the happy sensation of visual
renewal.   It was the best she could expect at this stage. With that, she
wandered down to the deli to celebrate somewhat with a decaf coffee. As much as she had
always loved the buzz of caffeine, her body was too weak to tolerate it yet. Pretend only for
now.
She crafted a confident list of targets and aims; a structured plan to commence when feeling
strong. Always the strategic planner; she vowed this time to put less pressure on herself.
Only make hay when the sun shines. No MUSTS, only HOPES.
She had by this point realized that it was best to pay heed to the advice of these knowing
folk….(who by all accounts appear labotomised at the best of times!)

– for health and inner harmony, one needs to **'stop thinking too much'** and go within,
trusting that the body instinctively knows how to process and amend damage done. The
complexity of life only serves to make us sick. Albeit a somewhat ludicrous concept to
accept, being a ***simpleton*** actually works…..its super smart for health!

Feeling positive and self-righteous, she returned to her villa and decided to take a walk down
to the pantai. The ocean was perhaps the most emotionally healing element available to
man, and it was a 10 min walk away for her here. She would get there a few times a week.
The intentions for more frequency were there, but alas, not the energy. Today however, she
was in a state of near-elation.

The cleaner was working on her room as she arrived. The girl grabbed her ipod, a towel and
her bikini; excused herself, and headed off with a light backpack. As she walked through the
gate, she turned back to wave to other staff. An immediate, uncontrollable wave of
spontaneous nervous tension struck her gut, but she blocked it. Today was a great day; all
negativity was to be ignored. It must just be the coffee she thought; too bitter perhaps……

She walked the familiar Seminyak street that wound down to the beach; listening to music
that suited her state, and waving to familiar faces on the way. The heat was intense as
always, but a gentle breeze softened the blow.
She knew the waves would cradle her and bring a sense of further renewal, as always. So
refreshing.   As she waded in, immense emotion struck her every time. It
unblocked the suppressed pain in waves; allowing it to be acknowledged and then finally
escape. The tears cascaded without self-conscious expression as she lay on her back in the
rippling grasp of the sea's motion. It was the only place she felt safe to cry. It was her doctor.
Her shrink.   Her god.
It forgave her and allowed her to be who she really was; in all the many guises.

This time, she cried both in sadness and joy. She felt the phoenix rising.
It was a sense that no matter what happened, she would survive. All doubts were gone.

Purging the demons that roared deep within, the calm relief that resulted was tinged with euphoria. During these seaside journeys, one by one they would rear their ugly heads. Dragons to be slayed. It is believed here that the dragon resides in the ocean. Hers escaped to join the foe, and award her degrees of peace. Yes it was therapy, but draining too.

One could sell their soul, as she had done many times over; surely it was possible to buy it back…. She must remain hopeful of that salvation.

She towelled off and as she slowly trudged back on the sand, her weary legs begged for some therapy. She decided to visit one of the spas she favoured nearby for a Balinese massage. Why not? There was no rush! Nobody else to return to.
Her solitude had awarded her the luxury of being allowed to listen to the bodies' messages; undistracted by external preoccupations. It was a blessing, and to be her healing salvation.

She knew she would have to ignore the reactions to her scrawny appearance by the healing hands of the masseuse. Albeit gracious, they were usually most concerned and inquisitive, which only served to distress her further.
She was ready; it would be water off a ducks' back today. She hadn't felt this positive in so long ~ since she couldn't remember when.

During the massage her mind drifted in a trance-like manner; and she wondered why she felt so amazing all of a sudden. There was a slight degree of concern now too; she had learnt of many situations where people came really good just before they crashed fatally. It was quantam physics; the way the pendulum swung………

Her protective mind came to her defense then, as she reminded herself that you cant please everyone. She was noticing a pattern. She had spent much of her life concerned with appeasing others and expressing generosity. However, it only seemed to instill dramas, and in effect, often backfire to create enemies! Altruistic behavior had been her own downfall. Any time she had pleased herself on the other hand, others resented her for it, and she suffered immense guilt.

One day she woke up to the revelation that it is, quite simply, a no-win situation. Trying to manage solutions was masochistic behavior; it only served to compromise her health.
For heavens' sake, just please yourself and SOMEONE be happy!! With that notion in mind, she drifted off again into the blissful state of semi-consciousness.

It was several hours later that she returned to the jalan of her villa, and she witnessed the sunset and darkness begin to appear. So lovely to have no curfew or commitments she thought. No one else to consider; manage or care for but herself. Just as well, since at this point in this life, it proved to be a full time occupation!
Her blood sugar required constant monitoring. She usually had a 10 minute window to replace fuel before she felt truly weak and shaky, as it plummeted. She was there now; it was time to prepare a healthy dinner quickly and retire for the evening. How she longed for the vigour of youth to return…

The staff had all gone for the day, and the landlord lady was watering her garden as usual. The only remaining person to be seen.

As she entered her room, it took several minutes for the realization to strike her, but the place appeared VERY clean. Unusually streamlined.

Still in a dazed state from the afternoon's activities, and requiring sustenance, she wasn't thinking clearly. She dropped her backpack on the bed and headed in to shower. In her room, one of the windows were open, and some items were on the floor; tissues, a scarf, some loose coins. They must have fluttered down from the cupboard in the wind, she thought. She closed the window and turned to the cupboard.

Where her handbag had been.

In which was her blackberry, mobile phone, money, jewellery, camera and Mont Blanc pen she had saved to do her special writing. They all stayed in her chanel bag; it was the grand total of her remaining luxuries from the past. Her little shrine.

The shelf was empty.

Robotically she moved to the main room where the beanbag she rested her pc on to charge sat alone, with only the indent of the computer all that remained. She had saved all her photos on it for the last decade; including the recent ones she had so passionately captured of life here.   It was the window to her past; the creative aesthetic collection of culture here, as well as her communication tool.

No, no, no, there must be some mistake. She had put everything somewhere else, surely. Like a trapped animal, she moved frantically now, opening and closing drawers and doors in a panicked state. The heart beat wildly in her chest, and she felt she would faint.

Though not much, it was all that she had, and needed for contact and survival. She was weak and alone, and now devoid of any possessions.

What happened next was to be the turning point for her. As she collapsed onto the floor in an exhausted heap, her mind shut down in survival mode. Like a computer at risk of losing all data, the automatic processes that are part of the sanity maintenance control procedure occurred.   She remained in childs' pose for an extended period, focusing on her breathing until the heartrate returned to normal.

She was in nothing but her t-shirt and underwear. The shirt on her back.

The essential list then drifted through her blank mind like a sky banner from a plane…

Passport. Check.

Place to stay. Check.

Food in the cupboard and water to drink. Check.

Then it went blank again. She was the quintessential list-writer, but this was her shortest to date.   Her alter ego then emerged protectively, and beckoned her to look for the silver lining; see the light.

No money…..No possessions….. ~ and since the computer had housed the window to the other lives; no past either.

(Bear in mind these were the days before she utilised dropbox and iCloud for data backup)

Focus on, and feel what remains…
A sense of glorious richness transpired like a warm glow of relief.
Profound irony.

All that she had initially valued was now truly gone. Money; lifestyle; looks; hair; material
possessions; control. All that was left was the body; mind and spirit. In essence, by LOSING
control, she had actually gained it. Stripped bare, she was master of her own destiny now.
The balls and chains had been severed.

As one of the hard truths of human existence, Buddhism teaches:
In order to gain anything, you must first lose everything…

With that in mind, she stood up and moved outside. She needed to be near nature. She
found a soft spot of grass under a frangipani tree, and crossed her legs in the yoga pose of
meditation. Would the natural world pay her homage and would she feel the sense of pure
joy that Siddharta experienced in this transitory world we are a part of? He had sat in this
manner, under the Bodhi tree, meditating. He intended to remain as such until he had
attained the supreme and final wisdom……

Only by removing the toxic boundaries of our past, can the secret visions of passion be
realized and come to fruition. They were shown the door to reality.
She was awarded the eye of perception, and had the sense now, more than ever before in
her life, that she was going to be okay.
Because she had just learnt to let it be.
To be her own light.
It was powerful and divine. Like the breath of life.
She needed nobody and nothing but herself. Dwelling in the here and now.
Retribution had become her Liberty.

It is a sad fact that one needs to go into an extremely dark place of personal distress for the
pheonix rising to occur…….

She knew however that, like the acquisition of health, this newfound mindset would require
constant monitoring to avoid slipping back into the vortex of fear. It was however, precious;
life-saving, and worth the efforts required for maintenance.

Immediate duties to attend to however; despite her complete lack of energy or strength. As
she trudged off to the owner's abode out back to inform of the disaster, she realised she had
no numbers to call either. The woman stopped what she was doing as she saw the sullen
victim emerge. "Are you alright? What's happened, you look terrible!!"
"Even more than usual today, Rosa.(?) Someone has broken in and taken everything I own"

" I don't understand……….this cannot be………only the staff here today, and they have
worked with me for years……" They returned to her room to inspect the scene.
She soothed Letha, rubbing her back as she scribbled down a list of the stolen items for the
police report. They then surveyed the villa for evidence of break-in as Rosa spoke to the
police on her mobile about the incident, and sure enough the kitchen window had been
yanked off its hinges.
Letha

detected something about Rosa's presence now that created an acidic heat sensation deep in her core. Alert. She was listening intently to every message her body sent her now. It told her to remove herself from this negative force. Change was needed.

Rosa sat down on the bed with Letha, and started to explain some concepts from the Koran. It was background white noise to Letha as she felt her body slump from post adrenal shock. The woman finished her spiel with a knowing smile; tinged with a sinister touch: "You must take comfort in the fact that these offerings have gone to a better cause now. You see, we must understand that someone else needed these things far more than you do"…

Letha's gut alerted her to suspicion as she reminded herself: trust absolutely nobody. Especially now in this stripped vulnerable state. See everyone as a villain but yourself as the safe-house.   Rosa handed her the phone and said "please use my phone to call anyone you like. Your family, your friends……."

With only her backpack remaining, she emptied the contents onto the table, and apart from towel, costume, ipod and a mass of sand, there was a card she had been given by a man she met in bintang supermarket the week before. Coincidentally, he had lost everything in bankruptcy in his other life, and had started up a 'lifecoach' business here. She took the phone and started to dial.

He was an ex-chiropractor in Canada, so this change of vocation was a somewhat radical one; as is often the case. He did however incorporate his knowledge and skills into his client programs.   These spinal adjustments served to rebalance the body; in addition to the mental/emotional counselling he provided. As the body regained a sense of equilibrium, the adjustments unblocked pockets of stagnant energy; along which emotional release often resulted too. It was all part of the healing process. Letha enlisted his support and he became somewhat of an assistant crutch to her on her path. His purpose was to reinforce what she already knew.

 In times of weakness, like a guardian angel, she now had the extra voice in her ear, until she was strong enough for her own intuition to resume the self-talk to her. He served to ameliorate the damage done.

His tool of assistance was a book based on 'the law of attraction', which she was already familiar with from her prior quantam physics research. Essentially: generate positive energy into the universe, and the same shall be bestowed back upon you. He was inspirational as he had used a negative situation in his own life to create a positive, healing one for others. This was obviously bringing him more satisfaction than all the acquisitions and trappings of wealth in his former life, and she found herself feeding off his enthusiasm and motivational guidance.

 She soon discovered that he was one of so many examples of this situation; ~ victims of life's challenges and disasters tended to flock to the island to resurrect their lives.
It was like a stirfry of such a vast array of fascinating ingredients!……

One of the beautiful things about here was the tremendous life-lessons that were 'shared' and passed on like folklore, if you opened your ears and your mind. She was learning so much from others and their little anecdotes and tales of tragedy, wonder and triumph.

The prevailing opinion by many; including her husband, was that it had been an 'inside job', concerning the theft: "I bet Rosa's son is doing his uni homework on your computer right now"......

Truth be known, Letha had by this stage processed most of the loss and was over it. The one thing that continued to break her heart was the loss of the Balinese children and wedding ceremony photos she had so passionately acquired. She had poured her heart and soul into those ventures, so it was the toughest remaining fragment to deal with.
She also remembered how many times Rosa had admired her special handbag. She had trusted the woman, and had befriended her to a degree, so it was another bitter pill to swallow.   Still, you cant saw sawdust as they say, and pondering the perils of the past only serves to compromise health now. Forward marching with blinkers on...

She sought a new location for residence, and one night, just packed what was left in her bag and left.

Some say that a passport, t'shirt and bikini was all you needed to survive in bali. She was certainly putting that concept to the test, and it wasn't too far from the truth!

All that is really needed, is contained within.

The life coach had insisted she keep a daily diary,- (a *'gratitude journal'* if you will); -as it assisted in putting things in perspective, and reinforcing the lessons he was preaching. It was at this time that she searched her memory bank for what had brought her happiness in the past. In fact, doing just what he had prescribed was one thing; she had always kept a personal diary for the various chapters of her life! Why had she stopped?
Life and its prevailing chaos and challenges had got in the way; she had neglected the expression from her heart.

Two healing processes were underway.
She did some more in depth research on the principles of Buddhism. And she got back into her writing. She professed that written brilliance seemed to coincide with tremendous mortal pain....

" Who you are; what you think of as yourself, is constantly changing. Like a river, endlessly flowing. One thing today; another tomorrow "..............(Buddha)
This reinforced her already existing thoughts on health: how it had an ebb and flow aspect about it.

In modern life, with the much greater toxic load we are forced to endure (even just through breathing in pollution), the body is under constant pressure with the detoxification process. Like waves, sensations of lethargy and body disharmony (or illness), alternate with energetic vitality;~ as the body processes, and eliminates the daily exposure. It is an unavoidable pattern. One cannot be in supreme health full time! Regardless of how healthy the lifestyle is, some days are great, others lackluster. Like quantum physics.

With this in mind, she devised a strategy to integrate into 'the real world' existence, with its prevailing pressures and indulgences.

She called it the 'day on, day off' principle.

Quite simply, it entailed abstaining from caffeine, alcohol, all forms of meat, sugars dairy and wheat on one day. Lots of water; vegetarian soups; fruit, vegetables, yoga and meditation. This was 'day off'.   The following day was 'day on'. There were no rules!! She encouraged 'listening to your body – it will tell you what it needs'. [She herself actually did day 'off' for 2 days before her 'day on' mostly, but she realized that in the real world, this actually created a kind of stress for many people, forced to be social and conform etc . Not everyone had the opportunity or constitution to wait more than a day for so called 'rewards'!). More consecutive 'days off' are of course recommended, but allowing the body at least a days' break in between indulgences gave it a little breathing space to process before re~toxing again.

Although difficult to adhere to at times, she knew that it obviously helped prevent illness and disease, and kept the immune system stronger. Like the other facets of her lifestyle, this took discipline and strength of will; - particularly in 'saying no' to people and invitations. It used to concern her, but now she no longer cared if she was perceived as an antisocial outcast. For it was the commitment she had made to HERSELF, and took precedence over all else.

Liko all tho difforont phasea we go through in life, one must be dynamic in the quest for a harmonious existence. Quite simply: survival of the fittest.

Unlike so-called ideal relationships, the body IS conditional:

Only when you worship and respect the body, will it love you back in return...

Chapter 24

THE DEATH OF TWENTY SEVEN ALIENS

She'd always lived two lives.

 Simultaneously.

Like faithful twins, they protected her from exposure in various ways.

There had been efforts to live one, but they nearly destroyed her.

Even here in Asia, she fluctuated between wholehearted assimilation into the Hindu people and their culture ~ and returning to the ingrained western mindset thinking.

Not exactly scitzofrenia, but dual identity, if you will.

It was a case of masks and mirrors:

The person that dwells within, versus the reflection you project for the world to see.

She had 2 passports with different names too, and this brought her comfort and a sense of safety.

She was both a married woman, and a single entity.

Furthermore, within those two different names were two entirely different lifestyles; the western shared one spent in a big city, the eastern single one on a tropical island.

As the Mrs she spoke English; as the single woman she spoke (as she progressively learnt) a foreign language.

On several occasions throughout her life she had received palm readings, and the same scenario played out each time. They were fascinated : "you are SUCH an old soul. So many past lives!"

They apparently just kept throwing her back, it seemed……

The number **twenty seven**……the day she was born in November.

She had encountered others of similar ilk and there appeared to be a common thread;

those born on this date were seemingly not of this world.

Perpetual aliens it appeared.

She shared her birthday with 2 others who were like family to her; their connection uncannily intertwined.

One she met in bizarre circumstances (during one of her 'dual personality' episodes), and the other was his daughter, who she had witnessed grow up.

They, like her were not normal……whatever normal was. The eternal mystery.

In any case, it was startlingly obvious that they were misfits; anomalies.

They could not integrate; it was a danger-zone.

They came undone.

Their curiosity lured them to venture out from time to time, to play in tho 'roal world' and frolick in its' gardens of sin. It was not where they belonged however, and it always ended badly, or tragically.

As a result of their dalliances, one ended up serving two hardcore prison sentences; one got so drastically sick she was near-death, and the other committed suicide.

The man's mother, too, had been cursed with the date and she fell victim to the fate of suicide also.

27/11s were meant to be alone. This is when they flourished and remained safe.

Yes, they had immersed themselves in the poisons of decadence, however in **solitude**.

A private indulgence was always key; for the worst toxin of all was other people……they were the furnace of fear to be avoided. The mantra: don't get too close to the fire.

A multitude of natural healers, mystics etc had professed her to be 'super sensitive' to the surrounding forces; people's negative energy etc – and that she had psychic abilities. She was advised to protect herself.

She knew it was a selfish admission, but she honestly felt that PEOPLE simply wasted your precious time and energy.

Likewise, she had low tolerance for those who weren't content with their own company. She considered an inability for solitude a sign of needy weakness.

Wherever she resided, she was intensely private, no doubt perceived as a recluse.

('Selalu sendirian'…. Always alone.)

Anonomity was more than a luxury to her; she thrived on it.

Familiarity, after all, breeds contempt…

[Bukowski captured her sentiments well in 'tales of ordinary madness':

"I know a man, a kind of intellectual-poet type, a lively life-filled sort who has a large sign attached to his front door. I do not remember it directly but it goes something like this (and done in a beautifully-printed hand):

to whom it may concern: please phone me for appointments when you want to see me. I will not answer unsolicited knocks upon the door. I need time to do my work. I will not allow you to murder my work. please understand that whatever keeps me alive will make me a better person toward and for you when we finally meet under easy and unrestrained conditions.

I admired this sign. I did not take it as a snobbery or an overvaluation of self. he was a good man in a good sense and had enough humour and courage to state his natural rights."]

Perhaps further influenced by her earlier education and multiple school-change days, she was, as the saying goes: 'a rolling stone'. She needed no moss!

She was notorious for being harsh with acquaintances, and gave no chances. Those who knew her held concern as they witnessed her wipe many a long-term association in an instant over disloyalty on their part.

Such is the curse of 27 – 11's.   People born on this date struggle immensely to cope with the real world; theirs' is one of lonesome fantasy.

She had given up long ago on the quest to 'fit in'. That was almost the antithesis of her purpose now.

So what were the *semantics* of the number twenty seven then?

The unknown implored her to investigate:

Well, from a spiritual standpoint, there were 27 signs of the zodiac in Indian astrology; and 27 is the highest level of knowledge in rupaloke (Buddhism).

There were 27 countries in the European Union!

In some mystical teachings of the number 27 is a hidden 9, which is a sign of darkness.

The very same sign of 27 – is a sign of a killer.

J. Boehme (a German mystic and theologian) calls this number "the death".

An unusual number of talented and famous rock/blues musos died at the age of 27; leading to their reference as ' the 27 club':

Jimi Hendrix; Janis Joplin; Jim Morrison: Kurt Cobain, and more recently Amy Winehouse, to name a few.

Frank Sinatra was arrested on 27th November, 1938. Not surprising for one of the gangsta rat pack.

*.... 'it has to do with the trinity 3 ^ 3 = 27;   the alpha and the omega'..... (?)

[-the first and the last.

"Alpha and Omega are the first and last letters of the classical (ionic) Greek alphabet. This would be similar to referring to someone in English as the 'A and the Z'.........the beginning and the end.]

This made sense to her. As three, she and her 'doppelgangers' were indeed a trinity; - and their nature was, without doubt, extremist; as in A & Z.

Always on the edge, her quest to find the 'middle ground' had failed; she saw that as a weakness.

The extreme highs and lows were disturbing. She'd researched 'quantum physics' in a quest to attain a more balanced perception of life.

Going from living full-speed ahead like a Ferrari, she was now seeking to master 'cruise-control'.

When she first learnt the story of Siddharta on his struggled mission to find his inner Buddha, she felt such a profound connection. She had in fact been on the Buddhist path her entire life!

Abstinence felt appropriate; and indeed the only option when embarking on a cleansed state of being. Monitored food and alcohol intake, limited possessions, solitude and celibacy is mandatory; and transports one effectively to a higher state of awareness.

She found a paper she had written years ago. It had faded yellow with age. She guessed it had been written in her teens. Concerning the correlation between age and fear. It is absent in glorious youth…

I often venture back in my minds' eye

to times of contentment and peace with the world;

fight pangs of envy for the pure happiness and excitement I could emanate

from the mere simplest of life's pleasures

What eats at man to the marrow and core

that we can no longer enjoy such spiritual luxuries anymore?

Age is a decaying demon

- who destroys not only flesh but substance, will and spirit.

Life has changed...from a gentle welcoming breeze on which to float with fancy..

to a fierce and tireless hurricane,

which batters and bruises all that it transports

through the progression of time and space.

The concept of fear becomes inevitable.....

Reading it she stifled a laugh…the young think they are 'old' before they hit 20! As she had.

And yet, the words are wise and true.

Anyway, I digress. Back to the present then.

She had returned from a stint of unavoidable global integration to gasps of horror at her withered appearance.

What had happened to the glowing girl that had left these tropical soils a mere 4 months ago?

This time however, she was aware of the symptoms – and knew the toolkit required to mend and repair.

For when exposed to the selfish ratrace of society, she always faded away; - literally melting like a candle……….

Her physical demise was a true reflection of the internal anguish.. When the transformation occurred it was remarkably evident.   The body never lies. She was an open book!   In fact, during these times when she was in a compromised state of health or illness of a more severe nature, she actually appeared *faded* in photo shots, as if she eventually would disappear… (and yes, the camera lense was clean; it was only the image of her that was blurry). It was a phenomenon she noticed and displayed to her mother on a few occasions. It was an indication she had to work on the self resurrection if she was to continue.

Her soul was starving, and the world could see.

She wished it wasn't this way, as it forced her into hiding; like a wounded animal.

 Away from prying eyes and left in peace to rejuvenate and self-nourish.

She had a generous nature, but she knew that when she gave of herself wholeheartedly, this internal death occurred. Her own needs were compromised and desperate measures had to then be taken to resurrect her soul. Reinvention.

 Man is not only a part of the macrocosmos, but is himself, a microcosmos. Maintaining balance and avoiding the influence of negative forces was key for survival.

It is a Hindu belief that illness is a manifestation of evil forces or spirits ('kala' or 'buta'); that have managed to 'disrupt the body's universe'.

Demons.

Death is : " permanent end of all functions of life in a person; destruction."

She had died many times, on various levels.

Sold her soul.

Emotionally,……… mentally,………… spiritually,………… physically,………

Literally.

Chapter 25

The Face behind the Mask

INSOMNIA is your subconscious

knocking at the door of your

conscious mind.

Something you must do.

Or something you did.

Or both.

Memories fleeting in and out,

knock, knock, knock………..

incessantly wielding "remember me?!"

The mind is complex –

constantly demanding attention.

There's no hiding from the raging beast that lies dormant in us all;

scratching at the undersurface.

She felt perpetually drained.

So many different characters and phases……

How to put them to sleep, and allow her soul to find peace?

Her retribution.

They would stalk and haunt her for years until she finally procured the solution.

The early mornings when they would pounce;

These too were the hours of heightened lucidity.

And so she attacked, and wrote them down.

Parodied accounts of memories unravelling.

One by one.

In no sequential order.

Random.

Scattered.

Like dreams……

She had found the weapon.

Her pen.

It became her voice; mode of expression.

She felt empowered.

Like peeling layers off an onion……

She gave each chapter and personality the attention it deserved.

Slowly; … nervously at first.

Then with more eloquence as she gained momentum.

Like an actress,

she relived every role in her head,

as they were played out via the pen.

And in so doing, she slowly exorcised the demons.

One by sordid one.

The god of written expression had found her!

She became the medium.

Words came from nowhere and flowed with intensity.

She determined that to adequately express yourself in this manner, one must be a recluse.

Isolation was imperitive.

Writing comes from the heart;

 interaction with others was a distracting influence on the portrayal.

Her spoken words became more seldom as her scribed ones gained precedence.

Write all the stories.

Pure and unadulterated.

The rescue was a slow; painstaking process.

Draining.

And she started to sleep.

Deep, deep......

like the dead.

The waves of relief were so refreshing;

uplifting;

intoxicating even.

Addictive......

Her obsessive, compulsive nature had found a new outlet.

Like ghosts, the fears subsided

and her body uncoiled to a natural; untortured state.

Live in the moment and look to the future.

That was the plan.

Unburden herself of past mistakes; conquests; wins and losses

and be done with them.

They no longer have the key to dwell here and unbalance her equilibrium.

Rebirth.

Reinvention.

She felt certain that once the final chapter was at last completed,

 she would gracefully float down to the waters' edge like a spiritual vision,

and literally submerse herself in the arms of the forgiving ocean......

Chapter 26

You Live and you Learn

" the person who has lived the most is not the one with the most years but the one with the richest experiences"....

Jean Jacques Rousseau.

It was during the most spectacularly near-fatal stint that Sapphire fled to the tropics to die in peace in paradise.

Bali was far removed from the rest of the world she felt. It was more like a separate planet!

Not surprisingly it was a mecca for those seeking healing and salvation.

It welcomed her with open arms:

Om Swastiastu!

Walaikum Salam!

Selamat Tinggal.

It became her sanctuary.

For Sapphire had retired at 27; been a millionaire by 30; lost everything at 35; been near death by 36, and meanwhile endured celibacy for a decade.

It was overdrive acceleration to the extreme, and she had burnt out big-time.

Being a naturally fast person (much to her detriment in the past), here, she was constantly reminded to slow down. The pace was dramatically slower; almost trance-like at times. As the locals say: "Hati-hati, pelan-pelan"............take care; slowly, slowly.

Her migration here was hence partly self-enforced. Fate had brought her.

Here was a land whose inhabitants were extremely moody and spiritual – with a most elaborate history of trials and tribulations. The lunar calendar dictates most of their lives; they are under constant influence of the phases of the moon! It wasn't for everyone, but it suited her temperament. Its' invaders never stayed long enough to be annoying; always fresh faces.

A comfort zone.

As was the case in Tenerife, she liked the constant influx of visiting foreigners; ~ also knowing they would disappear as fast as they emerged. Smiles always abound; - on the visitors because they had escaped their normal life for a spell, and on the locals because this paradise WAS their life!

She concurred with a comrade on some of his Spanish sayings, one of which was: "visitors are like fish. They are great when fresh at first, but after around 2 days, they start to smell"…

The only grumpiness tended to be in impatient ex-pats, or invading westerners -who just couldn't adapt to the pace as it was, and the prevailing frustrations. 'Jam karet'; ~ rubber time. It was the way of life here! Things happen.....eventually. You either get with the program, or suffer the enfuriating consequences of expecting things to be done on *your* clock! Half a life spent in a fast-paced and controlled environment will do that to one.

Some westerners got insulted by the barrage of questions that is the customary conversation here. The locals' incessant need to know your life story and every personal detail requires patience….it can easily be annoying, and misconstrued as intrusive!

That's not the intention of these people however; just a different culture's idiosyncrasies. It goes something like this:

" Mau kermana? (where are you going) ; asli darimana? (where are you from) ; berapa lama di bali? (how long will you stay/ have you been here) ; siapa nama anda? (what is your name) ; dimana tinggal disini? (where do you stay?) ; apa kamu punya bizness? (what is your line of work) berapa umur sekarang? (how old are you) ; punya anak? (do you have children – how many etc) ; suda menikah? (are you married) ; dimana suami? (well where is your husband)…..and so forth;

usually delivered in consecutive bullet fashion. Answer required!

It's <u>easy</u> to see why it is misinterpreted as nosy 'prying' into personal affairs! The etiquette of the western way deems this an invasive manner of inquisition.

Even it's position on the globe was compelling; situated on one of the two main energy flow intersection points of the planets' magnetic force grids. This location generated extroidinary sources of energy and knowledge, the principles of which are an ancient science known from the beginnings of civilization.   (She used to refer to Tenerife in the Canaries as a 'magnetic island'; - one that you were continually drawn to returning to, but this one literally took the cake.) More than a second home, her repeat trips here had reached an impressive tally.   'Sering kali kersini'

She affectionately referred to it as her 'playground'. Like the Japanese, the Indonesians were all children at heart! Life was a game. Don't take it too seriously or think too much. They kept you young.

It was impossible to maintain a gloomy outlook in this environment. Any clouds of depression were most certainly lifted. Legions of foreigners who have migrated permanently to these lush tropical soils can attest to that. The affinity with the ocean was also paramount to the contentment of many, including herself.

She had acquired body-art embellishments here, dedicated to the two locations she had considered home most: Japan and Bali.

The japanese branch of the tattoo was the 'sakura', cherry blossom; the Balinese one the 'kamboja' – frangipani. These branched out from a heart wrapped in thorned roses ~ her symbol of 'pembujangan'…celibacy.

She also now carried her 'address' on the back of her neck: the bali Om; - as in 'Om Swastiastu'. Like a 'return to sender' code! It was well welcomed by her people as tribal membership. Protection.

Perhaps the energy she might normally have projected towards the sensual union that she craved, was instead expressed through her fitness and writing? They say the two deliver a similar appeal via endorphins and joy.

It was here that a monumentally epic journey of self-recovery commenced, to find life again.

Her existence combined the spectacular tropical nature all around, and retreating to the serenity of her 'zen den'.

She often wondered: 'Am I ALLOWED to feel this happy and free??' It felt like tasting the forbidden fruits from the garden of Eden. A foreign sensation to the enforced conditioning of the 'other world'.

There were moments here that surprised her, when she was filled with emotion and overwhelming joy; - the likes of which she hadn't experienced since her childhood.

During one such time, she sat, in the delicious breeze on her porch and wrote a message to share:

WELCOME TO MY BALI, WHERE:

Every day is different, and special.

Events unfold like a mystery unraveling.

There is never a dull moment!

You can never predict anything...but can expect the unexpected.

The weather is always wonderfully warm.

The people are gloriously gracious.

 The wealthy whinge, and the destitute smile....(!)

The sun always shines

The birds always sing

The mozzies always bite (!)

The magnificent gardens bloom with splendour

The food is an adventure; - delicious and varied.

Every day guarantees you spontainaiety on some level,.... and at least one laugh!

The majestic ocean beckons; cradles and rebalances

The ceremonies and scenery enrich your life with a caleidescope of vibrant colour

~ Where things flourish and glow...

From her porch where she wrote, the distant drones of traditional Hindu and Muslim chanting could be heard often. The spiritual flavour of which made her skin tingle, and opened the recess chambers of her mind with serenity.

That with nature's audio of birdsong, gecko talk and duck noise here created a safe environment for her creative playground to come to life. Her mind would wander fearlessly, of its own accord.

Free spirit roaming.....

Although many disagree with the notion of having an 'addictive personality' disorder, she believed it to be true. And for those inflicted, it never leaves.

(Like her friend wrote in a helpful handbook on bali, referring to the entire island as her 'KETAGIHAN': bali <u>addiction</u>.)

With destructive pattern behaviour however, 'transference' of addiction was the only solution. The choice was generally to destruct or preserve. Selecting the latter, she had thrown herself wholeheartedly into health and fitness.

Sapphire worked on nurturing the trilogy of supreme health: mind, body and spirit.....the pursuit of which (like most things worth acquiring) demanded discipline and dedication.

For if even one of them was neglected, the pyramid collapsed.

She expressively wrote from the heart and studied language for the mind; exercised daily and received regular massage for the body; practiced yoga and attended hindu ceremonies for the spirit.

Meditation of course enhanced all three, but took many forms. She found the process of healthy cooking to be a meditative pursuit for example. As was gentle, rhythmic swimming, dance, etc. The power of the subconscience can be a brilliant thing – particularly for healing and self-preservation. In the past she had used drugs to untap it, but now she turned to meditative pursuits to let it shine.

She found the biggest relief of all in the expression of her writing when in a mindful, relaxed state. For she believed wholeheartedly that you had to

'turn it off to turn it on'.....

Bianca Bosker wrote it so well in her book 'CORK DORK' :

" *Empty your mind....*

Advanced martial-arts masters are said to enter a state of complete mental clarity, or "unconscious conshiousness", called **<u>mushin</u>** *meaning "no mind". They shed their thoughts, emotions, fears, and ego so that they are able to receive the experience before them in a pure way, free of interference.*

Mushin is often likened to the state **mizu no kokoro**, *or "mind like water" - in which the mind becomes still like the surface of a pond so it can reflect exactly what it's shown. Nerves and feelings create ripples.*

One of the local rag's professed: 'although India is the birthplace of the Hindu religion and yoga, Bali is perhaps now India's coming of age sister'.

 A saying she now came to understand was: "There is no yoga without Hinduism and no Hinduism without yoga".

Her inherent need to express her feminine side became apparent in the satisfaction she received from all the creative pursuits leaning towards that: art; decorating; sensual movement and dance (she later pursued pole-dancing classes); writing; etc. For in times of desperate survival mode, one naturally evolves to develop masculine traits. This denies the dying woman inside…

In fact, Sapphire had by this stage devised a strategy for personal balance that resulted in health in <u>all</u> areas of importance. It sounded easy in theory but proved to be, in fact, somewhat of a full-time job!

The ultimate challenge she confirmed, was being *allowed* to self-focus within this paradigm without the demands and distractions of life and people in general….

yes, it may be perceived as a narcissistic pursuit, and she recognized that. The fact remains however, it is the work one has to do to maintain equilibrium of self.

In the balance…..juggling 'the big 5":

She decided every day should contain a taste of all the following ingredients for a complete recipe of health and harmony:

1: physical/sensual/energy expenditure

2: intellectual stimulation

3: spiritual nurturing

4: culinary!…(this means learning to love <u>*healthy*</u> foods predominantly, and 'reward' oneself with regular treats. For life is empty if devoid of epicurean~fancy~fulfillment!)

5: artistic expression ~and some <u>spontanaeity.</u> (A rare talent in the modern world)

Her entire quest now was to reach a *natural* state of inner contentment, or **sentosa** ~ (a malay word meaning peace and tranquility). Or: to be 'content and at peace with what each day brings'. Easier said than done!

It often requires a paradigm shift in *perception* of life too….a positive attitude to life's dramas and problems is the ultimate control tactic.

In the past, Sapphires' initial trips to Bali had been hedonistic as hell! Then, it had been a party holiday location, and she burnt the candle at both ends madly. Now, her highs were natural. Like anything, one has to work hard to access results, but there was nothing like the surge of endorphins from an intense exercise session. It was euphoric. The body can give you the biggest buzz of all if you push it.

As quoted from the movie WTF - whisky tango foxtrot:

"The human body produces its' own heroin. In fact when the fight or flight instinct is activated in the hypothalamus, your body releases endorphins; dopamine and norapidaphine (that is - heroin, cocaine and amphetamine all at once.) There is a reason to believe that a person can get addicted to this type of high. Soldiers, athletes, (war reporters/ got it...) An addict always needs a greater and greater dose, and then people make mistakes. People get hurt..."

She had experienced the vast spectrum of healing treatments available here – namely Acupuncture; authentic Reflexology; all forms of massage including hot stone, shiatsu ,thai, shotaiho, aromatherapy, traditional Balinese etc, and had received chinese energy healing. Not only were they medicinal, but physical luxuries, and it simply didn't get better than here!

Human contact of some form is vital for survival…

She had long been opposed to western and associated pharmaceutical medicine……(it would not be exaggerating in fact to say that the more she learnt about it, the more it terrified her);-opting instead for alternative natural Eastern methods and naturopathy, homeopathy, aromatherapy etc. She had sampled a taste of everything possible on the extensive 'natural healing menu', in every country she visited or resided in. Here, it was referred to as 'jamu' - natural remedies that could be attained from little stores where the owner sells natural healing pills, rubs, teas, or mixes muddy concoctions with village eggs, sugar, and boiling water. It is followed by a ginger 'shooter' (to take the hideous taste from the mouth!) and a mint for the breath. Nothing chemical and a fraction of the cost. There was a store directly opposite her home here, where she referred to the owner as 'doctor suki' - for she would visit him for any ailment way before she considered any normal western doctor visit and/or associated toxic prescription. She took many others there who also swore by his powers of healing without repercussions.

'In traditional Chinese medicine, the state of mind of the patient is considered a critical factor in pathology.' It acknowledges that the five emotions impact on our health, with each one associated with a main body organ.

Anger is represented in the liver; joy in the heart; thinking with the spleen; grief with the lungs;   and fear with the kidneys.   Basically, the HEALTHY MIND = HEALTHY BODY equation rang true. Perfect mathematics. Similarly, energy in vs energy out, and so on.

The Chinese also ascertain the state of health by observing a persons' tongue; which they read like a map. This, in conjunction with pulse rate indicates an organs' disharmony – to which they treat with acupuncture and possibly herbs. Hence, no invasive tests or screens necessary. If a persons' 'chi' energy flow was blocked, the body's health was compromised.

The East often provides bizarre beliefs and natural healing methods, that are hard to fathom (or digest!) -particularly throughout Asia and the tropics; - but the proof has to lie in the pudding, as they say. If something has been known to work for centuries, then why go down the toxic path of drugs and create an environment for unabating ill health?

For example: she had met a fellow free spirited soul who had lived in many places on his journeys, and professed the benefits of *'eating yoghurt cultured by the urine of wild water buffalo'* as protection from malaria. (evidently the buffalo themselves were immune to the disease, and hence the enzymes they pass on to the culture provide the same deterrent results to those who injest it). *She would never entertain the thought of partaking, but each to their own!*

It became her conviction now, after all she'd learnt and witnessed, that survival is contained **in nature** first and foremost; not in the laboratory. Science has provided some amazing discoveries, no question, but mankind (referring predominantly here to the western world) has been conned into relying on it **entirely**. Seek first what is readily available here on earth...it should be pursued as a 'plan B' when the uninvasive natural methods have been trialled first.

She had never been a morning person, and here also, 'mornings were for the birds'....literally!

The sounds of nature. .....A blind man's clock......

~learn to listen :

at four in the morning the roosters would crow; at 5am the muslims would chant; at 7 -8 am the birdsong reached fever pitch – it was a hive of activity for all birdlife! Throughout the day at various intervals they would take turns with their unique varietal verbal shrills, but it was at peak levels in the morn.

At 5pm the ducks would squawk for feeding time.

In the evenings, the larger 'togay' lizards would take the stage with their characteristic 'gekko' – echo chant, in microphone-like intensity. (One who had annoyingly taken residence behind her fridge and refused to budge - preventing sleep most nights...)

She was strongly opposed to antibiotics, and their gross over-prescription and use. They were a temporary bandaid, that kept you coming back for more. The conspiracy theory....(the 'wellness' industry?!) Their consequent destruction of the good bacteria responsible for a healthy immune system, results in continued, unabating health issues….(keeps the medical staff payroll grooving!)   It becomes a vicious cycle.

Meanwhile, the underlying issues of the patient still remain, and result in further compromised health of a much grander magnitude.

There was one incident in another country where she had an extreme infection in her fingers after jamming them in the car boot, and it was insisted she see a doctor immediately for fear of gangrene setting in. She refused, and went to her Chinese herbalist - who bandaged it; gave her some herbal pills to take, and it was clear in 24 hours. Presto. No internal damage or disruption.

 As she had become more attuned to her bodies' state of being, she could now detect precisely the location of response the body gave when feeling unbalanced. It was an indication that a certain emotion had been in overdrive, or neglected or suppressed etc – and needed to be attended to. Time to zone in on the target with yoga, meditation and reviving breath channeling (prana) to the region. (Stress is often stored in the buttocks and hips for example; - life can quite literally become a pain in the arse!)

 Her time in Japan had also exposed her to their prolonging lifestyle tactics that had been proven for centuries. The miraculous stats on their mortality rate, despite chronically stressful and competitive lives, and a profound prevalence of smoking addiction were proof enough.

She had attended 'Qigong' sessions with a Taoist master; learning to harness the earths' energy as a revitalising force. It taught her that 'energy follows attention'; ~ where we place our conscious awareness ('qi') is where the energy will flow and gather. This cultivation of lifeforce energy is referred to as 'prana'. She had even used a pranic dentist, who used 'dolphin music' to assist in this process; avoiding toxic anaesthetic.

She had a jet-Spa installed in her previous house in Australia; designed for her specifically by an osteopath so that the massage jets hit the correct points, as aqua therapy.

There too, she would have at least 2 dry saunas a week; sweating expels toxins from the body and helps take the load off the kidneys.

She had undertaken several detoxes over the years; - a LIVER one in particular that she continued   twice   annually.
For optimal body functioning the liver is king, so it was only right to pay it homage as the organ of maintenance. Being the largest internal organ in the body, it performs over 30,000 enzymatic reactions per second to ensure metabolic harmony. Dr. Lewis Thomas, chancellor of the Cancer Centre wrote in 'The Lives of a Cell' that he :

`would rather be given the controls of a 747, knowing nothing about how to fly, than to be responsible for the functioning of his liver.`

In her serious detox phase, she had undergone a series of colonic irrigation. Ten to be exact; and regular ones thereafter. She knew the benefits of this; the thought of it was far worse than the procedure!

She learnt to administer her own vitamin B injections; which she continued every 2 weeks. In other countries, a doctors' appointment was necessary, to attain a script – to retrieve from the pharmacist, and return *again* for the injection to be given. All up : at least $120. They were easily accessible over the counter here, at a fraction of the cost, and more than twice the size.

Reiki healing was her therapy of choice in New York, to deal with the repressed emotions from the divorce of her parents. The result was a most cathartic effect.

She'd also had Iridology readings; done flotation tanks, had live-blood analysis.........the list goes on.

Suffice to say there was a whole other world out there for health options if one wished to support the body naturally, and avoid becoming a victim of 'the system'.

The 'balians' (traditional doctors; healers) here in Indonesia too, relied on nature as the medicine. They focused on the 'jamu' (powder mixes with water); fragranced oils; purification ceremonies and 'pijat' (massage). They managed to amend pain , ailments, and even avoid surgery through these methods.

When a girlfriend was struck with breast cancer, she incorporated daily fresh juices made by staff consisting of several fresh ingredients, including ginger but the most prominent one was KUNYIT (or 'kunir' in local bahasa Indonesia) as a treatment and preventative.   ~
Fresh TURMERIC.   It is
said to eradicate tumours, and prevent new ones from occurring.

One of the massage parlours she frequented was staffed entirely with BLIND masseuses. This of course made them far more adept at the skill of tactile healing; they instinctively zoned in on any areas or organs needing assistance, particularly via Reflexology. They read the body like a book from the heels of the feet! It was always an intensely painful experience, but there was no question that the results were detected immediately. She awarded them with 'talking watches', as a gift of appreciation.

An acupuncturist she favoured used ancestral Chinese techniques. Her grandfather had trained her in the skill of 'energy healing' – which was one of the most profound experiences to endure. After the acupuncture needles were removed, she would close her eyes to harness the earth's power, and run her hand over the skull and brain, neck and heart areas. The shock waves were astronomical; it was like being electrocuted!! An abundance of repressed emotions would be released, and bubble to the surface. The first time Sapphire experienced this, she apologised, as she held the therapists' hand and literally sobbed for

half an hour.   The second
time, she laughed hysterically! Again, a most painful exercise, but the relief was astounding.

So nature provides all necessary for healing.

As humans we are miraculous entities. The power is within us all to mend and repair. We need to respect and honour that gift, and get out of the way of our bodies' natural processes; stop interfering with it.

Nature too was medicinal in itself.

The majestic sunsets here were legendary; a tonic in themselves, and life tended to revolve somewhat around them for visitors and locals alike. There was nothing like witnessing the huge ball of fire as it descended off in the horizon at the end of every sun-kissed day.

She would often wander down to the 'pantai' and sit on the beach with lifeguards and locals; practicing her bahasa – usually as the magnificent 'masuk matahari', or 'tenggelam matahari' (sunset) occurred.

Frequenting the traditional 'pasar' (markets); she passionately devised wholesome meals from local, seasonal produce as opposed to foreign imports. In response to the immense volume of her purchases, it was assumed she ran a restaurant! She adored the folk who worked at her favourite venues; they were like her village; her people. She would scoop up their adorable baby; trotting around barefoot amongst the action, handing her all manner of vegetables   in   assistance.
Sometimes, as they weighed her stock via archaeic means, she would sit on a milk crate with pen and paper to hand for the days' lesson; she was becoming fluent in all to do with *green*! It was like being in another century here. Like the loot that she accrued, it was wholesome   to   the   max.
She consumed a wide variety of both cooked and raw vegetables to provide full enzyme count, and experimented with the food of the land: tofu and tempeh.

One of the local vendors she bought daily greens from would exclaim: "you – like rabbit!", and had her in stitches one day when he asked "are you a playboy bunny?".

She forged a close friendship with all the local supply vendors; there were a string of them on her nearby 'village walk'. They would contact her and put aside fresh supplies for her imminent arrival almost daily.

She attended a Balinese cooking course with her 'gay husband' on one of his visits ; (one of her dearest friends who she deeply adored.) It gave an insight into producing local cuisine, such as gado-gado etc, and she adopted 'healthier' versions of them to incorporate into her menus. She was aware of all the 'lokal' vegetables, and their names in bahasa , but was just bewildered as to what to do with them! (she had never encountered 'gambas', 'pakis' 'komangi' etc, but loved them even thrown in a salad, so now she extended her repoirtoire with the further knowledge she had gained)

She also did a *living food for healing and detox'* course with a girlfriend; hours away in the hinterland. It confirmed and reinforced her knowledge on harnessing maximum benefits from enzymes through careful treatment and preparation of nature's gifts.

She had a self-confessed addiction to papaya however; much to the puzzlement of many. Not only was it an utterly divine example of 'fruit of the gods', but it was a powerhouse of enzymatic functions –(particularly regarding digestion and detoxification); reduced bodily inflammation, **and** was natures' protection from parasites and germs. (If you wanted to know where to score papaya at 'lokal harga' (cheap price), she was your gal! She had fully sussed the market; always buying in volume for a better rate.) Christopher Columbus had actually reputably labeled them the 'fruit of the angels'. Gods, angels…. whatever, it was natures' gift to all things good and she took full advantage of it's benefits!

As she led a predominantly vegetarian existence, she attended a seminar on organic farming, where she was the only buleh (foreigner) present. She was keen to attain the truth about the possible use of toxic pesticides here. Like with most things, there was always conflicting reports depending on the source, but she ascertained that the local produce here was indeed MOSTLY organic – (you only had to observe the bugs present to know that was true !); the exception to this was during rainy season when human intervention came into play to compensate for crop damage. **Some** pesticides were then used; albeit not to the extent of other countries…. (in Australia, she learnt that, much to her horror, they permitted the usage of 120 toxic chemicals that were banned elsewhere worldwide.) She was a firm believer that pesticides had an immense contribution to disease. The key here was to avoid the foreign imports.

The organic virgin coconut oil here was marvelous for a myriad of purposes: for cooking and use in salads and also for body enhancement. When ingested, it stimulates the thyroid gland; lowers cholesterol and promotes good gut bacteria internally. The lauric acid content is converted to a substance that fights bacterial and viral infections in infants naturally, and serves to boost the immune system in adults. Externally, it serves as a skin moisturiser; stretch-mark or skin irritation treatment and hair protectant . She sent little gift bottles to all she cared for.

Even the coffee here had extra enzymes, and for a very special reason. 'Kopi Luwak adalah kopi paling langka di dunia!'….Civet coffee was the rarest coffee in the world.

[Known as 'cat poo coffee' it is produced from the dung of the civet cat. It selects the very finest beans; ingests them , and as it passes through their system, the coffee acquires the extra beneficial enzymes from the cats' digestive tract.] Now that's organic for you! She had a friend who knew a guy that exported the stuff, and he told her that his house was literally "full of bags of shit!"   Like her initial response, many others were (understandably) reluctant to try, but if you can get past the queezy concept and taste it, the proof is in the pudding, as they say. It truly is one of the finest tasting coffee she'd ever had. Each day now, she would 'wake up and smell the luwak'!

Here, if you were selective, it appeared to be the closest to 'the way nature intended' she had ever experienced.

So essentially, she herself cultivated a back to basics natural lifestyle.

The cleansing aspects of a minimalist existence too, was intensely liberating. Its amazing how little one really needs to live contently. Forcing oneself to 'make do unless absolutely necessary' was all part of a healing process. It served to prove how much clutter and unnecessary possessions people surround themselves with, to fill a void.

Stuff the stuff!

She had experienced greater joy with nothing than with immense wealth.

Oh – and the sleep had never been so deep. Definitely the elixir of youth.

She liked HERSELF here; she was at home in her body.

Being third world, it had taught her to appreciate the simple things in life, and reminded her not to take things for granted. Basic necessities like power and water could be depleted or 'kosong' in an instant.

(The frustration of which was medicinal to her, as patience was a virtue she knew nothing of!)

She took passion in seeking the native way here; how the locals themselves lived – away from the tourist hotspots.

Similarly, she honoured the hindu Balinese living concept of 'tri hita karana'. Their happiness relied on the harmonious balance between the people with their gods, the community, and nature.

She was determined to adhere to the 'when in Rome' principal.

They welcomed her curiosity warmly, however here too, she was still an Alien. But that, like her surrounds, was a homely state.

Yes, the Balinese were flawed. Beneath their veneer, and reputation as 'the nicest people on earth', they still fell victim to the evils of humanity. Western society had created greed, dishonesty and jealousy in them; most prominently in the city regions and those areas that foreigners are familiar with.

The untouched folk, who hadn't been poisoned by the presence of wasteful foreigners, reigned in the more remote outskirts. A close friend of hers had boutique villas out near

Tanah Lot, and had the rare luxury of being able to profess that his staff of 10 years were indeed like family. He trusted them implicitly to attend to all matters in his absence, and they had never once betrayed his confidence . This is virtually unheard of now days, sadly.

As a 'buleh', a well known fact amongst all expats was that it was difficult at times not to feel like you were considered a walking ATM machine. She was learning to exercise patience too, as there were days when the incessant enquiries of "mau kermana?" (where are you going?) would annoy her, and she had to resist the urge to respond: "none of your business!" It was an intrinsic part of their culture though, so she had no right to take offense. [It was actually akin to enquiring: "HOW're you going?", as we say in English.] One required a sense of humour, definitely!

She still stood by the opinion however that they were a far preferable race to her. As always, she was selective with social interaction; her learned intuition more acute to the 'darma dan adarma' (Hindu good vs bad folk).   Without question whatsoever, there was a definite **dark** side, to balance the score.....unavoidable qantum physics.

See only the positive though; a skill one needs for survival and peace. For the most part they were far more gracious, and their warm smiles and jokes could melt your heart.

They were her people now, and she chose only to acknowledge all their positive attributes, for there were many. She had learnt to recognise the genuine vs the masked avengers. (Truth be known, the only time her instincts had failed her here was with *western* folk – she had classified some as friends but they had proven her wrong. She had been in a weakened, 'unbalanced' state when she made that judgement, and they had taken advantage of her generous nature.)

Family, both blood and choosn remained the only constant.

In any case, wherever you are, its all about choices. Sapphires' life there was vastly different to most foreigners; she had crafted her own existence taking the best on offer, and avoiding the ugly. Selective hearing, seeing and doing.

She felt endebted to the land and its people for assisting her rescue. If there was any way she could somehow express that gratitude in the future, she vowed to do it. *(Here in the writing is payment for that!)*

She was however most concerned about the pollution and the prevailing oblivion to damage control. The toxic fumes from motorbikes was immense. The escalating 'macet' (traffic) and worsening roads over the years meant that there were days the air was so smog ridden that she could hardly breathe. Coupled with that was the ridiculous frequency with which they burnt off all the piles of rubbish, without an ounce of concern for the environment. One of their less attractive traits was their love of fire and noisy fireworks. Their ignorance of recycling and preserving the rapidly declining planet,(of which they were entitled the best part) was a major concern, and most primitive. Paradise lost…

It all came down to education. Third world. They were the most fortunate location-wise, but the most disadvantaged knowledge-wise. The horrific stats on motorbike fatalities were highest here. They displayed blatant disregard to all forms of danger or destruction. If there was some way to educate them on all the risks, it would be a god-send to all.

They were also blessed with, she believed, the best natural produce on the planet, but no concept of how to utilize its' health attributes ingestively. They were oblivious to the fact that deep-frying everything was not the way to cook, nor adding vast amounts of sugar and salt!

Always, dedication to their fundamental Hindu faith prevailed as priority, which was perhaps the protective mechanism from external influence. For these peoples' world had been rocked on more than one occasion; being targeted for terrorism, and through natural disaster; - (it was a seismic island after all .)

A mass of bad press concerning Australian drug smugglers and their plight in Kerobokan 'penjara'; prison, too had affected tourism and business for the people….(and further decimated Australians' reputation amongst all other races).

Hindu dharma: she liked the beliefs it entailed. Bottom line: it was about KARMA: 'a persons actions affecting his or her fate for the next reincarnation'.

Basic stuff. Be a good person, and wellbeing shall be bestowed back upon you.

Perfect mindset. This was as much of a 'religion' as she dared to accommodate-(along with all its associated GUILT.)

Essentially, she had taken her interpretation of the *principles of **many** religions;* selected those she deemed most advantageous to her, and in a sense, created her own personal 'designer' form of the term religion.

Then, in conjunction with other beliefs and lifestyle choices adopted through the experiences of her life thus far, she appointed her own faith.

Not commandments as such; nor a 'step program', but merely a listed guideline for a peaceful existence.

For religion, when dictated, is the ultimate crutch.

Each has dogmatic interpretations of worship to a higher being… – {except for Buddhism of course, where 'god' reigns supreme within us all. One just had to acknowledge the presence. Siddharta is me, you, the person you pass on the street..}

[In that sense, she supposed yoga was like a religion to her then, for in return, the physical self was rewarded, - and she did tend to rely on it for balance, wellbeing and serenity.]

The process mankind avoids at all costs is exposing oneself to the mirror, and being forced to fight the dragon, or demon that stares back.

Human behaviour is always to cower and hide; usually behind a mask of habits and addictions; ~ or religion.

And yes! Far be it for her to pronounce herself a hypocrite – she had fallen victim herself many times in a multitude of ways! She had immersed herself in the trappings of wealth and partaken in the poisonous illegal decadence akin to that.

Her lifelong rebellion to any form of authority or protocol had led her down many risky paths; the danger of which was an adrenalin rush for her.

Perhaps the thing that she should fear most, in retrospect of her life was HERSELF, and what she was capable of!

The fight against fear is the eternal struggle, and the war that must be waged for the entirety of existence in this life.

The dragon never ever leaves though.

He is always there. Very few have the strength, but if you can stare him down and lose the fear, he loses all power and you take the ultimate control. Life returns.

Fear. This is the death….of all things.

Propaganda: that's what it was all about in this world. The power of creating fear. Brainwashing the masses as a control mechanism.

Religion: breeds immense guilt = fear of retribution.

And terrorism. Back to fear.

Its virtually impossible to avoid becoming a victim of **fear** in the real world.

One has to find their own land of safety and strength of mind; freedom of opinion – untainted by what society deems to be the acceptable way, or the wrong one.

Otherwise, its just a plethora of corpses, going through the identical motions……

Deep introspection is required.

One must look in the mirror, and take off the mask.

She had found her ' Nirvana' ; - where it was all about nature and nurture in a nutshell.

Her heart was at home here, and her spirit was free. It was more the way life used to be, before man became a gadget fiend. Nature and man co-existed at a much more intimate level; harmoniously.

She felt that the key in this modern, chaotic world is to simplify; not complicate further. Get back to basics. For survival. And health.

It was here that, although it incessantly knocked, she learnt to close the door on the enemy: the ego.

She had deliberately shunned all forms of news and media for peace of mind; - mental liberation…. (good grief, this was a mind detox in itself! How can a person function on any constructive level, with mental clarity, when it is bombarded with unnecessary information overload and fear-inducing details on a daily basis?)

If there was something she needed to know, or that may affect her or her family directly, she was inevitably notified by sms or email. (these being the necessary evil mediums required for communication)

This was not ignorance; it was merely survival tactics.

However, she was painfully aware of how near impossible it was to protect "the promised land."

For it was constantly at threat of being under siege.

Hence, HER fear now was in having it all taken from her…

She'd had so many things taken from her in the past. Everything she valued.

And sadly, much of it was lost through her generosity to others.

Her strength now lay in her core beliefs.

When she strayed from them, homeostasis withered accordingly.

"Anging meng-gongong kafila berlalu"………..(bahasa Indonesia): { Let the dogs talk and hear them, but ultimately make up your own mind.} She was learning to block her ears to the 'white noise' of others.

Her beliefs gained clarity, but she was painfully aware that her opinions would be perhaps misinterpreted and/or challenged by folk. They would most surely receive retaliation. For she would profoundly *abjure* to her initial Christian upbringing.

She meant no offence however. Everyone was entitled to their own vista.

"Itu pendapat saya" – that's **my** opinion.

Her intention was not to inflict HER beliefs onto others, merely to freely express them.

It was her eye of perception…..

As she saw it, all religion was akin to a children's story book……fabulously conjured stories, with no absolute evidence of truth…. Fantasy! ~ As the comedian George Carlin flamboyantly expressed in his stand-up comedy routines, and in his books on the topic. Apparently humans needed some degree of that in their lives. So she decided to create/custom-design her own…..a sanctum of truth.

*(Not dissimilar to what Stephen R Covey describes as a 'personal mission statement' (or philosophy or creed); a personal constitution. (In his '7 habits of highly effective people' manual)

'It is the written standard, the key criterion by which everything else is evaluated and directed'

For it was imperitive that she remain true to <u>herself</u>, as dishonesty was most repugnant to her and she was devoid of tolerance for it.

Although the saying amongst mankind goes *"never say never"* the concept of breaking or bending the rules had been somewhat the theme of her entire life…..   And so in keeping with that she did say it.

As a promise to herself.   .
And in an obsessive compulsive manner, twenty seven times in fact!….

So…..this journey for Sapphire had been a long one; spanning several years………..but she finally arrived at <u>her</u> sanctum of truth :

"the <u>NEVER-NEVER LAND</u>"…………. the code of twenty seven:

Never say: 'never say never' (!)

Code 1: Never forget: be true to yourself. Nurture your mind, body and spirit. Make no excuses for being fit and healthy. You have none. Make supreme health a lifestyle choice; not merely a fad. Namaste.

Code 2: Never be too proud nor too confident. We are all equal.

Code 3: Never rest on your laurels; but don't allow others to dampen your spirits or destruct your confidence either. Jealousy and envy is all around us.

"insults are the arguments employed by those who are in the wrong" Jean Jacques Rousseau.

Code 4: Be open to possibilities; but remain protective, and never let your guard down. Never trust anyone but yourself..........but don't lose faith in mankind (that's a hard one!) Choose your friends wisely, for "the devil hath the power to assume a pleasing shape" (shakespearian quote: Hamlet)   If someone has let you down in the past, they will continue to do so; a leopard never changes its spots!!   See beyond the mask......

5: Be generous, but never at the expense of your own wellbeing. YOU deserve all that encompasses happiness.

6: Never dwell on the past. Live in the moment, but never forget or regret your past lives; journeys; successes and mistakes. It is how you evolve. Embrace the lot. They are the chapters of your book!

Know it. Own it.

7: We all, as humans contain many different personalities that have dominated different phases of our lives at different times. Each have certain attributes and flaws. Like Christie, Sapphire, Letha, Crystal, Lovisa, Barbara, Sarah, Livia etc.........recognize that they are all one and the same, and ultimately make up the grand total of you.

8: Never expect others to understand you - for each has their own profoundly unique, and personal story, which should never be judged. Never succumb to feeling ostracized by the fact that ... **nobody knows who you really are**......take *solace* in the fact! For it represents your supreme uniqueness.

9. Don't give up on the possibility of love; however brief the encounter - you never know when it may come knocking; ~nor from where.

10: Be self-sufficient, and you will never be let down. We are all-encompassing entities. You are born alone; some live alone, you die alone.

Fact.

11: Recognise that you will never be able to control most things. What will be will be...it is what it is.

12: Live now in this very moment; its all you've got. Pay attention! In a figurative and literal sense: stop and smell the roses. They are everywhere.

13: People may lie to you; and they inevitably do! The one thing that never will is your body. Get in tune and learn to 'listen'. Never ignore the messages your body sends.

14: Never allow yourself to wake up feeling that you NEED something or someone; as that is when you've hit despair. You alone are all you need. It is imperitive that you learn to love your own company. Time completely alone is vital for self-growth.

15: Love yourself first. Worship your body, mind and spirit. The temple is you, and 'god' reigns supreme within us all. Freedom and paradise is a place within. Stop looking externally…

16: Never hold onto anger or bitterness; it only makes you sick. Ask not what others can do for you, but what you can do for yourself (and others!)

17: At the end of every day, stop and count your blessings. Control the way your mind sees things; always look for the silver lining in every perceived disaster. Things usually happen for a reason. That's out of your control. Let it be. The eye of perception…

18: Never fall victim to the constraints of society. Be open-minded, but stay protected from external influence. Protocol is a myth now in this changing world.

19: Never continue company that doesn't *enhance* you. Life is too short to tolerate fools.

"The Key is to keep company only with people who uplift you, whose presence calls forth your best"   Epictetus, Greek philosopher.

20: ~Never make promises you can't keep, or you fail others – and yourself. Only commit if you are 100% sure.

"Those that are most slow in making a promise are the most faithful in the performance of it" Jean Jacques Rousseau.

21: Never remain in a miasma (unwholesome or foreboding atmosphere)>To be avoided at all costs…

22: Never lose sight of your dreams, however bizarre or resplendent they may be! Use creative visualization and positive affirmations to strengthen your resolve. The power of the mind is the most extroidinary tool you have…

23: Never forget how lucky you are. There is always someone worse off than yourself.

24: Never forget kindness or good deeds others have blessed you with. Intend to honour them with **reciprocation.**

25: Never stop learning, especially about yourself. Challenge yourself; confront your fears. Life experiences provide the best education of all.

#26: Seek not others' opinions, trust only in your own. Let your intuition guide you; never ignore it – for that's when mistakes are made. The 'gut-brain' trumps the head brain.

27...........

But above all, never, ever lose **hope**....

For that is death.

27th mantra code....the final boom.

Chapter 27

*Soul-selling. The revelation…

Forgive me.

For I have committed and witnessed unspeakable acts that I can't speak of……
ones I can only *write* about.

So many personalities and chapters.
Constantly evolving.
In a state of perpetual flux….
Stability and serenity have no access. Non-conformist alien soul.

Always looking over my shoulder. Adrenalin rushing. Need protection.

They say extreme athletes experience a sense of calm while embracing fear….

And to continue, one must REINVENT; REINCARNATE for the next life to commence.
For every time one chapter ends, a mini death occurs too.

I have died many times.

Sold my soul.

Mentally, physically, emotionally, spiritually…

literally.

"If you're losing your soul and you know it then you still have a soul left to lose...

...You have to die a few times before you can really live"

Bukowski.

Hold no regrets though, for they only make you sick. But honour the progression…..the past lives are like stepping stones to the promised land!

I have learnt that life is only lonely if you are not complete *within yourself*......

I have also learnt that the choices that generally piss *other people* off, are the ones that allow *me* to sleep at night......there is always a price to pay.

No matter your trauma, if you are a true survivor, the phoenix will rise from *deep* inside.

For to carry on living the life, one must sell their soul.

Im selling my soul to you now......

I wish I didn't have to expose my deepest, darkest secrets......but I have been left with no alternative, and it is called survival.

Life........heartache; hardship, pain and loss are all part of the bumpy journey.

Like the way I've lived my life, I write with *sheer abandon* and *no rules.*

The mantra for survival: YOU are all you have. Here and Now. Know it; Own it.

May former lives rest in peace.

And...........i live on..............

XOXOXOXOXOXOXOXXOXOXO

Afterword:

People change.

PLACES change.

The whole goddamn WORLD has changed. And lots of chapters have ended with it.

Mulai means to begin. *Selasai* means to end/finish.

I feel it is prudent to add my feelings now that a lot of what I've written no longer applies. Certainly not in the current world. Reading these chapters now feels like it's from another life…a different century. Its almost archaic in a lot of its detail - akin to a historical study of a different time and age. I don't want to be labelled a hypocrite!

The process of survival dictates that change is ever imminent. But the description of the strict denial and discipline once instilled sounds sanctimonious in comparison to the simpler, more flexible life I now lead.

My recent return venture to a land I once ecstatically embraced new feels somewhat tainted. There's a foreign feeling I can't describe….not loneliness, as I've always embraced that. It's like a long love affair has come to a bitter ending. The passion has gone; the original bright allure has faded to a shadow. I didn't think I would ever grow tired of it; and yet here I am exhausted!   The undercurrent of greed and subterfuge has always been there but now it is omnipresent. The world struggles to financially get back on its feet after covid decimation -sure, but this is next level. The selfish restrictions they now exhibit in force are a false economy as they are repelling those who have always been their salvation. Trust cannot reside in such a miasma.

I expressed my melancholy to my wise mother on the topic, and she replied : "but is WAS applicable at the time. An honest account of the era. It isn't a lie - a lot has changed in the world and this is the final instalment of the Bali chapter."

Loss pervades the soul on so many levels since 2020. For everybody. Its time we all commence new chapters with an open heart and a sense of hope....

*Acknowledgements :

I am profoundly blessed to have the most supportive parents and partner in this daring game of words.

My beautiful Mum Ros; ~ Garry and Michael : I couldn't have done it without your continued encouragement.

The more honest you are, the less true comrades you have. Fact. People come and go in life, but as a loner, you become more adept at determining the genuine from the phoney…these creatures are very rare! ~I seek only authentic folk who need no mask.

Joycee and Vicky-Lee: you proved friendship when it was needed the most. Thankyou to the sisterhood.

As forementioned, Mark and Robert are the souls I wanted to dedicate the project to. The most painful part of the process was knowing that they would never get to witness its completion. Life is too short to not pursue your wild ambitions.

There needs to be sincere gratitude shown to my marvellous editor _Andreea_ (or should I say co-pilot); without which, you would not be reading this now.

I gave her this document in a million pieces; warning her: 'it's challenging!' ~ as I was most adamant about the style and format of my writing. A pedantic client with a specific vision (!)

She accepted with much grace and confidence saying, quote:

"*I've got your back Sam!*"

I was nervous… dubious… doubtful.

But she certainly proved true to her word.

I'm a novice at this game, but I learnt a lot in the process.
There were multiple obstacles and setbacks, but I realise now it was all part
of the victorious journey. She took me under her wing and she flew me to the
finish line.

I respect and love her and I hope she takes on my future wild endeavours as
my pen continues to speak my voice....

*S*am xoxo

Samara Williams has dwelled in many places, but currently writes overlooking the city of London she calls home.

Masks and Mirrors is her first book, in which like the title suggests, she challenges the concept of fact and fiction. And finding the courage to speak your truth.

'Masks and Mirrors' is all about being real and raw. Sam Williams gives us a mix of fiction and jaw-dropping reality that hits you in the gut. From extreme highs to total wipeouts, these stories cover it all. It's like looking into a mirror of life and seeing the good, the bad, and the ugly.

*Ruby Garner, Linguistic Teacher **ACS International School Egham***

***

Sam Williams has put together a real thought-provoking collection in 'Masks and Mirrors.' It's all about life's ups and downs and how we live in the moment. The stories will make you think about things and leave you deep in thought. Totally relatable and eye-opening, you gotta give it a go!

Lily Bosch, History Student L'Ecole de Battersea

***

In 'Masks and Mirrors,' the author fearlessly challenges conventions, weaving together a sequence of bold and unconventional stories. With a unique blend of fact and fiction, she delves deep into the shadows of human existence. Each narrative exposes vulnerability and courage, painting an unforgettable picture of life's intricacies. A daring and audacious read that pushes the boundaries of storytelling.

*Coby Johnson, Teacher **ACS International School Hillingdon***

***

Sam Williams' collection of short stories offers a compelling exploration of life's complexities. From the thrill of pushing boundaries to the introspective peace that follows, each tale leaves an indelible mark on the reader's soul. It's a thought-provoking and deeply reflective read, definitely worth my time.

Mason Roberts, Automation Engineer JEF Automation LTD

***

I recently had the pleasure of reading Sam Williams' latest book, 'Masks and Mirrors,' and let me tell you, from the very first page, I was hooked. Each story in 'Masks and Mirrors' has a unique flavor that keeps you engaged and invested in the characters. You'll find yourself laughing, crying, and experiencing a myriad of emotions as you journey through the ups and downs of these captivating tales.

Chloe Clark, Chief Editor BWF Publishing